2.00

CLOAK and DAGGER

A Treasury of 35 Great Espionage Stories

ABOUT THE EDITORS

BILL PRONZINI is one of America's finest mystery/suspense writers, as well as one of its leading critics. He has published more than 30 novels and 280 short stories. He has edited or coedited more than 40 anthologies and, with Martin H. Greenberg, has coedited *101 Mystery Stories, Baker's Dozen™: 13 Short Mystery Stories, Manhattan Mysteries*, and others. A longtime resident of San Francisco, he possesses one of the larger collections of pulp magazines in the world.

MARTIN H. GREENBERG, who has been called "the King of the anthologists," now has some 200 to his credit. Greenberg is professor of regional analysis and political science at the University of Wisconsin-Green Bay, where he teaches a course in American foreign and defense policy. He has served as coeditor of many books with Bill Pronzini and is the editor of *On the Diamond, In the Ring*, and other anthologies.

CLOAK and DAGGER

A Treasury of 35 Great Espionage Stories

Edited by
Bill Pronzini
and
Martin H. Greenberg

AVENEL BOOKS
New York

Published in 1988 by Avenel Books
distributed by Crown Publishers, Inc.
225 Park Avenue South, New York, New York 10003

Manufactured in the United States of America
Library of Congress Cataloging-in-Publication Data

Cloak and dagger.

1. Spy stories, American.   2. Spy stories, English.
I. Pronzini, Bill.   II. Greenberg, Martin Harry.
PS648.S85C5   1988   813′.0872′08   87-19463

ISBN 0-517-65351-6
h g f e d c b a

Book design by Cynthia Dunne

ACKNOWLEDGMENTS

"A Man's Foes"—Copyright 1948 by Pearl S. Buck. Copyright renewed 1968 by Pearl S. Buck. Reprinted by permission of Harold Ober Associates, Inc.

"Strictly Diplomatic"—Copyright 1945 by John Dickson Carr. From *Ellery Queen's Mystery Magazine*. Reprinted by permission of Harold Ober Associates, Inc.

"The Army of the Shadows"—Copyright 1939 by Eric Ambler. Reprinted by permission of Campbell Thomson & McLaughlin Limited.

"Flight into Disaster"—Copyright 1952 by Erle Stanley Gardner. Reprinted by permission of Curtis Brown, Ltd.

"The Russian Prisoner"—Copyright © 1963 by Leslie Charteris. Reprinted by permission of the author.

"The Traitor"—Copyright © 1965 by Pamar Enterprises. Reprinted by permission of the Anita Diamant Agency.

"Cloak and Digger"—Copyright © 1961 by Fiction Publishing Company. First published as "Cloak and Dagger" in the February 1962 issue of *The Saint*. Reprinted by permission of the author.

"Cross-Over"—Copyright © 1973 by Michael Gilbert. Reprinted by permission of the author.

"To Slay an Eagle"—Copyright © 1965 by Universal Publishing and Distributing Corporation. Reprinted by permission of the author.

"The Little Green Book"—Copyright © 1966 by Pamar Publications. Reprinted by permission of Larry Sternig Literary Agency.

"S.P.Y. in the Sky"—Copyright © 1965 by Pamar Enterprises; originally published in *Intrigue Mystery Magazine*, January 1966. Reprinted by permission of the author.

"The Case of XX2"—Copyright 1951 by Julian Symons. Reprinted by permission of the author.

CONTENTS

INTRODUCTION

Cloak and Dagger brings together for the first time in book form more than two dozen outstanding spy and espionage stories by some of the finest and most accomplished writers in the field—both past and present.

These stories span more than a half-century of espionage writing in the United States and Great Britain and feature a variety of secret agents (male and female), double agents, counterspies, and saboteurs, all working in what has been called "the world's second oldest profession." These brave men and women work in diverse settings—in the United States, England, Europe, and, of course, behind the Iron Curtain. Taken together these stories demonstrate how the spy story (or spy fiction, as it is coming to be called) has evolved in form, structure, and content through this century and how the masters of this type of fiction have adapted to meet changing conditions, events, and technologies. Indeed, the spy story is closely tied to history; in this collection you will find tales set before and during World War I, the interwar period, World War II, during the continuing Cold War battle between agents of the East and West, and even in the struggle against the terrorists of today's headlines.

In these pages we offer you the best in espionage fiction written during the twentieth century. From the "Golden Age" of spy fiction we have authors such as W. Somerset Maugham, Richard Harding Davis, E. Phillips Oppenheim, Joseph Conrad (whose work, *The Secret Agent*, published in 1907, is considered the first great novel in the genre), John Dickson Carr, and Eric Ambler (whose story *A Coffin for Dimitrios*, 1939, was made into a notable spy film). The second group includes such masters as Leslie Charteris (whose character Simon Templar—"The Saint"—is one of the great literary creations of our time), the justly famous John Jakes, Michael Gilbert, Edward D. Hoch, Isaac Asimov, Brian Garfield, and, of course, Peter O'Donnell (here represented by his masterspy Modesty Blaise, the female James Bond).

The field of espionage is one that has attracted people from all walks of life, and also one that seems to have caught the fancy of talented writers, some of whom combined careers in the spy business with their writing endeavors. Examples include such stalwarts from across the Atlantic as W. Somerset Maugham, John Buchan, Graham Greene, Ian Fleming, John LeCarre, and A. E. W. Mason, and former American operatives such as E. Howard Hunt and William F. Buckley, Jr. The readers of spy fiction include people from truck drivers to presidents—for example, it was John F. Kennedy's affection for Ian Fleming's James Bond novels that helped make these books into super sellers.

Cloak and Dagger should provide something for every lover of espionage fiction—memorable stories by expert writers, some anthologized here for the first time since their original appearance in print. We hope you derive as much pleasure from reading these exciting and stimulating stories as we did from selecting them.

Bill Pronzini
Martin H. Greenberg
1987

CLOAK and DAGGER

A Treasury of 35 Great Espionage Stories

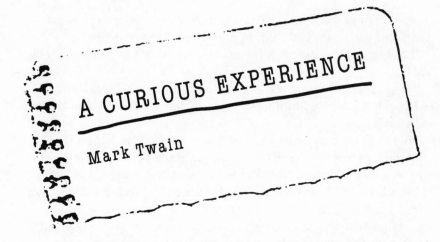

A CURIOUS EXPERIENCE

Mark Twain

THIS IS THE story which the Major told me, as nearly as I can recall it:

In the winter of 1862–63 I was commandant of Fort Trumbull, at New London, Conn. Maybe our life there was not so brisk as life at "the front"; still it was brisk enough, in its way—one's brains didn't cake together there for lack of something to keep them stirring. For one thing, all the Northern atmosphere at that time was thick with mysterious rumors—rumors to the effect that rebel spies were flitting everywhere, and getting ready to blow up our Northern forts, burn our hotels, send infected clothing into our towns, and all that sort of thing. You remember it. All this had a tendency to keep us awake, and knock the traditional dullness out of garrison life. Besides, ours was a recruiting station— which is the same as saying we hadn't any time to waste in dozing, or dreaming, or fooling around. Why, with all our watchfulness, fifty per-cent of a day's recruits would leak out of our hands and give us the slip the same night. The bounties were so prodigious that a recruit could pay a sentinel three or four hundred dollars to let him escape, and still have enough of his bounty-money left to constitute a fortune for a poor man. Yes, as I said before, our life was not drowsy.

Well, one day I was in my quarters alone, doing some writing, when a pale and ragged lad of fourteen or fifteen entered, made a neat bow, and said:

"I believe recruits are received here?"

"Yes."

"Will you please enlist me, sir?"

"Dear me, no! You are too young, my boy, and too small."

A disappointed look came into his face and quickly deepened into an

1

expression of despondency. He turned slowly away, as if to go; hesitated, then faced me again, and said, in a tone that went to my heart:

"I have no home, and not a friend in the world. If you *could* only enlist me!"

But of course the thing was out of the question, and I said so as gently as I could. Then I told him to sit down by the stove and warm himself, and added:

"You shall have something to eat, presently. You are hungry?"

He did not answer; he did not need to; the gratitude in his big, soft eyes was more eloquent than any words could have been. He sat down by the stove, and I went on writing. Occasionally I took a furtive glance at him. I noticed that his clothes and shoes, although soiled and damaged, were of good style and material. This fact was suggestive. To it I added the facts that his voice was low and musical; his eyes deep and melancholy; his carriage and address gentlemanly; evidently the poor chap was in trouble. As a result, I was interested.

However, I became absorbed in my work by and by, and forgot all about the boy. I don't know how long this lasted; but at length I happened to look up. The boy's back was toward me, but his face was turned in such a way that I could see one of his cheeks—and down that cheek a rill of noiseless tears was flowing.

"God bless my soul!" I said to myself; "I forgot the poor rat was starving." Then I made amends for my brutality by saying to him, "Come along, my lad; you shall dine with *me;* I am alone today."

He gave me another of those grateful looks, and a happy light broke in his face. At the table he stood with his hand on his chair-back until I was seated, then seated himself. I took up my knife and fork and—well, I simply held them, and kept still; for the boy had inclined his head and was saying a silent grace. A thousand hallowed memories of home and my childhood poured in upon me, and I sighed to think how far I had drifted from religion and its balm for hurt minds, its comfort and solace and support.

As our meal progressed I observed that young Wicklow—Robert Wicklow was his full name—knew what to do with his napkin; and—well, in a word, I observed that he was a boy of good breeding; never mind the details. He had a simple frankness, too, which won upon me. We talked mainly about himself, and I had no difficulty in getting his history out of him. When he spoke of his having been born and reared in Louisiana, I warmed to him decidedly, for I had spent some time down there. I knew all the "coast" region of the Mississippi, and loved it, and had not been long enough away from it for my interest in it to begin to pale. The very names that fell from his lips sounded good to me—so good that I steered the talk in directions that would bring them out: Baton Rouge, Plaquemine, Donaldsonville, Sixty-mile Point, Bonnet-Carré, the Stock Landing, Carrollton, the Steamship Landing, the Steamboat Landing, New Orleans, Tchoupitoulas Street, the Esplanade, the Rue des Bons Enfants, the St. Charles Hotel, the Tivoli Circle, the Shell Road, Lake Pontchartrain; and it was particularly delightful to me to hear once more of the *R. E. Lee,* the *Natchez,* the *Eclipse,* the *General Quitman,* the *Duncan F. Kenner,* and other old familiar steamboats. It was almost as good as being back there, these names so vividly reproduced in my mind the look of the things they stood for. Briefly, this was little Wicklow's history:

When the war broke out, he and his invalid aunt and his father were living near Baton Rouge, on a great and rich plantation which had been in the family for fifty years. The father was a Union man. He was persecuted in all sorts of ways, but clung to his principles. At last one night masked men burned his mansion down, and the family had to fly for their lives. They were hunted from place to place, and learned all there was to know about poverty, hunger, and distress. The invalid aunt found relief at last: misery and exposure killed her; she died in an open field, like a tramp, the rain beating upon her and the thunder booming overhead. Not long afterward the father was captured by an armed band; and while the son begged and pleaded, the victim was strung up before his face. [At this point a baleful light shone in the youth's eyes, and he said, with the manner of one who talks to himself: "If I cannot be enlisted, no matter—I shall find a way—I shall find a way."] As soon as the father was pronounced dead, the son was told that if he was not out of that region within twenty-four hours it would go hard with him. That night he crept to the riverside and hid himself near a plantation landing. By and by the *Duncan F. Kenner* stopped there, and he swam out and concealed himself in the yawl that was dragging at her stern. Before daylight the boat reached the Stock Landing and he slipped ashore. He walked the three miles which lay between that point and the house of an uncle of his in Good Children Street, in New Orleans, and then his troubles were over for the time being. But this uncle was a Union man, too, and before very long he concluded that he had better leave the South. So he and young Wicklow slipped out of the country on board a sailing vessel, and in due time reached New York. They put up at the Astor House. Young Wicklow had a good time of it for a while, strolling up and down Broadway, and observing the strange Northern sights; but in the end a change came—and not for the better. The uncle had been cheerful at first, but now he began to look troubled and despondent; moreover, he became moody and irritable; talked of money giving out, and no way to get more—"not enough left for one, let alone two." Then, one morning, he was missing—did not come to breakfast. The boy inquired at the office, and was told that the uncle had paid his bill the night before and gone away—to Boston, the clerk believed, but was not certain.

The lad was alone and friendless. He did not know what to do, but concluded he had better try to follow and find his uncle. He went down to the steamboat landing; learned that the trifle of money in his pocket would not carry him to Boston; however, it would carry him to New London; so he took passage for that port, resolving to trust to Providence to furnish him means to travel the rest of the way. He had now been wandering about the streets of New London three days and nights, getting a bite and a nap here and there for charity's sake. But he had given up at last; courage and hope were both gone. If he could enlist, nobody could be more thankful; if he could not get in as a soldier, couldn't he be a drummer-boy? Ah, he would work *so* hard to please, and would be so grateful!

Well, there's the history of young Wicklow, just as he told it to me, barring details. I said:

My boy, you are among friends now—don't you be troubled any more." How his eyes glistened! I called in Sergeant John Rayburn—he was from Hartford; lives in Hartford yet; maybe you know him—and said, "Rayburn, quarter this boy with the musicians. I am going to enroll him as a drummer-boy, and I want you to look after him and see that he is well treated."

Well, of course, intercourse between the commandant of the post and the drummer-boy came to an end now; but the poor little friendless chap lay heavy on my heart just the same. I kept on the lookout, hoping to see him brighten up and begin to be cheery and gay; but no, the days went by, and there was no change. He associated with nobody; he was always absentminded, always thinking; his face was always sad. One morning Rayburn asked leave to speak to me privately. Said he:

"I hope I don't offend, sir; but the truth is, the musicians are in such a sweat it seems as if somebody's *got* to speak."

"Why, what is the trouble?'"

"It's the Wicklow boy, sir. The musicians are down on him to an extent you can't imagine."

"Well, go on, go on. What has he been doing?"

"Prayin', sir."

"Praying!"

"Yes, sir; the musicians haven't any peace of their life for that boy's prayin'. First thing in the mornin' he's at it; noons he's at it; and nights— well, *nights* he just lays into 'em like all possessed! Sleep? Bless you, they *can't* sleep; he's got the floor, as the sayin' is, and then when he once gets his supplication-mill agoin' there just simply ain't any let-up *to* him. He starts in with the bandmaster, and he prays for him; next he takes the head bugler, and he prays for him; next the bass drum, and he scoops *him* in; and so on, right straight through the band, givin' them all a show, and takin' that amount of interest in it which would make you think he thought he warn't but a little while for this world, and believed he couldn't be happy in heaven without he had a brass band along, and wanted to pick 'em out for himself, so he could depend on 'em to do up the national tunes in a style suitin' to the place. Well, sir, heavin' boots at him don't have no effect; it's dark in there; and, besides, he don't pray fair, anyway, but kneels down behind the big drum; so it don't make no difference if they *rain* boots at him, *he* don't give a dern—warbles right along, same as if it was applause. They sing out, 'Oh, take a walk!' and all sorts of such things. But what of it? It don't faze him. *He* don't mind it." After a pause: "Kind of a good little fool, too; fits up in the mornin' and carts all that stock of boots back, and sorts 'em out and sets each man's pair where they belong. And they've been throwed at him so much now that he knows every boot in the band—can sort 'em out with his eyes shut."

After another pause, which I forbore to interrupt:

"But the roughest thing about it is that when he's done prayin'—when he ever *does* get done—he pipes up and begins to *sing*. Well, you know what a honey kind of voice he's got when he talks; you know how it would persuade a cast-iron dog to come down off of a doorstep and lick his hand. Now if you'll take my word for it, sir, it ain't a circumstance to his singin'! Flute music is harsh to that boy's singin'. Oh, he just gurgles it out so soft and sweet and low, there in the dark, that it makes you think you are in heaven."

"What is there 'rough' about that?"

"Ah, that's just it, sir. You hear him sing

'Just as I am—poor, wretched, blind'—

just you hear him sing that once, and see if you don't melt all up and the water come into your eyes! I don't care *what* he sings, it goes plum straight home to you—it goes deep down to where you *live*—and it fetches you every time! Just you hear him sing

'Child of sin and sorrow, filled with dismay,
Wait not till tomorrow, yield thee today;
Grieve not that love
Which, from above' —

and so on. It makes a body feel like the wickedest, ungratefulest brute
that walks. And when he sings them songs of his about home, and mother,
and childhood, and old memories, and things that's vanished, and old
friends dead and gone, it fetches everything before your face that you've
ever loved and lost in all your life—and it's just beautiful, it's just divine
to listen to, sir—but, Lord, Lord, the heartbreak of it! The band—well,
they all cry—every rascal of them blubbers, and don't try to hide it,
either; and first you know, that very gang that's been slammin' boots at
that boy will skip out of their bunks all of a sudden, and rush over in the
dark and hug him! Yes, they do—and slobber all over him, and call him
pet names, and beg him to forgive them. And just at that time, if a
regiment was to offer to hurt a hair of that cub's head, they'd go for that
regiment, if it was a whole army corps!"

Another pause.

"Is that all?" said I.

"Yes, sir."

"Well, dear me, what is the complaint? What do they want done?"

"Done? Why, bless you, sir, they want you to stop him from *singin'.*"

"What an idea! You said his music was divine."

"That's just it. It's *too* divine. Mortal man can't stand it. It stirs a body
up so; it turns a body inside out; it racks his feelin's all to rags; it makes
him feel bad and wicked, and not fit for any place but perdition. It keeps
a body in such an everlastin' state of repentin', that nothin' don't taste
good and there ain't no comfort in life. And then the *cryin',* you see—
every mornin' they are ashamed to look one another in the face."

"Well, this is an odd case, and a singular complaint. So they really
want the singing stopped?"

"Yes, sir, that is the idea. They don't wish to ask too much; they would
like powerful well to have the prayin' shut down on, or leastways trimmed
off around the edges; but the main thing's the singin'. If they can only
get the singin' chocked off, they think they can stand the prayin', rough
as it is to be bullyragged so much that way."

I told the sergeant I would take the matter under consideration. That
night I crept into the musicians' quarters and listened. The sergeant had
not overstated the case. I heard the praying voice pleading in the dark; I

heard the execrations of the harassed men; I heard the rain of boots whiz through the air, and bang and thump around the big drum. The thing touched me, but it amused, me, too. By and by, after an impressive silence, came the singing. Lord, the pathos of it, the enchantment of it! Nothing in the world was ever so sweet, so gracious, so tender, so holy, so moving. I made my stay very brief; I was beginning to experience emotions of a sort not proper to the commandant of a fortress.

Next day I issued orders which stopped the praying and singing. Then followed three or four days which were so full of bounty-jumping excitements and irritations that I never once thought of my drummer-boy. But now comes Sergeant Rayburn, one morning, and says:

"That new boy acts mighty strange, sir."

"How?"

"Well, sir, he's all the time writin'."

"Writing? What does he write—letters?"

"I don't know, sir; but whenever he's off duty, he is always pokin' and nosin' around the fort, all by himself—blest if I think there's a hole or corner in it he hasn't been into—and every little while he outs with pencil and paper and scribbles somethin' down."

This gave me a most unpleasant sensation. I wanted to scoff at it, but it was not a time to scoff at *anything* that had the least suspicious tinge about it. Things were happening all around us in the North then that warned us to be always on the alert, and always suspecting. I recalled to mind the suggestive fact that this boy was from the South—the extreme South, Louisiana—and the thought was not of a reassuring nature, under the circumstances. Nevertheless, it cost me a pang to give the orders which I now gave to Rayburn. I felt like a father who plots to expose his own child to shame and injury. I told Rayburn to keep quiet, bide his time, and get me some of those writings whenever he could manage it without the boy's finding it out. And I charged him not to do anything which might let the boy discover that he was being watched. I also ordered that he allow the lad his usual liberties, but that he be followed at a distance when he went out into the town.

During the next two days Rayburn reported to me several times. No success. The boy was still writing, but he always pocketed his paper with a careless air whenever Rayburn appeared in the vicinity. He had gone twice to an old deserted stable in the town, remained a minute or two, and come out again. One could not pooh-pooh these things—they had an evil look. I was obliged to confess to myself that I was getting uneasy. I went into my private quarters and sent for my second in command—an officer of intelligence and judgment, son of General James Watson Webb.

He was surprised and troubled. We had a long talk over the matter, and came to the conclusion that it would be worthwhile to institute a secret search. I determined to take charge of that myself. So I had myself called at two in the morning; and pretty soon after I was in the musicians' quarters, crawling along the floor on my stomach among the snorers. I reached my slumbering waif's bunk at last, without disturbing anybody, captured his clothes and kit, and crawled stealthily back again. When I got to my own quarters, I found Webb there, waiting and eager to know the result. We made search immediately. The clothes were a disappointment. In the pockets we found blank paper and a pencil; nothing else, except a jackknife and such queer odds and ends and useless trifles as boys hoard and value. We turned to the kit hopefully. Nothing there but a rebuke for us!—a little Bible with this written on the flyleaf: "Stranger, be kind to my boy, for his mother's sake."

I looked at Webb—he dropped his eyes; he looked at me—I dropped mine. Neither spoke. I put the book reverently back in its place. Presently Webb got up and went away, without remark. After a little I nerved myself up to my unpalatable job, and took the plunder back to where it belonged, crawling on my stomach as before. It seemed the peculiarly appropriate attitude for the business I was in.

I was most honestly glad when it was over and done with.

About noon next day Rayburn came, as usual, to report. I cut him short. I said:

"Let this nonsense be dropped. We are making a bugaboo out of a poor little cub who has got no more harm in him than a hymn book."

The sergeant looked surprised, and said:

"Well, you know it was your orders, sir, and I've got some of the writin'."

"And what does it amount to? How did you get it?"

"I peeped through the keyhole, and see him writin'. So, when I judged he was about done, I made a sort of a little cough, and I see him crumple it up and throw it in the fire, and look all around to see if anybody was comin'. Then he settled back as comfortable and careless as anything. Then I comes in, and passes the time of day pleasantly, and sends him on an errand. He never looked uneasy, but went right along. It was a coal fire and new built; the writin' had gone over behind a chunk, out of sight; but I got it out; there it is; it ain't hardly scorched, you see."

I glanced at the paper and took in a sentence or two. Then I dismissed the sergeant and told him to send Webb to me. Here is the paper in full:

FORT TRUMBULL, *the 8th.*
COLONEL *I was mistaken as to the caliber of the three guns I ended my list with. They are 18-pounders; all the rest of the armament is as I stated. The garrison remains as before reported, except that the two light infantry companies that were to be detached for service at the front are to stay here for the present—can't find out for how long, just now, but will soon. We are satisfied that, all things considered, matters had better be postponed un—*

There it broke off—there is where Rayburn coughed and interrupted the writer. All my affection for the boy, all my respect for him and charity for his forlorn condition, withered in a moment under the blight of this revelation of cold-blooded baseness.

But never mind about that. Here was business—business that required profound and immediate attention, too. Webb and I turned the subject over and over, and examined it all around. Webb said:

"What a pity he was interrupted! Something is going to be postponed until—when? And what *is* the something? Possibly he would have mentioned it, the pious little reptile!"

"Yes," I said, "we have missed a trick. And who is *'we'* in the letter? Is it conspirators inside the fort or outside?"

That "we" was uncomfortably suggestive. However, it was not worthwhile to be guessing around that, so we proceeded to matters more practical. In the first place, we decided to double the sentries and keep the strictest possible watch. Next, we thought of calling Wicklow in and making him divulge everything; but that did not seem wisest until other methods should fail. We must have some more of the writings; so we began to plan to that end. And now we had an idea: Wicklow never went to the post office—perhaps the deserted stable was his post office. We sent for my confidential clerk—a young German name Sterne, who was a sort of natural detective—and told him all about the case, and ordered him to go to work on it. Within the hour we got word that Wicklow was writing again. Shortly afterward word came that he had asked leave to go out into the town. He was detained awhile and meantime Sterne hurried off and concealed himself in the stable. By and by he saw Wicklow saunter in, look about him, then hide something under some rubbish in a corner, and take leisurely leave again. Sterne pounced upon the hidden article—a letter—and brought it to us. It had no superscription and no signature. It repeated what we had already read, and then went on to say:

We think it best to postpone till the two companies are gone. I mean the four inside think so; have not communicated with the others—afraid of attracting attention. I say four because we have lost two; they had hardly enlisted and got inside when they were shipped off to the front. It will be absolutely necessary to have two in their places. The two that went were the brothers from Thirty-mile Point. I have something of the greatest importance to reveal, but must not trust it to this method of communication; will try the other.

"The little scoundrel!" said Webb; "who *could* have supposed he was a spy? However, never mind about that; let us add up our particulars, such as they are, and see how the case stands to date. First, we've got a rebel spy in our midst, whom we know; secondly, we've got three more in our midst whom we don't know; thirdly, these spies have been introduced among us through the simple and easy process of enlisting as soldiers in the Union army—and evidently two of them have got sold at it, and been shipped off to the front; fourthly, there are assistant spies 'outside'—number indefinite; fifthly, Wicklow has very important matter which he is afraid to communicate by the 'present method'—will 'try the other.' That is the case, as it now stands. Shall we collar Wicklow and make him confess? Or shall we catch the person who removes the letters from the stable and make *him* tell? Or shall we keep still and find out more?"

We decided upon the last course. We judged that we did not need to proceed to summary measures now, since it was evident that the conspirators were likely to wait till those two light infantry companies were out of the way. We fortified Sterne with pretty ample powers, and told him to use his best endeavors to find out Wicklow's "other method" of communication. We meant to play a bold game; and to this end we proposed to keep the spies in an unsuspecting state as long as possible. So we ordered Sterne to return to the stable immediately, and, if he found the coast clear, to conceal Wicklow's letter where it was before, and leave it there for the consiprators to get.

The night closed down without further event. It was cold and dark and sleety, with a raw wind blowing; still I turned out of my warm bed several times during the night, and went the rounds in person, to see that all was right and that every sentry was on the alert. I always found them wide awake and watchful; evidently whispers of mysterious dangers had been floating about, and the doubling of the guards had been a kind of endorsement of those rumors. Once, toward morning, I encountered Webb, breasting his way against the bitter wind, and learned then that he, also, had been the rounds several times to see that all was going right.

Next day's events hurried things up somewhat. Wicklow wrote another letter; Sterne preceded him to the stable and saw him deposit it; captured it as soon as Wicklow was out of the way, then slipped out and followed the little spy at a distance, with a detective in plainclothes at his own heels, for we thought it judicious to have the law's assistance handy in case of need. Wicklow went to the railway station, and waited around till the train from New York came in, then stood scanning the faces of the crowd as they poured out of the cars. Presently an aged gentleman, with green goggles and a cane, came limping along, stopped in Wicklow's neighborhood, and began to look about him expectantly. In an instant Wicklow darted forward, thrust an envelope into his hand, then glided away and disappeared in the throng. The next instant Sterne had snatched the letter; and as he hurried past the detective, he said: "Follow the old gentleman—don't lose sight of him." Then Sterne scurried out with the crowd, and came straight to the fort.

We sat with closed doors, and instructed the guard outside to allow no interruption.

First we opened the letter captured at the stable. It read as follows:

HOLY ALLIANCE *Found, in the usual gun, commands from the Master, left there last night, which set aside the instructions heretofore received from the subordinate quarter. Have left in the gun the usual indication that the commands reached the proper hand—*

Webb, interrupting: "Isn't the boy under constant surveillance now?"

I said yes; he had been under strict surveillance ever since the capturing of his former letter.

"Then how could he put anything into a gun, or take anything out of it, and not get caught?"

Well," I said, "I don't like the look of that very well."

"I don't either," said Webb. "It simply means that there are conspirators among the very sentinels. Without their connivance in some way or other, the thing couldn't have been done."

I sent for Rayburn, and ordered him to examine the batteries and see what he could find. The reading of the letter was then resumed:

*The new commands are peremptory, and require that the MMMM shall
be FFFFF at 3 o'clock tomorrow morning. Two hundred will arrive, in
small parties, by train and otherwise, from various directions, and will
be at appointed place at right time. I will distribute the sign today.
Success is apparently sure, though something must have got out, for the
sentries have been doubled, and the chiefs went the rounds last night
several times. W. W. comes from southerly today and will receive secret
orders—by the other method. All six of you must be in 166 at sharp 2
A.M. You will find B. B. there, who will give you detailed instruction,
Passwords same as last time, only reversed—put first syllable last and
last syllable first. REMEMBER XXXX. Do not forget. Be of good heart;
before the next sun rises you will be heroes; your fame will be permanent;
you will have added a deathless page to history. AMEN.*

"Thunder and Mars," said Webb, "but we are getting into mighty hot
quarters, as I look at it!"

I said there was no question but that things were beginning to wear a
most serious aspect. Said I:

"A desperate enterprise is on foot, that is plain enough. Tonight is the
time set for it—that, also, is plain. The exact nature of the enterprise—I
mean the manner of it—is hidden away under those blind bunches of M's
and F's, but the end and aim, I judge, is the surprise and capture of the
post. We must move quick and sharp now. I think nothing can be gained
by continuing our clandestine policy as regards Wicklow. We *must* know,
and as soon as possible, too, where '166' is located, so that we can make
a descent upon the gang there at 2 A.M.; and doubtless the quickest way
to get that information will be to force it out of that boy. But first of all,
and before we make any important move, I must lay the facts before the
War Department, and ask for plenary powers."

The dispatch was prepared in cipher to go over the wires; I read it,
approved it, and sent it along.

We presently finished discussing the letter which was under consideration, and then opened the one which had been snatched from the lame
gentleman. It contained nothing but a couple of perfectly blank sheets of
notepaper! It was a chilly check to our hot eagerness and expectancy.
We felt as blank as the paper, for a moment, and twice as foolish. But it
was for a moment only; for, of course, we immediately afterward thought
of "sympathetic ink." We held the paper close to the fire and watched for

the characters to come out, under the influence of the heat; but nothing appeared but some faint tracings, which we could make nothing of. We then called in the surgeon, and sent him off with orders to apply every test he was acquainted with till he got the right one, and report the contents of the letter to me the instant he brought them to the surface. This check was a confounded annoyance, and we naturally chafed under the delay; for we had fully expected to get out of that letter some of the most important secrets of the plot.

Now appeared Sergeant Rayburn, and drew from his pocket a piece of twine string about a foot long, with three knots tied in it, and held it up.

"I got it out of a gun on the waterfront," said he. "I took the tompions out of all the guns and examined close; this string was the only thing that was in any gun."

So this bit of string was Wicklow's "sign" to signify that the "Master's" commands had not miscarried. I ordered that every sentinel who had served near that gun during the past twenty-four hours be put in confinement at once and separately, and not allowed to communicate with any one without my privity and consent.

A telegram now came from the Secretary of War. It read as follows:

Suspend habeas corpus. Put town under martial law. Make necessary arrests. Act with vigor and promptness. Keep the department informed.

We were now in shape to go to work. I sent out and had the lame gentleman quietly arrested and as quietly brought into the fort; I placed him under guard, and forbade speech to him or from him. He was inclined to bluster at first, but he soon dropped that.

Next came word that Wicklow had been seen to give something to a couple of our new recruits; and that, as soon as his back was turned, these had been seized and confined. Upon each was found a small bit of paper, bearing these words and signs in pencil:

EAGLE'S THIRD FLIGHT
REMEMBER XXXX
166

In accordance with instructions, I telegraphed to the Department, in cipher, the progress made, and also described the above ticket. We seemed to be in a strong enough position now to venture to throw off the mask as regarded Wicklow; so I sent for him. I also sent for and received back the letter written in sympathetic ink, the surgeon accompanying it with the information that thus far it had resisted his tests, but that there were others he could apply when I should be ready for him to do so.

Presently Wicklow entered. He had a somewhat worn and anxious look, but he was composed and easy, and if he suspected anything it did not appear in his face or manner. I allowed him to stand there a moment or two; then I said pleasantly:

"My boy, why do you go to that old stable so much?"

He answered, with simple demeanor and without embarrassment:

"Well, I hardly know, sir; there isn't any particular reason, except that I like to be alone, and I amuse myself there."

"You amuse yourself there, do you?"

"Yes, sir," he replied, as innocently and simply as before.

"Is that all you do there?"

"Yes, sir," he said, looking up with childlike wonderment in his big, soft eyes.

"You are *sure*?"

"Yes, sir, sure."

After a pause I said:

"Wicklow, why do you write so much?"

"I? I do not write much, sir."

"You don't?"

"No, sir. Oh, if you mean scribbling, I *do* scribble some, for amusement."

"What do you do with your scribblings?"

"Nothing, sir—throw them away."

"Never send them to anybody?"

"No, sir."

I suddenly thrust before him the letter to the "Colonel." He started slightly, but immediately composed himself. A slight tinge spread itself over his cheek.

"How came you to send *this* piece of scribbling, then?"

"I nev—never meant any harm, sir!"

"Never meant any harm! You betray the armament and condition of the post, and mean no harm by it?"

He hung his head and was silent.

"Come, speak up, and stop lying. Whom was this letter intended for?"

He showed signs of distress now; but quickly collected himself, and replied, in a tone of deep earnestness:

"I will tell you the truth, sir—the whole truth. The letter was never intended for anybody at all. I wrote it only to amuse myself. I see the error and foolishness of it now; but it is the only offense, sir, upon my honor."

"Ah, I am glad of that. It is dangerous to be writing such letters. I hope you are sure this is the only one you wrote?"

"Yes, sir, perfectly sure."

His hardihood was stupefying. He told that lie with as sincere a countenance as any creature ever wore. I waited a moment to soothe down my rising temper, and then said:

"Wicklow, jog your memory now, and see if you can help me with two or three little matters which I wish to inquire about."

"I will do my very best, sir."

"Then, to begin with—who is 'the Master'?"

It betrayed him into darting a startled glance at our faces, but that was all. He was serene again in a moment, and tranquilly answered:

"I do not know, sir."

"You do not know?"

"I do not know."

"You are *sure* you do not know?"

He tried hard to keep his eyes on mine, but the strain was too great; his chin sunk slowly toward his breast and he was silent; he stood there nervously fumbling with a button, an object to command one's pity, in spite of his base acts. Presently I broke the stillness with the question:

"Who are the 'Holy Alliance'?"

His body shook visibly, and he made a slight random gesture with his hands, which to me was like the appeal of a despairing creature for compassion. But he made no sound. He continued to stand with his face bent toward the ground. As we sat gazing at him, waiting for him to speak, we saw the big tears begin to roll down his cheeks. But he remained silent. After a little, I said:

"You must answer me, my boy, and you must tell me the truth. Who are the Holy Alliance?"

He wept on in silence. Presently I said, somewhat sharply:

"Answer the question!"

He struggled to get command of his voice; and then, looking up appealingly, forced the words out between his sobs:

"Oh, have pity on me, sir! I cannot answer it, for I do not know."

"What!"

"Indeed, sir, I am telling the truth. I never have heard of the Holy Alliance till this moment. On my honor, sir, this is so."

"Good heavens! Look at this second letter of yours; there, do you see those words, *'Holy Alliance'?* What do you say now?"

He gazed up into my face with the hurt look of one upon whom a great wrong had been wrought, then said, feelingly:

"This is some cruel joke, sir; and how could they play it upon me, who have tried all I could to do right, and have never done harm to anybody? Someone has counterfeited my hand; I never wrote a line of this; I have never seen this letter before!"

"Oh, you unspeakable liar! Here, what do you say to *this?*"—and I snatched the sympathetic-ink letter from my pocket and thrust it before his eyes.

His face turned white—as white as a dead person's. He wavered slightly in his tracks, and put his hand against the wall to steady himself. After a moment he asked, in so faint a voice that it was hardly audible:

"Have you—read it?"

Our faces must have answered the truth before my lips could get out a false "yes," for I distinctly saw the courage come back into that boy's eyes. I waited for him to say something, but he kept silent. So at last I said:

"Well, what have you to say as to the revelations in this letter?"

He answered, with perfect composure:

"Nothing, except that they are entirely harmless and innocent; they can hurt nobody."

I was in something of a corner now, as I couldn't disprove his assertion. I did not know exactly how to proceed. However, an idea came to my relief, and I said:

"You are sure you know nothing about the Master and the Holy Alliance, and did not write the letter which you say is a forgery?"

"Yes, sir—sure."

I slowly drew out the knotted twine string and held it up without speaking. He gazed at it indifferently, then looked at me inquiringly. My patience was sorely taxed. However, I kept my temper down, and said, in my usual voice:

"Wicklow, do you see this?"

"Yes, sir."

"What is it?"

"It seems to be a piece of string."

"*Seems?* It *is* a piece of string. Do you recognize it?

"No, sir," he replied, as calmly as the words could be uttered.

His coolness was perfectly wonderful! I paused now for several seconds, in order that the silence might add impressiveness to what I was about to say; then I rose and laid my hand on his shoulder, and said gravely:

"It will do you no good, poor boy, none in the world. This sign to the 'Master,' this knotted string, found in one of the guns on the waterfront—"

"Found *in* the gun! Oh, no, no, no! do not say *in* the gun, but in a crack in the tompion—it *must* have been in the crack!" and down he went on his knees and clasped his hands and lifted up a face that was pitiful to see, so ashy it was, and wild with terror.

"No, it was *in* the gun."

"Oh, something has gone wrong! My God, I am lost!" and he sprang up and darted this way and that, dodging the hands that were put out to catch him, and doing his best to escape from the place. But of course escape was impossible. Then he flung himself on his knees again, crying with all his might, and clasped me around the legs; and so he clung to me and begged and pleaded, saying, "Oh, have pity on me! Oh, be merciful to me! Do not betray me; they would not spare my life a moment! Protect me, save me, I will confess everything!"

It took us some time to quiet him down and modify his fright, and get him into something like a rational frame of mind. Then I began to question him, he answering humbly, with downcast eyes, and from time to time swabbing away his constantly flowing tears:

"So you are at heart a rebel?"

"Yes, sir."

"And a spy?"

"Yes, sir."

"And have been acting under distinct orders from outside?"

"Yes, sir."

"Willingly?"

"Yes, sir."

"*Gladly,* perhaps?"

"Yes, sir; it would do no good to deny it. The South is my country; my heart is Southern, and it is all in her cause."

"Then the tale you told me of your wrongs and the persecution of your family was made up for the occasion?"

"They—they told me to say it, sir."

"And you would betray and destroy those who pitied and sheltered you. Do you comprehend how base you are, you poor misguided thing?"

He replied with sobs only.

"Well, let that pass. To business. Who is the 'Colonel,' and where is he?"

He began to cry hard, and tried to beg off from answering. He said he would be killed if he told. I threatened to put him in the dark cell and lock him up if he did not come out with the information. At the same time I promised to protect him from all harm if he made a clean breast. For all answer, he closed his mouth firmly and put on a stubborn air which I could not bring him out of. At last I started with him; but a single glance into the dark cell converted him. He broke into a passion of weeping and supplicating, and declared he would tell everything.

So I brought him back, and he named the "Colonel," and described him particularly. Said he would be found at the principal hotel in the town, in citizen's dress. I had to threaten him again, before he would describe and name the "Master." Said the Master would be found at No. 15 Bond Street, New York, passing under the name of R. F. Gaylord. I telegraphed name and description to the chief of police of the metropolis, and asked that Gaylord be arrested and held till I could send for him.

"Now," said I, "it seems that there are several of the conspirators 'outside,' presumably in New London. Name and describe them."

He named and described three men and two women—all stopping at the principal hotel. I sent out quietly, and had them and the "Colonel" arrested and confined in the fort.

"Next, I want to know all about your three fellow-conspirators who are here in the fort."

He was about to dodge me with a falsehood, I thought; but I produced the mysterious bits of paper which had been found upon two of them, and this had a salutary effect upon him. I said we had possession of two of the men, and he must point out the third. This frightened him badly, and he cried out:

"Oh, please don't make me; he would kill me on the spot!"

I said that that was all nonsense; I would have somebody nearby to protect him, and, besides, the men should be assembled without arms. I ordered all the raw recruits to be mustered, and then the poor, trembling little wretch went out and stepped along down the line, trying to look as indifferent as possible. Finally he spoke a single word to one of the men, and before he had gone five steps the man was under arrest.

As soon as Wicklow was with us again, I had those three men brought in. I made one of them stand forward, and said:

"Now, Wicklow, mind, not a shade's divergence from the exact truth. Who is this man, and what do you know about him?"

Being "in for it," he cast consequences aside, fastened his eyes on the man's face, and spoke straight along without hesitation—to the following effect:

"His real name is George Bristow. He is from New Orleans; was second mate of the coast-packet *Capitol* two years ago; is a desperate character, and has served two terms for manslaughter—one for killing a deckhand named Hyde with a capstan-bar, and one for killing a roustabout for refusing to heave the lead, which is no part of a roustabout's business. He is a spy, and was sent here by the Colonel to act in that capacity. He was third mate of the *St. Nicholas* when she blew up in the neighborhood of Memphis, in '58, and came near being lynched for robbing the dead and wounded while they were being taken ashore in an empty wood-boat."

And so forth and so on—he gave the man's biography in full. When he had finished, I said to the man:

"What have you to say to this?"

"Barring your presence, sir, it is the infernalist lie that ever was spoke!"

I sent him back into confinement, and called the others forward in turn. Same result. The boy gave a detailed history of each, without ever hesitating for a word or a fact; but all I could get out of either rascal was the indignant assertion that it was all a lie.

They would confess nothing. I returned them to captivity, and brought out the rest of my prisoners, one by one. Wicklow told all about them—what towns in the South they were from, and every detail of their connection with the conspiracy.

But they all denied his facts, and not one of them confessed a thing. The men raged, the women cried. According to their stories, they were all innocent people from out West, and loved the Union above all things in this world. I locked the gang up, in disgust, and fell to catechizing Wicklow once more.

"Where is No. 166, and who is B. B.?"

But *there* he was determined to draw the line. Neither coaxing nor threats had any effect upon him. Time was flying—it was necessary to institute sharp measures. So I tied him up a-tiptoe by the thumbs. As the pain increased, it wrung screams from him which were almost more than I could bear. But I held my ground, and pretty soon he shrieked out:

"Oh, *please* let me down, and I will tell!"

"No—you'll tell *before* I let you down."

"Every instant was agony to him now, so out it came:

"No. 166, Eagle Hotel!"—naming a wretched tavern down by the water, a resort of common laborers, longshoremen, and less reputable folk.

So I released him, and then demanded to know the object of the conspiracy.

"To take the fort tonight," said he, doggedly and sobbing.

"Have I got all the chiefs of the conspiracy?"

"No. You've got all except those that are to meet at 166."

"What does 'Remember XXXX' mean?"

No reply.

"What is the password to No. 166?"

No reply.

"What do those bunches of letters mean—'FFFFF' and 'MMMM'? Answer! or you will catch it again."

"I never *will* answer! I will die first. Now do what you please."

"Think what you are saying, Wicklow. Is it final?"

He answered steadily, and without a quiver in his voice:

"It is final. As sure as I love my wronged country and hate everything this Northern sun shines on, I will die before I will reveal those things."

I tied him up by the thumbs again. When the agony was full upon him it was heartbreaking to hear the poor thing's shrieks, but we got nothing else out of him. To every question he screamed the same reply: "I can die, and I *will* die; but I will never tell."

Well, we had to give it up. We were convinced that he certainly would die rather than confess. So we took him down, and imprisoned him under strict guard.

Then for some hours we busied ourselves with sending telegrams to the War Department, and with making preparations for a descent upon No. 166.

It was stirring times, that black and bitter night. Things had leaked out, and the whole garrison was on the alert. The sentinels were trebled, and nobody could move, outside or in, without being brought to a stand with a musket leveled at his head. However, Webb and I were less concerned now than we had previously been, because of the fact that the conspiracy must necessarily be in a pretty crippled condition, since so many of its principals were in our clutches.

I determined to be at No. 166 in good season, capture and gag B. B., and be on hand for the rest when they arrived. At about a quarter past one in the morning I crept out of the fortress with half a dozen stalwart and gamy U. S. regulars at my heels, and the boy Wicklow, with his hands tied behind him. I told him we were going to No. 166, and that if I found he had lied again and was misleading us, he would have to show us the right place or suffer the consequences.

We approached the tavern stealthily and reconnoitered. A light was burning in the small barroom, the rest of the house was dark. I tried the front door; it yielded, and we softly entered, closing the door behind us. Then we removed our shoes, and I led the way to the barroom. The German landlord sat there, asleep in his chair. I woke him gently, and told him to take off his boots and precede us, warning him at the same time to utter no sound. He obeyed without a murmur, but evidently he was badly frightened. I ordered him to lead the way to 166. We ascended two or three flights of stairs as softly as a file of cats; and then, having arrived near the farther end of a long hall, we came to a door through the glazed transom of which we could discern the glow of a dim light from within. The landlord felt for me in the dark and whispered to me that that was 166. I tried the door—it was locked on the inside. I whispered an order to one of my biggest soldiers; we set our ample shoulders to the door, and with one heave we burst it from its hinges. I caught a half-glimpse of a figure in a bed—saw its head dart toward the candle; out went the light and we were in pitch darkness. With one big bound I lit on that bed and pinned its occupant down with my knees. My prisoner struggled fiercely, but I got a grip on his throat with my left hand, and that was a good assistance to my knees in holding him down. Then straightway I snatched out my revolver, cocked it, and laid the cold barrel warningly against his cheek.

"Now somebody strike a light!" said I. "I've got him safe."

It was done. The flame of the match burst up. I looked at my captive, and, by George, it was a young woman!

I let go and got off the bed, feeling pretty sheepish. Everybody stared stupidly at his neighbor. Nobody had any wit or sense left, so sudden and overwhelming had been the surprise. The young woman began to cry, and covered her face with the sheet. The landlord said, meekly:

"My daughter, she has been doing something that is not right, *nicht wahr?*"

"Your daughter? Is she your daughter?"

"Oh, yes, she is my daughter. She is just tonight come home from Cincinnati a little bit sick."

"Confound it, that boy has lied again. This is not the right 166; this is not B. B. Now, Wicklow, you will find the correct 166 for us, or—hello! where is that boy?"

Gone, as sure as guns! And, what is more, we failed to find a trace of him. Here was an awful predicament. I cursed my stupidity in not tying him to one of the men; but it was of no use to bother about that now. What should I do in the present circumstances?—that was the question. That girl *might* be B. B., after all. I did not believe it, but still it would not answer to take unbelief for proof. So I finally put my men in a vacant room across the hall from 166, and told them to capture anybody and everybody that approached the girl's room, and to keep the landlord with them, and under strict watch, until further orders. Then I hurried back to the fort to see if all was right there yet.

Yes, all was right. And all remained right. I stayed up all night to make sure of that. Nothing happened. I was unspeakably glad to see the dawn come again, and be able to telegraph the Department that the Stars and Stripes still floated over Fort Trumbull.

An immense pressure was lifted from my breast. Still I did not relax vigilance, of course, nor effort, either; the case was too grave for that. I had up my prisoners, one by one, and harried them by the hour, trying to get them to confess, but it was a failure. They only gnashed their teeth and tore their hair, and revealed nothing.

About noon came tidings of my missing boy. He had been seen on the road, tramping westward, some eight miles out, at six in the morning. I started a cavalry lieutenant and a private on his track at once. They came in sight of him twenty miles out. He had climbed a fence and was wearily dragging himself across a slushy field toward a large old-fashioned mansion on the edge of a village. They rode through a bit of woods, made a detour, and closed upon the house from the opposite side; then dismounted and skurried into the kitchen. Nobody there. They slipped into the next room, which was also unoccupied; the door from that room into the front or sitting room was open. They were about to step through it when they heard a low voice; it was somebody praying. So they halted reverently, and the lieutenant put his head in and saw an old man and an old woman kneeling in a corner of that sitting-room. It was the old man that was praying, and just as he was finishing his prayer, the Wicklow boy opened the front door and stepped in. Both of those old people sprang at him and smothered him with embraces, shouting:

"Our boy! our darling! God be praised. The lost is found! He that was dead is alive again!"

Well, sir, what do you think! That young imp was born and reared on that homestead, and had never been five miles away from it in all his life till the fortnight before he loafed into my quarters and gulled me with that maudlin yarn of his! It's as true as gospel. That old man was his father—a learned old retired clergyman; and that old lady was his mother.

Let me throw in a word or two of explanation concerning that boy and his performances. It turned out that he was a ravenous devourer of dime novels and sensation-story papers—therefore, dark mysteries and gaudy heroisms were just in his line. Then he had read newspaper reports of the stealthy goings and comings of rebel spies in our midst, and of their lurid purposes and their two or three startling achievements, till his imagination was all aflame on that subject. His constant comrade for some months had been a Yankee youth of much tongue and lively fancy, who had served for a couple of years as "mud clerk" (that is, subordinate purser) on certain of the packet-boats plying between New Orleans and points two or three hundred miles up the Mississippi—hence his easy facility in handling the names and other details pertaining to that region. Now I had spent two or three months in that part of the country before the war; and I knew just enough about it to be easily taken in by that boy, whereas a born Louisianian would probably have caught him tripping before he had talked fifteen minutes. Do you know the reason he said he would rather die than explain certain of his treasonable enigmas? Simply because he *couldn't* explain them!—they had no meaning; he had fired them out of his imagination without forethought or afterthought; and so, upon sudden call, he wasn't able to invent an explanation of them. For instance, he couldn't reveal what was hidden in the "sympathetic ink" letter, for the ample reason that there wasn't anything hidden in it; it was blank paper only. He hadn't put anything into a gun, and had never intended to—for his letters were all written to imaginary persons, and when he hid one in the stable he always removed the one he had put there the day before; so he was not acquainted with that knotted string, since he was seeing it for the first time when I showed it to him; but as soon as I had let him find out where it came from, he straightway adopted it, in his romantic fashion, and got some fine effects out of it. He invented the "Gaylord"; there wasn't any 15 Bond Street, just then—it had been pulled down three months before. He invented the "Colonel"; he invented the glib histories of those unfortunates whom I captured and confronted him with; he invented "B. B."; he even invented No. 166, one may say, for he didn't know there *was* such a number in the Eagle Hotel until we went there. He stood ready to invent anybody or anything whenever it was wanted. If I called for "outside" spies, he promptly described strangers whom he had seen at the hotel, and whose names he had happened to hear. Ah, he lived in a gorgeous, mysterious, romantic world during those few stirring days, and I think it was *real* to him, and that he enjoyed it clear down to the bottom of his heart.

But he made trouble enough for us, and just no end of humiliation. You see, on account of him we had fifteen or twenty people under arrest and confinement in the fort, with sentinels before their doors. A lot of the captives were soldiers and such, and to them I didn't have to apologize; but the rest were first-class citizens, from all over the country,

and no amount of apologies was sufficient to satisfy them. They just
fumed and raged and made no end of trouble! And those two ladies—one
was an Ohio Congressman's wife, the other a Western bishop's sister—
well, the scorn and ridicule and angry tears they poured out on me made
up a keepsake that was likely to make me remember them for considerable
time—and I shall. That old lame gentleman with the goggles was a
college president from Philadelphia, who had come up to attend his
nephew's funeral. He had never seen young Wicklow before, of course.
Well, he not only missed the funeral, and got jailed as a rebel spy, but
Wicklow had stood up there in my quarters and coldly described him as
a counterfeiter, nigger-trader, horse-thief, and firebug from the most
notorious rascal-nest in Galveston; and this was a thing which that poor
old gentleman couldn't seem to get over at all.

And the War Department! But, oh, my soul, let's draw the curtain over
that part!

NOTE: I showed my manuscript to the Major, and he said: "Your unfamiliarity
with military matters has betrayed you into some little mistakes. Still, they are
picturesque ones—let them go; military men will smile at them, the rest won't
detect them. You have got the main facts of the history right, and have set them
down just about as they occurred."   M.T.

THE STORY OF A CONSCIENCE

Ambrose Bierce

CAPTAIN PARROLL HARTROY stood at the advanced post of his picket-guard, talking in low tones with the sentinel. This post was on a turnpike which bisected the captain's camp, a half-mile in rear, though the camp was not in sight from that point. The officer was apparently giving the soldier certain instructions—was perhaps merely inquiring if all were quiet in front. As the two stood talking a man approached them from the direction of the camp carelessly whistling, and was promptly halted by the soldier. He was evidently a civilian—a tall person, coarsely clad in the homemade stuff of yellow-gray, called "butternut," which was men's only wear in the latter days of the Confederacy. On his head was a slouch felt hat, once white, from beneath which hung masses of uneven hair, seemingly unacquainted with either scissors or comb. The man's face was rather striking; a broad forehead, high nose, and thin cheeks, the mouth visible in the full dark beard, which seemed as neglected as the hair. The eyes were large and had that steadiness and fixity of attention which so frequently mark a considering intelligence and a will not easily turned from its purpose—so say those physiognomists who have that kind of eyes. On the whole, this was a man whom one would be likely to observe and be observed by. He carried a walking stick freshly cut from the forest and his ailing cowskin boots were white with dust.

"Show your pass," said the Federal soldier, a trifle more imperiously perhaps than he would have thought necessary if he had not been under the eye of his commander, who with folded arms looked on from the roadside.

"'Lowed you'd rec'lect me, Gineral," said the wayfarer tranquilly, while producing the paper from the pocket of his coat. There was something in his tone—perhaps a faint suggestion of irony—which made his elevation of his obstructor to exalted rank less agreeable to that worthy warrior than promotion is commonly found to be. "You-all have to be purty pertickler, I reckon," he added, in a more conciliatory tone, as if in half-apology for being halted.

Having read the pass, with his rifle resting on the ground, the soldier handed the document back without a word, shouldered his weapon, and returned to his commander. The civilian passed on in the middle of the road, and when he had penetrated the circumjacent Confederacy a few yards resumed his whistling and was soon out of sight beyond an angle in the road, which at that point entered a thin forest. Suddenly the officer undid his arms from his breast, drew a revolver from his belt and sprang forward at a run in the same direction, leaving his sentinel in gaping astonishment at his post. After making to the various visible forms of nature a solemn promise to be damned, that gentleman resumed the air of stolidity which is supposed to be appropriate to a state of alert military attention.

Captain Hartroy held an independent command. His force consisted of a company of infantry, a squadron of cavalry, and section of artillery, detached from the army to which they belonged, to defend an important defile in the Cumberland Mountains in Tennessee. It was a field officer's command held by a line officer promoted from the ranks, where he had quietly served until "discovered." His post was one of exceptional peril; its defense entailed a heavy responsibility and he had wisely been given corresponding discretionary powers, all the more necessary because of his distance from the main army, the precarious nature of his communications and the lawless character of the enemy's irregular troops infesting that region. He had strongly fortified his little camp, which embraced a village of a half-dozen dwellings and a country store, and had collected a considerable quantity of supplies. To a few resident civilians of known loyalty, with whom it was desirable to trade, and of whose services in various ways he sometimes availed himself, he had given written passes admitting them within his lines. It is easy to understand that an abuse of this privilege in the interest of the enemy might entail serious consequences. Captain Hartroy had made an order to the effect that anyone so abusing it would be summarily shot.

While the sentinel had been examining the civilian's pass the captain had eyed the latter narrowly. He thought his appearance familiar and had at first no doubt of having given him the pass which had satisfied the sentinel. It was not until the man had got out of sight and hearing that his identity was disclosed by a revealing light from memory. With soldierly promptness of decision the officer had acted on the revelation.

To any but a singularly self-possessed man the apparition of an officer of the military forces, formidably clad, bearing in one hand a sheathed sword and in the other a cocked revolver, and rushing in furious pursuit, is no doubt disquieting to a high degree; upon the man to whom the pursuit was in this instance directed it appeared to have no other effect than somewhat to intensify his tranquility. He might easily enough have escaped into the forest to the right or the left, but chose another course of action—turned and quietly faced the captain, saying as he came up: "I reckon ye must have something to say to me, which ye disremembered. What mout it be, neighbor?"

But the "neighbor" did not answer, being engaged in the unneighborly act of covering him with a cocked pistol.

"Surrender," said the captain as calmly as a slight breathlessness from exertion would permit, "or you die."

There was no menace in the manner of this demand; that was all in the matter and in the means of enforcing it. There was, too, something not altogether reassuring in the cold gray eyes that glanced along the barrel of the weapon. For a moment the two men stood looking at each other in silence; then the civilian, with no appearance of fear—with as great apparent unconcern as when complying with the less austere demand of the sentinel—slowly pulled from his pocket the paper which had satisfied that humble functionary and held it out, saying:

"I reckon this 'ere parss from Mister Hartroy is—"

"The pass is a forgery," the officer said, interrupting. "I am Captain Hartroy—and you are Dramer Brune."

It would have required a sharp eye to observe the slight pallor of the civilian's face at these words, and the only other manifestation attesting their significance was a voluntary relaxation of the thumb and fingers holding the dishonored paper, which, falling to the road, unheeded, was rolled by a gentle wind and then lay still, with a coating of dust, as in humiliation for the lie that it bore. A moment later the civilian, still looking unmoved into the barrel of the pistol, said:

"Yes, I am Dramer Brune, a Confederate spy, and your prisoner. I have on my person, as you will soon discover, a plan of your fort and its armament, a statement of the distribution of your men and their number, a map of the approaches, showing the positions of all your outposts. My life is fairly yours, but if you wish it taken in a more formal way than by your own hand, and if you are willing to spare me the indignity of marching into camp at the muzzle of your pistol, I promise you that I will neither resist, escape, nor remonstrate, but will submit to whatever penalty may be imposed."

The officer lowered his pistol, uncocked it, and thrust it into its place in his belt. Brune advanced a step, extending his right hand.

"It is the hand of a traitor and a spy," said the officer coldly, and did not take it. The other bowed.

"Come," said the captain, "let us go to camp; you shall not die until tomorrow morning."

He turned his back upon his prisoner, and these two enigmatical men retraced their steps and soon passed the sentinel, who expressed his general sense of things by a needless and exaggerated salute to his commander.

Early on the morning after these events the two men, captor and captive, sat in the tent of the former. A table was between them on which lay, among a number of letters, official and private, which the captain had written during the night, the incriminating papers found upon the spy. That gentleman had slept through the night in an adjoining tent, unguarded. Both, having breakfasted, were now smoking.

"Mr. Brune," said Captain Hartroy, "you probably do not understand why I recognized you in your disguise, nor how I was aware of your name."

"I have not sought to learn, Captain," the prisoner said with quiet dignity.

"Nevertheless I should like you to know — if the story will not offend. You will perceive that my knowledge of you goes back to the autumn of 1861. At that time you were a private in an Ohio regiment — a brave and trusted soldier. To the surprise and grief of your officers and comrades you deserted and went over to the enemy. Soon afterward you were captured in a skirmish, recognized, tried by court-martial and sentenced to be shot. Awaiting the execution of the sentence you were confined, unfettered, in a freight car standing on a side track of a railway."

"At Grafton, Virginia," said, Brune, pushing the ashes from his cigar with the little finger of the hand holding it, and without looking up.

"At Grafton, Virginia," the captain repeated. "One dark and stormy night a soldier who had just returned from a long, fatiguing march was put on guard over you. He sat on a cracker box inside the car, near the door, his rifle loaded and the bayonet fixed. You sat in a corner and his orders were to kill you if you attempted to rise."

"But if I *asked* to rise he might call the corporal of the guard."

"Yes. As the long silent hours wore away the soldier yielded to the demands of nature: he himself incurred the death penalty by sleeping at his post of duty."

"You did."

"What! you recognize me? you have known me all along?"

The captain had risen and was walking the floor of his tent, visibly excited. His face was flushed, the gray eyes had lost the cold, pitiless look which they had shown when Brune had seen them over the pistol barrel; they had softened wonderfully.

"I knew you," said the spy, with his customary tranquility, "the moment you faced me, demanding my surrender. In the circumstance it would have been hardly becoming in me to recall these matters. I am perhaps a traitor, certainly a spy; but I should not wish to seem a suppliant."

The captain had paused in his walk and was facing his prisoner. There was a singular huskiness in his voice as he spoke again.

"Mr. Brune, whatever your conscience may permit you to be, you saved my life at what you must have believed the cost of your own. Until I saw you yesterday when halted by my sentinel I believed you dead— thought that you had suffered the fate which through my own crime you might easily have escaped. You had only to step from the car and leave me to take your place before the firing squad. You had a divine compassion. You pitied my fatigue. You let me sleep, watched over me, and as the time drew near for the relief-guard to come and detect me in my crime, you gently waked me. Ah, Brune, Brune, that was well done—that was great—that—"

The captain's voice failed him; the tears were running down his face and sparkled upon his beard and his breast. Resuming his seat at the table, he buried his face in his arms and sobbed. All else was silence.

Suddenly the clear warble of a bugle was heard sounding the "assembly." The captain started and raised his wet face from his arms; it had turned ghastly pale. Outside, in the sunlight, were heard the stir of the men falling into line; the voices of the sergeants calling the roll; the tapping of the drummers as they braced their drums. The captain spoke again:

"I ought to have confessed my fault in order to relate the story of your magnanimity; it might have procured you a pardon. A hundred times I resolved to do so, but shame prevented. Besides, your sentence was just and righteous. Well, Heaven forgive me! I said nothing, and my regiment was soon afterward ordered to Tennessee and I never heard about you."

"It was all right, sir," said Brune; without visible emotion; "I escaped and returned to my colors—the Confederate colors. I should like to add that before deserting from the Federal service I had earnestly asked a discharge, on the ground of altered convictions. I was answered by punishment."

"Ah, but if I had suffered the penalty of my crime—if you had not generously given me the life that I accepted without gratitude you would not be again in the shadow and imminence of death."

The prisoner started slightly and a look of anxiety came into his face. One would have said, too, that he was surprised. At that moment a lieutenant, the adjutant, appeared at the opening of the tent and saluted. "Captain," he said, "the battalion is formed."

Captain Hartroy had recovered his composure. He turned to the officer and said: "Lieutenant, go to Captain Graham and say that I direct him to assume command of the battalion and parade it outside the parapet. This gentleman is a deserter and a spy; he is to be shot to death in the presence of the troops. He will accompany you, unbound and unguarded."

While the adjutant waited at the door the two men inside the tent rose and exchanged ceremonious bows, Brune immediately retiring.

Half an hour later an old Negro cook, the only person left in camp except the commander, was so startled by the sound of a volley of musketry that he dropped the kettle that he was lifting from a fire. But for his consternation and the hissing which the contents of the kettle made among the embers, he might also have heard, nearer at hand, the single pistol shot with which Captain Hartroy renounced the life which in conscience he could no longer keep.

In compliance with the terms of a note that he left for the officer who succeeded him in command, he was buried, like the deserter and spy, without military honors; and in the solemn shadow of the mountain which knows no more of war the two sleep well in long-forgotten graves.

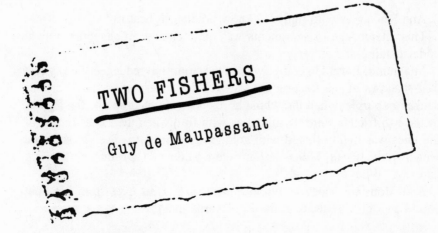

TWO FISHERS

Guy de Maupassant

PARIS WAS BLOCKADED—famished—at the point of death. Even the sparrows on the housetops were few and far between, and the very sewers were in danger of becoming depopulated. People ate anything they could get.

Monsieur Morisot, watchmaker by trade, was walking early one bright January morning down the Boulevards, his hands in the pockets of his overcoat, feeling hungry and depressed, when he unexpectedly ran into a friend. He recognized Monsieur Sauvage, an old-time chum of the riverside.

Every Sunday before the war Morisot used to start at daybreak with his bamboo fishing rod in his hand, his tin bait and tackle box upon his back. He used to take the train to Colombes, and to walk from there to the Island of Maranthe. No sooner had he arrived at the river than he used to begin to fish and continue fishing until evening. Here every Sunday he used to meet Monsieur Sauvage, a linen-draper from Paris, but stout and jovial withal, as keen a fisherman moreover as he was himself.

Often they would sit side by side, their feet dangling over the water for half a day at a time and say scarcely a word, yet little by little they became friends. Sometimes they never spoke at all. Occasionally they launched out into conversation, but they understood each other perfectly without its aid, for their tastes and ideas were the same.

On a spring morning in the bright sunshine, when the light and delicate mist hovered over the river, and these two mad fishermen enjoyed a foretaste of real summer weather, Morisot would say to his neighbour: "Hein! not bad, eh?"

And Sauvage would reply: "I know nothing to beat it."

This interchange of sentiments was quite enough to engender mutual understanding and esteem.

In autumn, toward evening, when the setting sun reddened the sky and cast shadows of the fleeting clouds over the water; when the river was decked in purple; when the whole horizon was lighted up and the figures of the two friends were illumined as with fire; when the russet-brown of the trees was lightly tinged with gold, and the trees themselves shivered with a wintry shake, Monsieur Sauvage would smile at Monsieur Morisot and say: "What a sight, eh?"

And Monsieur Morisot, without even raising his eyes from his float would answer: "Better than the Boulevards, hein!"

This morning, as soon as they had recognized each other they shook hands warmly, quite overcome at meeting again under such different circumstances.

Monsieur Sauvage sighed and murmured: "A nice state of things."

Monsieur Morisot, gloomy and sad, answered: "And what weather! Today is New Year's Day." The sky, in fact, was clear, bright and beautiful.

They began to walk along, sorrowful and pensive. Said Morisot: "And our fishing, eh? What times we used to have!"

Sauvage replied: "When shall we have them again?"

They went into a little café and had a glass of absinthe, and then started again on their walk.

They stopped at another café for another glass. When they came out again they were slightly dazed, like people who had fasted long and then partaken too freely.

It was lovely weather; a soft breeze fanned their faces. Monsieur Sauvage, upon whom the fresh air was beginning to take effect, suddenly said: "Suppose we were to go!"

"Go where?"

"Why, fishing!"

"But where?"

"To our island, of course. The French outposts are at Colombes. I know Colonel Dumoulin; he will let us pass through easily enough."

Morisot trembled with delight at the very idea: "All right, I'm your man."

They separated to fetch their rods.

An hour afterwards they were walking fast along the high road, towards the town commanded by Colonel Dumoulin. He smiled at their request but granted it, and they went on their way rejoicing in the possession of the password.

Soon they had crossed the lines, passed through deserted Colombes, and found themselves in the vineyard leading down to the river. It was about eleven o'clock.

On the other side the village of Argenteuil seemed as if it were dead. The hills of Orgremont and Saumons commanded the whole country round. The great plain stretching out as far as Nanterne was empty as air. Nothing in sight but cherry trees, and stretches of grey soil.

Monsieur Sauvage pointed with his finger to the heights above and said: "The Prussians are up there," and a vague sense of uneasiness seized upon the two friends.

The Prussians! They had never set eyes upon them, but for months past they had felt their presence near, encircling their beloved Paris, ruining their beloved France, pillaging, massacring, insatiable, invincible, invisible, all-powerful, and as they thought on them a sort of superstitious terror seemed to mingle with the hate they bore towards their unknown conquerors. Morisot murmured: "Suppose we were to meet them," and Sauvage replied, with the instinctive gallantry of the Parisian; "Well! we would offer them some of our fish for supper."

All the same they hesitated before venturing into the country, intimidated as they were by the all-pervading silence.

Eventually Monsieur Sauvage plucked up courage: "Come along, let's make a start; but we must be cautious."

They went through the vineyard, bent double, crawling along from bush to bush, ears and eyes upon the alert.

Only one strip of ground lay between them and the river. They began to run, and when they reached the bank they crouched down among the dry reeds for shelter.

Morisot laid his ear to the ground to listen for the sound of footsteps, but he could hear nothing. They were alone, quite alone; gradually they felt reassured and began to fish.

The deserted island of Maranthe hid them from the opposite shore. The little restaurant was closed, and looked as if it had been neglected for years.

Monsieur Sauvage caught the first gudgeon, Monsieur Morisot the second. And every minute they pulled up their lines with a little silver object dangling and struggling on the hook. Truly, a miraculous draught of fishes. As the fish were caught they put them in a net which floated in the water at their feet. They positively reveled in enjoyment of a long-forbidden sport. The sun shone warm upon their backs. They heard nothing—they though of nothing—the rest of the world was as nothing to them. They simply fished.

Suddenly a smothered sound, as it were underground, made the earth tremble. The guns had recommenced firing. Morisot turned his head, and saw above the bank, far away to the left, the vast shadow of Mont Valerien, and over it the white wreath of smoke from the gun which had just been fired. Then a jet of flame burst forth from the fortress in answer, a moment later followed by another explosion. Then others, till every second as it seemed the mountain breathed out death, and the white smoke formed a funeral pall above it.

Monsieur Sauvage shrugged his shoulders. "They are beginning again," he said.

Monsieur Morisot, anxiously watching his float bob up and down, was suddenly seized with rage against the belligerents and growled out: "How idiotic to kill one another like that."

Monsieur Sauvage: "It's worse than the brute beasts."

Monsieur Morisot, who had just hooked a bleak, said: "And to think that it will always be thus so long as there are such things as Governments."

Monsieur Sauvage stopped him: "The Republic would not have declared war."

Monsieur Morisot in his turn: "With Kings we have foreign wars, with the Republic we have civil wars."

Then in a friendly way they began to discuss politics with the calm common sense of reasonable and peace-loving men, agreeing on the one point that no one would ever be free. And Mont Valerien thundered unceasingly, demolishing with its cannonballs French houses, crushing out French lives, ruining many a dream, many a joy, many a hope deferred, wrecking much happiness, and bringing to the hearts of women, girls and mothers in France and elsewhere, sorrow and suffering which would never have an end.

"It's life," said Monsieur Morisot.

"Say rather that it's death," said Monsieur Sauvage.

They started, scared out of their lives, as they felt that someone was walking close behind them. Turning round, they saw four men, four tall, bearded men, dressed as servants in livery, and wearing flat caps upon their heads. These men were covering the two fishermen with rifles.

The rods dropped from their frightened hands, and floated aimlessly down the river. In an instant the Frenchmen were seized, bound, thrown into a boat, and ferried over to the island.

Behind the house they had thought uninhabited was a picket of Prussian soldiers. A hairy giant, who was sitting astride a chair, and smoking a porcelain pipe, asked them in excellent French if they had had good sport.

A soldier placed at the feet of the officer the net full of fish, which he had brought away with him.

"Not bad, I see. But we have other fish to fry. Listen, and don't alarm yourselves. You are a couple of French spies sent out to watch my movements, disguised as fishermen. I take you prisoners, and I order you to be shot. You have fallen into my hands—so much the worse for you. It is the fortune of war. Inasmuch, however, as you came through the lines you are certainly in possession of the password. Otherwise you could not get back again. Give me the word and I will let you go."

The two friends, livid with fear, stood side by side, their hands nervously twitching, but they answered not a word.

The officer continued: "No one need ever know it. You will go home quietly, and your secret will go with you. If you refuse it is death for you both, and that instantly. Take your choice."

They neither spoke nor moved.

The Prussian calmly pointed to the river and said: "Reflect, in five minutes you will be at the bottom of that water. I suppose you have families."

Mont Valerien thundered unceasingly.

The two Frenchmen stood perfectly still and silent.

The officer gave an order in German. Then he moved his chair farther away from the prisoners, and a dozen soldiers drew up in line twenty paces off.

"I will give you one minute," he said, "not one second more."

He got up leisurely and approached the two Frenchmen. He took Morisot by the arm and said, in an undertone: "Quick! Give me the word. Your friend will know nothing. I will appear to give way."

Monsieur Morisot did not answer.

The Prussian took Monsieur Sauvage aside and said the same thing to him.

Monsieur Sauvage did not answer.

They found themselves once more side by side.

The officer gave another order; the soldiers raised their guns.

By accident Morisot's glance fell upon the net full of fish on the ground a few steps off. A ray of sunshine lit up their glittering bodies, and a sudden weakness came over him. "Good-bye, Monsieur Morisot," replied Monsieur Sauvage. They pressed each other's hands, trembling from head to foot.

"Fire," said the officer.

Monsieur Sauvage fell dead on his face. Monsieur Morisot, of stronger build, staggered, stumbled, and then fell right across the body of his friend, with his face turned upwards to the sky, his breast riddled with balls.

The Prussian gave another order. His men dispersed for a moment, returning with cords and stones. They tied the stones to the feet of the dead Frenchmen, and carried them down to the river.

Mont Valerien thundered unceasingly.

Two soldiers took Morisot by the head and feet. Two others did the same to Sauvage. The bodies swung to and fro, were launched into space, described a curve, and plunged feet first into the river.

The water bubbled, boiled, then calmed down, and the little wavelets, tinged with red, circled gently towards the bank.

The officer, impassive as ever, said: "It is the fishes' turn now."

His eye fell upon the gudgeon lying on the grass. He picked them up and called out: "Wilhelm." A soldier in a white cap appeared. He threw the fish towards him.

"Fry these little animals for me at once, while they are still alive and kicking. They will be delicious."

Then he began smoking again.

THE TRAITOR

W. Somerset Maugham

WHEN ASHENDEN, GIVEN charge of a number of spies working from Switzerland, was first sent there, R., wishing him to see the sort of reports that he would be required to obtain, handed him the communications, a sheaf of typewritten documents, of a man known in the secret service as Gustav.

"He's the best fellow we've got," said R. "His information is always very full and circumstantial. I want you to give his reports your very best attention. Of course Gustav is clever little chap, but there's no reason why we shouldn't get just as good reports from the other agents. It's merely a question of explaining exactly what we want."

Gustav, who lived at Basle, represented a Swiss firm with branches at Frankfort, Mannheim and Cologne, and by virtue of his business was able to go in and out of Germany without risk. He traveled up and down the Rhine, and gathered material about the movement of troops, the manufacture of munitions, the state of mind of the country (a point on which R. laid stress) and other matters upon which the Allies desired information. His frequent letters to his wife hid an ingenious code and the moment she received them in Basle she sent them to Ashenden in Geneva, who extracted from them the important facts and communicated these in the proper quarter. Every two months Gustav came home and prepared one of the reports that served as models to the other spies in this particular section of the secret service.

His employers were pleased with Gustav and Gustav had reason to be pleased with his employers. His services were so useful that he was not only paid more highly than the others but for particular scoops had received from time to time a handsome bonus.

This went on for more than a year. Then something aroused R.'s quick suspicions: he was a man of an amazing alertness, not so much of mind, as of instinct. And he had suddenly a feeling that some hanky-panky was going on. He said nothing definite to Ashenden (whatever R. surmised he was disposed to keep to himself) but told him to go to Basle, Gustav being then in Germany, and have a talk with Gustav's wife. He left it to Ashenden to decide the tenor of the conversation.

Having arrived at Basle, and leaving his bag at the station, for he did not yet know whether he would have to stay or not, he took a tram to the corner of the street in which Gustav lived, and with a quick look to see that he was not followed, walked along to the house he sought. It was a block of flats that give you the impression of decent poverty and Ashenden conjectured that they were inhabited by clerks and small tradespeople. Just inside the door was a cobbler's shop and Ashenden stopped.

"Does Herr Grabow live here?" he asked in his none-too-fluent German.

"Yes, I saw him go up a few minutes ago. You'll find him in."

Ashenden was startled, for he had but the day before received through Gustav's wife a letter addressed from Mannheim in which Gustav by means of his code gave the numbers of certain regiments that had just crossed the Rhine. Ashenden thought it unwise to ask the cobbler the question that rose to his lips, so thanked him and went up to the third floor on which he knew already that Gustav lived. He rang the bell and heard it tinkle within. In a moment the door was opened by a dapper little man with a close-shaven round head and spectacles. He wore carpet slippers.

"Herr Grabow?" asked Ashenden.

"At your service," said Gustav.

"May I come in?"

Gustav was standing with his back to the light and Ashenden could not see the look on his face. He felt a momentary hesitation and gave the name under which he received Gustav's letters from Germany.

"Come in, come in. I am very glad to see you."

Gustav led the way into a stuffy little room, heavy with carved oak furniture, and on the large table covered with a tablecloth of green velveteen was a typewriter. Gustav was apparently engaged in composing one of his invaluable reports. A woman was sitting at the open window darning socks, but at a word from Gustav rose, gathered up her things and left. Ashenden had disturbed a pretty picture of connubial bliss.

"Sit down, please. How very fortunate that I was in Basle! I have long wanted to make your acquaintance. I have only just this minute returned from Germany." He pointed to the sheets of paper by the typewriter. "I think you will be pleased with the news I bring. I have some very valuable information." He chuckled. "One is never sorry to earn a bonus."

He was very cordial, but to Ashenden his cordiality rang false. Gustav kept his eyes, smiling behind the glasses, fixed watchfully on Ashenden and it was possible that they held a trace of nervousness.

"You must have traveled quickly to get here only a few hours after your letter, sent here and then sent on by your wife, reached me in Geneva."

"That is very probable. One of the things I had to tell you is that the Germans suspect that information is getting through by means of commercial letters and so they have decided to hold up all mail at the frontier for eight and forty hours."

"I see," said Ashenden amiably. "And was it on that account that you took the precaution of dating your letter forty-eight hours after you sent it?"

"Did I do that? That was very stupid of me. I must have mistaken the day of the month."

Ashenden looked at Gustav with a smile. That was very thin; Gustav, a business man, knew too well how important in his particular job was the exactness of a date. The circuitous routes by which it was necessary to get information from Germany made it difficult to transmit news quickly and it was essential to know precisely on what days certain events had taken place.

"Let me look at your passport a minute," said Ashenden.

"What do you want with my passport?"

"I want to see when you went into Germany and when you came out."

"But you do not imagine that my comings and goings are marked on my passport? I have methods of crossing the frontier."

Ashenden knew a good deal of this matter. He knew that both the Germans and the Swiss guarded the frontier with severity.

"Oh? Why should you not cross in the ordinary way? You were engaged because your connection with a Swiss firm supplying necessary goods to Germany made it easy for you to travel backwards and forwards without suspicion. I can understand that you might get past the German sentries with the connivance of the Germans, but what about the Swiss?"

Gustav assumed a look of indignation.

"I do not understand you. Do you mean to suggest that I am in the service of the Germans? I give you my word of honor . . . I will not allow my straightforwardness to be impugned."

"You would not be the only one to take money from both sides and provide information of value to neither."

"Do you pretend that my information is of no value? Why then have you given me more bonuses than any other agent has received? The Colonel has repeatedly expressed the highest satisfaction with my services."

It was Ashenden's turn now to be cordial.

"Come, come, my dear fellow, do not try to ride the high horse. You do not wish to show me your passport and I will not insist. You are not under the impression that we leave the statements of our agents without corroboration or that we are so foolish as not to keep track of their movements? Even the best of jokes cannot bear an indefinite repetition. I am in peacetime a humorist by profession and I tell you that from bitter experience." Now Ashenden thought the moment had arrived to attempt his bluff; he knew something of the excellent but difficult game of poker. "We have information that you have not been to Germany now, nor since you were engaged by us, but have sat here quietly in Basle, and all your reports are merely due to your fertile imagination."

Gustav looked at Ashenden and saw a face expressive of nothing but tolerance and good humor. A smile slowly broke on his lips and he gave his shoulders a little shrug.

"Did you think I was such a fool as to risk my life for fifty pounds a month? I love my wife."

Ashenden laughed outright.

"I congratulate you. It is not everyone who can flatter himself that he has made a fool of our secret service for a year."

"I had the chance of earning money without any difficulty. My firm stopped sending me into Germany at the beginning of the war, but I learned what I could from the other travelers, I kept my ears open in restaurants and beer cellars, and I read the German papers. I got a lot of amusement out of sending you reports and letters."

"I don't wonder," said Ashenden.

"What are you going to do?"

"Nothing. What can we do? You are not under the impression that we shall continue to pay you a salary?"

"No, I cannot expect that."

"By the way, if it is not indiscreet, may I ask if you have been playing the same game with the Germans?"

"Oh, no," Gustav cried vehemently. "How can you think it? My sympathies are absolutely pro-ally. My heart is entirely with you."

"Well, why not?" asked Ashenden. "The Germans have all the money in the world and there is no reason why you should not get some of it. We could give you information from time to time that the Germans would be prepared to pay for."

Gustav drummed his fingers on the table. He took up a sheet of the now useless report.

"The Germans are dangerous people to meddle with."

"You are a very intelligent man. And after all, even if your salary is stopped, you can always earn a bonus by bringing us news that can be useful to us. But it will have to be substantiated; in future we pay only by results."

"I will think of it."

For a moment or two Ashenden left Gustav to his reflections. He lit a cigarette and watched the smoke he had inhaled fade into the air. He thought too.

"Is there anything particular you want to know?" asked Gustav suddenly.

Ashenden smiled.

"It would be worth a couple of thousand Swiss francs to you if you could tell me what the Germans are doing with a spy of theirs in Lucerne. He is an Englishman and his name is Grantley Caypor."

"I have heard the name," said Gustav. He paused a moment. "How long are you staying here?"

"As long as necessary. I will take a room at the hotel and let you know the number. If you have anything to say to me you can be sure of finding me in my room at nine every morning and at seven every night."

"I should not risk coming to the hotel. But I can write."

"Very well."

Ashenden rose to go and Gustav accompanied him to the door.

"We part without ill-feeling then?" he asked.

"Of course. Your reports will remain in our archives as models of what a report should be."

Ashenden spent two or three days visiting Basle. It did not much amuse him. He passed a good deal of time in the bookshop turning over the pages of books that would have been worth reading if life were a thousand years long. Once he saw Gustav in the street. On the fourth morning a letter was brought up with his coffee. The envelope was that of a commercial firm unknown to him and inside it was a typewritten sheet. There was no address and no signature. Ashenden wondered if Gustav was aware that a typewriter could betray its owner as certainly as a handwriting. Having twice carefully read the letter, he held the paper up to the light to see the watermark (he had no reason for doing this except that the sleuths of detective novels always did it), then struck a match and watched it burn. He scrunched up the charred fragments in his hand.

He got up, for he had taken advantage of his situation to breakfast in bed, packed his bag and took the next train to Berne. From there he was able to send a code telegram to R. His instructions were given to him verbally two days later, in the bedroom of his hotel at an hour when no one was likely to be seen walking along a corridor, and within twenty-four hours, though by a circuitous route, he arrived at Lucerne.

Having taken a room at the hotel at which he had been instructed to stay Ashenden went out; it was a lovely day, early in August, and the sun shone in a unclouded sky. He had not been to Lucerne since he was a boy and but vaguely remembered a covered bridge, a great stone lion and a church in which he had sat, bored yet impressed, while they played an organ; and now wandering along a shady quay (and the lake looked just as tawdry and unreal as it looked on the picture postcards) he tried not so much to find his way about a half-forgotten scene as to reform in his mind some recollection of the shy and eager lad, so impatient for life (which he saw not in the present of his adolescence but only in the future of his manhood), who so long ago had wandered there. But it seemed to him that the most vivid of his memories was not of himself, but of the crowd; he seemed to remember sun and heat and people; the train was crowded and so was the hotel, the lake steamers were packed and on the quays and in the streets you threaded your way among the throng of holiday makers. They were fat and old and ugly and odd, and they stank. Now, in wartime, Lucerne was as Switzerland was the playground of Europe. Most of the hotels were closed, the streets were empty, the rowing boats for hire rocked idly at the water's edge and there was none to take them, and in the avenues by the lake the only persons to be seen were serious Swiss taking their neutrality, like a dachshund, for a walk with them. Ashenden felt exhilarated by the solitude, and sitting down on a bench that faced the water surrendered himself deliberately to the sensation. It was true that the lake was absurd, the water was too blue, the mountains too snowy, and its beauty, hitting you in the face, exasperated rather than thrilled; but all the same there was something pleasing in the prospect, an artless candor, like one of Mendelssohn's *Songs Without Words,* that made Ashenden smile with complacency. Lucerne reminded him of wax flowers under glass cases and cuckoo clocks and fancywork in Berlin wool. So long at all events as the fine weather lasted he was prepared to enjoy himself. He did not see why he should not at least try to combine pleasure to himself with profit to his country. He was traveling with a brand-new passport in his pocket, under a borrowed name, and this gave him an agreeable sense of owning a new personality. He was often slightly tired of himself, and it diverted him for a while to be merely a creature of R.'s facile invention. The experience he had just enjoyed appealed to his acute sense of the absurd. R., it is true, had not seen the fun of it: what humor R. possessed was of a sardonic turn and he had no facility for taking in good part a joke at his own expense. To do that you must be able to look at yourself from the outside and be at the same time spectator and actor in the pleasant comedy of life. R. was a soldier and regarded introspection as unhealthy, unenglish and unpatriotic.

Ashenden got up and strolled slowly to his hotel. It was a small German hotel, of the second class, spotlessly clean, and his bedroom had a nice view; it was furnished with brightly varnished pitch-pine and though on a cold wet day it would have been wretched, in that warm and sunny weather it was gay and pleasing. There were tables in the hall and he sat down at one of these and ordered a bottle of beer. The landlady was curious to know why in that dead season he had come to stay and he was glad to satisfy her curiosity. He told her that he had recently recovered from an attack of typhoid and had come to Lucerne to get back his strength. He was employed in the Censorship Department and was taking the opportunity to brush up his rusty German. He asked her if she could recommend to him a German teacher. The landlady was a blond and blowsy Swiss, good-humored and talkative, so that Ashenden felt pretty sure that she would repeat in the proper quarter the information he gave her. It was his turn now to ask a few questions. She was voluble on the subject of the war on account of which the hotel, in that month so full that rooms had to be found for visitors in neighboring houses, was nearly empty. A few people came in from outside to eat their meals *en pension,* but she had only two lots of resident guests. One was an old Irish couple who lived in Vevey and passed their summers in Lucerne and the other was an Englishman and his wife. She was a German and they were obliged on that account to live in a neutral country. Ashenden took care to show little curiosity about them—he recognized in the description Grantley Caypor—but of her own accord she told him that they spent most of the day walking about the mountains. Herr Caypor was a botanist and much interested in the flora of the country. His lady was a very nice woman and she felt her position keenly. Ah, well, the war could not last forever. The landlady bustled away and Ashenden went upstairs.

Dinner was at seven, and, wishing to be in the dining room before anyone else so that he could take stock of his fellow-guests as they entered, he went down as soon as he heard the bell. It was a very plain, stiff, whitewashed room, with chairs of the same shiny pitch-pine as in his bedroom, and on the walls were oleographs of Swiss lakes. On each little table was a bunch of flowers. It was all neat and clean and presaged a bad dinner. Ashenden would have liked to make up for it by ordering a bottle of the best Rhine-wine to be found in the hotel, but did not venture to draw attention to himself by extravagance (he saw on two or three tables half-empty bottles of table hock, which made him surmise that his fellow-guests drank thriftily), and so contented himself with ordering a pint of lager. Presently one or two persons came in, single men with some occupation in Lucerne and obviously Swiss, and sat down each at his own little table and untied the napkins that at the end of luncheon they had neatly tied up. They propped newspapers against their water jugs and read while they somewhat noisily ate their soup. Then entered a very old tall bent man, with white hair and a drooping white mustache, accompanied by a little old white-haired lady in black. These were certainly the Irish colonel and his wife of whom the landlady had spoken. They took their seats and the colonel poured out a thimbleful of wine for his wife and a thimbleful for himself. They waited in silence for their dinner to be served to them by the buxom, hearty maid.

At last the persons arrived for whom Ashenden had been waiting. He was doing his best to read a German book and it was only by an exercise of self-control that he allowed himself only for one instant to raise his eyes as they came in. His glance showed him a man of about forty-five with short dark hair, somewhat grizzled, of middle height, but corpulent, with a broad red clean-shaven face. He wore a shirt open at the neck, with a wide collar, and a grey suit. He walked ahead of his wife, and of her Ashenden only caught the impression of a German woman self-effaced and dusty. Grantley Caypor sat down and began in a loud voice explaining to the waitress that they had taken an immense walk. They had been up some mountain the name of which meant nothing to Ashenden but which excited in the maid expressions of astonishment and enthusiasm. Then Caypor, still in fluent German but with a marked English accent, said that they were so late they had not even gone up to wash, but had just rinsed their hands outside. He had a resonant voice and a jovial manner.

"Serve me quick, we're starving with hunger, and bring beer, bring three bottles. *Lieber Gott,* what a thirst I have!"

He seemed to be a man of exuberant vitality. He brought into that dull, overclean dining room the breath of life and everyone in it appeared on a sudden more alert. He began to talk to his wife, in English, and everything he said could be heard by all; but presently she interrupted him with a remark made in an undertone. Caypor stopped and Ashenden felt that his eyes were turned in his direction. Mrs. Caypor had noticed the arrival of a stranger and had drawn her husband's attention to it. Ashenden turned the page of the book he was pretending to read, but he felt that Caypor's gaze was fixed intently upon him. When he addressed his wife again it was in so low a tone that Ashenden could not even tell what language he used, but when the maid brought them their soup, Caypor, his voice still low, asked her a question. It was plain that he was inquiring who Ashenden was. Ashenden could catch of the maid's reply but the one word *länder*.

One or two people finished their dinner and went out picking their teeth. The old Irish colonel and his old wife rose from their table and he stood aside to let her pass. They had eaten their meal without exchanging a word. She walked slowly to the door; but the colonel stopped to say a word to a Swiss who might have been a local attorney, and when she reached it she stood there, bowed and with a sheeplike look, patiently waiting for her husband to come and open it for her. Ashenden realized that she had never opened a door for herself. She did not know how to. In a minute the colonel with his old, old gait came to the door and opened it; she passed out and he followed. The little incident offered a key to their whole lives, and from it Ashenden began to reconstruct their histories, circumstances and characters; but he pulled himself up: he could not allow himself the luxury of creation. He finished his dinner.

When he went into the hall he saw tied to the leg of a table a bullterrier and in passing mechanically put down his hand to fondle the dog's drooping, soft ears. The landlady was standing at the foot of the stairs.

"Whose is this lovely beast?" asked Ashenden.

"He belongs to Herr Caypor. Fritzi, he is called. Herr Caypor says he has a longer pedigree than the King of England."

Fritzi rubbed himself against Ashenden's leg and with his nose sought the palm of his hand. Ashenden went upstairs to fetch his hat, and when he came down saw Caypor standing at the entrance of the hotel talking with the landlady. From the sudden silence and their constrained manner he guessed that Caypor had been making inquiries about him. When he passed between them, into the street, out of the corner of his eye he saw Caypor give him a suspicious stare. That frank, jovial red face bore then a look of shifty cunning.

Ashenden strolled along till he found a tavern where he could have his coffee in the open and to compensate himself for the bottle of beer that his sense of duty had urged him to drink at dinner, ordered the best brandy the house provided. He was pleased at last to have come face to face with the man of whom he had heard so much and in a day or two hoped to become acquainted with him. It is never very difficult to get to know anyone who has a dog. But he was in no hurry; he would let things take their course: with the object he had in view he couldn't afford to be hasty.

Ashenden reviewed the circumstances. Grantley Caypor was an Englishman, born according to his passport in Birmingham, and he was forty-two years of age. His wife, to whom he had been married for eleven years, was of German birth and parentage. That was public knowledge. Information about his antecedents was contained in a private document. He had started life, according to this, in a lawyer's office in Birmingham and then had drifted into journalism. He had been connected with an English paper in Cairo and with another in Shanghai. There he got into trouble for attempting to get money on false pretenses and was sentenced to a short term of imprisonment. All trace of him was lost for two years after his release, when he reappeared in a shipping office in Marseilles. From there, still in the shipping business, he went to Hamburg, where he married, and to London. In London he set up for himself, in the export business, but after some time failed and was made a bankrupt. He returned to journalism. At the outbreak of war he was quietly with his German wife at Southampton. In the beginning of the following year he told his employers that owing to the nationality of his wife his position was intolerable; they had no fault to find with him and, recognizing that he was in an awkward fix, granted his request that he should be transferred to Genoa. Here he remained till Italy entered the war, but then gave notice and with his papers in perfect order crossed the border and took up his residence in Switzerland.

All this indicated a man of doubtful honesty and unsettled disposition, with no background and of no financial standing; but the facts were of no importance to anyone till it was discovered that Caypor, certainly from the beginning of the war and perhaps sooner, was in the service of the German Intelligence Department. He had a salary of forty pounds a month. But though dangerous and wily no steps would have been taken to deal with him if he had contented himself with transmitting such news as he was able to get in Switzerland. He could do no great harm there and it might even be possible to make use of him to convey information that it was desirable to let the enemy have. He had no notion that anything was known of him. His letters, and he received a good many, were closely censored; there were few codes that the people dealt with such matters could not in the end decipher and it might be that sooner or later through him it would be possible to lay hands on the organization that still flourished in England. But then he did something that drew R.'s attention to him. Had he known it none could have blamed him for shaking in his shoes; R. was not a very nice man to get on the wrong side of. Caypor scraped acquaintance in Zürich with a young Spaniard, Gomez by name, who had lately entered the British secret service, by his nationality inspired him with confidence, and managed to worm out of him the fact that he was engaged in espionage. Probably the Spaniard, with a very human desire to seem important, had done no more than talk mysteriously; but on Caypor's information he was watched when he went to Germany and one day caught just as he was posting a letter in a code that was eventually deciphered. He was tried, convicted and shot. It was bad enough to lose a useful and disinterested agent, but it entailed besides the changing of a safe and simple code. R. was not pleased. But R. was not the man to let any desire of revenge stand in the way of his main object and it occurred to him that if Caypor was merely betraying his country for money it might be possible to get him to take more money to betray his employers. The fact that he had succeeded in delivering into their hands an agent of the Allies must seem to them an earnest of his good faith. He might be very useful. But R. had no notion what kind of man Caypor was, he had lived his shabby, furtive life obscurely, and the only photograph that existed of him was one taken for a passport. Ashenden's instructions were to get acquainted with Caypor and see whether there was any chance that he would work honestly for the British: if he thought there was, he was entitled to sound him and if his suggestions were met with favor to make certain propositions. It was a task that needed tact and a knowledge of men. If on the other hand Ashenden came to the conclusion that Caypor could not be bought he was to watch and report his movements. The information he had obtained from Gustav was vague, but important; there was only one point in it that was interesting, and this was that the head of the German Intelligence Department in Berne was growing restive at Caypor's lack of activity. Caypor was asking for a higher salary and Major von P. had told him that he must earn it. It might be that he was urging him to go to England. If he could be induced to cross the frontier Ashenden's work was done.

"How the devil do you expect me to persuade him to put his head in a noose?" asked Ashenden.

"It won't be a noose, it'll be a firing squad," said R.

"Caypor's clever."

"Well, be cleverer, damn your eyes."

Ashenden made up his mind that he would take no steps to make Caypor's acquaintance, but allow the first advances to be made by him. If he was being pressed for results it must surely occur to him that it would be worthwhile to get into conversation with an Englishman who was employed in the Censorship Department. Ashenden was prepared with a supply of information that it could not in the least benefit the Central Powers to possess. With a false name and a false passport he had little fear that Caypor would guess that he was a British agent.

Ashenden did not have to wait long. Next day he was sitting in the doorway of the hotel, drinking a cup of coffee and already half asleep after a substantial *mittagessen,* when the Caypors came out of the dining room. Mrs. Caypor went upstairs and Caypor released the dog. The dog bounded along and in a friendly fashion leaped up against Ashenden.

"Come here, Fritzi," cried Caypor, and then to Ashenden: "I'm so sorry. But he's quite gentle."

"Oh, that's all right. He won't hurt me."

Caypor stopped at the doorway.

"He's a bullterrier. You don't often seen them on the Continent." He seemed while he spoke to be taking Ashenden's measure; he called to the maid, "A coffee, please, *fräulein*. You've just arrived, haven't you?"

"Yes, I came yesterday."

"Really? I didn't see you in the dining room last night. Are you making a stay?"

"I don't know. I've been ill and I've come here to recuperate."

The maid came with the coffee and seeing Caypor talking to Ashenden put the tray on the table at which he was sitting. Caypor gave a laugh of faint embarrassment.

"I don't want to force myself upon you. I don't know why the maid put my coffee on your table."

"Please sit down," said Ashenden.

"It's very good of you. I've lived so long on the Continent that I'm always forgetting that my countrymen are apt to look upon it as confounded cheek if you talk to them. Are you English, by the way, or American?"

"English," said Ashenden.

Ashenden was by nature a very shy person, and he had in vain tried to cure himself of a failing that at his age was unseemly, but on occasion he knew how to make effective use of it. He explained now in a hesitating and awkward manner the facts that he had the day before told the landlady and that he was convinced she had already passed on to Caypor.

"You couldn't have come to a better place than Lucerne. It's an oasis of peace in this war-weary world. When you're here you might almost forget that there is such a thing as a war going on. That is why I've come here. I'm a journalist by profession."

"I couldn't help wondering if you wrote," said Ashenden, with an eager timid smile.

It was clear that he had not learned that "oasis of peace in a war-weary world" at the shipping office.

"You see, I married a German lady," said Caypor gravely.

"Oh, really?"

"I don't think anyone could be more patriotic than I am, I'm English through and through and I don't mind telling you than in my opinion the British Empire is the greatest instrument for good that the world has ever seen, but having a German wife I naturally see a good deal of the reverse of the medal. You don't have to tell me that the Germans have faults, but frankly I'm not prepared to admit that they're devils incarnate. At the beginning of the war my poor wife had a very rough time in England and I for one couldn't have blamed her if she'd felt rather bitter about it. Everyone thought she was a spy. It'll make you laugh when you know her. She's the typical German *hausfrau* who cares for nothing but her house and her husband and our only child Fritzi." Caypor fondled his dog and gave a little laugh. "Yes, Fritzi, you are our child, aren't you? Naturally it made my position very awkward, I was connected with some very important papers, and my editors weren't quite comfortable about it. Well, to cut a long story short I thought the most dignified course was to resign and come to a neutral country till the storm blew over. My wife and I never discuss the war, though I'm bound to tell you that it's more on my account than hers, she's much more tolerant than I am and she's more willing to look upon this terrible business from my point of view than I am from hers."

"That is strange," said Ashenden. "As a rule women are so much more rabid than men."

"My wife is a very remarkable person. I should like to introduce you to her. By the way, I don't know if you know my name. Grantley Caypor."

"My name is Somerville," said Ashenden.

He told him then of the work he had been doing in the Censorship Department, and he fancied that into Caypor's eyes came a certain intentness. Presently he told him that he was looking for someone to give him conversation lessons in German so that he might rub up his rusty knowledge of the language; and as he spoke a notion flashed across his mind; he gave Caypor a look and saw that the same notion had come to him. It had occurred to them at the same instant that it would be a very good plan for Ashenden's teacher to be Mrs. Caypor.

"I asked our landlady if she could find me someone and she said she thought she could. I must ask her again. It ought not to be very hard to find a man who is prepared to come and talk German to me for an hour a day."

"I wouldn't take anyone on the landlady's recommendation," said Caypor. "After all you want someone with a good north German accent and she only talks Swiss. I'll ask my wife if she knows anyone. My wife's a very highly educated woman and you could trust her recommendation."

"That's very kind of you."

Ashenden observed Grantley Caypor at his ease. He noticed how the small, grey-green eyes, which last night he had not been able to see, contradicted the red good-humored frankness of the face. They were quick and shifty, but when the mind behind them was seized by an unexpected notion they were suddenly still. It gave one a peculiar feeling of the working of the brain. They were not eyes that inspired confidence; Caypor did that with his jolly, good-natured smile, the openness of his broad, weather-beaten face, his comfortable obesity and the cheeriness of his loud, deep voice. He was doing his best now to be agreeable. While Ashenden talked to him, a little shyly still but gaining confidence from that breezy, cordial manner, capable of putting anyone at his ease, it intrigued him to remember that the man was a common spy. It gave a tang to his conversation to reflect that he had been ready to sell his country for no more than forty pounds a month. Ashenden had known Gomez, the young Spaniard whom Caypor had betrayed. He was a high-spirited youth, with a love of adventure, and he had undertaken his dangerous mission not for the money he earned by it, but from a passion for romance. It amused him to outwit the clumsy German and it appealed to his sense of the absurd to play a part in a shilling shocker. It was not very nice to think of him now six feet underground in a prison yard. He was young and he had a certain grace of gesture. Ashenden wondered whether Caypor had felt a qualm when he delivered him up to destruction.

"I suppose you know a little German?" asked Caypor, interested in the stranger.

"Oh, yes, I was a student in Germany, and I used to talk it fluently, but that is long ago and I have forgotten. I can still read it very comfortably."

"Oh, yes, I noticed you were reading a German book last night."

Fool! It was only a little while since he had told Ashenden that he had not seen him at dinner. He wondered whether Caypor had observed the slip. How difficult it was never to make one! Ashenden must be on his guard; the thing that made him most nervous was the thought that he might not answer readily enough to his assumed name of Somerville. Of course there was always the chance that Caypor had made the slip on purpose to see by Ashenden's face whether he noticed anything. Caypor got up.

"There is my wife. We go for a walk up one of the mountains every afternoon. I can tell you some charming walks. The flowers even now are lovely."

"I'm afraid I must wait till I'm a bit stronger," said Ashenden, with a little sigh.

He had naturally a pale face and never looked as robust as he was. Mrs. Caypor came downstairs and her husband joined her. They walked down the road, Fritzi bounding round them, and Ashenden saw that Caypor immediately began to speak with volubility. He was evidently telling his wife the results of his interview with Ashenden. Ashenden looked at the sun shining so gaily on the lake; the shadow of a breeze fluttered the green leaves of the trees; everything invited to a stroll: he got up, went to his room and throwing himself on his bed had a very pleasant sleep.

He went into dinner that evening as the Caypors were finishing, for he had wandered melancholy about Lucerne in the hope of finding a cocktail that would enable him to face the potato salad that he foresaw, and on their way out of the dining room Caypor stopped and asked him if he would drink coffee with them. When Ashenden joined them in the hall Caypor got up and introduced him to his wife. She bowed stiffly and no answering smile came to her face to respond to Ashenden's civil greeting. It was not hard to see that her attitude was definitely hostile. It put Ashenden at his ease. She was a plainish woman, nearing forty, with a muddy skin and vague features; her drab hair was arranged in a plait round her head like that of Napoleon's Queen of Prussia; and she was squarely built, plump rather than fat, and solid. But she did not look stupid; she looked on the contrary a woman of character and Ashenden, who had lived enough in Germany to recognize the type, was ready to believe that though capable of doing the housework, cooking the dinner and climbing a mountain, she might be also prodigiously well informed. She wore a white blouse that showed a sunburned neck, a black skirt and heavy walking boots. Caypor addressing her in English told her in his jovial way, as though she did not know it already, what Ashenden had told him about himself. She listened grimly.

"I think you told me you understood German," said Caypor, his big red face wreathed in polite smiles but his little eyes darting about restlessly.

"Yes, I was for some time a student in Heidelberg."

"Really? said Mrs. Caypor in English, an expression of faint interest for a moment chasing away the sullenness from her face. "I know Heidelberg very well. I was at school there for one year."

Her English was correct, but throaty, and the mouthing emphasis she gave her words was disagreeable. Ashenden was diffuse in praise of the old university town and the beauty of the neighborhood. She heard him, from the standpoint of her Teutonic superiority, with toleration rather than with enthusiasm.

"It is well known that the valley of the Neckar is one of the beauty places of the whole world," she said.

"I have not told you, my dear," said Caypor then, "that Mr. Somerville is looking for someone to give him conversation lessons while he is here. I told him that perhaps you could suggest a teacher."

"No, I know no one whom I could conscientiously recommend," she answered. "The Swiss accent is hateful beyond words. It could do Mr. Somerville only harm to converse with a Swiss."

"If I were in your place, Mr. Somerville, I would try and persuade my wife to give you lessons. She is, if I may say so, a very cultivated and highly educated woman."

"*Ach,* Grantley, I have not the time. I have my own work to do."

Ashenden saw that he was being given his opportunity. The trap was prepared and all he had to do was fall in. He turned to Mrs. Caypor with a manner that he tried to make shy, deprecating and modest.

"Of course it would be too wonderful if you would give me lessons. I should look upon it as a real privilege. Naturally I wouldn't want to interfere with your work, I am just here to get well, with nothing in the world to do, and I would suit my time entirely to your convenience."

He felt a flash of satisfaction pass from one to the other and in Mrs. Caypor's blue eyes he fancied that he saw a dark glow.

"Of course it would be a purely business arrangement," said Caypor. "There's no reason that my good wife shouldn't earn a little pin money. Would you think ten francs an hour too much?"

"No," said Ashenden, "I should think myself lucky to get a first-rate teacher for that."

"What do you say, my dear? Surely you can spare an hour, and you would be doing this gentleman a kindness. He would learn that all Germans are not the devilish fiends that they think them in England."

On Mrs. Caypor's brow was an uneasy frown and Ashenden could not but think with apprehension of that hour's conversation a day that he was going to exchange with her. Heaven only knew how he would have to rack his brain for subjects of discourse with that heavy and morose woman. Now she made a visible effort.

"I shall be very pleased to give Mr. Somerville conversation lessons."

"I congratulate you, Mr. Somerville," said Caypor noisily. "You're in for a treat. When will you start, tomorrow at eleven?"

"That would suit me very well if it suits Mrs. Caypor."

"Yes, that is as good an hour as another," she answered.

Ashenden left them to discuss the happy outcome of their diplomacy. But when, punctually at eleven next morning, he heard a knock at his door (for it had been arranged that Mrs. Caypor should give him his lesson in his room) it was not without trepidation that he opened it. It behooved him to be frank, a trifle indiscreet, but obviously wary of a German woman, sufficiently intelligent, and impulsive. Mrs. Caypor's face was dark and sulky. She plainly hated having anything to do with him. But they sat down and she began, somewhat peremptorily, to ask him questions about his knowledge of German literature. She corrected his mistakes with exactness and when he put before her some difficulty in German construction explained it with clearness and precision. It was obvious that though she hated giving him a lesson she meant to give it conscientiously. She seemed to have not only an aptitude for teaching, but a love of it, and as the hour went on she began to speak with greater earnestness. It was already only by an effort that she remembered that he was a brutal Englishman. Ashenden, noticing the unconscious struggle within her, found himself not a little entertained; and it was with truth that, when later in the day Caypor asked him how the lesson had gone, he answered that it was highly satisfactory; Mrs. Caypor was an excellent teacher and a most interesting person.

"I told you so. She's the most remarkable woman I know."

And Ashenden had a feeling that when in his hearty, laughing way Caypor said this he was for the first time entirely sincere.

In a day or two Ashenden guessed that Mrs. Caypor was giving him lessons only in order to enable Caypor to arrive at a closer intimacy with him, for she confined herself strictly to matters of literature, music and painting; and when Ashenden, by way of experiment, brought the conversation round to the war, she cut him short.

"I think that is a topic that we had better avoid, Herr Somerville," she said.

She continued to give her lessons with the greatest thoroughness, and he had his money's worth, but every day she came with the same sullen face and it was only in the interest of teaching that she lost for a moment her instinctive dislike of him. Ashenden exercised in turn, but in vain, all his wiles. He was ingratiating, ingenious, humble, grateful, flattering, simple and timid. She remained coldly hostile. She was a fanatic. Her patriotism was aggressive, but disinterested, and obsessed with the notion of the superiority of all things German she loathed England with a virulent hatred because in that country she saw the chief obstacle to their diffusion. Her ideal was a German world in which the rest of the nations under a hegemony greater than that of Rome should enjoy the benefits of German science and German art and German culture. There was in the conception a magnificent impudence that appealed to Ashenden's sense of humor. She was no fool. She had read much, in several languages, and she could talk of the books she had read with good sense. She had a knowledge of modern painting and modern music that impressed Ashenden. It was amusing once to hear her before luncheon play one of those silvery little pieces of Debussy: she played it disdainfully because it was French and so light, but with an angry appreciation of its grace and gaiety. When Ashenden congratulated her she shrugged her shoulders.

"The decadent music of a decadent nation," she said. Then with powerful hands she struck the first resounding chords of a sonata by Beethoven; but she stopped. "I cannot play, I am out of practice, and you English, what do you know of music? You have not produced a composer since Purcell!"

"What do you think of that statement?" Ashenden, smiling, asked Caypor who was standing near.

"I confess its truth. The little I know of music my wife taught me. I wish you could hear her play when she is in practice." He put his fat hand, with its square, stumpy fingers, on her shoulder. "She can wring your heartstrings with pure beauty."

"*Dummer Kerl,*" she said, in a soft voice. "Stupid fellow," and Ashenden saw her mouth for a moment quiver, but she quickly recovered.

"You English, you cannot paint, you cannot model, you cannot write music."

"Some of us can at times write pleasing verses," said Ashenden, with good humor, for it was not his business to be put out, and, he did not know why, two lines occurring to him he said them:

"Whither, O splendid ship, thy white sails crowding,
Leaning across the bosom of the urgent West."

"Yes," said Mrs. Caypor, with a strange gesture, "you can write poetry. I wonder why."

And to Ashenden's surprise she went on, in her guttural English, to recite the next two lines of the poem he had quoted.

"Come, Grantley, *mittagessen* is ready, let us go into the dining room."

They left Ashenden reflective.

Ashenden admired goodness, but was not outraged by wickedness.

People sometimes thought him heartless because he was more often interested in others than attached to them, and even in the few to whom
he was attached his eyes saw with equal clearness the merits and the
defects. When he liked people it was not because he was blind to their
faults, he did not mind their faults but accepted them with a tolerant
shrug of the shoulders, or because he ascribed to them excellencies that
they did not possess; and since he judged his friends with candor they
never disappointed him and so he seldom lost one. He asked from none
more than he could give. He was able to pursue his study of the Caypors
without prejudice and without passion. Mrs. Caypor seemed to him more
of a piece and therefore the easier of the two to understand; she obviously
detested him; though it was so necessary for her to be civil to him her
antipathy was strong enough to wring from her now and then an expression of rudeness; and had she been safely able to do so she would have
killed him without a qualm. But in the pressure of Caypor's chubby hand
on his wife's shoulder and in the fugitive trembling of her lips Ashenden
had divined that this unprepossessing woman and that mean fat man were
joined together by a deep and sincere love. It was touching. Ashenden
assembled the observations that he had been making for the past few days
and little things that he had noticed but to which he had attached no
significance returned to him. It seemed to him that Mrs. Caypor loved
her husband because she was of a stronger character than he and because
she felt his dependence on her; she loved him for his admiration of her,
and you might guess that till she met him this dumpy, plain woman with
her dullness, good sense and want of humor could not have much enjoyed
the admiration of men; she enjoyed his heartiness and his noisy jokes,
and his high spirits stirred her sluggish blood; he was a great big bouncing
boy and he would never be anything else and she felt like a mother
towards him; she had made him what he was, and he was her man and
she was his woman, and she loved him, notwithstanding his weakness
(for with her clear head she must always have been conscious of that),
she loved him, *ach*, *was*, as Isolde loved Tristan. But then there was the
espionage. Even Ashenden with all his tolerance for human frailty could
not but feel that to betray your country for money is not a very pretty
proceeding. Of course she knew of it, indeed it was probably through
her that Caypor had first been approached; he would never have undertak-
en such work if she had not urged him to it. She loved him and she was
an honest and an upright woman. By what devious means had she persuaded herself to force her husband to adopt so base and dishonorable a
calling? Ashenden lost himself in a labyrinth of conjecture as he tried to
piece together the actions of her mind.

Grantley Caypor was another story. There was little to admire in him, but at that moment Ashenden was not looking for an object of admiration; but there was much that was singular and much that awas unexpected in that gross and vulgar fellow. Ashenden watched with entertainment the suave manner in which the spy tried to inveigle him in his toils. It was a couple of days after his first lesson that Caypor, after dinner, his wife having gone upstairs, threw himself heavily into a chair by Ashenden's side. His faithful Fritzi came up to him and put his long muzzle with its black nose on his knee.

"He has no brain," said Caypor, "but a heart of gold. Look at those little pink eyes. Did you ever see anything so stupid? And what an ugly face, but what incredible charm!"

"Have you had him long? asked Ashenden.

"I got him in 1914 just before the outbreak of war. By the way, what do you think of the news today? Of course my wife and I never discuss the war. You can't think what a relief to me it is to find a fellow country-man to whom I can open my heart."

He handed Ashenden a cheap Swiss cigar and Ashenden, making a rueful sacrifice to duty, accepted it.

"Of course they haven't got a chance, the Germans," said Caypor, "not a dog's chance. I knew they were beaten the moment we came in."

His manner was earnest, sincere and confidential. Ashenden made a commonplace rejoinder.

"It's the greatest grief of my life that owing to my wife's nationality I was unable to do any war work. I tried to enlist the day war broke out, but they wouldn't have me on account of my age, but I don't mind telling you, if the war goes on much longer, wife or no wife, I'm going to do something. With my knowledge of languages I ought to be of some service in the Censorship Department. That's where you were, wasn't it?"

That was the mark at which he had been aiming and in answer now to his well-directed questions Ashenden gave him the information that he had already prepared. Caypor drew his chair a little nearer and dropped his voice.

"I'm sure you wouldn't tell me anything that anyone shouldn't know, but after all these Swiss are absolutely pro-German and we don't want to give anyone the chance of overhearing."

Then he went on another tack. He told Ashenden a number of things that were of a certain secrecy.

"I wouldn't tell this to anybody else, you know, but I have one or two friends who are in pretty influential positions, and they know they can trust me."

Thus encouraged Ashenden was a little more deliberately indiscreet and when they parted both had reason to be satisfied. Ashenden guessed that Caypor's typewriter would be kept busy next morning and that that extremely energetic Major in Berne would shortly receive a most interesting report.

One evening, going upstairs after dinner, Ashenden passed an open bathroom. He caught sight of the Caypors.

"Come in," cried Caypor in his cordial way. "We're washing our Fritzi."

The bullterrier was constantly getting himself very dirty, and it was Caypor's pride to see him clean and white. Ashenden went in. Mrs. Caypor with her sleeves turned up and a large white apron was standing at one end of the bath, while Caypor, in a pair of trousers and a singlet, his fat, freckled arms bare, was soaping the wretched hound.

"We have to do it at night," he said, "because the Fitzgeralds use this bath and they'd have a fit if they knew we washed the dog in it. We wait till they go to bed. Come along, Fritzi, show the gentleman how beautifully you behave when you have your face scrubbed."

The poor brute, woebegone but faintly wagging his tail to show that however foul was this operation performed on him he bore no malice to the god who did it, was standing in the middle of the bath in six inches of water. He was soaped all over and Caypor, talking the while, shampooed him with his great fat hands.

"Oh, what a beautiful dog he's going to be when he's as white as the driven snow. His master will be as proud as Punch to walk out with him and all the little lady-dogs will say: good gracious, who's that beautiful aristocratic-looking bullterrier walking as though he owned the whole of Switzerland? Now stand still while you have your ears washed. You couldn't bear to go out into the street with dirty ears, could you? Like a nasty little Swiss schoolboy. *Noblese oblige*. Now the black nose. Oh, and all the soap is going into his little pink eyes and they'll smart."

Mrs. Caypor listened to this nonsense with a good-humored sluggish smile on her broad, plain face, and presently gravely took a towel.

"Now he's going to have a ducking. Upsie-daisy."

Caypor seized the dog by the forelegs and ducked him once and ducked him twice. There was struggle, a flurry and a splashing. Caypor lifted him out of the bath.

"Now go to mother and she'll dry you."

Mrs. Caypor sat down and taking the dog between her strong legs rubbed him till the sweat poured off her forehead. And Fritzi, a little shaken and breathless, but happy it was all over stood, with his sweet stupid face, white and shining.

"Blood will tell," cried Caypor exultantly. "He knows the names of no less than sixty-four of his ancestors, and they were all nobly born."

Ashenden was faintly troubled. He shivered a little as he walked upstairs.

Then, one Sunday, Caypor told him that he and his wife were going on an excursion and would eat their luncheon at some little mountain restaurant; and he suggested that Ashenden, each paying his share, should come with them. After three weeks at Lucerne Ashenden thought that his strength would permit him to venture the exertion. They started early, Mrs. Caypor businesslike in her walking boots and Tyrolese hat and alpenstock, and Caypor in stockings and plus-fours looking very British. The situation amused Ashenden and he was prepared to enjoy his day; but he meant to keep his eyes open; it was not inconceivable that the Caypors had discovered what he was and it would not do to go too near a precipice: Mrs. Caypor would not hesitate to give him a push and Caypor for all his jolliness was an ugly customer. But on the face of it there was nothing to mar Ashenden's pleasure in the golden morning. The air was fragrant. Caypor was full of conversation. He told funny stories. He was gay and jovial. The sweat rolled off his great red face and he laughed at himself because he was so fat. To Ashenden's astonishment he showed a peculiar knowledge of the mountain flowers. Once he went out of the way to pick one he saw a little distance from the path and brought it back to his wife. He looked at it tenderly.

"Isn't it lovely?" he cried, and his shifty grey-green eyes for a moment were as candid as a child's. "It's like a poem by Walter Savage Landor."

"Botany is my husband's favorite science," said Mrs. Caypor. "I laugh at him sometimes. He is devoted to flowers. Often when we have hardly had enough money to pay the butcher he has spent everything in his pocket to bring me a bunch of roses."

"*Qui fleurit sa maison fleurit son coeur,*" said Grantley Caypor.

Ashenden had once or twice seen Caypor, coming in from a walk, offer Mrs. Fitzgerald a nosegay of mountain flowers with an elephantine courtesy that was not entirely displeasing; and what he had just learned added a certain significance to the pretty little action. His passion for flowers was genuine and when he gave them to the old Irish lady he gave her something he valued. It showed a real kindness of heart. Ashenden had always thought botany a tedious science, but Caypor, talking exuberantly as they walked along, was able to impart to it life and interest. He must have given it a good deal of study.

"I've never written a book," he said. "There are too many books already and any desire to write I have is satisfied by the more immediately profitable and quite ephemeral composition of an article for a daily paper. But if I stay here much longer I have half a mind to write a book about the wildflowers of Switzerland. Oh, I wish you'd been here a little earlier. They were marvelous. But one wants to be a poet for that, and I'm only a poor newspaper man."

It was curious to observe how he was able to combine real emotion with false fact.

When they reached the inn, with its view of the mountains and the lake, it was good to see the sensual pleasure with which he poured down his throat a bottle of ice-cold beer. You could not but feel sympathy for a man who took so much delight in simple things. They lunched deliciously off scrambled eggs and mountain trout. Even Mrs. Caypor was moved to an unwonted gentleness by her surroundings; the inn was in an agreeably rural spot, it looked like a picture of a Swiss châlet in a book of early nineteenth-century travels; and she treated Ashenden with something less than her usual hostility. When they arrived she had burst into loud German exclamations on the beauty of the scene, and now, softened perhaps too by food and drink, her eyes, dwelling on the grandeur before her, filled with tears. She stretched out her hand.

"It is dreadful and I am ashamed, notwithstanding this horrible and unjust war I can feel in my heart at the moment nothing but happiness and gratitude."

Caypor took her hand and pressed it and, an unusual thing with him, addressing her in German, called her little pet-names. It was absurd, but touching. Ashenden, leaving them to their emotions, strolled through the garden and sat down on a bench that had been prepared for the comfort of the tourist. The view was of course spectacular, but it captured you; it was like a piece of music that was obvious and meretricious, but for the moment shattered your self-control.

And as Ashenden lingered idly in that spot he pondered over the mystery of Grantley Caypor's treachery. If he liked strange people he had found in him one who was strange beyond belief. It would be foolish to deny that he had amiable traits. His joviality was not assumed, he was without pretence a hearty fellow, and he had real good nature. He was always ready to do a kindness. Ashenden had often watched him with the old Irish Colonel and his wife who were the only other residents of the hotel; he would listen good-humoredly to the old man's tedious stories of the Egyptian war, and he was charming with her. Now that Ashenden had arrived at terms of some familiarity with Caypor he found that he regarded him less with repulsion than with curiosity. He did not think that he had become a spy merely for the money; he was a man of modest tastes and what he had earned in a shipping office must have sufficed to so good a manager as Mrs. Caypor; and after war was declared there was no lack of remunerative work for men over the military age. It might be that he was one of those men who prefer devious ways to straight for some intricate pleasure they get in fooling their fellows; and that he had turned spy, not from hatred of the country that had imprisoned him, not even from love of his wife, but from a desire to score off the bigwigs who never even knew of his existence. It might be that it was vanity that impelled him, a feeling that his talents had not received the recognition they merited, or just a puckish, impish desire to do mischief. He was a crook. It is true that only two cases of dishonesty had been brought home to him, but if he had been caught twice it might be surmised that he had often been dishonest without being caught. What did Mrs. Caypor think of this? They were so united that she must be aware of it. Did it make her ashamed, for her own uprightness surely none could doubt, or did she accept it as an inevitable kink in the man she loved? Did she do all she could to prevent it or did she close her eyes to something she could not help?

How much easier life would be if people were all black or all white and how much simpler it would be to act in regard to them! Was Caypor a good man who loved evil or a bad man who loved good? And how could such unreconcilable elements exist side by side and in harmony within the same heart? For one thing was clear, Caypor was disturbed by no gnawing of conscience; he did his mean and despicable work with gusto. He was a traitor who enjoyed his treachery. Though Ashenden had been studying human nature more or less consciously all his life, it seemed to him that he knew as little about it now in middle age as he had done when he was a child. Of course R. would have said to him: why the devil do you waste your time with such nonsense? The man's a dangerous spy and your business is to lay him by the heels.

That was true enough. Ashenden had decided that it would be useless to attempt to make any arrangement with Caypor. Though doubtless he would have no feeling about betraying his employers he could certainly not be trusted. His wife's influence was too strong. Besides, notwithstanding what he had from time to time told Ashenden, he was in his heart convinced that the Central Powers must win the war, and he meant to be on the winning side. Well, then Caypor must be laid by the heels, but how he was to effect that Ashenden had no notion. Suddenly he heard a voice.

"There you are. We've been wondering where you had hidden yourself."

He looked round and saw the Caypors strolling towards him. They were walking hand in hand.

"So this is what has kept you so quiet," said Caypor as his eyes fell on the view. "What a spot!"

Mrs. Caypor clasped her hands.

"Ach Gott, wie schön!" she cried. *"Wie schön.* When I look at that blue lake and those snowy mountains I feel inclined, like Goëthe's Faust, to cry to the passing moment: tarry."

"This is better than being in England with the excursions and alarms of war, isn't it?" said Caypor.

"Much," said Ashenden.

"By the way, did you have any difficulty in getting out?"

"No, not the smallest."

"I'm told they make rather a nuisance of themselves at the frontier nowadays."

"I came through without the smallest difficulty. I don't fancy they bother much about the English. I thought the examination of passports was quite perfunctory."

A fleeting glance passed between Caypor and his wife. Ashenden wondered what it meant. It would be strange if Caypor's thoughts were occupied with the chances of a journey to England at the very moment when he was himself reflecting on its possibility. In a little while Mrs. Caypor suggested that they had better be starting back and they wandered together in the shade of trees down the mountain paths.

Ashenden was watchful. He could do nothing (and his inactivity irked him) but wait with his eyes open to seize the opportunity that might present itself. A couple of days later an incident occurred that made him certain something was in the wind. In the course of his morning lesson Mrs. Caypor remarked:

"My husband has gone to Geneva today. He had some business to do there."

"Oh," said Ashenden, "will he be gone long?"

"No, only two days."

It is not everyone who can tell a lie and Ashenden had the feeling, he hardly knew why, that Mrs. Caypor was telling one then. Her manner perhaps was not quite as indifferent as you would have expected when she was mentioning a fact that could be of no interest to Ashenden. It flashed across his mind that Caypor had been summoned to Berne to see the redoubtable head of the German secret service. When he had the chance he said casually to the waitress:

"A little less work for you to do, *fraülein*. I hear that Herr Caypor has gone to Berne."

"Yes. But he'll be back tomorrow."

That proved nothing, but it was something to go upon. Ashenden knew in Lucerne a Swiss who was willing on emergency to do odd jobs and, looking him up, asked him to take a letter to Berne. It might be possible to pick up Caypor and trace his movements. Next day Caypor appeared once more with his wife at the dinner table, but merely nodded to Ashenden and afterwards both went straight upstairs. They looked troubled. Caypor, as a rule so animated, walked with bowed shoulders and looked neither to the right nor to the left. Next morning Ashenden received a reply to his letter: Caypor had seen Major von P. It was possible to guess what the Major had said to him. Ashenden well knew how rough he could be: he was a hard man and brutal, clever and unscrupulous and he was not accustomed to mince his words. They were tired of paying Caypor a salary to sit still in Lucerne and do nothing; the time was come for him to go to England. Guesswork? Of course it was guesswork, but in that trade it mostly was: you had to deduce the animal from its jawbone. Ashenden knew from Gustav that the Germans wanted to send someone to England. He drew a long breath; if Caypor went he would have to get busy.

When Mrs. Caypor came in to give him his lesson she was dull and listless. She looked tired and her mouth was set obstinately. It occurred to Ashenden that the Caypors had spent most of the night talking. He wished he knew what they had said. Did she urge him to go or did she try to dissuade him? Ashenden watched them again at luncheon. Something was the matter, for they hardly spoke to one another and as a rule they found plenty to talk about. They left the room early, but when Ashenden went out he saw Caypor sitting in the hall by himself.

"Hulloa," he cried jovially, but surely the effort was patent, "how are you getting on? I've been to Geneva."

"So I heard," said Ashenden.

"Come and have your coffee with me. My poor wife's got a headache. I told her she'd better go and lie down." In his shifty green eyes was an expression that Ashenden could not read. "The fact is, she's rather worried, poor dear; I'm thinking of going to England."

Ashenden's heart gave a sudden leap against his ribs, but his face remained impassive.

"Oh, are you going for long? We shall miss you."

"To tell you the truth, I'm fed up with doing nothing. The war looks as though it were going on for years and I can't sit here indefinitely.

Besides, I can't afford it, I've got to earn my living. I may have a German wife, but I am an Englishman, hang it all, and I want to do my bit. I could never face my friends again if I just stayed here in ease and comfort till the end of the war and never attempted to do a thing to help the country. My wife takes her German point of view and I don't mind telling you she's a bit upset. You know what women are."

Now Ashenden knew what it was that he saw in Caypor's eyes. Fear. It gave him a nasty turn. Caypor didn't want to go to England, he wanted to stay safely in Switzerland; Ashenden knew now what the major had said to him when he went to see him in Berne. He had got to go or lose his salary. What was it that his wife had said when he told her what had happened? He had wanted her to press him to stay, but, it was plain, she hadn't done that; perhaps he had not dared tell her how frightened he was; to her he had always been gay, bold, adventurous and devil-may-care; and now, the prisoner of his own lies, he had not found it in him to confess himself the mean and sneaking coward he was.

"Are you going to take your wife with you?" asked Ashenden.

"No, she'll stay here."

It had been arranged very neatly. Mrs. Caypor would receive his letters and forward the information they contained to Berne.

"I've been out of England so long that I don't quite know how to set about getting war work. What would you do in my place?"

"I don't know; what sort of work are you thinking of?"

"Well, you know, I imagine I could do the same thing as you did. I wonder if there's anyone in the Censorship Department that you could give me a letter of introduction to."

It was only by a miracle that Ashenden saved himself from showing by a smothered cry or by a broken gesture how startled he was; but not by Caypor's request, by what had just dawned upon him. What an idiot he had been! He had been disturbed by the thought that he was wasting his time at Lucerne, he was doing nothing, and though in fact, as it turned out, Caypor was going to England it was due to no cleverness of his. He could take to himself no credit for the result. And now he saw that he had been put in Lucerne, told how to describe himself and given the proper information, so that what actually had occurred should occur. It would be a wonderful thing for the German secret service to get an agent into the Censorship Department; and by a happy accident there was Grantley Caypor, the very man for the job, on friendly terms with someone who had worked there. What a bit of luck! Major von P. was a man of culture, and rubbing his hands, he must surely have murmured: *stultum facit fortuna quem vult perdere*. It was a trap of that devilish R. and the grim major at Berne had fallen into it. Ashenden had done his work just by sitting still and doing nothing. He almost laughed as he thought what a fool R. had made of him.

"I was on very good terms with the chief of my department, I could give you a note to him if you liked."

"That would be just the thing."

"But of course I must give the facts. I must say I've met you here and only known you a fortnight."

"Of course. But you'll say what else you can for me, won't you?"

"Oh, certainly."

"I don't know yet if I can get a visa. I'm told they're rather fussy."

"I don't see why. I shall be very sick if they refuse me one when I want to go back."

"I'll go and see how my wife is getting on," said Caypor suddenly, getting up. "When will you let me have that letter?"

"Whenever you like. Are you going at once?"

"As soon as possible."

Caypor left him. Ashenden waited in the hall for a quarter of an hour so that there should appear in him no sign of hurry. Then he went upstairs and prepared various communications. In one he informed R. that Caypor was going to England; in another he made arrangements through Berne that wherever Caypor applied for a visa it should be granted to him without question; and these he dispatched forthwith. When he went down to dinner he handed Caypor a cordial letter of introduction.

Next day but one Caypor left Lucerne.

Ashenden waited. He continued to have his hour's lesson with Mrs. Caypor and under her conscientious tuition began now to speak German with ease. They talked of Goëthe and Winckelmann, of art and life and travel. Fritzi sat quietly by her chair.

"He misses his master," she said, pulling his ears. "He only really cares for him, he suffers me only as belonging to him."

After his lesson Ashenden went every morning to Cook's to ask for his letters. It was here that all communications were addressed to him. He could not move till he received instructions, but R. could be trusted not to leave him idle long; and meanwhile there was nothing for him to do but have patience. Presently he received a letter from the consul in Geneva to say that Caypor had there applied for his visa and had set out for France. Having read this Ashenden went on for a little stroll by the lake and on his way back happened to see Mrs. Caypor coming out of Cook's office. He guessed that she was having her letters addressed there too. He went up to her.

"Have you had news of Herr Caypor?'" he asked her.

"No," she said. "I suppose I could hardly expect to yet."

He walked along by her side. She was disappointed, but not yet anxious; she knew how irregular at that time was the post. But next day during the lesson he could not but see that she was impatient to have done with it. The post was delivered at noon and at five minutes to she looked at her watch and him. Though Ashenden knew very well that no letter would ever come for her he had not the heart to keep her on tenterhooks.

"Don't you think that's enough for the day? I'm sure you want to go down to Cook's," he said.

"Thank you. That is very amiable of you."

Later he went there himself and he found her standing in the middle of the office. Her face was distraught. She addressed him wildly.

"My husband promised to write from Paris. I am sure there is a letter for me, but these stupid people say there's nothing. They're so careless, it's a scandal."

Ashenden did not know what to say. While the clerk was looking through the bundle to see if there was anything for him she came up to the desk again.

"When does the next post come in from France?" she asked.

"Sometimes there are letters about five."

"I'll come then."

She turned and walked rapidly away. Fritzi followed her with his tail between his legs. There was no doubt of it, already the fear had seized her that something was wrong. Next morning she looked dreadful; she could not have closed her eyes all night; and in the middle of the lesson she started up from her chair.

"You must excuse me, Herr Somerville, I cannot give you a lesson today. I am not feeling well."

Before Ashenden could say anything she had flung nervously from the room, and in the evening he got a note from her to say that she regretted that she must discontinue giving him conversation lessons. She gave no reason. Then Ashenden saw no more of her; she ceased coming in to meals; except to go morning and afternoon to Cook's she spent apparently the whole day in her room. Ashenden thought of her sitting there hour after hour with that hideous fear gnawing at her heart. Who could help feeling sorry for her? The time hung heavy on his hands too. He read a good deal and wrote a little, he hired a canoe and went for long leisurely paddles on the lake; and at last one morning the clerk at Cook's handed him a letter. It was from R. It had all the appearance of a business communication, but between the lines he read a good deal.

Dear Sir, it began, *The goods, with accompanying letter, dispatched by you from Lucerne have been duly delivered. We are obliged to you for executing our instructions with such promptness.*

It went on in this strain. R. was exultant. Ashenden guessed that Caypor had been arrested and by now had paid the penalty of his crime. He shuddered. He remembered a dreadful scene. Dawn. A cold, grey dawn, with a drizzling rain falling. A man, blindfolded, standing against a wall, an officer very pale giving an order, a volley, and then a young soldier, one of the firing party, turning round and holding on to his gun for support, vomiting. The officer turned paler still, and he, Ashenden, feeling dreadfully faint. How terrified Caypor must have been! It was awful when the tears ran down their faces. Ashenden shook himself. He went to the ticket office and obedient to his orders bought himself a ticket for Geneva.

As he was waiting for his change Mrs. Caypor came in. He was shocked at the sight of her. She was blowsy and disheveled and there were heavy rings round her eyes. She was deathly pale. She staggered up to the desk and asked for a letter. The clerk shook his head.

"I'm sorry, madam, there's nothing yet."

She gave a hoarse cry of despair and her face was distorted with anguish.

"Oh, God, oh, God," she moaned.

She turned away, the tears streaming from her weary eyes, and for a moment she stood there like a blind man groping and not knowing which way to go. Then a fearful thing happened. Fritzi, the bullterrier, sat down on his haunches and threw back his head and gave a long, long melancholy howl. Mrs. Caypor looked at him with terror; her eyes seemed really to start from her head. The doubt, the gnawing doubt that had tortured her during those dreadful days of suspense, was a doubt no longer. She knew. She staggered blindly into the street.

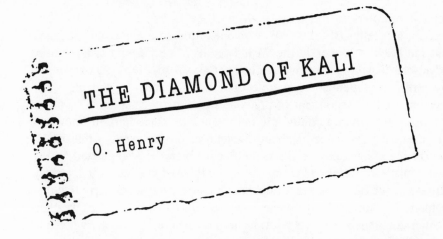

THE DIAMOND OF KALI

O. Henry

THE ORIGINAL NEWS item concerning the diamond of the goddess Kali was handed in to the city editor. He smiled and held it for a moment above the wastebasket. Then he laid it back on his desk and said: "Try the Sunday people; they might work something out of it."

The Sunday editor glanced the item over and said: "H'm!" Afterward he sent for a reporter and expanded his comment.

"You might see General Ludlow," he said, "and make a story out of this if you can. Diamond stories are a drug; but this one is big enough to be found by a scrubwoman wrapped up in a piece of newspaper and tucked under the corner of the hall linoleum. Find out first if the General has a daughter who intends to go on the stage. If not, you can go ahead with the story. Run cuts of the Kohinoor and J. P. Morgan's collection, and work in pictures of the Kimberley mines and Barney Barnato. Fill in with a tabulated comparison of the values of diamonds, radium, and veal cutlets since the meat strike; and let it run to a half page."

On the following day the reporter turned in his story. The Sunday editor let his eye sprint along its lines. "H'm!" he said again. This time the copy went into the wastebasket with scarcely a flutter.

The reporter stiffened a little around the lips; but he was whistling softly and contentedly between his teeth when I went over to talk with him about an hour later.

"I don't blame the 'old man,' " said he, magnanimously, "for cutting it out. It did sound like funny business; but it happened exactly as I wrote it. Say, why don't you fish that story out of the w.b., and use it? Seems to me it's as good as the tommyrot you write."

I accepted the tip, and if you read further you will learn the facts about the diamond of the goddess Kali as vouched for by one of the most reliable reporters on the staff.

Gen. Marcellus B. Ludlow lives in one of those decaying but venerated old red-brick mansions in the West Twenties. The General is a member of an old New York family that does not advertise. He is a globe-trotter by birth, a gentleman by predilection, a millionaire by the mercy of Heaven, and a connoisseur of precious stones by occupation.

The reporter was admitted promptly when he made himself known at the General's residence at about eight thirty on the evening that he received the assignment. In the magnificent library he was greeted by the distinguished traveler and connoisseur, a tall, erect gentleman in the early fifties, with a nearly white mustache, and a bearing so soldierly that one perceived in him scarcely a trace of the national Guardsman. His weather-beaten countenance lit up with a charming smile of interest when the reporter made known his errand.

"Ah, you have heard of my latest find. I shall be glad to show you what I conceive to be one the six most valuable blue diamonds in existence."

The General opened a small safe in a corner of the library and brought forth a plush-covered box. Opening this, he exposed to the reporter's bewildered gaze a huge and brilliant diamond—nearly as large as a hailstone.

"This stone," said the General, "is something more than a mere jewel. It once formed the central eye of the three-eyed goddess Kali, who is worshipped by one of the fiercest and most fanatical tribes of India. If you will arrange yourself comfortably I will give your a brief history of it for your paper."

General Ludlow brought a decanter of whisky and glasses from a cabinet, and set a comfortable armchair for the lucky scribe.

"The Phansigars, or Thugs, of India," began the General, "are the most dangerous and dreaded of the tribes of North India. They are extremists in religion, and worship the horrid goddess Kali in the form of images. Their rites are interesting and bloody. The robbing and murdering of travelers are taught as a worthy and obligatory deed by their strange religious code. Their worship of the three-eyed goddess Kali is conducted so secretly that no traveler has ever heretofore had the honor of witnessing the ceremonies. That distinction was reserved for myself.

"While at Sakaranpur, between Delhi and Khelat, I used to explore the jungle in every direction in hope of learning something new about these mysterious Phansigars.

"One evening at twilight I was making my way through a teakwood forest, when I came upon a deep circular depression in an open space, in the center of which was a rude stone temple. I was sure this was one of the temples of the Thugs, so I concealed myself in the undergrowth to watch.

"When the moon rose the depression in the clearing was suddenly filled with hundreds of shadowy, swiftly gliding forms. Then a door opened in the temple, exposing a brightly illuminated image of the goddess Kali, before which a white-robed priest began a barbarous incantation, while the tribe of worshippers prostrated themselves upon the earth.

"But what interested me the most was the central eye of the huge wooden idol. I could see by its flashing brilliancy that it was an immense diamond of the purest water.

"After rites were concluded the Thugs slipped away into the forest as silently as they had come. The priest stood for a few minutes in the door of the temple enjoying the cool of the night before closing his rather warm quarters. Suddenly a dark, lithe shadow slipped down into the hollow, leaped upon the priest, and struck him down with a glittering knife. Then the murderer sprang at the image of the goddess like a cat and pried out the glowing central eye of Kali with his weapon. Straight toward me he ran with his royal prize. When he was within two paces I rose to my feet and struck him with all my force between the eyes. He rolled over senseless and the magnificent jewel fell from his hand. That is the splendid blue diamond you have just seen—a stone worthy of a monarch's crown."

"That's a corking story," said the reporter. "That decanter is exactly like the one that John W. Gates always sets out during an interview."

"Pardon me," said General Ludlow, "for forgetting hospitality in the excitement of my narrative. Help yourself."

"Here's looking at you," said the reporter.

"What I am afraid of now," said the General, lowering his voice, "is that I may be robbed of the diamond. The jewel that formed the eye of their goddess is their most sacred symbol. Somehow the tribe suspected me of having it; and members of the band have followed me half around the earth. They are the most cunning and cruel fanatics in the world, and their religious vows would compel them to assassinate the unbeliever who has desecrated their sacred treasure.

"Once in Lucknow three of their agents, disguised as servants in a hotel, endeavored to strangle me with a twisted cloth. Again, in London, two Thugs, made up as street musicians, climbed into my window at night and attacked me. They have even tracked me to this country. My life is never safe. A month ago, while I was at a hotel in the Berkshires, three of them sprang upon me from the roadside weeds. I saved myself by my knowledge of their customs."

"How was that, General?" asked the reporter.

"There was a cow grazing nearby," said General Ludlow, "a gentle Jersey cow. I ran to her side and stood. The three Thugs ceased their attack, knelt and struck the ground thrice with their foreheads. Then, after many respectful salaams, they departed."

"Afraid the cow would hook?" asked the reporter.

"No; the cow is a sacred animal to the Phansigars. Next to their goddess they worship the cow. They have never been known to commit any deed of violence in the presence of the animal they reverence."

"It's a mighty interesting story," said the reporter. "If you don't mind I'll take another drink, and then a few notes."

"I will join you," said General Ludlow, with a courteous wave of his hand.

"If I were you," advised the reporter, "I'd take that sparkler to Texas. Get on a cow ranch there, and the Pharisees—"

"Phansigars," corrected the General.

"Oh yes; the fancy guys would run up against a long horn every time they made a break."

General Ludlow closed the diamond case and thrust it into his bosom.

"The spies of the tribe have found me out in New York," he said, straightening his tall figure. "I'm familiar with the East Indian cast of countenance, and I know that my every movement is watched. They will undoubtedly attempt to rob and murder me here."

"Here?" exclaimed the reporter, seizing the decanter and pouring out a liberal amount of its contents.

"At any moment," said the General. "But as a soldier and a connoisseur I shall sell my life and my diamond as dearly as I can."

At this point of the reporter's story there is a certain vagueness, but it can be gathered that there was a loud crashing at the rear of the house they were in. General Ludlow buttoned his coat closely and sprang for the door. But the reporter clutched him firmly with one hand, while he held the decanter with the other.

"Tell me before we fly," he urged, in voice thick with inward turmoil, "do any of your daughters contemplate going on the stage?"

"I have no daughters—fly for your life—the Phansigars are upon us!" cried the General.

The two men dashed out of the front door of the house.

The hour was late. As their feet struck the sidewalk strange men of dark and forbidding appearance seemed to rise up out of the earth and encompass them. One with Asiatic features pressed close to the General and droned in a terrible voice:

"Buy cast clo'!"

Another, dark-whiskered and sinister, sped lithely to his side and began in a whining voice:

"Say, mister, have yer got a dime fer a poor feller what—"

They hurried on, but only into the arms of a black-eyed, dusky-browed being, who held out his hat under their noses, while a confederate of Oriental hue turned the handle of a street organ nearby.

Twenty steps farther on General Ludlow and the reporter found themselves in the midst of a half-dozen villainous-looking men with high-turned coat collars and faces bristling with unshaven beards.

"Run for it!" hissed the General. "They have discovered the possessors of the diamond of the goddess Kali."

The two men took to their heels. The avengers of the goddess pursued.

"Oh, Lordy!" groaned the reporter, "there isn't a cow this side of Brooklyn. We're lost!"

When near the corner they both fell over an iron object that rose from the sidewalk close to the gutter. Clinging to it desperately, they awaited their fate.

"If I only had a cow!" moaned the reporter—"or another nip from that decanter, General!"

As soon as the pursuers observed where their victims had found refuge they suddenly fell back and retreated to a considerable distance.

"They are waiting for reinforcements in order to attack us," said General Ludlow.

But the reporter emitted a ringing laugh, and hurled his hat triumphantly into the air.

"Guess again," he shouted, and leaned heavily upon the iron object. "Your old fancy guys or thugs, whatever you call 'em, are up to date. Dear General, this is a pump we're stranded upon—same as a cow in New York (hic!) see? Thas'h why the 'nfuriated smoked guys don't attack us—See? Sacred an'mal, the pump in N' York, my dear General!"

But further down in the shadows of Twenty-eighth Street the marauders were holding a parley.

"Come on, Reddy," said one. "Let's go frisk the old 'un. He's been showin' a sparkler as big as a hen egg all around Eighth Avenue for two weeks past."

"Not on your silhouette," decided Reddy. "You see 'em rallyin' round The Pump? They're friends of Bill's. Bill won't stand for nothin' of this kind in his district since he got that bid to Esopus."

This exhausts the facts concerning the Kali diamond. But it is deemed not inconsequent to close with the following brief (paid) item that appeared two days later in a morning paper.

"It is rumored that a niece of Gen. Marcellus B. Ludlow, of New York City, will appear on the stage next season.

"Her diamonds are said to be extremely valuable and of much historic interest."

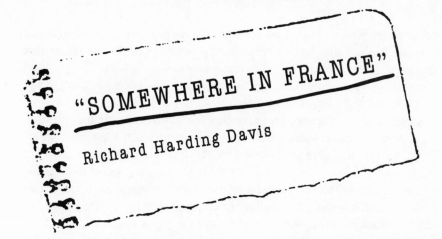

"SOMEWHERE IN FRANCE"

Richard Harding Davis

MARIE GESSLER, KNOWN as Marie Chaumontel, Jeanne d'Avrechy, the Countess d'Aurillac, was German. Her father, who served through the Franco-Prussian War, was a German spy. It was from her mother she learned to speak French sufficiently well to satisfy even an Academician and, among Parisians, to pass as one. Both her parents were dead. Before they departed, knowing they could leave their daughter nothing save their debts, they had her trained as a nurse. But when they were gone, Marie in the Berlin hospitals played politics, intrigued, indiscriminately misused the appealing, violet eyes. There was a scandal; several scandals. At the age of twenty-five she was dismissed from the Municipal Hospital, and as now — save for the violet eyes — she was without resources, as a *compagnon de voyage* with a German doctor she traveled to Monte Carlo. There she abandoned the doctor for Henri Ravignac, a captain in the French Aviation Corps, who, when his leave ended, escorted her to Paris.

The duties of Captain Ravignac kept him in barracks near the aviation field, but Marie he established in his apartments on the Boulevard Haussmann. One day he brought from the barracks a roll of blueprints, and as he was locking them in a drawer, said: "The Germans would pay through the nose for those!" The remark was indiscreet, but then Marie had told him she was French, and any one would have believed her.

The next morning the same spirit of adventure that had exiled her from the Berlin hospitals carried her with the blueprints to the German embassy. There, greatly shocked, they first wrote down her name and address, and then, indignant at her proposition, ordered her out. But the day following a strange young German who was not at all indignant, but, on the contrary, quite charming, called upon Marie. For the blueprints he offered her a very large sum, and that same hour with them and Marie departed for Berlin. Marie did not need the money. Nor did the argument that she was serving her country greatly impress her. It was rather that she loved intrigue. And so she became a spy.

Henri Ravignac, the man she had robbed of the blueprints, was tried by court-martial. The charge was treason, but Charles Ravignac, his younger brother, promised to prove that the guilty one was the girl, and to that end obtained leave of absence and spent much time and money. At the trial he was able to show the record of Marie in Berlin and Monte Carlo; that she was the daughter of a German secret agent; that on the afternoon the prints disappeared Marie, with an agent of the German embassy had left Paris for Berlin. In consequence of this the charge of selling military secrets was altered to one of "gross neglect," and Henri Ravignac was sentenced to two years in the military prison at Tours. But he was of an ancient and noble family, and when they came to take him from his cell in the Cherche-Midi, he was dead. Charles, his brother, disappeared. It was said he also had killed himself; that he had been appointed a military attaché in South America; that to revenge his brother he had entered the secret service; but whatever became of him no one knew. All that was certain was that, thanks to the act of Marie Gessler, on the rolls of the French army the ancient and noble name of Ravignac no longer appeared.

In her chosen profession Marie Gessler found nothing discreditable. Of herself her opinion was not high, and her opinion of men was lower. For her smiles she had watched several sacrifice honor, duty, loyalty; and she held them and their kind in contempt. To lie, to cajole, to rob men of secrets they thought important, and of secrets the importance of which they did not even guess, was to her merely an intricate and exciting game.

She played it very well. So well that in the service her advance was rapid. On important missions she was sent to Russia, through the Balkans; even to the United States. There, with credentials as an army nurse, she inspected our military hospitals and unobstrusively asked many innocent questions.

When she begged to be allowed to work in her beloved Paris, "they" told her when war came "they" intended to plant her inside that city, and that, until then, the less Paris knew of her the better.

But just before the great war broke, to report on which way Italy might jump, she was sent to Rome, and it was not until September she was recalled. The telegram informed her that her Aunt Elizabeth was ill, and that at once she must return to Berlin. This, she learned from the code book wrapped under the cover of her thermos bottle, meant that she was to report to the general commanding the German forces at Soissons.

From Italy she passed through Switzerland, and, after leaving Basle, on military trains was rushed north to Luxemburg, and then west to Laon. She was accompanied by her companion, Bertha, an elderly and respectable, even distinguished-looking female. In the secret service her number was 528. Their passes from the war office described them as nurses of the German Red Cross. Only the Intelligence Department knew their real mission. With her also, as her chauffeur, was a young Italian soldier of fortune, Paul Anfossi. He had served in the Belgian Congo, in the French Foreign Legion in Algiers, and spoke all the European languages. In Rome, where as a wireless operator he was serving a commercial company, in selling Marie copies of messages he had memorized, Marie had found him useful, and when war came she obtained for him, from the Wilhelmstrasse, the number 292. From Laon, in one of the automobiles of the General Staff, the three spies were driven first to Soissons, and then along the road to Meaux and Paris, to the Village of Neufchelles. They arrived at midnight, and in a château of one of the champagne princes, found the colonel commanding the Intelligence Bureau. He accepted their credentials, destroyed them, and replaced them with a *laisser-passer* signed by the mayor of Laon. That dignitary, the colonel explained, to citizens of Laon fleeing to Paris and the coast had issued many passes. But as now between Laon and Paris there were three German armies, the refugees had been turned back and their passes confiscated.

"From among them," said the officer, "we have selected one for you. It is issued to the wife of Count d'Aurillac, a captain of reserves, and her aunt, Madame Benet. It asks for those ladies and their chauffeur, Briand, a safe-conduct through the French military lines. If it gets you into Paris you will destroy it and assume another name. The Count d'Aurillac is now with his regiment in that city. If he learned of the presence there of his wife, he would seek her, and that would not be good for you. So, if you reach Paris, you will become a Belgian refugee. You are high-born and rich. Your château has been destroyed. But you have money. You will give liberally to the Red Cross. You will volunteer to nurse in the hospitals. With your sad story of ill treatment by us, with your high birth, and your knowledge of nursing, which you acquired, of course, only as an amateur, you should not find it difficult to join the Ladies of France, or the American Ambulance. What you learn from the wounded English and French officers and the French doctors you will send us through the usual channels."

"When do I start?" asked the woman.

"For a few days," explained the officer, "you remain in this château.

You will keep us informed of what is going forward after we withdraw."

"Withdraw?" It was more of an exclamation than a question. Marie was too well trained to ask questions.

"We are taking up a new position," said the officer, "on the Aisne."

The woman, incredulous, stared.

"And we do not enter Paris?"

"You do," returned the officer. "That is all that concerns you. We will join you later—in the spring. Meanwhile, for the winter we intrench ourselves along the Aisne. In a chimney of this château we have set up a wireless outfit. We are leaving it intact. The chauffeur Briand—who, you must explain to the French, you brought with you from Laon, and who has been long in your service—will transmit whatever you discover. We wish especially to know of any movement toward our left. If they attack in front from Soissons, we are prepared; but of any attempt to cross the Oise and take us in flank, you must warn us."

The officer rose and hung upon himself his field glasses, map cases, and side arms.

"We leave you now," he said. "When the French arrive you will tell them your reason for halting at this château was that the owner, Monsieur Iverney, and his family are friends of your husband. You found us here, and we detained you. And so long as you can use the wireless, make excuses to remain. If they offer to send you on to Paris, tell them your aunt is too ill to travel."

"But they will find the wireless," said the woman. "They are sure to use the towers for observation, and they will find it."

"In that case," said the officer, "you will suggest to them that we fled in such haste we had no time to dismantle it. Of course, you had no knowledge that it existed, or, as a loyal French woman, you would have at once told them." To emphasize his next words the officer pointed at her: "Under no circumstances," he continued, "must you be suspected. If they should take Briand in the act, should they have even the least doubt concerning him, you must repudiate him entirely. If necessary, to keep your own skirts clear, it would be your duty yourself to denounce him as a spy."

"Your first orders," said the woman, "were to tell them Briand had been long in my service; that I brought him from my home in Laon."

"He might be in your service for years," returned the colonel, "and you not know he was a German agent."

"If to save myself I inform upon him," said Marie, "of course you know you will lose him."

The officer shrugged his shoulders. "A wireless operator," he retorted, "we can replace. But for you, and for the service you are to render in Paris, we have no substitute. You must not be found out. You are invaluable."

The spy inclined her head. "I thank you," she said.

The officer sputtered indignantly.

"It is not a compliment," he exclaimed; "it is an order. You must not be found out!"

Withdrawn some two hundred yards from the Paris road, the château stood upon a wooded hill. Except directly in front, trees of great height surrounded it. The tips of their branches brushed the windows; interlacing, they continued until they overhung the wall of the estate. Where it ran with the road the wall gave way to a lofty gate and iron fence, through which those passing could see a stretch of noble turf, as wide as a polo field, borders of flowers disappearing under the shadows of the trees; and the château itself, with its terrace, its many windows, its high-pitched, sloping roof, broken by towers and turrets.

Through the remainder of the night there came from the road to those in the château the roar and rumbling of the army in retreat. It moved without panic, disorder, or haste, but unceasingly. Not for an instant was there a breathing-spell. And when the sun rose, the three spies—the two women and the chauffeur—who in the great château were now alone, could see as well as hear the gray column of steel rolling past below them.

The spies knew that the gray column had reached Claye, had stood within fifteen miles of Paris, and then upon Paris had turned its back. They knew also that the reverberations from the direction of Meaux, that each moment grew more loud and savage, were the French "seventy-fives" whipping the gray column forward. Of what they felt the Germans did not speak. In silence they looked at each other, and in the eyes of Marie was bitterness and resolve.

Toward noon Marie met Anfossi in the great drawing room that stretched the length of the terrace and from the windows of which, through the park gates, they could see the Paris road.

"This, that is passing now," said Marie, "is the last of our rear guard. Go to your tower,'" she ordered, "and send word that except for stragglers and the wounded our column has just passed through Neufchelles, and that any moment we expect the French." She raised her hand impressively. "From now," she warned, "we speak French, we think French, we are French!"

Anfossi, or Briand, as now he called himself, addressed her in that language. His tone was bitter. "Pardon my lese-majesty," he said, "but this chief of your Intelligence Department is a *dummer Mensch*. He is throwing away a valuable life."

Marie exclaimed in dismay. She placed her hand upon his arm, and the violet eyes filled with concern.

"Not yours!" she protested.

"Absolutely!" returned the Italian. "I can send nothing by this knapsack wireless that they will not learn from others; from airmen, Uhlans, the peasants in the fields. And certainly I will be caught. Dead I am dead, but alive and in Paris the opportunities are unending. From the French Legion Etranger I have my honorable discharge. I am an expert wireless operator and in their Signal Corps I can easily find a place. Imagine me, then, on the Eiffel Tower. From the air I snatch news from all of France, from the Channel, the North Sea. You and I could work together, as in Rome. But here, between the lines, with a pass from a village *sous préfet*, it is ridiculous. I am not afraid to die. But to die because some one else is stupid, that is hard."

Marie clasped his hand in both of hers.

"You must not speak of death," she cried; "you know I must carry out my orders, that I must force you to take this risk. And you know that thought of harm to you tortures me!"

Quickly the young man disengaged his hand. The woman exclaimed with anger.

"Why do you doubt me?" she cried.

Briand protested vehemently.

"I do not doubt you."

"My affection, then?" In a whisper that carried with it the feeling of a caress Marie added softly: "My love?"

The young man protested miserably. "You make it very hard, mademoiselle," he cried. "You are my superior officer, I am your servant. Who am I that I should share with others—"

The woman interrupted eagerly.

"Ah, you are jealous!" she cried. "Is that why you are so cruel? But when I *tell* you I love you, and only you, can you not *feel* it is the truth?"

The young man frowned unhappily.

"My duty, mademoiselle!" he stammered.

With an exclamation of anger Marie left him. As the door slammed behind her, the young man drew a deep breath. On his face was the expression of ineffable relief.

In the hall Marie met her elderly companion, Bertha, now her aunt, Madame Benet.

"I heard you quarrelling," Bertha protested. "It is most indiscreet. It is not in the part of the Countess d'Aurillac that she makes love to her chauffeur."

Marie laughed noiselessly and drew her farther down the hall. "He is imbecile!" she exclaimed. "He will kill me with his solemn face and his conceit. I make love to him—yes—that he may work the more willingly. But he will have none of it. He is jealous of the others."

Madame Benet frowned.

"He resents the others," she corrected. "I do not blame him. He is a gentleman!"

"And the others," demanded Marie; "were they not of the most noble families of Rome?"

"I am old and I am ugly," said Bertha, "but to me Anfossi is always as considerate as he is to you who are so beautiful."

"An Italian gentleman," returned Marie, "does not serve in Belgian Congo unless it is the choice of that or the marble quarries."

"I do not know what his past may be," sighed Madame Benet, "nor do I ask. He is only a number, as you and I are only numbers. And I beg you to let us work in harmony. At such a time your love affairs threaten our safety. You must wait."

Marie laughed insolently. "With the Du Barry," she protested, "I can boast that I wait for no man."

"No," replied the older woman; "you pursue him!"

Marie would have answered sharply, but on the instant her interest was diverted. For one week, by day and night, she had lived in a world peopled only by German soldiers. Beside her in the railroad carriage, on the station platforms, at the windows of the trains that passed the one in which she rode, at the grade crossings, on the bridges, in the roads that paralleled the tracks, choking the streets of the villages and spread over the fields of grain, she had seen only the gray-green uniforms. Even her professional eye no longer distinguished regiment from regiment, dragoon from grenadier, Uhlan from Hussar or Landsturm. Stripes, insignia, numerals, badges of rank, had lost their meaning. Those who wore them no longer were individuals. They were not even human. During the three last days the automobile, like a motorboat fighting the tide, had crept through a gray-green river of men, stained, as though from the banks, by mud and yellow clay. And for hours, while the car was blocked, and in fury the engine raced and purred, the gray-green river had rolled past her, slowly but as inevitably as lava down the slope of a volcano, bearing on its surface faces with staring eyes, thousands and thousands of eyes, some fierce and bloodshot, others filled with weariness, homesickness, pain. At night she still saw them: the white faces under the sweat and dust, the eyes dumb, inarticulate, asking the answer. She had been suffocated by German soldiers, by the mass of them, engulfed and smothered; she had stifled in a land inhabited only by gray-green ghosts.

And suddenly, as though a miracle had been wrought, she saw upon the lawn, riding toward her, a man in scarlet, blue, and silver. One man riding alone.

Approaching with confidence, but alert; his reins fallen, his hands nursing his carbine, his eyes searched the shadows of the trees, the empty windows, even the sun-swept sky. His was the new face at the door, the new step on the floor. And the spy knew had she beheld an army corps it would have been no more significant, nor more menacing, than the solitary *chasseur à cheval* scouting in advance of the enemy.

"We are saved!" exclaimed Marie, with irony. "Go quickly," she commanded, "to the bedroom on the second floor that opens upon the staircase, so that you can see all who pass. You are too ill to travel. They must find you in bed."

"And you?" said Bertha.

"I," cried Marie rapturously, "hasten to welcome our preserver!"

The preserver was a peasant lad. Under the white dust his cheeks were burned a brown-red, his eyes, honest and blue, through much staring at the skies and at horizon lines, were puckered and encircled with tiny wrinkles. Responsibility had made him older than his years, and in speech brief. With the beautiful lady who with tears of joy ran to greet him, and who in an ecstasy of happiness pressed her cheek against the nose of his horse, he was unimpressed. He returned to her her papers and gravely echoed her answers to his questions. "This château," he repeated, "was occupied by their General Staff; they have left no wounded here; you saw the last of them pass a half-hour since." He gathered up his reins.

Marie shrieked in alarm. "You will not leave us?" she cried.

For the first time the young man permitted himself to smile. "Others arrive soon," he said.

He touched his shako, wheeled his horse in the direction from which he had come, and a minute later Marie heard the hoofs echoing through the empty village.

When they came, the others were more sympathetic. Even in times of war a beautiful woman is still a beautiful woman. And the staff officers who moved into the quarters so lately occupied by the enemy found in the presence of the Countess d'Aurillac nothing to distress them. In the absence of her dear friend, Madame Iverney, the châtelaine of the château, she acted as their hostess. Her chauffeur showed the company cooks the way to the kitchen, the larder, and the charcoal-box. She, herself, in the hands of General Andre placed the keys of the famous wine cellar, and to the surgeon, that the wounded might be freshly bandaged, intrusted those of the linen closet. After the indignities she had suffered while "detained" by *les Boches,* her delight and relief at again finding herself under the protection of her own people would have touched a heart of stone. And the hearts of the staff were not of stone. It was with regret they gave the countess permission to continue on her way. At this she exclaimed with gratitude. She assured them, were her aunt able to travel, she would immediately depart.

"In Paris she will be more comfortable than here," said the kind surgeon. He was a reservist, and in times of peace a fashionable physician and as much at his ease in a boudoir as in a field hospital. "Perhaps if I saw Madame Benet?"

At the suggestion the countess was overjoyed. But they found Madame Benet in a state of complete collapse. The conduct of the Germans had brought about a nervous breakdown.

"Though the bridges are destroyed at Meaux," urged the surgeon, "even with a detour, you can be in Paris in four hours. I think it is worth the effort."

But the mere thought of the journey threw Madame Benet into hysterics. She asked only to rest, she begged for an opiate to make her sleep. She begged also that they would leave the door open, so that when she dreamed she was still in the hands of the Germans, and woke in terror, the sound of the dear French voices and the sight of the beloved French uniforms might reassure her. She played her part well. Concerning her Marie felt not the least anxiety. But toward Briand, the chauffeur, the new arrivals were less easily satisfied.

The general sent his adjutant for the countess. When the adjutant had closed the door General Andre began abruptly:

"The chauffeur Briand," he asked, "you know him; you can vouch for him?"

"But, certainly!" protested Marie. "He is an Italian."

As though with sudden enlightenment, Marie laughed. It was as if now in the suspicion of the officer she saw a certain reasonableness. "Briand was so long in the Foreign Legion in Algiers," she explained, "where my husband found him, that we have come to think of him as French. As much French as ourselves, I assure you."

The general and his adjutant were regarding each other questioningly.

"Perhaps I should tell the countess," began the general, "that we have learned—"

The signal from the adjutant was so slight, so swift, that Marie barely intercepted it.

The lips of the general shut together like the leaves of a book. To show the interview was at an end, he reached for a pen.

"I thank you," he said.

"Of course," prompted the adjutant, "Madame d'Aurillac understands the man must not know we inquired concerning him."

General Andre frowned at Marie.

"Certainly not!" he commanded. "The honest fellow must not know that even for a moment he was doubted."

Marie raised the violet eyes reprovingly.

"I trust," she said with reproach, "I too well understand the feelings of a French soldier to let him know his loyalty is questioned."

With a murmur of appreciation the officers bowed and with a gesture of gracious pardon Marie left them.

Outside in the hall, with none but orderlies to observe, like a cloak the graciousness fell from her. She was drawn two ways. In her work Anfossi was valuable. But Anfossi suspected was less than of no value; he became a menace, a death-warrant.

General Andre had said, "We have learned—" and the adjutant had halted him. What had he learned? To know that, Marie would have given much. Still, one important fact comforted her. Anfossi alone was suspected. Had there been concerning herself the slightest doubt, they certainly would not have allowed her to guess her companion was under surveillance; they would not have asked one who was herself suspected to vouch for the innocence of a fellow conspirator. Marie found the course to follow difficult. With Anfossi under suspicion his usefulness was for the moment at an end; and to accept the chance offered her to continue on to Paris seemed most wise. On the other hand, if, concerning Anfossi, she had succeeded in allaying their doubts, the results most to be desired could be attained only by remaining where they were.

Their position inside the lines was of the greatest strategic value. The rooms of the servants were under the roof, and that Briand should sleep in one of them was natural. That to reach or leave his room he should constantly be ascending or descending the stairs also was natural. The field-wireless outfit, or, as he had disdainfully described it, the "knapsack" wireless, was situated not in the bedroom he had selected for himself, but in one adjoining. At other times this was occupied by the maid of Madame Iverney. To summon her maid Madame Iverney, from her apartment on the second floor, had but to press a button. And it was in the apartment of Madame Iverney, and on the bed of that lady, that Madame Benet now reclined. When through the open door she saw an officer or soldier mount the stairs, she pressed the button that rang a bell in the room of the maid. In this way, long before whoever was ascending the stairs could reach the top floor, warning of his approach came to Anfossi. It gave him time to replace the dustboard over the fireplace in which the wireless was concealed and to escape into his own bedroom. The arrangement was ideal. And already information picked up in the halls below by Marie had been conveyed to Anfossi to relay in a French cipher to the German General Staff at Rheims.

Marie made an alert and charming hostess. To all who saw her it was evident that her mind was intent only upon the comfort of her guests. Throughout the day many came and went, but each she made welcome; to each as he departed she called *"bonne chance."* Efficient, tireless, tactful, she was everywhere: in the dining room, in the kitchen, in the bedrooms, for the wounded finding mattresses to spread in the gorgeous salons of the champagne prince; for the soldier-chauffeurs carrying wine into the courtyard, where the automobiles panted and growled, and the arriving and departing shrieked for right of way. At all times an alluring person, now the one woman in a tumult of men, her smart frock covered by an apron, her head and arms bare, undismayed by the sight of the wounded or by the distant rumble of the guns, the Countess d'Aurillac was an inspiring and beautiful picture. The eyes of the officers, young and old, informed her of that fact, one of which already she was well aware. By the morning of the next day she was accepted as the owner of the château. And though continually she reminded the staff she was present only as the friend of her schoolmate, Madame Iverney, they deferred to her as to a hostess. Many of them she already saluted by name, and to those who with messages were constantly motoring to and from the front at Soissons she was particularly kind. Overnight the legend of her charm, of her devotion to the soldiers of all ranks, had spread from Soissons to Meaux, and from Meaux to Paris. It was noon of that day when from the window of the second story Marie saw an armored automobile sweep into the courtyard. It was driven by an officer, young and appallingly good-looking, and, as was obvious by the way he spun his car, one who held in contempt both the law of gravity and death. That he was some one of importance seemed evident. Before he could alight the adjutant had raced to meet him. With her eye for detail Marie observed that the young officer, instead of importing information, received it. He must, she guessed, have just arrived from Paris, and his brother officer either was telling him the news or giving him his orders. Whichever it might be, in what was told him the new arrival was greatly interested. One instant in indignation his gauntleted fist beat upon the steering-wheel, the next he smiled with pleasure. To interpret this pantomime was difficult; and, the better to inform herself, Marie descended the stairs.

As she reached the lower hall the two officers entered. To the spy the man last to arrive was always the one of greatest importance; and Marie assured herself that through her friend, the adjutant, to meet with this one would prove easy.

But the chauffeur commander of the armored car made it most difficult. At sight of Marie, much to her alarm as though greeting a dear friend, he snatched his kepi from his head and sprang toward her.

"The major," he cried, "told me you were here, that you are Madame d'Aurillac." His eyes spoke his admiration. In delight he beamed upon her. "I might have known it!" he murmured. With the confidence of one who is sure he brings good news, he laughed happily. "And I," he cried, "am 'Pierrot'!"

Who the devil "Pierrot" might be the spy could not guess. She knew only that she wished by a German shell "Pierrot" and his car had been blown to tiny fragments. Was it a trap, she asked herself, or was the handsome youth really someone the Countess d'Aurillac should know. But, as from his introducing himself it was evident he could not know that lady very well, Marie took courage and smiled.

"*Which* 'Pierrot'?" she parried.

"Pierre Thierry!" cried the youth.

To the relief of Marie he turned upon the adjutant and to him explained who Pierre Thierry might be.

"Paul d'Aurillac," he said, "is my dearest friend. When he married this charming lady I was stationed in Algiers, and but for the war I might never have met her."

To Marie, with his hand on his heart in a most charming manner, he bowed. His admiration he made no effort to conceal.

"And so," he said, "I know why there is war!"

The adjutant smiled indulgently, and departed on his duties, leaving them alone. The handsome eyes of Captain Thierry were raised to the violet eyes of Marie. They appraised her boldly and as boldly expressed their approval.

In burlesque the young man exclaimed indignantly: "Paul deceived me!" he cried. "He told me he had married the most beautiful woman in Laon. He has married the most beautiful woman in France!"

To Marie this was not impertinence, but gallantry.

This was a language she understood, and this was the type of man, because he was the least difficult to manage, she held most in contempt.

"But about you, Paul did not deceive me," she retorted. In apparent confusion her eyes refused to meet his. "He told me 'Pierrot' was a most dangerous man!"

She continued hurriedly. With wifely solicitude she asked concerning Paul. She explained that for a week she had been a prisoner in the château, and, since the mobilization, of her husband save that he was with his regiment in Paris she had heard nothing. Captain Thierry was able to give her later news. Only the day previous, on the boulevards, he had met Count d'Aurillac. He was at the Grand Hôtel, and as Thierry was at once motoring back to Paris he would give Paul news of their meeting. He hoped he might tell him that soon his wife also would be in Paris. Marie explained that only the illness of her aunt prevented her from the same day joining her husband. Her manner became serious.

"And what other news have you?" she asked. "Here on the firing line we know less of what is going forward than you in Paris."

So Pierre Thierry told her all he knew. They were preparing despatches he was at once to carry back to the General Staff, and, for the moment, his time was his own. How could he better employ it than in talking of the war with a patriotic and charming French woman?

In consequence Marie acquired a mass of facts, gossip, and guesses. From these she mentally selected such information as, to her employers across the Aisne, would be of vital interest.

And to rid herself of Thierry and on the fourth floor seek Anfossi was now her only wish. But, in attempting this, by the return of the adjutant she was delayed. To Thierry the adjutant gave a sealed envelope.

"Thirty-one, Boulevard des Invalides," he said. With a smile he turned to Marie. "And you will accompany him!"

"I!" exclaimed Marie. She was sick with sudden terror.

But the tolerant smile of the adjutant reassured her.

"The count, your husband," he explained, "has learned of your detention here by the enemy, and he has besieged the General Staff to have you convoyed safely to Paris." The adjutant glanced at a field telegram he held open in his hand. "He asks," he continued, "that you be permitted to return in the car of his friend, Captain Thierry, and that on arriving you join him at the Grand Hôtel."

Thierry exclaimed with delight.

"But how charming!" he cried. "Tonight you must both dine with me at La Rue's." He saluted his superior officer. "Some petrol, sir," he said. "And I am ready." To Marie he added: "The car will be at the steps in five minutes." He turned and left them.

The thoughts of Marie, snatching at an excuse for delay, raced madly. The danger of meeting the Count d'Aurillac, her supposed husband, did not alarm her. The Grand Hôtel has many exits, and, even before they reached it, for leaving the car she could invent an excuse that the gallant Thierry would not suspect. But what now concerned her was how, before she was whisked away to Paris, she could convey to Anfossi the information she had gathered from Thierry. First, of a woman overcome with delight at being reunited with her husband she gave an excellent imitation; then she exclaimed in distress: "But my aunt, Madame Benet!" she cried. "I cannot leave her!"

"The sisters of St. Francis," said the adjutant, "arrive within an hour to nurse the wounded. They will care also for your aunt."

Marie concealed her chagrin. "Then I will at once prepare to go," she said.

The adjutant handed her a slip of paper. "Your *laisser-passer* to Paris," he said. "You leave in five minutes, madame!"

As temporary hostess of the château Marie was free to visit any part of it, and as she passed her door a signal from Madame Benet told her that Anfossi was on the fourth floor, that he was at work, and that the coast was clear. Softly, in the felt slippers she always wore, as she explained, in order not to disturb the wounded, she mounted the staircase. In her hand she carried the housekeeper's keys, and as an excuse it was her plan to return with an armful of linen for the arriving Sisters. But Marie never reached the top of the stairs. When her eyes rose to the level of the fourth floor she came to a sudden halt. At what she saw terror gripped her, bound her hand and foot, and turned her blood to ice.

At her post for an instant Madame Benet had slept, and an officer of the staff, led by curiosity, chance, or suspicion, had, unobserved and unannounced, mounted to the fourth floor. When Marie saw him he was in front of the room that held the wireless. His back was toward her, but she saw that he was holding the door to the room ajar, that his eye was pressed to the opening, and that through it he had pushed the muzzle of his automatic. What would be the fate of Anfossi Marie knew. Nor did she for an instant consider it. Her thoughts were of her own safety; that she might live. Not that she might still serve the Wilhelmstrasse, the Kaiser, or the Fatherland; but that she might live. In a moment Anfossi would be denounced, the château would ring with the alarm, and, though she knew Anfossi would not betray her, by others she might be accused. To avert suspicion from herself she saw only one way open. She must be the first to denounce Anfossi.

Like a deer she leaped down the marble stairs and, in a panic she had no need to assume, burst into the presence of the staff.

"Gentlemen!" she gasped, "my servant—the chauffeur—Briand is a spy! There is a German wireless in the château. He is using it! I have seen him." With exclamations, the officers rose to their feet. General Andre alone remained seated. General Andre was a veteran of many Colonial Wars: Cochin-China, Algiers, Morocco. The great war, when it came, found him on duty in the Intelligence Department. His aquiline nose, bristling white eyebrows, and flashing, restless eyes gave him his nickname of *l'Aigle*.

In amazement, the flashing eyes were now turned upon Marie. He glared at her as though he thought she suddenly had flown mad.

"A German wireless!" he protested. "It is impossible!"

"I was on the fourth floor," panted Marie, "collecting linen for the Sisters. In the room next to the linen closet I heard a strange buzzing sound. I opened the door softly. I saw Briand with his back to me seated by an instrument. There were receivers clamped to his ears! My God! The disgrace. The disgrace to my husband and to me, who vouched for him to you!" Apparently in an agony of remorse, the fingers of the woman laced and interlaced. "I cannot forgive myself!"

The officers moved toward the door, but General Andre halted them. Still in a tone of incredulity, he demanded: "When did you see this?"

Marie knew the question was coming, knew she must explain how she saw Briand, and yet did not see the staff officer who, with his prisoner, might now at any instant appear. She must make it plain she had discovered the spy and left the upper part of the house before the officer had visited it. When that was she could not know, but the chance was that he had preceded her by only a few minutes.

"When did you see this?" repeated the general.

"But just now," cried Marie; "not ten minutes since."

"Why did you not come to me at once?"

"I was afraid," replied Marie. "If I moved I was afraid he might hear me, and he, knowing I would expose him, would kill me—and so *escape you!*" There was an eager whisper of approval. For silence, General Andre slapped his hand upon the table.

"Then," continued Marie, "I understood with the receivers on his ears he could not have heard me open the door, nor could he hear me leave, and I ran to my aunt. The thought that we had harbored such an animal sickened me, and I was weak enough to feel faint. But only for an instant. Then I came here." She moved swiftly to the door. "Let me show you the room," she begged; "you can take him in the act." Her eyes, wild with the excitement of the chase, swept the circle. "Will you come?" she begged.

Unconscious of the crisis he interrupted, the orderly on duty opened the door.

"Captain Thierry's compliments," he recited mechanically, "and is he to delay longer for Madame d'Aurillac?"

With a sharp gesture General Andre waved Marie toward the door. Without rising, he inclined his head. "Adieu, madame," he said. "We act at once upon your information. I thank you!"

As she crossed from the hall to the terrace, the ears of the spy were assaulted by a sudden tumult of voices. They were raised in threats and curses. Looking back, she saw Anfossi descending the stairs. His hands were held above his head; behind him, with his automatic, the staff officer she had surprised on the fourth floor was driving him forward. Above the clenched fists of the soldiers that ran to meet him, the eyes of Anfossi were turned toward her. His face was expressionless. His eyes neither accused nor reproached. And with the joy of one who has looked upon and then escaped the guillotine, Marie ran down the steps to the waiting automobile. With a pretty cry of pleasure she leaped into the seat beside Thierry. Gayly she threw out her arms. "To Paris!" she commanded. The handsome eyes of Tierry, eloquent with admiration, looked back into hers. He stooped, threw in the clutch, and the great gray car, with the machine gun and its crew of privates guarding the rear, plunged through the park.

"To Paris!" echoed Thierry.

In the order in which Marie had last seen them, Anfossi and the staff officer entered the room of General Andre, and upon the soldiers in the hall the door was shut. The face of the staff officer was grave, but his voice could not conceal his elation.

"My general," he reported, "I found this man in the act of giving information to the enemy. There is a wireless—"

General Andre rose slowly. He looked neither at the officer nor at his prisoner. With frowning eyes he stared down at the maps upon his table.

"I know," he interrupted. "Some one has already told me." He paused, and then, as though recalling his manners, but still without raising his eyes, he added: "You have done well, sir."

In silence the officers of the staff stood motionless. With surprise they noted that, as yet, neither in anger nor curiosity had General Andre glanced at the prisoner. But of the presence of the general the spy was most acutely conscious. He stood erect, his arms still raised, but his body strained forward, and on the averted eyes of the general his own were fixed.

In an agony of supplication they asked a question.

At last, as though against his wish, toward the spy the general turned his head, and their eyes met. And still General Andre was silent. Then the arms of the spy, like those of a runner who has finished his race and breasts the tape exhausted, fell to his sides. In a voice low and vibrant he spoke his question.

"It has been so long, sir," he pleaded. "May I not come home?"

General Andre turned to the astonished group surrounding him. His voice was hushed like that of one who speaks across an open grave.

"Gentlemen," he began, "my children," he added. "A German spy, a woman, involved in a scandal your brother-in-arms, Henri Ravignac. His honor, he thought, was concerned, and without honor he refused to live. To prove him guiltless his younger brother Charles asked leave to seek out the woman who had betrayed Henri, and by us was detailed on secret service. He gave up home, family, friends. He lived in exile, in poverty, at all times in danger of a swift and ignoble death. In the War Office we know him as one who has given to his country services she cannot hope to reward. For she cannot return to him his brother. But she can and will clear the name of Henri Ravignac, and upon his brother Charles bestow promotion and honors."

The general turned and embraced the spy. "My children," he said, "welcome your brother. He has come home."

Before the car had reached the fortifications, Marie Gessler had arranged her plan of escape. She had departed from the château without even a handbag, and she would say that before the shops closed she must make purchases.

Le Printemps lay in their way, and she asked that, when they reached it, for a moment she might alight. Captain Thierry readily gave permission.

From the department store it would be most easy to disappear, and in anticipation Marie smiled covertly. Nor was the picture of Captain Thierry impatiently waiting outside unamusing.

But before Le Printemps was approached, the car turned sharply down a narrow street. On one side, along its entire length, ran a high gray wall, grim and forbidding. In it was a green gate studded with iron bolts. Before this the automobile drew suddenly to a halt. The crew of the armored car tumbled off the rear seat, and one of them beat upon the green gate. Marie felt a hand of ice clutch at her throat. But she controlled herself.

"And what is this?" she cried gayly.

At her side Captain Thierry was smiling down at her, but his smile was hateful.

"It is the prison of St. Lazare," he said. "It is not becoming," he added sternly, "that the name of the Countess d'Aurillac should be made common as the Paris road!"

Fighting for her life, Marie thrust herself against him; her arm that throughout the journey had rested on the back of the driving-seat caressed his shoulders; her lips and the violet eyes were close to his.

"Why should you care?" she whispered fiercely. "You have *me!* Let the Count d'Aurillac look after the honor of his wife himself."

The charming Thierry laughed at her mockingly.

"He means to," he said. "I *am* the Count d'Aurillac!"

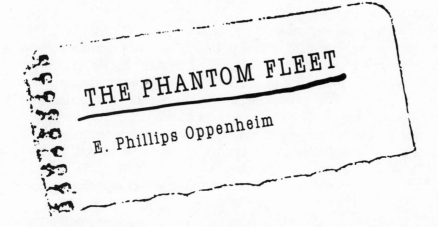

THE PHANTOM FLEET

E. Phillips Oppenheim

IT WAS DURING the service of *apéritifs* before a men's dinner at Monte Carlo, the annual dinner of an old-established and highly popular club there. The Comte de Wrette, a well-known Belgian millionaire, who was numbered amongst the guests, turned to his sponsor.

"Tell me again," he asked curiously, "the name of the gentleman to whom I was just presented?"

His friend promptly acquiesced.

"That is one of our very popular residents," he confided. "General Besserley, an American. He is one of our oldest members, too—came to the inaugural meeting and joined the club right away."

"General Besserley," the other repeated thoughtfully, "of the American Army?"

His host shrugged his shoulders.

"At one time or other, one presumes so," he assented. "Besserley very seldom talks about himself, but I have heard that he commanded a brigade during the war, was one of the first wounded and went straight back to the Secret Service in Washington—where he really belonged."

"That is very interesting," the Comte de Wrette declared.

The two men sat at opposite ends of the table and did not happen to come into contact again until the close of the evening when, the speeches all concluded and a sufficiency of wine consumed, the proceedings broke up in a mist of alcoholic good humor. It was then that Besserley, stepping into his automobile, glanced around and saw the Count under the portico of the hotel, eyeing with distaste the spattering raindrops.

"Give you a lift?" General Besserley asked.

"You are awfully kind," the other replied. "Are you going by any chance to the Sporting Club?"

The General smiled.

"By a very singular chance," he admitted, "I am. Get in, please."

The two men drove off together. De Wrette was a man of medium height but of quiet, rather undistinguished, appearance. He was neither tall nor short, stout nor thin. He wore a slight black mustache and a small, very closely cropped imperial. He was of pallid complexion with gray, secretive eyes. Besserley, a man built on a larger scale altogether, tapped a cigarette upon the case which he passed to his companion.

"Going to join the club?" he inquired. "It isn't a bad place."

"It would give me much pleasure," the Count replied, "but I doubt whether I am often enough in these parts. I have recently joined a business house in Paris and I find many demands upon my time."

"Curious thing," Besserley reflected, "how few French or Belgian people we see down here."

"You are likely to see more, if things continue as they are at present."

"What do you mean?"

De Wrette shrugged his shoulders.

"Well, it really seems as though all the money in the world were drifting into French hands," he observed. "They do not want it—I always think too much money is one of the first signs of decay in any nation. I think their present prosperity is to be regretted. It is, none the less, however, an obvious fact."

"You should consider yourself lucky that you have French connections," General Besserley said carelessly. "It is not so pleasant for us others to see our money decrease in value every day."

"The whole thing is rather chimerical," De Wrette pointed out. "We are no longer at the mercy of real events. We are at the mercy of what the world calls currencies."

The two men entered the club together but separated on the first floor with a few courteous words. De Wrette mounted to the gambling rooms, Besserley stopped to speak to a few acquaintances. He waited a reasonable time, then descended the stairs and made his way by the underground passage back to the Hôtel de Paris. He collected two or three cable forms from the hall porter and retired to his apartments. Arrived there, he unlocked a somewhat formal-looking dispatch box, which had the air of not having been opened for months, and drew from it a small leather-bound code book. With it by his side he set to work to concoct a cablegram. The task was evidently an unfamiliar one to him, for it took him the best part of an hour. Just as he had finished, there was a knock at the door. He turned the form over on its face and answered the summons.

"Come in," he invited.

It was a very obvious fellow-countryman who made his appearance. An American businessman—suave, confident, with ingratiating manners and friendly smile. Besserley had been out of America just long enough to forget what was expected in the way of a handshake and he rather winced after the formality had been concluded.

"James Brogden's my name, General," the newcomer announced, presenting a card. "I'm a Philadelphia man—Brogden and Biddle. Real estate and a sideshow of banking. I'm glad to meet you, sir."

"I am always glad to meet a fellow-countryman," the General declared slowly, opening and closing his fingers. "Step in, won't you."

He ushered Mr. Brogden into his *salon*. A tentative inquiry as to refreshments brought an enthusiastic assent. The waiter appeared and departed with an order. Mr. Brogden fingered his tie.

"F.I.C.O.," he said.

"I have not been out of the game long enough to have forgotten that," the General replied. "I am wondering, though, whether there has been any mistake. You understand that I am on the full retired list?"

"This is a special job."

"I can guess the nature of it already," the General continued. "Of course, I will do what I can. It is not an easy situation, though. Mine was a genuine retirement. I am well known here for just what I am. If I get into any trouble, there is no one at the back of me."

Brogden shrugged his shoulders.

"Washington doesn't take too much stock in that," he remarked. "I suppose they reckon even if we retire from the service we stay good Americans. They have always run anything they have had in the shape of Secret Service by trained amateurs and I'll say that they've done pretty well by it."

"I suppose you have some sort of communication for me?" Besserley queried.

Mr. Brogden nodded. He lifted his rather long, double-breasted coat and disclosed the hip pocket with three buttons in a line and an ominous little bulge. After fingering about for some time he produced a letter.

"You kept your Angier code?" he asked, with a flash of anxiety.

The General nodded.

"Yes. We are all supposed to keep that, unless we are dismissed from the service," he reminded his visitor.

"There's your letter, then, and I guess when you have it in your hand and I have drunk that Scotch," Mr. Brogden added, as the door opened and a waiter appeared, carrying a tray, "the sooner I get going the better."

"Things shaping well at home?" the General asked amiably.

"Business is foul. Boost it as much as you like, you still have to come back to the same thing—business is foul. I have a client to see over in London. I think I'll fly from Cannes tomorrow morning. I have not got enough of the holiday spirit left for this place. They tell me you are one of the big sports here."

"I don't know about that," Besserley answered, "but if you were staying for a few days, I might have made it agreeable for you."

"Better not," was the frank reply. "They have got stiffer and stiffer about that since your day. They keep to the same principle—business men who can be trusted—out-and-out Americans. We're the stuff they trust for any work that's got to be done. But they don't like it mixed up with the social side as they do over here. I've done my job with you, General, and I'm thankful to say that I've got through with it pretty quickly. There's the letter in your hand. I came over on one of these round-the-world-trip steamers and there isn't a soul who tumbled to it that I was carrying a warrant to bring you back into the game again. A clean job and finished. I'll bid you good day, sir."

The General held out his hand and Mr. Brogden, of Brogden and Biddle, Philadelphia, clasped it. This time, however, it was the General who provided the muscular force. With an old trick of his college days, he swung his visitor, who was by no means an undersized man, round by the wrist till he called out in agony. Another moment and he was lying on his back on the sofa and the small lumpy article which had a few seconds ago been in his hip pocket was in Besserley's hands. The latter, with his feet planted squarely upon the carpet, stood a couple of yards away.

"Gone out of your senses, Besserley?" the man on the couch gasped.

"Perhaps so," was the steady reply. "Not quite so badly as you think, though. I may be a bit rusty, but I haven't forgotten all the old tricks. Have you seen the wireless this evening? There's a sheet hanging up in the hall."

The man on the couch made no reply. He ventured to raise himself a little. His knuckles showed white, where he was gripping the side of the couch. He was breathing fast. He had the air of a man afraid.

"What do you mean—wireless?" he demanded.

"Mr. James Brogden of Brogden and Biddle, land and real estate agents of Philadelphia, was reported missing from the *Homeric* last night, under mysterious circumstances," the General confided. "You know what that generally means? Murder. You and I, assisted perhaps by the Commissaire of Police, Mr. Brogden, will have to have a little conversation before you make the next move in the game. You may be in it all right, but I imagine you are on the other side."

The stranger in the room shivered as he looked up at the towering figure dominating him.

"General," he said, "I don't see how they ever let you get on the retired list."

"I don't want any flattery," was the curt reply. "What became of Brogden?"

"He was—dealt with."

"By you?"

The pseudo Mr. Brogden, of Brogden and Biddle, Philadelphia, shook his head vigorously.

"I am a Number Seven man," he protested. "They don't ask that of us. They do it themselves, and pretty neat they are too. Those Japs can do almost anything with a knife."

"The newspaper report is that he is missing," Besserley observed.

"Knifed first and pushed overboard. There were three of them in it, all in the second class. They had been waiting for a chance all the way from New York."

"Nice bright lads," General Besserley commented. "Where are they now?"

"Oh, they're around," the other answered cheerfully. "Guess they're in Nice at the present moment."

"And what's the idea of trying to work something on me?" the General asked.

Mr. Brogden coughed.

"That accursed wireless," he complained, "has got in with the news twenty-four hours too soon. Now that you know I am not Mr. Brogden of Brogden and Biddle, staff Number Seven F.I.C.O., we're through with the idea. Pretty slick idea, too. But then, these chaps are a slick race. I think I won't waste any more of your time, so long as there's nothing doing."

General Besserley raised his eyebrows.

"So you think I am going to let you go?"

"I'm sure you are," was the cool rejoinder. "There's nothing you can do about it. Nothing you can keep me for. I have not stolen anything of yours, I have not threatened you, I have not broken the law. I called to do a little business with you, but it was business which only Mr. Brogden of Brogden and Biddle could have handled."

The General paused to consider the situation.

"You admit," he said, "that you—posing on the boat, no doubt, as a reputable American—are concerned with these three Japs in the murder of James Brogden—"

"Not so fast," the other interrupted. "I do not admit anything of the sort. I am not in that branch of the game. I had nothing whatever to do with that trouble."

"But you know who did it?"

"I can guess. That wouldn't be any use to anybody."

"You know where they are hiding?"

"I know where they are. That wouldn't help anyone, either. There's not a scrap of evidence against them and I'm not the sort of fool who would risk having his throat cut giving them away."

"Your idea is, then," Besserley pointed out, "that having failed in your mission with me—whatever it may have been—you will walk out of this room and get on with the dirty work of betraying your own country to her natural enemies?"

"There is not a darn soul who could stop me!"

Besserley reflected.

"No," he admitted, "I don't suppose there is. I should like very much to know, though, under what name you traveled on the *Homeric*."

His visitor smiled.

"I don't see how you are going to find that out," he said, "and so far as I am concerned, you never will."

"The Commissaire of Police—" the General began.

The other, however, shook his head.

"My dear friend," he remonstrated, "don't try any bluff of that sort on me. I have committed no extraditable offense, and you know it. You also know that you haven't the right to detain me here a single moment longer than I care to stay."

Besserley threw open the door.

"Then get out," he ordered brusquely.

The three men were probably the filthiest-looking objects to be met with in a quarter of the town consecrated to vice and uncleanliness. Their black hair was matted, their features were almost invisible with dried coal dust and dirt. They wore the disreputable slops of stokers on a tramp steamer. They sat together at a corner table in one of the worst cafés of the worst quarter in Nice—the region which lies in the heart of the old town—a region seldom penetrated by the most intrepid of slum seekers and which even a gendarme approaches with hesitation. That they were Orientals was apparent, but of what nationality it was hard to say. They talked together in some foreign gibberish and they were drinking some repulsive looking liquid, the nature of which was concealed by the fact that they drank it out of cups. Occasionally one of them would stagger to the counter, holding out his cup, watch whilst it was filled with more noxious-looking liquor from a black bottle by a disreputable-looking barman, pay for it with a crumpled note and stagger back to his place. There were stains on the floor and stains on the marble-topped table around which the three were crouching. They had the sleight of hand of most Oriental races, and there was no one amongst the half-drunken company, gradually becoming fewer in number, who noticed the final destination of the cups full of liquor . . . . A stranger stumbled into the café, followed by a growl of curses from outside. From the clatter upon the pavement, it appeared that he had upset a table in his clumsy progress. A vicious-looking waiter, in a singlet and the remains of a pair of trousers, followed him truculently. With shaking fingers the newcomer pressed a note into the man's hand.

"That will pay for the drinks," he muttered in broken French. "My friends there," he went on, pointing to the three men. "Shipmates—dirty little rats."

He reeled to the table, dragging a chair with him. Not one of the three turned their heads but they seemed to be conscious of his approach. He dragged his chair up to the table and took a genuine drink from the glass of brandy which the waiter brought him. Afterwards a curious thing happened. A conversation between the four men was started and carried on—in English.

"Got book?" one of the three asked.

The new arrival was wearing a soiled and stained suit of blue serge of nautical cut and was without shirt or collar. His appearance seemed to be well in keeping with the men he had claimed as shipmates.

"The old cuss tumbled to me," he scowled. "I got away. All I could do."

"No book," one of the others murmured softly.

"No book," his neighbor repeated, almost in a whisper.

The newcomer, who in features bore a singular resemblance to the pseudo Mr. Brogden, of Brogden and Biddle, spat on the floor.

"It's this bloody wireless," he confided. "There it was in the hall—suspicious disappearance of Brogden overboard. After that, all I could do was to quit."

"Very unpleasant," one of the three little men murmured. "You read papers—yes? They say a search is being made in Nice for some Japanese who were traveling second class. Very unpleasant. He ask you any questions, this General?"

From outside came a crazy sound of shouting from a drunken Neapolitan, essaying a song in praise of the sun. Two women were quarreling violently in high-pitched falsetto voices. A table with its load of glasses was thrown over on the pavement. The three men who were dressed as ship's stokers rose to their feet.

"There will be more gendarmes here soon," one of them said. "We mount to our rooms. We will have a little talk with Mr. Brogden there."

The latter rose to his feet unwillingly. He finished his brandy.

"Anything to drink up there?" he asked.

"Plenty drink everywhere—plenty drink," one of the men assured him coaxingly.

"I wouldn't trust you," Brogden declared. "You were drinking water all the time on the steamer. A lily-livered drink—water."

One of the three men whispered to another, who took a bill from his pocket and went to the bar. They all passed on into the rear premises of the place in solemn procession, the last one carrying a bottle of cheap brandy. The leader unlatched a door and they mounted the stone steps. On the first landing a man was lying asleep, groaning stertorously. The three Orientals walked meticulously around him. Their companion stepped over him with a curse. On the next landing a man and a woman, half-undressed and quite drunk, were leaning with their backs to a door which apparently they had been unable to open. From behind other closed doors came an orgy of sound—shouting, quarrelling, cursing. In one room a fight was going on. On the third landing, Brogden stopped to wipe the sweat off his forehead.

"I've had enough of this," he muttered. "I'm going to leave you guys right here."

"We have arrived," one of the three men assured him. "This is our room here opposite. Two questions we have to ask. It is very little. Perhaps some more money for expenses—yes?"

Brogden looked them all three over.

"Say, I'm damned if I know how you fellows get all this money you handle."

There was a thin, strained smile on the lips of the one of the three who did most of the talking.

"There is always money for our honorable friends," he said.

Brogden leaned against the wall. The brandy was very crude, poor stuff.

"Don't look as though you owned a dollar between the three of you," he declared.

They half insinuated, half pushed him through a door close at hand. There was no electric light, but a ghastly corner of moonshine stole through the dust-encrusted window. Brogden put his hand to the back of his neck.

"What's that?" he called out sharply.

No one answered. There was no need. Three inches of blue steel were already quivering in the middle of his neck. He collapsed, a crumpled-up heap upon the bare floor.

They belonged to a methodical race indeed, those three. One by one they stripped stark naked, stepped into the middle of the pewter bowl and washed their bodies inch by inch. As each one finished, they threw the water of their ablutions out of the window, down the three stories into a broad river with a narrow path alongside, which ran below—the river with a dry bed for many months of the year but swollen now with recent rains. One of the three had dragged out a suitcase from underneath the neatly turned-over bed. The first man was soon attired—a neat, dapper little gentleman, with his clean collar and brightly polished shoes. The second followed suit, but the last of the three, before he stepped into his basin of water, dragged what remained of Brogden to the low windowsill, peered down below and, scorning help from the others, flung his burden into the gulf of darkness. He listened to the thud and the splash, nodded his head gravely and then he, too, stepped into the water and washed and dried himself. There were no signs of blood in the room when they had finished. They had known where to strike. Out of the window went their soiled and miserable garments. Then, with reverent fingers, one of the three placed a little brown box upon the mantelpiece and opened it, disclosing a small statue of the Japanese Buddha. One by one they took their turn in front of it. For several unhurried minutes their heads were bowed, their lips moved without sound. Then they closed the box. One of them carried it under his arm. Through the window went the suitcase— a cheap affair of canvas. After it went three rolls of stokers' overalls. They patted the bed and looked around, then one by one they left the room. They passed down the unlit staircase, passed the drunken man still snoring, passed the man and the woman, now asleep. Passed the shadows of others stealing up and down, each with that furtive air of secrecy. The café was deserted. There was a line of white light in the sky. The three Japanese parted outside. One made his way towards the station, another towards the port, the third disappeared into the deeper shadows of the neighborhood. There was an empty room in the lofty tenement house above the Café des Etrangers; the unrecognizable remains of a human being floated and bobbed amongst the stones towards the arches of the Pont des Sept Arcs, and some miscellaneous articles of miserable clothing had gone their way towards the rubbish heap of the city.

For once General Besserley varied his usual morning program. He occupied his accustomed seat at the Royalty Bar for only a quarter of an hour and, just as the little crowd of habitués were beginning to stream in, he finished his solitary cocktail, descended the steps into the Boulevard des Moulins and entered the bank. Chudleigh, the manager, came forward to meet him.

"Want any money, General?"

Besserley shook his head.

"Just a word in your office," he said. "I shan't keep you. I have a very simple commission for you."

The manager led the way. Besserley seemed, for him, to be in a curiously suspicious frame of mind. He not only waited until the door was closed, but he looked carefully around the room, as though to assure himself that there were no listeners. Then he drew from his pocket two long envelopes, each sealed in three places.

"My dear Chudleigh," he began, "are your new vaults in action?"

"For the last two months," was the prompt reply. "Like to look over them?"

The General shook his head.

"Is my box moved there?" he asked.

"You have a niche all to yourself," the bank manager reminded him.

The General handed over the envelopes.

"There you are, Chudleigh," he siad. "I may not require you to take care of them for more than twenty-four hours."

"But during those twenty-four hours they will be as safe as in the Bank of England," the other assured him. "Do you want me to deposit them now?"

"Just what I am waiting for you to do. As soon as you come up and tell me that they are safe, I will give you final instructions."

Mr. Chudleigh who, except that the General was an old friend, thought that he might have trusted a subordinate with so ordinary a transaction, hurried off and returned in a few minutes.

"Until you release them," he announced, "there is no person in the world could get at those envelopes."

"Capital," Besserley replied. "What time do you close?"

"Four o'clock as usual," was the somewhat surprised reply.

"Then between half-past three and four I shall be up again," Besserley told him. "If by any chance—come this way a minute, Chudleigh," he broke off suddenly.

"One moment," the bank manager begged, spotting an important client. "Step into my room."

The General did as he was bidden, but not before he had waved his hand and spoken a word of salutation to the Comte de Wrette. He had barely entered the manager's parlor before Chudleigh followed him. Besserley closed the door.

"This may sound a little melodramatic, Chudleigh," he said, "but if I am not in before closing time, you have a commission to perform, and I want your word that you will perform it."

"My dear fellow," Chudleigh assured him. "Anything in the world."

"You yourself go down to the vaults, you bring out those envelopes and you hand them over to your most trusted clerk who can be spared for forty-eight hours. Here is my open cheque for ten thousand francs. With that you hire an escort for your clerk—you can arrange that with the Commissaire—and see that he travels to Paris by the Blue Train tonight. He goes straight to the United States Embassy and he hands over that envelope. He catches the same train at the Gare du Nord and hands over the other one to our Ambassador in London."

The manager's perpetual smile had faded.

"This sounds like serious business, General," he observed.

Besserley shrugged his shoulders.

"It is very likely," he confesssed, "a mare's nest. On the other hand, it might be of the greatest possible importance. We have talked of currencies and the European conditions until we are both pretty well sick of it. What would another war mean between two first-class powers?"

"The end of the world," Chudleigh groaned.

"Well, it might mean that," Besserley said, "if anything happened to me and those envelopes were not delivered."

For a moment or two Mr. Chudleigh wondered whether his old client and friend had suddenly taken leave of his senses. He looked carefully into his face and he saw the lines there which belonged to the man of whom rumor still told strange stories.

"You may rely upon me, sir," he promised. "If it would make you any easier, I have imminent business myself in Paris and I will take them myself."

The General shook him by the hand.

"That's very good of you, Chudleigh," he acknowledged. "You need not pack your bag just yet, though. You will almost certainly see me back again before four."

The General paused on the top of the stone steps to light a cigarette. This was an old trick of his when he wanted to make quite sure whether or not he was being followed.

There was consternation in the picturesque entrance gardens of the famous Beaulieu restaurant. The *maître d' hôtel,* hurrying up from the restaurant to the small chalet-like hotel in the grounds, paused abruptly and in obvious discomfiture. The commissionaire, in magnificent uniform, who threw open the door of Besserley's car with a broad smile, paused in the middle of his bow and the welcoming words faded away upon his lips. The concierge at the door hastened to put on his glasses. The proprietor, with his flowing tie, hurrying up to welcome a distinguished client, stopped short in surprise. The whole trouble was that General Besserley, one of their most esteemed patrons, had ordered a marvelous luncheon in a private room in a place notorious for its private rooms, its excellent food, wonderful wines and perfect service—and the General had arrived alone. Besserley descended from the car and, as a man of the world, he was quick to grasp the situation. For the first time that morning he smiled.

"I am expecting a guest," he announced, "perhaps two. You have my usual suite on the first floor?"

"Everything is prepared, sir," the *maître d' hôtel* assured him. "If Monsieur will give himself the trouble to mount."

Besserley shook hands with *Monsieur le patron* and mounted. By degrees the consternation faded away. The guests were to arrive. There were many explanations of such a situation. Besserley was ushered into a very pleasant sitting room with a wonderful view of the sea on one side and the gardens on the other. The table was beautifully decorated with roses, the linen and glass were, as always, perfection. There was a slight film upon the decanter of vodka, which was as it should be. He scrutinized the labels on the Montrachet and Chambertin and discovered that they were of the right vintage, the Montrachet in its lightly filled ice pail, and the Chambertin reposing in its basket.

"Everything," General Besserley declared, "is perfect, as usual, Louis. Be so good as to bring me at once a dry martini cocktail in the shaker. I am a little in advance of my time."

"Monsieur is expecting, perhaps?" Louis asked with a little cough.

"Two gentlemen," Besserley announced firmly. "One is Monsieur le Comte de Wrette. He is doubtless known to you. The other is Professor Kralin. They may arrive together or separately. Show them up at once."

All excitement died away. The Comte de Wrette was a famous Belgian millionaire and a valued client. Mr. Kralin was unknown. Two ordinary guests. The romance had passed from this little luncheon party. Madame, when she was told by her husband, sighed and regretted the changed times. Madame, her sister-in-law behind the desk, shook her head and also dreamt of the past. The violinist, who was hoping for an invitiation across the gardens to the chalet, packed away his favorite violin and resumed his ordinary instrument. He, too, sighed. And amidst it all a very beautiful car turned into the grounds and two gentlemen inquired at the chalet for General Besserley and were ushered into the sitting room . . . .

If General Besserley, for once, when giving a party, was a trifle ill-at-ease, he showed no signs of it. He shook hands with the Count, he shook hands also with Professor Kralin, a tall man with gross features, a prominent forehead and piercing eyes, and he noticed with a sigh of relief that both men seemed attracted by the preparations for the feast. They accepted easy chairs on the balcony and cocktails served in beautiful glasses.

"It is not my custom," Professor Kralin remarked, "to spoil such excellent wine as I see on the sideboard by drinking cocktails, but a speedy opportunity to wish for your better acquaintance, my host," he added, with a little bow to Besserley, "cannot be neglected."

"I, alas," the Comte de Wrette confessed with a sigh, "am an *apéritif* worshipper. Like a great many men who seem to be idlers but who find every hour of their day occupied, I am always just a trifle exhausted when the time comes for luncheon or dinner. I need the slight impetus of alcohol to clear my brain."

"The European world," General Besserley remarked, with a smile, "has formed its own opinion on that score. However, I, in my idleness, have never outgrown my American tastes."

The smiling face of the *maître d' hôtel* appeared at the French windows. *"Monsieur le général est servi,"* he announced.

The three men sat at a round table of ample dimensions and both the service of luncheon and the luncheon itself were as near perfection as possible. The conversation seemed a little elusive. They talked of Einstein, the internal condition of Germany, the ebb and flow of art and religion in the cultured countries of the world. They talked as men of intelligence who are used to the exercise of their brains. But with all three there was a general understanding that this conversation was nothing but the flashes of lightning before the storm on the stillness of a summer night. Everything had been perfectly arranged. With the service of coffee and the warming of the glasses for the old brandy, the *maître d' hôtel* and his myrmidons faded from the place. General Besserley rose from his chair. He closed the window leading out on to the balcony. He crossed the room and locked the door. There was a little twitch about the lips of De Wrette and his hand moved slightly towards his pocket. Besserley, with a genial smile, laid the key by his side.

"My two guests—" he said, "I hope I may say my friends—these precautions are for you and not for me. I have a few words to say which I fancy you would wish spoken without the risk of eavesdroppers."

"Let us have those words," the Professor begged, lighting his cigar. "I am in the hands of my friend De Wrette and De Wrette brought me here. Why—I do not know. But whatever may happen from now on, I have eaten a most excellent luncheon and drunk some wonderful wines. You are a great host, General."

The General bowed. He resumed his place between the two men.

"I have a few gifts in life," he said. "The gift of expression is not one of them. The remarks I have to make may sound almost crude."

The General also lit a cigar. He served the brandy.

"Comte de Wrett," he went on, "I have lived in Europe for twelve years. You have filled a great place in European society for about the same time. You must give me credit for one thing—there is a certain freemasonry amongst those who have served behind the scenes in every country of the world. I am one of the few breathing who know that you, with a Belgian mother, are a Japanese by birth, the son of the famous Baron Nyashi, who was the greatest diplomat your country ever possessed. I have never mentioned the fact to a living soul."

The eyelids of De Wrette never flickered.

"I have no remark to make," he said, after a brief pause. "There are cemeteries in many countries of the world where repose the bones of those who have even hinted at the fact which you have just stated."

"Naturally," Besserley agreed, "but we have passed those times. The lives and deaths of individuals seldom have any effect upon the wheel of history. I have asked you here because I want to tell you both that I have discovered—by accident, if you will, not by means of my own intelligence—the secret of your wonderful scheme, De Wrette, of which I propose to be a cog in the wheel. I shall now prove my knowledge. Only a few months ago the finest Japanese fleet that has ever sailed out of harbor steamed proudly into the Pacific, into new waters. There came a protest from my country. Whether it was well advised or not it is futile to discuss. The reply from Tokyo was the reply that a proud and successful nation was bound to send. Your country has made great history within the last ten years, De Wrette. It has nothing further to learn from the West. It has no need to stand bareheaded before the presidents or the monarchs of any country. Still, you lack a little of that complete strength upon the seas which you crave. You, De Wrette, discovered how to atone for that."

A look flashed from Kralin to De Wrette. For the first time there was a gleam of something which might be counted emotion in the former's face.

"De Wrette," Besserley went on, "I was a soldier during the early part of the war, but I passed into the Secret Service at Washington within a few months. For one year I had to work on naval matters. It was just at the time of the Russian *débâcle* that I met a cousin of the first man who tried to restore order to your country. Never mind his name. From him I learnt what had been kept a profound secret. In your naval docks at St. Petersburg a small but complete fleet was in course of building. In another two years these ships would have been ready for action. There was a plan—but that does not concern us. There came the revolution. There came the new Russia. What happened to those ships no one knew, for even to their hulls they were disguised, the great gates of the navy dockyards were sealed, and the prison burying grounds had been heaped with the bodies of those who had whispered. Only within the last eighteen months has the roar of hammers and machinery reawakened with the silent coming and going of a multitude of work-people."

"From what province in fairyland has such a story reached you, General?" Kralin asked.

"You may well ask," Besserley replied gravely, "for I will admit the censorship inaugurated by your dictator has been almost impenetrable. Yet, if you wish to know, the hint of what was happening reached me from a so-called Mr. Brogden of Brogden and Biddle, land agents of Philadelphia."

No word. The smoke from the cigars was curling upward. It was almost impossible to hear the breathing of either of the two men who sat with their eyes fixed upon Besserley. Once more De Wrette's hand had stolen downwards.

"It is true," the host of the party went on, "that the gentleman bearing that name met with an unfortunate accident on the *Homeric*. He made friends with one or two tourists from your country, De Wrette, and I think we all three know what became of him. But he was a man of careful habits, and two days after the news of the fatal accident to him was published I received a letter in an old cipher written in indelible pencil and posted in Southampton by a steward off the *Homeric*. An ignominious way of learning a great historical fact, but there it is. The man whom you sent to me, De Wrette, although I imagine you scarcely trouble yourself about such trifles, and who posed as being Mr. Brogden of

Brogden and Biddle, and wished for a little information I could have given him, or rather a codebook I possessed, was too obvious an impostor. He went back to Nice to report to your three Japanese friends, and I have an idea somehow or other that we shall not hear much of him again. To proceed. For how much money I do not know, but you, De Wrette, have made a perfectly legitimate deal with Professor Kralin of Leningrad, of whose official position I will not speak, to buy those recently completed ships. They have been cunningly and marvelously completed and by skillful handling in camouflage would probably make the long voyage into the Pacific in safety. The only condition that was necessary for the success of your scheme was secrecy. You have now lost that necessary condition."

Still there was silence. Neither man spoke, but Besserley knew that never in his life had he been nearer death.

"I am no longer a man of affairs," he went on. "I am a retired servant of my Government, but I have seen the agony of war. I have seen its futility and if my life can hinder another one, it is cheerfully offered."

He raised his glass to his lips, threw his head back and drank slowly the remainder of his brandy. Still there was silence from his two guests.

"If those ships ever leave port and come in touch with your fleet, De Wrette, there will be war, and such a war as will shake the world. Therefore that thing must not happen. It is one of those incidents—this bargain between you, Professor, on behalf of your Government which needs so badly the money, and you, De Wrette—or shall I call you for once Nyashi?—representing Japan, of which no one knows. I honestly believe that we three are the only living persons who are acquainted with the full details."

"The only three alive," De Wrette said ominously.

"Exactly," Besserley went on. "But although I would offer my life willingly, if it were necessary, my life if I lost it within the next thirty seconds," he added, with a glance at De Wrette's right hand, "would never alter the course of history. At a certain hour tomorrow the whole story will be simultaneously in the hands of the American Ambassadors in Paris and in London, but if we shake hands across this table, and if this bargain is forgotten, and we each go our own ways, no word of it will ever pass my lips. If the packets which I left behind me and which even all the wit of a De Wrette could never intercept, be read by the two men to whom they are addressed, there must be war just as surely as though your scheme had succeeded. Not such sudden war, perhaps, but war which would come of smouldering anger, of righteous anger, on the part of my country-people."

Besserley wondered afterwards what means those two men found to convey the one to the other their secret thoughts. Yet in some measure they succeeded. De Wrette rose to his feet. His hand was no longer in his right-hand pocket. He moved towards the bell.

"You permit us, General, to ask for our car?"

"By all means," was the courteous response. "Unless I can persuade you to have half a glass more brandy?"

"That will I do," the Professor said, helping himself liberally.

De Wrette unlocked the door. The *maître d' hôtel* appeared. Orders were given. The sound of wheels was heard below. De Wrette held out his hand.

"I must thank you, General," he said, "for the most wonderful luncheon and the most entertaining hour of my life."

"It was a very good luncheon," Professor Kralin declared. "It was wonderful food and wonderful wine. And as for you, my host—a little drama—shall we call it that?"

"Some touch of the film about it," De Wrette observed.

"A slight lacking in reality," the Professor agreed.

"The three men shook hands. De Wrette, at the last moment, turned back. He poured out a little more of the brandy and he raised his glass to Besserley. No words passed. The toast, whatever it may have been, was a silent one. A moment or two later the sound of a motor horn was heard and the car crawled out of the gardens. The *maître d' hôtel* bowed inquiringly to his distinguished patron.

"The lunch, I trust, was satsifactory, General?" he asked.

"As always—wonderful," Besserley declared, passing his handkerchief lightly across his forehead. "The bill, if you please, Louis."

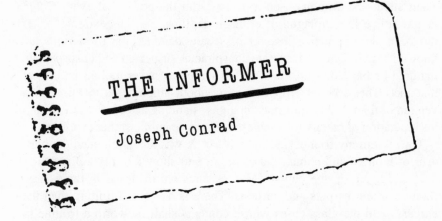

THE INFORMER

Joseph Conrad

MR. X CAME to me, preceded by a letter of introduction from a good friend of mine in Paris, specifically to see my collection of Chinese bronzes and porcelain.

My friend in Paris is a collector, too. He collects neither porcelain, nor bronzes, nor pictures, nor medals, nor stamps, nor anything that could be profitably dispersed under an auctioneer's hammer. He would reject, with genuine surprise, the name of a collector. Nevertheless, that's what he is by temperament. He collects acquaintances. It is delicate work. He brings to it the patience, the passion, the determination of a true collector of curiosities. His collection does not contain any royal personages. I don't think he considers them sufficiently rare and interesting; but, with that exception, he has met with and talked to everyone worth knowing on any conceivable ground. He observes them, listens to them, penetrates them, measures them, and puts the memory away in the galleries of his mind. He has schemed, plotted, and traveled all over Europe in order to add to his collection of distinguished personal acquaintances.

As he is wealthy, well connected, and unprejudiced, his collection is pretty complete, including objects (or should I say subjects?) whose value is unappreciated by the vulgar, and often unknown to popular fame. Of those specimens my friend is naturally the most proud.

He wrote to me of X: "He is the greatest rebel (*révolté*) of modern times. The world knows him as a revolutionary writer whose savage irony has laid bare the rottenness of the most respectable institutions. He has scalped every venerated head, and has mangled at the stake of his wit every received opinion and every recognized principle of conduct and policy. Who does not remember his flaming red revolutionary pamphlets?

Their sudden swarmings used to overwhelm the powers of every Continental police like a plague of crimson gadflies. But this extreme writer has been also the active inspirer of secret societies, the mysterious unknown Number One of desperate conspiracies suspected and unsuspected, matured or baffled. And the world at large has never had an inkling of that fact! This accounts for him going about amongst us to this day, a veteran of many subterranean campaigns, standing aside now, safe within his reputation of merely the greatest destructive publicist that ever lived."

Thus wrote my friend, adding that Mr. X was an enlightened connoisseur of bronzes and china, and asking me to show him my collection.

X turned up in due course. My treasures are disposed in three large rooms without carpets and curtains. There is no other furniture than the *étagères* and the glass cases whose contents shall be worth a fortune to my heirs. I allow no fires to be lighted, for fear of accidents, and a fireproof door separates them from the rest of the house.

It was a bitter cold day. We kept on our overcoats and hats. Middle-sized and spare, his eyes alert in a long, Roman-nosed countenance, X walked on his neat little feet, with short steps, and looked at my collection intelligently. I hope I looked at him intelligently, too. A snow-white mustache and imperial made his nut-brown complexion appear darker than it really was. In his fur coat and shiny tall hat that terrible man looked fashionable. I believe he belonged to a noble family, and could have called himself Vicomte X de la Z if he chose. We talked nothing but bronzes and porcelain. He was remarkably appreciative. We parted on cordial terms.

Where he was staying I don't know. I imagine he must have been a lonely man. Anarchists, I suppose, have no families—not, at any rate as we understand that social relation. Organization into families may answer to a need of human nature, but in the last instance it is based on law, and therefore must be something odious and impossible to an anarchist. But, indeed, I don't understand anarchists. Does a man of that—of that—persuasion still remain an anarchist when alone, quite alone and going to bed, for instance? Does he lay his head on the pillow, pull his bedclothes over him, and go to sleep with the necessity of the *chambardement général,* as the French slang has it, of the general blow-up, always present to his mind? And if so how can he? I am sure that if such a faith (or such a fanaticism) once mastered my thoughts I would never be able to compose myself sufficiently to sleep or eat or perform any of the routine acts of daily life. I would want no wife, no children; I could have no friends, it seems to me; and as to collecting bronzes or china, that, I should say, would be quite out of the question.

But I don't know. All I know is that Mr. X took his meals in a very good restaurant which I frequented also.

With his head uncovered, the silver top-knot of his brushed-up hair completed the character of his physiognomy, all bony ridges and sunken hollows, clothed in a perfect impassiveness of expression. His meagre brown hands emerging from large white cuffs came and went breaking bread, pouring wine, and so on, with quiet mechanical precision. His head and body above the tablecloth had a rigid immobility. This firebrand, this great agitator, exhibited the least possible amount of warmth and animation. His voice was rasping, cold, and montonous in a low key. He could not be called a talkative personality; but with his detached calm manner he appeared as ready to keep the conversation going as to drop it at any moment.

And his conversation was by no means commonplace. To me, I own, there was some excitement in talking quietly across a dinner table with a man whose venomous pen-stabs had sapped the vitality of at least one monarchy. That much was a matter of public knowledge. But I knew more. I knew of him—from my friend—as a certainty what the guardians of social order in Europe had at most only suspected, or dimly guessed at.

He had had what I may call his underground life. And as I sat, evening after evening, facing him at dinner, a curiosity in that direction would naturally arise in my mind. I am a quiet and peaceable product of civilization, and know no passion other than the passion for collecting things which are rare, and must remain exquisite even if approaching to the monstrous. Some Chinese bronzes are monstrously precious. And here (out of my friend's collection), here I had before me a kind of rare monster. It is true that this monster was polished and in a sense even exquisite. His beautiful unruffled manner was that. But then he was not of bronze. He was not even Chinese, which would have enabled one to contemplate him calmly across the gulf of racial difference. He was alive and European; he had the manner of good society, wore a coat and hat like mine, and had pretty near the same taste in cooking. It was too frightful to think of.

One evening he remarked, casually, in the course of conversation, "There's no amendment to be got out of mankind except by terror and violence."

You can imagine the effect of such a phrase out of such a man's mouth upon a person like myself, whose whole scheme of life had been based upon a suave and delicate discrimination of social and artistic values. Just imagine! Upon me, to whom all sorts and forms of violence appeared as unreal as the giants, ogres, and seven-headed hydras whose activities affect, fantastically, the course of legends and fairy tales!

I seemed suddenly to hear above the festive bustle and clatter of the brilliant restaurant the mutter of a hungry and seditious multitude.

I suppose I am impressionable and imaginative. I had a disturbing vision of darkness, full of lean jaws and wild eyes, amongst the hundred electric lights of the place. But somehow this vision made me angry, too. The sight of that man, so calm, breaking bits of white bread, exasperated me. And I had the audacity to ask him how it was that the starving proletariat of Europe to whom he had been preaching revolt and violence had not been made indignant by his openly luxurious life. "At all this," I said, pointedly, with a glance round the room and at the bottle of champagne we generally shared between us at dinner.

He remained unmoved.

"Do I feed on their toil and their heart's blood? Am I a speculator or a capitalist? Did I steal my fortune from a starving people? No! They know this very well. And they envy me nothing. The miserable mass of the people is generous to its leaders. What I have acquired has come to me through my writings; not from the millions of pamphlets distributed gratis to the hungry and the oppressed, but from the hundreds of thousands of copies sold to the well-fed bourgeois. You know that my writings were at one time the rage, the fashion—the thing to read with wonder and horror, to turn your eyes up at my pathos . . . or else, to laugh in ecstasies at my wit."

"Yes," I admitted. "I remember, of course; and I confess frankly that I could never understand that infatuation."

"Don't you know yet," he said, "that an idle and selfish class loves to see mischief being made, even if it is made at its own expense? Its own life being all a matter of pose and gesture, it is unable to realize the power and the danger of a real movement and of words that have no sham meaning. It is all fun and sentiment. It is sufficient, for instance, to point out the attitude of the old French aristocracy towards the philosophers whose words were preparing the Great Revolution. Even in England, where you have some common sense, a demagogue has only to shout loud enough and long enough to find some backing in the very class he is shouting at. You, too, like to see mischief being made. The demagogue carries the amateurs of emotion with him. Amateurism in this, that, and the other thing is a delightfully easy way of killing time, and feeding one's own vanity—the silly vanity of being abreast with the ideas of the day after tomorrow. Just as good and otherwise harmless people will join you in ecstasies over your collection without having the slightest notion in what its marvelousness really consists."

I hung my head. It was a crushing illustration of the sad truth he advanced. The world is full of such people. And that instance of the French aristocracy before the Revolution was extremely telling, too. I could not traverse his statement, though its cynicism—always a distasteful trait—took off much of its value to my mind. However, I admit I was impressed. I felt the need to say something which would not be in the nature of assent and yet would not invite discussion.

"You don't mean to say," I observed, airily, "that extreme revolutionists have ever been actively assisted by the infatuation of such people?"

"I did not mean exactly that by what I said just now. I generalized. But since you ask me, I may tell you that such help has been given to revolutionary activities, more or less consciously, in various countries. And even in this country."

"Impossible!" I protested with firmness. "We don't play with fire to that extent."

"And yet you can better afford it than others, perhaps. But let me observe that most women, if not always ready to play with fire, are generally eager to play with a loose spark or so."

"Is this a joke?" I asked, smiling.

"If it is, I am not aware of it," he said, woodenly. "I was thinking of an instance. Oh! mild enough in a way . . . ."

I became all expectation at this. I had tried many times to approach him on his underground side, so to speak. The very word had been pronounced between us. But he had always met me with his impenetrable calm.

"And at the same time," Mr. X continued, "it will give you a notion of the difficulties that may arise in what you are pleased to call underground work. It is sometimes difficult to deal with them. Of course there is no hierarchy amongst the affiliated. No rigid system."

My surprise was great, but short-lived. Clearly, amongst extreme anarchists there could be no hierarchy; nothing in the nature of a law of precedence. The idea of anarchy ruling among anarchists was comforting, too. It could not possibly make for efficiency.

Mr. X startled me by asking, abruptly, "You know Hermione Street?"

I nodded doubtful assent. Hermione Street has been, within the last three years, improved out of any man's knowledge. The name exists still, but not one brick or stone of the old Hermione Street is left now. It was the old street he meant, for he said:

"There was a row of two-storied brick houses on the left, with their backs against the wing of a great public building—you remember. Would it surprise you very much to hear that one of these houses was for a time the center of anarchist propaganda and of what you would call underground action?"

"Not at all," I declared. Hermione Street had never been particularly respectable, as I remembered it.

"The house was the property of a distinguished government official," he added, sipping his champagne.

"Oh, indeed!" I said, this time not believing a word of it.

"Of course he was not living there," Mr. X continued. "But from ten till four he sat next door to it, the dear man, in his well-appointed private room in the wing of the public building I've mentioned. To be strictly accurate, I must explain that the house in Hermione Street did not really belong to him. It belonged to his grown-up children—a daughter and a son. The girl, a fine figure, was by no means vulgarly pretty. To more personal charm than mere youth could account for, she added the seductive appearance of enthusiasm, of independence, of courageous thought. I suppose she put on these appearances as she put on her picturesque dresses and for the same reason: to assert her individuality at any cost. You know, women would go to any length almost for such a purpose. She went to great length. She had acquired all the appropriate gestures of revolutionary convictions—the gestures of pity, of anger, of indignation against the antihumanitarian vices of the social class to which she belonged herself. All this sat on her striking personality as well as her slightly original costumes. Very slightly original; just enough to mark a protest against the philistinism of the overfed taskmasters of the poor. Just enough, and no more. It would not have done to go too far in that direction—you understand. But she was of age, and nothing stood in the way of her offering her house to the revolutionary workers."

"You don't mean it!" I cried.

"I assure you," he affirmed, "that she made that very practical gesture. How else could they have got hold of it? The cause is not rich. And, moreover, there would have been difficulties with any ordinary house-agent, who would have wanted references and so on. The group she came in contact with while exploring the poor quarters of the town (you know the gesture of charity and personal service which was so fashionable some years ago) accepted with gratitude. The first advantage was that Hermione Street is, as you know, well away from the suspect part of the town, specially watched by the police.

"The ground floor consisted of a little Italian restaurant, of the flyblown sort. There was no difficulty in buying the proprietor out. A woman and a man belonging to the group took it on. The man had been a cook. The comrades could get their meals there, unnoticed amongst the other customers. This was another advantage. The first floor was occupied by a shabby Variety Artists' Agency—an agency for performers in inferior music halls, you know. A fellow called Bomm, I remember. He was not disturbed. It was rather favorable than otherwise to have a lot of foreign-looking people, jugglers, acrobats, singers of both sexes, and so on, going in and out all day long. The police paid no attention to new faces, you see. The top floor happened, most conveniently, to stand empty then."

X interrupted himself to attack impassively, with measured movements, a *bombe glacée* which the waiter had just set down on the table. He swallowed carefully a few spoonfuls of the iced sweet, and asked me, "Did you ever hear of Stone's Dried Soup?"

"Hear of *what?*"

"It was," X pursued, evenly, "a comestible article once rather prominently advertised in the dailies, but which never, somehow, gained the favor of the public. The enterprise fizzled out, as you say here. Parcels of their stock could be picked up at auctions at considerably less than a penny a pound. The group bought some of it, and an agency for Stone's Dried Soup was started on the top floor. A perfectly respectable business. The stuff, a yellow powder of extremely unappetizing aspect, was put up in large square tins, of which six went to a case. If anybody ever came to give an order, it was, of course, executed. But the advantage of the powder was this, that things could be concealed in it very conveniently. Now and then a special case got put on a van and sent off to be exported abroad under the very nose of the policeman on duty at the corner. You understand?"

"I think I do," I said, with an expressive nod at the remnants of the *bombe* melting slowly in the dish.

"Exactly. But the cases were useful in another way, too. In the basement, or in the cellar at the back, rather, two printing presses were established. A lot of revolutionary literature of the most inflammatory kind was got away from the house in Stone's Dried Soup cases. The brother of our anarchist young lady found some occupation there. He wrote articles, helped to set up type and pull off the sheets, and generally assisted the man in charge, a very able young fellow called Sevrin.

"The guiding spirit of that group was a fanatic of social revolution. He is dead now. He was an engraver and etcher of genius. You must have seen his work. It is much sought after by certain amateurs now. He began by being revolutionary in his art, and ended by becoming a revolutionist, after his wife and child had died in want and misery. He used to say that the bourgeois, the smug, overfed lot, had killed them. That was his real belief. He still worked at his art and led a double life. He was tall, gaunt, and swarthy, with a long, brown beard and deep-set eyes. You must have seen him. His name was Horne."

At this I was really startled. Of course years ago I used to meet Horne about. He looked like a powerful, rough gypsy, in an old top hat, with a red muffler round his throat and buttoned up in a long, shabby overcoat. He talked of his art with exaltation, and gave one the impression of being strung up to the verge of insanity. A small group of connoisseurs appreciated his work. Who would have thought that this man . . . . Amazing! And yet it was not, after all, so difficult to believe.

"As you see," X went on, "this group was in a position to pursue its work of propaganda, and the other kind of work, too, under very advantageous conditions. They were all resolute, experienced men of a superior stamp. And yet we became struck at length by the fact that plans prepared in Hermione Street almost invariably failed."

"Who were 'we'?" I asked, pointedly.

"Some of us in Brussels—at the center," he said, hastily. "Whatever vigorous action originated in Hermione Street seemed doomed to failure. Something always happened to baffle the best-planned manifestations in every part of Europe. It was a time of general activity. You must not imagine that all our failures are of a loud sort, with arrests and trials. That is not so. Often the police work quietly, almost secretly, defeating our combinations by clever counter plotting. No arrests, no noise, no alarming of the public mind and inflaming the passions. It is a wise procedure. But at that time the police were too uniformly successful from Mediterranean to the Baltic. It was annoying and began to look dangerous. At last we came to the conclusion that there must be some untrustworthy elements amongst the London groups. And I came over to see what could be done quietly.

"My first step was to call upon our young Lady Amateur of anarchism at her private house. She received me in a flattering way. I judged that she knew nothing of the chemical and other operations going on at the top of the house in Hermione Street. The printing of anarchist literature was the only 'activity' she seemed to be aware of there. She was displaying very strikingly the usual signs of severe enthusiasm, and had already written many sentimental articles with ferocious conclusions. I could see she was enjoying herself hugely, with all the gestures and grimaces of deadly earnestness. They suited her big-eyed, broad-browed face and the good carriage of her shapely head, crowned by a magnificent lot of brown hair done in an unusual and becoming style. Her brother was in the room, too, a serious youth, with arched eyebrows and wearing a red necktie, who struck me as being absolutely in the dark about everything in the world, including himself. By and by a tall young man came in. He was clean-shaved with a strong bluish jaw and something of the air of a taciturn actor or of a fanatical priest: the type with thick black eyebrows—you know. But he was very presentable indeed. He shook hands at once vigorously with each of us. The young lady came up to me and murmured sweetly, 'Comrade Sevrin.'

"I had never seen him before. He had little to say to us, but sat down by the side of the girl, and they fell at once into earnest conversation. She leaned forward in her deep armchair, and took her nicely rounded chin in her beautiful white hand. He looked attentively into her eyes. It was the attitude of love making, serious, intense, as if on the brink of the grave. I suppose she felt it necessary to round and complete her assumption of advanced ideas, of revolutionary lawlessness, by making believe to be in love with an anarchist. And this one, I repeat, was extremely presentable, notwithstanding his fanatical black-browed aspect. After a few stolen glances in their direction, I had no doubt that he was in earnest. As to the lady, her gestures were unapproachable, better than the very thing itself in the blended suggestion of dignity, sweetness, condescension, fascination, surrender, and reserve. She interpreted her conception of what that precise sort of love making should be with consummate art. And so far, she, too, no doubt, was in earnest. Gestures— but perfect!

"After I had been left alone with our Lady Amateur I informed her guardedly of the object of my visit. I hinted at our suspicions. I wanted to hear what she would have to say, and half expected some perhaps unconscious revelation. All she said was, 'That's serious,' looking delightfully concerned and grave. But there was a sparkle in her eyes which meant plainly, 'How exciting!' After all, she knew little of anything except of words. Still, she undertook to put me in communication with Horne, who was not easy to find unless in Hermione Street, where I did not wish to show myself just then.

"I met Horne. This was another kind of a fanatic altogether. I exposed to him the conclusion we in Brussels had arrived at, and pointed out the significant series of failures. To this he answered with irrelevant exaltation:

"'I have something in hand that shall stike terror into the heart of these gorged brutes.'

"And then I learned that, by excavating in one of the cellars of the house, he and some companions had made their way into the vaults under the great public building I have mentioned before. The blowing up of a whole wing was a certainty as soon as the materials were ready.

"I was not so appalled at the stupidity of that move as I might have been had not the usefulness of our center in Hermione Street become already very problematical. In fact, in my opinion it was much more of a police trap by this time than anything else.

"What was necessary now was to discover what, or rather who, was wrong, and I managed at last to get that idea into Horne's head. He glared, perplexed, his nostrils working as if he were sniffing treachery in the air.

"And here comes a piece of work which will no doubt strike you as a sort of theatrical expedient. And yet what else could have been done? The problem was to find out the untrustworthy member of the group. But no suspicion could be fastened on one more than another. To set a watch upon them all was not very practicable. Besides, that proceeding often fails. In any case, it takes time, and the danger was pressing. I felt certain that the premises in Hermione Street would be ultimately raided, though the police had evidently such confidence in the informer that the house, for the time being, was not even watched. Horne was positive on that point. Under the circumstances it was an unfavorable symptom. Something had to be done quickly.

"I decided to organize a raid myself upon the group. Do you understand? A raid of other trusty comrades personating the police. A conspiracy within a conspiracy. You see the object of it, of course. When apparently about to be arrested I hoped the informer would betray himself in some way or other; either by some unguarded act or simply by his unconcerned demeanor, for instance. Of course there was the risk of complete failure and the no lesser risk of some fatal accident in the course of resistance, perhaps, or in the efforts at escape. For, as you will easily see, the Hermione Street group had to be actually and completely taken unawares, as I was sure they would be by the real police before very long. The informer was amongst them, and Horne alone could be let into the secret of my plan.

"I will not enter into the detail of my preparations. It was not very easy to arrange, but it was done very well, with a really convincing effect. The sham police invaded the restaurant, whose shutters were immediately put up. The surprise was perfect. Most of the Hermione Street party were found in the second cellar, enlarging the hole communicating with the vaults of the great public building. At the first alarm, several comrades bolted through impulsively into the aforesaid vault, where, of course, had this been a genuine raid, they would have been hopelessly trapped. We did not bother about them for the moment. They were harmless enough. The top floor caused considerable anxiety to Horne and myself. There, surrounded by tins of Stone's Dried Soup, a comrade, nicknamed the Professor (he was an ex-science student), was engaged in perfecting some new detonators. He was an abstracted, self-confident, sallow little man, armed with large round spectacles, and we were afraid that under a mistaken impression he would blow himself up and wreck the house about our ears. I rushed upstairs and found him already at the door, on the alert, listening, as he said, to 'suspicious noises down below.' Before I had quite finished explaining to him what was going on he shrugged his shoulders disdainfully and turned away to his balances and test tubes. His was the true spirit of an extreme revolutionist. Explosives were his faith, his hope, his weapon, and his shield. He perished a couple of years afterwards in a secret laboratory through the premature explosion of one of his improved detonators.

"Hurrying down again, I found an impressive scene in the gloom of the big cellar. The man who personated the inspector (he was no stranger to the part) was speaking harshly, and giving bogus orders to his bogus subordinates for the removal of his prisoners. Evidently nothing enlightening had happened so far. Horne, saturnine and swarthy, waited with folded arms, and his patient, moody expectation had an air of stoicism well in keeping with the situation. I detected in the shadows one of the Hermione Street group surreptitiously chewing up and swallowing a small piece of paper. Some compromising scrap, I suppose; perhaps just a note of a few names and addresses. He was a true and faithful 'companion.' But the fund of secret malice which lurks at the bottom of our sympathies caused me to feel amused at that perfectly uncalled-for performance.

In every other respect the risky experiment, the theatrical *coup,* if you like to call it so, seemed to have failed. The deception could not be kept up much longer; the explanation would bring about a very embarrassing and even grave situation. The man who had eaten the paper would be furious. The fellows who had bolted away would be angry, too.

"To add to my vexation, the door communicating with the other cellar, where the printing presses were, flew open, and our young lady revolutionist appeared, a black silhouette in a close-fitting dress and a large hat, with the blaze of gas flaring in there at her back. Over her shoulder I perceived the arched eyebrows and the red necktie of her brother.

"The last people in the world I wanted to see then! They had gone that evening to some amateur concert for the delectation of the poor people, you know; but she had insisted on leaving early, on purpose to call in Hermione Street on the way home, under the pretext of having some work to do. Her usual task was to correct the proofs of the Italian and French editions of the *Alarm Bell* and the *Firebrand*. . . ."

"Heavens!" I murmured. I had been shown once a few copies of these publications. Nothing, in my opinion, could have been less fit for the eyes of a young lady. They were the most advanced things of the sort; advanced, I mean, beyond all bounds of reason and decency. One of them preached the dissolution of all social and domestic ties; the other advocated systematic murder. To think of a young girl calmly tracking printers' errors all along the sort of abominable sentences I remembered was intolerable to my sentiment of womanhood. Mr. X, after giving me a glance, pursued steadily.

"I think, however, that she came mostly to exercise her fascinations upon Sevrin, and to receive his homage in her queenly and condescending way. She was aware of both—her power and his homage—and enjoyed them with, I dare say, complete innocence. We have no ground in expediency or morals to quarrel with her on that account. Charm in woman and exceptional intelligence in man are a law unto themselves. It is not so?"

I refrained from expressing my abhorrence of that licentious doctrine because of my curiosity.

"But what happened then?" I hastened to ask.

X went on crumbling slowly a small piece of bread with a careless left hand.

"What happened, in effect," he confessed, "is that she saved the situation."

"She gave you an opportunity to end your rather sinister farce," I suggested.

"Yes," he said, preserving his impassive bearing. "The farce was bound to end soon. And it ended in a very few minutes. And it ended well. Had she not come in, it might have ended badly. Her brother, of course, did not count. They had slipped into the house quietly some time before. The printing cellar had an entrance of its own. Not finding any one there, she sat down to her proofs, expecting Sevrin to return to his work at any moment. He did not do so. She grew impatient, heard through the door the sounds of a disturbance in the other cellar and naturally came in to see what was the matter.

"Sevrin had been with us. At first he had seemed to me the most amazed of the whole raided lot. He appeared for an instant as if paralyzed with astonishment. He stood rooted to the spot. He never moved a limb. A solitary gas-jet flared near his head; all the other lights had been put out at the first alarm. And presently, from my dark corner, I observed on his shaven actor's face an expression of puzzled, vexed watchfulness. He knitted his heavy eyebrows. The corners of his mouth dropped scornfully. He was angry. Most likely he had seen through the game, and I regretted I had not taken him from the first into my complete confidence.

"But with the appearance of the girl he became obviously alarmed. It was plain. I could see it grow. The change of his expression was swift and startling. And I did not know why. The reason never occurred to me. I was merely astonished at the extreme alteration of the man's face. Of course he had not been aware of her presence in the other cellar; but that did not explain the shock her advent had given him. For a moment he seemed to have been reduced to imbecility. He opened his mouth as if to shout, or perhaps only to gasp. At any rate, it was somebody else who shouted. This somebody else was the heroic comrade whom I had detected swallowing a piece of paper. With laudable presence of mind he let out a warning yell.

"'It's the police! Back! Back! Run back, and bolt the door behind you.'"

"It was an excellent hint; but instead of retreating the girl continued to advance, followed by her long-faced brother in his knickerbocker suit, in which he had been singing comic songs for the entertainment of a joyless proletariat. She advanced not as if she had failed to understand—the word 'police' has an unmistakable sound—but rather as if she could not help herself. She did not advance with the free gait and expanding presence of a distinguished amateur anarchist amongst poor, struggling professionals, but with slightly raised shoulders, and her elbows pressed close to her body, as if trying to shrink within herself. Her eyes were fixed immovably upon Sevrin. Sevrin the man, I fancy; not Sevrin the anarchist. But she advanced. And that was natural. For all their assumption of independence, girls of that class are used to the feeling of being specially protected, as, in fact, they are. This feeling accounts for nine-tenths of their audacious gestures. Her face had gone completely colorless. Ghastly. Fancy having it brought home to her so brutally that she was the sort of person who must run away from the police! I believe she was pale with indignation, mostly, though there was, of course, also the concern for her intact personality, a vague dread of some sort of rudeness. And, naturally, she turned to a man, to the man on whom she had a claim of fascination and homage—the man who could not conceivably fail her at any juncture."

"But," I cried, amazed at this analysis, "if it had been serious, real, I mean—as she thought it was—what could she expect him to do for her?"

X never moved a muscle of his face.

"Goodness knows. I imagine that this charming, generous, and inde-

pendent creature had never known in her life a single genuine thought; I
mean a single thought detached from small human vanities, or whose
source was not in some conventional perception. All I know is that after
advancing a few steps she extended her hand towards the motionless
Sevrin. And that at least was no gesture. It was a natural movement. As
to what she expected him to do, who can tell? The impossible. But
whatever she expected, it could not have come up, I am safe to say, to
what he had made up his mind to do, even before that entreating hand
had appealed to him so directly. It had not been necessary. From the
moment he had seen her enter that cellar, he had made up his mind to
sacrifice his future usefulness, to throw off the impenetrable, solidly
fastened mask it had been his pride to wear—"

"What do you mean?" I interrupted, puzzled. "Was it Sevrin, then,
who was—"

"He was. The most persistent, the most dangerous, the craftiest, the
most systematic of informers. A genius amongst betrayers. Fortunately
for us, he was unique. The man was a fanatic, I have told you. Fortunately, again, for us, he had fallen in love with the accomplished and
innocent gestures of that girl. An actor in desperate earnest himself, he
must have believed in the absolute value of conventional signs. As to the
grossness of the trap into which he fell, the explanation must be that two
sentiments of such absorbing magnitude cannot exist simultaneously in
one heart. The danger of that other and unconscious comedian robbed
him of his vision, of his perspicacity, of his judgment. Indeed, it did at
first rob him of his self-possession. But he regained that through the
necessity—as it appeared to him imperiously—to do something at once.
To do what? Why, to get her out of the house as quickly as possible. He
was desperately anxious to do that. I have told you he was terrified. It
could not be about himself. He had been surprised and annoyed at a move
quite unforeseen and premature. I may even say he had been furious. He
was accustomed to arrange the last scene of his betrayals with a deep,
subtle art which left his revolutionist reputation untouched. But it seems
clear to me that at the same time he had resolved to make the best of it,
to keep his mask resolutely on. It was only with the discovery of her
being in the house that everything—the forced calm, the restraint of his
fanaticism, the mask—all came off together in a kind of panic. Why
panic, do you ask? The answer is very simple. He remembered—or, I
dare say, he had never forgotten—the Professor alone at the top of the
house, pursuing his researches, surrounded by tins upon tins of Stone's
Dried Soup. There was enough in some few of them to bury us all where
we stood under a heap of bricks. Sevrin, of course, was aware of that.

And we must believe, also, that he knew the exact character of the man. He had gauged so many such characters! Or perhaps he only gave the Professor credit for what he himself was capable of. But, in any case, the effect was produced. And suddenly he raised his voice in authority.

"'Get the lady away at once.'

"It turned out that he was as hoarse as a crow; result, no doubt, of the intense emotion. It passed off in a moment. But these fateful words issued forth from his contracted throat in a discordant, ridiculous croak. They required no answer. The thing was done. However, the man personating the inspector judged it expedient to say roughly:

" 'She shall go soon enough, together with the rest of you.'

"These were the last words belonging to the comedy part of this affair.

"Oblivious of everything and everybody, Sevrin strode towards him and seized the lapels of his coat. Under his thin bluish cheeks one could see his jaws working with passion.

" 'You have men posted outside. Get the lady taken home at once. Do you hear? Now. Before you try to get hold of the man upstairs.'

" 'Oh! There is a man upstairs,' scoffed the other, openly. 'Well, he shall be brought down in time to see the end of this.'

"But Sevrin, beside himself, took no heed of the tone.

"'Who's the imbecile meddler who sent you blundering here? Didn't you understand your instructions? Don't you know anything? It's incredible. Here—'

"He dropped the lapels of the coat and, plunging his hand into his breast, jerked feverishly at something under his shirt. At last he produced a small square pocket of soft leather, which must have been hanging like a scapulary from his neck by the tape whose broken ends dangled from his fist.

"'Look inside,' he spluttered, flinging it in the other's face. And instantly he turned round towards the girl. She stood just behind him, perfectly still and silent. Her set, white face gave an illusion of placidity. Only her staring eyes seemed bigger and darker.

"He spoke rapidly, with nervous assurance. I heard him distinctly promise her to make everything as clear as daylight presently. But that was all I caught. He stood close to her, never attempting to touch her even with the tip of his little finger—and she stared at him stupidly. For a moment, however, her eyelids descended slowly, pathetically, and then, with the long black eyelashes lying on her white cheeks, she looked ready to fall down in a swoon. But she never even swayed where she stood. He urged her loudly to follow him at once, and walked towards the door at the bottom of the cellar stairs without looking behind him.

And, as a matter of fact, she did move after him a pace or two. But, of course, he was not allowed to reach the door. There were angry exclamations, a short, fierce scuffle. Flung away violently, he came flying backwards upon her, and fell. She threw out her arms in a gesture of dismay and stepped aside, just clear of his head, which struck the ground heavily near her shoe.

"He grunted with the shock. By the time he had picked himself up, slowly, dazedly, he was awake to the reality of things. The man into whose hands he had thrust the leather case had extracted therefrom a narrow strip of bluish paper. He held it up above his head, and, as after the scuffle an expectant uneasy stillness reigned once more, he threw it down disdainfully with the words, 'I think, comrades, that this proof was hardly necessary.'

"Quick as thought, the girl stooped after the fluttering slip. Holding it spread out in both hands, she looked at it; then, without raising her eyes, opened her fingers slowly and let it fall.

"I examined that curious document afterwards. It was signed by a very high personage, and stamped and countersigned by other high officials in various countries of Europe. In his trade—or shall I say, in his mission?—that sort of talisman might have been necessary, no doubt. Even to the police itself—all but the heads—he had been known only as Sevrin the noted anarchist.

"He hung his head, biting his lower lip. A change had come over him, a sort of thoughtful, absorbed calmness. Nevertheless, he panted. His sides worked visibly, and his nostrils expanded and collapsed in weird contrast with his somber aspect of a fanatical monk in a meditative attitude, but with something, too, in his face of an actor intent upon the terrible exigencies of his part. Before him Horne declaimed, haggard and bearded, like an inspired denunciatory prophet from a wilderness. Two fanatics. They were made to understand each other. Does this surprise you? I suppose you think that such people would be foaming at the mouth and snarling at each other?"

I protested hastily that I was not surprised in the least; that I thought nothing of the kind; that anarchists in general were simply inconceivable to me mentally, morally, logically, sentimentally, and even physically. X received this declaration with his usual woodenness and went on.

"Horne had burst out into eloquence. While pouring out scornful invective, he let tears escape from his eyes and roll down his black beard unheeded. Sevrin panted quicker and quicker. When he opened his mouth to speak, everyone hung on his words.

"'Don't be a fool, Horne,' he began. 'You know very well that I have done this for none of the reasons you are throwing at me.' And in a moment he became outwardly as steady as a rock under the other's lurid stare. 'I have been thwarting, deceiving, and betraying you—from conviction.'

"He turned his back on Horne, and addressing the girl, repeated the words: 'From conviction.'

"It's extraordinary how cold she looked. I suppose she could not think of any appropriate gesture. There can have been few precedents indeed for such a situation.

"'Clear as daylight,' he added. 'Do you understand what that means? From conviction.'

"And still she did not stir. She did not know what to do. But the luckless wretch was about to give her the opportunity for a beautiful and correct gesture.

"'I have felt in me the power to make you share this conviction,' he protested, ardently. He had forgotten himself; he made a step towards her—perhaps he stumbled. To me he seemed to be stooping low as if to touch the hem of her garment. And then the appropriate gesture came. She snatched her skirt away from his polluting contact and averted her head with an upward tilt. It was magnificently done, this gesture of conventionally unstained honor, of an unblemished high-minded amateur.

"Nothing could have been better. And he seemed to think so, too, for once more he turned away. But this time he faced no one. He was again panting frightfully, while he fumbled hurriedly in his waistcoat pocket, and then raised his hand to his lips. There was something furtive in this movement, but directly afterwards his bearing changed. His labored breathing gave him a resemblance to a man who had just run a desperate race; but a curious air of detachment, of sudden and profound indifference, replaced the strain of the striving effort. The race was over. I did not want to see what would happen next. I was only too well aware. I tucked the young lady's arm under mine without a word, and made my way with her to the stairs.

"Her brother walked behind us. Halfway up the short flight she seemed unable to lift her feet high enough for the steps, and we had to pull and push to get her to the top. In the passage she dragged herself along, hanging on my arm, helplessly bent like an old woman. We issued into an empty street through a half-open door, staggering like besotted revelers. At the corner we stopped a four-wheeler, and the ancient driver looked round from his box with morose scorn at our efforts to get her in. Twice during the drive I felt her collapse on my shoulder in a half faint. Facing us, the youth in knickerbockers remained as mute as a fish, and, till he jumped out with the latchkey, sat more still than I would have believed it possible.

"At the door of their drawing room she left my arm and walked in first, catching at the chairs and tables. She unpinned her hat, then, exhausted with the effort, her cloak still hanging from her shoulders, flung herself into a deep armchair, sideways, her face half buried in a cushion. The good brother appeared silently before her with a glass of water. She motioned it away. He drank it himself and walked off to a distant corner — behind the grand piano, somewhere. All was still in this room where I had seen, for the first time, Sevrin, the antianarchist, captivated and spellbound by the consummate and hereditary grimaces that in a certain sphere of life take the place of feelings with an excellent effect. I suppose her thoughts were busy with the same memory. Her shoulders shook violently. A pure attack of nerves. When it quieted down she affected firmness, 'What is done to a man of that sort? What will they do to him?'

"'Nothing. They can do nothing to him,' I assured her, with perfect truth. I was pretty certain he had died in less than twenty minutes from the moment his hand had gone to his lips. For if his fanatical antianarchism went even as far as carrying poison in his pocket, only to rob his adversaries of legitimate vengeance, I knew he would take care to provide something that would not fail him when required.

"She drew an angry breath. There were red spots on her cheeks and a feverish brilliance in her eyes.

"'Has ever any one been exposed to such a terrible experience? To think that he had held my hand! That man!' Her face twitched, she gulped down a pathetic sob. 'If I ever felt sure of anything, it was of Sevrin's high-minded motives.'

"Then she began to weep quietly, which was good for her. Then through her flood of tears, half resentful, 'What was it he said to me? — "From conviction!" It seemed a vile mockery. What could he mean by it?'

"'That, my dear young lady,' I said, gently, 'is more than I or anybody else can ever explain to you.'"

Mr. X flicked a crumb off the front of his coat.

"And that was strictly true as to her. Though Horne, for instance, understood very well; and so did I, especially after we had been to Sevrin's lodging in a dismal back street of an intensely respectable quarter. Horne was known there as a friend, and we had no difficulty in being admitted, the slatternly maid merely remarking, as she let us in, that 'Mr. Sevrin had not been home that night.' We forced open a couple of drawers in the way of duty, and found a little useful information. The most interesting part was his diary; for this man, engaged in such deadly work, had the weakness to keep a record of the most damnatory kind. There were his acts and also his thoughts laid bare to us. But the dead don't mind that. They don't mind anything.

"'From conviction.' Yes. A vague but ardent humanitarianism had urged him in his first youth into the bitterest extremity of negation and revolt. Afterwards his optimism flinched. He doubted and became lost. You have heard of converted atheists. These turn often into dangerous fanatics, but the soul remains the same. After he had got acquainted with the girl, there are to be met in that diary of his very queer politico-amorous rhapsodies. He took her sovereign grimaces with deadly seriousness. He longed to convert her. But all this cannot interest you. For the rest, I don't know if you remember—it is a good many years ago now—the journalistic sensation of the 'Hermione Street Mystery'; the finding of a man's body in the cellar of an empty house; the inquest; some arrests; many surmises—then silence—the usual end for many obscure martyrs and confessors. The fact is, he was not enough of an optimist. You must be a savage, tyrannical, pitiless, thick-and-thin optimist, like Horne, for instance, to make a good social rebel of the extreme type."

He rose from the table. A waiter hurried up with his overcoat; another held his hat in readiness.

"But what became of the young lady?" I asked.

"Do you really want to know?" he said, buttoning himself in his fur coat carefully. "I confess to the small malice of sending her Sevrin's diary. She went into retirement; then she went to Florence; then she went into retreat in a convent. I can't tell where she will go next. What does it matter? Gestures! Gestures! Mere gestures of her class."

He fitted on his glossy high hat with extreme precision, and casting a rapid glance round the room, full of well-dressed people, innocently dining, muttered between his teeth:

"And nothing else! That is why their kind is fated to perish."

I never met Mr. X again after that evening. I took to dining at my club. On my next visit to Paris I found my friend all impatience to hear of the effect produced on me by this rare item of his collection. I told him all the story, and he beamed on me with the pride of his distinguished specimen.

"Isn't X well worth knowing?" he bubbled over in great delight. "He's unique, amazing, absolutely terrific."

His enthusiasm grated upon my finer feelings. I told him curtly that the man's cynicism was simply abominable.

"Oh, abominable! abominable!" assented my friend, effusively. "And then, you know, he likes to have his little joke sometimes," he added in a confidential tone.

I fail to understand the connection of this last remark. I have been utterly unable to discover where in all this the joke comes in.

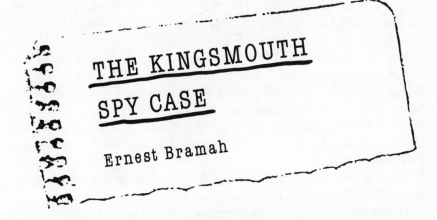

THE KINGSMOUTH SPY CASE

Ernest Bramah

"NOT GUILTY, MY Lord!" There was a general laugh in the lounge of the "Rose and Plumes", the comfortable old Cliffhurst hotel that upheld the ancient traditions unaffected by the flaunting rivalry of Grand or Metropole. The jest hidden in the retort was a small one but it was at the expense of a pompous, pretentious bore, and the speaker was a congenial wag who had contrived in the course of a few weeks to win a facile popularity on all sides.

Across the room one of the later arrivals—"the blind gentleman", as he was sympathetically alluded to, for few had occasion to learn his name—turned slightly towards the direction of the voice and added a pleasantly appreciative smile at the common tribute. Then his attention again settled on the writing-table at which he sat, and for the next few minutes his pencil traveled smoothly, with an occasional pause for consideration, over the block of telegraphic forms that he had picked out. At the end of ten minutes he rang for a waiter and directed that his own man should be sent to him.

"Here are three telegrams to go off, Parkinson," he said in the suave, agreeable voice that scarcely ever varied, no matter what the occasion might be. "You will take them yourself at once. After that I shall not require you again tonight."

The attendant thanked him and withdrew. The blind man closed his letter-case, retired from the writing-table to the obscurity of a sequestered corner and sat unnoticed with his sightless eyes, that always seemed to be quietly smiling, looking placidly into illimitable space as he visualized the scene before him, and the laughter, the conversation and the occasional whisper went on unchecked around.

Max Carrados had journeyed down to Cliffhurst a few days previously, good-naturedly but without any enthusiasm. Indeed, it had needed all Mr. Carlyle's persuasive eloquence to move him.

"The Home Office, Max," urged the inquiry agent, "one of the premier departments of the State! Consider the distinction! Surely you will not refuse a commission of that nature direct from the Government?" Carrados, looking a little deeper than a Melton overcoat and a glossy silk hat, had once declared his friend to be the most incurably romantic of idealists. He now took a malicious pleasure in reducing the situation to its crudest terms.

"Why can't the local police arrest a solitary inoffensive German spy themselves?" he inquired.

"To tell the truth, Max, I believe that there are two or three fingers in that pie at the present moment," replied Mr. Carlyle confidentially. "It doesn't concern the Home Office alone. And after that Guitry Bay fiasco and the unmerciful chaffing that we got in the German papers—with rather a nasty rap or two over the knuckles from the *Kolnische Zeitung*— both Whitehall and Downing Street are in a blue funk lest they should do the wrong thing, either let the man slip away with the papers or arrest him without them."

"Contingencies with which I am sure you could grapple successfully, Louis."

Mr. Carlyle's bland complacency did not suggest that he, at any rate, had any doubt on that score.

"But, you know, Max, I am pledged to carry through the Vandeeming affair here in town. And—um—well, the Secretary did make a point of you being the man they relied on."

"Oh, someone there must read the papers, Louis! But I wonder . . . why they did not communicate with me direct?"

Mr. Carlyle contrived to look extremely ingenuous. Even he occasionally forgot that looks went for nothing with Carrados.

"I imagine that they thought that a friendly intermediary—or something of that sort."

"Possibly Inspector Beedel hinted to the Commissioner that you would have more influence with me than a whole Government Department?" smiled Carrados. "And so you have, Louis; so you have. If it's your ambition to get the Government on your books you can tell your clients that I'll take on their job!"

"By Jupiter, Max, you are a good fellow if ever there was one!" exclaimed Mr. Carlyle with gentlemanly emotion. "But I owe too much to you already."

"This won't make it any more, then. I have another reason, quite different, for going."

"Of course you have," assented the visitor heartily. "You are not one to talk about partriotism, and all that, but you can't hoodwink me with your dilettantish pose, Max, and I know that deep down in your nature there is a passionate devotion to your country—"

"Thank you, Louis," interrupted Carrados. "It is very nice to learn that. But I am really going to Kingsmouth because there's a man there—a curate—who has the second-best private collection in Europe of autonomous coins of Thessaly."

For a few seconds Mr. Carlyle looked his unutterable feelings. When he did speak it was with crushing deliberation.

"'Mrs. Carrados,' I shall say—if ever there is a Mrs. Carrados, Max—Mrs. Carrados, two things are necessary for your domestic happiness. In the first place, pack up your husband's tetradrachms in a brown-paper parcel and send them with your compliments to the British Museum. In the second, at the earliest possible opportunity, exact from him an oath that he will never touch another Greek coin as long as you both live.'"

"If ever there is a Mrs. Carrados," was the quick retort, "I shall probably be independent of the consolation of Greek coins as, also, Louis, of the distraction of criminal investigation. In the meantime, what are you going to tell me about this case?"

Mr. Carlyle at once became alert. He would have become absolutely professional had not Carrados tactfully obtruded the cigar box. The digression, and the pleasant aroma that followed it, brought him back again to the merely human.

"It began, like a good many other cases, with an anonymous letter." He took a slip of paper from his pocket-book and handed it to Carrados. "Here is a copy."

"A copy!" The blind man ran his finger lightly along the lines and read aloud what he found there:

> "A friend warns you that an attempt is being successfully
> made on behalf of another Power to obtain naval information
> of vital importance. You have a traitor within your gates."

Then he crumpled up the paper and dropped it half-contemptuously into the wastepaper basket. "A copy is no use to us, Louis," he remarked. "Indeed, it is worse than useless; it is misleading."

"That is all they had here. The original was addressed to the Admiral-Superintendent at the Kingsmouth Dockyard. This was sent up with the report. But I am assured that the other contained no clue to the writer's identity."

"Not even a watermark, 'Jones, stationer, High Street, Kingsmouth'!" said Carrados dryly. "Really, Louis! Every piece of paper contains at least four palpable clues."

"And what are they, pray?"

"A smell, a taste, an appearance and a texture. This one, in addition, bears ink, and with it all the characteristics of an individual handwriting."

"In capitals, Max," Mr. Carlyle reminded him. "Our anonymous friend is up to that."

"Yes; I wonder who first started that venerable illusion."

"Illusion?"

"Certainly an illusion. Capitals, or 'printed handwriting', as one sees them called, are just as idiomorphic as a cursive form."

"But much less available for comparison. How are you going to obtain a specimen of anyone's printed handwriting for comparison?"

Carrados reflected silently for a moment.

"I think I should ask anyone I suspected to do one for me," he replied.

Carlyle resisted the temptation to laugh outright, but mordacity lurked in his voice.

"And you imagine that the writer of this, who evidently has good reason for anonymity, will be simple enough to comply?"

"I think so; if I ask him nicely."

"Look here, Max, I will bet you a box of any cigars you care to name—"

"Yes, Louis?"

Mr. Carlyle had hesitated. He was recalling one or two things from the past, and on those occasions his friend's unemotional face had looked just as devoid of guile as it did now.

"No, Max, I won't bet this time, but I should like to send across a small box of Monterrey Coronas for Parkinson to pack among your things. Well, so much for the letter."

"Not quite all," interposed Carrados. "I must have the original."

The visitor made a note in his pocket diary.

"It shall be sent to you at once. I stipulated an absolutely free hand for you. Oh, I took a tolerably high tone, I can assure you, Max. You will find everything at Kingsmouth very pleasant, and there, of course, you will learn all the details. Here they don't seem to know very much. I was not informed whether the dockyard authorities had already had their suspicions aroused or whether the letter was the first hint. At all events they acted with tolerable promptness. The letter, you will see, is undated, but it was delivered on the seventeenth—last Thursday. On Friday they put their hands on a man in the construction department—a fellow called Brown. He made no fight of it when he was cornered, but although he owned up to the charge of betraying information, there was one important link that he could not supply and one that he would not. He could not tell them who the spy collecting the information was, because there was an intermediary; and he would not betray the intermediary on any terms. And, by gad, I for one can't help respecting the beggar for that remnant of loyalty."

"A woman?" suggested Carrados.

"Even that, I believe, is not known, but very likely you have hit the mark. A woman would explain the element of chivalry that prompts Brown's attitude. He is under open arrest now—nobody outside is supposed to know, but of course he can't buy an evening paper without it being noted. They are in hope of something more definite turning up. At present they have pitched their suspicions on a German visitor staying at Cliffhurst."

"Why?"

"I don't know, Max. They must fix on someone, you know. It's expected. All the same, they are deucedly nervous at this end about the outcome."

"Did they say what Brown had given away?"

"Yes, egad! Do you know anything of the Croxton-Delahey torpedo?"

"A little," admitted Carrados.

"What does it do?" asked Mr. Carlyle, with the rather sublime air of casual interest which he attached to any subject outside his own knowledge.

"It's rather an ingenious contrivance. It is fired like any other uncontrolled torpedo. At the end of a straight run—anything up to ten thousand yards at fifty-five knots with the superheated system—the diabolical creature stops and begins deliberately to slash a zigzag course over any area you have set it for. If in its roving it comes within two hundred feet of any considerable mass of iron it promptly makes for it, cuts its way through torpedo-netting if any bars its progress, explodes its three hundred-weight of gun-cotton and finishes its existence by firing a twenty-four-pound thorite shell through the breach it has made."

"'Um," mused Mr. Carlyle; "I don't like the weapon, Max, but I would rather that we kept it to ourselves. Well, Mr. Brown has given away the plans."

Carrados disposed of the end of his cigar and crossed the room to his open desk. From its appointed place he took a book inscribed "Engagements", touched a few pages and scribbled a line of comment here and there. Then he turned to his guest again.

"All right. I'll go down to Kingsmouth by the 12:17 tomorrow morning," he said. "Now I want you to look up the following points for me and let me have the particulars before I go."

Mr. Carlyle again took out his pocket diary and beamed approvingly.

As a matter of fact the tenor of the replies he received influenced Carrados to make some change in his plans. Accompanied by Parkinson he left London by the appointed train on the next day, but instead of proceeding to Kingsmouth he alighted at Cliffhurst, the pretty little seaside resort some five miles east of the great dockport. After securing rooms at the "Rose and Plumes"—an easy enough matter in October—he directed his attendant to take him to a sheltered seat on the winding paths below the promenade and there leave him for an hour.

"Very nicely kept, these walks and shrubberies, sir," remarked an affable voice from the other end of the bench. A leisurely pedestrian whose clothes and manner proclaimed him to be an aimless holiday-maker had sauntered along and, after a moment's hesitation, had sat down on the same form.

"Yes, Inspector," replied Carrados genially. "Almost up to the standard of our own Embankment Gardens, are they not?"

Detective Inspector Tapling of New Scotland Yard went rather red and then laughed quietly.

"I wasn't quite sure at first if it was you, Mr. Carrados," he apologized, moving nearer and lowering his voice. "I was to report to you here, sir, and to give you any information and assistance you might require."

"How are you getting on?" inquired Carrados.

"We think that we have got hold of the right man, sir; but for reasons that you can guess the Chief is very anxious to have no mistake this time."

"Muller?"

"Yes, sir. He has a furnished villa here in Cliffhurst and is very open-handed. The time he came fits in, so far as we can tell, with the beginning of the inquiries in Kingsmouth. Then, whatever his real name is, it isn't Muller."

"He is a German?"

"Oh yes; he's German right enough, sir. We've looked up telegrams to him from Lübeck—nothing important though—and he has changed German notes in Kingsmouth. He spends a lot of time over there—says the fishing is better, but that's all my eye, only the Kingsmouth boatmen get hold of the dockyard talk and know more of the movements than the men about here. Then there's a lady."

"The intermediary?"

"That's futher than we can go at the moment, but there is a lady at the furnished villa. She's not exactly Mrs. Muller, we believe, but she lives there, if you understand what I mean, sir."

"Perfectly," acquiesced Carrados in the same modest spirit.

"So that all the necessary conditions can be shown to exist," concluded Tapling.

"But so far you have not a single positive fact connecting Muller with Brown?"

The Inspector admitted that he had not, but added hopefully that he was in immediate expectation of information that would enable him to link up the detached surmises into a conclusive chain of direct evidence.

"And if I might ask the favor of you, sir," he continued, "you would be doing us a great service if you would allow us to continue our investigation for another twenty-four hours. I think that by then we shall be able to show something solid. And if you certify what we have done, that's all to our credit, whereas if you take it out of our hands now— You see what I mean, Mr. Carrados; but of course it lies entirely with you."

Carrados assented with his usual good nature. His actual business was only to examine the evidence before the arrest was made and to guarantee that the Home Office should not be involved in another spy-scare fiasco. He knew Tapling to be reliable officer, and he did not doubt that the line he was working was the correct one. Least of all did he wish to deprive the man of his due credit.

"I can very well put in a day on my own account," he accordingly replied. "And so long as Muller is here there does not appear to be any special urgency. I suppose the odds are that the papers have been got away before you began to watch?"

"There is just a chance yet, we believe, sir; and the Admiralty is very keen on recovering those torpedo plans if it's to be done. Some of these foreign spies like to keep the thing as much as posible in their own hands. There's more credit to it, and more cash, too, at headquarters if they do. Then if it comes to a matter of touch and go, a letter, and especially a letter from abroad, may be stopped on the way. You will say that a man may be, for that matter, but there's been another reason against posting valuable papers about here for the past week."

"Of course," assented Carrados with enlightenment. "The Suffragettes down here are out."

"I never thought to have any of that lot helping," said the Inspector, absentmindedly stroking his right shin; "but they may have turned the scale for us this time. There isn't a posting-place from a rural pillar-box to the head office at Kingsmouth that has been really safe from them. They've even got at the registered letters in the sorting-rooms somehow. That's why I think there's a chance still."

Parkinson's approaching figure announced that an hour had passed. Carrados and the Inspector rose to walk away in different directions but before they parted the blind man put a question that had confronted him several times, although he had as yet given only a glancing attention to the case.

"Now that Muller has got the plans of the torpedo, Inspector, why is he remaining here?"

It was a simple and an obvious inquiry, but before he replied Inspector Tapling looked round suspiciously. Then he further reduced the distance between them and dropped his voice to a whisper.

St. Ethelburga's boasted the most tin-potty bell and the highest ritual of any church in Kingsmouth. Outside it resembled a brick barn, inside a marble palace, and its ministration overworked a vicar and two enthusiastic curates. It stood at the corner of Jubilee Street and Lower Dock Approach, a conjunction that should render further description of the neighborhood superfluous.

The Rev. Byam Hosier, the senior curate, whose magnetic eloquence filled St. Ethelburga's from chancel steps to porch, lodged in Jubilee Street, and there Mr. Carrados found him at ten o'clock on the following morning. The curate had just finished his breakfast and the simultaneous correction of a batch of exercise-books. He apologized for the disorder without justifying himself by explaining the cause, for instead of being a laggard Mr. Hosier had already taken an early celebration, and afterwards allowed himself to be intercepted on his way back to attend to a domestic quarrel, a lost cat, and the arrangements for a funeral.

"I got your note last night, Mr. Carrados," he said, after guiding his guest to a seat, for Parkinson had been dismissed to make himself agreeable elsewhere. "I am glad to show you my small collection, and still more so to have an opportunity of thanking you for the help you have given me from time to time."

Carrados lightly disclaimed the obligation. It was the first time the two had met, though, as the outcome of a review article, they had frequently corresponded. The clergyman went to his single cabinet, took out the top tray and put it down before his visitor on the now available table.

"Pherae," he said.

"May I touch the surfaces?" asked the blind man.

"Oh, certainly. Pray do. I am sorry—" He did not quite know what to say before the spectacle of the blind expert, with his eyes fixed elsewhere, passing a critical touch over the details that he himself loved to gaze upon.

In this one thing the Rev. Byam was fastidious. His clothes were generally bordering on the shabby, and he allowed himself to wear boots that shocked or amused the feminine element in the first half-dozen pews of St. Ethelburga's. He might—as he frequently did, indeed—make a breakfast of weak tea, bread and butter and marmalade without any sense of deficiency, but in the matter of Greek coins his taste was exacting and his standard exact. His one small mahogany cabinet was pierced for five hundred specimens, and it was far from full, but every coin was the exquisite production of the golden era of the world's creative art.

It did not take Carrados three minutes to learn this. Occasionally he dropped a word of comment or inquiry, but for the most part tray succeeded tray in fascinated silence.

"Still Larissa," announced the clergyman, sliding out the last tray.

Under each coin was a circular ticket with written particulars of the specimen accompanying it. For some time Carrados took little interest in these commentaries, but presently Hosier noticed that his guest was submitting many of them to a close but quiet scrutiny.

"Excuse my asking, Mr. Carrados," he said at length, "but are you quite blind?"

"Quite," was the unconcerned reply. "Why?"

"Because I noticed that you held some of the labels close to your eyes and I fancied that perhaps—"

"It is my way."

"Forgive my curiosity—"

"I can assure you, Mr. Hosier, that other people are much more touchy about my blindness than I am. Now will you do me a kindness? I should like a copy of the inscriptions on half a dozen of these gems."

"With pleasure." The curate discovered pen and ink and paper and waited.

"This didrachm of the nymph Larissa wearing earrings; this of Artemis and the stag; this, and this, and this." The trays had been left displayed upon the table and Carrados's hand selected from them with unerring precision.

Hosier took the chosen coins and noted down the legends in their bold Greek capitals. "Shall I describe the type of each as well?" he asked.

"Thank you," assented his visitor. "If you don't mind writing that also in capitals and not blotting I shall read it so much the easier."

He accepted the sheet of paper and delicately touched the lettering along each line.

"I have a friend who will be equally interested in this," he remarked, taking out his pocket-book.

The clergyman had turned to remove a tray from the table when a sheet of paper, fluttering to the ground, caught his eye. He picked it up and was returning it into the blind man's hand when he stopped in a sudden arrest of every movement.

"Good heavens, Mr. Carrados," he exclaimed in an agitated voice, "how does this come in your possession?"

"Your note?"

"You know that it is mine?"

"Yes—now," replied Carrados quietly. "It was sent to me by the Admiral-Superintendent of the Yard here. He wished to communicate with the writer."

"I am bewildered at the suddenness of this," protested the poor young man in some distress. "Let me tell you the circumstances—such at least as do not violate my promise."

He procured himself a glass of water from the sideboard, drank half of it and began to pace the room nervously as he talked.

"On Wednesday last, after taking Evensong at the church, I was leaving the vestry when a lady stepped forward and asked if she might speak to me privately. It is a request which a clergyman cannot refuse, Mr. Carrados, but I endeavored first to find out what she required, because people frequently come to one or another of us on business that really has to do with the clerk, or the organist, or something of that sort.

"She assured me that it was a personal matter and that no other official would do.

"The lights had by this time been extinguished in the church, and doubtless the apparitor had left. I gave her my address here and asked her if she would call in ten or twenty minutes. I preferred that she should present herself in the ordinary way.

"There is no need to go into extraneous details. The unhappy lady wished to unburden her conscience by making explicit confession, and she had come to me in consequence of a sermon which she had heard me preach on the Sunday before.

"It is not expedient to weigh considerations of time or circumstance in such a case. I allowed her to proceed, and she made her confession under the seal of inviolable confidence. It involved other persons besides herself. I besought her to undo as far as possible the great harm she had done by making a full statement to the authorities, but this she was too weak—too terrified—to do. This clumsy warning of mine"—he pointed to the paper now lying on the table between them—"was the utmost concession that I could wring from her."

He stopped and looked at his visitor with a troubled face that seemed to demand some sort of assent to the dilemma.

"You are an Englishman, Mr. Hosier, and you know what this might mean in a conflict—you know that one of our most formidable weapons has been annexed."

"My dear sir," rapped out the distressed curate, "don't you think that I haven't worried about that? But behind the Englishman stands something more primitive, more just—the man. I gave my assurance as a man, and the Admiralty can go hang!

"Besides," he added, in petulant reaction, "the poor woman is dying, and then everyone can know. Of course, it may be too late."

"Do you mind telling me if the lady gave you the names of her accomplices?"

"How can I tell you, Mr. Carrados? It may identify her in some way. I am too confounded by your unexpected appearance in the affair to know what is important and what is not."

"It will not implicate her. I have no concern there."

"Then, yes, she did. She gave me every detail."

"I ask because a man is suspected and on the point of arrest. He may be innocent. I have no deeper motive, but if the one for whom she is working is not a German called, or passing as, Muller, you might have some satisfaction in exonerating him."

The curate reflected a moment.

"He is not, Mr. Carrados," he replied decidedly. "But please don't ask me anything more."

"Very well, I won't," said Carrados, rising. "Our numismatic conversation has taken a strange turn, Mr. Hosier. There is a text for you—Money at the root of everything! By the way, I can do you one trifling service." He picked up the anonymous letter, tore it across and held it out. "You have done all you could. Burn this and then you are clear of the matter."

"Thanks, thanks. But won't it get you into trouble with the Admiralty?"

"I make my own terms," replied Carrados. "Now, Mr. Hosier, I have been an ill-omened bird, but I had no suspicion of this when I came. The 'long arm' has landed us this time. Will you come and dine with me one day this week, and I promise you not a single reference to this troublesome business?"

"You are very good," assented Hosier.

"I am at Cliffhurst—"

"Cliffhurst?" was Hosier's quick exclamation.

"Yes, at the 'Rose and Plumes'."

"I—I am very sorry, Mr. Carrados," stammered the curate, "but, after all, I am afraid that I must cry off. This week—"

"If the distance takes up too much of your time, may I send a car?"

"No, no, it isn't that—at least, of course, one has to consider time and work. Thank you, Mr. Carrados; you are very kind, but, really, if you don't mind—"

Carrados courteously accepted the refusal without further pressure. He turned the momentary embarrassment by hoping that Hosier would not fail to call on him when next in London, and the curate availed himself of the compromise to protest the pleasure that it would afford him. Parkinson was summoned and the strangely developed visit came to an end.

Parkinson doubtless found his master a dull companion on the way back. Carrados had to rearrange his ideas from the preconception which he had so far tentatively based on Inspector Tapling's report, and he was faced by the necessity of discovering whose presence made the Rose and Plumes Hotel inexplicably distasteful to Mr. Hosier just then. Only two flashes of conversation broke the journey, both of which may be taken as showing the trend of Max Carrados's mind, and demonstrating the sound common sense exhibited by his henchman.

"It is a mistake they often make, Parkinson, to begin looking with a fixed idea of what they are going to find."

"Yes, sir."

And, ten minutes later:

"But I don't know that it would be safe yet to ignore the obvious altogether."

"No, sir," replied Parkinson.

"Not guilty, my lord!"

That was the link for which Carrados had been waiting patiently each day since his visit to Kingsmouth; or, more exactly, since the sound of a voice heard in the hotel on his return had stirred a memory that he could not materialize. Parkinson had described the man with photographic exactness, and still recognition was balked. Tapling, who found himself at a deadlock before the furnished villa, both by reason of his want of progress and at Carrados's recommendation, contributed his observation, which was guardedly negative. Everyone about knew Mr. Slater—"a pleasant, openhanded gentleman, with a word and a joke for all"—but no one knew anything of him, as, indeed, who should know of a leisurely bird of passage staying for a little time at a seaside hotel?

Then across the lounge rang the mock-serious repartee, and enlightenment cut into the patient listener's brain like a flash of inspiration.

These were the three telegrams which immediately came into existence
as a result of that ray, deciphered here from their code obscurity:

TO GREATOREX, TURRETS, RICHMOND, SURREY.

EXTRACT "TIMES" FULL REPORT TRIAL HENRY
FRANKWORTH, CONVICTED EMBEZZLEMENT EARLY 1906,
AND FORWARD EXPRESS. — CARRADOS

TO WRATTESLEY, HOME OFFICE, WHITEHALL, S.W.

WILL YOU PLEASE HAVE LINCOLN AUTHORITIES IN-
STRUCTED TO SEND ME CONFIDENTIAL REPORT ANTECE-
DENTS HENRY FRANKWORTH. EMBEZZLER, NATIVE
TRUDSTONE THAT COUNTY. URGENT. — WYNN CARRADOS

TO CARLYLE, 72A BAMPTON ST., W.C.

MY DEAR LOUIS. — WHY NOT COME DOWN WEEKEND
TALK THINGS OVER? MEANWHILE MAKE EVERY EFFORT
DISCOVER SUBSEQUENT HISTORY HENRY FRANKWORTH
CONVICTED EMBEZZLEMENT CENTRAL CRIMINAL COURT
EARLY 1906. BEEDEL WILL FURNISH POLICE RECORDS.
PRESSING. — MAX.

On his way upstairs a few hours later Carrados looked in at the reception office to inquire if there were any letters.

"By the by," he remarked, after he had turned to leave, "I wonder if you happen to have a room a little—just a little—farther away from the drawing room?"

"Certainly, sir," replied the clerk. "Does the playing annoy you? They
do keep it up rather late sometimes, don't they?"

"No, it doesn't annoy me," admitted Carrados; "on the contrary, I am
passionately fond of it. But it tempts me into lying awake listening when
I ought to be asleep."

The young lady laughed pleasantly. It was her business to be agreeable.

"You are considerate!" she rippled. "Well, there's the further corridor;
or, of course, a floor above—"

"The floor above would do nicely. Not on the front if possible. The
sea is rather noisy."

"Second floor, west corridor." She glanced at her keyboard. "No. 15?"

"Is that the side overlooking the—?"

"The High Street," she prompted.

"I am such a poor sleeper," he apologized.

"No. 21 on the other side, overlooking the gardens?" she suggested.

"I am sure that will do admirably," he said, with the gratitude that is always so touching from the blind. "Thank you for taking so much trouble to pick it for me. Good night."

"I will have your things transferred tomorrow," she nodded after him.

An hour later Mr. Slater, generally the last man to leave the lounge, strolled across to the office for his key.

"No. 22, sir, isn't it?" she hazarded, unhooking it without waiting for the number.

"Good little girl," he assented approvingly. "What a brain beneath that fascinating aureola. *Eh bien, au revoir, petite!* You ought to be about snuffing the candle yourself, my dear."

The young lady laughed just as pleasantly. It was her business to be equally agreeable to all.

Mr. Carrados was sitting in an alcove of the lounge on the following morning when Parkinson brought him a letter. It proved to be the extract from *The Times,* written on the special typewriter. The day was bright and inviting and the room was deserted. On his master's instruction Parkinson sat down and waited while the blind man rapidly deciphered the half-dozen sheets of typewriting.

"You have been with me to the Old Bailey several times," remarked Carrados as he slowly replaced the document. "Do you remember an occasion in February, 1906?"

Parkinson looked unnecessarily wise, but was unable to acquiesce. Carrados gave him another guide.

"A man named Frankworth was sentenced to eighteen months' imprisonment for an ingenious system of theft. He had also fraudulently disposed of information to trade rivals of his employer."

"I apprehend the circumstances now, sir."

"Can you recall the appearance of the prisoner?"

Parkinson thought that he could, but he did not rise to the suggestion, and Carrados was obliged to follow the direct line.

"Have you seen anyone lately—here in the hotel—who might be Frankworth?"

"I can't say that I have, sir."

"Take Mr. Slater now. Shake off his beard and mustache."

Parkinson began to look respectfully uncomfortable.

"Do you mean, sir—"

"By an effort of the imagination, Parkinson. Close your eyes and picture Mr. Slater as a clean-shaven man, some years younger, standing in the dock—"

"Yes, sir. There is a distinct resemblance."

With this Max Carrados had to be satisfied for the time. Long memory was not Parkinson's strong point, but he had his own preeminent gift, and of this his master was to have an immediate example that outweighed every possible deficiency.

"Speaking of Mr. Slater, sir, I noticed a curious thing that I intended to mention, as you told me to be particularly observant."

Carrados nodded encouragingly.

"I was talking to Herbert early this morning as he cleaned the boots. He is a very bigoted Free Trader, sir, and is thinking of becoming a Mormon, and I was speaking to him about it. Presently he came to No. 22's—Mr. Slater's. They were muddy, for Mr. Slater went out for a walk last night—I saw him as he returned. But the boots that Mr. Slater put out to be cleaned last night were not the boots that he went out in and got wet, although they were exactly the same make."

"That is certainly curious," admitted Carrados slowly. "There was only one pair put out?"

"That is all, sir; and they were not the boots that Mr. Slater has worn every day since I began to notice him particularly. He always does wear the same pair, morning, noon and night."

"Wait," said Carrados briskly. An idea bordering on the fantastic flashed between a sentence in the report which he had just been reading and Parkinson's discovery. He took out the sheets, ran his finger along the lines and again read—"stated that the prisoner was the son of a respectable bootmaker, and had followed the occupation himself." "I know how accurate you are, Parkinson, but this may be of superlative importance. You see that?"

"I had not contemplated it in that light, sir."

"But what did the incident suggest to you?"

"I inferred, sir, that Mr. Slater must have had some reason for going out again after the hotel was closed."

"Yes, that might explain half; but what if he did not?" persisted Carrados.

Parkinson wisely dismissed the intellectual problem as outside his sphere.

"Then I am unable to suggest why the gentleman cleaned his muddy boots himself and muddied his clean boots, sir."

"Yes, that is what it comes to. He is wearing the same pair again this morning?"

"Yes, sir. The boots that were dirty at ten o'clock last night."

"Pay particular attention to Mr. Slater's boots in future. I have transferred to No. 21, so you will have every opportunity. Talk to Herbert about Tariff Reform tomorrow morning. In the meanwhile— Are they any particular make?"

"'Moorland handmade waterproof', a heavy shooting-boot, sir. Size 7. Rossiter, of Kingsmouth, is the maker."

"In the meantime go to Kingsmouth and buy an identical pair. Before you go, cut the sole off one of your oldest boots and bring me a piece about three inches square. Buy yourself another pair. Here is a note. Do you know which chambermaid has charge of No. 21?"

"I could ascertain, sir."

"It would be as well. You might buy her a bangle out of the change—if you have no personal objection to the young lady's society. And, Parkinson—"

"Yes, sir?"

"I know you to be discreet and reliable. The work we are engaged on here is exceptionally important and equally honorable. A mistake might ruin it. That is all."

"Thank you, sir." Parkinson marched away with his head a little higher for the guarded compliment. It was the essence of the man's extraordinary value to his master that while on some subjects he thought deeply, on others he did not think at all; and he contrived automatically to separate everything into its proper compartment.

"Here is what you require, sir," he said, returning with the square of leather.

"Come across to the fireplace," said Carrados. "There is still no one else in the lounge?"

"No, sir."

"Who would be the last servant to see to this room at night—to leave the fire safe and the windows fastened?"

"The hall porter, sir."

"Where is he now?"

"In the outer hall."

Carrados bent towards the fire. "It's a million-to-one chance," he thought, "but it's worth trying." He dropped the leather on to the red coals, waited until it began to smoke fiercely, and then, lifting it out with the tongs, he allowed the pungent aromatic odor to diffuse into the air for a few seconds. A minute later the charred fragment had lost its identity among the embers.

"Go now, and on your way tell the hall porter that I want to speak to him."

The hall porter came, a magnificent being, but full of affable condescension.

"You sent for me, sir?"

Carrados was sitting at a table near the fire.

"Yes. I am a little nervous. Do you smell anything burning?"

The porter sniffed the air—superfluously but loudly, so that the blind gentleman should hear that he was not failing in his duty. Then he looked comprehensively around.

"There certainly is a sort of hottish smell somewhere, sir," he admitted.

"It isn't any woodwork about the fireplace scorching? We blind are so helpless."

"That's all right, sir." He laid a broad hand on the mantelpiece and then rapped it reassuringly. "Solid marble that, sir. You needn't be afraid; I'll give a look across now and then."

"Thank you, if you will," said Carrados, with relief in his voice. "And, by the way, will you ring for Maurice as you go?"

A distant bell churred. Across the room, like a strangely balancing bird, skimmed a waiter.

"Sair?"

"Oh, is that you, Maurice? I want— By the way, what's that burning?"

"Burning, sair?"

"Yes; don't you smell anything?"

"There is an odor of smell," admitted Maurice sagely, "but it is nothing to see."

"You don't know the smell?"

The waiter shook his head and looked vague. Carrados divined perplexity.

"Oh, I dare say it's nothing," he declared carelessly. "Will you get me a sherry and khoosh?"

The million-to-one chance had failed.

"Sherry and bittaire, sair."

Maurice deposited the glass with great precision, regarded it sadly and then moved it three inches to the right.

"I 'ave recollect this odor, sair," he remarked, "although I cannot give actuality. I 'ave met him here before, but—less—less forcefully."

"When?"

"Oh, one week since, perhaps."

"Something in the coals?" suggested Carrados.

"I imagine yes," pondered Maurice conscientiously. "I was 'brightening up', as you say, for the night, and the fire was low down. I squash it with the poker still more for safety."

"Oh, then the lounge would be empty?"

"Yes—of people. Only Mr. Slataire already departing."

Carrados indicated that he did not want the change and dismissed the subject.

"So long as nothing's on fire," he said with indifference.

"Thank you, sair."

The million-to-one chance had come off after all.

Two days later, walking beyond the usual limit of the conventional promenade, Carrados reached a rough wooden hut such as contractors erect during the progress of their work. Having accompanied his master to the door, Parkinson returned towards the promenade and sat down to admire the seascape from the nearest bench.

Inside the hut three men had been waiting. One of the trio, a tall, military-looking man with the air of a personage, had been sitting on a whitewash-splashed trestle reading *The Times*. Of the others, one was Inspector Tapling, and the third a dwarfish, wizened creature with the air of a converted ostler. He had passed the time by watching the Cliffhurst side through a knothole in a plank. With the entrance of Carrados the tall man folded his newspaper and a period of expectancy seemed to have come to an end.

"Good morning, Colonel, Inspector, and you there, Bob."

"You found your way, Mr. Carrados?" remarked the Colonel.

"Yes; it is not really I who am late. I had a letter this morning from Wrattesley holding me up for a wire at 10:30. It did not arrive till 10:45."

"Ah, it did come! Then we may regard everything as settled?"

"No, Colonel. On the contrary, we must accept everything as upset."

"What, sir?"

Carrados took out the slim pocket-book, extracted a telegram and held it out.

"What is this?" demanded the Colonel, peering through his glasses in the indifferent light. "'Laburnum edifice plaster dark dark late herald same dome aurora dark vitiate camp encase.' I don't know the code."

"Oh, it's Westneath's arrangement," explained Carrados. "'The individual with whom we are concerned must not be arrested on charge, but it is of the gravest importance that the papers in question be recovered. There must be no public proceedings even if conviction assured.'"

There was a moment of stupefaction.

"This—this is a bombshell!" exclaimed the Colonel. "What does it mean?"

"Politics," replied Carrados tersely.

"Ah!" soliloquized Tapling, walking to the door and looking sympathetically out at the gloomy prospect of sea and sky.

"But I've had no notification," protested the Colonel. "Surely, Mr. Carrados—"

"The wire is probably at the station."

"True; you said 10:45. Well, what do you propose doing now?"

"Scrapping all our arrangements and recovering the papers without arresting Slater."

"In what way?"

"At the moment I have not the faintest idea."

The Inspector left the door and came back moodily to his old position.

"We have reason to think that he is becoming suspicious, Mr. Carrados," he remarked. "He may decide to go any hour."

"Then the sooner we act the better."

The stunted pygmy in the background had been listening to the conversation with rapt attention, fastening his eyes unwinkingly on each face in turn. He now glided forward,

"Listen to me, gents," he said, throwing round a cunning leer. "How does this sound? This afternoon . . ."

That afternoon Mr. Slater had been for what he termed "a blow of the briny", as his custom was on a fine day. He was returning in the dusk and had crossed the spacious promenade when, at a corner, he almost ran into the broad figure of a policeman who stood talking to a woman on the path.

"That's the man!" exclaimed the woman wth almost vicious certainty.

Mr. Slater fell back a step in momentary alarm; then, recovering his self-control, he went forward with admirable composure.

"Beg pardon, sir," explained the constable, "but this young lady has just lost her purse. She says she was sitting next to you on a seat—"

"And the minute after he had gone—the very minute—my bag was open like you see it now and my purse vanished," interposed the lady volubly.

"On the seat by the lifeboat where I passed you, sir," amplified the constable.

"This is ridiculous," said Mr. Slater with a breath of relief. "I am a gentleman and I have no need to steal purses. My name is Slater, and I am staying at the 'Rose and Plumes'."

"Yes, sir," assented the policeman respectfully. "I know you by sight, sir, and have seen you go there. You hear what the gentleman says, miss?"

"Gentleman or no gentleman, I know my purse has gone," snapped the girl. "If he hasn't got it why did it vanish—where is it now? That's all I ask—where is it now?"

"You've seen nothing of it, I take it, sir?"

"No, of course I haven't," retorted the gentleman contemptuously. "I was sitting on a seat. The woman may have sat next to me—someone reading certainly did. Then I got up, walked once or twice up and down and came across. That's all."

"What was in the purse, miss?" inquired the constable.

"A postal order for a pound—and, thank the Lord, I've got the tag of it—a half-crown, two shillngs and a few coppers, a Kruger sixpence with a hole through, a gold gypsy ring with pearls, the return half of my ticket, some hairpins and a few recipes, a book of powder papers, a pocket mirror—"

"That ought to be enough to identify it by," said the constable, catching Mr. Slater's eye in humorous sympathy. "Well, miss, you'd better come to the station and report the loss. Perhaps you'll look in as well, sir?"

"Does that mean," demanded Mr. Slater with a dark gleam, "that I am to be charged with theft?"

"Bless you, no, sir," was the easy reassurance. "We couldn't take a charge in the circumstances—not with a gentleman of respectable position and known address. But it might save you some inquiry and bother later, and if it was myself I should like to get it done with while it was red-hot, so to speak."

"I will go now," decided Mr. Slater. "Do I walk with—?"

"Just as you like sir. You can go before or follow on. It's only just down Bank Street."

The two went on and the gentleman followed at a few yards' interval. Three minutes and a blue lamp indicated their destination. No other pedestrian was in sight; the door stood hospitably open and Mr. Slater walked in.

The Station Inspector was seated at a desk when they entered and a couple of other officials stood about the room. The policeman explained the circumstances of the loss, the Inspector noting the details in the record-book.

"This gentleman voluntarily accompanied us as he had been brought into the case," concluded the policeman.

"Here is my card, Superintendent," said Mr. Slater with some importance. He had determined to be agreeable but dignified, and to enlist the Inspector on his side. "I am staying at the 'Rose and Plumes'. It's deuced unpleasant, you know, for a gentleman in my position to have to answer to a charge like this. That's why I came at once to clear the matter up."

"Quite so, sir," replied the Inspector; "but there is no charge at present." He turned to the girl. "You understand that if you sign the charge-sheet and it turns out that you are mistaken it may be a serious matter?"

"I only want my purse and money back," replied the young woman mulishly.

"We will try to find it for you; but there is nothing beyond your suspicion that this gentleman has ever seen it. Probably, sir, you don't possess a pound postal order, or a Kruger coin, or any of the other articles, even of your own?"

"I don't," replied Mr. Slater. "Except, of course, some silver and copper. If it will satisfy you I will turn out my pockets."

The Inspector looked at the complainant.

"You hear that, miss?"

"Oh, very well," she retorted. "If he really hasn't got it I shall be the one to look silly, shan't I?"

"On this encouragement Mr. Slater made a display of his various possessions, turning out each pocket as he emptied it. The contents were laid before the Inspector, who satisfied himself by a glance of their innocent nature.

"I should warn you that I am going to bring out a loaded revolver," said Mr. Slater when he came to his hip pocket. "I travel a good deal abroad and often in wild parts, where it is necessary to carry a pistol for protection."

The Inspector nodded and examined the weapon with a knowing touch. The last pocket was displayed.

"That's not what I mean," objected the girl with a dogged air, as everyone began to regard her in varying degrees of inquiry. "You don't suppose that anyone would keep the things in their pocket, do you? I thought you meant properly."

The Inspector addressed himself to Mr. Slater again in a matter-of-fact, business manner.

"Perhaps you would like one of my men to put his hand over you to settle the matter, sir?" he asked.

For just a couple of seconds there was the pause of hesitation.

"If nothing is found you withdraw all imputation against this gentleman?" demanded the Inspector of the girl.

"Suppose I must," she admitted with an admirable pose of sulky acquiescence. In less exciting moments the young lady was a valued member of the Kingsmouth Amateur Dramatic Society.

"Oh, all right," assented Mr. Slater. "Only get it over."

"You quite understand that the search is entirely voluntary on your part, sir. Hilldick!"

One of the other policemen came forward.

"You can stand where you are, sir," he directed. With the practiced skill of, say, a Customs House officer from Kingsmouth, he used his fingers dexterously about the gentleman's clothing. "Now, sir, will you sit down and remove your boots for a moment?"

"My boots!" The man's eyes narrowed and his mouth took another line. He glanced at the Inspector. "Is it really necessary —?"

"That's it!" came from the girl in a fiercely exultant whisper. "He's slipped them in his boots!"

"Idiot!" commented Mr. Slater. He sat down and slowly drew slack the laces.

"Thank you," said Hilldick. He picked up both boots and with them turned to the table underneath the light. The next moment there was a sound like the mainspring of a clock going wrong and the sole and the upper of one boot came violently apart.

"You scoundrel!" screamed Slater, leaping from the chair.

But the grouping of the room had undergone a quiet change. Two men closed in on his right and left, and Mr. Slater sat down again. The Inspector opened the desk, dropped in the revolver and turned the key. Then all eyes went again to Hilldick and saw — nothing.

"The other boot," came in a quiet voice from the doorway to the inner room. "But just let me have it for a second."

It was put into his hands, and Carrados examined it in unmoved composure, while unpresentable words flowed in a blistering stream from Slater's lips.

"Yes, it is very good workmanship, Mr. Frankworth," remarked the blind man. "You haven't forgotten your early training. All right, Hilldick."

The tool cut and rasped again and the stitches flew. But this time from the opening, snugly lying in a space cut out among the leathers, a flat packet slid down to the ground.

Someone tore open the oiled silk covering and spread out the contents. Six sheets of fine tracing paper, each covered with signs and drawings, were disclosed.

The finality of the discovery acted on the culprit like a douche of water. He ceased to revile, and a white and deadly calm came over him.

"I don't know who is responsible for this atrocious outrage," he said between his clenched teeth, "but everyone concerned shall pay dearly for it. I am a naturalized Frenchman, and my adopted country will demand immediate satisfaction."

"Your adopted country is welcome to you, and it's going to have you back again," said the Inspector grimly. "Here is a pair of boots exactly like your own—we only retain the papers, which do not belong to you. You are allowed twenty-four hours to be clear of the country. If you have not sailed by this time tomorrow you will be arrested as Henry Frankworth for failing to report yourself when on license and sent to serve the unexpired portion of your sentence. If you return at any time the same course will be followed. Inspector Tapling, here is the warrant. You will keep Frankworth under observation and act as the circumstances demand."

Henry Frankworth glared round the room vindictively, drew himself up and clenched his fists. Then his figure drooped, and he turned and walked dully out into the darkening night.

"So you let the German spy slip through your fingers after all," protested Mr. Carlyle warmly. "I know that it was on instructions, and not your doing, Max; but why, why on earth, why?"

Carrados smiled and pointed to the heading of a column in an evening paper that he picked up from his side.

"There is your answer, Louis," he replied.

"'POSITION OF THE ENTENTE. WHAT DOES FRANCE MEAN?'" read the gentleman. "What has that got to do with it?"

"Your German spy was a French spy, Louis, and just at this moment a certain section of the public, led by a certain gang of politicians and aided by a certain interest in the Press, is doing its best to imperil the Entente. The Government has no desire to have the Entente imperiled. Hence your wail. If the dear old emotional, pig-headed, Rule Britannia! public had got it that French spies were stalking thorugh the land at this crisis, then, indeed, the fat would have been in the fire!"

"But, upon my soul, Max—Well, well; I hope that I am the last man to be led by newspaper claptrap, but I think that it's a deuced queer proceeding all the same. Why should our ally want our secret plans?"

"Why not, if he can get them?" demanded Max Carrados philosophically. "One never knows what may happen next. We ought to have plans and knowledge of all the French strategic positions as well as of the German. I hope that we have, but I doubt it. It would be a guarantee of peace and good relations."

"There are times, Max," declared Mr. Carlyle severely, "when I suspect you of being—er—paradoxical."

"Can you imagine, Louis, an Archbishop of Canterbury, or a Poet Laureate, or a Chancellor of the Exchequer being friendly—perhaps even dining—with the editor of *The Times*?"

"Certainly; why not?"

"Yet in the editor's office, drawn up by his orders, there is probably a three-column obituary notice of each of those impersonalities. Does it mean that the editor wishes them to die—much less has any intention of poisoning their wine? Ridiculous! He merely, as a prudent man, prepares for an eventuality, so as not to be caught unready by a misfortune which he sincerely hopes will never take place—in his time, that is to say."

"Well, well," said Mr. Carlyle benignantly—they were lunching together at Vitet's, on Carrados's return—"I am glad that we got the papers. One thing I cannot understand. Why didn't the fellow get clear as soon as he had the plans?"

"Ah," admitted the blind man, "why not, indeed? Even Inspector Tapling bated his breath when he suggested the reason to me."

"And what was that?" inquired Carlyle with intense interest.

Mr. Carrados looked extremely mysterious and half reluctant for a moment. Then he spoke.

"Do you know, Louis, of any great secret military camp where a surprise fleet of dirigibles and flying-machines of a new and terrible pattern is being formed by a far-seeing Government as a reserve against the day of Armageddon?"

"No," admitted Mr. Carlyle, with staring eyes, "I don't."

"Nor do I," contributed Carrados.

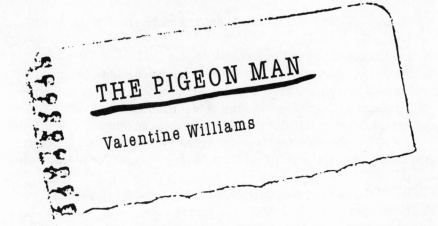

THE PIGEON MAN

Valentine Williams

FLANDERS IN '18, and March coming in like a lion. With a purr that, nearer the front, might have been confused with the thudding of distant drumfire the icy rain beat against the panes. At the streaming window of a dingy bedroom of the Hôtel du Commerce a girl stood gazing listlessly into the street below. Outside, over the gleaming cobbles of the little Belgian town, the great grey lorries, splashed hood-high with Flanders mud, slithered along in an endless train, swerving from the road's gray crown only to make way for the snorting Staff cars that, freighted with begoggled officers in field-grey, from time to time came roaring down the street. In and out of the traffic, despatch-riders on motorcycles whirled and rattled, staying their progress with trailing, gaitered leg to inquire the location of Operations or Intelligence offices of the Corps established there. In the hotel bedroom the crockery on the washstand jingled to the din of the street.

Without turning round from her observation post, the girl flung a question across her shoulder. She was tall, and the black frock she wore emphasized her slimness. Her shining red hair, loosely coiled about her well-shaped head, was the only blur of positive color among the neutral shades of the room.

"Am I to wait the convenience of the Corps Intelligence office all day?" she demanded sullenly.

At a table against the wall an officer in field-grey sat reading the *Kölnische Zeitung*. He did not lift his eyes from his newspaper at the girl's question.

"Such were Colonel von Trompeter's orders, *meine Gnädige*," he retorted.

She stamped her foot and faced the speaker. "This room stifles me, do you hear?" she exclaimed tensely. "I don't mind the rain: I'm going out!"

"No!" said the officer.

"Do I understand that I'm a prisoner?"

The officer shrugged his shoulders as, stretching forth his arms, he folded back the paper. "You're of the Service, Fraulein Sylvia," he rejoined placidly. "You've got to obey orders like the rest of us!"

"Agreed," she cried. "But they can trust me, can't they?"

The officer shrugged his shoulders again. "Doubtless the Colonel had his reasons for not wishing civilians to roam about Corps Headquarters. . . ."

"Bah!" she broke in contemptuously. "Do you think I'm blind? Do you really imagine, Captain Pracht, that I don't know"—she waved a slim hand towards the window and the sounding street beyond—"what all this movement means? Every railhead from the North Sea to the Vosges is pouring forth men and guns; your troops released by the Russian Revolution are gathering to deal the Allies the final—"

Pracht sprang to his feet. *"Um Gottes Willen,* mind what you're saying! You speak of things that are known to but a handful of us—"

"Quite so, my friend. But will you please remember that I am of that handful? My sources in Brussels are excellent—" She broke off and contemplated her companion's face. "Why has Colonel von Trompeter sent for me?"

"There I can answer you quite frankly," said the Captain. "I don't know."

"And if you did, you wouldn't tell me?"

The officer bowed. "It would be hard to refuse so charming a lady anything. . . ."

She shook herself impatiently. "Words, merely words!" she cried.

She let her eyes rest meltingly on his face. They were strange eyes, madder-brown under dark lashes. "Have you ever been in love, Captain Pracht?"

The officer's face set doggedly, so that two small vertical lines appeared on either side of his thin lips under the clipped brown mustache. "Never on duty, *Gnädiges Fraulein*—that is"—he paused, then added—"unless commanded."

"Why, then," she put in merrily, "I might have spared myself the trouble of locking my door last night."

Captain Pracht flushed darkly, and a little pulse began to beat at his temple.

She looked at him fixedly and laughed. "You have a charming métier, Herr Hauptmann!"

An ugly look crept into his face. "The same as yours, *meine Gnädige!*"

A patch of color crept into her pale cheeks. "Not quite!" Her voice vibrated a little. "Men know how to protect themselves. They go into these things with their eyes open. But almost every woman, even in the Secret Service, is blinded by love . . . once . . . ." She sighed and added, "The first time . . ."

"The gracious lady speaks from personal experience, no doubt," the officer hazarded. His manner was unpleasant.

With calm disdain she looked him up and down. "Yes," she answered simply.

"I have always said," the Captain announced ponderously, "that women were too emotional for Secret Service work. Especially foreigners."

"Rumanians, for instance?" suggested the girl sweetly.

"I was not speaking personally," retorted the officer huffily. "If we must have women spies, they why not Germans? Our German women have an ingrained sense of discipline, a respect for orders . . . ."

The girl's gurgling laugh pealed through the room. "But their taste in nighties is dreadful," she broke in. "You must remember, my dear Captain Pracht, that our battlefield is the boudoir—"

At that moment the door was flung back. An orderly, in a streaming cape, stood there. "Colonel von Trompeter's compliments," he bawled out of a wooden face, saluting with a stamp that shook the floor, "and will the Herr Hauptmann bring Fraulein Averescu to the office immediately."

"The trouble about this job of ours, young Horst," said Colonel von Trompeter, "is to recognize the truth when you find it!"

A heavy man, the Herr Oberst, but handsome still with his fearless eyes of the brightest blue, straight nose, and trim white mustache. The blue-and-silver Hussar cap which, in defiance of all clothing regulations, he insisted on wearing with his Staff uniform, was the only evidence that he had started his army career in the light cavalry, for advancing years had endowed him with the body of a heavy dragoon. His big form, muscular yet under its swelling curves, was moulded in his well-fitting service dress of grey, frogged with the brandenbourgs of the Hussar, and the broad pink stripe of the Great General Staff, together with the glossy brown field-boot into which it disappeared, set off admirably his length of leg.

A fine blade, the Herr Oberst, with a naturally intuitive mind sharpened by the intensive training of War School and Great General Staff, a gift of lightning decision and a notable aptitude for languages. But, more

than this, he was a man of rugged character, of unflinching moral courage, and as such ranged head and shoulders above the swarm of silver-
laced sycophants at Headquarters who assiduously lick-spittled to His
Excellency Lieutenant-General Baron Haase von dem Hasenberg, the
Corps Commander. For His Excellency, a choleric old party with the
brains of a louse and the self-control of a gorilla, was His Majesty's
friend who with supple spine had genuflected his way up the rough road
of promotion under the approving eye of the All-Highest War Lord.

His Excellency detested his Chief of Intelligence. He might have for-
given Colonel von Trompeter his outstanding ability, for brains are an
asset on the staff of a Corps Commander when awkward incidents have
to be covered up; and Baron Haase had not been a lucky leader. But His
Excellency was enraged by the Colonel's habit of invariably speaking his
mind. It infuriated him that Colonel von Trompeter should have made his
career in spite of his brutal candor. When only a Major, acting as assistant
umpire at Kaiser maneuvers, had he not curtly replied to the Emperor
himself, enthusiastically seeking praise for a cavalry charge led in the
All-Highest Person against a nest of machine-guns: "All dead to the last
horse, Your Majesty!" and been promptly exiled to an East Prussian
frontier garrison for his pains?

Yet, although the victim of the All-Highest displeasure had lived the
incident down, he had learned nothing by experience. To the Corps Commander's resentful fury, he flatly refused to curry favor with his immediate chief by lending himself to the great conspiracy of eyewash by
means of which, in war as in peace, the War Lord was justified of his
appointments to the high commands.

And so a state of open warfare existed between His Excellency—and
that signified the bulk of the Headquarters Staff—and his Chief of Intelligence. Only the Intelligence Staff, who worshipped Trompeter to a
man, less for his brilliant ability than for his sturdy championship of his
subordinates even in the face of the epileptic ravings of His Excellency,
stood by their chief. For the rest, every imaginable form of chicane and
sabotage was employed in the attempt to drive Colonel von Trompeter
into seeking a transfer. In almost every branch of Corps Headquarters,
save only the Intelligence, it became as important to defeat Colonel von
Trompeter and his assistants as to beat the English who held the line in
this part of Flanders. And His Excellency proclaimed at least thrice a day
to all who would hear him that Trompeter was *"ein taktloser Keri."*

When, therefore, on this wet March morning, "the old man," as his
staff called Trompeter, delivered himself of the apothegm set forth above,
Lieutenant Horst, his youngest officer, who was examining a sheaf of

aeroplane photographs at his desk in a corner of the office, glanced up with troubled eyes. It was rare, indeed, that "the old man" allowed the daily dose of pinpricks to get under his skin. But today the Chief was restless. Ever since breakfast he had been pacing like a caged lion up and down the wet track left by the boots of visitors on the strip of matting between the door and his desk.

"Operations are making trouble about the shelling of the 176th divisional area last night," the Colonel continued.

"With permission, Herr Oberst," Horst put in diffidently "these fresh troops carry on as though they were still in Russia. Their march discipline is deplorable. They were probably spotted by aircraft—"

The Herr Oberst shook his grizzled poll. "Won't wash, my boy. They went in after dark. That explanation we put up to Operations when the 58th Division had their dumps shelled last week. Operations won't swallow it again. Humph—"

He grunted and turned to stare out into the rain. A battalion was passing up the street, rank on rank of soaked and weary men. Their feet hammered out a melancholy tattoo on the cobbles. There was no brave blare of music to help them on their way. The band marched in front with instruments wrapped up against the wet. "Fed—up, fed—up," the crunching feet seemed to say.

The Colonel's voice suddenly cut across the rhythmic tramping. "What time is Ehrhardt arriving with that prisoner from the 91st Division?" he asked.

"He was ordered for eleven, Herr Oberst!"

"It's after that now—"

"The roads are terribly congested, Herr Oberst!"

The Colonel made no reply. His fingers drummed on the windowpane. Then he said: "Our English cousins are concentrating on the Corps area, young Horst. They've got a pigeon man out. That much was clear when that basket of pigeons was picked up in Fleury Wood last week."

"A pigeon man, Herr Oberst?"

"I was forgetting; you're new to the game. So you don't know what a pigeon man is, young Horst?"

"No, Herr Oberst!"

"Then let me tell you something: if you ever meet a pigeon man, you can safely take your hat off to him, for you're meeting a hero. It's a job that means almost certain death. A pigeon man is a Secret Service officer who's landed by an aeroplane at some quiet spot in the enemy lines with a supply of carrier pigeons. His job is to collect the reports which spies have already left for him at agreed hiding places. He fastens these messages to the legs of his birds and releases them to fly back to their loft. . . ."

"Does the aeroplane wait, Herr Oberst?"

The Colonel laughed shortly, *"I wo!* The pigeon man has to make his way home the best he can. They usually head for the Dutch frontier. . . ."

"He's in plain clothes, then?"

"Of course. That's why I say the job means almost certain death. Even we Huns, as they call us, are justified in shooting an officer caught in plain clothes behind our lines."

The young man pursed up his lips in a silent whistle. "Brave fellows! Do we send out pigeon men too, Herr Oberst?"

His Chief shook his head. "They wouldn't stand an earthly. The pigeon man can operate successfully only among a friendly civilian population— Well?"

An orderly had bounced into the office, and, stiff as a ramrod, now fronted the Colonel. "Hauptmann Ehrhardt is here to report to the Herr Oberst."

The clear blue eyes snapped into alertness. "Has he brought a prisoner with him, Reinhold?"

"Jawohl, Herr Oberst."

"Send him in! Prisoner and escort remain outside." He turned to Horst as the orderly withdrew. "Herr Lieutenant, a certain lady is waiting at the Hôtel du Commerce in charge of Captain Pracht, of the Brussels command. I may ask you to send for her presently. You will not say anything to her about this prisoner, and you will be responsible to me that no one approaches him in the meantime. And see that I'm not disturbed."

Then with bowed head the Colonel resumed his pacing up and down.

"As the Herr Oberst will see for himself," said Ehrhardt, rocking slightly as he stood stiffly at attention before his chief—he was a secondary school teacher in civil life and the military still overawed him—"the prisoner is practically a half-wit. If you speak to him, he only grins idiotically and dribbles. He looks half-starved, and as for his body—well, with respect, he's fairly crawling. God knows how long he's been wandering about the Bois des Corbeaux, where the fatigue party ran across him in the early hours of this morning. According to the Herr Oberst's orders, I had advised all units that any civilian caught in our lines was to be brought straightway to me at the Divisional Intelligence office. When this man was sent in, I rang the Herr Oberst up at once. I haven't overlooked the possibility that the fellow may be acting a part; but I'm bound to say that he seems to me to be what he looks like—a half-witted Flemish peasant. Speaking ethnologically—"

A brusque gesture cut short the imminent deadly treatise on the psychology of the Flemings. The Colonel pointed to a chair beside the desk and pushed across a box of cigars.

"Ehrhardt," said he, "information of the most exact description is being sent back regularly. Our troop movements are known. The 176th Division had two hundred casualties getting into their billeting area last night. These are no haphazard notes of regimental numbers jotted down at railway stations, or of movements of isolated units strung together by ignorant peasants. They are accurate reports prepared with intelligence by someone with a thorough grasp of the military situation. The English have a star man operating on this front. Who he is or what he looks like we don't know; but what we do know is that correspondence of a very secret nature which fell into the hands of one of our agents at The Hague speaks with enthusiasm of the accuracy of the reports sent by an unnamed agent concerning our present troop movements in Belguim. You are aware of my belief that an English pigeon man has been at work here"— he bent his white-tufted brows at his companion, who was gazing intently at him through gold-rimmed spectacles. "Supposing our friend outside is the man I'm looking for . . . ."

Very positively Captain Ehrhardt shook his head. "Of course," he said in his pedantic fashion, "I must bow to the Herr Oberst's experience in these matters. But for me the hypothesis is out of the question. This fellow may be a spy; but in that case he's an agent of the lowest order, a brutish Belgian peasant—not a man of the calibre you mention, an educated individual, possibly a regular officer."

"Certainly a regular officer," the Colonel's calm voice broke in.

"*Ausgeschlossen,* Herr Oberst! The thing's impossible, as at least by repute from prewar days. We never managed to ascertain his name or get his photograph; but we know him for a man who is a marvelous linguist, with a most amazing knowledge of the Continent and Continental peoples. Dialect is one of his specialties. What is more to the point, he is a magnificent actor, and his skill in disguises is legendary. Again and again we were within an ace of catching him, but he always contrived to slip through our fingers. We used to call him *N*, the unknown quantity. Do you see what I'm driving at?"

"*Gewiss, gewiss,* Herr Oberst!" Ehrhardt wagged his head dubiously. "But this lout is no English officer."

"Well," said the Colonel, "let's look at him, anyway," He pressed a button on the desk, and presently, between two stolid figures in field-grey, a woebegone and miserable-looking tramp shambled in.

His clothes were a mass of rags. On his head a torn and shapeless cloth cap was stuck askew, and from beneath its tattered peak a pair of hot, dark eyes stared stupidly out of a face that was clotted with grime and darkened, as to the lower part, with a stiff growth of beard. A straggling mustache trembled above a pendulous underlip that gleamed redly through bubbles that frothed at the mouth and dripped down the chin. His skin glinted yellowly through great rents in jacket and trousers, and his bare feet were thrust into clumsy, broken boots, one of which was swathed round with a piece of filthy rag. As he stood framed between the fixed bayonets of the escort, long shudders shook him continually.

Without looking up, the Colonel scribbled something on a writing-pad, tore off the slip and gave it to Horst. "Let the escort remain outside," he ordered. Horst and the guards clumped out. Then only did Trompeter, screwing his monocle in his eye, favor the prisoner with a long and challenging stare. The man did not budge. He continued to gaze into space, with his head rocking slightly to and fro and the saliva running down his chin.

The Colonel spoke in an aside to Ehrhardt. "You say you found nothing on him when you searched him?"

"Only a clasp-knife, some horse-chestnuts, and a piece of string, Herr Oberst."

"No papers?"

"No, Herr Oberst."

The Colonel addressed the prisoner in French. "Who are you and where do you come from?" he demanded.

Very slowly the man turned his vacuous gaze towards the speaker. He smiled feebly and dribbled, but did not speak.

"It struck me that he might be dumb." Ehrhardt whispered across the desk, "although he seems to hear all right."

"Wait!" Trompeter bade him. He spoke to the prisoner again. "Any civilian found wandering in the military zone without proper papers is liable to be shot," he said sternly. "Do you realize that?"

The tramp grinned feebly and made a gurgling noise like an infant. The Colonel repeated his warning in Flemish.

"Grr . . . goo . . . grr!" gibbered the prisoner.

Trompeter went round the desk and looked the man in the eye. "See his hands, Herr Oberst," said Ehrhardt in an undertone. The tramp's hands were coarse and horny, with blackened and broken nails. "Are those the hands of an officer?"

The Colonel grunted, but made no other comment.

There was a smart rap at the door. Reinhold, the orderly, appeared with a tray. On it were set out a pot of coffee, a jug of milk, sugar, a plate of ham, and a hunk of greyish war bread. The Colonel signed to the man to put the tray down on a side table. Then he turned to the prisoner. "Eat!" he bade him.

The idiot grinned broadly and broke into a cackling laugh. Then, while the two officers watched him from a distance, he fell upon the victuals. It was horrible to see him wolf the food. He tore the ham with his hands and thrust great fragments into his mouth: he literally buried his face in the bread, wrenching off great lumps with his teeth: he emptied the milkpot at a draught, spilling a good deal of the milk down his jacket in the process. He made animal noises as he ate and drank, stuffing himself until he gasped for breath.

"Could an officer eat like that?" Ehrhardt whispered in his chief's ear. But again the Colonel proffered no remark.

When the last of the food had disappeared he said to his subordinate: "Take the prisoner outside now, and when I ring three times send him in—alone. Alone, do you understand?"

"*Zu Befel,* Herr Oberst!"

Left alone, Colonel von Trompeter strode across to the window and stood for an instant looking out. In the street a gang of British prisoners of war, their threadbare khaki sodden with the rain, scraped away at the mud with broom and spade. A voice at the door brought the Colonel about. Horst was there.

"Herr Oberst, the lady has arrived!"

"She's not seen the prisoner, I trust?"

"No, Herr Oberst, I put her to wait in the orderlies' room."

Trompeter nodded approval. "Good. I'll see her at once . . . alone."

As Horst went away, he moved to the desk and turned the chair which Ehrhardt had vacated so that it faced the door. He himself remained standing, his hands resting on the desk at his back. With his long fingers he made sure that the bell-push in its wooden bulb was within his reach.

It was commonly said of Colonel von Trompeter that he had a card-index mind. He forgot no name, no face, no date, that came into his day's work, and he had an uncanny facility at need of opening, as it were, a drawer in his brain and drawing forth a file of data.

As he helped Sylvia Averescu out of her wrap and invited her to be seated, he was mentally glancing over her record. Nineteen hundred and twelve it had been when Steuben had bought her away from the Russians at Bucharest and installed her at Brussels, that clearinghouse of international espionage. For a woman, the Colonel condescendingly reflected, she had proved her worth. That affair of the signaling-book of H.M.S. *Queen* had been her doing; and it was she who had laid the information which had led to the arrest of the English spy, Barton, at Wilhelmshaven.

"Madame," was Trompeter's opening when he had given her a cigarette, "I have ventured to bring you out from Brussels in this terrible weather because I need your help."

Sylvia Averescu looked at him coldly. Her wait in a freezing cubbyhole full of damp and strongly flavored orderlies had not improved her temper. She had entered the room resolved to give this Colonel von Trompeter a piece of her mind. Yet, somehow, his personality cowed her. Against her will she was favorably impressed by his direct gaze, good looks, and charming manners. She saw at once that he was a regular officer of the old school, a man of breeding, not a commercial traveler stuffed into uniform, like Pracht. She was flattered by the way he handed her to a chair and assisted her out of her furs as though she were a Duchess. And the Latin in her, which had always squirmed at the "Frau" and "Fraulein" of her German associates, was grateful for "Madame" as a form of address.

Still, the recollection of that icy vigil yet grated on her, and she replied rather tartly, "I don't know in what way I can be of any assistance to you, Herr Oberst."

The Colonel's blue eyes rested for an instant on her handsome, rather discontented face. Then, brushing the ash from the end of his cigarette, he said: "When you were in Brussels before the War, you knew the British Secret Service people pretty well, I believe?"

She shrugged her shoulders. "It was what I was paid for."

"You were acquainted with some of their principal agents, I take it: the star turns, I mean—men like Francis Okewood or Philip Brewster, or"—he paused—"even our friend *N,* the mysterious Unknown Quantity?"

She laughed on a hard note. "If you'll tell me who *N* was—or is," she returned, "I'll tell you if I knew him. I've met the other two you mentioned." She leaned back in her chair and blew out luxuriously a cloud of smoke. "'Unknown Quanitity,' eh? What a dance he led you, Colonel! I've often wondered which of the boys he was."

The Colonel's hand groped behind him until he found the bell. Thrice his thumb pushed the button. His eyes were on the woman as she reclined gracefully in her chair staring musingly at the ceiling. His watchful gaze did not quit her face even when the door was suddenly thrust open and a tatterdemalion figure hobbled into the room.

Trompeter, his face a mask of steel, saw how, at the sound of the door closing, the woman at his side looked up—saw, too, the little furrow of perplexity that suddenly appeared between her narrow, arching eyebrows. But the swift, suspicious glance she shot at her companion found him apparently intent on studying the end of his cigarette, yet even as her gaze switched back to the outcast, cowering in forlorn abandonment in the center of the floor, the Colonel's bright blue eyes were quick to note the expression of horror-struck amazement which for one fleeting instant flickered across her regular features.

But the next moment she was bored and listless as before. So swift was her reaction that it was as though her face had never lost its wonted air of rather sulky indifference. She darted an amused glance at the impassive visage gazing down upon her and laughed.

"You have some queer visitors, Herr Oberst," she said. "Tell me"—she indicated the tramp with a comic movement of the head—"is he one of us?"

"No," replied Trompeter, with quiet emphasis.

"Then who is he?"

"I was hoping you would be able to tell me that."

She stared at him for a moment, then suddenly broke into a peal of merry laughter.

"Oh, my dear Colonel," she exclaimed, "you do their ingenuity too much honor."

"And yet," observed Trompeter quietly, "he's one of their star men." His eyes were on the prisoner as he spoke. But the tramp, leering idiotically, stared into space and dribbled feebly.

Sylvia Averescu laughed incredulously. "Then they've changed their methods. All the British Secret Service aces I've known were serving officers, or ex-officers. You're not going to claim that this miserable creature is an English gentleman, Colonel. Why, his hands alone give you the lie!"

"Specially roughened for the job!"

"What job?"

But the Colonel left the question unanswered. "The English are devilish thorough," he added. "I'll grant them that!"

The woman left her chair and went boldly up to the idiot. With a pointing finger she indicated a V of yellow skin that appeared below his uncollared neck between the lapels of his jacket.

"Look," she vociferated in disgust, "the man's filthy. He hasn't had a bath for years!" She turned about to face Trompeter, who had followed her. "If this man is what you say, he would have white skin, a properly tended body, under his rags. But this creature is disgusting!"

Trompeter stepped swiftly up to the prisoner and with brutal hands ripped the ragged jacket apart. The man wore no shirt; his coat was buttoned across his naked body. The Colonel recoiled a pace and clapped his handkerchief to his nose. *"Bfui Deibel!"* he muttered.

Something had rattled smartly on the floor. Trompeter stooped quickly with groping fingers; then, drawing himself erect, stared fixedly at the prisoner. The outside pocket of the idiot's jacket had been almost ripped away in the vigor of the Colonel's action and hung lamentably down. Trompeter's hand darted into the torn pocket and explored the lining. His fingers dredged up some tiny invisible thing which he transferred to the palm of his other hand.

With an air of triumph he swung round to the woman. "Well," he remarked roughly, "he's in for it, anyway. If he were a friend of yours, I should tell you to kiss him good-bye."

At that she faltered ever so slightly. "What do you mean?" her voice was rather hoarse.

"What I mean," Trompeter gave her back brutally, "is that he's the pigeon man we've been looking for. He'll go before the court in the morning, and by noon he'll be snugly under the sod!"

So saying, he unfolded his clenched hand and thrust it close under her face. Two little shining yellow grains reposed in the open palm. "Maize," he announced grimly. "Food for the birds. Pigeon men always carry it."

With that, he shut his hand and joined it to its fellow behind his back, while he dropped his square chin on his breast and sternly surveyed her.

"And do you mean to say," she questioned unsteadily, "that the military court would send him to his death on no other evidence than that?"

"Certainly. There was an identical case last month. Two English flying officers. They shot them in the riding school at Charleroi. Game lads they were, too!"

"But this poor devil may have picked up some maize somewhere and kept it for food. He looks half-starved, anyway."

Trompeter shrugged his shoulders. "That's his lookout. We're not taking any chances on pigeon men. They're too dangerous, my dear. Not that I want the poor devil shot. I'd rather have him identified."

The woman raised her head and gazed curiously at the Colonel. "Why?" she asked, almost in a whisper.

Trompeter drew her to the window, out of earshot of the prisoner. Outside, the whole town seemed to reverberate to the passage of heavy guns, monsters, snouting under their tarpaulins, that thundered by in the wake of their tractors.

"Because," he said in an undertone, "I can use him to mislead the enemy. Our dear English cousins shall get their pigeon service all right, but after this the birds will carry my reports instead of our friend's. For this I must have the fellow's name." He paused and bent his bushy eyebrows at her. "You know this man?"

"Wait," she bade him, rather breathless. "Let us get this clear. If this man were identified, you would spare his life?"

The Colonel nodded curtly. His eyes never left her face.

"What guarantee have I that you will keep your word?"

"I shall hand over to you the only evidence there is against him."

"You mean the maize?"

"Yes."

She cast a timorous glance across the room to where the prisoner was standing, his head lolling on his shoulder. He had not changed his position. His eyes were half closed and his tongue hung out under the ragged mustache. The reek of him was pungent in the room.

Silently she held out her hand to Trompeter. Without hesitation he dropped the two grains of maize into the slender palm. She ran to the stove and dropped them in. Impassively the Colonel watched her from the window. The maps on the walls trembled in the din of gun-wheels in the street.

Slowly the woman returned to the Colonel's side. He noticed how pale her face appeared against the flame of her hair. She looked at him intently, then said, in a sort of breathless whisper, "You're right, I know him."

A steely light glittered in the quick blue eyes. "Ah! Who is it?"

"Dunlop. Captain Dunlop."

Trompeter leaned forward swiftly. "Not 'The Unknown Quantity'?"

She made a little movement of the shoulders. "I can't tell you. He never attempted to disguise himself with me."

"Did you meet him in Brussels?"

She nodded. "He used to come over from London almost every weekend . . . ."

The Colonel grunted assent. "Yes, that was the way they did it before the War." He flashed her a scrutinizing glance. "Did you know him well? You're sure you're not making a mistake?"

She shook her head, and there was something wistful in the gesture. "He was my lover . . . ."

Trompeter smiled broadly. "Ah," he murmured, "Steuben always managed that sort of thing so cleverly . . . ."

"Steuben had nothing to do with it," came back her hot whisper. "No one knew him for a secret agent—at least, not until I found him out. He told me he was an English engineer who came to Brussels on business: I was jealous of him, and one day I discovered he was visiting another woman, a Belgian. Then—then I followed things up and found out the rest. He was frank enough when I confronted him—the English are, you know. He told me he had only been carrying out his orders. And I"—she faltered—"I was part of those orders too . . . ."

She clenched her hands tensely, and turned to stare forlornly out at the rain.

"You were fond of him, Madame?"

"My feelings have nothing to do with the business between you and me, Colonel," she told him glacially over her shoulder.

He bowed. "I beg your pardon. And you have told me all you know. What is his full name?"

"James, I think. I called him Jimmy."

"How did he sign his reports? Can you tell me that?"

She nodded. "'J. Dunlop,'" she answered.

"How do you know this?"

"Because I made it my business to find out . . . afterwards!" she answered passionately, and was silent.

"And he is a regular officer?"

"Of the Royal Engineers." She turned to the Colonel. "And now, if you don't mind, I should like to go back to my hotel. I—I don't feel very well. I expect I must have caught a chill. This awful weather . . . ."

The Colonel rang. "I'll send for Captain Pracht—"

Like a fury she rounded on him. "For the love of God!" she burst forth, "am I never to be left alone again? Can't I go back to the hotel by myself?"

Trompeter bowed. "Certainly, if you promise to go straight there. It's in your own interest I say it. The P.M. is very strict about civilians just now."

"I'll go straight back," she retorted impatiently. "And you'll keep to our bargain, Colonel?"

The officer inclined his head.

"What—what will you do with *him?*" she asked, rather unsteadily.

"Oh, prisoners of war camp, I suppose," was the brisk answer.

She said no more, but moved slowly towards the door. There she paused and let her eyes rest for an instant on the scarecrow shape that mowed and gibbered between them. The Colonel saw her put forth one little hand towards the pigeon man and stand thus as though she hoped that he might turn and greet her. But the tramp with his melancholy imbecile stare paid no heed. She seemed to droop as she turned and passed out.

Then Trompeter went up to the prisoner and clapped him encouragingly on the shoulder. "It's a wonderful disguise, Dunlop," he said pleasantly and in flawless English, "and I don't mind telling you that you nearly took me in. But the game's up, my friend! You're spotted. Let's have a friendly talk. I don't expect you to give anything away, but I'm anxious for news of Colonel Ross, my esteemed opposite number on the other side of No Man's Land. I heard he'd been down with this damnable grippe . . . ."

"Goo . . . !" mumbled the tramp, and the bubbles frothed at his mouth. The telephone on the desk rang. The colonel left the prisoner to answer it. A well-bred voice said: "His Excellency desires to speak with Colonel von Trompeter." The next instant a high-pitched, furious voice came ringing over the wire.

"Is that Trompeter? So, Herr Oberst, a new division can't come into the Corps area without being shelled to ribbons! What the devil are your people doing? What's that you say? You're investigating. Investigating be damned! I want action—action, do you understand? The whole Corps knows that there's a spy in the area sending information back, and when I ask you what you propose to do about it, you tell me you're investigating! *Verdammt nochmal!* What I expect you to do is to catch the lousy fellow and shoot him, and, by God, if you don't, I'll have the collar off your back, and don't you forget it! *Himmelkreuzsakrament!* I'll show you who's in command here, you and your investigation! You'll report to me in person at six o'clock this afternoon, and I shall expect to hear then that you've laid hands on this spy. If you fail me this time, Herr Oberst, I give you fair warning that I'll get somebody I can rely upon to carry out my wishes. And you are to understand that the General is extremely dissatisfied with you. Is that clear?"

"Zu Befehl, Excellenz!" replied the Colonel stiffly, and hung up the receiver. He lit a cigarette and sat at the desk for a full minute, contemplating through a swathe of blue smoke the wretched-looking outcast before him.

"Sorry, Dunlop," he said at last. "I'd have saved you if I could, but charity begins at home. My General demands a victim, and my head is the price. I'm a poor man, my friend, with no private means and a family to support. I've got powerful enemies, and if I lose this job my career's over. As God is my judge, Dunlop, I can't afford to keep my pledged word." He paused and pressed his handkerchief to his lips. "If there's anything I can do about letting your people know . . ."

He broke off expectantly, but the pigeon man made no sign. With his head cocked in the air his whole attention appeared to be directed to a fly buzzing round the wire of the elecric light.

"You'll at least give me the honor," Trompeter went on rather tremulously, "of shaking hands with a brave man?"

But the pigeon man did not even look at him. His grimy right hand stole furtively under his tattered jacket and he writhed beneath his verminous rags. His gaze remained immutably distant, as though he were peering down some long vista. Slowly the grizzled head at the desk drooped and there was a moment's pregnant hush in the room.

Then the Colonel stood up, a stalwart figure, and moved resolutely to a press in the wall. He opened the door and disclosed, neatly hung on pegs. his steel helmet, revolver, Thermos flask, map-case, and saddlebags. He unstrapped one of the saddlebags, and, dipping in his hand, brought away in his fingers a few shining orange grains. Then he rang and told the orderly to send in Captain Ehrhardt. The officer recoiled at the grim severity of his chief's expression.

"*Also,* Herr Hauptmann," was the Colonel's greeting, "you searched the prisoner, did you?"

"*Jawohl,* Herr Oberst!" said Ehrhardt, in a quaking voice.

"And found nothing, I think you told me?"

"Nothing—that is, except the articles I enumerated, Herr Oberst, namely—"

The stern voice interrupted him. "Would it surprise you to learn that I discovered maize in the prisoner's pocket when I searched him? See!" The Colonel's hand opened and spilled a few grains of maize on the blotter. "It appears to me, Herr Hauptmann, that you have grossly neglected your duty. You've got to wake yourself up, or one of these mornings you'll find yourself back in the trenches with your regiment. Now pay attention to me! The prisoner goes before the tribunal tomorrow. You will have him washed and disinfected and issued with clean clothes immediately, and hand him over to the Provost Marshal. Horst will warn the P.M. The prisoner can have anything he likes in the way of food or drink or smokes. Your evidence will be required at the trial, so you'll have to stay the night. See Horst about a bed. March the prisoner out!"

The door shut and the escort's ringing tramp died away. Grimly the Colonel shook his balled fist at the telephone.

"Break me, would you, you old sheepshead!" he muttered through his teeth. "But my pigeon man will spike your guns, my boy! *Verdammt,* though, the price is high!"

Then, drawing himself up to his full height, he brought his heels together with a jingle of spurs and gravely saluted the door through which the pigeon man had disappeared between the fixed bayonets of his guards.

A week later, in an unobtrusive office off Whitehall, high above the panorama of London threaded by the silver Thames, a large, quiet man sat at his desk and frowned down at a typewritten sheet he held in his hand.

"Well," he said, addressing an officer in khaki who stood in an expectant attitude before him, "they've nabbed Tony, Carruthers!"

"Oh, sir!" ejaculated Carruthers in dismay. "You were right, then?"

"'Fraid so. I knew they'd pinched him when Corps forwarded those Dunlop messages that kept reachin' 'em by pigeon. Prendergast, of Rotterdam, says here he has word from a trustworthy source in Belgium that at Roulers on the 6th the Boches shot a half-witted tramp on a charge of espionage. The trial, of course, was held in secret, but the rumor in the town is that the tramp was a British officer. That'd be Tony, all right. God bless my soul, what an actor the fellow was! I'd never have lent him for this job, only G.H.Q. were so insistent. Well, he had a good run for his money, anyway. Our friends on the other side used to call him *N*, "The Unknown Quantity." They never managed to identify him, you see. My hat! Old Tony must be smilin' to think that he managed to take his *incognito* down to the grave with him."

"But did he?"

"Obviously, otherwise the old Boches would have signed his real name to those pigeon messages of theirs which have so much amused Ross and his young men at Corps Headquarters."

"But why 'Dunlop,' sir?"

The large man smiled enigmatically. "Ah," he remarked, "you weren't in the Service before the War, Carruthers, or you'd have known that 'Dunlop' was one of our accommodation names in the office. Most of us were Captain Dunlop at one time or another. I've been Captain Dunlop myself. We run up against some rum coves in this business, and it ain't a bad plan to have a sort of general alias. It prevents identification and all manner of awkwardness, when the double-crossin' begins." He broke off to chuckle audibly. "Let's see, it's old Trompeter on that front, ain't it? I wonder where he got hold of the office *alias,* the foxy old devil! He's probably put up another Iron Cross over this! He'd be kickin' himself if he knew the truth. That's the catch about this job of ours, my boy—to recognize the truth when you find it!"

So saying, the large man unlocked his desk and, taking out a book, turned to a list of names. With the red pencil he scored out, slowly and methodically, a name that stood there.

THE HAIRLESS MEXICAN

W. Somerset Maugham

"Do you like macaroni?" said R.

"What do you mean by macaroni?" answered Ashenden. "It is like asking me if I like poetry. I like Keats and Wordsworth and Verlaine and Goethe. When you say macaroni, do you mean spaghetti, tagliatelli, rigatoni, vermicelli, fettucini, tufali, farfalli, or just macaroni?"

"Macaroni," replied R., a man of few words.

"I like all simple things, boiled eggs, oysters and caviar, truite au bleu, grilled salmon, roast lamb (the saddle by preference), cold grouse, treacle tart and rice pudding. But of all simple things the only one I can eat day in and day out, not only without disgust but with the eagerness of an appetite unimpaired by excess, is macaroni."

"I am glad of that because I want you to go down to Italy."

Ashenden had come from Geneva to meet R. at Lyons and having got there before him had spent the afternoon wandering about the dull, busy and prosaic streets of that thriving city. They were sitting now in a restaurant on the place to which Ashenden had taken R. on his arrival because it was reputed to give you the best food in that part of France. But since in so crowded a resort (for the Lyonese like a good dinner) you never knew what inquisitive ears were pricked up to catch any useful piece of information that might fall from your lips, they had contented themselves with talking of indifferent things. They had reached the end of an admirable repast.

"Have another glass of brandy?" said R.

"No, thank you," answered Ashenden, who was of an abstemious turn.

"One should do what one can to mitigate the rigors of war," remarked R. as he took the bottle and poured out a glass for himself and another for Ashenden.

171

Ashenden, thinking it would be affectation to protest, let the gesture pass, but felt bound to remonstrate with his chief on the unseemly manner in which he held the bottle.

"In my youth I was always taught that you should take a woman by the waist and a bottle by the neck," he murmured.

"I am glad you told me. I shall continue to hold a bottle by the waist and give women a wide berth."

Ashenden did not know what to reply to this and so remained silent. He sipped his brandy and R. called for his bill. It was true that he was an important person, with power to make or mar quite a large number of his fellows, and his opinions were listened to by those who held in their hands the fate of empires; but he could never face the business of tipping a waiter without an embarrassment that was obvious in his demeanor. He was tortured by the fear of making a fool of himself by giving too much or of exciting the waiter's icy scorn by giving too little. When the bill came he passed some hundred-franc notes over Ashenden, and said:

"Pay him, will you? I can never understand French figures."

The groom brought them their hats and coats.

"Would you like to go back to the hotel?" asked Ashenden.

"We might as well."

It was early in the year, but the weather had suddenly turned warm, and they walked with their coats over their arms. Ashenden, knowing that R. liked a sitting room, had engaged one for him and to this, when they reached the hotel, they went. The hotel was old-fashioned and the sitting room was vast. It was furnished with a heavy mahogany suite upholstered in green velvet and the chairs were set primly round a large table. On the walls, covered with a dingy paper, were large steel engravings of the battles of Napoleon, and from the ceiling hung an enormous chandelier once used for gas, but now fitted with electric bulbs. It flooded the cheerless room with a cold, hard light.

"This is very nice," said R., as they went in.

"Not exactly cozy," suggested Ashenden.

"No, but it looks as though it were the best room in the place. It all looks very good to me."

He drew one of the green velvet chairs away from the table and, sitting down, lit a cigar. He loosened his belt and unbuttoned his tunic.

"I always thought I liked a cheroot better than anything," he said, "but since the war I've taken quite a fancy to Havanas. Oh, well, I suppose it can't last forever." The corners of his mouth flickered with the beginning of a smile. "It's an ill wind that blows nobody any good."

Ashenden took two chairs, one to sit on and one for his feet, and when

R. saw him he said: "That's not a bad idea," and swinging another chair out from the table with a sigh of relief put his boots on it.

"What room is that next door?" he asked.

"That's your bedroom."

"And on the other side?"

"A banqueting hall."

R. got up and strolled slowly about the room and when he passed the windows, as though in idle curiosity, peeped through the heavy rep curtains that covered them, and then returning to his chair once more comfortably put his feet up.

"It's just as well not to take any more risk than one need," he said.

He looked at Ashenden reflectively. There was a slight smile on his thin lips, but the pale eyes, too closely set together, remained cold and steely. R.'s stare would have been embarrassing if Ashenden had not been used to it. He knew that R. was considering how he would broach the subject that he had in mind. The silence must have lasted for two or three minutes.

"I'm expecting a fellow to come and see me tonight," he said at last. "His train gets in about ten." He gave his wristwatch a glance. "He's known as the Hairless Mexican."

"Why?"

"Because he's hairless and because he's a Mexican."

"The explanation seems perfectly satisfactory," said Ashenden.

"He'll tell you all about himself. He talks nineteen to the dozen. He was on his uppers when I came across him. It appears that he was mixed up in some revolution in Mexico and had to get out with nothing but the clothes he stood up in. They were rather the worse for wear when I found him. If you want to please him you call him General. He claims to have been a general in Huerta's army, at least I think it was Huerta; anyhow he says that if things had gone right he would be minister of war now and no end of a big bug. I've found him very useful. Not a bad chap. The only thing I really have against him is that he will use scent."

"And where do I come in?" asked Ashenden.

"He's going down to Italy. I've got rather a ticklish job for him to do and I want you to stand by. I'm not keen on trusting him with a lot of money. He's a gambler and he's a bit too fond of the girls. I suppose you came from Geneva on your Ashenden passport."

"Yes."

"I've got another for you, a diplomatic one, by the way, in the name of Somerville with visas for France and Italy. I think you and he had better travel together. He's an amusing cove when he gets going, and I think you ought to get to know one another."

"What is the job?"

"I haven't yet quite made up my mind how much it's desirable for you to know about it."

Ashenden did not reply. They eyed one another in a detached manner, as though they were strangers who sat together in a railway carriage and each wondered who and what the other was.

"In your place I'd leave the General to do most of the talking. I wouldn't tell him more about yourself than you find absolutely necessary. He won't ask you any questions, I can promise you that, I think he's by way of being a gentleman after his own fashion."

"By the way, what is his real name?"

"I always call him Manuel, I don't know that he likes it very much, his name is Manuel Carmona."

"I gather by what you have not said that he's an unmitigated scoundrel."

R. smiled with his pale blue eyes.

"I don't know that I'd go quite so far as that. He hasn't had the advantages of a public school education. His ideas of playing the game are not quite the same as yours or mine. I don't know that I'd leave a gold cigarette case about when he was in the neighborhood, but if he lost money to you at poker and had pinched your cigarette case he would immediately pawn it to pay you. If he had half a chance he'd seduce your wife, but if you were up against it he'd share his last crust with you. The tears will run down his face when he hears Gounod's 'Ave Maria' on the gramophone, but if you insult his dignity he'll shoot you like a dog. It appears that in Mexico it's an insult to get between a man and his drink and he told me himself that once when a Dutchman who didn't know passed between him and the bar he whipped out his revolver and shot him dead."

"Did nothing happen to him?"

"No, it appears that he belongs to one of the best families. The matter was hushed up and it was announced in the papers that the Dutchman had committed suicide. He did practically. I don't believe the Hairless Mexican has a great respect for human life."

Ashenden who had been looking intently at R. started a little and he watched more carefully than ever his chief's tired, lined and yellow face. He knew that he did not make this remark for nothing.

"Of course a lot of nonsense is talked about the value of human life. You might just as well say that the counters you use at poker have an intrinsic value, their value is what you like to make it; for a general giving battle men are merely counters and he's a fool if he allows himself for sentimental reasons to look upon them as human beings."

"But, you see, they're counters that feel and think and if they believe they're being squandered they are quite capable of refusing to be used any more."

"Anyhow that's neither here nor there. We've had information that a man called Constantine Andreadi is on his way from Constantinople with certain documents that we want to get hold of. He's a Greek. He's an agent of Enver Pasha and Enver has great confidence in him. He's given him verbal messages that are too secret and too important to be put on paper. He's sailing from Piraeus, on a boat called the *Ithaca,* and will land at Brindisi on his way to Rome. He's to deliver his dispatches at the German embassy and impart what he has to say personally to the ambassador."

"I see."

At this time Italy was still neutral; the Central Powers were straining every nerve to keep her so; the Allies were doing what they could to induce her to declare war on their side.

"We don't want to get into any trouble with the Italian authorities, it might be fatal, but we've got to prevent Andreadi from getting to Rome."

"At any cost?" asked Ashenden.

"Money's no object," answered R., his lips twisting into a sardonic smile.

"What do you propose to do?"

"I don't think you need bother your head about that."

"I have a fertile imagination," said Ashenden.

"I want you to go down to Naples with the Hairless Mexican. He's very keen on getting back to Cuba. It appears that his friends are organizing a show and he wants to be as near at hand as possible so that he can hop over to Mexico when things are ripe. He needs cash. I've brought money down with me, in American dollars, and I shall give it to you tonight. You'd better carry it on your person."

"Is it much?"

"It's a good deal, but I thought it would be easier for you if it wasn't bulky, so I've got it in thousand-dollar notes. You will give the Hairless Mexican the notes in return for the documents that Andreadi is bringing."

A question sprang to Ashenden's lips, but he did not ask it. He asked another instead.

"Does this fellow understand what he has to do?"

"Perfectly."

There was a knock at the door. It opened and the Hairless Mexican stood before them.

"I have arrived. Good evening, Colonel. I am enchanted to see you."

R. got up.

"Had a nice journey, Manuel? This is Mr. Somerville who's going to Naples with you. General Carmona."

"Pleased to meet you, sir."

He shook Ashenden's hand with such force that he winced.

"Your hands are like iron, General," he murmured.

The Mexican gave them a glance.

"I had them manicured this morning. I do not think they were very well done. I like my nails much more highly polished."

They were cut to a point, stained bright red, and to Ashenden's mind shone like mirrors. Though it was not cold the General wore a fur coat with an astrakhan collar and with his every movement a wave of perfume was wafted to your nose.

"Take off your coat, General, and have a cigar," said R.

The Hairless Mexican was a tall man, and though thinnish gave you the impression of being very powerful; he was smartly dressed in a blue serge suit, with a silk handkerchief neatly tucked in the breast pocket of his coat, and he wore a gold bracelet on his wrist. His features were good, but a little larger than life-size, and his eyes were brown and lustrous. He was quite hairless. His yellow skin had the smoothness of a woman's and he had no eyebrows nor eyelashes; he wore a pale brown wig, rather long, and the locks were arranged in artistic disorder. This and the unwrinkled sallow face, combined with his dandified dress, gave him an appearance that was at first glance a trifle horrifying. He was repulsive and ridiculous, but you could not take your eyes from him. There was a sinister fascination in his strangeness.

He sat down and hitched up his trousers so that they should not bag at the knees.

"Well, Manuel, have you been breaking any hearts today?" said R. with his sardonic joviality.

The General turned to Ashenden.

"Our good friend, the Colonel, envies me my success with the fair sex. I tell him he can have just as many as I if he will only listen to me. Confidence, that is all you need. If you never fear a rebuff you will never have one."

"Nonsense, Manuel, one has to have your way with the girls. There's something about you that they can't resist."

The Hairless Mexican laughed with a self-satisfaction that he did not try to disguise. He spoke English very well, with a Spanish accent, but with an American intonation.

"But since you ask me, Colonel, I don't mind telling you that I got into conversation on the train with a little woman who was coming to Lyons to see her mother-in-law. She was not very young and she was thinner than I like a woman to be, but she was possible, and she helped me to pass an agreeable hour."

"Well, let's get to business," said R.

"I am at your service, Colonel." He gave Ashenden a glance. "Is Mr. Somerville a military man?"

"No," said R., "he's an author."

"It takes all sorts to make a world, as you say. I am happy to make yoru acquaintance, Mr. Somervile. I can tell you many stories that will interest you; I am sure that we shall get on well together. You have a sympathetic air. I am very sensitive to that. To tell you the truth I am nothing but a bundle of nerves and if I am with a person who is antipathetic to me I go all to pieces."

"I hope we shall have a pleasant journey," said Ashenden.

"When does our friend arrive at Brindisi?" asked the Mexican, turning to R.

"He sails from the Piraeus on the *Ithaca* on the fourteenth. It's probably some old tub, but you'd better get down to Brindisi in good time."

"I agree with you."

R. got up and with his hands in his pockets sat on the edge of the table. In his rather shabby uniform, his tunic unbuttoned, he looked a slovenly creature beside the neat and well-dressed Mexican.

"Mr. Somerville knows practically nothing of the errand on which you are going and I do not desire you to tell him anything. I think you had much better keep your own counsel. He is instructed to give you the funds you need for your work, but your actions are your own affair. If you need his advice of course you can ask for it."

"I seldom ask other people's advice and never take it."

"And should you make a mess of things I trust you to keep Mr. Somerville out of it. He must on no account be compromised."

"I am a man of honor, Colonel," answered the Hairless Mexican with dignity, "and I would sooner let myself be cut in a thousand pieces than betray my friends."

"That is what I have already told Mr. Somerville. On the other hand if everything pans out O.K. Mr. Somerville is instructed to give you the sum we agreed on in return for the papers I spoke to you about. In what manner you get them is no business of his."

"That goes without saying. There is only one thing I wish to make quite plain; Mr. Somerville understands of course that I have not accepted the mission with which you have entrusted me on account of the money?"

"Quite," replied R., gravely, looking him straight in the eyes.

"I am with the Allies body and soul, I cannot forgive the Germans for outraging the neutrality of Belgium, and if I accept the money that you have offered me it is because I am first and foremost a patriot. I can trust Mr. Somerville implicitly, I suppose?"

R. nodded. The Mexican turned to Ashenden.

"An expedition is being arranged to free my unhappy country from the tyrants that exploit and ruin it and every penny that I receive will go on guns and cartridges. For myself I have no need of money; I am a soldier and I can live on a crust and a few olives. There are only three occupations that befit a gentleman, war, cards and women: it costs nothing to sling a rifle over your shoulder and take to the mountains—and that is real warfare, not this maneuvering of battalions and firing of great guns—women love me for myself, and I generally win at cards."

Ashenden found the flamboyance of this strange creature, with his scented handkerchief and his gold bracelet, very much to his taste. This was far from being just the man in the street (whose tyranny we rail at but in the end submit to) and to the amateur of the baroque in human nature he was a rarity to be considered with delight. He was a purple patch on two legs. Notwithstanding his wig and his hairless big face he had undoubtedly an air; he was absurd, but he did not give you the impression that he was a man to be trifled with. His self-complacency was magnificent.

"Where is your kit, Manuel?" asked R.

It was possible that a frown for an instant darkened the Mexican's brow at the abrupt question that seemed a little contemptuously to brush to one side his eloquent statement, but he gave no other sign of displeasure. Ashenden suspected that he thought the Colonel a barbarian insensitive to the finer emotions.

"I left it at the station."

"Mr. Somerville has a diplomatic passport so that he can get it through with his own things at the frontier without examination if you like."

"I have very little, a few suits and some linen, but perhaps it would be as well if Mr. Somerville would take charge of it. I bought half a dozen suits of silk pajamas before I left Paris."

"And what about you?" asked R., turning to Ashenden.

"I've only got one bag. It's in my room."

"You'd better have it taken to the station while there's someone about. Your train goes at one-ten."

"Oh?"

This was the first Ashenden had heard that they were to start that night.

"I think you'd better get down to Naples as soon as possible."

"Very well."

R. got up.

"I'm going to bed. I don't know what you fellows want to do."

"I shall take a walk about Lyons," said the Hairless Mexican. "I am interested in life. Lend me a hundred francs, Colonel, will you? I have no change on me."

R. took out his pocketbook and gave the General the note he asked for. Then to Ashenden:

"What are you going to do? Wait here?"

"No," said Ashenden, "I shall go to the station and read."

"You'd both of you better have a whisky and soda before you go, hadn't you? What about it, Manuel?"

"It is very kind of you, but I never drink anything but champagne and brandy."

"Mixed?" asked R. drily.

"Not necessarily," returned the other with gravity.

R. ordered brandy and soda and when it came, whereas he and Ashenden helped themselves to both, the Hairless Mexican poured himself out three parts of a tumbler of neat brandy and swallowed it in two noisy gulps. He rose to his feet and put on his coat with the astrakhan collar, seized in one hand his bold black hat and, with the gesture of a romantic actor giving up the girl he loved to one more worthy of her, held out the other to R.

"Well, Colonel, I will bid you goodnight and pleasant dreams. I do not expect that we shall meet again so soon."

"Don't make a hash of things, Manuel, and if you do keep your mouth shut."

"They tell me that in one of your colleges where the sons of gentlemen are trained to become naval officers it is written in letters of gold: there is no such word as impossible in the British Navy. I do not know the meaning of the word failure."

"It has a good many synonyms," retorted R.

"I will meet you at the station, Mr. Somerville," said the Hairless Mexican, and with a flourish left them.

R. looked at Ashenden with that little smile of his that always made his face look so dangerously shrewd.

"Well, what d'you think of him?"

"You've got me beat," said Ashenden. "Is he a mountebank? He seems as vain as a peacock. And with that frightful appearance can he really be the lady's man he pretends? What makes you think you can trust him?"

R. gave a low chuckle and he washed his thin, old hands with imaginary soap.

"I thought you'd like him. He's quite a character, isn't he? I think we can trust him." R.'s eyes suddenly grew opaque. "I don't believe it would pay him to double cross us." He paused for a moment. "Anyhow we've got to risk it. I'll give you the tickets and the money and then you can take yourself off; I'm all in and I want to go to bed."

Ten minutes later Ashenden set out for the station with his bag on a porter's shoulder.

Having nearly two hours to wait he made himself comfortable in the waiting room. The light was good and he read a novel. When the time drew near for the arrival of the train from Paris that was to take them direct to Rome and the Hairless Mexican did not appear Ashenden, beginning to grow a trifle anxious, went out on the platform to look for him. Ashenden suffered from that distressing malady known as train fever: an hour before his train was due he began to have apprehensions lest he should miss it; he was impatient with the porters who would never bring his luggage down from his room in time and he could not understand why the hotel bus cut it so fine; a block in the street would drive him to frenzy and the languid movements of the station porters infuriated him. The whole world seemed in a horrid plot to delay him; people got in his way as he passed through the barriers; others, a long string of them, were at the ticket-office getting tickets for other trains than his and they counted their change with exasperating care; his luggage took an interminable time to register; and then if he was traveling with friends they would go to buy newspapers, or would take a walk along the platform and he was certain they would be left behind, they would stop to talk to a casual stranger or suddenly be seized with a desire to telephone and disappear at a run. In fact the universe conspired to make him miss every train he wanted to take and he was not happy unless he was settled in his corner, his things on the rack above him, with a good half hour to spare. Sometimes by arriving at the station too soon he had caught an earlier train than the one he had meant to, but that was nerve-racking and caused him all the anguish of very nearly missing it.

The Rome express was signaled and there was no sign of the Hairless Mexican, it came in and he was not to be seen. Ashenden became more and more harassed. He walked quickly up and down the platform, looked in all the waiting rooms, went to the consigne where the luggage was left; he could not find him. There were no sleeping-cars, but a number of people got out and he took two seats in a first-class carriage. He stood at the door, looking up and down the platform and up at the clock; it was useless to go if his traveling companion did not turn up and Ashenden made up his mind to take his things out of the carriage as the porter cried *en voiture;* but, by George! he would give the brute hell when he found him. There were three minutes more, then two minutes, then one; at that late hour there were few persons about and all who were traveling had taken their seats. Then he saw the Hairless Mexican, followed by two porters with his luggage and accompanied by a man in a bowler-hat, walk leisurely on to the platform. He caught sight of Ashenden and waved to him.

"Ah, my dear fellow, there you are, I wondered what had become of you."

"Good God, man, hurry up or we shall miss the train."

"I never miss a train. Have you got good seats? The chief *de gare* has gone for the night; this is his assistant."

The man in the bowler-hat took it off when Ashenden nodded to him.

"But this is an ordinary carriage. I am afraid I could not travel in that." He turned to the station master's assistant with an affable smile. "You must do better for me than that, *mon cher.*"

"*Certainement, mon général,* I will put you into the *salon-lit.* Of course."

The assistant station master led them along the train and put them in an empty compartment where there were two beds. The Mexican eyed it with satisfaction and watched the porters arrange the luggage.

"That will do very well. I am much obliged to you." He held out his hand to the man in the bowler hat. "I shall not forget you and next time I see the Minister I will tell him with what civility you have treated me."

"You are too good, General. I shall be very grateful."

A whistle was blown and the train started.

"This is better than an ordinary first-class carriage, I think, Mr. Somerville," said the Mexican. "A good traveler should learn how to make the best of things."

But Ashenden was still extremely cross.

"I don't know why the devil you wanted to cut it so fine. We should have looked a pair of damned fools if we'd missed the train."

"My dear fellow, there was never the smallest chance of that. When I arrived I told the stationmaster that I was General Carmona, Commander-in-Chief of the Mexican Army, and that I had to stop off in Lyons for a few hours to hold a conference with the British Field Marshal, I asked him to hold the train for me if I was delayed and suggested that my government might see its way to conferring an order on him. I have been to Lyons before, I like the girls here; they have not the chic of the Parisians, but they have something, there is no denying that they have something. Will you have a mouthful of brandy before you go to sleep?"

"No, thank you," said Ashenden morosely.

"I always drink a glass before going to bed, it settles the nerves."

He looked in his suitcase and without difficulty found a bottle. He put it to his lips and had a long drink, wiped his mouth with the back of his hand and lit a cigarette. Then he took off his boots and lay down. Ashenden dimmed the light.

"I have never yet made up my mind." said the Hairless Mexican reflectively, "whether it is pleasanter to go to sleep with the kisses of a beautiful woman on your mouth or with a cigarette between your lips. Have you ever been to Mexico? I will tell you about Mexico tomorrow. Goodnight."

Presently Ashenden heard from his steady breathing that he was asleep and in a little while himself dozed off. Presently he woke. The Mexican, deep in slumber, lay motionless; he had taken off his fur coat and was using it as a blanket; he still wore his wig. Suddenly there was a jolt and the train with a noisy grinding of brakes stopped; in the twinkling of an eye, before Ashenden could realize that anything had happened, the Mexican was on his feet with his hand to his hip.

"What is it?" he cried.

"Nothing. Probably only a signal against us."

The Mexican sat down heavily on his bed. Ashenden turned on the light.

"You wake quickly for such a sound sleeper," he said.

"You have to in my profession."

Ashenden would have liked to ask him whether this was murder, conspiracy or commanding armies, but was not sure that it would be discreet. The General opened his bag and took out the bottle.

"Will you have a nip?" he asked. "There is nothing like it when you wake suddenly in the night."

When Ashenden refused he put the bottle once more to his lips and poured a considerable quantity of liquor down his throat. He sighed and lit a cigarette. Although Ashenden had seen him now drink nearly a bottle of brandy and it was probable that he had had a good deal more when he was going about the town he was certainly quite sober. Neither in his manner nor in his speech was there any indication that he had drunk during the evening anything but lemonade.

The train started and soon Ashenden again fell asleep. When he awoke it was morning and turning round lazily he saw that the Mexican was awake too. He was smoking a cigarette. The floor by his side was strewn with burnt-out butts and the air was thick and grey. He had begged Ashenden not to insist on opening a window, for he said the night air was dangerous.

"I did not get up, because I was afraid of waking you. Will you do your toilet first or shall I?"

"I'm in no hurry," said Ashenden.

"I am an old campaigner, it will not take me long. Do you wash your teeth every day?"

"Yes," said Ashenden.

"So do I. It is a habit I learned in New York. I always think that a fine set of teeth are an adornment to a man."

There was a washbasin in the compartment and the General scrubbed his teeth, with gurglings and garglings, energetically. Then he got a bottle of eau-de-cologne from his bag, poured some of it on a towel and rubbed it over his face and hands. He took a comb and carefully arranged his wig; either it had not moved in the night or else he had set it straight before Ashenden awoke. He got another bottle out of his bag, with a spray attached to it, and squeezing a bulb covered his shirt and coat with a fine cloud of scent, did the same to his handkerchief, and then with a beaming face, like a man who has done his duty by the world and is well pleased, turned to Ashenden and said:

"Now I am ready to brave the day. I will leave my things for you, you need not be afraid of the eau-de-cologne, it is the best you can get in Paris."

"Thank you very much," said Ashenden. "All I want is soap and water."

"Water? I never use water except when I have a bath. Nothing can be worse for the skin."

When they approached the frontier, Ashenden, remembering the General's instructive gesture when he was suddenly awakened in the night, said to him:

"If you've got a revolver on you I think you'd better give it to me. With my diplomatic passport they're not likely to search me, but they might take it into their heads to go through you and we don't want to have any bothers."

"It is hardly a weapon, it is only a toy," returned the Mexican, taking out of his hip pocket a fully loaded revolver of formidable dimensions. "I do not like parting with it even for an hour, it gives me the feeling that I am not fully dresssed. But you are quite right, we do not want to take any risks; I will give you my knife as well. I would always rather use a knife than a revolver; I think it is a more elegant weapon."

"I daresay it is only a matter of habit," answered Ashenden. "Perhaps you are more at home with a knife."

"Anyone can pull a trigger, but it needs a man to use a knife."

To Ashenden it looked as though it were in a single movement that he tore open his waistcoat and from his belt snatched and opened a long knife of murderous aspect. He handed it to Ashenden with a pleased smile on his large, ugly and naked face.

"There's a pretty piece of work for you, Mr. Somerville. I've never seen a better bit of steel in my life, it takes an edge like a razor and it's strong; you can cut a cigarette paper with it and you can hew down an oak. There is nothing to get out of order and when it is closed it might be the knife a schoolboy uses to cut notches in his desk."

He shut it with a click and Ashenden put it along with the revolver in his pocket.

"Have you anything else?"

"My hands," replied the Mexican with arrogance, "but those I daresay the custom officials will not make trouble about."

Ashenden remembered the iron grip he had given him when they shook hands and slightly shuddered. They were large and long and smooth; there was not a hair on them or on the wrists, and with the pointed, rosy, manicured nails there was really something sinister about them.

Ashenden and General Carmona went through the formalities at the frontier independently and when they returned to their carriage Ashenden handed back to his companion the revolver and the knife. He sighed.

"Now I feel more comfortable. What do you say to a game of cards?"

"I should like it," said Ashenden.

The Hairless Mexican opened his bag again and from a corner extracted a greasy pack of French cards. He asked Ashenden whether he played écarté and when Ashenden told him that he did not suggested piquet. This was a game that Ashenden was not unfamiliar with so they settled the stakes and began. Since both were in favor of quick action they played the game of four hands, doubling the first and last. Ashenden had good enough cards, but the General seemed notwithstanding always to have better. Ashenden kept his eyes open and he was not careless of the possibility that his antagonist might correct the inequalities of chance, but he saw nothing to suggest that everything was not above board. He lost game after game. He was capotted and rubiconed. The score against him mounted up and up till he had lost something like a thousand francs, which at the time was a tidy sum. The General smoked innumerable cigarettes. He made them himself with a twist of the finger, a lick of his tongue and incredible celerity. At last he flung himself against the back of his seat.

"By the way, my friend, does the British Government pay your card losses when you are on a mission?" he asked.

"It certainly doesn't."

"Well, I think you have lost enough. If it went down on your expense account I would have proposed playing till we reached Rome, but you are sympathetic to me. If it is your own money I do not want to win any more of it."

He picked up the cards and put them aside. Ashenden somewhat ruefully took out a number of notes and handed them to the Mexican. He counted them and with his usual neatness put them carefully folded into his pocketbook. Then, leaning forward, he patted Ashenden almost affectionately on the knee.

"I like you, you are modest and unassuming, you have not the arrogance of your countrymen, and I am sure that you will take my advice in the spirit in which it is meant. Do not play piquet with people you don't know."

Ashenden was somewhat mortified and perhaps his face showed it, for the Mexican seized his hand.

"My dear fellow, I have not hurt your feelings? I would not do that for the world. You do not play piquet worse than most piquet players. It is not that. If we were going to be together longer I would teach you how to win at cards. One plays cards to win money and there is no sense in losing."

"I thought it was only in love and war that all things were fair," said Ashenden, with a chuckle.

"Ah, I am glad to see you smile. That is the way to take a loss. I see that you have good humor and good sense. You will go far in life. When I get back to Mexico and am in possession of my estates again you must come and stay with me. I will treat you like a king. You shall ride my best horses, we will go to the bullfights together, and if there are girls you fancy you have only to say the word and you shall have them."

He began telling Ashenden of the vast territories, the haciendas and the mines in Mexico, of which he had been dispossessed. He told him of the feudal state in which he lived. It did not matter whether what he said was true or not, for those sonorous phrases of his were fruity with the rich-distilled perfumes of romance. He described a spacious life that seemed to belong to another age and his eloquent gestures brought before the mind's eye tawny distances and vast green plantations, great herds of cattle, and in the moonlit night the song of the blind singers that melted in the air and the twanging of guitars.

"Everything I lost, everything. In Paris I was driven to earn a pittance by giving Spanish lessons or showing Americans—*Americanos del Norte,* I mean—the night life of the city. I who have flung away a thousand duros on a dinner have been forced to beg my bread like a blind Indian. I who have taken pleasure in clasping a diamond bracelet round the wrist of a beautiful woman have been forced to accept a suit of clothes from a hag old enough to be my mother. Patience. Man is born to trouble as the sparks fly upward, but misfortune cannot last forever. The time is ripe and soon we shall strike our blow."

He took up the greasy pack of cards and set them out in a number of little piles.

"Let us see what the cards say. They never lie. Ah, if I had only had greater faith in them I should have avoided the only action of my life that has weighed heavily on me. My conscience is at ease. I did what any man would do under the circumstances, but I regret that necessity forced upon me an action that I would willingly have avoided."

He looked through the cards, set some of them on one side on a system Ashenden did not understand, shuffled the remainder and once more put them in little piles.

"The cards warned me, I will never deny that, their warning was clear and definite. Love and a dark woman, danger, betrayal and death. It was as plain as the nose on your face. Any fool would have known what it meant and I have been using the cards all my life. There is hardly an action that I make without consulting them. There are no excuses. I was besotted. Ah, you of the Northern races do not know what love means, you do not know how it can prevent you from sleeping, how it can take your appetite for food away so that you dwindle as if from a fever, you do not understand what a frenzy it is so that you are like a madman and you will stick at nothing to satisfy your desire. A man like me is capable of every folly and every crime when he is in love, *si,* Señor, and of heroism. He can scale mountains higher than Everest and swim across seas broader than the Atlantic. He is god, he is devil. Women have been my ruin."

Once more the Hairless Mexican glanced at the cards, took some out of the little piles and left others in. He shuffled them again.

"I have been loved by multitudes of women. I do not say it in vanity. I offer no explanation. It is mere matter of fact. Go to Mexico City and ask them what they know of Manuel Carmona and his triumphs. Ask them how many women have resisted Manuel Carmona."

Ashenden, frowning a little, watched him reflectively. He wondered whether R., that shrewd fellow who chose his instruments with such a sure instinct, had not this time made a mistake, and he was uneasy. Did the Hairless Mexican really believe that he was irresistible or was he merely a blatant liar? In the course of his manipulations he had thrown out all of the cards in the pack but for four and these now lay in front of him face downwards and side by side. He touched them one by one but did not turn them up.

"There is fate," he said, "and no power on earth can change it. I hesitate. This is a moment that ever fills me with apprehension and I have to steel myself to turn over the cards that may tell me that disaster awaits me. I am a brave man, but sometimes I have reached this stage and not had the courage to look at the four fatal cards."

Indeed now he eyed the backs of them with an anxiety he did not try to hide.

"What was I saying to you?"

"You were telling me that women found your fascinations irresistible," replied Ashenden dryly.

"Once all the same I found a woman who resisted me. I saw her first in a house, a *casa de mujeres* in Mexico City. She was going down the stairs as I went up; she was not very beautiful, I had had a hundred more beautiful, but she had something that took my fancy and I told the old woman who kept the house to send her to me. You will know her when you go to Mexico City; they call her La Marqueza. She said that the girl was not an inmate, but came there only from time to time and had left. I told her to have her there next evening and not to let her go till I came. But I was delayed and when I arrived La Marqueza told me that the girl had said she was not used to being kept waiting and had gone. I am a good-natured fellow and I do not mind if women are capricious and teasing, that is part of their charm, so with a laugh I sent her a note of a hundred duros and promised that on the following day I would be punctual. But when I went, on the minute, La Marqueza handed me back my hundred duros and told me the girl did not fancy me. I laughed at her impertinence. I took off the diamond ring I was wearing and told the old woman to give her that and see whether it would induce her to change her mind. In the morning La Marqueza brought me in return for my ring—a red carnation. I did not know whether to be amused or angry. I am not used to being thwarted in my passions. I never hesitate to spend money (what is it for but to squander on pretty women?), and I told La Marqueza to go to the girl and say that I would give her a thousand duros to dine with me that night. Presently she came back with the answer that the girl would come on the condition that I allowed her to go home immediately after dinner. I accepted with a shrug of the shoulders. I did not think she was serious. I thought that she was saying that only to make herself more desired. She came to dinner at my house. Did I say she was not beautiful? She was the most beautiful, the most exquisite creature I had ever met. I was intoxicated. She had charm and she had wit. She had all the *gracia* of the Andalusian. In one word she was adorable. I asked her why she had treated me so casually and she laughed in my face. I laid myself out to be agreeable. I exercised all my skill. I surpassed myself. But when we finished dinner she rose from her seat and bade me goodnight. I asked her where she was going. She said I had promised to let her go and she trusted me as a man of honor to keep my word. I expostulated, I reasoned, I raved, I stormed. She held me to my word. All I could induce her to do was to consent to dine with me the following night on the same terms.

"You would have thought that I should be angry with her. For seven days I paid her a thousand silver duros to dine with me. Every evening I waited for her with my heart in my mouth, as nervous as a *novillero* at his first bullfight, and every evening she played with me, laughed at me, coquetted with me and drove me frantic. I was madly in love with her. I have never loved anyone so much before or since. I could think of nothing else. I was distracted. I neglected everything. I am a patriot and I love my country. A small band of us had got together and made up our minds that we could no longer put up with the misrule from which we were suffering. All the lucrative posts were given to other people, we were being made to pay taxes as though we were tradesmen, and we were exposed to abominable affronts. We had money and men. Our plans were made and we were ready to strike. I had an infinity of things to do, meetings to go to, ammunition to get, orders to give; I was so besotted over this woman that I could attend to nothing.

"You would have thought that I should be angry with her for making such a fool of me, me who had never known what it was not to gratify my smallest whim; I did not believe that she refused me to inflame my desires, I believe that she told the plain truth when she said that she would not give herself to me until she loved me. She said it was for me to make her love me. I thought her an angel. I was ready to wait. My passion was so consuming that sooner or later, I felt, at last it must communicate itself to her; it was like a fire on the prairie that devours everything around it; and at last—at last she said she loved me. My emotion was so terrific that I thought I should fall down and die. Oh, what rapture, oh, what madness! I would have given her everything I possessed in the world, I would have torn down the stars from heaven to deck her hair. I wanted to do something to prove to her the extravagance of my love, I wanted to do the impossible, the incredible. I wanted to give her myself, my soul, my honor, all, all I had and all I was; and that night when she lay in my arms I told her of our plot and who we were that were concerned in it. I felt her body stiffen with attention, I was conscious of a flicker of her eyelids, there was something, I hardly knew what, the hand that stroked my face was dry and cold; a sudden suspicion seized me and all at once I remembered what the cards had told me: love and a dark woman, danger, betrayal and death. Three times they'd said it and I wouldn't heed. I made no sign that I had noticed anything. She nestled up against my heart and told me that she was frightened to hear such things and asked me if so and so was concerned. I answered her. I wanted to make sure. One after the other, with infinite cunning, between her kisses she cajoled me into giving every detail of the plot, and now I was certain, as certain as I am that you sit before me, that she was a spy. She was a spy of the president's and she had been set to allure me with her devilish charm, and now she had wormed out of me all our secrets. The lives of all of us were in her hands and I knew that if she left that room in twenty-four hours we should be dead men. And I loved her, I loved her; oh, words cannot tell you the agony of desire that burned my heart; love like that is no pleasure, it is pain, pain, but the exquisite pain that transcends all pleasure. It is that heavenly anguish that the saints speak of when they are seized with a divine ecstasy. I knew that she must not leave the room alive and I feared that if I delayed my courage would fail me.

"'I think I shall sleep,' she said.

"'Sleep, my dove,' I answered.

"'*Alma de mi corazón,*' she called me. 'Soul of my heart.' They were the last words she spoke. Those heavy lids of hers, dark like a grape and faintly humid, those heavy lids of hers closed over her eyes and in a little while I knew by the regular movement of her breast against mine that she slept. You see, I loved her, I could not bear that she should suffer, she was a spy, yes, but my heart bade me spare her the terror of knowing what must happen. It is strange, I felt no anger because she had betrayed me. I only felt that my soul was enveloped in night. Poor thing, poor thing, I could have cried for pity for her. I drew my arm very gently from around her, my left arm that was, my right was free, and raised myself on my hand. But she was so beautiful that I turned my face away when I drew the knife with all my strength across her lovely throat. Without awakening she passed from sleep to death."

He stopped and stared frowning at the four cards that still lay, their backs upward, waiting to be turned up.

"It was in the cards. Why did I not take their warning? I will not look at them. Damn them. Take them away."

With a violent gesture he swept the whole pack on to the floor.

"Though I am a freethinker I had masses said for her soul." He leaned back, and rolled himself a cigarette. He inhaled a long breathful of smoke. He shrugged his shoulders. "The colonel said you were a writer. What do you write?"

"Stories," replied Ashenden.

"Detective stories?"

"No."

"Why not? They are the only ones I read. If I were a writer I should write detective stories."

"They are very difficult. You need an incredible amount of invention. I devised a murder story once, but the murder was so ingenious that I could never find a way of bringing it home to the murderer, and after all, one of the conventions of the detective story is that the mystery should in the end be solved and the criminal brought to justice."

"If your murder is as ingenious as you think, the only means you have of proving the murderer's guilt is by the discovery of his motives. When once you have found a motive the chances are that you will hit upon evidence that until then had escaped you. If there is no motive the most damning evidence will be inconclusive. Imagine for instance that you went up to a man in a lonely street on a moonless night and stabbed him to the heart. Who would ever think of you? But if he was your wife's lover, or your brother, or had cheated or insulted you, then a scrap of paper, a bit of string or a chance remark would be enough to hang you. What were your movements at the time he was killed? Are there not a dozen people who saw you before and after? But if he was a total stranger you would never for a moment be suspected. It was inevitable that Jack the Ripper should escape unless he was caught in the act."

Ashenden had more than one reason to change the conversation. They were parting at Rome and he thought it necessary to come to an understanding with his companion about their respective movements. The Mexican was going to Brindisi and Ashenden to Naples. He meant to lodge at the Hotel de Belfast, which was a large second-rate hotel near the harbor frequented by commercial travelers and the thriftier kind of tripper. It would be as well to let the General have the number of his room so that he could come up if necessary without inquiring of the porter, and at the next stopping place Ashenden got an envelope from the station-buffet and made him address it in his own writing to himself at the post office in Brindisi. All Ashenden had to do then was to scribble a number on a sheet of paper and post it.

The Hairless Mexican shrugged his shoulders.

"To my mind all these precautions are rather childish. There is absolutely no risk. But whatever happens you may be quite sure that I will not compromise you."

"This is not the sort of job which I'm very familiar with," said Ashenden. "I'm content to follow the Colonel's instructions and know no more about it than it's essential I should."

"Quite so. Should the exigencies of the situation force me to take a drastic step and I get into trouble I shall of course be treated as a political prisoner. Sooner or later Italy is bound to come into the war on the side of the Allies and I shall be released. I have considered everything. But I beg you very seriously to have no more anxiety about the outcome of our mission than if you were going for a picnic on the Thames."

But when at last they separated and Ashenden found himself alone in a carriage on the way to Naples he heaved a great sigh of relief. He was glad to be rid of that chattering, hideous and fantastic creature. He was gone to meet Constantine Andreadi at Brindisi and if half of what he had told Ashenden was true, Ashenden could not but congratulate himself that he did not stand in the Greek spy's shoes. He wondered what sort of a man he was. There was a grimness in the notion of his coming across the blue Ionian, with his confidential papers and his dangerous secrets, all unconscious of the noose into which he was putting his head. Well, that was war, and only fools thought it could be waged with kid gloves on.

Ashenden arrived in Naples and, having taken a room at the hotel, wrote its number on a sheet of paper in block letters and posted it to the Hairless Mexican. He went to the British Consulate where R. had arranged to send any instructions he might have for him and found that they knew about him and everything was in order. Then he put aside these matters and made up his mind to amuse himself. Here in the South the spring was well advanced and in the busy streets the sun was hot. Ashenden knew Naples pretty well. The Piazza di San Ferdinando, with it bustle, the Piazza del Plebiscito, with its handsome church, stirred in his heart pleasant recollections. The Strada di Chiara was as noisy as ever. He stood at corners and looked up the narrow alleys that climbed the hill precipitously, those alleys of high houses with the washing set out to dry on lines across the street like pennants flying to mark a feast-day; and he sauntered along the shore, looking at the burnished sea with Capri faintly outlined against the day, till he came to Posilippo where there was an old, rambling and bedraggled palazzo in which in his youth he had spent many a romantic hour. He observed the curious little pain with which the memories of the past wrung his heartstrings. Then he took a fly drawn by a small and scraggy pony and rattled back over the stones to the Galleria where he sat in the cool and drank an *americano* and looked at the people who loitered there, talking, forever talking, with vivacious gestures, and, exercising his fancy, sought from their appearance to divine their reality.

For three days Ashenden led the idle life that fitted so well the fantastical, untidy and genial city. He did nothing from morning till night but wander at random, looking, not with the eye of the tourist who seeks for what ought to be seen, nor with the eye of the writer who looks for his own (seeing in a sunset a melodious phrase or in a face the inkling of a character), but with that of the tramp to whom whatever happens is absolute. He went to the museum to look at the statue of Agrippina the Younger, which he had particular reasons for remembering with affection, and took the opportunity to see once more the Titian and the Brueghel in the picture gallery. But he always came back to the church of Santa Chiara. Its grace, its gaiety, the airy persiflage with which it seemed to treat religion and at the back of this its sensual emotion; its extravagance, its elegance of line; to Ashenden it seemed to express, as it were in one absurd and gradiloquent metaphor, the sunny, dusty, lovely city and its bustling inhabitants. It said that life was charming and sad; it's a pity one hadn't any money, but money wasn't everything, and anyway why bother when we are here today and gone tomorrow, and it was all very exciting and amusing, and after all we must make the best of things: *facciamo una piccola combinazione*.

But on the fourth morning, when Ashenden, having just stepped out of his bath, was trying to dry himself on a towel that absorbed no moisture, his door was quickly opened and a man slipped into his room.

"What'd you want?" cried Ashenden.

"It's all right. Don't you know me?"

"Good Lord, it's the Mexican. What have you done to yourself?"

He had changed his wig and wore now a black one, close cropped, that fitted on his head like a cap. It entirely altered the look of him and though this was still odd enough, it was quite different from that which he had worn before. He wore a shabby grey suit.

"I can only stop a minute. He's getting shaved."

Ashenden felt his cheeks suddenly redden.

"You found him then?"

"That wasn't difficult. He was the only Greek passenger on the ship. I went on board when she got in and asked for a friend who had sailed from the Piraeus. I said I had come to meet a Mr. George Diogenidis. I pretended to be much puzzled at his not coming and I got into a conversation with Andreadi. He's traveling under a false name. He calls himself Lombardos. I followed him when he landed and do you know the first thing he did? He went into a barber's and had his beard shaved. What do you think of that?"

"Nothing. Anyone might have his beard shaved."

"That is not what I think. He wanted to change his appearance. Oh, he's cunning. I admire the Germans, they leave nothing to chance, he's got his whole story pat, but I'll tell you that in a minute."

"By the way, you've changed your appearance too."

"Ah yes, this is a wig I'm wearing; it makes a difference, doesn't it?"

"I should never have known you."

"One has to take precautions. We are bosom friends. We had to spend the day in Brindisi and he cannot speak Italian. He was glad to have me help him and we traveled up together. I have brought him to this hotel. He says he is going to Rome tomorrow, but I shall not let him out of my sight; I do not want him to give me the slip. He says that he wants to see Naples and I have offered to show him everything there is to see."

"Why isn't he going to Rome today?"

"That is part of the story. He pretends he is a Greek businessman who had made money during the war. He says he was the owner of two coasting steamers and had just sold them. Now he means to go to Paris and have his fling. He says he has wanted to go to Paris all his life and at last has a chance. He is close. I tried to get him to talk. I told him I was Spaniard and had been to Brindisi to arrange communications with Turkey about war material. He listened to me and I saw he was interested, but he told me nothing and of course I did not think it wise to press him. He had the papers on this person."

"How do you know?"

"He is not anxious about his grip, but he feels every now and then round his middle, they're either in a belt or in the lining of his vest."

"Why the devil did you bring him to this hotel?"

"I thought it would be more convenient. We may want to search his luggage."

"Are you staying here too?"

"No, I am not such a fool as that, I told him I was going to Rome by the night train and would not take a room. But I must go. I promised to meet him outside the barber's in fifteen minutes."

"All right."

"Where shall I find you tonight if I want you?"

Ashenden for an instant eyed the Hairless Mexican, then with a slight frown looked away.

"I shall spend the evening in my room."

"Very well. Will you just see that there's nobody in the passage."

Ashenden opened the door and looked out. He saw no one. The hotel in point of fact at that season was nearly empty. There were few foreigners in Naples and trade was bad.

"It's all right," said Ashenden.

The Hairless Mexican walked boldly out. Ashenden closed the door behind him. He shaved and slowly dressed. The sun was shining as brightly as usual on the square and the people who passed, the shabby little carriages with their scrawny horses, had the same air as before, but they did not any longer fill Ashenden with gaiety. He was not comfortable. He went out and called as was his habit as the Consulate to ask if there was a telegram for him. Nothing. Then he went to Cook's and looked out the trains to Rome; there was one soon after midnight and another at five in the morning. He wished he could catch the first. He did not know what were the Mexican's plans; if he really wanted to get to Cuba he would do well to make his way to Spain, and, glancing at the notices in the office, Ashenden saw that next day there was a ship sailing from Naples to Barcelona.

Ashenden was bored with Naples. The glare in the streets tired his eyes, the dust was intolerable, the noise was deafening. He went to the Galleria and had a drink. In the afternoon he went to a cinema. Then, going back to his hotel, he told the clerk that since he was starting so early in the morning he preferred to pay his bill at once, and he took his luggage to the station, leaving in his room only a dispatch-case in which were the printed part of his code and a book or two. He dined. Then returning to the hotel, he sat down to wait for the Hairless Mexican. He could not conceal from himself the fact that he was exceedingly nervous. He began to read, but the book was tiresome, and he tried another; his attention wandered and he glanced at his watch. It was desperately early; he took up his book again, making up his mind that he would not look at his watch till he had read thirty pages, but though he ran his eyes conscientiously down one page after another he could not tell more than vaguely what it was he read. He looked at the time again. Good God, it was only half-past ten. He wondered where the Hairless Mexican was, and what he was doing; he was afraid he would make a mess of things. It was a horrible business. Then it struck him that he had better shut the window and draw his curtains. He smoked innumerable cigarettes. He looked at his watch and it was a quarter past eleven. A thought struck him and his heart began to beat against his chest; out of curiosity he counted his pulse and was surprised to find that it was normal. Though it was a warm night and the room was stuffy his hands and feet were icy. What a nuisance it was, he reflected irritably, to have an imagination that conjured up pictures of things that you didn't in the least want to see! From his standpoint as a writer he had often considered murder, and his mind went to that fearful description of one in *Crime and Punishment*. He did not want to think of this topic, but it forced itself upon him; his book dropped to his knees and staring at the wall in front of him (it had a brown wallpaper with a pattern of dingy roses) he asked himself how, if one had to, one would commit a murder in Naples. Of course there was the Villa, the great leafy garden facing the bay in which stood the aquarium; that was deserted at night and very dark; things happened there that did not bear the light of day and prudent persons after dusk avoided its sinister paths. Beyond Posilippo the road was very solitary and there were byways that led up the hill in which by night you would never meet a soul, but how would you induce a man who had any nerves to go there? You might suggest a row in the bay, but the boatman who hired the boat would see you; it was doubtful indeed if he would let you go on the water alone. There were disreputable hotels down by the harbor where no questions were asked of persons who arrived late at night without luggage; but here again the waiter who showed you your room had the chance of a good look at you and you had on entering to sign an elaborate questionnaire.

Ashenden looked once more at the time. He was very tired. He sat now not even trying to read, his mind a blank.

Then the door opened softly and he sprang to his feet. His flesh crept. The Hairless Mexican stood before him.

"Did I startle you?" he asked smiling. "I thought you would prefer me not to knock."

"Did anyone see you come in?"

"I was let in by the night watchman; he was asleep when I rang and didn't even look at me. I'm sorry I'm so late, but I had to change."

The Hairless Mexican now wore the clothes he had traveled down in and his fair wig. It was extraordinary how different he looked. He was bigger and more flamboyant; the very shape of his face was altered. His eyes were shining and he seemed in excellent spirits. He gave Ashenden a glance.

"How white you are, my friend! Surely you're not nervous?"

"Have you got the documents?"

"No. He hadn't got them on him. This is all he had."

He put down on the table a bulky pocketbook and a passport.

"I don't want them," said Ashenden quickly. "Take them."

With a shrug of the shoulders the Hairless Mexican put the things back in his pocket.

"What was in his belt? You said he kept feeling round his middle."

"Only money. I've looked through the pocketbook. It contains nothing but private letters and photographs of women. He must have locked the documents in his grip before coming out with me this evening."

"Damn," said Ashenden.

"I've got the key of his room. We'd better go and look through his luggage."

Ashenden felt a sensation of sickness in the pit of his stomach. He hesitated. The Mexican smiled not unkindly.

"There's no risk, *amigo*," he said, as though he were reassuring a small boy, "but if you don't feel happy, I'll go alone."

"No, I'll come with you," said Ashenden.

"There's no one awake in the hotel and Mr. Andreadi won't disturb us. Take off your shoes if you like."

Ashenden did not answer. He frowned because he noticed his hands were slightly trembling. He unlaced his shoes and slipped them off. The Mexican did the same.

"You'd better go first," he said. "Turn to the left and go straight along the corridor. It's number thirty-eight."

Ashenden opened the door and stepped out. The passage was dimly lit. It exasperated him to feel so nervous when he could not but be aware that his companion was perfectly at ease. When they reached the door the Hairless Mexican inserted the key, turned the lock and went in. He switched on the light. Ashenden followed him and closed the door. He noticed that the shutters were shut.

"Now we're all right. We can take our time."

He took a bunch of keys out of his pocket, tried one or two and at last hit upon the right one. The suitcase was filled with clothes.

"Cheap clothes," said the Mexican contemptuously as he took them out. "My own principle is that it's always cheaper in the end to buy the best. After all one is a gentleman or one isn't a gentleman."

"Are you obliged to talk?" asked Ashenden.

"A spice of danger affects people in different ways. It only excites me, but it puts you in a bad temper, *amigo*."

"You see I'm scared and you're not," replied Ashenden with candor.

"It's merely a matter of nerves."

Meanwhile he felt the clothes, rapidly but with care, as he took them out. There were no papers of any sort in the suitcase. Then he took out his knife and slit the lining. It was a cheap piece and the lining was gummed to the material of which the suitcase was made. There was no possibility of anything being concealed in it.

"They're not here. They must be hidden in the room."

"Are you sure he didn't deposit them in some office? At one of the consulates for example?"

"He was never out of my sight for a moment except when he was getting shaved."

The Hairless Mexican opened the drawers and the cupboard. There was no carpet on the floor. He looked under the bed, in it, and under the mattress. His dark eyes shot up and down the room looking for a hiding place, and Ashenden felt that nothing escaped him.

"Perhaps he left them in charge of the clerk downstairs."

"I should have known it. And he wouldn't dare. They're not here. I can't understand it."

He looked about the room irresolutely. He frowned in the attempt to guess at a solution of the mystery.

"Let's get out of here," said Ashenden.

"In a minute."

The Mexican went down on his knees, quickly and neatly folded the clothes, and packed them up again. He locked the bag and stood up. Then, pulling out the light, he slowly opened the door and looked out. He beckoned to Ashenden and slipped into the passage. When Ashenden had followed him he stopped and locked the door, put the key in his pocket and walked with Ashenden to his room. When they were inside it and the bolt drawn Ashenden wiped his clammy hands and his forehead.

"Thank God, we're out of that!"

"There wasn't really the smallest danger. But what are we to do now? The Colonel will be very angry that the papers haven't been found."

"I'm taking the five o'clock train to Rome. I shall wire for instructions there."

"Very well, I will come with you."

"I should have thought it would suit you better to get out of the country more quickly. There's a boat tomorrow that goes to Barcelona. Why don't you take that and if necessary I can come to see you there?"

The Hairless Mexican gave a little smile.

"I see that you are anxious to be rid of me. Well, I won't thwart a wish that your inexperience in these matters excuses. I will go to Barcelona.

I have a visa for Spain."

Ashenden looked at his watch. It was a little after two. He had nearly three hours to wait. His companion comfortably rolled himself a cigarette.

"What do you say to a little supper?" he asked. "I'm as hungry as a wolf."

The thought of food sickened Ashenden, but he was terribly thirsty. He did not want to go out with the Hairless Mexican, but neither did he want to stay in that hotel by himself.

"Where could one go at this hour?"

"Come along with me. I'll find you a place."

Ashenden put on his hat and took his dispatch case in his hand. They went downstairs. In the hall the porter was sleeping soundly on a mattress on the floor. As they passed the desk, walking softly in order not to wake hm, Ashenden noticed in the pigeonhole belonging to his room a letter. He took it out and saw that it was addressed to him. They tiptoed out of the hotel and shut the door behind them. Then they walked quickly away. Stopping after a hundred yards or so under a lamppost Ashenden took the letter out of his pocket and read it; it came from the Consulate and said: "The enclosed telegram arrived tonight and in case it is urgent I am sending it round to your hotel by messenger." It had apparently been left some time before midnight while Ashenden was sitting in his room. He opened the telegram and saw that it was in code.

"Well, it'll have to wait," he said, putting in back in his pocket.

The Hairless Mexican walked as though he knew his way through the deserted streets and Ashenden walked by his side. At last they came to a tavern in a blind alley, noisome and evil, and this the Mexican entered.

"It's not the Ritz," he said, "but at this hour of the night it's only in a place like this that we stand a chance for getting something to eat."

Ashenden found himself in a long sordid room at one end of which a wizened young man sat at a piano; there were tables standing out from the wall on each side and against them benches. A number of persons, men and women, were sitting about. They were drinking beer and wine. The women were old, painted, and hideous; and their harsh gaiety was at once noisy and lifeless. When Ashenden and the Hairless Mexican came in they all stared, and when they sat down at one of the tables Ashenden looked away in order not to meet the leering eyes, just ready to break into a smile, that sought his insinuatingly. The wizened pianist strummed a tune and several couples got up and began to dance. Since there were not enough men to go round some of the women danced together. The General ordered two plates of spaghetti and a bottle of Capri wine. When the wine was brought he drank a glassful greedily and then, waiting for the pasta, eyed the women who were sitting at the other tables.

"Do you dance?" he asked Ashenden. "I'm going to ask one of these girls to have a turn with me."

He got up and Ashenden watched him go up to one who had the least flashing eyes and white teeth to recommend her; she rose and he put his arm around her. He danced well. Ashenden saw him begin talking; the woman laughed and presently the look of indifference with which she had accepted his offer changed to one of interest. Soon they were chatting gaily. The dance came to an end and putting her back at her table he returned to Ashenden and drank another glass of wine.

"What do you think of my girl?" he asked. "Not bad, is she? It does one good to dance. Why don't you ask one of them? This is a nice place, is it not? You can always trust me to find anything like this. I have an instinct."

The pianist started again. The woman looked at the Hairless Mexican and when with his thumb he pointed to the floor she jumped up with alacrity. He buttoned up his coat, arched his back and standing by the side of the table waited for her to come to him. He swung her off, talking, smiling, and already he was on familiar terms wth everyone in the room. In fluent Italian, with his Spanish accent, he exchanged badinage with one and the other. They laughed at his sallies. Then the waiter brought two heaped platefuls of macaroni and when the Mexican saw them he stopped dancing without ceremony and, allowing his partner to get back to her table as she chose, hurried to his meal.

"I'm ravenous," he said. "And yet I ate a good dinner. Where did you dine? You're going to eat some macaroni, aren't you?"

"I have no appetite," said Ashenden.

But he began to eat and to his surprise found that he was hungry. The Hairless Mexican ate with huge mouthfuls, enjoying himself vastly; his eyes shone and he was loquacious. The woman he had danced with had in that short time told him all about herself and he repeated now to Ashenden what she had said. He stuffed huge pieces of bread into his mouth. He ordered another bottle of wine.

"Wine?" he cried scornfully. "Wine is not a drink, only champagne; it does not even quench your thirst. Well, *amigo,* are you feeling better?"

"I'm bound to say I am," smiled Ashenden.

"Practice, that is all you want, practice."

He stretched out his hand to pat Ashenden on the arm.

"What's that?" cried Ashenden with a start. "What's that stain on your cuff?"

"That? Nothing. It's only blood. I had a little accident and cut myself."

Ashenden was silent. His eyes sought the clock that hung over the door.

"Are you anxious about your train? Let me have one more dance and then I'll accompany you to the station."

The Mexican got up and with his sublime self-assurance seized in his arms the woman who sat nearest to him and danced away with her. Ashenden watched him moodily. He was a monstrous, terrible figure with that blond wig and his hairless face, but he moved with a matchless grace; his feet were small and seemed to hold the ground like the pads of a cat or a tiger; his rhythm was wonderful and you could not but see that the bedizened creature he danced with was intoxicated by the gestures. There was music in his toes and in the long arms that held her so firmly, and there was music in those long legs that seemed to move strangely from the hips. Sinister and grotesque though he was, there was in him now a feline elegance, even something of beauty, and you felt a secret, shameful fascination. To Ashenden he suggested one of those sculptures of the pre-Aztec hewers of stone in which there is barbarism and vitality, something terrible and cruel, and yet withal a brooding and signficant loveliness. All the same he would gladly have left him to finish the night by himself in that sordid dance hall, but he knew that he must have a business conversation with him. He did not look forward to it without misgiving. He had been instructed to give Manuel Carmona certain sums in return for certain documents. Well, the documents were not forthcoming, and as for the rest—Ashenden knew nothing about that; it was no business of his. The Hairless Mexican waved gaily as he passed him.

"I will come the moment the music stops. Pay the bill and then I shall be ready."

Ashenden wished he could have seen into his mind. He could not even make a guess at its workings. Then the Mexican, with his scented handkerchief wiping the sweat from his brow, came back.

"Have you had a good time, General?" Ashenden asked him.

"I always have a good time. Poor white trash, but what do I care? I like to feel the body of a woman in my arms and see her eyes grow languid and her lips part as her desire for me melts the marrow in her bones like butter in the sun. Poor white trash, but women."

They sallied forth. The Mexican proposed that they should walk and in that quarter, at that hour, there would have been little chance of finding a cab; but the sky was starry. It was a summer night and the air was still. The silence walked beside them like the ghost of a dead man. When they neared the station the houses seemed on a sudden to take on a greyer, more rigid line, and you felt that the dawn was at hand. A little shiver trembled through the night. It was a moment of apprehension and the soul for an instant was anxious; it was as though, inherited down the years in their countless millions, it felt a witless fear that perhaps another day would not break. But they entered the station and the night once more enwrapped them. One or two porters lolled about like stagehands after the curtain has rung down and the scene is struck. Two soldiers in dim uniforms stood motionless.

The waiting room was empty, but Ashenden and the Hairless Mexican went to sit in the most retired part of it.

"I still have an hour before my train goes. I'll just see what this cable's about."

He took it out of his pocket and from the dispatch case got his code. He was not then using a very elaborate one. It was in two parts, one contained in a slim book and the other, given him on a sheet of paper and destroyed by him before he left allied territory, committed to memory. Ashenden put on his spectacles and set to work. The Hairless Mexican sat in a corner of the seat, rolling himself cigarettes and smoking; he sat there placidly, taking no notice of what Ashenden did, and enjoyed his well-earned repose. Ashenden deciphered the groups of numbers one by one and as he got it jotted down each word on a piece of paper. His method was to abstract his mind from the sense till he had finished, since he had discovered that if you took notice of the words as they came along you often jumped to a conclusion and sometimes were led into error. So he translated quite mechanically, without paying attention to the words as he wrote them one after the other. When at last he had done he read the complete message. It ran as follows:

> *Constantine Andreadi has been detained by illness at Piraeus.*
> *He will be unable to sail. Return Geneva and await instruc-*
> *tions.*

At first Ashenden could not understand. He read it again. He shook from head to foot. Then, for once robbed of his self-possession, he blurted out, in a hoarse, agitated and furious whisper:

"You bloody fool, you've killed the wrong man."

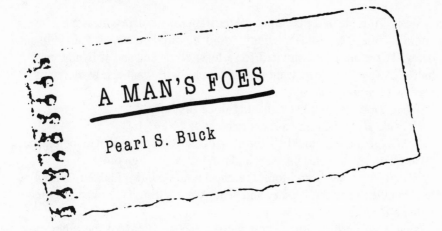

A MAN'S FOES

Pearl S. Buck

MARTIN LIU WAS bewildered as he stepped out of the train at the railroad station in Peking. Nothing was changed, it was exactly as he had remembered it for the seven years he had been abroad. But he had so long looked forward to this moment of homecoming that now it was come it was unreal.

He stood, looking about him, and at that instant saw Wang Ting, his father's chief secretary, and his own sister Siu-li. They were looking in the crowd for him and he now saw them first. He shouted and Siu-li saw him and waved a gay pink handkerchief. She came toward him eagerly, the elderly secretary following her. Martin had not seen this twin sister of his all these years. He had thought of her much and though he had seen many pictures of her he was not quite prepared for this extremely pretty and poised young woman who put out her hand.

"Elder Brother!" she cried in a soft voice. He was older than she by two hours.

"Is this you, Siu-li?" he inquired, unbelieving.

"It is no other, certainly," she replied, smiling. "But here's Wang Ting, too."

Wang Ting came bowing and Martin bowed. He remembered with affection this man who had stood as his father's deputy as long as he could remember. That Wang Ting was here now meant that his father was not. He was disappointed, though he had known his father might not come to meet him. Still, after seven years, and he an only son—

"Is Father well?" he asked Siu-li.

He noticed the smallest of hesitations before she answered.

"Yes, he is well. Today it happens he has important business or he would have come."

Wang Ting cleared his throat. "Your father sent every message of welcome by me," he said solemnly. "And he says he hopes you will not delay. There are guests invited for a feast at seven, and it is now nearly half past five. You will want to rest and he will want a few moments at least with you alone."

Wang Ting stepped back, having done his duty.

"Thank you," Martin said courteously.

"Let's go home quickly," Siu-li said with an unexpected petulance. "Wang Ting, you see to his bags and trunks. We will go on."

Wang Ting bowed and took the checks that Martin handed to him. A few minutes later the brother and sister were sitting side by side in their father's car.

They said nothing for a short while. Each was shy of the other, now that they were alone. Though they were fully aware of their relation, still it remained true that they were a young man and a young woman, strange to each other. Then Martin forgot himself.

"I don't remember this road," he remarked. "I thought we used to go to the right."

"We always did until the Japanese came," Siu-li said. "Now we go this way so as to avoid their chief barracks."

"I see," Martin said. He knew that the Japanese had full possession of Peking. Even if his father and sister had not written him of it he would have known it from reading the newspapers in New York, where he had been a student. At first he had expected every letter to tell him that his family had moved away, but as time went on and this did not happen he began to believe that things had not changed so much as he had feared they would. Evidently it was still possible for proud Chinese like his father to live under a Japanese flag, although of course it would be only temporary. It was unthinkable that the Japanese would continue to rule in China. That was why he had come back to China with only a master's degree. His father had urged, indeed, had commanded him to remain abroad for two more years at least and if possible longer in order to get practical experience in his chosen field of metallurgy.

"China needs men of the highest training," his father had written.

But Martin, reading in the American newspapers about the way Japanese soldiers were behaving in his country, could not keep his blood calm enough to sit studying.

"I must come back and do what I can now against the enemy," he wrote his father. And without waiting for reply he had drawn his next term's expense money out of the bank and bought a ticket for China. He had expected questions and even trouble at the port; but when he had given his father's name there had been no trouble and the questions had ceased.

"Do the Japanese annoy you on the street?" he asked his sister now.

Again there was that faint but unmistakable hesitation in her answer. Then she said:

"Sometimes—no, not if they know who I am." Her face shadowed. "But I hate them!" she said in a low voice. "I want to avoid them!"

"Of course," he agreed. He was glad to avoid them, too, and he said nothing when the chauffeur drove slowly through small winding alleys instead of the wide main streets of the city.

When the car drew up finally before the gate of his father's home, his throat tightened. He was really home at last!

"It looks just the same," he said, gazing at it.

It was just the same, the wide wooden gates painted vermillion red and set in the thick brick wall and over the wall the old twin pomegranate trees of the entrance court.

"How the trees have grown!" he said.

"Seven years," Siu-li said smiling. "I've grown, too, and so have you."

"Yes," he said.

Then he saw something was changed after all. Instead of the one watchman he had been used to see at his father's gate, he now saw two soldiers, uniformed, their bayonets fixed. They presented arms smartly as he stepped from the car and he was embarrassed.

"What's this?" he whispered to Siu-li when he had returned their salute.

"Father has to have a bodyguard just now," she said in a voice whose quality confounded him. It was angry with scorn.

But she led the way quickly into the gate and there was no time for questions. The first courtyard was full of eager servants, waiting to welcome home the son of the house. Firecrackers exploded and banners waved. He had to speak to all the old ones and to acknowledge the bows of the new. Even his old wet nurse was there, come in from the country for this day. His mother had died at the birth of the twins, and while Siu-li her own nurse, Ling Ma had fed Martin and taken care of him when he was too big to suckle. Everyone had expected his father to take another wife but he had never done so.

"But where is Father?" he asked his sister when it was over at last.

"He seems not to have come home yet," she replied. She hesitated, then went on. "Why don't you go to your room and change your things? By then surely he will be back."

"I will," he replied.

They stood a moment, he feeling that she was about to speak of something. But she did not. She touched his hand merely.

"It is very good to have you home again," she said and left him.

His own room was not changed at all. Its wide paper-latticed window looked out into his own small courtyard. The bamboos, the pine, were the same. Bamboos attained their growth in a single year and seven years were nothing to the pine, already two centuries old.

"Japan and China," he thought, and was pleased with his comparison.

The door opened and Ling Ma came, her face all loving solicitude.

"Now, heart of my flesh, you are not to touch anything. I will unpack your garments and fold them away."

"Foreign suits must be hung, not folded, Ling Ma," he said.

"Then show me one and I will do the others," she said. "You must rest yourself, you must eat and sleep and play after all these years of study. You are too thin." She came close and searched his face. "You didn't take a foreign wife!"

Martin laughed at her. "No, no wife!"

She nodded her satisfaction. "Then we must see to it. I will talk with your father myself."

Martin sat down in his foreign easy chair. "I haven't seen my father yet," he said.

"Oh, he's busy—very busy—" Ling Ma said. She had her face deep in one of his trunks. He could only see her stout back.

"I never knew my father to be busy," he remarked. He could say things to Ling Ma that he could say to no one else.

"He's very busy now," Ling Ma's voice came out of the trunk.

A sudden thought struck him. He put it away and then returned to it. After all, it was only Ling Ma.

"He's not getting married again, is he?" The thought was repulsive, but his father was only fifty years old and it was possible.

"Don't ask me!" Ling Ma's voice was suddenly snappish. She came out of the trunk and her face was very red from bending so long. "Don't ask me anything, Young Master! I don't know anything. If anybody asks me anything about this house, I don't know. I live in the country now with my son and I only came back to welcome you home, heart of my body."

He was used to outbursts from Ling Ma, for she was a woman of impetuous temper. Now he hardly knew whether there was truth in his suspicion or whether she was angry because she had been treated in some way she considered unfair. Ling Ma had quarreled often over his father's decrees during his childhood, and it might be her old jealousy against authority over the child in her care.

"Did my father treat your unjustly?" he inquired.

She laughed loudly. "Me, little heart? No, I left this house of my own accord. He even invited me to stay and await your coming. But no, I would not. No, it was nothing he did to *me!*"

Ling Ma pursed her lips and looked solemn. He was about to put another question to her. Then he decided against it. He did not wish to resume with Ling Ma the old affectionate childish relationship that gave her power over him. He was a man, now. So he said a little coldly:

"That is well, for if he had not given you your due, I should have felt I ought to make amends."

She felt the difference in him and gave way to it at once. "From you I expect only what is good," she said, and then spoke no more, but crept about with her silent solid tread, putting his things right. Then she went away and he was alone.

The house was very still. He had not in years heard such stillness. New York was full of noise, and in its own way, so was the ocean. But this was the stillness of centuries. He felt it around him a protection of strength. What could the enemy do against a great, silent old country?

"They are like swallows attacking a snow-capped mountain," he thought proudly.

At that moment to his astonishment the door opened abruptly, and his father came in.

"Father!" he cried with joy.

"My son," his father replied. He came forward and seized Martin's two hands and held them closely and gazed into his face.

And Martin, receiving that earnest, questioning gaze, felt suddenly shy. Why had his father done so strange a thing as to come to him in his own room? It was not like the austere man he remembered so to step aside from custom. He had been prepared to go to his father when summoned, to stand while his father sat, to answer when he was questioned. But instead here his father was, an eager, even importunate look upon his aging face. He had aged very much. Martin drew back. Instantly his father loosed his hands and the look disappeared.

"Are you well?" he inquired.

"Quite well," Martin replied. He hurried on, anxious for talk. "I hope you are not angry that I disobeyed you, my father. I felt I must come home now — for two reasons. The first is that I want to be of what use I can against the enemy. The second is that I was honestly ashamed to be living abroad in ease and at study as though my country were not suffering."

His father stood looking at him. "I am not angry," he said. "It would be of little use if I were. This generation does what it pleases."

"No, Father, don't speak so," Martin cried. "It makes me feel you are angry!"

His father shook his head. "No, only certain of your misunderstanding," he said in a low voice.

"Father, how can you say that?" Martin demanded. "I am your son!"

But his father only gave him a melancholy smile. "We will see," he said gently. "Meanwhile, it is time for our guests." He glanced at his son's clothing. "What are you wearing?" he inquired.

"What do you wish?" Martin asked, surprised. He had imagined a dinner of old friends, informal and gay, and he had thought with pleasure of a soft silk robe, easy and cool, and which he had not been able to wear for a long time.

"Wear your formal foreign evening clothes," his father said. "And what badges have you? Put on the gold key the gave you, and any other thing you have."

He met his son's stare of astonishment. "I want to be proud of you before my—my friends," he said, and then looked at his watch. "It's late," he muttered and hurried away.

In his room alone Martin dressed himself carefully in his best, stiff shirt, silk vest, tailed coat. He had not worn them since the formal college banquet of his graduation day. He had thought then that he would never wear them again—certainly not in his father's home. More mystified than ever, he put on his Phi Beta Kappa key, and his gold signet ring, and his diamond-studded fraternity pins, one Greek letter and the other the honor society of his profession.

"I have nothing more," he thought. Then he remembered a small pin Siu-li had sent him once in play. It had been attached to the first page of a letter. It was made of silver and enameled in the design of the Chinese flag. Half in fun he took it from the box with his cuff links and pinned it to his lapel.

"Why not?" he thought. "I'm a good Chinese and I'll let the world know it."

He went out of his room, whistling an American tune under his breath. There was no one about, and he sauntered in the direction of the main hall. Then he heard voices and he hurried his steps slightly. It was half an hour beyond seven but he had not expected anyone before eight. If he knew his China no one came on time to a dinner. The noise now was that of many voices. It sounded as though everyone had come.

He drew aside the red satin curtain hanging in the door and looked.

The room was large, but there were many there, between thirty and forty, his eye guessed. And then he saw something else. He could not believe it, but it was true. Three-fourths of the guests were Japanese! Then his father saw him.

"Come in, my son," he said.

There was nothing for him to do except to obey.

"You should have warned me," he said to Siu-li.

He had come straight to her room after the interminable dinner was over.

"What do I know to tell you?" she retorted.

The years they had been parted were vanished. His anger and dismay had demanded frankness between them, and she had expected him. When he went to her court the light was shining like moonbeams through the opaqueness of the rice paper lattice, and he saw the shadow of her head bent over a book.

"You should have told me what people are saying," he replied.

"What are people saying except what they, too, do not know?" she retorted again.

"At least you should have told me that my father has Japanese friends," he said.

"But he has always had friends among foreigners in Peking," she said stubbornly. "And some have always been Japanese. The Baron Muraki has been his lifelong friend and you know it."

Yes, he knew it. When he was a little boy Baron Muraki, even then a kindly, aging man, used to bring him miniature rickshas and animals and tiny fish of gold-washed silver. Nevertheless he said, "No one can have Japanese friends now."

"I have told Father that, too," Siu-li said quietly.

"What did he say?" Martin demanded.

"That he had seen too many wars to allow them to change his friendships," she replied.

They looked at each other with the tragic and absolute despair of the young.

"It is such men who will lose our country for us," Martin cried, "and I shall tell him so!"

"You will tell Father that?" she cried.

"I'm not afraid of him, any more, not after tonight," he told her. "If you could have seen him, Siu-li, bowing to those strutting little men, the gold on their uniforms like scabs! And calling them carefully by their titles, General This and General That! And pressing the best of everything on them and watching them grow drunk as though they were doing him a favor. I could scarcely swallow, though I've been thinking for years of eating sharks fins again and spit-roasted duck!" His young face gloomed at her, and she cried:"

"Ah, it is hateful, but how can you say anything to Father?"

"I can," he retorted. "These are not the times of Confucius."

He strode away on this strength to his father's court. But it was now very late. The rooms were dark around the large silent court where his father lived so much alone. He hesitated and knew he dared not knock in spite of his angry courage.

"I will wait until tomorrow," he thought, and tiptoed away. It would be all the better to wait, he told himself, back in his own room He could speak calmly and reasonably in the morning. After all, his father was an old man and it was possible that he did not know what he was doing. It was hard to imagine that the keen eyes of his father did not see all that went on before them, but the time must come for him to fail as for all men. He sighed, tried to sleep, and could not until it was nearly dawn. Then he slept long and extravagantly, and it was noon when he was awakened by Wang Ting, standing by his bed.

"Your father commands your presence," Wang Ting said.

And out of old habit Martin leaped to his feet.

What he must remember, he told himself an hour later, in his father's study was that old bonds were broken between a man and his son. What the revolution had begun this war had finished. Everywhere young men and women were telling their parents that their country must come first. "Patriotism is higher than filial duty," they were telling old people who felt themselves deserted.

He struggled against the bonds still strong between himself and this tall, slender, silk-robed man. It was hard to believe so dignified a gentleman had been the one he had watched last night. When Martin thought of this his will hardened. His father had been that man, nevertheless.

"Sit down, my son," his father told him.

He sat down, not cornerwise as he had been taught to sit in an elder's presence but as one man sits in the presence of another. If his father noticed this, he made no sign of it.

"There are many things between us for talk," his father said. "And yesterday I was busy."

"Your time is no longer your own," Martin said boldly.

His father threw him a sharp look. "It is true I am busy," he said smoothly. Something crept over his face like a veil, leaving it expressionless. Against it Martin suddenly rebelled. The last seven years had been spent among frank and impulsive foreigners, and he would not return to careful speech.

"I shall speak plainly," he told his father. "I was surprised to see our enemies in this house."

"Baron Muraki—" his father began.

But Martin interrupted him. "The Baron was only one of nearly a score."

The look on his father's face grew closer.

"Do you accuse me?" he asked gently.

"I do," Martin said. His eyes were steady upon his father's face. But his father's eyes did not turn either.

"Does it occur to you that I may have my reasons?" he asked.

"There can be no reason, now," Martin declared. Small things he had forgotten were coming back to him. In New York a Chinese classmate had suddenly declined further friendship with him. When Martin pressed him one day with an invitation the young man had said curtly, before he turned away:

"My father does not know your father."

It had seemed foolish then to give as cause against friendship that a Chinese merchant in New York had not known a Chinese gentleman in Peking.

"That can scarcely be expected," Martin had said haughtily and thereafter had ignored the man. Now he understood.

And Ling Ma last night—now he understood her hints.

"Do you know, Father, what people are saying about you?" he demanded.

"I have never known what they say, because I have not cared," his father said calmly.

"You must care now—they are saying you are a friend of the Japanese." He watched his father's face. It did not change.

"I have always had my friends among the Japanese," he said.

"They are saying you are a traitor," Martin rose to his feet.

His father's face did not quiver. "Do you believe them?" he asked.

Martin saw curiosity in his look—nothing else. He was suddenly full of angry certainty. Nobody, he thought, had ever known his father well. He had come and gone in this house, a cold and dignified figure whom they had all feared.

"I do not know what to believe," he said.

There was a long pause, then his father spoke:

"You will believe what you want to believe," he said. "That is the habit of the young."

"And is that all you will say?" Martin demanded.

"That is all," his father replied.

They were both very angry, and Martin was the more angry because he was less able to control himself than his father.

"I cannot stay in a house where enemies are accepted as friends," he said proudly.

"Do you mean my house?" his father inquired.

His blandness drove Martin to his last step.

"Yes," he said.

He rushed from the room. He had exiled himself the day after he had come home. Where now could he go? Siu-li must know. She must help him. He went to find her. She was in her courtyard sprinkling small gray orchids in the rocks, her fingers dipping in and out of a pewter bowl she held.

"I have told Father I cannot stay," he said to her.

She turned, and the bowl dropped from her hand.

"You have quarreled with him!"

"Yes—forever," he said. "And you must come, too, Siu-li. Only traitors can live in this house. You must come!" he insisted when he saw her face. "I can't leave you if Japanese men are to be allowed to come and go here. But where shall we go?"

She stooped and picked up the bowl.

"I have it already long planned," she said softly. She glanced about the small courtyard. "Twice—I didn't know whether I could stay. There is an old general—did you see him last night? The one with the small white mustache?"

"Yes," he said, and his gorge rose.

"Well, that one—once he saw me, and he asked for me to be brought in." Disgust was dark upon her face.

"Did Father send for you?" Martin cried.

"Yes—I didn't know why, or I would not have gone. When I entered the main hall the old general was there."

"But—but—what did Father say?" Martin was bewildered. This was not like father!

"He said he thought modern young women could take care of themselves," Siu-li said. A slight pink rose in her cheeks and she went on. "The truth is we had quarreled the day before, Father and I. He did not want me to go to a dance at the Grand Hotel. I wanted to go and I went. So perhaps he was punishing me."

"It was not suitable punishment," Martin cried.

They stood full of a mutual anger.

"We must go," he repeated.

"It could be to the northwest," she said. "I have a friend who knows the way—a girl—soldier."

"Communist?" he asked.

"Guerilla," she amended.

"Where?"

"I can send her a message for tonight. She comes and goes," Siu-li replied. "She is here now in the city. When she goes back we can go with her. She has ways."

He thought hard for a moment. Into the northwest! It was the birthplace of bandits and warlords in the old days, the stronghold of Communists in the new. He had seen men from the northwest, camel drivers and traveling merchants, soldiers and wandering priests. They spoke with a burr upon their tongues that was foreign to him and they were more foreign to him than the Americans among whom he had lived. And he was loath to leave this home to which he had looked with longing all his years away from it. Life in Peking was easy and beautiful.

"But not now," he thought; and aloud he said, "It may as well be there as anywhere."

Siu-li wavered one moment before she spoke, but only one.

"I also," she said firmly. She looked down and saw the pewter bowl in her hand and in a gesture of recklessness she lifted it up and threw it over the wall.

He was forever after to divide his life into two parts, that before he knew Meng-an, and all that which came to him afterwards. The question which he put to himself often was why he did not at once see her for what she was. But he did not. On the day on which he and Siu-li left their home with her, he saw his sister's friend as a small inconspicuous creature, so like a young boy in her peasant garb that it took faith to believe her a girl. He had seen plenty of girls in America, athletic girls, boyish girls, strongbodied and clear-eyed girls. But one always knew they were girls. Meng-an was without sex, he thought, looking at her again and again, even that first day.

"Though why did I look at her so often?" he inquired of memory.

She was not beautiful. An earnest face, a square, an unchanging mouth with small full lips, eyes very black and white, short shining black hair, skin as brown as a peasant's and a slim breastless body, carried like the soldier she was, though she wore no uniform now. He said for days of hard journeying, always westward, that there was no allure in this little creature. She seldom talked and when she did she seemed purposely brusque and plain. But though she was small, she was merciless in her strength. She could walk endlessly and ride anything of a beast. Once she leaped astride a farmer's ox as it pulled a wooden cart. And she had refused the motorcar Siu-li had suggested bringing the day they started.

"Why trouble ourselves with a machine we can use only for a few miles?" she said scornfully.

He did not at that moment realize all that her words meant. They had left home quite openly one clear summer's day. Each carried a knapsack and no more. Their father never rose until noon, and Wang Ting meeting them at the gate smiled and bowed and said, as he hurried on:

"You have a lucky day for your holiday."

They had looked at each other and smiled behind his back.

"A long holiday," Martin had said.

They had not walked more than half a day before Siu-li was exhausted. The sun grew hot. Meng-an, springing along, her cloth shoes silent in the dust, was merciful.

"You will be able to walk more tomorrow," she said.

She kept watching for a vehicle and in a little while she stopped a farmer returning from market with his wheelbarrow empty and asked for a ride. He was willing enough, but when Meng-an bade Siu-li seat herself he was less willing.

"I thought it was to be you, girl soldier," he complained.

"It is the same—she is my friend," Meng-an replied calmly, and so the farmer pushed Siu-li as far as he was going.

"Why was he willing for you?" Martin inquired, curious to know this small creature's power.

"He knows we work for them," Meng-an answered vaguely. "And I pass here often."

Everywhere it was the same. With an assurance that might have been impudent in another, Meng-an asked and was given. Village bakers gave her bread, at teashops she was given a pot of tea, and anywhere a small traveling restaurant keeper stirred up a bowl of noodles and vegetable oil and shook his head when she held out the cash.

"We all work for the country," he would say, a little pompously.

They depended on Meng-an for everything and the more as they came into the northwest where she knew all and they knew nothing. By now Siu-li wore man's clothing that she might walk more freely, and Martin wore peasant's garments, and Meng-an wore the ragged boy's clothing that she always put on when she entered land held by the enemy. They walked until noon, ate, slept by the roadside, and walked again until midnight. This they did day after day until it became the habit of their lives. Every other thing they had once done now grew dreamlike in their memories.

"I wonder if Father minds that we are gone?" Siu-li said one day as they rested for a moment.

"He knows why we went," Martin replied.

Meng-an's eyes were upon the bare and distant hills.

"I have not seen my parents for six years," she said suddenly.

"Do you long for them?" Siu-li asked.

"Sometimes," Meng-an said. "Then I remember that if I return to them I return to all the old life—marriage to a man I do not know, a courtyard with the gates locked. And then I get up and go on."

She had never said so much. There was a flicker in her eyes as she spoke but no more. But Martin thought to himself that this small creature had felt things that he did not know.

"Were you early betrothed?" he asked.

She nodded, but did not speak, and he could not for decency ask again.

All these days they had been walking through enemy-held country. Had they been without Meng-an they would have been stopped before this by enemy soldiers. But Meng-an knew how to come and go as a mouse does in a crowded house. Everywhere she was told by someone, a beggar, a farmer, a priest, if there were enemy soldiers near, and then she led them differently, by secret devious ways of her own. Never once did they meet the enemy face-to-face.

"Though sometimes I do," she told them.

"What then?" Martin asked. He watched her while she answered. Upon that small inscrutable face he was beginning to discern changes, slight to an unseeing eye but vivid to him. This girl could feel.

"I always pretend to be a fool," she said. "Like this—"

By some trick she threw her lower jaw crooked and crossed her eyes and looked an idiot. She straightened herself again.

"Then they let me pass."

"I should think so," Siu-li said laughing.

But Martin said nothing. At this moment he was not sure whether a girl should be like this Meng-an. There she sat, on a side of the dusty road where they had stopped for a rest. Her hair was brown with dust, and dust lay in shadows on her face.

"She is not beautiful," he thought, "though brave."

And then that night they passed out of enemy-held country and into their own. He could feel the difference, or thought he could, even in the twilight air. Certainly people were more free in their talk and their laugh-

ter at the inn where they lodged, and there was much boasting of how
this one and that had crept in and out of the enemy line. But Meng-an
was the most changed of all. When they reached the inn she went into
one room a while. A little later she came out for the evening meal. Martin
had washed himself and changed his garments. But he was not prepared
for what he now saw. A slim young soldier came out of the room Siu-li
and Meng-an shared, a soldier in a clean khaki uniform, belted and
buttoned and with a small pistol at the waist. It was Meng-an. When she
saw him she saluted and gave him the smallest of smiles. It was the first
she had ever given him.

"You must go to our general," Meng-an told him. Three days more had
brought them to the stronghold of this Chinese army to which she belonged. For three days they had walked among a tranquil people, tilling
and working the land as though war were in another world. Night brought
them to the camp itself, where he would go to the men's division and
Siu-li and Meng-an to the women's. They halted at the gate of the temple
compound where guards stood. Once inside they must part. Thus Meng-
an had paused to speak.

"I will see him tonight," she went on, "and when I have given him
my secret messages from the old city, I will tell him of you. He will be
glad, for he needs men like you."

Now Martin did not want to part from her.

"When shall we see each other?" he said boldly.

"The flicker in her eyes he could discern but not its meaning. Was it
feeling for him or against him? He did not know.

"There are many meetings for us all," she said, and whether it was
promise or evasion he still did not know. And she gave him no time to
think. She led the way inside the gate and they were parted. He was given
food and a bed and by dark he slept as all slept, because light at night
meant oil and oil was money, and money must be spent on bullets for
the enemy.

At dawn he rose, called by a bugle, and after food Martin was summoned by a young man so carelessly clothed as a soldier that on the upper
part of him he wore a farmer's coat.

"Are you the son of Liu Ming Chen?" he inquired abruptly of Martin.

"How do you know my father's name?" Martin asked.

"We all know it," the man replied.

Martin was silenced by fear. Why should all here know the name of
his quiet scholar father in Peking except now as a traitor? He said nothing.

"The general calls you," the man said. "Follow me."

Without hesitation Martin followed and found himself in the doorway of the cave house where the general lived at the back of the temple as many did here, among these high barren mountains. But this room was comfortable with furniture and the floor was rock swept clean. The general was not a fat old man but a young thin-bodied man in faded uniform. No one could have said he was anything more than another, except agile and clever, relentless if he were an enemy.

"One tells me you know metals," he said to Martin without greeting.

That one, Martin knew, was Meng-an. He wondered jealously if she knew this man well and if they were friends. He had missed her already, for when he woke he wondered if today he would see her and how and when.

"It is true," he replied.

The young general looked at him shrewdly.

"You left your father," he said.

"Yes," Martin said. The man knew that!

"Many leave their parents these days," the general said gravely. "Once when I was a child I was sent to a Christian school. In their sacred book I found one day by chance words like this: 'And a man's foes shall be they of his own household.' I who had been taught the doctrine of Wu Wei, I thought, 'How evil are these Christians not to know filial duty!' But the days are come." He paused a second, "I, too, left my parents. We must seek a new foundation for the state, lest we be lost."

The general's accent was not that of a peasant.

"Did you go abroad?" Martin asked.

"Yes—who told you?" the general replied.

"No one—but where?" Martin asked again.

"To Harvard and to Leipzig," the general said.

"And you are here," Martin said. It was wonder enough,

"I would be nowhere else," the general said. He hesitated a moment, and then went on. "Out of these inner regions will come those who will take back the land."

"But do these people know they are being attacked?" Martin asked. "They are so calm and they work in their fields as they always have."

"By day," the general broke in. "By night they put down their hoes and take their guns. But by what good luck you came I cannot say. We lack iron, and there is ore in these hills. The rocks shine when they are split. Is that iron? If it is, I will set about mining it out. It may be silver—and it is not so quickly useful. Do you see your task?"

"Yes," Martin said. He was looking at the seamed side of the cave as he answered. In the rocks was his task. He must find iron to make bullets for the enemy.

"Have you any message for your father?" the general asked abruptly. "Meng-an will start for Peking tonight."

"She goes back?" Martin cried.

"It is her work—to slip between the enemy armies and find out everything and bring me word."

"She told you of my father," Martin said.

The general nodded.

"No, I have no message for him," Martin said.

The general nodded again. "Then you may go," he told him.

He did not see Meng-an again. When he reached his tent six men were waiting. When they saw him they saluted.

"We are to go with you into the hills," they said.

By some means they had with them the few tools he needed—pick-axes, baskets for rock fragments, materials for mapping, and rolls of bedding.

"At once?" he asked.

"It is so ordered," they replied.

"But I must see someone before I go," he protested.

"We will wait a few minutes," a soldier said, "at your command."

"Let it not be longer, sir," another said. "The general does not like delay."

No, he would not, Martin knew, thinking of that firm young figure. He had turned away and at the door of the women's barracks he asked the girl soldier on guard for Siu-li, and was told to wait.

She came a few moments later and quickly he told her his orders.

"And you? he asked.

"I am to go into training, merely," she said.

"And Meng-an?" he asked, wanting only to hear of her and knowing very well that he knew more than Siu-li did.

"I have not seen her," Siu-li replied.

He knew he should tell nothing he had been told and yet he wanted some communication with that small creature slipping her lonely way among the enemy. He said in a low voice, too low for the waiting guard to hear:

"If you see her today, tell her I said to take care for herself as she goes." And then when he saw the astonishment in Siu-li's eyes he added quickly, "She is more value than you know—to the cause, I mean."

But Siu-li was shrewd with the shrewdness of a woman.

"I was about to ask you now that we are here if you regret coming, but I think I need not," she said.

He laughed sheepishly, feeling himself grow red.

"No, you need not," he agreed. "I am not sorry."

Weeks passed him, and he spent them day upon day in searching the barren hills. They were not barren, he was beginning to discover. Under their sandy tawny surfaces there was rock and in the seams of the rock minerals. He walked up the steep beds of mountain streams, his eyes upon every glint and glitter. The men with him were well chosen, for they were men who belonged to the hills, who had spent their youth washing the streams for silver.

"But is there iron?" he asked them as he asked the hills themselves.

"That we don't know, for we never looked for it when there was silver," they said.

In their fashion they had mined some parts of the hills, and they led him to shallow pits they had dug. These he tapped and examined and tested the fragments he chose. There was silver everywhere, but he could not find iron.

"We may have to make our bullets of silver," he thought grimly.

The strange hills surrounded him, and silence was their atmosphere. There seemed no life in them, and yet sometimes he came upon a monastery built out of sandy rock and seeming in its shape and color so like a cliff that only a gate told the difference. Inside the priests lived, silent so long that they could scarcely speak when he spoke, men whom the mountain winds had dried and beaten upon and bleached until they too were sand-colored. And yet everyone of them when he told them his task, were eager to help him and to show him certain dark ledges they had seen. Everyone of them knew that they had an enemy.

Everywhere they knew. In the night under the endless clear skies and beneath the sharp stars he thought of those who were farmers by day and soldiers by night, and he thought of priests who wanted no peace, and of his sister, who had been so tenderly reared, learning to march long hours and to fire a gun, and most of all and longest he thought of Meng-an making her lonely way in and out among the enemy.

"She has the hardest and most dangerous work of us all," he thought. When he thought of this his bitterness against his father heaped itself up with gall. "He betrays every one of us," he thought.

The filial piety he had been taught he put from him forever, that ancient teaching which had tied together the generations of his people.

"I am no more his son," he thought. And he thought, "We must build a new country, and every generation must be its own lawmaker."

"There is no iron," he told the general.

"There must be," the general said. "Go back."

The hills were bitterly cold now with autumn. The foolish silver was rich everywhere. But the hills held nothing more. He had stayed a month, and then the cold rain had driven him down from the summit. And then it had seemed he must make report of having found nothing. And he knew, too—the long silent nights and the hot moons had told him—that he longed to see Meng-an. Had she come and gone safely? He must know or thought he must. And so he had come down. He had gone at once to Siu-li. But Siu-li was not there. She had been sent the day before with her regiment to a village to the east to make forays by night against an enemy garrison. He was sick with alarm when he heard it, and then dismayed because since she was gone there was no one he could ask of Meng-an. Everyone went about his business here, and it was no one's business to speak of Meng-an. And he had had to go then to the general.

"Go back," the general said now.

And against his look there was no hope of refusal. Besides how could he say, "I cannot, until I have seen a certain woman," and how could he even say, "I must hear first if Meng-an is safe?"

The general saw his hesitation. "We are still at war," he said. "Why you delay?"

"I do not," Martin said doggedly.

He went back that same day.

He had lived in the hills so long now that when he thought of cities and of people they were words and nothing more. Had he once seen ships and trains and traveled upon them? Even his memories of them were gone. He had for companions these men as dogged as himself and for his strength his own determination that if there was iron in these hills he would find it. And if he had needed a spur to prod him he had it. One day when in an October as cold as winter where he was, he sat on a rock near a summit eating his bread and salt fish, at noon, he saw even there an airplane. It flew well above the mountain top and yet close enough for him to see it. It was an enemy plane! He could see its markings clearly above him as he looked up at it. It sank a little as though it saw him, then rose and sped on. An enemy plane over these far, inner mountains! He swallowed his food quickly and called his men. They were eating fifty feet below him in a shallow valley. He had climbed out of it to see the hills while he ate.

"Come on!" he cried, and when they were come he said, "We must make haste if the enemy has flown as far as this."

They had worked longer after that, and every day they searched the skies. There were no planes for ten days more, and then eleven planes flew over them like wild geese.

That was the day he found iron. He found it early in the morning, low, near the base of the peak upon which he had spent uselessly nearly fifteen days. He had gone too high. The iron was old, and aeons had driven the deposits deep into the bowels of the mountains.

"Have I been looking too high, everywhere?" he asked himself.

He was so excited by this possible thing that he went no higher. He covered half the base of the mountain by noon and in seven places he found signs of iron, whether it was seven different places or all one great rich vein he did not know. But when he sat down at noon, he ate his bread in such excitement that he could scarcely swallow.

Then it was he heard the planes, and looking up he saw their geeselike passage. The sight might only yesterday have filled him with despair. But today he shook his fist at them and with his mouth filled with bread he shouted:

"We have our bullets for you!"

Now he could go back with good news. He was even glad that he had found iron in autumn instead of spring. Soon it would be too cold for the enemy planes to fly over the inland, and during the winter months the mines could be planned and made ready. He had long talks about machinery with his men. When he thought of machinery for mines he was troubled. How could they construct and haul and place those great masses? But these men had been miners without such aid. Bamboo and ropes and wooden buckets were their utensils, and Martin listened to them. "A little more than they have had and it will be much," he thought as they went on.

Everywhere through the countryside there were signs of autumn. The harvests were good, and the farmers grew bold to reap them, because few airplanes came now to bomb.

"In the summer we spend half the day in our bomb huts," they told Martin. "Well, it's cool there!" they said, grinning with mischief. "Well, we have had bandits of many kinds," another said. Wherever he went. there was no talk of hardship or surrender, only of how work could be done, whether the enemy came or not.

"I wish my father could be here," he thought. "If he saw these people, could he still betray them?"

The thought of his father was like a sore in his heart. Whatever he did, he thought, it would not be enough to atone for his father. And when he thought of Meng-an he asked himself what right he had, the son of a traitor, to think of her.

In this mood he walked the miles back to the encampment and, without asking of his sister or Meng-an, he went, dusty as he was, to report to the general. In his hand he carried the fragments of rock and he laid them upon the table.

"I have found iron," he said simply, "and plenty of it." The news was enough of itself.

"The general took up the rocks as though they were gold.

"Better than gold," he said. And then when he had examined them he looked up at Martin. "When can you go back?" he asked.

"Today, if you bid me," Martin replied steadily.

But the general laughed. "Now you are taught," he said. "It is the answer I wanted. But you shall not go today. We must make our plans."

"There is not much time before winter comes down," Martin said doggedly.

"Not much, but a day or two," the general said, "and that is long enough for everything. I have news for you. Do you remember my little spy?"

"Meng-an?" Her name flew out of Martin's mouth like a bird from a cage.

The general nodded. "How did you know her name?" he asked, surprised.

"She brought my sister and me here," Martin said.

"Do you have a sister?" the general demanded of him. "And if you have, why did you not tell me?"

"There was no need," Martin said.

But the general struck a bell on his table. "She must come here, too," he said. "This news is for both of your father's children."

A soldier appeared.

"Go and fetch—what is her name?"

"Siu-li," Martin said. "Of the Third Regiment."

"Surname Liu, name Siu-li, of the Third Regiment," the general ordered. "And tell Meng-an to come also."

"So!" the soldier cried as he had been taught, and saluting he hurried away.

At the mention of his father Martin was afraid. What would the general call good news except that a traitor had been killed? If this was the news he must warn Siu-li first. They must show no grief. He thought quickly.

"Sir," he asked, "may I speak first with my sister? If something has befallen our father, it will be better to prepare her for it."

"Nothing has befallen him," the general replied. He was turning the fragments of rocks over in his hands, dreaming of the precious stuff they held.

So there was nothing to do except to wait.

"Sit down," the general said and he sat down. It was very hard to wait. The general was looking at the rock now through a small hand microscope.

Then in a while they heard the light quick tread of feet trained to march, the feet of girl soldiers. The general put down his microscope and looked up. The door curtains opened. Two straight slender girls in uniform stood there. They saluted and stood at attention, Meng-an and Siu-li. Martin smiled at Siu-li and looked at Meng-an. His heart rose on a great wave of pride. These two girls in the old days would have been sheltered, helpless creatures behind a courtyard wall; Siu-li even a few months ago had been in her way useless.

"Is this your sister?" the general asked of Martin, but gazing at Siu-li.

"It is she," Martin said, rising to his feet.

"Be at ease, all of you," the general said. He seemed to have forgotten why he had called Meng-an here. "Be seated," he told Siu-li, without taking his eyes from her face. "I have not seen you before," he said.

Siu-li blushed a little. The uniform, her straight-cut hair, the pistol at her belt, her feet in hard leather shoes, none of these could hide what she was, a soft-eyed girl. Those large soft eyes she now turned upon the young general as full of coquetry as though she wore a silk robe and had jewels in her hair.

"I did not know you wished it," she said demurely.

"But I do," the general said.

Meng-an looked at Martin. In her eyes he saw that flickering—it was laughter, surely. He smiled to answer it. It was pleasant to communicate thus with her over those other two. Then Meng-an coughed a small dry cough, and the general glanced at her and remembered.

"Ah, you also," he said, but his voice was very different to her. "Yes, and now repeat what you told me. Who told you that the enemy is about to march southward and how we can surprise that march?"

"Wang Ting," Meng-an replied.

"Wang Ting!" Siu-li cried. "But he is my father's secretary!"

Meng-an did not turn her head. She continued to make report, her eyes upon the general's face. "He is sent by his master. Of himself he knows nothing, but his master is in a position to know much and will be as long as his life is spared by the enemy. If they find out he will die. But until that time, I go to a certain small teashop and there I can be told."

All this Meng-an said in her even voice as though what she said was nothing.

"If I had known there was also you," the general said to Siu-li as though she were the only one in the room, "I would have told you at once what your father was. He has been for us since the city fell. Why do you think this little spy comes and goes except to bring me news from your father?"

Now Siu-li turned upon Meng-an. "And you did not tell me!"

"How did I know what you thought of your father?" Meng-an retorted. "And I have my orders against talk about him with anyone," she added.

"And you," the general said to Martin, "you I wanted to try, to see if you were fit to be your father's son. When you did not give up until you found the iron we need, I said, 'He is fit.'"

"You know I doubted my father?" Martin asked slowly.

"Your father begged me in a letter to tell you what he was, when I saw the time was right," the general replied.

They sat, these impetuous two, the modern son and daughter of an old Confucian scholar, and humbled themselves in their knowledge. Then suddenly Siu-li began to weep. She turned to Martin.

"We—we were very unjust!" she whispered.

"Yes," Martin said in a daze, "yes, we were." He thought of his old father in the midst of the comings and goings of the enemy in his house, holding his life as lightly as a toy in his hands, and he cleared his throat. "I wish we could tell him so," he said.

"I will tell him," Meng-an said calmly.

"Don't cry!" the general said suddenly to Siu-li.

She looked at him, her great eyes dewy with tears and very beautiful.

"How can I help it?" she said piteously. "I have been a wicked daughter. I ought to have known my father couldn't—be what we thought he was!"

"I say you are not to weep any more!" the general shouted. "I cannot bear it," he added in a gentler voice.

And then Martin felt his own eyes caught by someone's gaze, and looked up, and there were Meng-an's eyes holding his, and this time it was as though their hands clasped. And suddenly his heart inquired, "Is there any reason now?" and then answered itself, "There is no reason."

"Now this is all settled," the general said hastily, "and it is time we went back to our work." His eyes took leave of Siu-li's soft black ones, though unwillingly. "Let us proceed," he said sharply. "Soldiers, attention!"

Martin rose, Siu-li and Meng-an leaped to their feet, saluted, wheeled, and marched out.

The general stared after them and sighed. Then he smiled at Martin.

"You are in love with that little spy of mine," he said.

"How—who—?" Martin stammered.

"Ah, I saw it," the general said calmly. "Well, why not? Everything must go on the same in wartime. Well, you may have my little spy. Tell her so. But she must go on workng. We must all go on working."

"Yes, sir," Martin said. He was dazed with the general's calmness over the most enormous thing in the world. Then even as he looked at the general he saw a strange thing happening. Over that firm stern young face he saw a soft sheepish smile appear that turned the general at once into an ordinary young man such as may be seen any spring day in any country.

"Your sister has very fine eyes," he said abruptly.

"They have been so considered," Martin replied.

The general looked startled. "I suppose so," he said unwillingly. He reflected a moment, still staring at Martin without seeing him.

"Why not?" he demanded after a moment.

"Why not, indeed?" Martin replied, "As you said, sir, even in war everything must go on as usual."

They looked at each other for the least part of a moment longer and suddenly they laughed, and then, sharing this laughter in their youth like a cup of wine between them, they laughed again for pure pleasure.

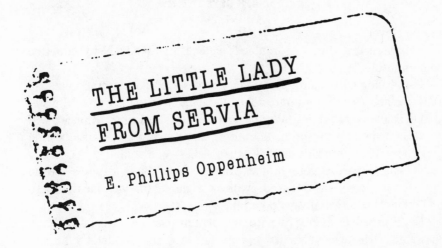

THE LITTLE LADY FROM SERVIA

E. Phillips Oppenheim

WESTWARD SPED THE little electric brougham, driven without regard to police regulations or any rule of the road: silent and swift, wholly regardless of other vehicles—as though, indeed, its occupants were assuming to themselves the rights of Royalty. Inside, Peter Ruff, a little breathless, was leaning forward, tying his white cravat with the aid of the little polished mirror set in the middle of the dark green cushions. At his right hand was Lady Mary, watching his proceedings with an air of agonised impatience.

"Let me tell you—" she begged.

"Kindly wait till I have tied this and put my studs in," Peter Ruff interrupted. "It is impossible for me to arrive at a ball in this condition, and I cannot give my whole attention to more than one thing at a time."

"We shall be there in five minutes!" she exclaimed. "What is the good, unless you understand, of you coming at all?"

Peter Ruff surveyed his tie critically. Fortunately, it pleased him. He began to press the studs into their places with firm fingers. Around them surged the traffic of Piccadilly; in front, the gleaming arc of lights around Hyde Park Corner. They had several narrow escapes. Once the brougham swayed dangerously as they cut in on the wrong side of an island lamppost. A policeman shouted after them, another held up his hand—the driver of the brougham took no notice.

"I am ready," Peter Ruff said, quietly.

"My younger brother—Maurice," she began, breathlessly—"you've never met him, I know, but you've heard me speak of him. He is private secretary to Sir James Wentley—"

"Minister for Foreign Affairs?" Ruff asked, swiftly.

"Yes! Maurice wants to go in for the Diplomatic Service. He is a dear, and so clever!"

"Is it Maurice who is in trouble?" Peter Ruff asked. "Why didn't he come himself?"

"I am trying to explain," Lady Mary protested. "This afternoon he had an important paper to turn into cipher and hand over to the Prime Minister at the Duchess of Montford's dance tonight. The Prime Minister will arrive in a motorcar from the country at about two o'clock and the first thing he will ask for will be that paper. It has been stolen!"

"At what time did your brother finish copying it, and when did he discover its loss?" Ruff asked, with a slight air of weariness. These preliminary inquiries always bored him.

"He finished it in his own rooms at half-past seven," Lady Mary answered. "He discovered its loss at eleven o'clock—directly he had arrived at the ball."

"Why didn't he come to me himself?" Peter Ruff asked. "I like to have these particulars at first hand."

"He is in attendance upon Sir James at the ball," Lady Mary answered. "There is trouble in the East, as you know, and Sir James is expecting dispatches tonight. Maurice is not allowed to leave."

"Has he told Sir James yet?"

"He had not when I left," Lady Mary answered. "If he is forced to do so, it will be ruin! Mr. Ruff, you must help us. Maurice is such a dear, but a mistake like this, at the very beginning of his career, would be fatal. Here we are. That is my brother waiting just inside the hall."

A young man came up to them in the vestibule. He was somewhat pale, but otherwise perfectly self-possesed. From the shine of his glossy black hair to the tips of his patent boots he was, in appearance, everything that a young Englishman of birth and athletic tastes could hope to be. Peter Ruff liked the look of him. He waited for no introduction, but laid his hand at once upon the young man's shoulder.

"Between seven-thirty and arriving here," he said, drawing him on one side—"quick! Tell me, whom did you see? What opportunities were there of stealing the paper, and by whom?"

"I finished it at five and twenty past seven," the young man said, "sealed it in an official envelope, and stood it up on my desk by the side of my coat and hat and muffler, which my servant had laid there, ready for me to put on. My bedroom opens out from my sitting room. While I was dressing, two men called for me—Paul Jermyn and Count von Hern. They walked through to my bedroom first, and then sat together in the sitting room until I came out. The door was wide open and we talked all the time."

"They called accidentally?" Peter Ruff asked.

"No—by appointment," the young man replied. "We were all coming on here to the dance, and we had agreed to dine together first at the Savoy."

"You say that you left the paper on your desk with your coat and hat?" Peter Ruff asked. "Was it there when you came out?"

"Apparently so," the young man answered. "It seemed to be standing in exactly the same place as where I had left it. I put it into my breast pocket, and it was only when I arrived here that I fancied the envelope seemed lighter. I went off by myself and tore it open. There was nothing inside but half a newspaper!"

"What about the envelope?" Peter Ruff asked. "That must have been the same sort of one as you had used or you would have noticed it?"

"It was," the Honorable Maurice answered.

"It was a sort which you kept in your room?"

"Yes!" the young man admitted.

"The packet was changed, then, by some one in your room, or some one who had access to it," Peter Ruff said. "How about your servant?"

"It was his evening off. I let him put out my things and go at seven o'clock."

"You must tell me the nature of the contents of the packet," Peter Ruff declared. "Don't hesitate. You must do it. Remember the alternative."

The young man did hesitate for several moments, but a glance into his sister's appealing face decided him.

"It was our official reply to a secret communication from Russia respecting—a certain matter in the Balkans."

Peter Ruff nodded.

"Where is Count von Hern?" he asked abruptly.

"Inside, dancing."

"I must use a telephone at once," Peter Ruff said. "Ask one of the servants here where I can find one."

Peter Ruff was conducted to a gloomy waiting room, on the table of which stood a small telephone instrument. He closed the door, but he was absent for only a few minutes. When he rejoined Lady Mary and her brother they were talking together in agitated whispers. The latter turned towards him at once.

"Do you mean that you suspect Count von Hern?" he asked, doubtfully. "He is a friend of the Danish Minister's, and every one says that he's such a good chap. He doesn't seem to take the slightest interest in politics—spends nearly all his time hunting or playing polo."

"I don't suspect any one," Peter Ruff answered. "I only know that

Count von Hern is an Austrian spy, and that he took your paper! Has he been out of your sight at all since you rejoined him in the sitting room? I mean to say—had he any opportunity of leaving you during the time you were dining together, or did he make any calls *en route*, either on the way to the Savoy or from the Savoy here?"

The young man shook his head.

"He has not been out of my sight for a second."

"Who is the other man—Jermyn?" Peter Ruff asked. "I never heard of him."

"An American—cousin of the Duchess. He could not have had the slightest interest in the affair."

"Please take me into the ballroom," Peter Ruff said to Lady Mary. Your brother had better not come with us. I want to be as near the Count von Hern as possible."

They passed into the crowded rooms, unnoticed, purposely avoiding the little space where the Duchess was still receiving the latecomers among her guests. They found progress difficult, and Lady Mary felt her heart sink as she glanced at the little jeweled watch which hung from her wrist. Suddenly Peter Ruff came to a standstill.

"Don't look for a moment," he said, "but tell me as soon as you can—who is that tall young man, like a Goliath, talking to the little dark woman? You see whom I mean?"

Lady Mary nodded, and they passed on. In a moment or two she answered him.

"How strange that you should ask!" she whispered in his ear. "That is Mr. Jermyn."

They were on the outskirts now of the ballroom itself. One of Lady Mary's partners came up with an open programme and a face full of reproach.

"Do please forgive me, Captain Henderson," Lady Mary begged. "I have hurt my foot, and I am not dancing any more."

"But surely I was to take you in to supper?" the young officer protested, good-humoredly. "Don't tell me that you are going to cut that?"

"I am going to cut everything tonight with everybody," Lady Mary said. "Please forgive me. Come to tea tomorrow and I'll explain."

The young man bowed, and, with a curious glance at Ruff, accepted his dismissal. Another partner was simply waved away.

"Please turn round and come back," Peter Ruff said. "I want to see those two again."

"But we haven't found Count von Hern yet," she protested. "Surely that is more important, is it not? I believe that I saw him dancing just now—there, with the tall girl in yellow."

"Never mind about him, for the moment," Ruff answered. "Walk down this corridor with me. Do you mind talking all the time, please? It will sound more natural, and I want to listen."

The young American and his partner had found a more retired seat now, about three quarters of the way down the pillared vestibule which bordered the ballroom. He was bending over his companion with an air of unmistakable devotion, but it was she who talked. She seemed, indeed, to have a good deal to say to him. The slim white fingers of one hand played all the time with a string of magnificent pearls. Her dark, soft eyes—black as aloes and absolutely un-English—flashed into his. A delightful smile hovered at the corners of her lips. All the time she was talking and he was listening. Lady Mary and her partner passed by unnoticed. At the end of the vestibule they turned and retraced their steps. Peter Ruff was very quiet—he had caught a few of those rapid words. But the woman's foreign accent had troubled him.

"If only she would speak in her own language!" he muttered.

Lady Mary's hand suddenly tightened upon his arm.

"Look!" she exclaimed. "That is Count von Hern!"

A tall, fair young man, very exact in his dress, very stiff in his carriage, with a not unpleasant face, was standing talking to Jermyn and his companion. Jermyn, who apparently found the intrusion an annoyance, was listening to the conversation between the two, with a frown upon his face and a general attitude of irritation. As Lady Mary and her escort drew near, the reason for the young American's annoyance became clearer—his two companions were talking softly, but with great animation, in a foreign language, which it was obvious that he did not understand. Peter Ruff's elbow pressed against his partner's arm, and their pace slackened. He ventured even, to pause for a moment, looking into the ballroom as though in search of some one, and he had by no means the appearance of a man likely to understand Hungarian. Then, to Lady Mary's surprise, he touched the Count von Hern on the shoulder and addressed him.

"I beg your pardon, sir," he said, "but I fancy that we accidentally exchanged programs, a few minutes ago, at the buffet. I have lost mine and picked up one which does not belong to me. As we were standing side by side, it is possibly yours."

"I believe not, sir," he answered, with that pleasant smile which had gone such a long way toward winning him the reputation of being "a good fellow" amongst a fairly large circle of friends. "I believe at any rate," he added, glancing at his programme, "that this is my own. You mistake me, probably, for some one else."

Peter Ruff, without saying a word, was actor enough to suggest that he was unconvinced. The Count good-humoredly held out his program.

"You shall see for yourself," he remarked. "That is not yours, is it? Besides, I have not been to the buffet at all this evening."

Peter Ruff cast a swift glance down the program which the Count had handed him. Then he apologized profusely.

"I was mistaken," he admitted. "I am very sorry."

The Count bowed.

"It is of no consequence, sir," he said, and resumed his conversation.

Peter Ruff passed on with Lady Mary. At a safe distance, she glanced at him inquiringly.

"It was his program I wanted to see," Peter Ruff explained. "It is as I thought. He has had four dances with the Countess—"

"Who is she?" Lady Mary asked, quickly.

"The little dark lady with whom he is talking now," Peter Ruff continued. "He seems, too, to be going early. He had no dances reserved after the twelfth. We will go downstairs at once, if you please. I must speak to your brother."

"Have you been able to think of anything?" she asked, anxiously. "Is there any chance at all, do you think?"

"I believe so," Peter Ruff answered. "It is most interesting. Don't be too sanguine, though. The odds are against us, and the time is very short. Is the driver of your electric brougham to be trusted?"

"Absolutely," she assured him. "He is an old servant."

"Will you lend him to me?" Peter Ruff asked, "and tell him that he is to obey my instructions absolutely?"

"Of course," she answered. "You are going away, then?"

Peter Ruff nodded. He was a little sparing of words just then. The thoughts were chasing one another through his brain. He was listening, too, for the sweep of a dress behind.

"Is there nothing I can do?" Lady Mary begged, eagerly.

Peter Ruff shook his head. In the distance he saw the Honorable Maurice come quickly toward them. With a firm but imperceptible gesture he waved him away.

"Don't let your brother speak to me," he said. "We can't tell who is behind. What time did you say the Prime Minister was expected?"

"At two o'clock," Lady Mary said, anxiously.

Peter Ruff glanced at his watch. It ws already half an hour past midnight.

"Very well," he said, "I will do what I can. If my theory is wrong, it will be nothing. If I am right—well, there is a chance, anyhow. In the meantime—"

"In the meantime?" she repeated, breathlessly.

"Take your brother back to the ballroom," Peter Ruff directed. "Make him dance—dance yourself. Don't give yourselves away by looking anxious. When the time is short—say at a quarter to two—he can come down here and wait for me."

"If you don't come!" she exclaimed.

"Then we shall have lost," Peter Ruff said, calmly. "If you don't see me again tonight, you had better read the newspapers carefully for the next few days."

"You are going to do something dangerous!" she protested.

"There is danger in interfering at all in such a matter as this," he answered, "but you must remember that it is not only my profession—it is my hobby. Remember, too," he added, with a smile, "that I do not often lose!"

For twenty minutes Peter Ruff sat in the remote corner of Lady Mary's electric brougham, drawn up at the other side of the Square, and waited. At last he pressed a button. They glided off. Before them was a large, closed motorcar. They started in discreet chase.

Fortunately, however, the chase was not a long one. The car which Peter Ruff had been following was drawn up before a plain, solid-looking house, unlit and of gloomy appearance. The little lady with the wonderful eyes was already halfway up the flagged steps. Hastily lifting the flap and looking behind as they passed, her pursuer saw her open the door with a latchkey, and disappear. Peter Ruff pulled the checkstring and descended. For several moments he stood and observed the house into which the lady whom he had been following had disappeared. Then he turned to the driver.

"I want you to watch that house," he said, "never to take your eyes off it. When I reappear from it, if I do at all, I shall probably be in a hurry. Directly you see me be on your box ready to start. A good deal may depend upon our getting away quickly."

"Very good, sir," the man answered. "How long am I to wait here for you?"

Peter Ruff's lips twisted into a curious little smile.

"Until two o'clock," he answered. "If I am not out by then, you needn't bother any more about me. You can return and tell your mistress exactly what has happened."

"Hadn't I better come and try and get you out, sir?" the man asked. "Begging your pardon, but her Ladyship told me that there might be queer doings. I'm a bit useful in a scrap, sir," he added. "I do a bit of sparring regularly."

Peter Ruff shook his head.

"If there's any scrap at all," he said, "you had better be out of it. Do as I have said."

The motorcar had turned around and disappeared now, and in a few moments Peter Ruff stood before the door of the house into which the little lady had disappeared. The problem of entrance was already solved for him. The door had been left unlatched; only a footstool had been placed against it inside. Peter Ruff, without hesitation, pushed the door softly open and entered, replaced the footstool in its former position, and stood with his back to the wall, in the darkest corner of the hall, looking around him—listening intently. Nearly opposite the door of a room stood ajar. It was apparently lit up, but there was no sound of any one moving inside. Upstairs, in one of the rooms on the first floor, he could hear light footsteps—a woman's voice humming a song. He listened to the first few bars, and understanding became easier. Those first few bars were the opening ones of the Servian national anthem!

With an effort, Peter Ruff concentrated his thoughts upon the immediate present. The little lady was upstairs. The servants had apparently retired for the night. He crept up to the half-open door and peered in. The room, as he had hoped to find it, was empty, but Madame's easy chair was drawn up to the fire, and some coffee stood upon the hob. Stealthily Peter Ruff crept in and glanced around, seeking for a hiding place. A movement upstairs hastened his decision. He pushed aside the massive curtains which separated this from a connecting room. He had scarcely done so when light footsteps were heard descending the stairs.

Peter Ruff found his hiding place all that could have been desired. This secondary room itself was almost in darkness, but he was just able to appreciate the comforting fact that it possessed a separate exit into the hall. Through the folds of the curtain he had a complete view of the further apartment. The little lady had changed her gown of stiff white satin for one of flimsier material, and, seated in the easy chair, she was busy pouring herself out some coffee. She took a cigarette from a silver box, and lighting it, curled herself up in the chair and composed herself as though to listen. To her as well as to Peter Ruff, as he crouched in his hiding place, the moments seemed to pass slowly enough. Yet, as he realized afterward, it could not have been ten minutes before she sat upright in a listening attitude. There was some one coming! Peter Ruff, too, heard a man's firm footsteps come up the flagged stones.

The little lady sprang to her feet.

"Paul!" she excalimed.

Paul Jermyn came slowly to meet her. He semed a little out of breath. His tie was all disarranged and his collar unfastened. The little lady, however, noticed none of these things. She looked only into his face.

"Have you got it?" she asked, eagerly.

He thrust his hand into his breast coat pocket, and held an envelope out toward her.

"Sure!" he answered. "I promised!"

She gave a litle sob, and with the packet in her hand came running straight toward the spot where Peter Ruff was hiding. He shrank back as far as possible. She stopped just short of the curtain, opened the drawer of a table which stood there, and slipped the packet in. Then she came back once more to where Paul Jermyn was standing.

"My friend!" she cried, holding out her hands—"my dear, dear, friend! Shall I ever be able to thank you enough?"

"Why, if you try," he answered, smiling, "I think that you could!"

She laid her hand upon his arm—a little caressing, foreign gesture.

"Tell me," she said, "how did you manage it?"

"We left the dance together," Jermyn said. "I could see that he wanted to get rid of me, but I offered to take him in my motorcar. I told the man to choose some back streets, and while we were passing through one of them, I took Von Hern by the throat. We had a struggle, of course, but I got the paper."

"What did you do with Von Hern?" she asked.

"I left him on his doorstep," the young American answered. "He wasn't really hurt, but he was only half conscious. I don't think he'll bother any one tonight."

"You dear, brave man!" she murmured. "Paul, what am I to say to you?"

He laughed.

"That's what I'm here to ask," he declared. "You wouldn't give me my answer at the ball. Perhaps you'll give it me now?"

They sprang apart. Ruff felt his nerves stiffen—felt himself constrained to hold even his breath as he widened a little the crack in the curtains. This was no stealthy entrance. The door had been flung open. Von Hern, his dress in wild disorder, pale as a ghost, and with a great bloodstain upon his cheek, stood confronting them.

"When you have done with your lovemaking," he called out, "I'll trouble you to restore my property!"

The electric light gleamed upon a small revolver which flashed out toward the young American. Paul Jermyn never hesitated for a moment.

He seized the chair by his side and flung it at Von Hern. There was a shot, the crash of the falling chair, a cry from Jermyn, who never hesitated, however, in his rush. The two men closed. A second shot went harmlessly to the ceiling. The little lady stole away—stole softly across the room toward the table. She opened the drawer. Suddenly the blood in her veins was frozen into fear. From nowhere, it seemed to her, came a hand which held her wrists like iron!

"Madam," Peter Ruff whispered from behind the curtain, "I am sorry to deprive you of it, but this is stolen property."

Her screams rang though the room. Even the two men released one another.

"It is gone!" she cried. "Some one was hiding in the room! Quick!"

She sprang into the hall. The two men followed her. The front door was slammed. They heard flying footsteps outside. Von Hern was out first, clearing the little flight of steps in one bound. Across the road he saw a flying figure. A level stream of fire poured from his hand—twice, three times. But Peter Ruff never faltered. Round the corner he tore. The man had kept his word—the brougham was already moving slowly.

"Jump in, sir," the man cried. "Throw yourself in. Never mind about the door."

They heard the shouts behind. Peter Ruff did as he was bid, and sat upon the floor, raising himself gradually to the seat when they had turned another corner. Then he put his head out of the window.

"Back to the Duchess of Montford's!" he ordered.

The latest of the guests had ceased to arrive—a few were already departing. It was an idle time, however, with the servants who loitered in the vestibules of Montford House, and they looked with curiosity upon this strange guest who arrived at five minutes to two, limping a little, and holding his left arm in his right hand. One footman on the threshold nearly addressed him, but the words were taken out of his mouth when he saw Lady Mary and her brother—the Honorable Maurice Sotherest—hasten forward to greet him.

Peter Ruff smiled upon them benignly.

"You can take the paper out of my breast-coat pocket," he said.

The young man's fingers gripped it. Through Lady Mary's great thankfulness, however, the sudden fear came shivering.

"You are hurt!" she whispered. "There is blood on your sleeve."

"Just a graze," Peter Ruff answered. "Von Hern wasn't much good at a running target. Back to the ballroom, young man," he added. "Don't you see who's coming?"

The Prime Minister came up the tented way into Montford House. He, too, wondered a little at the man whom he met on his way out, holding his left arm, and looking more as though he had emerged from a street fight than from the Duchess of Montford's ball. Peter Ruff went home smiling.

A TALL STORY

G. K. Chesterton

THEY HAD BEEN discussing the new troubles in Germany; the three old friends, Sir Hubert Wotton, the famous official; Mr. Pond, the obscure official; and Captain Gahagan, who never did a stroke of work in the way of putting pen to paper, but liked making up the most fantastic stories on the spur of the moment. On this occasion, however, the group was increased to four; for Gahagan's wife was present, a candid-looking young woman with light brown hair and dark brown eyes. They had only just recently been married; and the presence of Joan Gahagan still stimulated the Captain to rather excessive flights of showing-off.

Captain Gahagan looked like a Regency buck; Mr. Pond looked like a round-eyed fish, with the beard and brow of Socrates; Sir Hubert Wotton looked like Sir Hubert Wotton—it summed up a very sound and virile quality in him, for which his friends had a great respect.

"It's an infernal shame," Wotton was saying, "the way these fellows have treated the Jews: perfectly decent and harmless Jews, who were no more Communists than I am; little men who'd worked their way up by merit and industry, all kicked out of their posts without a penny of compensation. Surely you agree with that, Gahagan?"

"Of course I do," replied Gahagan. "I never kicked a Jew. I can distinctly remember three and a half occasions on which I definitely refrained from doing so. As for all those hundreds and thousands of poor little fiddlers and actors and chess players, I think it was a damned shame that they should be kicked out or kicked at all. But I fancy they must be kicking themselves, for having been so faithful to Germany and even, everywhere else, pretty generally pro-German."

"Even that can be exaggerated," said Mr. Pond. "Do you remember the case of Carl Schiller, that happened during the War? It was all kept rather quiet, as I have reason to know; for the thing happened, in some sense, in my department. I have generally found spy stories the dullest of all forms of detective fiction; in my own modest researches into the light literature of murder, I invariably avoid them. But this story really did have an unexpected and rather astonishing ending. Of course, you know that in wartime the official dealing with these things is very much exposed to amateurs, as the Duke of Wellington was exposed to authors. We persecuted the spies; and the spy-maniacs persecuted us. They were always coming to us to say they had seen certain persons who looked like spies. We vainly assured them that spies do not look like spies. As a matter of fact, the enemy was pretty ingenious in keeping the really suspicious character just out of sight; sometimes by his being ordinary; sometimes actually by his being extraordinary; one would be too small to be noticed, another too tall to be seen; one was apparently paralyzed in a hospital and got out of the window at night—"

Joan looked across at him with a troubled expression in her honest brown eyes.

"Please, Mr. Pond, do tell us what you mean by a man being too tall to be seen."

Gahagan's spirits, already high, soared into laughter and light improvisation.

"These things do happen, my dear girl," he said. "I can throw out a thousand instances that would meet the case. Take, for example, the case of my unfortunate friends the Balham-Browns who lived at Muswell Hill. Mr. Balham-Brown had just come home from the office (of the Imperial and International Lead-Piping Company) and was exercising the lawn mower in the usual manner, when he noticed in the grass a growth not green but reddish brown and resembling animal hair; nay, even human hair. My friend Mr. Pond, whose private collection of Giant Whiskers is unrivaled (except of course, by the unique collection of Sir Samuel Snodd) was able to identify it with the long hair of the Anakin; and judged by its vigor, the son of Anak was buried but still alive. With the spitefulness of the scientific world, Professor Pooter countered with the theory that Jupiter buried the Titans, one under Etna, another under Ossa, and a third under Muswell Hill. Anyhow, the villa of my ill-fated friends the Balham-Browns was ruined, and the whole suburb overturned as by an earthquake, in order to excavate the monster. When his head alone emerged, it was like a colossal sphinx; and Mrs. Balham-Brown complained to the authorities that the face frightened her, because it was too large. Mr. Pond, who happened to be passing at the moment, immediately produced a paradox (of which he always carries a small supply) and said that, on the contrary, they would soon find that the face was too small. To cut a long story short—"

"Or a tall story shorter," said Joan in a trenchant manner.

"When the Titan was extricated, he was so tall that by the common converging laws of perspective, his head in the remote sky was a mere dot. It was impossible to discern or recall one feature of that old familiar face. He strode away; and fortunately decided to walk across the Atlantic, where even he was apparently submerged. It is believed that the unfortunate creature was going to give lectures in America; driven by that mysterious instinct which leads any person who is notorious for any reason to adopt that course."

"Well, have you done?" demanded Joan. "We know all about you and your yarns; and they don't mean anything. But when Mr. Pond says that somebody was too tall to be seen, he does mean something. And what can he possibly mean?"

"Well," said Mr. Pond, coughing slightly, "it was really a part of the story to which I was alluding just now. I did not notice anything odd about the expression when I used it; but I recognize, on second thought, that it is, perhaps, a phrase requiring explanation." And he proceeded, in his slightly pedantic way to narrate the story which is now retold here.

It all happened in a fashionable watering place, which was also a famous seaport, and, therefore, naturally a place of concentration for all the vigilance against spies, whether official or amateur. Sir Hubert Wotton was in general charge of the district, but Mr. Pond was in more practical though private occupation of the town, watching events from a narrow house in a back street, an upper room of which had been unobtrusively turned into an office; and he had two assistants under him; a sturdy and very silent young man named Butt, bull-necked and broad-shouldered, but quite short; and a much taller and more talkative and elegant government-office clerk named Travers, but referred to by nearly everybody as Arthur. The stalwart Butt commonly occupied a desk on the ground floor, watching the door and anyone who entered it; while Arthur Travers worked in the office upstairs, where there were some very valuable State papers, including the only plan of the mines in the harbor.

Mr. Pond himself always spent several hours in the office, but he had more occasion than the others to pay visits in the town, and had a general grasp of the neighborhood. It was a very shabby neighborhood; indeed, it consisted of a few genteel, old-fashioned houses, now mostly shuttered and empty, standing on the very edge of a sort of slum of small houses, at that time riddled with what is called Unrest in a degree very dangerous, especially in time of war. Immediately outside his door, he found but few things that could be called features in that featureless street; but there was an old curiosity shop opposite, with a display of ancient Asiatic weapons; and there was Mrs. Hartog-Haggard next door, more alarming than all the weapons of the world.

Mrs. Harton-Haggard was one of those persons, to be found here and there, who look like the conventional caricature of the spinster, though they are in fact excellent mothers of families. Rather in the same way she looked very like the sort of lady who is horribly in earnest at Pacifist meetings; yet, as a matter of fact, she was passionately patriotic, not to say militaristic. And, indeed, it is often true that those two extremes lend themselves to the same sort of fluent fanaticism. Poor Mr. Pond had reason to remember the woeful day when he first saw her angular and agitated figure darkening his doorway as she entered out of the street, peering suspiciously through her curious square spectacles. There was apparently some slight delay about her entrance; some repairs were being done to the porch and some loose board or pole was not removed sufficiently promptly from her path: was, in fact, as she declared, removed reluctantly and in a grumbling spirit by the workmen employed on the job; and by the time she had reached the responsible official, a theory had fully formed and hardened in her mind.

"That man is a *Socialist*, Mr. Pond," she declared in the ear of that unfortunate functionary. "I heard him with my own ears mutter something about what his Trade Union would say. What is he doing so near to your office?"

"We must distinguish," said Mr. Pond. "A Trade Unionist, even a militant Trade Unionist, is not necessarily a Socialist; a Socialist is not necessarily a Pacifist, still less a Pro-German. In my opinion, the chief S.D.F. men are the most extreme Marxians in England; and they are all out for the Allies. One of the Dock Strike leaders is in a mood to make recruiting speeches all over the Empire."

"I'm sure he's not English; he doesn't look a bit English," said the lady, still thinking of her wicked proletarian without.

"Thank you, Mrs. Hartog-Haggard," said Pond, patiently. "I will certainly make a note of your warning and see that inquiries are made about it."

And so he did, with the laborious precision of one who could not leave any loophole unguarded. Certainly the man did not look very English; though perhaps rather Scandinavian than German. His name was Peterson; it was possible that it was really Petersen. But that was not all. Mr. Pond had learned the last lesson of the wise man; that the fool is sometimes right.

He soon forgot the incident in the details of his work; and next day it was with a start that he looked up from his desk, or rather from Mr. Butt's desk which he was using at the moment, and saw once again the patriotic lady hovering like an avenging shadow in the doorway. This time she glided swiftly in, unchecked by any Socialist barricade, and warned him that she had news of the most terrible kind. She seemed to have forgotten all about her last suspicions; and, in truth, her new ones were naturally more important to her. This time she had warmed the viper on her own hearth. She had suddenly become conscious of the existence of her own German governess, whom she had never especially noticed before. Pond himself had noticed the alien in question with rather more attention; he had seen her, a dumpy lady with pale hair, returning with Mrs. Hartog-Haggard's three little girls and one little boy from the pantomime of Puss-in-Boots that was being performed on the pier. He had even heard her instructing her charges, and saying something educational about a folktale; and had smiled faintly at that touch of Teutonic pedandry that talks about a folktale when we would talk about a fairy tale. But he knew a good deal about the lady; and saw no reason to move in the matter.

"She shuts herself up for hours in her room and won't come out," Mrs. Hartog-Haggard was already breathing hoarsely in his ear. "Do you think she is signaling, or does she climb down the fire escape? What do you think it means, Mr. Pond?"

"Hysterics," said Mr. Pond. "What, do you think the poor lady cannot be hysterical, because she does not scream the house down? But any doctor will tell you that hysteria is mostly secretive and silent. And there really is a vein of hysteria in a great many of the Germans; it is at the very opposite extreme to the external excitability of the Latins. No, madam, I do not think she is climbing down the fire escape. I think she is saying that her pupils do not love her, and thinking about *welt-schmerz* and suicide. And really, poor woman, she is in a very hard position."

"She won't come to family prayers," continued the patriotic matron, not to be turned from her course, "because we pray for a British victory."

"You had better pray," said Mr. Pond, "for all the unhappy English women stranded in Germany by poverty or duty or dependence. If she loves her native land, it only shows she is a human being. If she expresses it by ostentatious absences or sulks or banging doors, that may show she is too much of a German. It also shows she is not much of a German spy."

Here again, however, Mr. Pond was careful not to ignore or entirely despise the warning; he kept an eye on the German governess, and even engaged that learned lady in talk upon some trivial pretext—if anything she touched could remain trivial.

"Your study of our national drama," he said gravely, "must sometime recall to you the greatest and noblest work that ever came out of Germany."

"You refer to Goethe's *Faust,* I presume," she replied.

"I refer to Grimm's Fairy Tales," said Mr. Pond. "I fear I have forgotten for the moment whether the story we call *Puss-in-Boots* exists in Grimm's collection in the same form; but I am pretty certain there is some variant of it. It always seems to me about the best story in the world."

The German governess obliged him with a short lecture on the parallelism of folklore; and Pond could not help feeling faintly amused at the idea of this enthnological and scientific treatment of a folktale which had just been presented on the pier by Miss Patsy Pickles, in tights and various other embellishments, supported by that world-famed comedian who called himself Alberto Tizzi and was born in the Blackfriars Road.

When he returned to his office at twilight, and, turning, beheld the figure of Mrs. Hartog-Haggard again hovering without, Mr. Pond began to think he was in a nightmare. He wondered wildly whether she had drawn some dark conclusions from his own meeting with the Teutonic teacher of youth. Perhaps he, Mr. Pond, was a German spy, too. But he ought to have known his neighbor better; for when Mrs. Hartog-Haggard spoke she had once again forgotten, for the moment, her last cause of complaint. But she was more excited than ever; she ducked under the frame of scaffolding and darted into the room, crying out as she came:

"Mr. Pond, do you know what is right opposite your own house?"

"Well, I think so," said Mr. Pond, doubtfully, "more or less."

"I never read the name over the shop before!" cried the lady. "You know it is all dark and dirty and obliterated—that curiosity shop, I mean; with all the spears and daggers. Think of the impudence of the man! He's actually written up his name there: 'C Schiller.'"

"He's written up C. Schiller; I'm not so sure he's written up his name," said Mr. Pond.

"Do you mean," she cried, "that you actually know he goes by two names? Why, that makes it worse than ever!"

"Well," said Mr. Pond, rising suddenly, and with a curtness that cut all his own courtesy, "I'll see what I can do about it."

And for the third time did Mr. Pond take some steps to verify the Hartog-Haggard revelations, He took the ten or twelve steps necessary to take him across the road and into the shop of C. Schiller, amid all the shining sabres and yataghans. It was a very peaceable-looking person who waited behind all this array of arms; not to say a rather smooth and sleek one; and Pond, leaning across the counter, addressed him in a low and confidential voice.

"Why the dickens do you people do it? It will be more than half your own fault if there's a row of some kind and a Jingo mob comes here and breaks your windows for your absurd German name. I know very well this is no quarrel of yours. I am well aware," Mr. Pond continued with an earnest gaze, "that you never invaded Belgium. I am fully conscious that your national tastes do not lie in that direction. I know you had nothing to do with burning the Louvain Library or sinking the *Lusitania*. Then why the devil can't you say so? Why can't you call yourself Levy, like your fathers before you—your fathers who go back to the most ancient priesthood of the world? And you'll get into trouble with the Germans, too, some day, if you go about calling yourself Schiller. You might as well go and live in Stratford-on-Avon and call yourself Shakespeare."

"There'th a lot of prejudith againth my rathe," said the warden of the armory.

"There'll be a lot more, unless you take my advice," said Mr. Pond with unusual brevity; and left the shop to return to the office.

The square figure of Mr. Butt, who was sitting at the desk looking towards the doorway, rose at his entrance, but Pond waved him to his seat again and, lighting a cigarette, began to moon about the room in a rather moody fashion. He did not believe that there was anything very much in any of the three avenues of suspicion that had been opened to him; though he owned that there were indirect possibilities about the last. Mr. Levy was certainly not a German; and it was very improbable that he was a real enthusiast for Germany; but it was not altogether impossible to suppose, in the tangle and distraction of all the modern international muddle, that he might be some sort of tool, conscious or unconscious, of a real German conspiracy. So long as that was possible, he must be watched. Mr. Pond was very glad that Mr. Levy lived in the shop exactly opposite.

Indeed, he found himself gazing across the street in the gathering dusk with feelings which he found it hard to analyze. He could still see the shop, with its pattern of queer, archaic weapons, through the frame of the last few poles left in the low scaffolding round the porch; for the workmen's business had been entirely limited to the porch itself and the props were mostly cleared away, the work being practically over; but there was just enough suggestion of a cluster or network of lines to confuse the prospect at that very confusing turn of the twilight. Once he fancied he saw something flicker behind them, as if a shadow had shifted;

and there arose within him the terror of Mrs. Hartog-Haggard, which is the terror of boredom and a sort of paralyzed impatience, one of the worst of the woes of life.

Then he saw that the shifting shadow must have been produced by the fact that the lights had been turned up in the shop opposite; and he saw again, and now much more clearly, the queer outline of all those alien Asiatic weapons, the crooked darts and monstrous missiles, the swords with a horrid resemblance to hooks or the blades that bent back and forth like snakes of iron. . . . He became dreamily conscious of the chasm between Christendom and that greater other half of human civilization; so dreamily that he hardly knew which was a torture implement and which was a tool. Whether the thought was mingled with his own belief that he was fighting a barbarism at heart as hostile, or whether he had caught a whiff of the strange smell of the East from that apparently harmless human accident who kept the shop, he could hardly be certain himself; but he felt the peculiar oppression of his work as he had never felt it before.

Then he shook himself awake, telling himself sharply that his business was working and not worrying about the atmosphere of the work; and that he should be ashamed to idle when his two subordinates were still busy, Butt behind him, and Travers in the office above. He was all the more surprised, when he turned sharply around, to find that Butt was not working at all; but, like himself, was staring, not to say glaring, as in a congested mystification, into the twilight. Butt was commonly the most calm and prosaic of subordinates; but the look on his face was quite enough to prove that something was really the matter.

"Is anything bothering you?" asked Pond, in a gentle voice which people found very encouraging.

"Yes, sir," said Mr. Butt. "I'm bothering about whether I'm going to be a beast or not. It's a beastly caddish thing to say a word, or hint a word, against your comrades or anybody connected with them. But after all — well, sir, there is the country, isn't there?"

"There is certainly the country," said Mr. Pond, very seriously.

"Well," Butt blurted out at last, "I'm not a bit comfortable about Arthur."

Then, after a sort of gasp, he tried again: "At least, it isn't so much Arthur as Arthur's . . . what Arthur's doing. It makes it all the nastier to have to put it like that. But you know he got engaged last week. Have you met his fiancé, sir?"

"I have not yet had the honor," replied Pond, in his punctilious way.

"Well, sir, Arthur brought her in here today while you were out; he'd just taken her to the pantomime of Puss-in-Boots on the pier, and they were laughing like anything. Of course, that's quite all right; it was his time off; but it seemed to me it wasn't quite all right that she walked straight upstairs without any invitation, even from him, to the private office where we don't allow visitors to go. Of course, that's about the only possible case where I could hardly prevent it. In the ordinary way, we're perfectly safe; I mean the documents are perfectly safe. There's only one door, and you or I are always sitting bang in front of it; and there's only one staircase, and nobody uses it but we three. Of course, she might have done it in all innocence; that's what made it seem quite too ghastly to snub her. And yet. . . . Well, she's a very nice-looking girl, and no doubt a very nice girl; but somehow that's just the one word that wouldn't jump to my mind about her—innocence."

"Why, what sort of a girl is she?" asked Pond.

"Well," said Mr. Butt, gloomily seeking words, "we all know that making-up and even dyeing your hair doesn't mean what it once did; lots of women do it who are perfectly decent; but not those who are—well, utterly inexperienced. It seemed to me that, while she might be perfectly honest, she would know very decidedly whether a thing is done or not."

"If she is engaged to him," said Pond, with a rather unusual severity, "she must know that he is here on highly confidential work, and she must be as anxious to protect his honor as we are. I'm afraid that I shall have to ask you for some sort of description."

"Well," said Butt, "she's very tall and elegant, or . . . no, elegant is exactly the word. She has beautiful golden hair—very beautiful golden hair—and very beautiful long dark eyes that make it look rather like a gilded wig. She has high cheekbones, not in the way that Scotch girls have, but somehow as if it were part of the shape of the skull; and though she's not at all long in the tooth, in any sense, her teeth are just a little to the fore."

"Did he meet her in Besançon, near Belfort?"

"Pretty rum you should say that," said Butt, miserably; "because he did."

Mr. Pond received the news in silence.

"I hope, sir, you won't assume anything against Arthur," said Butt, huskily. "I'm sure I'd do anything to clear him of any—"

As he spoke, the ceiling above them shook with a thud like thunder; then there was a sound of scampering feet; and then utter stillness. No one acquainted with Mr. Pond's usual process of ambulation could have believed that he flew up the staircase as he did just then.

They flung open the door, and they saw all that was to be seen. All that was to be seen was Arthur Travers stretched out face downwards on the ground, and between his shoulder blades stood out the very long hilt of a very strange-looking sword. Butt impetuously laid hold of it, and was startled to find that it was sunk so deep in the corpse and the carpeted floor that he could not have plucked it out without the most violent muscular effort. Pond had already touched the wrist and felt the rigidity of the muscles and he waved his subordinate away.

"I am sorry to say that our friend is certainly dead," he said steadily. "In that case, you had better not touch things till they can be properly examined." Then, looking at Butt very solemnly, he added:

"You said you would do anything to clear him. One thing is certain: that he is quite cleared."

Pond then walked in silence to the desk, which contained the secret drawer and the secret plan of the harbor. He only compressed his lips when he saw that the drawer was empty.

Pond walked to the telephone and issued orders to about six different people. He did about twenty things, but he did not speak again for about three-quarters of an hour. It was only about the same time that the stunned and bewildered Butt stumbled into speech.

"I simply can't make head or tail of anything. That woman had gone; and, besides, no woman could have nailed him to the floor like that."

"And with such an extraordinary nail," said Pond, and was silent once more.

And indeed the riddle revolved more and more on the one thing that thief and murderer had left behind him; the enormous misshapen weapon. It was not difficult to guess why he had left it behind; it was so difficult to tug out of the floor that he probably had not time to try effectually, hearing Pond clattering up the stairs; he thought it wiser to escape some-how, presumably through the window. But about the nature of the thing itself it was hard to say anything, for it seemed quite abnormal. It was as long as a claymore; yet it was not upon the pattern of any known sword. It had no guard or pommel of any kind. The hilt was as long as the blade; the blade was twice as broad as the hilt; at least, at its base, whence it tapered to a point in a sort of right-angled triangle, only the outer edge or hypotenuse being sharpened. Pond gazed musingly at this uncouth weapon, which was made very rudely of iron and wood painted with garish colors; and his thoughts crept slowly back to that shop across the road that was hung with strange and savage weapons. Yet this seemed to be in a somewhat cruder and gaudier style. Mr. Schiller-Levy naturally denied all knowledge of it, which he would presumably have done in any case; but what was much more cogent, all the real authorities on such barbaric or Oriental arms said that they had never seen such a thing before.

Touching many other things, the darkness began to thin away to a somewhat dreary dawn. It was ascertained that poor Arthur's equivocal fiancee had indeed fled; very possibly in company with the missing plan. She was known by this time to be a woman quite capable of stealing a document or even stabbing a man. But I was doubtful whether any woman was capable of stabbing a man, with that huge and heavy and clumsy instrument, so as to fix him to the floor; and quite impossible to imagine why she should select it for the purpose.

"It would all be as clear as death," said Mr. Butt, bitterly, "except for that lumbering, long-hilted short-sword, or whatever it is. It never was in Levy's shop. It never was in Asia or Africa or any of the tribes the learned jossers tell us about. It's the real remaining mystery of the whole thing."

Mr. Pond seemed to be waking up slowly from a trance of hours or days.

"Oh, *that,*" he said, "that's the only thing about it I'm really beginning to understand."

It has been hinted, with every delicacy, we may hope, that the attitude of Mr. Pond towards the visits of Mrs. Hartog-Haggard was, perhaps, rather passive than receptive; that he did not look forward to them as pants the hart for cooling streams; and that for him they rather resembled getting into hot water. It is all the more worthy of record that, on the last occasion of her bringing him a new tale of woe, he actually leapt to his feet with an air of excitement and even of triumph. He had been right in his premonitions about the wisdom of folly; and the triumph was truly the triumph of the fool. Mrs. Hartog-Haggard gave him the clue after all.

She darted in under the scaffolding by the doorway, the same dark and almost antic figue. Full of the Cause, she was utterly oblivious of such trifles as the murder of his friend. She had now reverted to her original disapproval of her own governess. She had altered nothing, except all her reasons for disapproving of her governess. On the former occasion she had appeared to claim the fairy tale used for pantomines as exclusively English and part of the healthy innocence of the stately homes of England. Now she was denouncing the German woman for taking the children to the pantomime at all; regarding it as a ruse for filling them with the gruesome tales of Grimm and the terrors of the barbaric forest.

"They're *sent* to do that," she repeated in the fierce, confidential voice she used in such cases. "They're sent here to undermine all our children's nerves and minds. Could any other nation be such fiends, Mr. Pond?

She's been poisoning their poor little minds with horrors about magicians and magic cats; and now the worst has happened, as I knew it would. Well—*you* haven't done anything to stop it; and my life is simply ruined. My three girls are all twittering with terror; and my boy is mad."

The symptoms of Mr. Pond were still mainly those of fatigue; and she rapped out a repetition.

"He is *mad*, I tell you, Mr. Pond; he is actually *seeing* things out of those horrible German fairy tales; says he saw a giant with a great knife walking through the town by moonlight . . . a *giant*, Mr. Pond."

Mr. Pond staggered to his feet and for once really goggled and gulped like a fish. Mrs. Hartog-Haggard watched him with wild eyes, intermittently exclaiming: "Have you no word of consolation for a mother?"

Mr. Pond controlled himself and managed to recapture, at least, a hazy courtesy.

"Yes, madam," he said. "I have the best possible consolation for a mother. Your son is not mad."

He looked more judicial, and even severe, when he next sat in consultation with Mr. Butt, Sir Hubert Wotton, and Inspector Grote, the leading detective of the district.

"What it comes to is this," said Mr. Pond, very sternly: "that you do not really know the story of Puss-in-Boots. And they talk about this as an epoch of Education."

"Oh, I know it's about a clever cat and all the rest of it," said Butt, vaguely. "A cat that helps its master to get things—"

The Inspector smote his knee with a smack that rang through the office.

"A cat burglar!" he cried. "So that's what you mean. I fancied at first there was something wrong about that bit of scaffolding round the door; but I soon saw it was far too low and small for anybody to climb up to the window by it. But, of course, if we're talking about a really clever cat burglar, there's always some chance that—"

"Pardon me," said Mr. Pond, "does a cat burglar, or for that matter any burglar, any more than any cat, load himself with a gigantic knife rather bigger than a garden spade? Nobody carries a gigantic knife except a giant. This crime was committed by a giant."

They all stared at him; but he resumed with the same air of frigid rebuke:

"What I remark upon, what I regret and regard as symptomatic of serious intellectual decay, is that you apparently do not know that the story of Puss-in-Boots includes a giant. He is also a magician; but he is always depicted, in pictures and pantomimes, as an ogre with a large knife. Signor Alberto Tizzi, that somewhat dubious foreign artist, enacts the part on the pier by the usual expedient of walking on very high stilts, covered by very long trousers. But he sometimes walks about on the stilts and dispenses with the trousers; taking a walk through the almost entirely deserted streets at night. Just round here, especially, the chances are against his being even seen; all the big houses are shut up, except ours and Mrs. Hartog-Haggard's, which only looks on the street through a landing window; through which her little boy (probably in his nightgown) peered and beheld a real ogre, with a great gory knife, and, perhaps, a great grinning mask, walking majestically under the moon—rather a fine sight to put among the memories of childhood. For the rest, all the poor houses are low houses of one story; and the people would see nothing but his legs, or rather his stilts, even if they did look out; and they probably didn't. The really native poor, in these seaport towns, have country habits; and generally go to bed early. But it wouldn't really have been fatal to his plans even if he had been seen. He was a recognized public entertainer, dressed in his recognized part; and there is nothing illegal in walking about on stilts. The really clever part of it was the trick by which he could leave the stilts standing, and climb out of them on to any ledge or roof or other upper level. So he left them standing outside our doorway, among the poles of the little scaffolding, while he climbed in at the upper window and killed poor Travers."

"If you are sure of this," cried Sir Hubert Wotton, starting to his feet hastily, "you ought to act on it at once!"

"I did act on it at once," replied Pond, with a slight sigh. "This morning two or three clowns with white faces were going about on stilts on the beach, distributing leaflets of the pantomime. One of them was arrested and found to be Signor Tizzi. He was also found, I am glad to say, to be still in possession of the plans." But he sighed again.

"For after all," as Mr. Pond observed, in telling the tale long after, "though we did manage to save the secret plans, the incident was much more of a tragedy than a triumph. And what I most intensely disliked about the tragedy was the irony—what I believe is called the tragic irony, or, alternatively, the Greek irony. We felt perfectly certain we were guarding the only entrance to the office, because we sat staring at the street between two little clusters of sticks, which we knew were a temporary part of the furniture. We didn't count the sticks; we didn't know when there happened to be two more wooden poles standing up among the other wooden poles. We certainly had no notion of what was on top of these two poles; nor would our fancy have easily entertained the idea that it was a pantomime giant. We ought to have seen him—only," said Mr.

Pond, ending, as he had begun, with an apologetic little laugh, "he was too tall to be seen."

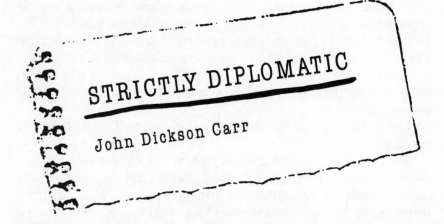

STRICTLY DIPLOMATIC

John Dickson Carr

NOW THAT HE was nearly at the end of his rest cure, Dermot had never felt so well in his life.

He leaned back in the wicker chair, flexing his muscles. He breathed deeply. Below him the flattish lands between France and Belgium sloped to the river: a slow Flemish river dark green with the reflection of its banks. Half a mile away he could see the houses of the town, with the great glass roof of the spa smoky in autumn sunshine. Behind him—at the end of the arbor—was the back of the hotel, now denuded of its awnings.

They had taken down the awnings; they were closing up many of the bedrooms. Only a few guests now pottered about the terrace. A crisp tang had come into the air; work, and the thunder of London again, now loomed up as a pleasant prospect. Once, hardly a month ago, it had been a nightmare of buses charging straight at you, like houses loose; a place where nerves snapped, and you started to run.

Even with that noise in his ears, he had not wanted to go away.

"But I can't take a holiday now!" he had told the doctor.

"Holiday?" snorted the doctor. "Do you call it a holiday? Your trouble is plain overwork, a complaint we don't often get nowadays. Why don't you relax? Not hard up, are you?"

"No, it isn't that."

"You're too conscientious," the doctor had said, rather enviously.

"No. It's not a virtue," said Dermot, as honestly as he could. "I can't help it. Every second I'm away from work, I'm worrying about it until I get back. I'm built like that. I can't relax. I can't even get drunk."

The doctor grunted.

"Ever try falling in love?"

"Not since I was nineteen. And, anyway, it's not something you can take down like a box of pills and dose yourself with. Or at least I can't."

"Well," said the doctor, surveying him, "I know a rising barrister who's going to come a cropper unless you get out of this. Now I warn you. You get off to the Continent this week. There's a spa I know—Ile St. Cathérine. The waters won't do you any harm; and the golf will do you good."

Here the doctor, who was an old friend of Andrew Dermot's, grinned raffishly.

"What you want," he added, "is adventure. In the grand manner. I hear there's a fenced-off area near Ile St. Cathérine, bayonets and all. The casino is probably full of beautiful slant-eyed spies with jade earrings. Forget you're turning into such a mossback. Pick up one of the beautiful slant-eyed spies, and go on the razzle-dazzle with her. It'll do you all the good in the world."

Alone on the lawn behind his hotel, Dermot laughed aloud. Old Foggy had been right, in a way. But he had gone one less or one better than that. He had fallen in love.

Anyone less like a slant-eyed spy than Betty Weatherill would be difficult to imagine. In fact even the tension which tauntened nerves in the rest of Europe did not exist in Ile St. Cathérine. It was a fat, friendly, rather stodgy sort of place. Looking round the spa—where fountains fell, and people got very excited on the weighing machines—Dermot wondered at old Foggy's notion of bayonets. He felt soothed, and free. Bicycle bells tinkled in the streets under once-gilded houses. At night, when you ordered thin wine by the glass, a band played beneath lights in the trees. A mild flutter in roulette at the casino caused excitement; and one Belgian burgher was caught bringing his supper in a paper packet.

Dermot first saw Betty Weatherill on the morning after his arrival.

It was at breakfast. There were not many guests at the hotel: a fat Dutchman eating cheese for breakfast, half a dozen English people, a foreign envoy, a subdued French couple. And, of course, the sturdy girl who sat alone at the sun-steeped table by the windows.

Dermot's nerves were still raw from the journey. When he first saw her he felt a twinge of what he thought was envy at her sheer health. It flashed out at him. He had an impression of a friendly mouth, a suntanned complexion; of eagerness, and even naïveté. It disturbed him like the clattering coffee cups. He kept looking round at her, and looking round again, though he did not understand why.

He played execrable golf that day.

He saw her again next morning. They ran into each other buying stamps at the cash desk. They both smiled slightly, and Dermot felt embarrassed. He had been trying to remember whether the color of her hair was fair or chestnut; it was, he saw, a light brown. That afternoon his golf was even worse. It was absurd that he, thirty-five years old, should seem as stale and crumpled as an old poster against a wall. He was a nerve-ridden fool. And he fell to thinking of her again.

On the following day they went so far as to say good morning. On the third day he took his nerve in both hands, and plumped down at the breakfast table next to hers.

"I *can't* do it," he heard her say, half laughing.

The words gave him a start. Not a ladies' man, this move of his had struck him as distinctly daring. Yet he felt the communication between them, an uncomfortable awareness of each other's presence. He looked up, to find her eyes fixed on him.

"Do what?" he asked quickly.

"Manage Continental breakfasts," she answered, as though they were old friends discussing a problem of mutual importance. "I know I shouldn't, but every day I order bacon and eggs."

After that their acquaintance was off at a gallop.

Her name was Betty Weatherill. She was twenty-eight, and came from Brighton. She had been a schoolmistress (incongruous idea); but she had come into a small inheritance and, as she confessed, was blowing part of it. He had never met a girl who seemed so absolutely right: in what she said, in what she did, in her response to any given remark.

That afternoon they went to the fair and ate hot dogs and rode round and round on the wooden horses to the panting music of an electric piano. That night they dressed for the casino; and Andrew Dermot, shuffling roulette counters, felt no end of an experienced gay dog. And the knowledge came to him, with a kind of shock, "Good lord, I'm alive."

Betty was popular at the hotel. The proprietor, Monsieur Gant, knew her quite well and was fond of her. Even the fat Dr. Vanderver, of the Sylvanian Embassy, gave her a hoarse chuckle of appreciation whenever she went by. Not that she had no difficulties. There was, it appeared, some trouble about her passport. She had several times to go to the prefecture of police—from which she emerged flushed, and as near angry as it was possible for her to be.

As for Dermot, he was in love and he knew it. That was why he exulted when he sat by the tea table on the lawn behind the hotel, at half-past five on that lazy, veiled autumn afternoon, waiting for Betty to join him. The lawn was dotted with little tables, but he was alone. The remains of tea and sandwiches were piled on a tray. Dermot was replete; no outside alarms troubled Ile St. Cathérine; no black emblems threw shadows.

This was just before he received the greatest shock of his life.

"Hello!" said Betty. "Sorry I'm late." She came hurrying out of the arbor, with the breathless smile she always wore when she was excited. She glanced quickly round the lawn, deserted except for a waitress slapping at crumbs. Dermot got up.

"You're not late," he told her. "But you swore to me you were going to have tea in town, so I went ahead." He looked at her suspiciously. "Did you?"

"Did I what?"

"Have tea."

"Yes, of course."

For no reason that he could analyze, a chill of uneasiness came to Dermot. His nightmares were cured. But it was as though an edge of the nightmare returned. Why? Only because the atomosphere suddenly seemed wrong, because the expression of her eyes was wrong. He drew out a chair for her.

"Sure you wouldn't like another cup? Or a sandwich?"

"Well—"

Now he thought he must be a fool reading huge meanings into trifles. But the impression persisted. He gave an order to the waitress, who removed the tea tray and disappeared into the arbor. Betty had taken a cigarette out of her handbag; but, when he tried to light it for her, the cigarette slipped out of her fingers, and rolled on the table.

"Oh, damn," she whispered. Now he was looking into her eyes from a short distance away; they seemed the eyes of a slightly older, wiser woman. They were hazel eyes, the whites very clear against a suntanned face. The heavy lids blinked.

"I want to know what's wrong," Dermot said.

"There's nothing wrong," said Betty, shaking her head. "Only—I wanted to talk to you. I'm afraid I've got to leave here."

"When?"

"Tonight."

Dermot sat up. It seemed to him that there was a stranger sitting across from him, and that all his plans were toppling.

"If you must, you must," he said. "But I've got to go myself at the beginning of the week. I thought we were going to leave together."

"I can't. Very shortly"—she spoke with some intensity—"I hope I can explain to you what a beast I am. All I can tell you now is that it's not altogether safe for me to be here."

"Safe? In this place?"

Betty was not listening. She was wearing white, as he always remembered afterwards. With a white handbag. Again she had opened this handbag, and was going through it in something of a hurry.

"Derry." She spoke sharply. "You haven't seen my compact, have you? The white ivory one with the red band?" She looked round. "It didn't fall out when I opened my handbag before?"

"No, I don't think so. I didn't see it."

"I must have left it back in my room. Please excuse me. I'll be back in half a tick."

And she got to her feet, snapped shut the catch of the handbag.

Dermot also got up. It would not be fair to say that he exploded. He was a mild-mannered man who arrived at all emotions with difficulty. But in the past few minutes he felt that a door had opened on a world he could not understand.

"Look here, Betty," he said. "I don't know what's got into you; but I insist on knowing. If there's anything wrong, just tell me and we'll put it right. If—"

"I'll be back in a moment," she assured him.

And, disregarding the hand he put out, she hurried back through the arbor.

Dermot sat down heavily, and stared after her. A veiled sun had turned the sky to gray, making dingy the cloths of the little tables on the lawn. The cloths fluttered under a faint breeze.

He contemplated the arbor, which was a very special sort of arbor. Monsieur Gant, the proprietor of the Hotel Suchard, had imported it from Italy and was very proud of it. Stretching back a full twenty yards to the rear terrace of the hotel, it made a sort of tunnel composed of tough interlaced vines which in summer were heavy with purplish-pink blossoms. A line of tables ran beside it, with lights from above. Inside the arbor, at night, Chinese latterns hung from the roof. It was one of the romantic features of the hotel. But at the moment—cramped, unlighted, hooded with thick foliage—it was a tunnel which suggested unpleasant images.

"A good place for a murder," Betty had once laughed.

Andrew Dermot could hear his watch ticking. He wished she would come back.

He lit a cigarette and smoked it to a stump; but she had not returned. He got to his feet, stamping on the chilling grass. For the first time he glanced across the tea table at Betty's empty chair. It was a wicker chair.

And, lying on the seat in plain view, was a white ivory compact with a red band.

So that was it! She had been too much upset to notice the compact, of course. She was probably still searching her room for it.

He picked up the compact and went after her.

Inside the arbor it was almost dark, but chinks and glimmers of light flickered through interlaced vines and showed him an arched tunnel some ten feet high, with a floor of packed sand. There was a stagnant smell of dying blossom; the Judas tree, did they call it? Obscurely, he was relieved to find the gnat-stung arbor empty. He hurried along its length to the arch of light at the end, and emerged on a red-tiled terrace where there were more tables under the windows.

"Good eefening, Mr. Dermot," said an affable voice.

Dermot checked his rush.

He almost stumbled over Dr. Henrik Vanderver of the Sylvanian Embassy, who was sitting near the arbor, smoking a cigar with relish, and looking at him through thick-lensed spectacles.

"Ha, ha, ha!" said Dr. Vanderver, laughing uproariously and for no apparent reason, as was his custom.

"Good evening, Dr. Vanderver," said Dermot. His uneasiness had gone; he felt again a nerve-ridden fool. "Sorry to barge into you like that. Is Miss Weatherill down yet?"

Dr. Vanderver was proud of his English.

"Down?" he repeated, drawing down his eyebrows as though to illustrate.

"From her room, I mean."

"De young lady," said Vanderver, "iss with you. I have seen her go through dere"—he pointed to the arbor—"fifteen, twenty minutes ago."

"Yes, I know. But she came back here to get a compact."

Vanderver was now anxious about his English.

"Please?" he prompted, cupping his hand behind his ear.

"I said she came back here to get a compact. You know. This kind of thing." Dermot held it up. "She walked back through the arbor—"

"My friend," said Vanderver with sudden passion, "I do not know if I have understood you. Nobody has come back through this arbor while I am sitting here."

"But that's impossible."

"Please?"

Dermot thought he saw the explanation. "You mean you haven't been sitting here all the time?"

"My friend," said Vanderver, taking out a watch and shaking it, "I am sitting here one hour more—more!—where I sit always and smoke my cigar before I dress. Yes?"

"Well, Doctor?"

"I have seen the young lady go through, yes. But I have not seen her come back. I haf not seen nobody. In all dat time the only liffing soul I see on this terrace is the maid which gather up your tea-tray and bring it back here."

The terrace, always dark in the shadow of the arbor, was growing more dusky.

"Dr. Vanderver, listen to me." Dermot spoke coldly and sharply; he found Vanderver's thick-lensed spectacles turning on him with hypnotic effect. "That is not what I mean. I remember the maid going back through the arbor with the tray. But Miss Weatherill was with me then. I mean later. L-a-t-e-r, several minutes later. You saw Miss Weatherill come out through here about ten minutes ago, didn't you?"

"No."

"But you must have! I saw her go into the arbor on my side, and I never took my eyes off the entrance. She isn't in the arbor now; see for yourself. She must have come out here."

"So!" said Vanderver, tapping the table with magnificent dignity. "Now I tell you something. I do not know what you think has happened to the young lady. Perhaps de goblins ketch her, yes? Perhaps she dissolved to electrons and dust, yes?" Dark blood suffused his face. "Now I will haf no more of this. I settle it. I tell you." He thrust out his thick neck. "Nobody," he said flatly, "hass come back through this arbor at all."

By nine o'clock that night, terror had come to the Hotel Suchard.

Until then Monsieur Gant, the manager, had refrained from summoning the police. At first Monsieur Gant appeared to think that everybody was joking. He only began to gesticulate, and to run from room to room, when it became clear that Betty Weatherill was not to be found either in the hotel or in the grounds. If the testimony were to be believed—and neither Dermot nor Vanderver would retract one word—then Betty Weatherill had simply walked into the arbor, and there had vanished like a puff of smoke.

It was certain that she had not left the arbor by, say, getting out through the vines. The vines grew up from the ground in a matted tangle like a wire cage, so trained around their posts from floor to arch that it would be impossible to penetrate them without cutting. And nowhere were they disturbed in any way. There was not—as one romantic underporter suggested—an underground passage out of the tunnel. It was equally certain that Betty could not have been hiding in the arbor when Dermot walked through it. There was no place there to hide in.

This became only too clear when the Chinese lanterns were lighted in the greenish tunnel, and Monsieur Gant stood on a stepladder to shake frantically at the vine-walls—with half the domestic staff twittering behind him. This was a family matter, in which everybody took part.

Alys Marchand, in fact, was the backstairs-heroine of the occasion. Alys was the plump waitress who had been sent to fetch fresh tea and sandwiches not fifteen minutes before Betty's disappearance, but who had not brought them back because of a disagreement with the cook as to what hours constituted feev-o'clock-tay.

Apart from Dermot, Alys had been the last person to see Betty Weatherill in the flesh. Alys had passed unscathed through the arbor. To Monsieur Gant she described, with a wealth of gesture, how she had taken the order for tea and sandwiches from Monsieur Dermot. She showed how she had picked up the big tray, whisking a cloth over its debris like a conjuror. A pink-cheeked brunette, very neat in her black frock and apron, she illustrated how she had walked back through the arbor towards the hotel.

Had she seen Dr. Vanderver on this occasion?

She had.

Where was he?

At the little table on the terrace. He was smoking a cigar, and sharpening a big horn-handled knife on a small whetstone block he carried in his pocket.

"That," interposed Vanderver, in excellent French, "is a damned lie."

It was very warm in the arbor, under the line of Chinese lanterns. Vanderver stood against the wall. He seemed less bovine when he spoke French. But a small bead of perspiration had appeared on his forehead, up by the large vein near the temple; and the expression of his eyes behind the thick spectacles turned Andrew Dermot cold.

"It is true as I tell you," shrieked Alys, turning round her dark eyes. "I told my sister Clothilde, and Gina and Odette too, when I went to the kitchen. He thrusts it into his pocket—quick, so—when he sees me."

"There are many uses for knives," said Monsieur Gant, hastily and nervously. "At the same time, perhaps it would be as well to telephone the police. You are an advocate, Monsieur Dermot. You agree?"

Dermot did agree.

He had been keeping tight hold of his nerves. In fact, he found the cold reason of his profession returning to him; and it was he who directed matters. Instead of bringing back the nightmare, this practical situation steadied him. He saw the issue clearly now. It became even more clear when he arrived, amid a squad of plainclothes men, none other than Monsieur Lespinasse, the *juge d'instruction*.

After examining the arbor, M. Lespinasse faced them all in the manager's office. He was a long, lean, melancholy man with hollow cheeks, and the Legion of Honor in his buttonhole. He had hard uncomfortable eyes, which stared down at them.

"You understand," said Lespinasse, "we appear to have here a miracle. Now I am a realist. I do not believe in miracles."

"That is good," said Dermot grimly, in his careful French. "You have perhaps formed a theory?"

"A certainty," said Lespinasse.

The hard uncomfortable eyes turned on Dermot.

"From our examination," said Lespinasse, "it is certain that Mlle. Weatherill did not leave the arbor by any secret means. You, monsieur, tell one story." He looked at Vanderver. "You, monsieur, tell another." He looked back at Dermot. "It is therefore evident that one of you must be telling a lie."

Vanderver protested at this.

"I remind you," Vanderver growled, with signficant look, "that it will be unwise for you to make mistakes. As an acting representative of His Majesty the King of Sylvania, I enjoy immunities. I enjoy privileges—"

"Diplomatic privileges," said Monsieur Lespinasse. "That is no concern of mine. My concern is that you do not break the civil law."

"I have broken no law!" said Vanderver, purple in the face. "I have told no lie!"

The *juge d'instruction* held up his hand.

"And I tell you in return," he said sharply, "that either your story or Monsieur Dermot's must be untrue. Either the young lady never went into the arbor, in which case Monsieur Dermot is telling a falsehood. Or else she did go in, and for some reason you choose to deny that you saw her come out. In which case—" Again he held up his hand. "It is only fair to warn you, Dr. Vanderver, that Miss Weatherill told me you might try to kill her."

They could hear a clock ticking in the overcrowded room.

"Kill?" said Vanderver.

"That is what I said."

"But I did not know her!"

"Evidently she knew you," answered M. Lespinasse. His sallow face was alive with bitterness; he fingered the rosette in his buttonhold. Then he took a step forward. "Miss Weatherill several times came to me at the prefecture of police. She told me of your—murderous activities in the past. I did not choose to believe her. It was too much of a responsibility. Responsibility! Now this happens, and I must take the responsibility for it at least. One more question, if you please. What have you to say to the maid's story of the horn-handled knife?"

Vanderver's voice was hoarse. "I never owned such a knife. I never saw one. I call you a son of—"

"It will not be necessary to finish," said the *juge d'instruction*. "On the contrary, we shall finish." He snapped his fingers, and one of the plainclothes men brought into the room an object wrapped in a newspaper.

"Our search of the arbor," continued M. Lespinasse, "was perhaps more thorough than that of Monsieur Gant. This was found buried in the sand floor only a few feet away from where monsieur was sitting."

There were more than damp stains of sand on the bright, wafer-thin blade in the newspaper; there were others. Monsieur Lespinasse pointed to them.

"Human blood," he said.

At eleven o'clock Andrew Dermot was able to get out of the room.

They told him afterwards that he had made an admirable witness; that his replies had been calm, curt, and to the point; and that he had even given sound advice on details of legal procedure, contrasting those of England with those of the present country.

He did not remember this. He knew only that he must get out into the air and stop himself from thinking of Betty.

He stood on the front terrace of the hotel, as far removed as possible from the arbor in whose floor the knife had been buried. Half a mile away the light of the principal street in the town, the Promenade des Français, twinkled with deathly pallor. A cool wind swept the terrace.

They took Vanderver down the front steps and bundled him into a car. There was a chain round Vanderver's wrists; his legs shook so that they had to push him up into the car. The car roared away, with a puff of smoke from the exhaust—carbon monoxide , which meant death—and only the *juge d'instruction* remained behind searching Vanderver's room for some clue as to why a sudden, meaningless murder had been done at dusk beside a commonplace hotel.

Andrew Dermot put his hands to his temples, pressing hard.

Well, that was that.

He sat down on the terrace. The little round tables had red tops, and the color did not please him, but he remained. He ordered brandy, which he could not taste. The brandy was brought to him by the same underporter who had suggested an underground passage in the arbor, and who, agog, seemed to want to entertain him with speculations about motives for murder. Dermot chased him away.

But if Betty had to go—"go" was hardly the word for that—where was the sense in it? Why? Why? Vanderver was presumably not a homicidal maniac. Besides, all Dermot's legal instincts were bewildered by so clumsy a crime. If Vanderver were guilty, why had he from the first persisted in that unnecessary lie of saying Betty had never come out of the arbor? Why hadn't he simply faded away, never professing to have seen anything at all? Why thrust himself at that entrance as though determined to ensure suspicion for himself?

What Dermot had not permitted himself to wonder was where Betty herself might be.

But suppose Vanderver had been telling the truth?

Nonsense! Vanderver could not be telling the truth. People do not vanish like soap bubbles out of guarded tunnels.

Presently they would be turning out the lights here on this windy, deserted terrace. The Hotel Suchard was ready, in any case, to close its doors for the winter; it would close its doors very early tonight. Behind him, in lighted windows, glowed the lounge, the smoking room, the dining room where he had first seen Betty. The head porter, his footsteps rapping on hardwood, darkened first the dining room and then the lounge. Dermot would have to go upstairs to his room and try to sleep.

Getting to his feet, he walked through the thick carpeted hall. But he could not help it. He must have one more look at the arbor.

It was a veritable tunnel now: a black shape inside which, for twenty yards, Chinese lanterns glowed against the roof. The sand was torn where the knife had been dug out. Near that patch two shovels had been propped against the wall in readiness for deeper excavations next morning. It was when he noted those preparations, and realized what they meant, that Dermot's mind turned black; he had reached his lowest depth.

He was so obsessed by it that he did not, at first, hear footfalls on the tiled terrace. He turned round. Two persons had come out to join him— but they came by different windows, and they stopped short and stared at each other as much as they stared at him.

One of these persons was M. Lespinasse, the *juge d'instruction*.

The other was Betty Weatherill.

"And now, mademoiselle," roared Lespinasse, "perhaps you will be good enough to explain the meaning of this ridiculous and indefensible trick?"

M. Lespinasse, his cheekbones were more formidable, was carrying a briefcase and a valise. He let both fall to the floor.

"I had to do it," said Betty, addressing Dermot. "I *had* to do it, my dear."

She was not smiling at him. Dermot felt that presently, in the sheer relief of nerves, they would both be shouting with laughter. At the moment he only knew that she was there, and that he could touch her.

"One moment," said Lespinasse, coldly interrupting what was going on. "You do well, Monsieur Dermot, to demand an explanation—"

"But I don't. So long as she's—"

"—of this affair." The *juge d'instruction* raised his voice. "I can now tell you, in fact I came downstairs to tell you, *how* Miss Weatherill played this trick. What I do not know is why she did it."

Betty whirled round. "You know how?"

"I know, mademoiselle," snapped the other, "that you planned this foolishness and carried it out with the assistance of Alys Marchand, who deserves a formidable stroke of the boot behind for her part in the affair. When I found Alys ten minutes ago capering round her room waving a packet of thousand-franc notes, her behavior seemed to call for some explanation." He looked grim. "Alys was very shortly persuaded to give one."

Then he turned to Dermot.

"Let me indicate what happened, and you shall confirm it! Miss Weatherill asked you to meet her here, even specifying the table you were to occupy, and said she would arrive after tea?"

"Yes," said Dermot.

"At half-past five she came through the arbor—first making certain that Dr. Vanderver was on the terrace in the place he always occupied, every day, to smoke a cigar at that hour?"

"I—yes."

"Miss Weatherill was easily persuaded to have a fresh cup of tea?"

"Well, I asked her to."

"The waitress, Alys, was then pottering round for no apparent reason among otherwise deserted tables?"

"She was."

"You gave the order to Alys," said Monsieur Lespinasse grimly. "She picked up your tray—a big tray—whisking over it a large cloth to cover the dishes? Just as we later saw her do?"

"I do admit it."

"Alys then walked away from you through the arbor. As she did so," leered Lespinasse, so intent that he made a face, "Miss Weatherill distracted your attention by gettng a light for her cigarette. And kept your attention fixed on herself by dropping the cigarette, and pretending an agitation she did not feel."

Dermot gave a quick look at Betty. Whatever else this might be, it was not a hoax or a joke. Betty's face was white.

"Miss Weatherill held your attention," said Lespinasse, "so that Alys could slip back out of the arbor unnoticed. *Alys did not really go through the arbor at all!* Carrying the tray, she merely darted round the side of the arbor and returned unseen to the hotel by another way.

"Miss Weatherill was then ready to play the rest of the comedy. 'Discovering' the loss of her compact, *she* enters the arbor. Halfway up, in the darkness, is lying a stage property these two have already left there. This is another tray: like the first, and covered with a cloth. But this cloth does not cover dishes. It covers—" Monsieur Lespinasse broke off.

He looked flustered and dishevelled, but in his wicked eye there was a gleam of admiration.

"Monsieur Dermot, I tell you a psychological truth. The one person in this world whose features nobody can remember are those of a waitress. You see her at close range; yet you do not see her. Should you doubt this, the next time in your abominable London you go into a Lyons or an A.B.C., try calling for your bill in a hurry and see if you can identify the particular young lady who served you with a cup of tea. I know it. So did Miss Weatherill.

"She was already wearing a thin black frock under her white one. The tray in the arbor contained the other properties by which a blonde is changed into a brunette, white stockings and shoes change to black, a tanned complexion is heightened to a vivid ruddiness. It was the clumsiest possible disguise because it needed to be no more. Dr. Vanderver never glanced twice at the black-clad figure in cap and apron who walked out of the arbor carrying a tray. He saw no black wig; he saw no false complexion; he saw nothing. In his mind there registered, 'waitress-has-passed': no more. Thus Miss Weatherill, inexpertly got up as Alys, passed safely thorugh the dense shadow which the arbor casts on the terrace— carrying before her the tray whose cloth neatly hid the discarded white dress, stockings, and shoes."

The *juge d'instruction* drew a deep, whistling breath.

"Very well!" he said. "But what I wish to know is: *why?*"

"You don't see it even yet?" asked Betty.

"My deepest apologies," said Lespinasse, "if I am dense. But I do not see it. You cannot have liked cutting yourself so that you might get real blood to put on the knife you buried. But why? How does all this nonsense help us, when Dr. Vanderver has committed no crime?"

"Because he's Embassy," answered Betty simply.

"Mademoiselle?"

"He has diplomatic immunity," said Betty. "The government can't search him; can't even touch him. And so, you see, I had to get him arrested by the *civil* authorities so that his papers could be searched."

She turned to Dermot.

"Derry, I'm sorry," she went on. "That is, I'm sorry I'm not quite the candid-camera schoolmistress burbling to high heaven that I pretended to be. But I want to be just that. I want to enjoy myself. For the first time in all my life, I've enjoyed myself in the last month. What I mean is: I want to be with you, that's all. So, now that I'm chucking the beastly job—"

Monsieur Lespinasse swore softly. After remaining rigid for a moment, he picked up the briefcase and the valise he had dropped. Both were in green leather stamped in gold with the royal arms of Sylvania.

"—and of course," Betty was saying almost wildly, "the fellow's name wasn't 'Dr. Vanderver,' and he's no more a neutral than I am. Only he'd got that job on forged credentials, and he was safe. So I had to keep telling the *juge d'instruction* I suspected him of being a murderer. His real name is Karl Heinrich von Arnheim; and when Sir George—you know to whom I refer, Monsieur Lespinasse—asked me to go after him—"

Monsieur Lespinasse could not break the lock of the briefcase. So he opened a wicked-looking knife of his own to slit the leather; and so he found the secret.

"The English," he said, "are not bad." He waved the knife, which glittered against the light from the windows. "Dr. Vanderver will not, I think, leave the police station after all." He swept Betty Weatherill a profound bow. "The complete plans," he added, "of the underground fortifications whose fall would break the whole line of defense along this front."

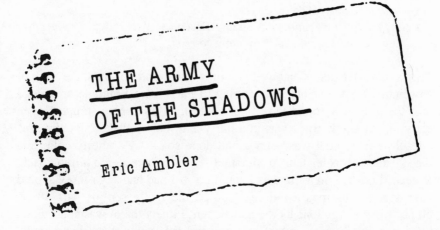

THE ARMY OF THE SHADOWS

Eric Ambler

It is three years since Llewellyn removed my appendix; but we still meet occasionally. I am dimly related to his wife: that, at least, is the pretext for the acquaintanceship. The truth is that, during my convalescence, we happened to discover that we both like the same musicians. Before the war we usually met when there was some Sibelius being played and went to hear it together. I was a little puzzled when, about three weeks ago, he telephoned with the suggestion that I should dine at his house that night. There was not, I knew, a concert of any sort in London. I agreed, however, to grope my way round to Upper Wimpole Street shortly before eight o'clock.

It was not until he had presented me with a brandy that I found out why I had been invited to dinner.

"Do you remember," he said suddenly, "that I spent a week or so in Belgrade last year? I missed Beecham doing the Second through it. There was one of those international medical bun fights being held there, and I went to represent the Association. My German is fairly good, you know. I motored. Can't stick trains. Anyway, on the way back a very funny thing happened to me. Did I ever tell you about it?"

"I don't think so."

"I thought not. Well"—he laughed self-consciously—"it was so funny now there's a war on that I've been amusing myself by writing the whole thing down. I wondered whether you'd be good enough to cast a professional eye over it for me. I've tried"—he laughed again—"to make a really literary job of it. Like a story, you know."

His hand had been out of sight behind the arm of his chair, but now it emerged from hiding holding a wad of typewritten sheets.

"It's typed." he said, planking it down on my knees. And then, with a theatrical glance at his watch, "Good Lord, it's ten. There's a telephone call I must make. Excuse me for a minute or two, will you?"

He was out of the room before I could open my mouth to reply. I was left *alone with the manuscript.*

I picked it up. It was entitled A Strange Encounter. *With a sigh, I turned over the title page and began, rather irritably, to read:*

THE STELVIO PASS is snowed up in winter, and towards the end of November most sensible men driving to Paris from Belgrade or beyond take the long way round via Milan rather than risk being stopped by an early fall of snow. But I was in a hurry and took a chance. By the time I reached Bolzano I was sorry I had done so. It was bitterly cold, and the sky ahead was leaden. At Merano I seriously considered turning back. Instead, I pushed on as hard as I could go. If I had had any sense I should have stopped for petrol before I started the really serious part of the climb. I had six gallons by the gauge then. I knew that it wasn't accurate, but I had filled up early that morning and calculated that I had enough to get me to Sargans. In my anxiety to beat the snow I overlooked the fact that I had miles of low-gear driving to do. On the Swiss side and on the Sargans road where it runs within a mile or two of the Rhàtikon part of the German frontier, the car spluttered to a standstill.

For a minute or two I sat there swearing at and to myself and wondering what on earth I was going to do. I was, I knew, the only thing on the road that night for miles.

It was about eight o'clock, very dark and very cold. Except for the faint creaking of the cooling engine and the rustle of the breeze in some nearby trees, there wasn't a sound to be heard. Ahead, the road in the headlights curved away to the right. I got out the map and tried to find out where I was.

I had passed through one village since I left Klosters, and I knew that it was about ten kilometres back. I must, therefore, either walk back ten kilometres to that village, or forward to the next village, whichever was the nearer. I looked at the map. It was of that useless kind that they sell to motorists. There was nothing marked between Klosters and Sargans. For all I knew, the next village might be fifteen or twenty kilometers away.

An Alpine road on a late November night is not the place to choose if you want to sleep in your car. I decided to walk back the way I had come.

I had a box of those small Italian waxed matches with me when I started out. There were, I thought, about a hundred in the box, and I calculated that, if I struck one every hundred metres, they would last until I reached the village.

That was when I was near the lights of the car. When I got out of sight of them, things were different. The darkness seemed to press against the backs of my eyes. It was almost painful. I could not even see the shape of the road along which I was walking. It was only by the rustling and the smell of resin that I knew that I was walking between fir trees. By the time I had covered a mile I had six matches left. Then it began to snow.

I say "snow." It had been snow; but the Sargans road was still below the snow line, and the stuff came down as a sort of half-frozen mush that slid down my face into the gap between my coat collar and my neck.

I must have done about another mile and a half when the real trouble began. I still had the six matches, but my hands were too numb to get them out of the box without wetting them, and I had been going forward blindly, sometimes on the road and sometimes off it. I was wondering whether I would get along better if I sang, when I walked into a telegraph post.

It was precast concrete and the edge was as sharp as a razor. My face was as numb as my hands and I didn't feel much except a sickening jar; but I could taste blood trickling between my teeth and found that my nose was bleeding. It was as I held my head back to stop it that I saw the light, looking for all the world as if it were suspended in midair above me.

It wasn't suspended in midair, and it wasn't above me. Darkness does strange things to perspective. After a few seconds I saw that it was showing through the trees on the hillside, up off the right of the road.

Anyone who has been in the sort of mess that I was in will know exactly how my mind worked at that moment. I did not speculate as to the origin of that God-forsaken light or as to whether or not the owner of it would be pleased to see me. I was cold and wet, my nose was bleeding, and I would not have cared if someone had told me that behind the light was a maniac with a machine gun. I knew only that the light meant that there was some sort of human habitation near me and that I was going to spend the night in it.

I moved over to the other side of the road and began to feel my way along the wire fence I found there. Twenty yards or so farther on, my hands touched a wooden gate. The light was no longer visible, but I pushed the gate open and walked on into the blackness.

The ground rose steeply under my feet. It was a path of sorts, and soon I stumbled over the beginnings of a flight of log steps. There must have been well over a hundred of them. Then there was another stretch of path, not quite so steep. When I again saw the light, I was only about twenty yards from it.

It came from an oil reading-lamp standing near a window. From the shape of the window and the reflected light of the lamp, I could see that the place was a small chalet of the kind usually let to families for the summer season or for the winter sports. That it should be occupied at the end of November was curious. But I didn't ponder over the curiosity: I had seen something else through the window besides the lamp. The light from a fire was flickering in the room.

I went forward up the path to the door. There was no knocker. I hammered on the wet, varnished wood with my fist and waited. There was no sound from inside. After a moment or two I knocked again. Still there was no sign of life within. I knocked and waited for several minutes. Then I began to shiver. In desperation I grabbed the latch of the door and rattled it violently. The next moment I felt it give and the door creaked open a few inches.

I think that I have a normal, healthy respect for the property and privacy of my fellow creatures; but at that moment I was feeling neither normal nor healthy. Obviously, the owner of the chalet could not be far away. I stood there for a moment or two, hesitating. I could smell the wood smoke from the fire, and mingled with it a bitter oily smell which seemed faintly familiar. But all I cared about was the fire. I hesitated no longer and walked in.

As soon as I was inside I saw that there was something more than curious about the place, and that I should have waited.

The room itself was ordinary enough. It was rather larger than I had expected, but there were the usual pinewood walls, the usual pinewood floor, the usual pinewood staircase up to the bedrooms, and the usual tiled fireplace. There were the usual tables and chairs, too: turned and painted nonsense of the kind that sometimes finds its way into English tea shops. There were red gingham curtains over the windows. You felt that the owner probably had lots of other places just like it, and that he made a good thing out of letting them.

No, it was what had been added to the room that was curious. All the furniture had been crowded into one half of the space. In the other half, standing on linoleum and looking as if it were used a good deal, was a printing press.

The machine was a small treadle platten of the kind used by jobbing printers for running off tradesmen's circulars. It looked very old and decrepit. Alongside it on a trestle table were a case of type and a small proofing press with a locked-up form in it. On a second table stood a pile of interleaved sheets, beside which was a stack of what appeared to be some of the same sheets folded. The folding was obviously being done by hand. I picked up one of the folded sheets.

It looked like one of those long, narrow business promotion folders issued by travel agencies. The front page was devoted to the reproduction, in watery blue ink, of a linocut of a clump of pines on the shore of a lake, and the display of the word "TITISEE." Page two and the page folded in to face it carried a rhapsodical account in German of the beauties of Baden in general and Lake Titisee in particular.

I put the folder down. An inaccessible Swiss chalet was an odd place to choose for printing German travel advertisements; but I was not disposed to dwell on its oddity. I was cold.

I was moving towards the fire when my eye was caught by five words printed in bold capitals on one of the unfolded sheets on the table: "DEUTSCHE MÄNNER UND FRAUEN, KAMERADEN."

I stood still. I remember that my heart thudded against my ribs as suddenly and violently as it had earlier that day on the Stelvio when some crazy fool in a Hispano had nearly crowded me off the road.

I leaned forward, picked the folder up again, and opened it right out. The message began on the second of the three inside pages.

"GERMAN MEN AND WOMEN, COMRADES! We speak to you with the voice of German Democracy, bringing you news. Neither Nazi propaganda nor the Gestapo can silence us, for we have an ally which is proof against floggings, an ally which no man in the history of the world has been able to defeat. That ally is Truth. Hear then, people of Germany, the Truth which is concealed from you. Hear it, remember it, and repeat it. The sooner the Truth is known, the sooner will Germany again hold up its head among the free nations of the world."

Then followed a sort of news bulletin consisting of facts and figures (especially figures) about the economic condition of Germany. There was also news of a strike in the Krupp works at Essen and a short description of a riot outside a shipyard in Hamburg.

I put it down again. Now I knw why these "travel advertisements" were being printed in an inaccessible Swiss chalet instead of in Germany itself. No German railway official would distribute these folders. That business would be left to more desperate men. These folders would not collect dust on the counters of travel agencies. They would be found in trains and in trams, in buses and in parked cars, in waiting rooms and in bars, under restaurant plates and inside table napkins. Some of the men that put them there would be caught and tortured to betray their fellows; but the distribution would go on. The folders would be read, perhaps furtively discussed. A little more truth would seep through Goebbels' dam of lies to rot still further the creaking foundation of Nazidom.

Then, as I stood there with the smell of wood smoke and printing ink in my nostrils, as I stood staring at that decrepit little machine as if it were the very voice of freedom, I heard footsteps outside.

I suppose that I should have stood my ground. I had, after all, a perfectly good explanation of my presence there. My car and the blood from my nose would confirm my story. But I didn't reason that way. I had stumbled on a secret, and my first impulse was to try to hide the fact from the owner of the secret. I obeyed that impulse.

I looked round quickly and saw the stairs. Before I had even begun to wonder if I might not be doing something excessively stupid, I was up the stairs and opening the first door I came to on the landing. In the half-light I caught a glimpse of a bed; then I was inside the room with the door slightly ajar. I could see across the landing and through the wooden palings along it to the top of the window at the far side of the room below.

I knew that someone had come in: I could hear him moving about. He lit another lamp. There was a sound from the door and a second person entered.

A woman's voice said in German, "Thank God, Johann has left a good fire."

There was an answering grunt. It came from the man. I could almost feel them warming their hands.

"Get the coffee, Freda," said the man suddenly. "I must go back soon."

"But Bruno is there. You should take a little rest first."

"Bruno is a Berliner. He is not as used to the cold as I am. If Kurt should come now he would be tired. Bruno could only look after himself."

There was silence for a moment. Then the woman spoke again.

"Do you really think that he will come now, Stephan? It is so late." She paused. Her voice had sounded casual, elaborately casual; but now, as she went on, there was an edge to it that touched the nerves. "I can keep quite calm about it you see, Stephan. I wish to believe, but it is so late, isn't it? You don't think he will come now, do you? Admit it."

He laughed, but too heartily. "You are too nervous, Freda. Kurt can take care of himself. He knows all the tricks now. He may have been waiting for the first snow. The frontier guards would not be so alert on a night like this."

"He should have been back a week ago. You know that as well as I do, Stephan. He has never been delayed so long before. They have got him. That is all. You see, I can be calm about it even though he is my dear husband." And then her voice broke. "I knew it would happen sooner or later. I knew it. First Hans, then Karl, and now Kurt. Those swine, those—"

She sobbed and broke suddenly into passionate weeping. He tried helplessly to comfort her.

I had heard enough. I was shaking from head to foot: but whether it was the cold or not, I don't know. I stood back from the door. Then, as I did so, I heard a sound from behind me.

I had noticed the bed as I had slipped into the room, but the idea that there might be someone in it had not entered my head. Now, as I whipped round, I saw that I had made a serious mistake.

Sitting on the edge of the bed in which he had been lying was a very thin, middle-aged man in a nightshirt. By the faint light from the landing I could see his eyes, bleary from sleep, and his grizzled hair standing ludicrously on end. But for one thing I should have laughed. That one thing was the large automatic pistol which he held pointed at me. His hand was as steady as a rock.

"Don't move," he said. He raised his voice. "Stephan! Come quickly!"

"I must apologize . . ." I began in German.

"You will be allowed to speak later."

I heard Stephan dash up the stairs.

"What is it, Johann?"

"Come here."

The door was pushed open behind me. I heard him draw in his breath sharply.

"Who is it?"

"I do not know. I was awakened by a noise. I was about to get up when this man came into the room. He did not see me. He has been listening to your conversation. He must have been examining the plant when he heard you returning."

"If you will allow me to explain. . . ."

"You may explain downstairs," said the man called Stephan. "Give me the pistol, Johann."

The pistol changed hands and I could see Stephan, a lean, rawboned fellow with broad, sharp shoulders and dangerous eyes. He wore black oilskins and gum boots. I saw the muscles in his cheeks tighten.

"Raise your hands and walk downstairs. Slowly. If you run, I shall shoot immediately. March."

I went downstairs.

The woman, Freda, was standing by the door, staring blankly up at me as I descended. She must have been about thirty and had that soft rather matronly look about her that is characteristic of so many young German women. She was short and plump, and as if to accentuate the fact, her straw-colored hair was plaited across her head. Wisps of the hair had become detached and clung wetly to the sides of her neck. She too wore a black oilskin coat and gum boots.

The grey eyes, red and swollen with crying, looked beyond me.

"He was hiding upstairs."

We had reached the foot of the stairs. He motioned me away from the door and towards the fire. "Now, we will hear your explanation."

I gave it with profuse apologies. I admitted that I had examined the folders and read on. "It seemed to me," I concluded, "that my presence might be embarrassing to you. I was about to leave when you returned. Then, I am afraid, I lost my head and attempted to hide."

Not one of them was believing a word that I was saying: I could see that from their faces. "I assure you," I went on in exasperation, "that what I am telling . . . ."

"What nationality are you?"

"British. I. . . ."

"Then speak English. What were you doing on this road?"

"I am on my way home from Belgrade. I crossed the Yugoslav frontier yesterday and the Italian frontier at Stelvio this afternoon. My passport was stamped at both places if you wish to. . . ."

"Why were you in Belgrade?"

"I am a surgeon. I have been attending an international medical convention there."

"Let me see your passport, please."

"Certainly. I have. . . ." And then with my hand in my inside pocket, I stopped. My heart felt as if it had come right into my throat. In my haste to be away after the Italian Customs had finished with me, I had thrust my passport with the Customs carnet for the car into the pocket beside me on the door of the car.

They were watching me with expressionless faces. Now, as my hand reappeared empty, I saw Stephan raise his pistol.

"Well?"

"I am sorry." Like a fool I had begun to speak in German again. "I find that I have left my passport in my car. It is several kilometres along the road. If. . . ."

And then the woman burst out as if she couldn't stand listening to me any longer.

"Don't you see? Don't you see?" she cried. "It is quite clear. They have found out that we are here. Perhaps after all these months Hans or Karl has been tortured by them into speaking. And so they have taken Kurt and sent this man to spy upon us. It is clear. Don't you see?"

She turned suddenly, and I thought she was going to attack me. Then Stephan put his hand on her arm.

"Gently, Freda." He turned to me again, and his expression hardened. "You see, my friend, what is in our minds? We know our danger, you see. The fact that we are in Swiss territory will not protect us if the Gestapo should trace us. The Nazis, we know, have little respect for frontiers. The Gestapo have none. They would murder us here as confidently as they would if we were in the Third Reich. We do not underrate their cunning. The fact that you are not a German is not conclusive. You may be what you say you are: you may not. If you are, so much the better. If not, then, I give you fair warning, you will be shot. You say that your passport is in your car several kilometres along the road. Unfortunately, it is not possible for us to spare time tonight to see if that is true. Nor is it possible for one of us to stand guard over you all night. You have already disturbed the first sleep Johann has had in twenty-four hours. There is only one thing for it, I'm afraid. It is undignified and barbaric; but I see no other way. We shall be forced to tie you up so that you cannot leave."

"But this is absurd," I cried angrily. "Good heavens man, I realize that I've only myself to blame for being here; but surely you could have the common decency to . . . ."

"The question," he said sternly, "is not of decency, but of necessity. We have no time tonight for six-kilometre walks. One of our comrades has been delivering a consignment of these folders to our friends in Germany. We hope and believe that he will return to us across the frontier tonight. He may need our help. Mountaineering in such weather is exhausting. Freda, get me some of the cord we use for tying the packages."

I wanted to say something, but the words would not come. I was too angry. I don't think that I've ever been so angry in my life before.

She brought the cord. It was thick grey stuff. He took it and gave the pistol to Johann. Then he came towards me.

I don't think they liked the business any more than I did. He had gone a bit white and he wouldn't look me in the eyes. I think that I must have been white myself; but it was anger with me. He put the cord under one of my elbows. I snatched it away.

"You had better submit," he said harshly.

"To spare your feelings? Certainly not. You'll have to use force, my friend. But don't worry. You'll get used to it. You'll be a good Nazi yet. You should knock me down. That'll make it easier."

What color there was left in his face went. A good deal of my anger evaporated at that moment. I felt sorry for the poor devil. I really believe that I should have let him tie me up. But I never knew for certain; for at that moment there was an interruption.

It was the woman who heard it first—the sound of someone running up the path outside. The next moment a man burst wildly into the room.

Stephan had turned. "Bruno! What is it? Why aren't you at the hut?"

The man was striving to get his breath, and for a moment he could hardly speak. His face above the streaming oilskins was blue with cold. Then he gasped out.

"Kurt! He is at the hut! He is wounded—badly!"

The woman gave a little whimpering cry and her hands went to her face. Stephan gripped the newcomer's shoulder.

"What has happened? Quickly!"

"It was dark. The Swiss did not see him. It was one of our patrols. They shot him when he was actually on the Swiss side. He was wounded in the thigh. He crawled on to the hut, but he can go no further. He . . . "

But Stephan had ceased to listen. He turned sharply. "Johann, you must dress yourself at once. Bruno, take the pistol and guard this man. He broke in here. He may be dangerous. Freda, get the cognac and the iodine. We shall need them for Kurt."

He himself went to a cupboard and got out some handkerchiefs, which he began tearing feverishly into strips, which he knotted together. Still gasping for breath, the man Bruno had taken the pistol and was staring at me with a puzzled frown. Then the woman reappeared from the kitchen carrying a bottle of cognac and a small tube of iodine of the sort that is sold for dabbing at cut fingers. Stephan stuffed them in his pockets with the knotted handkerchiefs. Then he called up the stairs, "Hurry, Johann. We are ready to leave."

It was more than I could hear. Professional fussiness, I suppose.

"Has any one of you," I asked loudly, "ever dealt with a bullet wound before?"

They stared at me. Then Stephan glanced at Bruno.

"If he moves," he said, "shoot." He raised his voice again. "Johann!"

There was an answering cry of reassurance.

"Has it occurred to you," I persisted, "that even if you get him here alive, which I doubt, as you obviously don't know what you're doing, he will need immediate medical attention? Don't you think that one of you had better go for a doctor? Ah, but of course: the doctor would ask questions about a bullet wound, wouldn't he? The matter would be reported to the police."

"We can look after him," he grunted. "Johann! Hurry!"

"It seems a pity," I said reflectively, "that one brave man should have to die because of his friends' stupidity." And then my calm deserted me. "You damn fool," I shouted. "Listen to me. Do you want to kill this man? You're going about it the right way. I'm a surgeon, and this is a surgeon's business. Take that cognac out of your pocket. We shan't need it. The iodine too. And those pieces of rag. Have you got two or three clean towels?"

The woman nodded stupidly.

"Then get them, please, and be quick. And you said something about some coffee. Have you a flask for it? Good. Then we shall take that. Put plenty of sugar in it. I want blankets, too. Three will be enough, but they must be kept dry. We shall need a stretcher. Get two poles or broomsticks and two old coats. We can make a stretcher of sorts by putting the poles through the sleeves of them. Take this cord of yours too. It will be useful to make slings for the stretcher. And hurry! The man may be bleeding to death. Is he far away?"

The man was glowering at me. "Four kilometres. In a climbing hut in the hills this side of the frontier." He stepped forward and gripped my arm. "If you are tricking us . . ." he began.

"I'm not thinking about you." I snapped. "I'm thinking about a man who's been crawling along with a bullet in his thigh and a touching faith in his friends. Now get those poles, and hurry."

They hurried. In three minutes they had the things collected. The exhausted Bruno's oilskins and gum boots had, at my suggestion, been transferred to me. Then I tied one of the blankets round my waist under my coat, and told Stephan and Johann to do the same.

"I" said the woman, "will take the other things."

"You," I said, "will stay here, please."

She straightened up at that. "No," she said firmly, "I will come with you. I shall be quite calm. You will see."

"Nevertheless," I said rather brutally, "you will be more useful here. A bed must be ready by the fire here. There must also be hot bricks and plenty of blankets. I shall need, besides, both boiled and boiling water. You have plenty of ordinary salt, I suppose?"

"Yes, *Herr Doktor.* But . . ."

"We are wasting time."

Two minutes later we left.

I shall never forget that climb. It began about half a mile along the road below the chalet. The first part was mostly up narrow paths between trees. They were covered with pine needles and, in the rain, as slippery as the devil. We had been climbing steadily for about half an hour when

Stephan, who had been leading the way with a storm lantern, paused.

"I must put out the light here," he said. "The frontier is only three kilometres from here, and the guards patrol to a depth of two kilometres. They must not see us." He blew out the lamp. "Turn round," he said then. "You will see another light."

I saw it, far away below us, a pinpoint.

"That is our light. When we are returning from Germany, we can see it from across the frontier and know that we are nearly home and that our friends are waiting. Hold on to my coat now. You need not worry about Johann behind you. He knows the path well. This way, *Herr Doktor.*"

It was the only sign he gave that he had decided to accept me for what I said I was.

I cannot conceive of how anyone could know that path well. The surface soon changed from pine needles to a sort of rocky rubble, and it twisted and turned like a wounded snake. The wind had dropped, but it was colder than ever, and I found myself crunching through sugary patches of half-frozen slush. I wondered how on earth we were going to bring down a wounded man on an improvised stretcher.

We had been creeping along without the light for about twenty minutes when Stephan stopped and, shielding the lamp with his coat, relit it. I saw that we had arrived.

The climbing hut was built against the side of an overhanging rock face. It was about six feet square inside, and the man was lying diagonally across it on his face. There was a large bloodstain on the floor beneath him. He was semiconscious. His eyes were closed, but he mumbled something as I felt for his pulse.

"Will he live?" whispered Stephan.

I didn't know. The pulse was there, but it was feeble and rapid. His breathing was shallow. I looked at the wound. The bullet had entered on the inner side of the left thigh just below the groin. There was a little bleeding, but it obviously hadn't touched the femoral artery and, as far as I could see, the bone was all right. I made a dressing with one of the towels and tied it in place with another. The bullet could wait. The immediate danger was from shock aggravated by exposure. I got to work with the blankets and the flask of coffee. Soon the pulse strengthened a little, and after about half an hour I told them how to prepare the stretcher.

I don't know how they got him down that path in the darkness. It was all I could do to get down by myself. It was snowing hard now in great fleecy chunks that blinded you when you moved forward. I was prepared for them to slip and drop the stretcher; but they didn't. It was slow work, however, and it was a good forty minutes before we got to the point where it was safe to light the lamp.

After that I was able to help with the stretcher. At the foot of the path up to the chalet, I went ahead with the lantern. The woman heard my footsteps and came to the door. I realized that we must have been gone for the best part of three hours.

"They're bringing him up," I said. "He'll be all right. I shall need your help now."

She said, "The bed is ready." And then, "Is it serious, *Herr Doktor?*"

"No." I didn't tell her then that there was a bullet to be taken out.

It was a nasty job. The wound itself wasn't so bad. The bullet must have been pretty well spent, for it had lodged up against the bone without doing any real damage. It was the instruments that made it difficult. They came from the kitchen. He didn't stand up to it very well, and I wasn't surprised. I didn't feel so good myself when I'd finished. The cognac came in useful after all.

We finally got him to sleep about five.

"He'll be all right now," I said.

The woman looked at me and I saw the tears begin to trickle down her cheeks. It was only then that I remembered that she wasn't a nurse, but his wife.

It was Johann who comforted her. Stephan came over to me.

"We owe you a great debt, *Herr Doktor,*" he said. "I must apologize for our behavior earlier this evening. We have not always been savages, you know. Kurt was a professor of zoology. Johann was a master printer. I was an architect. Now we are those who crawl across frontiers at night and plot like criminals. We have been treated like savages, and so we live like them. We forget sometimes that we were civilized. We ask your pardon. I do not know how we can repay you for what you have done. We . . ."

But I was too tired for speeches. I smiled quickly at him.

"All that I need by way of a fee is another glass of cognac and a bed to sleep in for a few hours. I suggest, by the way, that you get a doctor in to look at the patient later today. There will be a little fever to treat. Tell the doctor he fell upon his climbing axe. He won't believe you, but there'll be no bullet for him to be inquisitive about. Oh, and if you could find me a little petrol for my car . . . ."

It was five in the afternoon and almost dark again when Stephan woke me. The local doctor, he reported, as he set an enormous tray of food down beside the bed, had been, dressed the wound, prescribed, and gone. My car was filled up with petrol and awaited me below if I wished to drive to Zurich that night. Kurt was awake and could not be prevailed upon to sleep until he had thanked me.

They were all there, grouped about the bed, when I went downstairs. Bruno was the only one who looked as if he had had any sleep.

He sprang to his feet. "Here, Kurt," he said facetiously, "is the *Herr Doktor*. He is going to cut your leg off."

Only the woman did not laugh at the jest. Kurt himself was smiling when I bent over to look at him.

He was a youngish-looking man of about forty with intelligent brown eyes and a high, wide forehead. The smile faded from his face as he looked at me.

"You know what I wish to say, *Herr Doktor?*"

I took refuge in professional brusqueness. "The less you say, the better," I said, and felt for his pulse. But as I did so his fingers moved and gripped my hand.

"One day soon," he said, "England and the Third Reich will be at war. But you will not be at war with Germany. Remember that, please, *Herr Doktor*. Not with Germany. It is people like us who are Germany, and in our way we shall fight with England. You will see."

I left soon after.

At nine that night I was in Zurich.

Llewellyn was back in the room. I put the manuscript down. He looked across at me.

"Very interesting," I said.

"I'd considered sending it up to one of these magazines that publish short stories," he said apologetically. "I thought I'd like your opinion first, though. What do you think?"

I cleared my throat. "Well, of course, it's difficult to say. Very interesting, as I said. But there's no real point to it, is there? It needs something to tie it all together."

"Yes, I see what you mean. It sort of leaves off, doesn't it? But that's how it actually happened." He looked disappointed. "I don't think I could invent an ending. It would be rather a pity, wouldn't it? You see, it's all true."

"Yes, it would be a pity."

"Well, anyway, thanks for reading it. Funny thing to happen. I really only put it down on paper for fun. Have another brandy?" He got up. "Oh, by the way. I was forgetting. I heard from those people about a week after war broke out. A letter. Let's see now, where did I put it? Ah, yes."

He rummaged in a drawer for a bit, and then, tossing a letter over to me, picked up the brandy bottle.

The envelope bore a Swiss stamp and the postmark was Klosters, September

4th, 1939. The contents felt bulky. I drew them out.

The cause of the bulkiness was what looked like a travel agent's folder doubled up to fit the envelope. I straightened it. On the front page was linocut of a clump of pines on the shore of a lake and the word "TITISEE." I opened out the folder.

"GERMAN MEN AND WOMEN, COMRADES!" *The type was worn and battered.* "Hitler has led you into war. He fed you with lies about the friendly Polish people. In your name he has now committed a wanton act of aggression against them. As a consequence, the free democracies of England and France have declared war against Germany. Comrades, right and justice are on their side. It is Hitler and National Socialism who are the enemies of peace in Europe. Our place as true Germans is at the side of the democracies *against* Hitler, *against* National Socialism. Hitler cannot win this war. But the people of Germany must act. All Germans, Catholics, Protestants, and Jews, must act now. Our Czech and Slovak friends are already refusing to make guns for Hitler. Let us stand by their sides. Remember. . . ."

I was about to read on when I saw that the letter which accompanied the folder had fluttered to the carpet. I picked it up. It consisted of a few typewritten lines on an otherwise blank sheet of paper.

"Greetings, *Herr Doktor.* We secured your address from the Customs carnet in your car and write now to wish you good luck. Kurt, Stephan, and Bruno have made many journeys since we saw you and returned safely each time. Today, Kurt leaves again. We pray for him as always. With this letter we send you Johann's newest work so that you shall see that Kurt spoke the truth to you. We are of the army of the shadows. We do not fight for you against our countrymen; but we fight with you against National Socialism, our common enemy.

"Auf Wiedersehen.

"FREDA, KURT, STEPHEN, JOHANN, AND BRUNO."

Llewellyn put my glass down on the table beside me. "Help yourself to a cigarette. What do you think of that? Nice of them, wasn't it?" *he added.* "Sentimental lot, these Germans."

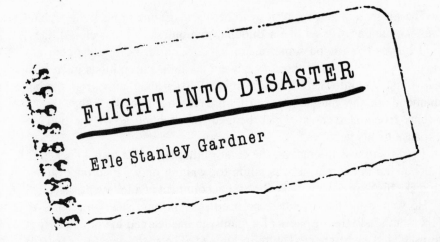

FLIGHT INTO DISASTER

Erle Stanley Gardner

ONLY ONCE BEFORE had the woman in the club car ever known panic—not merely fear but the real panic which paralyzes the senses.

That had been in the mountains when she had tried to take a shortcut to camp. When she realized she was lost there was a sudden overpowering desire to run. What was left of her sanity warned her, but panic made her feel that only by flight could she escape the menace of the unknown. The silent mountains, the somber woods, had suddenly become enemies, leering in hostility. Only by running did she feel she could escape—by running—the very worst thing she could have done.

Now, surrounded by the luxury of a crack transcontinental train, she again experienced that same panic. Once more there was that overpowering desire to run.

Someone had searched her compartment while she had been at dinner. She knew it was a man. He had tried to leave things just as he had found them, but there were little things that a woman would have noticed that the man didn't even see. Her plaid coat, which had been hung in the little steel closet so that the back was to the door, had been turned so the buttons were toward the door. A little thing, but a significant thing which had been the first to catch her attention, leaving her, for the moment, cold and numb. Now, seated in the club car, she strove to maintain an attitude of outward calm by critically inspecting her hands. Actually she was taking stock of the men who were in the car.

Her problem was complicated by the fact that she was compactly formed young woman, with smooth lines, clear eyes, a complete quota of curves, and under ordinary circumstances, a latent smile always quivering at the corners of her mouth. It was, therefore, only natural that every male animal in the club car sat up and took notice.

The fat man across the aisle who held a magazine in his pudgy hands was not reading. He sat like a Buddha, motionless, his half-closed, lazy-lidded eyes fixed upon some imaginary horizon far beyond the confines of the car—yet she felt those eyes were taking a surreptitious interest in eveything she did. There was something sinister about him, from the big diamond on the middle finger of his right hand to the rather ornate twenty-five-dollar cravat which begged for attention above the bulging expanse of his vest.

Then there was the man in the chair on her right. He hadn't spoken to her but she knew that he was going to, waiting only for an opportunity to make his remark sound like the casual comment of a fellow passenger.

He was in his late twenties, bronzed by exposure, steely-blue of eye. His mouth held the firmness of a man who has learned to command first himself and then others. The train lurched. The man's hand reached for the glass on the little stand between them. He glanced apprehensively at her skirt.

"Sorry," he said.

"It didn't spill," she replied almost automatically.

"I'll lower the danger point," he said, raising the glass to his lips. "Going all the way through? I'm getting off at six o'clock in a cold Wyoming morning."

For a moment her panic-numbed brain failed to appreciate the full significance of his remark, then she experienced a sudden surge of relief. Here, then, was one man whom she could trust. She knew that the man who had searched her baggage hadn't found what he wanted because she had it with her, neatly folded, fastened to the bottom of her left foot by strong adhesive tape. Therefore the enemy would stay on the train as long as she was on it, waiting, watching, growing more and more desperate, until at last, perhaps in the dead of night, he would . . . She knew only too well that he would stop at nothing. One murder had already been committed.

But now she had found one person whom she could trust, a man who had no interest in the thing she was hiding, a man who might well be a possible protector.

He seemed mildly surprised at her sudden friendliness.

"I didn't know this train stopped anywhere at that ungodly hour," she ventured, smiling.

"A flag stop," he explained.

Across the aisle the fat man had not moved a muscle, yet she felt absolutely certain that those glittering eyes were concentrating on her and that he was listening as well was watching.

"You live in Wyoming?" she asked.

"I did as a boy. Now I'm going back. I lived and worked on my uncle's cattle ranch. He died and left it to me. At first I thought I'd sell it. It would bring a small fortune. But now I'm tired of the big cities, I'm going back to live on the ranch."

"Won't it be frightfully lonely?"

"At times."

She wanted to cling to him now, dreading the time when she would have to go back to her compartment.

She felt the trainmen must have a master key which could open even a bolted door—in the event of sickness, or if a passenger rang for help. There *must* be a master key which would manipulate even a bolted door. And if trainmen had such a key, the man who had searched her compartment would have one.

Frank Hardwick, before he died, had warned her. "Remember," he had said, "they're everywhere. They're watching you when you don't know you're being watched. When you think you're running away and into safety, you'll simply be rushing into a carefully laid trap."

She hoped there was no trace of the inner tension within her as she smiled at the man on her right. "Do tell me about the cattle business," she said . . . .

All night she had crouched in her compartment, watching the door, waiting for that first flicker of telltale motion which would show the doorknob was being turned. Then she would scream, pound on the walls of the compartment, make sufficient commotion to spread an alarm.

Nothing had happened. Probably that was the way "they" had planned it. They'd let her spend one sleepless night, then when fatigue had numbed her senses . . .

The train abruptly slowed. She glanced at her wristwatch, saw that it was 5:55, and knew the train was stopping for the man who had inherited the cattle ranch. Howard Kane was the name he had given her after she had encouraged him to tell her all about himself. Howard Kane, twenty-eight, unmarried, presumably wealthy, his mind scarred by battle experiences, seeking the healing quality of the big, silent places, the one man on the train whom she knew she could trust.

There was a quiet competency about him, one felt he could handle any situation—and now he was getting off the train.

Suddenly a thought gripped her—"They" would hardly be expecting her to take the initiative. "They" always kept the initiative—that was why they always seemed so damnably efficient, so utterly invincible.

They chose the time, the place and the manner—give them that advantage, and . . . .

There wasn't time to reason the thing out. She jerked open the door of the little closet, whipped out her plaid coat, turned the fur collar up around her neck, and, as the train eased to a creaking stop, opened the door of her compartment and thrust out a cautious head.

The corridor was deserted.

She could hear the vestibule door being opened at the far end of the Pullman.

She ran to the opposite end of the car, fumbled for a moment with the fastenings of the vestibule door on the side next to the double track, then got it open and raised the platform.

Cold morning air, tanged with high elevation, rushed in to meet her, dispelling the train atmosphere, stealing the warmth from her garments.

The train started to move. She scrambled down the stairs, jumped for the graveled roadbed by the side of the track.

The train gathered speed. Dark, silent cars whizzed past her with continuing acceleration until the noise of the wheels became a mere hum. The steel rails readjusted themselves to the cold morning air, giving cracking sounds of protest. Overhead, stars blazed in steady brilliance. To the east was the first trace of daylight.

She looked for a town. There was none.

She could make out the faint outlines of a loading corral and cattle chute. Somewhere behind her was a road. An automobile was standing on this road, the motor running. Headlights sent twin cones of illumination knifing the darkness, etching into brilliance the stunted sagebrush shivering nervously under the impact of a cold north wind.

Two men were talking. A door slammed. She started running frantically.

"Wait!" she called. "Wait for me!"

Back on the train the fat man, fully dressed and shaved, contemplated the open vestibule door, then padded back to the recently vacated compartment and walked in.

He didn't even bother to search the baggage that had been left behind. Instead he sat down in the chair, held a telegraph blank against a magazine, and wrote out his message:

THE BUNGLING SEARCH TRICK DID THE JOB. SHE'S LEFT
THE TRAIN. IT ONLY REMAINS TO CLOSE THE TRAP. I'LL GET
OFF AT THE FIRST PLACE WHERE I CAN RENT A PLANE
AND CONTACT THE SHERIFF.

Ten minutes later the fat man found the porter. "I find the elevation bothering me," he said. "I'm going to have to leave the train. Get the conductor."

"You won't get no lower by gettin' off," the porter said.

"No, but I'll get bracing fresh air and a doctor who'll give me a heart stimulant. I've been this way before. Get the conductor."

This time the porter saw the twenty-dollar bill in the fat man's fingers.

Seated between the two men in the warm interior of the car, she sought to concoct a convincing story.

Howard Kane said, by way of introduction, "This is Buck Doxey. I'm afraid I didn't catch your name last night."

"Nell Lindsay," she said quickly.

Buck Doxey, granite-faced, kept one hand on the steering wheel while he doffed a five-gallon hat. "Pleased to meet yuh, ma'am."

She sensed his cold hostility, his tight-lipped disapproval.

Howard Kane gently prodded for an explanation.

"It was a simple case of cause and effect," she said, laughing nervously. "It was so stuffy in the car I didn't sleep at all.

"So," she went on quickly, "I decided that I'd get out for a breath of fresh air. When the train slowed and I looked at my wristwatch I knew it was your stop and . . . . Well, I expected the train would be there for at least a few minutes. I couldn't find a porter to get the vestibule open, so I did it myself, and jumped down to the ground. That was where I made my mistake."

"Go on," he said.

"At a station you step down to a platform that's level with the tracks. But here I jumped onto a slanting shoulder of gravel, and sprawled flat. When I got up, the step of the car was so far above me. . . . Well, you have to wear skirts to understand what I mean."

Kane nodded gravely. Buck turned his head and gave Kane a quartering glance.

She said, "I guess I could have made it at that if I'd had sense enough to pull my skirt all the way up to the hips, but I couldn't make it on that first try and there wasn't time for a second one. The train started to move. Good heavens, they must have just *thrown* you off!"

"I'm traveling light," Kane said.

"Well," she told him, "that's the story. Now just what do I do?"

"Why, you accept our hospitality, of course."

"I couldn't . . . couldn't wait here for the next rain?"

"Nothing stops here except to discharge passengers coming from a division point," he said.

"But there's a . . . station there. Isn't there someone on duty?"

"Only when cattle are being shipped," Buck Doxey explained. "This is a loading point."

"Oh."

She settled back against the seat, and was conscious of a reassuring masculine friendship on her right side, a cold detachment on her left side.

"I suppose it's horribly ravenous of me, but do we get to the ranch for breakfast?"

"I'm afraid not," Kane said. "It's slow going. Only sixty feet of the road is paved."

"Sixty feet?"

"That's right. We cross the main transcontinental highway about five miles north of here."

"What *do* we do about breakfast?"

"Well," Kane said, "in the trunk of the car there's a coffee pot and a canteen of water. I'm quite certain Buck brought along a few eggs and some ham . . . ."

"You mean you stop right out here in the open and cook?"

"When yuh stop here, you're in the open, ma'am," Buck said and somehow made it seem his words were in answer to some unjustified criticism.

She gave him her best smile. "Would it be impertinent to ask when?"

"In this next coulee . . . right here . . . right now."

The road slanted down to a dry wash that ran east and west. The perpendicular north bank broke the force of the north wind. Buck attested to the lack of traffic on the road by stopping the car squarely in the ruts.

They watched the sun rise over the plateau country, and ate breakfast. She hoped that Buck Doxey's cold disapproval wouldn't communicate itself to Howard Kane.

When Buck produced a battered dishpan, she said, "As the only woman present I claim the right to do the dishes."

"Women," Buck said, "are . . ." and abruptly checked himself.

She laughingly pushed him aside and rolled up her sleeves. "Where's the soap?"

As she was finishing the last dish she heard the motor of the low-flying plane.

All three looked up.

The plane, which had been following the badly rutted road, banked into a sharp turn.

"Sure givin' us the once over," Buck said, his eyes steady on Kane's face. "One of 'em has binoculars and he's as watchful as a cattle buyer at a loading chute. Don't yuh think it's about time we find out what we've got into, Boss?"

"I suppose it is," Kane said. Before her startled mind could counter his action, Buck Doxey picked up the purse which she had left lying on the running board of the car.

She flew toward him

Doxey's bronzed, steel fingers wrapped around her wet wrist. "Take it easy, ma'am," he said. "Take it easy."

He pushed her back, found her driving license. "The real name," he drawled, "seems to be Jane Marlow."

"Anything else?" Kane asked.

"Gobs of money, lipstick, keys and . . . Gosh, what a bankroll."

She went for him blindly.

Doxey said, "Now, ma'am, I'm goin to have to spank yuh if yuh keep on like this."

The plane circled, its occupants obviously interested in the scene on the ground below.

"Now—here's something else," Doxey said, taking out a folded newspaper clipping.

She suddenly went limp. There was no use in further pretense.

Doxey read aloud, "'Following the report of an autopsy surgeon, police, who had never been entirely satisfied that the unexplained death of Frank Hardwick was actually a suicide, are searching for his attractive secretary, Jane Marlow. The young woman reportedly had dinner with Hardwick in a downtown restaurant the night of his death.

"'Hardwick, after leaving Miss Marlow, according to her story, went directly to the apartment of Eva Ingram, a strikingly beautiful model who has, however, convinced police that she was dining out. Within a matter of minutes after entering the Ingram apartment, Hardwick either jumped or fell from the eighth-story window.

"'With the finding of a witness who says Frank Hardwick was accompanied at least as far as the apartment door by a young woman whose description answers that of Jane Marlow, and evidence indicating several thousand dollars was removed from a concealed floor safe in Hardwick's office, police are anxious once more to question Miss Marlow. So far their efforts have definitely not been crowned with success.'

"And here's a picture of this young lady," Buck said, "With some more stuff under it.

"'Jane Marlow, secretary of scientist who jumped from apartment window to his death, is now sought by police after witness claims to have seen her arguing angrily with Frank Hardwick when latter was ringing bell at front door of apartment house from which Hardwick fell or jumped to sidewalk.'"

Overhead, the plane suddenly ceased its circling and took off in a straight line to the north.

As the car proceeded northward, Buck put on speed, deftly avoiding the bad places in the road.

Jane Marlow, who had lapsed into hopeless silence, tried one more last desperate attempt when they crossed the paved road. "Please," she said, "let me out here. I'll catch a ride back to Los Angeles and report to the police."

Kane's eyes asked a silent question of the driver.

"Nope," Buck said decisively. "That plane was the sheriff's scout plane. He'll expect us to hold you. I don't crave to have no more trouble over women."

"All right," Jane said in a last burst of desperation, "I'll tell you the whole story. Then I'll leave it to your patriotism. I was secretary to Frank Hardwick. He was working on something that had to do with cosmic rays."

"I know," Doxey interrupted sarcastically. "And he dictated his secret formula to you."

"Don't be silly," she said, "but he *did* know that he was in danger. He told me that if anything happened to him, to take something, which he gave me, to a certain individual."

"Just keep on talking," Buck said. "Tell us about the money."

Her eyes were desperate. "Mr. Hardwick had a concealed floor safe in the office. He left reserve cash there for emergencies. He gave me the combination, told me that if anything happened to him, I was to go to that safe, take the money and deliver it and certain a paper to a certain scientist in Boston."

Buck's smile of skepticism was certain to influence Kane even more than words.

"Frank Hardwick never jumped out of any window," she went on. "They were waiting for him, and they threw him out."

"Or," Buck said, "a certain young lady became jealous, followed him, got him near an open window and then gave a sudden, unexpected shove. It *has* been done, you know."

"And people *have* told the truth," she blazed, "*I* don't enjoy what I'm doing. I consider it a duty to my country—and I'll probably be murdered, just as Frank Hardwick was."

"Now listen," Kane said. "Nice little girls don't jump off trains before daylight in the morning and tell the kind of stories you're telling. You got off that train because you were running away from someone."

She turned to Kane. "I was hoping that *you* would understand."

"He understands," Buck said, and laughed.

After that she was silent . . . .

Overhead, from time to time, the plane came circling back. Once it was gone for nearly forty-five minutes and she dared to hope they had thrown it off the track, but later she realized it had only gone to refuel and then it was back above them once more.

It was nearly nine when Buck turned off the rutted road and headed toward a group of unpainted, squat, log cabins which seemed to be bracing themselves against the cold wind while waiting for the winter snow. Back of the building were timbered mountains.

The pilot of the plane had evidently spotted the ranch long ago. Hardly had Buck turned off the road than the plane came circling in for a landing.

Jane Marlow had to lean against the cold wind as she walked from the car to the porch of the cabin. Howard Kane held the door open for her, and she found herself inside a cold room which fairly reeked of masculine tenancy, with a paper-littered desk, guns, deer and elk horns.

Within a matter of seconds she heard the pound of steps on the porch, the door was flung open, and the fat man and a companion stood on the threshold.

"Well, Jane," the fat man said, "you gave us quite a chase, didn't you?" He turned to the others.

"Reckon I'd better introduce myself, boys." He reached in his pocket, then took out a wallet and tossed it carelessly on the desk.

"I'm John Findlay of the FBI," he said.

"That's a lie," she said. "Can't you understand? This man is an enemy. Those credentials are forged."

"Well, ma'am," the other newcomer said, stepping forward, "there ain't nothing wrong with my credentials. I'm the sheriff here, and I'm taking you into custody."

He took her purse, said, "You just might have a gun in here."

He opened the purse. Findlay leaned over to look, said, "It's all there."

"Come on, Miss Marlow," the sheriff said, "You're going back in that plane."

"That plane of yours holds three people?" Findlay asked.

The sheriff looked appraisingly at the fat man. "Not us three."

"I can fly the crate," Findlay said. "I'll take the prisoner in, lock her up and then fly back for you and . . . ."

"No, no, no!" Jane Marlow screamed. "Don't you see, can't you realize, this man isn't an officer. I'd never get there. He . . . ."

"Shut up," the sheriff said.

"Sheriff, please! You're being victimized. Call up the FBI and you'll find out that . . . ."

"I've already called up the Los Angeles office of the FBI," the sheriff said.

Kane's brows leveled. "Was that because you were suspicious, Sheriff?"

"Findlay himself suggested it."

Jane was incredulous. "You mean they told you that. . . ?"

"They vouched for him in every way," the sheriff said. "They told me he'd been sent after Jane Marlow, and to give him every assistance. Now I've got to lock you up and . . . ."

"She's my responsibility, Sheriff," Findlay said.

The sheriff frowned, then said. "Okay, I'll fly back and send a deputy out with a car."

"Very well," Findlay agreed. "I'll see that she stays put."

Jane Marlow said desperately, "I presume that when Mr. Findlay told you to call the FBI office in Los Angeles, he gave you the number so you wouldn't have to waste time getting it through an operator, didn't he?"

"Why not?" the sheriff said, smiling good-humoredly. "He'd be a hell of an FBI man if he didn't know his own telephone number."

The fat man fished a cigar from his pocket. Biting off the end and scraping a match into flame, he winked at the sheriff.

Howard Kane said to Findlay, "Mind if I ask a question?"

"Hell no. Go right ahead."

"I'd like to know something of the facts in this case. If you've been working on the case you'd know . . . ."

"Sure thing," Findlay agreed, getting his cigar burning evenly. "She worked for Hardwick, who was having an affair with a model. We followed him to the model's apartment. They had a quarrel. Hardwick's supposed to have jumped out of the window. She went to his office and took five thousand dollars out of the safe. The money's in her purse."

"So she was jealous?"

"Jealous and greedy. Don't forget she got five grand out of the safe."

"I was following my employer's specific instructions in everything I did," Jane said.

Findlay grinned.

"What's more," she blazed, "Frank Hardwick wasn't having any affair with that model. He was lured to her apartment. It was a trap and he walked right in."

Findlay said, "Yeah. The key we found in his vest pocket fitted the apartment door. He must have found it on the street and was returning it to the owner as an act of gallantry."

The sheriff laughed.

Howard Kane glanced speculatively at the very young woman. "She doesn't look like a criminal."

"Oh, thank you!" she blazed.

Findlay's glance was patronizing. "How many criminals have you seen, buddy?'

Doxey rolled a cigarette. His eyes narrowed against the smoke as he squatted down cowboy fashion on the backs of his high-heeled riding boots. "Ain't no question but what she's the one who jimmied the safe, is there?"

"The money's in her purse," Findlay said.

"Any accomplices?" Buck asked.

"No. It was a combination of jealousy and greed." Findlay glanced inquiringly at the sheriff.

"I'll fly in and send that car out," the sheriff said.

"Mind if I fly in with yuh and ride back with the deputy, Sheriff?" Buck asked eagerly. "I'd like to see this country from the air once. there's a paved road other side of that big mountain where the ranger has his station. I'd like to look down on it. Some day they'll connect us up. Now it's an hour's ride by horse . . . ."

"Sure," the sheriff agreed. "Glad to have you."

"Just give me time enough to throw a saddle on a horse," Doxey said. "Kane might want to ride out and look the ranch over. Yuh won't mind, Sheriff?"

"Make it snappy," the sheriff said.

Buck Doxey went to the barn and after a few minutes returned leading a dilapidated-looking range pony saddled and bridled. He casually dropped the reins in front of the ranch "office," and called inside:

"Ready any time you are, Sheriff."

They started for the airplane. Buck stopped at the car to get a map from the glove compartment, then hurried to join the sheriff. The propeller of the plane gave a half-turn, stopped, gave another half-turn, the motor sputtered, then roared into action. A moment later the plane became the focal point of a trailing dust cloud, then raised and swept over the squat log buildings in a climbing turn and headed south.

Jane Marlow and Kane watched it through the window until it became but a speck.

Howard Kane said, "Now, Mr. Findlay, I'd like to ask you a few questions."

"Sure, go right ahead."

"You impressed the sheriff very cleverly," Kane said, "but I'd like to have you explain . . . "

"Now that it's too late," Jane Marlow blazed indignantly. "You've let him . . ."

Kane motioned her to silence. "Don't you see, Miss Marlow, I had to get rid of the sheriff. He represents the law, right or wrong. But if this man is an imposter, I can protect you against him."

Findlay's hand moved with such rapidity that the big diamond made a streak of glittering light.

"Okay, wise guy," he said. "Try protecting her against this."

Kane rushed the gun.

Sheer surprise slowed Findlay's reaction time. Kane's fist flashed out in a swift arc, just before the gun roared.

The fat man moved with amazing speed. He rolled with the punch, spun completely around on his heel and jumped back, the automatic held to his body, his eyes glittering with rage.

"Get 'em up," he said.

The cold animosity of his tone showed that this time there would be no hesitancy.

Slowly Kane's hands came up.

"Turn around," Findlay said. "Move over by that window. Press your face against the wall. Give me your right hand, Kane. . . . Now the left hand."

A smooth leather thong, which had been deftly knotted into a slipknot, was jerked tight, then knotted into a quick half hitch.

The girl, taking advantage of Findlay's preoccupation, flung herself on him.

The bulk of Findlay's big shoulders absorbed the onslaught without making him even shift the position of his feet. He jerked the leather thong into a last knot, turned and struck the girl in the pit of the stomach.

She wobbled about for a moment on rubber legs, then fell to the floor.

"Now, young lady," Findlay said, "you've caused me a hell of a lot of trouble. I'll just take the thing you're carrying in your left shoe. I could tell from the way you were limping there was something. . . ."

He jerked off the shoe, looked inside, seemed puzzled, then suddenly grabbed the girl's stockinged foot.

She kicked and tried to scream, but the wind had been knocked out of her.

Findlay reached casual hands up to the top of her stocking, jerked it loose without bothering to unfasten the garters, pulled the adhesive tape off the bottom of the girl's foot, ran out to the car, and jumped in.

"Well, what do you know!" he exclaimed. "The damn yokel took the keys with him. . . . So there's a paved road on the other side of the mountains, is there?

"Come on, horse, I guess there's a trail we can find. If we can't they'll never locate us in all that timber."

Moving swiftly, the fat man ran over to where the horse was standing on three legs, drowsing in the sunlight.

Findlay gathered up the reins, thrust one foot in the stirrup, grabbed the saddle, front and rear, and swung himself awkwardly into position.

Jane heard a shrill animal squeal of rage. The sleepy looking horse transformed into a bundle of dynamite, heaved himself into the air, ears laid back along his neck.

The fat man, grabbing the horn of the saddle, clung with frenzied desperation.

"Well," Kane asked, "are you going to untie me, or just stand there gawking?"

She ran to him then, frantically tugging at the knot.

The second his hands were freed Kane went into action.

Findlay, half out of the saddle, clung drunkenly to the pitching horse for a moment, then went into the air, turned half over and came down with a jar that shook the earth.

Kane emerged from the cabin holding a rifle.

"All right, Findlay, it's my turn now," Kane said. "Don't make a move for that gun."

The shaken Findlay seemed to have trouble orienting himself. He turned dazedly toward the sound of the voice, clawed for his gun.

Kane, aiming the rifle carefully, shot it out of his hand.

"Now, ma'am," Kane said, "if you want to get that paper out of his pocket. . . ."

She ran to Findlay, her feet fairly flying over the ground despite the fact that she was wearing only one shoe and the other foot had neither shoe nor stocking. . . .

Shortly before noon Jane Marlow decided to invade the sacred precincts of Buck Doxey's thoroughly masculine kitchen to prepare lunch. Howard Kane showed his respect for Findlay's resourcefulness by keeping him covered despite the man's bound wrists.

"Buck is going to hate me for this," she said. "Not that he doesn't hate me enough already—and I don't know why."

"Buck's soured on women," Kane explained. "I tried to tip you off.

He was engaged to a girl in Cheyenne. No one knows exactly what happened, but they split up. I think she's as miserable as he is, but neither one will make the first move. But for heaven's sake don't try to rearrange his kitchen according to ideas of feminiine efficiency. Just open a can of something and make coffee."

Findlay said, "I don't suppose there's any use trying to make a deal with you two."

Kane scornfully sighted along the gun by way of answer.

Jane, opening drawers in the kitchen, trying to locate the utensils, inadvertently stumbled on Buck Doxey's private heartache. A drawer containing letters, and the photograph of a girl.

The photograph had been torn into several pieces, and then laboriously pasted together and covered with Cellophane.

The front of the picture was inscribed "To Buck with all my heart, Pearl."

Jane felt a surge of guilt at even having opened the drawer, but feminine curiosity caused her to hesitate long enough before closing it to notice Pearl's return address in the upper left-hand corner of one of the envelopes addressed to Buck Doxey . . . .

It was as they were finishing lunch that they heard the roar of the plane.

They went to the door to watch it turn into the teeth of the cold north wind, settle to a landing, then taxi up to the low log buildings.

The sheriff and Buck Doxey started running toward the cabins, and it was solace to Jane Marlow's pride to see the look of almost comic relief on the face of the sheriff as he saw Kane with the rifle and Findlay with bound wrists.

Jane heard the last part of Doxey's hurried explanation to Kane.

"Wouldn't trust a woman that far but her story held together and his didn't. I thought you'd understand what I was doing. I flew in with the sheriff just so I could call the FBI in Los Angeles. What do you know? Findlay is a badly wanted enemy spy. They want him bad as . . . How did *you* make out?"

Kane grinned. "I decided to give Findlay a private third-degree. He answered my questions with a gun. If it hadn't been for that horse . . . ."

Buck's face broke into a grin. "He fell for that one?"

"Fell for it, and off it," Kane said.

"If he hadn't been a fool tenderfoot he'd have noticed that I led the horse out from the corral instead of riding him over. Old Fox is a rodeo horse, one of the best bucking broncs in Wyoming. Perfectly gentle until he feels it's time to do his stuff, and then he gives everything he has until he hears the ten-second whistle. I sort of figured Findlay might try something before I could sell the sheriff a bill of goods and get back."

It had been sheer impulse which caused Jane Marlow to leave the train early in the morning.

It was also sheer impulse which caused her to violate the law by forging Pearl's name to a telegram as she went through Cheyenne.

The telegram was addressed to Buck Doxey, care of the Forest Ranger Station and read:

BUCK I AM SO PROUD OF YOU PEARL.

Having started the message on its way, Jane looked up Pearl and casually told her of the torn picture which had been so laboriously pasted together.

Half an hour later Jane was once more speeding East aboard the sleek streamliner, wondering whether her efforts on behalf of Cupid had earned her the undying enmity of two people, or had perhaps been successful.

When she reached Omaha two telegrams were delivered. One was from Howard Kane and read simply:

YOU WERE SO RIGHT. IT GETS TERRIBLY LONELY AT TIMES. HOLD A DINNER DATE OPEN FOR TONIGHT. YOU NEED A BODYGUARD ON YOUR MISSION AND I AM FLYING TO CHICAGO TO MEET YOU AT TRAIN AND DISCUSS THE WYOMING CLIMATE AS A PERMANENT PLACE OF RESIDENCE. LOVE, HOWARD

The second telegram was the big surprise. It read:

I GUESS I HAD IT COMING. PEARL AND I BOTH SEND LOVE. I GUESS I JUST NEVER REALIZED WOMEN ARE LIKE THAT, YOURS HUMBLY, BUCK DOXEY.

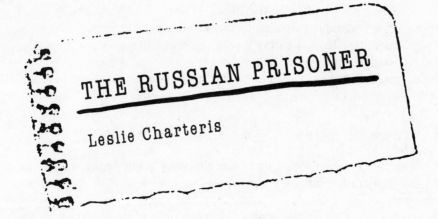

THE RUSSIAN PRISONER

Leslie Charteris

"EXCUSE ME. YOU are the Saint. You must help me."

By that time Simon Templar thought he must have heard all the approaches, all the elegant variations. Some were amusing, some were insulting, some were unusual, most were routine, a few tried self-consciously to be original and attention-getting. He had, regrettably, become as accustomed to them as any Arthurian knight-errant must eventually have become. After all, how many breeds of dragons were there? And how many different shapes and colorations of damsels in distress?

This one would have about chalked up her first quarter-century, and would have weighed in at about five pounds per annum—not the high-fashion model's ration, but more carnally interesting. She had prominent cheekbones to build shadow frames around blindingly light blue eyes, and flax-white hair that really looked as if it had been born with her and not processed later. She was beautiful like some kind of mythological ice maiden.

And she had the distinction of having condensed a sequence of inescapable clichés to a quintessence which could only have been surpassed by a chemical formula.

"Do sit down," Simon said calmly. "I'm sure your problem is desperate, or you wouldn't be bringing it to a perfect stranger—but have you heard of an old English duck called Drake? When they told him the Spanish Armada was coming, he insisted on finishing his game of bowls before he'd go out to cope with it. I've got a rather nice bowl here myself, and it would be a shame to leave it."

He carefully fixed a cube of coarse farmhouse bread on the small tines of his long shafted fork, and dipped it in the lucious goo that barely bubbled in the chafing dish before him. When it was soaked and coated

299

to its maximum burthen, he transferred it neatly to his mouth. Far from being an ostentatious vulgarity, this was a display of epicurean technique and respect, for he was eating *fondue*—perhaps the most truly national of Swiss delectables, that ambrosial blend of melted cheese perfumed with kirsch and other things, which is made nowhere better than at the Old Swiss House in Lucerne, where he was lunching.

"I like that," she said.

He pushed the bread plate towards her and offered a fork, hospitably.

"Have some."

"No, thank you. I meant that I like the story about Drake. And I like it that you are the same—a man who is so sure of himself that he does not have to get excited. I have already had lunch. I was inside, and I could see you through the window. Some people at the next table recognized you and were talking about you. I heard the name, and it was like winning a big prize which I had not even hoped for."

She spoke excellent English, quickly, but in a rather stilted way that seemed to have been learned from books or vocal drill rather than light conversation, with an accent which he could not place immediately.

"A glass of wine, then? Or a liqueur?"

"A Benedictine, if you like. And some coffee, may I?"

He beckoned a waitress who happened to come out, and gave the order.

"You seem to know something about me," he said, spearing another piece of bread. "Is one supposed to know something about you, or are you a Mystery Woman?"

"I am Irma Jorovitch."

"Good for you. It doesn't have to be your real name, but at least it gives me something to call you." He speared another chunk of bread. "Now, you tell me your trouble. It's tedious, but we have to go through this in most of my stories, because I'm only a second-rate mind reader."

"I am Russian, originally," she said. "My family are from the part of Finland where the two countries meet, but since nineteen-forty it has been all Soviet. My father is Karel Jorovitch, and he was named for the district we came from. He is a scientist."

"Any particular science, or just a genius?"

"I don't know. He is a professor at the University of Leningrad. Of physics, I think. I do not remember seeing him except in pictures. During the war, my mother was separated from him, and she escaped with me to Sweden."

"You don't have a Swedish accent."

"Perhaps because I learnt English first from her, and I suppose she had a Finnish or a Russian accent. Then there were all sorts of teachers in

Swedish schools. I speak everything like a mixture. But I learnt enough languages to get a job in a travel agency in Stockholm. My father could not get permission to leave Russia after the war, and my mother had learned to prefer the capitalist life and would not go back to join him. I don't think she was too much in love with him. At last there was a divorce, and she married a man with a small hotel in Göteborg, who adopted me so that I could have a passport and travel myself. But soon after, they were both killed in a car accident."

"I see . . . or do I? Your problem is that you don't know how to run a hotel?"

"No, that is for his own sons. But I thought that my father should be told that she was dead. I wrote to him, and somehow he received the letter—he was still at the University. He wrote back, wanting to know all about me. We began to write often. Now I didn't even have a mother, I had nobody, it was exciting to discover a real father and try to find out all about him. But then, one day, I got another letter from him which had been smuggled out, which was different from all the others."

The Saint sipped his wine. It was a native Johannesberg Rhinegold, light and bone-dry, the perfect punctuation for the glutinous goodness into which he was dunking.

"How different?"

"He said he could not stand it any more, the way he was living and what he was doing, and he wished he could escape to the West. He asked if I would be ready to help him. Of course I said yes. But how? We exchanged several letters, discussing possibilities, quite apart from the other letters which he went on writing for the censors to read."

"How did you work that?"

"Through the travel agency, it was not so hard to find ways. And at last the opportunity came. He was to be sent to Geneva, to a meeting of the disarmament conference—not to take part himself, but to be on hand to advise the Soviet delegate about scientific questions. It seemed as if everything was solved. He only had to get out of the Soviet embassy, here in Switzerland, and he would be free."

The Saint's gaze was no longer gently quizzical. His blue eyes, many southern shades darker than hers, had hardened as if sapphires were crystallizing in them. He was listening now with both ears and all his mind; but he went on eating with undiminished deference to the cuisine.

"So what's the score now?"

"I came here to meet him with some money, and to help him. When he escaped, of course, he would have nothing. And he speaks only Russian and Finnish . . . . But something went wrong."

"What, exactly?"

"I don't know."

Until then, she had been contained, precise, reciting a synopsis that she must have vowed to deliver without emotion, to acquit herself in advance of the charge of being just another hysterical female with helpful hallucinations. But now she was leaning across the table towards him, twisting her fingers together, and letting her cold lovely face be twisted into unbecoming lines of tortured anxiety.

"Someone betrayed us. We had to trust many people who carried our letters. Who knows which one? I only know that yesterday, when he was to do it, I waited all day up the street where I could watch the entrance, in a car which I had hired, and in the evening he came out. But not by himself, as we had planned. He was driven out in an embassy car, sitting between two men who looked like gangsters—the secret police! I could only just recognize him, from a recent photograph he had sent me, looking around desperately as if he hoped to see me, as if I could have rescued him."

Her coffee and Benedictine arrived, and Simon said to the waitress: "You can bring me the same, in about five minutes."

He harpooned a prize corner crust, and set about mopping the dish clean of the last traces of *fondue*. He said: "You should have got here sooner. There's an old Swiss tradition which says that when *fondue* is being eaten, anyone who loses the bread off their fork has to kiss everyone else at the table. It must make for a nice sociable eating . . . So what happened?"

"I followed them. It was all I could think of. If I lost him then, I knew I would lose him for ever. I thought at first they were taking him to the airport, to send him back to Russia, and I could make a fuss there. But no. They went to Lausanne, then on to here, and then still farther, to a house on the lake, with high walls and guards and they took him in. . . . Then I went to the police."

"And?"

"They told me they could do nothing. It was part of the Soviet embassy, officially rented for diplomatic purposes, and it could not be touched. The Russians can do whatever they like there, as if they were in Russia. And I know what they are doing. They are keeping my father there until they can send him back to Moscow—and then to Siberia. Unless they kill him first."

"Wouldn't that have been easier from Geneva?"

"There is another airport at Zürich, almost as close from this house, and without the newspaper men who will be at Geneva for the conference."

Letting his eyes wander around the quiet little square, Simon thought that you really had to have a paperback mind to believe tales like that in such a setting. The table where they sat outside the restaurant was under the shade of the awning, but he could have stretched a hand out into the sunshine which made it the kind of summer's day that travel brochures are always photographed on. And gratefully enjoying their full advertised money's worth, tourists of all shapes and sizes and nationalities were rambling back and forth, posing each other for snapshots, plodding in and out of the domed Panorama building opposite to peer (for reasons comprehensible only to tourists and the entrepreneurs who provide such attractions for them) at its depiction of the French general Bourbaki's entry into Switzerland in 1871 on a scale that seems somewhat disproportionate to the historic importance of that event, or trudging up the hill to gawk at the Lion Memorial carved in the rock to commemorate the Swiss mercenaries who died in Paris with unprofitable heroism defending the Tuileries against the French Revolution, or to the Glacier Garden above that which preserves the strange natural sculpture of much more ancient turnings—all with their minds happily emptied of everything but the perennial vacation problem of paying for their extra extravagances and souvenirs. Not one of them, probably, would have believed in this plot unless they saw it at home on television. But the Saint knew perhaps better than any man living how thinly the crust of peace and normalcy covered volcanic lavas everywhere in the modern world.

He turned back to Irma Jorovitch, and his voice was just as tolerantly good-humored as it had been ever since she had intruded herself with her grisly reminder of what to him were only the facts of life. He said: "And you think it should be a picnic for me to rescue him."

She said: "Not a picnic. No. But if any man on earth can do it, you can."

"You know, you could be right. But I was trying to take a holiday from all that."

"If you would want money," she said, "I have nothing worth your time to offer. But I could try to get it. I would do anything—*anything!*"

It was altogether disgraceful, he admitted, but he could do nothing to inhibit an inward reflex of response except try not to think about it.

"Gentleman adventurers aren't supposed to take advantage of offers like that," he said, with unfeigned regret.

"You must help me," she said again. "Please."

He sighed.

"All right," he said. "I suppose I must."

Her face lit up with a gladness that did the same things for it that the Aurora Borealis does to the arctic snows. It was a reaction that he had seen many times, as if his mere consent to have a bash had vaporized all barriers. It would have been fatally intoxicating if he ever forgot how precariously, time after time, he had succeeded in justifying so much faith.

"It isn't done yet, darling," he reminded her. "Tell me more about this house."

It was on the southern shore of the Vierwaldstättersee, he learned, the more rugged and less accessible side which rises to the mingled tripper-traps and tax-dodger chalets of Bürgenstock, and by land it was reachable only by a second-to-secondary road which served nothing but a few other similarly isolated hermitages. Although it was dark when she passed it, she was sure there was no other residence nearby, so that anyone approaching in daylight would certainly be under observation long before he got close. The walls around the grounds were about seven feet high, topped with barbed wire, but with slits that the inmates could peep through—to say nothing of what electronic devices might augment their vigilance. Added to which, she had heard dogs barking as she drove past.

"Nothing to it," said the Saint—"if I hadn't forgotten to bring my invisible and radar-proof helicopter."

"You will think of something," she said with rapturous confidence.

He lighted a cigarette and meditated for almost a minute.

"You say this house is right on the lake?"

"Yes. Because at the next turning after I passed, my headlights showed the water."

"Do you think you could recognize it again, from the lake side?"

"I think so."

"Good. Then let's take a little boat ride."

He paid his bill, and finished his coffee while he waited for the change. Then they walked down the Löwenstrasse and across the tree-shaded promenades of the Nationalquai to the lake front. Just a few yards to the left there was a small marina offering a variety of water craft for hire, which he had already casually scouted without dreaming that he would ever use it in this way. With the same kind of companionship, perhaps, but not for this kind of mission. . . .

The Saint chose a small but comfortably upholstered runabout, the type of boat that would automatically catch the eye of a man who was out to impress a pretty girl—and that was precisely how he wanted them to be categorized by anyone who had a motive for studying them closely. Taking advantage of the weather and the informal customs of the country, he was wearing only a pair of light slacks and a tartan sport shirt, and Irma was dressed in a simple white blouse and gaily patterned dirndl, so that there was nothing except their own uncommon faces to differentiate them from any other holiday-making twosome.

And as he aimed the speedboat diagonally southeastwards across the lake, with the breeze of their own transit tousling her short white-blond hair and moulding the filmy blouse like a tantalizing second skin against the thrusting mounds of her breasts, he had leisure to wish that they had been brought together by nothing more pre-emptive than one of those random holiday magnetisms which provide inexhaustible grist for the world's marriage and divorce mills in self-compensating proportions.

She had put on a pair of sunglasses when they left the restaurant, and out on the water the light was strong enough for Simon to take out a pair of his own which had been tucked in his shirt pocket. But they would be useful for more than protection against the glare.

"Get the most out of these cheaters when we start looking for the house," he told her as he put them on. "Don't turn your head and look at anything directly: just turn your eyes and keep facing somewhere else. Behind the glasses, anybody watching us won't be able to tell what we're really looking at."

"You think of everything. I will try to remember."

"About how far did you drive out of Lucerne to this house?"

"I cannot be sure. It seemed quite far, but the road was winding."

This was so femininely vague that he resigned himself to covering the entire southern shore if necessary. On such an afternoon, and with such a comely companion, it was a martyrdom which he could endure with beatific stoicism. Having reached the nearest probable starting point which he had mentally selected, he cut the engine down to a smooth idling gait and steered parallel to the meandering coast line, keeping a distance of about a hundred yards from the shore.

"Relax, Irma," he said. "Any house that's on this stretch of lake, we'll see. Meanwhile, we should look as if we're just out for the ride."

To improve this visual effect, he lowered himself from his hot-water-rodder's perch on the gunwhale to the cushion behind the wheel, and she snuggled up to him.

"Like this?" she asked seriously.

"More or less," he approved, with fragile gravity, and slipped an arm around her shoulders.

It was only when they had passed Kehrsiten, the landing where the funicular takes off up the sheer palisade to the hotels of Bürgenstock on its crest, that he began to wonder if she had overestimated her ability to identify the house to which Karel Jorovitch had been taken from an aspect which she had never seen. But he felt no change of tension in her as the boat purred along for some kilometers after that, until suddenly she stiffened and clutched him—but with the magnificent presence of mind to turn towards him instead of to the shore.

"There, I have seen it!" she gasped. "The white house with the three tall chimneys! I remember them!"

He looked to his right, over her flaxen head which had a disconcertingly pure smell which reminded him somehow of new-mown hay, and saw the only edifice she could have been referring to.

The tingle that went through him was an involuntary psychosomatic acknowledgement that the adventure had now become real, and he was well and truly hooked.

In order to study the place thoroughly and unhurriedly, he turned towards Irma, folded her tenderly in his arms, and applied his lips to hers. In that position, he could continue to keep his eyes on the house whilst giving the appearance of being totally preoccupied with radically unconnected pursuits.

It was surprisingly unpretentious, for a diplomatic enclave. He would have taken it for a large old-fashioned family house—or a house for a large old-fashioned family, according to the semantic preference of the phrasemaker. At any rate, it was not a refurbished mansion or a small reconverted hotel. Its most unusual feature was what she had already mentioned: the extraordinarily high wire-topped garden walls which came down at a respectable distance on both sides of it—not merely to the lake edge, but extending about twelve feet out into the water. And for the further discouragement of anyone who might still have contemplated going around them, those two barriers were joined by a rope linking a semicircle of small bright red buoys such as might have marked the limits of a safe bathing area, but which also served to bar an approach to the shore by boat—even if they were not anchored to some underwater obstruction which would have made access altogether impossible.

And on the back porch of the house, facing the lake, a square-shouldered man in a deck chair raised a pair of binoculars and examined them lengthily.

Simon was able to make all these observations in spite of the fact that Irma Jorovitch was cooperating in his camouflage with an ungrudging enthusiasm which was no aid at all to concentration.

Finally they came to a small headland beyond which there was a cove into which he could steer the boat out of sight of the watcher on the porch. Only then did the Saint release her, not without reluctance, and switched off the engine to become crisply businesslike again.

"Excuse the familiarity," he said. "But you know why I had to do it."

"I liked it, too," she said demurely.

As the boat drifted to a stop, Simon unstrapped his wrist watch and laid it on the deck over the dashboard. He held his pen upright beside it to cast a shadow from the sun, and turned the watch to align the hour hand with the shadow, while Irma watched fascinated.

"Now, according to my boy-scout training, halfway between the hour hand and twelve o'clock on the dial is due south," he explained. "I need a bearing on this place to be able to come straight to it next time—and at night."

From there, he could no longer see anything useful of Lucerne. But across the lake, on the north side, he spotted the high peaked roof of the Park Hotel at Viznau, and settled on that as a landmark with multiple advantages. He sighted on it several times, until he was satisfied that he had established an angle accurately enough for any need he would have.

"This is all we can do right now," he said. "In broad daylight, we wouldn't have a prayer of getting him out. I don't even know what the odds will be after dark, but I'll try to think of some way to improve them."

The beautiful cold face—which he had discovered could be anything but cold at contact range—was strained and entreating.

"But what if they take him away before tonight?"

"Then we'll have lost a bet," he said grimly. "We could hustle back to Lucerne, get a car, come back here by road—I could find the place now, all right—and mount guard until they try to drive away with him. Then we could try an interception and rescue—supposing he isn't already gone, or they don't take him away even before we get back. On the other hand, they might keep him here for a week, and how could we watch all that time? Instead of waiting, we could be breaking in tonight . . . . It's the kind of choice that generals are paid and pilloried for making."

She held her head in her hands.

"What can I say?"

Simon Templar prodded the starter button, and turned the wheel to point the little speedboat back towards Lucerne.

"You'll have to make up your own mind, Irma," he said relentlessly. "It's your father. You tell me, and we'll play it in your key."

There was little converstion on the return drive. The decision could only be left to her. He did not want to influence it, and he was glad it was not up to him, for either alternative seemed to have the same potentiality of being as catastrophically wrong as the other.

When he had brought the boat alongside the dock and helped her out, he said simply: "Well?"

"Tonight," she replied resolutely. "That is the way it must be."

"How did you decide?"

"As you would have, I think. If the nearest man on the dock when we landed wore a dark shirt, I would say 'Tonight'. It was a way of tossing up, without a coin. How else could I choose?"

Simon turned to the man in the blue jersey who was nearest, who was securing the boat to its mooring rings.

"Could we reserve it again tonight?" he inquired in German. "The Fräulein would like to take a run in the moonlight."

"At what time?" asked the attendant, unmoved by romantic visions. "Usually I close up at eight."

"At about nine," said the Saint, ostentatiously unfolding a hundred-franc note from his wad. "I will give you two more of these when I take the boat, and you need not wait for us. I will tie it up safely when we come back."

"*Jawohl mein Herr!*" agreed the man, with alacrity. "Whenever you come, at nine or later, I shall be here."

Simon and Irma walked back over the planking to the paved promenade where natives and visitors were now crisscrossing, at indicatively different speeds, on their homeward routes. The sun had already dropped below the high horizons to the west, snd the long summer twilight would soon begin.

"Suppose we succeed in this crazy project," he said. "Have you thought about what we do next?"

"My father will be free. I will book passage on a plane and take him back to Sweden with me."

"Your father will be free, but will you? And will I? Or for how long? Has it occurred to you, sweetheart, that the Swiss government takes a notoriously dim view of piratical operations on their nice neutral soil, even with the best of motives? And the Russkis won't hesitate to howl their heads off at this violation of their extraterritorial rights."

Her step faltered, and she caught his arm.

"I am so stupid," she said humbly. "I should have thought of that. Instead, I was asking you to become a criminal, to the Swiss Government, instead of a hero. Forgive me." Then she looked up at him in near terror. "Will you give it up because of that?"

He shook his head, with a shrug and a wry smile.

"I've been in trouble before. I'm always trying to keep out of it, but Fate seems to be agin me."

"Through the travel agency, perhaps I can arrange something to help us to get away. Let me go back to my hotel and make some telephoning."

"Where are you staying?"

"A small hotel, down that way." She pointed vaguely in the general direction of the Schwanenplatz and the older town which lies along the river under the ancient walls which protected it five centuries ago. "It is all I can afford," she said defensively. "I suppose you are staying here? Or at the Palace?"

They were at the corner of the Grand National Hotel and the Haldenstrasse.

"Here. It's the sort of place where travel bureaux like yours send people like me," he murmured. "So you go home and see what you can organize, and I'll see what I can work out myself. Meet me back here at seven. I'm in room 129." He flagged a taxi which came cruising by. "Dress up prettily for dinner, but nothing fussy—and bring a sweater, because it'll be chilly later on that thar lake."

This time he didn't have to take advantage of a situation. She put up her lips with a readiness which left no doubt as to how far she would have been willing to develop the contact in a less public place.

"See you soon," he said, and closed the taxi door after her, thoughtfully.

He had a lot to think about.

Without unchivalrously depreciating the value of any ideas she might have or phone calls she could make, he would not have been the Saint if he could have relied on them without some independent backing of his own. He had softened in many ways, over the years, but not to the extent of leaving himself entirely in the hands of any female, no matter how entrancing.

By seven o'clock, when she arrived, he had some of the answers; but his plan only went to a certain point and he could not project beyond that.

"I think I've figured a way to get into that house," he told her. "And if the garrison isn't too large and lively we may get out again with your father. But what happens after that depends on how hot the hue and cry may be."

She put down her sweater and purse on one of the beds—she had found her way to his room unannounced, and knocked on the door, and when he opened it she had been there.

"I have been telephoning about that, as I promised," she said. "I have arranged for a hired car and a driver to be waiting for us at Brunnen—that is at the other end of the lake, closer to the house than this, and just about as close to Zürich. He will drive us to the airport. Then, I have ordered through the travel agency to have a small private plane waiting to fly us all out."

"A private charter plane—how nice and simple," he murmured. "But can you afford it?"

"Of course not. I told them it was for a very rich invalid, with his private nurse and doctor. That will be you and I. When we are in Sweden and they give us the bill I shall have to explain everything, and I shall lose my job, but my father will be safe and they cannot bring us back."

He laughed with honest admiration.

"You're quite amazing."

"Did I do wrong?" She was crestfallen like a child that has been suddenly turned on, in fear of a slap.

"No, I mean it. You worked all that out while you were changing your clothes and fixing your hair, and you make it sound so easy and obvious. Which it is—now you've told me. But I recognize genius when I see it. And what a lot of footling obstacles disappear when it isn't hampered by scruples!"

"How can I have them when I must save my father's life? But what you have to do is still harder. What is your plan?"

"I'll tell you at dinner."

In an instant she was all femininity again.

"Do I look all right?"

She invited inspection with a ballerina's pirouette. She had put on a simple wool dress that matched her eyes and moulded her figure exactly where it should, wihout vulgar ostentation but clearly enough to be difficult to stop looking at. The Saint did not risk rupturing himself from such an effort.

"You're only sensational," he assured her. "If you weren't, I wouldn't be hooked on this caper."

"Please?"

"I wouldn't be chancing a bullet or a jail sentence to help you."

"I know. How can I thank you?" She reached out and took his right hand in both of hers. "Only to tell you my heart will never forget."

With an impulsively dramatic gesture, she drew his hand to her and placed it directly over her heart. The fact that a somewhat less symbolic organ intervened did not seem to occur to her, but it imposed on him some of the same restraint that a seismograph would require to remain unmoved at the epicenter of an earthquake.

"Don't I still have to earn that?" said the Saint, with remarkable mildness.

When they got to the Mignon Grill at the Palace Hotel on the other

side of the Kursaal ("I promised Dino last night I'd come in for his special
Lobster Thermidor, before I had any idea what else I'd be doing tonight,"
Simon explained, "but anyhow we should have one more good meal
before they put us on bread and water.") he told her how he was hoping
to carry out the abduction; and once again she was completely impersonal
and businesslike, listening with intense attention.

"I think it could work," she said at the end, nodding with prenatural
gravity. "Unless . . . There is one thing you may not have thought of."

"There could be a dozen," he admitted. "Which one have you spotted?"

"Suppose they have already begun to brainwash him—so that he does
not trust us."

Simon frowned.

"Do you think they could?"

"You know how everyone in a Soviet trial always pleads guilty and
begs to be punished? They have some horrible secret method . . . . If they
have done it to him, he might not even want to be rescued."

"That would make it a bit sticky," he said reflectively. "I wonder how
you un-brainwash somebody?"

"Only a psychologist would know. But first we must get him to one.
If it is like that, you must not hesitate because of me. If you must knock
him out, I promise not to become silly and hysterical."

"That'll help, anyway," said the Saint grimly.

The baby lobster were delicious, and he was blessed with the neverless
appetite to enjoy every bite. In fact, the prospect that lay ahead was a
celestial seasoning that no chef could have concocted from all the herbs
and spices in his pharmacopeia.

But the time came when anticipation could not be prolonged any more,
and had to attain reality. They walked back to the Grand National, and
he picked up a bag which he had left at the hall porter's desk when they
went out. It was one of those handy zippered plastic bags with a shoulder
strap which airlines emblazon with their insignia and distribute to overseas passengers to be stuffed with all those odds and ends which travelers
never seem able to get into their ordinary luggage, and Simon had packed
it with certain requisites for their expedition which would have been fatal
to the elegant drape of his coat if they had tried to crowd all of them into
various pockets. The boat was waiting at the marina, and in a transition
that seemed to flow with the smoothness of a cinematic effect they were
aboard and on their way into the dark expanse of the lake.

Simon followed the shoreline to Viznau before he turned away to the
right. From his bag he had produced a hiker's luminous compass, with
the aid of which he was able to set a sufficiently accurate course to retrace

the makeshift bearing he had taken that afternoon between his wrist-watch and the sun. He opened the throttle, and the boat lifted gently and skimmed. Irma Jorovitch put on her cardigan and buttoned it, keeping down in the shelter of the windshield. They no longer talked, for it would only have been idle chatter.

The water was liquid glass, dimpling lazily to catch the reflection of a light or a star, except where the wake stretched behind like a trail of swift-melting snow. Above the blackness ahead, the twinkling façades of Bürgenstock high against the star-powdered sky were a landmark this time to be kept well towards the starboard beam. Halfway across, as best he could judge it, he broke the first law by switching off the running lights, but there were no other boats out there to threaten a collision. Then when the scattered lights on the shore ahead drew closer he slackened speed again to let the noise sink to a soothing purr that would have been scarcely audible from the shore, or at least vague enough to seem distant and unalarming.

He thought he should have earned full marks for navigation. The three tall chimneys that he had to find rose black against the Milky Way as he came within perception range of curtained windows glowing dimly over the starboard bow, and he cruised softly on beyond them into the cove where he had paused on the afternoon reconnaissance.

This time, however, he let the boat drift all the way in to the shore where his cat's eyes could pick out a tiny promontory that was almost as good as a private pier. He jumped off as the bow touched, carrying the anchor, which he wedged down into a crevice to hold the boat snugly against the land.

Back in the boat, he stripped quickly down to the swimming trunks which he had worn under his clothes. From the airline bag he took a pair of wire-cutting pliers, and one of those bulky "pocket" knives equipped with a small-tool shop of gadgets besides the conventional blades, which he stuffed securely under the waistband of his trunks. Then came a flashlight, which he gave to Irma, and a small automatic pistol.

"Do you know how to use this, if you have to?" he asked.

"Yes. And I shall not be afraid to. I have done a lot of shooting—for sport."

"The safety catch is here."

He gave her the gun and guided her thumb to feel it.

She put it in her bag, and then he helped her ashore.

"The road has to be over there," he said, "and it has to take you to the gates which you saw from your car. You can't possibly go wrong. And you remember what we worked out. Your car has broken down, and you want to use their phone to call a garage."

"How could I forget? And when they don't want to let me in, I shall go on talking and begging as long as I can."

"I'm sure you can keep them listening for a while, at any rate. Is your watch still the same as mine?" They put their wrists together and she turned on the flashlight for an instant. "Good. Just give me until exactly half-past before you go into action . . . Good luck!"

"Good luck," she said; and her arms went around him and her lips searched for his once more before he turned away.

The water that he waded into was cold enough to quench any wistful ardor that might have distracted his concentration from the task ahead. He swam very hard, to stimulate his circulation, until his system had struck a balance with the chill, out and around the western arm of the little bay; and then as he curved his course towards the house with the three chimneys he slackened his pace to reduce the churning sounds of motion, until by the time he was within earshot of anyone in the walled garden he was sliding through the water as silently as an otter.

By that time his eyes had accommodated to the darkness so thoroughly that he could see one of the dogs sniffing at a bush at one corner of the back porch, but he did not see any human sentinel. And presently the dog trotted off around the side of the house without becoming aware of his presence.

Simon touched the rope connecting two of the marker buoys enclosing the private beach, feeling around it with a touch like a feather, but he could detect no wire intertwined with it. If there were any alarm device connected with it, therefore, it was probably something mechanically attached to the ends which would be activated by any tug on the rope. The Saint took great care not to do this as he cut though it with the blade of his boy-scout knife. But hardly a hand's breadth below the surface of the water, making the passage too shallow to swim through his delicately exploring fingers traced a barrier of stout wire netting supported by the buoys and stretched between their moorings, which would have rudely halted any small boat that tried to shoot in to the shore. He could feel that the wire was bare, apparently not electrified, but just in case it might also be attached to some warning trigger he touched it no less gingerly as he used his wire-cutters to snip out a section large enough to let him float through.

The luminous dial of his watch showed that he still had almost five minutes to spare from the time he had allowed himself. He waited patiently, close to the projecting side wall, until the first dog barked on the other side of the house.

A moment later, the other one chimed in.

A man came out of the back door and descended the verandah steps, peering to left and right in the direction of the lake. But coming from the lighted house, it would have to take several minutes for his pupils to dilate sufficiently for his retinas to detect a half-submerged dark head drifting soundlessly shorewards in the star-shadow of the wall. Secure in that physiological certainty, the Saint paddled silently on into the lake bank, using only his hands like fins and making no more disturbance than a roving fish.

Apparently satisfied that there was no threat from that side, the man turned and started back up the porch steps.

Simon slithered out of the water as noiselessly as a snake, and darted after him. The man had no more than set one foot on the verandah when the Saint's arm whipped around his throat from behind, and tightened with a subtle but expert pressure . . .

As the man went limp, Simon lowered him quietly to the boards. Then he swiftly peeled off his victim's jacket and trousers and put them on himself. They were a scarecrow fit, but for that nonce the Saint was not thinking of appearances: his main object was to confuse the watchdogs' sense of smell.

The back door was still slightly ajar, and if there were any alarms wired to it the guard must have switched them off before he opened it. The Saint went through without hesitation, and found himself in a large old-fashioned kitchen. Another door on the opposite side logically led to the main entrance hall. Past the staircase was the front door of the house, which was also ajar, meaning that another guard had gone out to investigate the disturbance at the entrance gate. The Saint crossed the hall like a hasty ghost and went on out after him.

The dogs were still barking vociferously in spite of having already aroused the attention they were supposed to, as is the immoderate habit of dogs, and their redundant clamor was earsplitting enough to have drowned much louder noises than the Saint's barefoot approach. One of them did look over its shoulder at him as he came down the drive, but was deceived as he had hoped it would be by the familiar scent of his borrowed clothing and by the innocuous direction from which he came; it turned and resumed its blustering baying at Irma, who was pleading with the burly man who stood inside the gate.

The whole scene was almost too plainly illuminated under the glare of an overhead floodlight; but the man was completely preoccupied with what was in front of him, doubtfully twirling a large iron key around a stubby forefinger, as Simon came up behind him and slashed one hand down on the back of his neck with a sharp smacking sound. The man started to turn, from pure reflex, and could have seen the Saint's hand raised again for a lethal follow-up before his eyes rolled up and he crumpled where he stood. The dogs stopped yapping at last and licked him happily, enjoying the game, as Simon took the key from him and put it in the massive lock. Antique as it looked, its tumblers turned with the smoothness of fresh oil, and Simon pulled the gate open.

"How wonderful!" she breathed. "I was afraid to believe you could really do it."

"I wasn't certain myself, but I had to find out."

"But why—" She fingered the sleeve that reached only halfway between his elbow and his wrist.

"I'll explain another time," he said. "Come on—but be quiet, in case there are any more of them."

She tiptoed with him back to the house. The hallway was deathly still, the silent emptiness of the ground floor emphasized by the metronome ticking of a clock. Simon touched her and pointed upwards, and she climbed the stairs behind him.

The upper landing was dark, so that a thin strip of light underlining one door helpfully indicated the only occupied room. The Saint took out his knife again and opened the longest blade, holding it ready for lightning use as a silent weapon if the door proved to be unlocked—which it did. He felt no resistance to a tentative fractional pressure after he had stealthily turned the doorknob. He balanced himself, flung it open, and went in.

The only occupant, a pale shock-headed man in trousers and shirtsleeves, shrank back in the chair where he sat, staring.

"Professor Jorovitch, I presume?" said the Saint unoriginally.

Irma brushed past him.

"Papa!" she cried.

Jorovitch's eyes dilated, fixed on the automatic which Simon had lent her, which waved in her hand as if she had forgotten she had it. Bewilderment and terror were the only expressions on his face.

Irma turned frantically to the Saint.

"You see, they have done it!" she wailed. "Just as I was afraid. We must get him away. Quick—do what you have to!"

Simon Templar shook his head slowly.

"No," he said. "I can't do that."

She stared at him.

"Why? You promised—"

"No, I didn't, exactly. But you did your best to plant the idea in my head. Unfortunately, that was after I'd decided there was something wrong with your story. I was bothered by the language you used, like 'the capitalist life', and always carefully saying 'Soviet' where most people say 'Russian', and saying that hearing my name was 'like winning a big prize' instead of calling it a miracle or an answer to prayer, as most people brought up on this side of the Curtain would do. And being so defensive about your hotel. And then when we came over this afternoon I noticed there was no Russian flag flying here, as there would be on diplomatic property."

"You're mad," she whispered.

"I was, rather," he admitted, "when I suspected you might be trying to con me into doing your dirty work for you. So I called an old acquaintance of mine in the local police, to check on some of the facts."

The gun in her hand leveled and cracked.

The Saint blinked, but did not stagger. He reached out and grabbed her hand as she squeezed the trigger again, and twisted the automatic out of her fingers.

"It's only loaded with blanks," he explained apologetically. "I thought it was safer to plant that on you, rather than risk having you produce a gun of you own, with real bullets in it."

"A very sensible precaution," said a gentle new voice.

It belonged to a short rotund man in a porkpie hat, with a round face and round-rimmed glasses, who emerged with as much dignity as possible from the partly open door of the wardrobe.

Simon said: "May I introduce Inspector Oscar Kleinhaus? He was able to tell me the true story—that Karel Jorovitch had already defected, weeks ago, and had been given asylum without any publicity, and that he was living here with a guard of Swiss security officers until he completed all the information he could give about the Russian espionage apparatus in Switzerland. Oscar allowed me to go along with your gag for a while—partly to help you convict yourself beyond any hope of a legal quibble, and partly as an exercise to check the protection arrangements."

"Which apparently leave something to be desired," Kleinhaus observed mildly.

"But who would have thought it'd be me they had to keep out?" Simon consoled him magnanimously.

The two guards from the back and the front of the house came in from the landing, looking physically none the worse for wear but somewhat sheepish—especially the one who was clad in his underthings.

"They weren't told anything about my plan, only that they were going to be tested," Simon explained, as he considerately shucked off and returned the borrowed garments. "But they were told that if I snuck close enough to grab them or slap them they were to assume they could just as well have been killed, and to fall down and play dead. We even thought of playing out the abduction all the way to Zürich."

"That would have been going too far," Kleinhaus said. "But I would like to know what was to happen if you got away from here."

"She said she'd arrange for a car to pick us up at Brunnen, and there would be a light plane waiting for a supposed invalid at the Zürich airport—which would have taken him at least as far as East Germany."

"They will be easy to pick up," Kleinhaus sighed. "Take her away."

She spat at the Saint as the guards went to her, and would have clawed out his eyes if they had not held her efficiently.

"I'm sorry, darling," the Saint said to her. "I'm sorry it had to turn out like this. I liked your story much better."

The irony was that he meant it. And that she would never believe him.

THE TRAITOR

Lawrence G. Blochman

TOSKER STOOD ON the steps of the Sub-Collector's bungalow and rattled the door impatiently. A dark face and white turban loomed at the screen, then vanished. Tosker swore and rattled the door again. He was a slim man of about thirty-five, dark and confidently dapper despite the fact that his travel-stained whites were drenched. The hot rain was running off his topee in streams.

A grey-haired Bengali babu came to the door.

"Five thousand pardons, sar," said the babu, "but are you wishing for something in particular?"

"Yes, of course, dammit!" said Tosker. "I want to see the Sub-Collector Sahib."

The babu looked over the visitor's shoulder to the road, where a tonga stood. The pony's head drooped dejectedly in the rain.

"You had better continue to *dak* bungalow," said the babu, wagging his big head once to the right. "Mr. Craven is not able to receive you at this time."

"He'll see me," Tosker insisted. "Just tell him Ben Tosker is here. And let me in out of the rain."

The babu opened the door.

"You will please be waiting on veranda," he said, "while I am informing Mr. Craven."

Tosker pushed past him and strode boldly into the bungalow.

"Please, sar! Please and wait, sar!" Distress wrinkled the babu's brown moon face as he waddled after the visitor, plucking at his sleeve.

"Take your hands off me!" ordered Tosker, striding into the next room.

He stopped just inside the threshold, nodded, and smiled expectantly while the babu was stammering explanations to the man seated behind a desk.

Gerald Craven, I.C.S., D.S.O., Sub-Collector for the *tahsil* of Gorapur, Bengal Presidency, British India, waved away the babu. He did not get up, but sat grasping the edge of his desk with both hands. His delicate fingers seemed almost transparent as they clutched the dark wood. "Hello, Tosker," he said, taking a deep, difficult breath. "What are you doing here?"

"I was in the neighborhood, so I thought I'd drop in to say hello." He hung his dripping topee on the back of a chair and sat down. "Heard from my sister Frances these days?"

"I hear frequently," said Craven. His hair was pure white, although he was still in his late thirties. His eyes seemed very old and wise, and as unhappy as if they had looked upon all the tragedy of forty centuries.

"Then you didn't divorce her after all?"

"You evidently don't correspond with Frances."

"I've been rather out of touch with things at home," said Tosker, crossing his legs. "I've . . . I've been forced to do considerable traveling these last few years. What about Frances?"

"There was no need of a divorce," said Craven. "I have no intention of marrying again. I'm fairly happy out here. Frances has her job cut out for her, bringing up the children at home. . . ."

"So you're letting her save her face, are you—as a reward for keeping her mouth shut about the death of Major Frick?" Tosker chuckled as he lighted a cigarette.

Craven's lips parted, then set in a firm, straight line. "That Frick matter has been settled for years."

"I know." And Tosker smiled knowingly through the smoke. "Death from a broken neck, caused by a fall from a third-story window, probably while intoxicated. That was the coroner's verdict, wasn't it, after the autopsy showed alcohol in the blood? But you seem to forget, Craven, that I was the one who drove you to Frick's apartment about five minutes before his death; that you were in a murderous mood; that you had a strong motive for wanting to kill Major Frick."

"Damn it! I didn't kill Frick!" protested Craven. "When he saw me arrive, he may have thought I'd come to kill him. He hit me and I grabbed hold of him. He was quite drunk. When I released my hold, he backed away in such a hurry that he lost his balance and went through the window."

"Strange, isn't it?" said Tosker, still smiling, "that in view of the purely accidental circumstances, you didn't come forward during the investigation to tell the coroner that you were in the major's apartment at the time of the—accident."

"Don't be a fool, Tosker. You know very well it was needless to expose Frances to the publicity of such a mess. We'd both suffered quite enough on account of Frick. She was completely frank with me. I offered to give her her freedom to marry Frick. But Frick, of course, had no such intentions."

"In view of which fact," said Tosker, waving away a cloud of smoke from before his eyes, "no jury in the world would believe that you didn't throw the major out of the third-story window to kill him."

Craven got to his feet. Perspiration glistened on his chin.

"Are you trying to blackmail me?" he demanded.

"I am," said Tosker, uncrossing his legs.

"You know a Sub-Collector's salary, don't you?"

"I don't want money," said Tosker jauntily.

"What do you want, then?"

"I have launched upon a—well, a rather risky undertaking in this general vicinity," said Tosker. "Fate has put you in a position—officially and geographically—of being able to help me. In view of my discreet silence for three years, I know you won't refuse. Sit down and I'll tell you about it."

Craven sank heavily into a chair.

"For the last several months," said Tosker, "there's been a silly ass of an engineer tramping around the hills of the theoretically independent state on our northern frontier, making military surveys. Last week he finished. Day before yesterday he left Bhutiabad, bound south with his little maps. Now it happens that being a Union of Soviet Socialist Republics hasn't made Russia any less interested in the northern frontiers of India than she was under the Tsar. In fact, there's a Russian gentleman in Calcutta—with a Bulgarian passport, I believe—who is so interested that he's going to pay me fifty thousand rupees for these maps. Now—"

"So you've stolen the maps?"

"Oh, dear no," said Tosker with a gesture of mock innocence. "Not I! But there's a very astute Parsee innkeeper a day's journey up the road, who is rather clever at putting just the right amount of veronal or some such stuff into a man's drink. By the time the man wakes up the Parsee would have had time to hand me—who just happened to be passing—a packet of maps in return for a few hundred rupee notes."

"Tosker," said Craven, "you've always bluffed your way through life with more or less success. But you can't bluff me into—"

"The matter would have been quite simple," Tosker broke in, "if it weren't for these floods that cut Gorapur off from the railway. I might not even have had to call on you. As it is, I'm likely to be held up here, and the mapmaker is only a few hours behind me—if he's that far. I'll want your car, Craven."

Craven sprang up. His lips were colorless as he advanced toward Tosker. Tosker did not move from his chair.

"You can't do this," said Craven in a tight voice.

"Don't be an ass," said Tosker, crossing his legs again. "You don't seem to understand me. Let me put it this way. Unless I get to Calcutta safely and without interference, you'll go home to stand trial for the murder of Major Frick. Is that clear?"

Craven stood above Tosker, looking down at him, breathing heavily. His fingers opened and closed at his sides.

"And suppose," he began slowly, "you should suddenly—drop dead before you got to Calcutta?"

"That won't help you a bit," said Tosker, with a pitying smile. "You'd stand trial anyhow. Read this. It's a carbon copy of a statement I left in a similar sealed envelope with my solicitor in Calcutta. It gives a pretty clear picture of the motives and circumstances surrounding the death of Major Frick. The solicitor has instructions to open it in case of my death. And if I should happen to be murdered, too—the contents might indicate the motive. . . ."

Tosker tendered a long manila envelope with a flat blob of vermilion sealing wax closing the flap. Craven stared at the envelope for several seconds, but made no move to take it. Tosker's upper lip curled a trifle more. He sniffed confidently as he replaced the envelope in his pocket.

Craven's hands stopped working. His fingers became claws, gripping Tosker's shoulders with the suddenness of an eagle swooping down on a lamb. He lifted Tosker off the floor, shaking him furiously. He shook him until his teeth rattled, until his dangling legs knocked against a chair, kicked it over. Then Tosker's arm swung out. That flat of his hand smacked resoundingly against the side of Craven's face. Craven released his hold. Tosker dropped to his feet, pale but sneering. He readjusted his damp, rumpled clothes. The two men stared at each other in silence. The punkah swished faintly overhead—faintly, lazily, as though the coolie boy at the end of the rope outside were going to sleep.

"You—you—indescribable—" Craven choked to a stop, unable to find proper epithets to apply to Tosker.

"That all you've got to say?" asked Tosker in injured tones.

Craven did not reply.

Tosker shrugged, picked up his topee from the floor and started out. Craven let him get as far as the door, then called: "Tosker!"

Tosker turned, bowed low in mock humility.

"At your service," he said.

"Just exactly what do you want of me?" demanded Craven.

"Now you're coming to your senses," said Tosker as he walked back into the room, righted the chair, and sat down again. "First of all you'll give me a letter. Just a chit on your official letterpress, reading something like this: 'To whom it may concern—The bearer of this letter, Ben Tosker, Esquire, is in my service as an emergency messenger, and his progress to Calcutta should be aided and expedited by all civil servants. . . .' "

"My car mired in up to the hubs down the road a mile this afternoon," said Craven, as though talking to himself.

"You'll have it dug out," said Tosker. "It shouldn't take more than a few hours at most."

"You can't get south of Gorapur in anything short of a boat," said Craven.

"How about the road a mile back, the one that runs along the *terai*? It's a long detour, but it follows high ground. I could reach the Eastern Bengal branch line by morning."

"There's a bridge out at Nallah."

"Yes, I know. I inquired about that. They're working on it, and cars may be able to get through tomorrow. We'll find out if a first car might not be able to get through tonight."

"The wires are down between here and Nallah."

"Very well. We'll send a messenger." Tosker leaned forward to touch a bell on Craven's desk. When the grey-haired Bengali appeared, Tosker said: "Babu, the Sub-Collector wants you to send a *chokra* on a bicycle to Nallah at once. He's to find out the very earliest that traffic can pass over the bridge they're repairing. Mr. Craven has urgent need of sending a car through tonight. How soon can you get word back?"

The babu wagged his head.

"Roads are extremely muddish," he said. "Bicycling being slipperishly difficult, *chokra* will probably not be returning before ten-thirty this nighttime."

"Tell him to pedal like hell," said Tosker, "and the instant he gets back he's to bring word to me here."

"Not here," corrected Craven. "He can report to me here, but Mr. Tosker will be stopping at the *dak* bungalow."

"Yes, sar," said the babu, withdrawing.

"And now get out of here," said Craven to Tosker. "The sooner the better."

"For a man who's deeply in debt to me," said Tosker, "you're not very hospitable. At least you'll offer me a drink."

"Get out!" said Craven, raising his voice. "I may have to submit to your blackmail, but I'll be damned if I have to put up with your company."

"Very well." Tosker got up. "I'll wait at the *dak* bungalow for word about that bridge until ten-thirty. You'd better plan to send your car for me at the same time. But I want that chit I mentioned before I leave this house."

"Get out of here!" repeated Craven.

Chuckling confidently, Tosker left the room.

Craven paced the floor for two minutes, then, as though all his energy had been spent, he dropped limply into his chair. He yanked out a drawer of his desk and stared down at a revolver lying there in its thin coating of grease. He slammed the drawer shut and stared through wide, unfocused eyes at a map of India on the wall opposite. A chameleon, running along the top bar of the map, halted, its head poised, stalking a mosquito. Craven picked up a pen, fingered it nervously, dipped it into ink, wrote furiously for a moment. He paused, read what he had written, tore the sheet of paper into bits, swept the scraps to the floor. Again he picked up the pen, hesitated, then hurled the pen across the room. It struck the map. The chameleon scampered up the wall and across the ceiling. Craven watched the penholder quiver as the point transfixed the heart of Kashmir.

"Please, sar." The babu coughed apologetically in the doorway.

"Yes," Craven, startled, faced him.

"Gentleman is waiting impatiently for chit to be written, sar," said the babu.

Craven started looking through his desk for another pen.

Tosker's tonga rolled downhill from the Sub-Collector's bungalow, rattled through dreary streets of one-story rain-soaked mud houses. On the opposite side of the town he stopped in front of the *dak* bungalow—one of the government's rest-houses maintained in out-of-the-way spots in India for the comfort—if it can be called that—of the occasional traveler.

There was danger of an unwelcome meeting in the *dak* bungalow, although it was probable that the man whose maps now reposed between Tosker's shirt and skin would go directly to the Sub-Collector instead of the *dak* bungalow. Anyhow, Tosker was armed with Craven's letter, which practically guaranteed him at least temporary immunity from danger. And in a few hours he would have Craven's car. There was no doubt in Tosker's mind now that Craven, having capitulated in the matter of the letter, would go through with his bargain. Until ten-thirty, Tosker was confident that he could bluff his way through any situation that might arise.

He stepped from the tonga and stood a moment framed by the two mango trees that guarded the front of the *dak* bungalow.

Tosker walked into the bungalow—a small structure with mildewed walls.

Three travelers were sitting at a table of the dining room in the gloomy interior. One of them was a plump, partly bald man in a fresh suit of tussah silk. Beside him was a tall, sandy-haired youth with a slightly undershot jaw. He wore khaki shorts. Tosker's eyes widened almost imperceptibly as they beheld the third man—a red-faced, broad-shouldered person with the general build of an ox. He also wore khaki. From the rain-soaked *terai* hat hanging on the wall, Tosker could draw the double conjecture that one of the men in khaki was a planter and had just come in.

The partly bald man got to his feet and extended a fat hand.

"Welcome, stranger, welcome," he exclaimed. "Shake hands with Henry Clay Judd."

"Good evening," said Tosker, with quiet superiority.

"And this," continued Henry Clay Judd, making a gesture towards the youth, "is Frank Sloan, big colong and pekoe man from the sea gardens. The gentleman across the table might be John Bull himself, but the name on his luggage is 'Hewett.' Hope you folks don't mind my being informal, but as long as we're all marooned together like this, I say we may as well be friendly . . ."

Sloan and Hewett nodded briefly to Tosker, both obviously embarrassed by Judd's heartiness.

"Might as well have a drink," Judd continued, addressing Tosker. "I don't know if they'll be able to find a bed for you. There's only three rooms in the place. Funny Gorapur doesn't have a bigger *dak* bungalow, with all the principal hill roads coming through here. I suppose people usually push on to the railway when the road's not under water. You going to Calcutta, too?"

"Eventually," said Tosker.

"Sloan here tells me he was on his way to Calcutta for his semiannual spree," said Judd.

"Just my luck," said the sandy-haired youth, moved to words at last. "I've got ten days' holiday and I thought I'd go down now while the Barrackpore races are on. I suppose I shall be lucky to get to Calcutta at all, the way things are. . . ."

"Cheer up," said Henry Clay Judd, mopping his bald spot with a blue-bordered silk handkerchief. "The Collector promised to let me know tomorrow if we can get through on that detour. . . . By the way, I didn't give you my card. As you see, I'm Far Eastern manager for Drake and Bean, purveyors of find foodstuffs. In our sunlit kitchens at home, we're making better curries than the Indians themselves can make. You'll note I'm also Oriental agent for Killskeet, most modern and scientific insecticide made. Then I'm representative in India, Burma and Ceylon for International Motors, although you wouldn't have guessed it to see me arriving here in one of those pony tongas. But it won't be long now before we get some real roads in this part of the country, and then—"

"If you'll pardon me," interrupted Tosker, "I'm going to change my clothes before dinner."

"Change in my room if you like," said Sloan.

"Thanks," said Tosker. "I'll promise not to steal anything."

During dinner Tosker noticed Hewett watching him constantly. He could not lift his eyes from his plate without meeting the steady, cold gaze of the red-faced man across the table. Henry Clay Judd was still doing all the talking, but Tosker was not listening to him. Tosker was thinking about Craven, and concocting a plan of action against the one chance in a hundred that Craven should disappoint. . . .

Henry Clay Judd was talking about the great demand for Killskeet, the modern insecticide, in Madras.

"India is a God-made market for scientific insecticide," he said, indicating the winged cloud buzzing about the kerosene lamp. "Now with automobiles it's different. It takes real salesmanship to unload motors, but I'm doing it. International Motors will be tickled to death when they hear of the deal I made with the Maharajah of Bhutiabad—"

"I drove—and slid—from the tea gardens in one of your cars, Mr. Judd," said Sloan.

"The dickens you say!" said Judd, beaming. "What model?"

"About 1865, I should imagine," said Sloan, "but it serves to get around the estates."

Tosker was leaning across the table, suddenly interested. He saw an emergency avenue of escape opening to him.

"Drive it down yourself?" he inquired.

"I've got a syce along, of course," said Sloan. "He'll take the car back, if we can get to the railway."

"He's probably taking the village belles riding tonight," said Tosker.

"No fear," said Sloan, patting his breast pocket. "I keep the keys with me."

"I didn't notice your car when I arrived," said Tosker.

"I've got it parked in a shed in the rear of the bungalow," said Sloan.

After dinner the four perspiring men sat drinking port that tasted of the cork.

At a quarter to ten Henry Clay Judd interrupted himself to say:

"Well, gents, I'm going to hit the hay. I'm piling out at sun-up to see if I can get through on that detour, and I've got to have my sleep. Did you ask the *khansama* about getting you a bed, young fellow?"

"I don't need a bed," said Tosker. "I'll sleep out here in one of these lounge chairs."

At ten o'clock Tosker was alone. He sat on the edge of a chair and turned down the lamp. Nervously he smoked three cigarettes, lighting one from the butt of the other. He looked about him uneasily. Cracks of light lay under two doors. Judd's lamp was already out.

Tosker got up and walked to the door of the bungalow with the vain idea of getting a breath of air. He put his hand inside his shirt to touch a thin packet of paper—the maps that the Parsee innkeeper had stolen for him. There was no reason why they should not be there, of course, but Tosker was jumpy. He was worried by the passive, silent hostility of Hewett.

He told himself that he had no reason to expect a great hullabaloo over the theft of the maps, because a man on a secret military mission would not immediately broadcast the loss of his secrets without first making efforts of his own at recovery. Then Tosker's own part in the affair was probably effectively hidden by the intermediary of the Parsee innkeeper.

Tosker brought the glowing stub of his cigarette close to the dial of his watch. Not quite ten-thirty. The babu had said the cyclist oculd not get back with news of the Nallah bridge until ten-thirty. Craven would not send the car before the cyclist came back—if he sent it at all. He would wait until eleven o'clock—not a minute longer. Then he would steal Sloan's keys and make his getaway in Sloan's car.

He walked back into the bungalow. Two doors were now dark. There was still a crack of light under Hewett's door.

Tosker stood on a straight chair, took out a pocket knife, and cut down a length of rope that ran from the punkah to a hole in the wall. He stepped to the floor, made a coil of the rope, and stretched himself out in a long wicker chair. He examined his gun, toyed with the safety, assured himself again that it was loaded.

A slight sound made him turn his head. The light had vanished from under Hewett's door. He listened. A mosquito whined in his ear. He replaced his gun in his pocket, got up, walked softly about he room, stopping briefly before each bedroom door. Hearty snores emerged from the room of Henry Clay Judd. The other two rooms were silent.

Tosker wiped the perspiration from his forehead. He sat down, leaned back. He could wait a little longer.

Eleven o'clock. No word from Craven. Tosker arose, tiptoed to Sloan's room, tried the door. It was unlocked. The hinges creaked as the door swung inward. Tosker stood motionless, held his breath. He listened for Sloan's measured breathing, heard nothing. Cautiously he approached the cot, bent over.

With a startled grunt, the tea planter sat up.

Tosker's right arm moved in a swift arc. The barrel of his gun thudded against Sloan's sandy hair. The planter silently fell back.

Quickly Tosker looped the punkah rope over and under the bed frame. Five, six turns and the unconscious youth was lashed secretly to the cot.

Tosker found the planter's shirt on a chair, fumbled for the keys to his car. He stuffed the sleeve of the shirt into Sloan's mouth to prevent a premature alarm. Then he started from the room.

As he reached the doorway, a blinding light leaped to his eyes. He blinked through the glare, saw the scowling, red face of Hewett, saw that he was fully dressed, saw the glint of gun metal.

Instantly he lunged forward, lifted his knee sharply into Hewitt's groin.

Hewett stumbled backward. His gun flung roaring flame at the ceiling. A bullet ripped though the roof, whining and clattering through the tiles.

Hewett's electric torch rolled to a stop along the floor. The cone of light illuminated Hewett's gun, almost at Tosker's feet. Tosker kicked the gun through the outer door, saw it sink into the mud.

"Up with your hands!" Tosker ordered as Hewett rose to his knees.

Another door opened, framing a corpulent figure in blue silk pajamas.

"What's the row?" asked Henry Clay Judd querulously. "What the—?"

"You, too! Up with your hands!"

Tosker backed toward the outer door, brandishing his gun. His left hand explored nervously behind him, seeking the key that would lock Sloan, Hewett and Judd inside the *dak* bungalow while he made good his escape in Sloan's car. . . .

It was two minutes past eleven o'clock when the babu brought word to the Sub-Collector Sahib that the bridge at Nallah had been repaired, that the road was open.

Craven was sitting at the desk which symbolized his career, the new life he had built for himself in the East. It was all crumbling about his ears now—unless he paid Tosker's price. Well, he could hesitate no longer. There was no choice between Tosker's alternatives now. The road was open. He must act.

"Motorcar is outside, Sahib," said the babu. "Syce is waiting."

"Tell the syce to go home," said Craven. "I'll drive myself."

When the babu had gone, he opened the desk drawer, took out the revolver that lay there, pocketed it. He walked from the bungalow with heavy, reluctant tread. He had a queer, cold, numb feeling inside his breast as he got into his car, started down the narrow, muddy road though the bazaar. He was crossing the square with the deserted markets under the banyan tree when he heard the report of a pistol shot.

His foot bore down on the accelerator. The car leaped ahead, hurtling through the night towards the sound of the shot, toward the *dak* bungalow. Still a furlong from the bungalow Craven shut off the motor, threw out the clutch. The car coasted ahead with undiminished speed, rushing toward the moment which was to destroy either his career or his sense of honor. He applied the brakes, drew his gun, jumped from the car and hurried over the gentle slope between the two mango trees.

In the entrance to the *dak* bungalow Craven almost collided with Tosker backing out, gun in his right hand, fumbling for the key with his left.

The flashlight on the floor illuminated the overturned furniture, the smashed lamp, the dark, spreading patch of oil on the cement, Hewett and Judd with their arms upraised.

"Drop that gun, Tosker!" ordered Craven.

Tosker froze into immobility. He did not turn around—and he did not drop his gun.

"Hello, Craven," he said. He tried to speak with his old self-assertion, but the ring was gone from his voice. "These men attacked me without provocation, Craven. Tell them about the special mission you're sending me on to Calcutta. . . ."

"Drop that gun!" Craven repeated mechanically.

"Tell them," insisted Tosker. "Or I'll tell them who *you* are, Craven."

"I'll tell you who I am," snapped Craven. "I'm Sub-Collector for this *tahsil*, with full police powers. You're under arrest, Tosker, for violation of the Defense of the Realm Act. Drop that gun!"

"You won't shoot me, Craven."

"I should dislike shooting you in the back, Tosker." The words came from Craven with difficulty. "I shall give you just three seconds to disarm."

Tosker sneered for the benefit of Hewett and Judd, who had not yet dared to lower their hands; but his white pasty face dripped perspiration of an animal at bay.

"One!" counted Craven.

"You can't shoot, Craven!" croaked Tosker. "You can't! There's—that envelope—at my solicitor's. . . ."

"Two!" said Craven.

Tosker's jaws worked spasmodically. His fingers tightened on the grip of his pistol. He spun about, leaped towards Craven.

Two detonations beat upon the air. Two jagged blades of fire slashed at each other.

With grotesque tempo of a slow-motion picture Tosker sank to his knees. He coughed twice, pitched forward on his face.

Craven stood with his legs far apart. He lowered his gun, a pale curl of vapor melting from the muzzle. A long crimson furrow on his left cheek dripped blood to his shoulder.

Henry Clay Judd laughed with nervous relief and mopped his brow with his blue pajama sleeve.

Hewett stepped into the next room to untie Sloan. When he returned, Craven was bending over Tosker's body, going through his pockets.

"Nice work Mr. Craven," said Hewett. "You gave him every chance. Did he hurt you badly?"

"Hurt me?" Craven looked up at Hewett uncomprehendingly. He was oblivious of the gash in his cheek. He was aware only of the long manila envelope which he held between his trembling fingers.

A frightened *khansama* came in with a new lamp.

Craven thrust the manila envelope into his pocket, resumed his search. He ripped open Tosker's shirt. From under the belt he removed a compact sheaf of papers.

As he unfolded the papers, Sloan, Judd and Hewett crowded near to peer over his shoulders. They saw topographical maps of a mountainous region, with heavy red tracings in red ink squirming up the valleys where the contour lines were far apart. Here and there were other red markings.

"Holy jumping Hoboken!" exclaimed Henry Clay Judd, slapping his ample blue thigh. "My maps! Where the—?"

"*Your* maps?" Craven interrupted.

"My road maps!" gasped Judd. "I just closed a deal with the Maharajah of Bhutiabad. He's granting International Motors a sales monopoly in his state, on condition that we finance the building of a road system. These are the highways him and me worked out together. Get the idea? First we build roads, then we sell cars to run on the roads. But how the—?"

A tremendous peal of laughter drowned his words. Craven was standing with his head thrown back, laughing loudly, bitterly, ironically. He had shot a man for treason—and a tricky Parsee innkeeper had forestalled him, made the treason meaningless. He had condemned himself to ruin— for a road map!

Hewett went back across the village with the Sub-Collector. Over two *chota pegs* in perspiring glasses, he showed Craven his credentials as colonel in the Royal Engineers. He would have paid his respects officially, he said, were it not that his mission was confidential and he was avoiding all official contacts.

"I'll go to the District Magistrate with you tomorrow, Mr. Craven," said Col. Hewett, "to testify that you shot in self-defense. I suppose you know that this chap Tosker was a secret agent of a foreign power. Calcutta warned me about him, and I've been dodging him for the past week. Last night he tried to bribe a Parsee innkeeper to put drops in my whisky and steal the survey maps I'd been making. Luckily the Parsee happened to be in our pay—although from the looks of things he took Tosker's bribe and made off with Judd's maps instead."

Hewett talked on and on. Craven listened but heard nothing. He did not even touch his drink. He sat numbly at his desk, staring at the map of India with the pen spearing the heart of Kashmir. The chameleon was back on the crossbar stalking mosquitoes . . .

Automatically Craven told Hewett goodnight.

He took the long manila envelope from his pocket. He turned it over, looking for a full minute at the vermilion sealing wax on the back. His hands were perfectly steady as he picked up a paper-knife to slit the envelope. He was quite resigned now, and only mildly curious regarding Tosker's damning interpretation of the circumstantial evidence in the death of Major Frick in London. He would await with complete calm the revelation of Tosker's posthumous accusation by the solicitor in Calcutta.

Craven drew the papers from the envelope, unfolded what Tosker had described as carbon copies of his accusing, compromising statement:

A croak of grim amusement escaped his lips.

Tosker had died as he had lived—bluffing!

The papers in the envelope were blank.

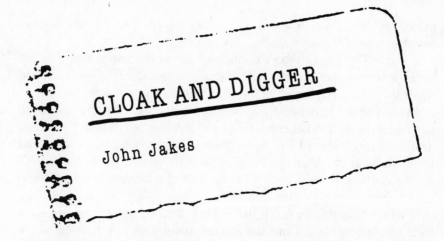

CLOAK AND DIGGER

John Jakes

ROGER GUESSED THAT the opposite side had got on to his mission when a black Citroen roared into the street and three men armed with Sten guns leaped out and began shooting at him simultaneously.

Bullets lacerated the stones of the car wall. Roger's head had been in front of this spot a moment before. As the slugs whined murderously in the twilight air, Roger crawled on hands and knees between the hems of the checked tablecloths.

He heard a great crashing above his own panicky breath. French curses, liquid and rapid, punctuated the bursts of gunfire. Spasmodically the shooting stopped twenty seconds after it had begun.

But by that time Roger had already crawled into the shadows of the cafe, bowled over the mustached proprietor and raced up rickety stairs to the second floor. He went out through a trapdoor to the slate roof.

Clinging dizzily to a chimney pot, he looked down. A flock of geese which had been strolling through the cobbled main street of the tiny village of St. Vign flew every which way, honking at the Citroen which nearly ran over them as it gathered speed and rolled away. Then, with a tight-lipped gasp of relief, Roger located the source of the crash which had saved him—an overturned vintner's cart. He vaguely remembered the cart being unloaded before the shooting started, as he sat sipping Coca-Cola, reading the pamphlet in his pocket, *A New Glossary of Interesting Americanisms,* and trying to look like a tame philologist in horn-rimmed spectacles.

He had failed miserably, he thought. In the disguise, that is. But then, the opposite side always had first-rate intelligence. Lucky the vintner's cart had gotten in the line of fine. The poor vintner was drawing a crowd of people as he sobbed over his dribbling and bullet-riddled casks and cursed off would-be drinkers. The whine of the Citroen had died altogether.

It was chilly, hanging on the chimney pot in the wind. Below in the street a nun in the crowd pointed up at Roger. Quickly he scrambled down the slates. He leaped to the adjoining roof in the amber dusk.

As he went skulking across the rooftops, one thought came up paramount in his mind after his shock and surprise had passed: his still-urgent need to get aboard *The Silver Mistral Express* which was scheduled to go through St. Vign on its way to Paris in—Roger consulted his shockproof watch while resting on the roof of a laundry—exactly forty-eight minutes.

His first task was to reach the railway station, hoping the assassins would be frightened off making another attempt on him because of the notoriety their first failure caused. Sliding, Roger dropped into an alley and began to run through the grape-fragrant French twilight.

As he ran he heard a number of whistles and saw several gendarmes pedalling frantically on bicycles. Good, he thought, puffing. Wonderful. If they keep the Citroen holed up in some garage for—again the watch—thirty-two minutes, I'll make it.

Reaching the depot without incident, he paced restlessly along the platform, trying to read his pamphlet. At last, up the track, a light shone and an air horn cried out stridently.

When the crack train from the south of France pulled to a hissing halt in response to the ticket seller's signal lantern, Roger leaped aboard with the pamphlet of Americanisms still clutched in one hand. The conductor badgered him in French for disturbing the schedule as the express began to roll. Roger ignored him. He held up the pamphlet in the vestibule light. On the inside front cover a car and compartment number had been noted in ballpoint. Roger turned to the right, stepped through a velvet padded door, then hastily backed out again. He had gone the wrong way. The private saloon car was filled with men and women in formal clothes, opera capes and evening growns.

"What's that?" Roger asked the trainman sourly. "A masked ball?"

"An opera troupe, *Anglais*. Returning from a triumphant engagement in the South," replied the trainman, kissing his fingertips. Then he scowled. "Let me see your ticket, please."

Roger handed it over.

"How far is compartment seven, car eleven-twelve?"

"Four cars to the rear," said the trainman without interest, turning his back on Roger and beginning to whistle an operatic aria. Roger kicked open the door on his left. He hurried, walking as fast as he dared. The cars were dimly lit, most of the doors closed. The wheels of the train clicked eerily from the shadows. Roger shivered. He felt for his automatic under his coat.

Finally he found the right car. Putting his pamphlet in his pocket, Roger knocked at compartment seven.

"Dozier? Open up."

Mouth close to the wood, Roger whispered it again:

"Dozier! For God's sake, man, open—"

With a start Roger realized the sliding door was unlocked.

He stepped quickly into the darkened carriage, blinked, and uttered a sigh of disgust. He might have known.

Wasn't this precisely why he had been sent to board the train in such haste? Because the agent—some agent, Roger thought, staring at the compartment's lone occupant—was one of the worst bunglers in the trade. An IBM machine had slipped a cog or something, dispensing the wrong punch card when the escort was being selected for the vital mission of accompanying Sir Stafford Runes from Cairo to Paris. At the last moment, higher-ups had caught the error and dispatched Roger by 707 to catch the train at St. Vign and see that no fatal damage had been done.

The agent in question, actually a coder from London who doubled in ladies' ready-to-wear, and who had no business at all in the field, was a fat, pot-bellied bald man with the first name Herschel. At the moment he was snoring contentedly with his hands twined over his Harris-tweeded paunch. Roger shook him.

"Dozier, wake up. Do you hear me? What's the matter with you, Dozier?"

Sniffing, Roger realized dismally that brandy had aided Herschel Dozier's slumber. With each valuable minute spent attempting to wake the slumbering cowlike fellow, Sir Stafford Runes sat alone, undoubtedly in the next compartment. Disgusted, Roger slid back into the corridor.

Which compartment, right or left?

He tried the one on the right, tapping softly. A feminine giggle came back, together with some sounds which indicated that if an archaeologist was inside, he was a young, lively archaeologist, not the red-haired, vain, aging Runes.

Moving back along the carpeted corridor to the other door, Roger hesitated, his knuckles an inch from the panel.

The compartment door stood open perhaps a thirty-second of an inch, allowing a hairline of light to fall across Roger's loafers.

Sweat came cold on his palm. He drew hs automatic.

Was someone from the opposite side in there?

Runes, on an underground exploration in the vicinity of Nisapur, had unearthed what headquarters described only as a "vital plan" belonging to the opposite side. The plan, apparently, was so important that higher-ups had ordered Runes to discontinue his valuable role as a double agent at once and return to home base as fast as he could while still avoiding danger. Now Roger smelled danger like burning insulation on a wire.

Drawing a tight breath, he cursed the faulty IBM machine, gripped the door handle, and yanked.

The first thing he saw was the corpse of Sir Stafford Runes.

It sprawled doll-fashion on the seat, an ivory knife-hilt poking from the waistcoat. Against the talcumed whiteness of the dead man's puffy old features, the carrot brightness of his thick red hair looked gruesome.

Then Roger's eyes were torn to the tall man who stood calmly in the center of the compartment, eyeing him with a stainless-steel gaze from under the rim of a shining top hat. From the man's lean shoulders fell the shimmering folds of an opera cape, which showed a flashing hint of blood-red satin lining as he raised one white-gloved hand in a vicious little salute. Roger slammed the door shut as the man said:

"Is it really you, Roger?" His voice was clipped, educated. "I'd thought they took care of you in St. Vign."

"No such luck."

Covering the gaunt man with his automatic, Roger nodded down at the dead body. The express train's horn howled in the night.

"So you did this, you rotten bastard. Just the way you ran over Jerry Pitts with the road grader in Liberia and fed Mag Busby that lye soup in Soho." A vein in Roger's temple began to hammer. "You rotten bastard," he repeated. "Someone should have squashed you a long time ago. But what are you doing in that get-up, Victor? Traveling with that opera company?"

"Of course, dear boy," the other purred. "I'm representing them on this tour. I schedule performances wherever duty calls. Such as in Paris. Most convenient." A white glove indicated the speeding motion of the train, but for all the man's casualness there was glacial chill in his calculating eyes. "It appears that this time, however, with you as relief man, I've landed in a spot of trouble. I'd thought all I had to worry about was that fool asleep next door."

"This time, Foxe-Craft," Roger said quietly, "you've got a bullet to worry about."

"A bullet?" The urbane man's eyebrow lifted. "Oh, now, really, old chap, so *brutal?*"

"Did you think about brutality when you fed Mag the lye soup? Listen, mister, for ten years we've wanted you. You and your fancy gloves and your code name." A line of derision twisted Roger's wirelike mouth. "*Elevenfingers.* Proud of that name, aren't you? One up on the rest of us, and all that. Well, tonight, I think I'll take those fingers off. One at a time."

With a stab of satisfaction Roger saw a dollop of sweat break out on Foxe-Craft's upper lip. Roger made a sharp gesture with the automatic.

"All right, Elevenfingers—"

"Don't make it sound cheap," Foxe-Craft said, dangerously soft. "Not theatrical, I warn you."

"Where's the folio Runes was carrying?"

Hastily Roger searched the archaeologist's corpse. He performed the same action on the person of his enemy, a shred of doubt beginning to worry him as he completed the task, unsuccessfully. Apart from the usual innocuous card cases, visas, antipersonnel fountain pen bombs and other personal effects, neither dead researcher nor live agent possessed a single item remotely resembling the flat, eight-and-a-half by eleven series of sheets, blank to the eye but inked invisibly, which Runes was carrying back from Nisapur. Roger raised the automatic again.

"Take a long look down the muzzle, friend. See the message? I can put some bullets in places that'll hurt like hell. And I don't care if I wake the whole damned train doing it. But you're going to tell me where the folio is. You're going to give it to me, or I'll blow you into an assortment of pieces no doctor on the Continent can put together." Desperate, angry, Roger added: "In five seconds."

Foxe-Craft shrugged.

"Very well."

As Foxe-Craft consulted a timetable card riveted to the compartment wall his eyes glinted maliciously for a moment. Then the toe of his dancing pump scraped a worn place in the carpeting. Looking at his wristwatch, the man who liked to call himself Elevenfingers said: "You're an American. Look under the rug."

"I'll just do that."

Carefully Roger knelt, keeping the automatic in a position to fire at the slightest sign of movement in the corner of his eyes. Roger probed at the frayed edges of the hole in the carpeting. And at that precise instant, the game turned against him; *The Silver Mistral Express* whipped around a curve and into a tunnel.

There was a scream of horn, a sudden roar of wheels racketing off walls. Roger swayed, off balance.

A tasseled pump caught him in the jaw, exploding roman candles behind his eyes a moment after he caught a fragmentary glimpse of traces of ash beneath the carpet.

Foxe-Craft *couldn't* have burned the folio, Roger thought wildly as he fell backward, flailing. I didn't smell anything—and that means *Runes* burned it because he knew they were on to us, but why did he burn the only copy in existence—?

No answer came except the roar of wheels and another brutal smash of a pump instep on his jaw, smacking Roger's head against the side of the compartment, sending him to oblivion.

Through his pain he had dim recollections of the next hour—hands lifting him, a fall through space, a jolt, the *clacka-clacka-clacka* of wheels gathering speed, then the chirruping of night insects. And silence.

Bruised, disappointed, briar-scratched and burr-decorated, Roger woke sometime before dawn, lying in a ditch a few hundred yards south of another railway depot, this one bearing a signboard naming the town as St. Yar.

Roger picked himself up and tried to wipe the humiliation of failure from his mind. In another two hours Foxe-Craft—and the train—would be in Paris, doubtless with the vital material in his hands.

Roger felt, somehow, that it still existed; that Elevenfingers had tricked him. But how? Starting off, Roger noticed his ubiquitous pamphlet in the weeds. He stared at it dully, finally putting it back in his pocket as he passed a sign pointing the way to a French military aerodrome two kilometers away.

Trudging into the village, Roger located an inn and ordered a glass of wine. The proprietor treated him with the respect given by all Frenchmen to those who look like confirmed alcoholics—torn clothes and hangdog expression. Dispiritedly Roger sat at a street-side table as the sun rose. Bells chimed in the cathedral. A French jet lanced the sky overhead.

To kill the futility of it all, Roger bought a paper at a kiosk and sat by a fountain reading. At a town quite a distance south, the wet-inked lead story ran, an unidentified bald man had been found in a ditch by railway inspectors.

Poor Herschel Dozier, Roger thought. It would be just like Elevenfingers to finish the sleeping agent, just for amusement. Another knife in the guts from nothing . . .

When he had finished the paper, he dragged out the pamphlet to try to dull his mind.

"What the hell do *I* care about Interesting Americanisms?" he said, blinking in the sun. And then, as pigeons cooed around his feet and a postcard seller passed by hawking indecent views, the depth of his blunder made itself known.

Foxe-Craft's remark flashed like a bomb. With a whoop, Roger leaped up and ran to the cafe.

"Where can I get a taxi to the military aerodrome? I have to get a helicopter to Paris right away!"

The baffled proprietor gave him directions. Roger's identification papers, concealed in his heels, served him well. Within an hour he stood on the noisy platform as *The Silver Mistral Express* chugged in along the arrival track.

Roger felt for the automatic in his pocket, grinning tensely. Of *course* Runes had burned the folio. Too obvious. But if Roger was right, there was another copy—*had* to be!

Down the platform trouped the formally dressed opera company, Foxe-Craft in their midst. When he saw Roger he turned and tried to walk in the opposite direction. Roger raced after him. He gouged the automatic in the agent's ribs.

"*Really,* old fellow—" Foxe-Craft began.

"Shut up," Roger said. "You egotistical bastard. Think you're so damn clever. One up. Well, you shouldn't have opened your precise mouth, Elevenfingers, because now you're going to be tagged with a killing. I thought it was Dozier in the ditch. But it wasn't. It was Runes, Bald, vain Runes."

Roger dug into the writing agent's pocket, came up with his prize, carrot-red.

"First we'll go wake up Dozier. Probably he's still asleep."

Roger turned his find over, noted minute markings which looked like ink on the inner, rather burlaplike surface.

"Then," Roger added, gagging his captive, "we'll have the lab blow up the stuff that's written here. Inside old Sir Stafford's—

A crowd began to gather. The divas and tenors of Elevenfinger's now-defunct opera troupe clucked curiously. Roger held up the carrot-colored wig and finished:

"—inside, or under—as we Americans say—his rug."

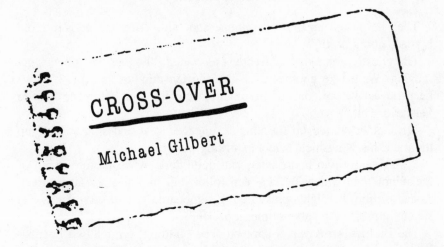

CROSS-OVER

Michael Gilbert

MR. CALDER SAT behind the wheel of his old Ford Zodiac and stared out at the sodden world. It was four o'clock on a February afternoon and visibility was down to a hundred yards. It would decrease still further as afternoon fell away into evening.

Ahead of him, a length of white road crawled up toward the skyline, running with water in all its ruts. To left and right stretched unfenced moorland. The rain covered everything in a slowly moving pall.

A high-pitched whistling noise made him look down.

Headphones hung over the back of the passenger seat, the cushion of which had been taken out. In the open space where the seat should have been was a black, ebonite-fronted box. It had two tuning knobs and a single large dial graduated in degrees, on which a needle was rotating slowly.

The whistling stopped. The needle on the dial steadied and the voice of Mr. Behrens, distorted but clearly recognizable, spoke from the headset.

"Seventeen, eighteen, nineteen. Back to eighteen. Steady on eighteen. Over to you."

Mr. Calder put his thumb on the "speak" switch of the microphone and said, "Two-hundred and thirteen. I shall have to replot. Out for a moment."

The map on his knees was mounted on plywood and covered with isinglass. He took a protractor from the pocket of the car, aligned it carefully on the isinglass and marked four points. Then he picked up a graduated ruler and joined the points so that they formed two intersecting lines. He peered down at the map. It was now so dark that he needed a torch, and it took a minute to get it out of the car locker and focus it.

Then he picked up the microphone and said, "He's on the Nettlefold byroad, going north."

The ghostly voice of Mr. Behrens answered, "I agree. We'd better get moving. We'll take another cross-bearing ten minutes from now. If we keep on as we are, one of us ought to cut him off before he gets to Felshead. Out."

Mr. Calder started up the engine, engaged gear and splashed off up the road, his windshield wipers working busily . . .

It was nearly two hours later, and quite dark, when he turned out of the minor road which he had been following, into a rather larger road. Ahead of him, his lights picked out a signboard. "This looks like it," he said to himself. "And about time, too."

The Bailiffs Arms was a dark crooked building, originally a posting-house, now a small residential hotel. Mr. Calder steered his car into the yard. There were two other cars parked there already. One was a Morris station wagon and belonged, he knew, to his friend, Mr. Behrens. The other was an old but solid-looking Mercedes.

Mr. Calder parked his own car, locked all the doors carefully and made his way through the back door of the hotel into the smoking room. A bright fire was blazing in the hearth. On one side of it Mr. Behrens was seated. On the other chair he recognized, with some surprise, the angular figure of Mr. Fortescue, who combined the offices of manager of the Westminster branch of the London and Home Counties Bank and of head of the Joint Services Standing Intelligence Committee.

Mr. Fortescue, who made few sartorial concessions, was dressed in the same black coat and striped trousers that he would have worn in his banker's parlor.

"I didn't know, sir, that it was you who was playing hare to our hounds," said Mr. Calder.

"It's the first time we've given the apparatus a field trial," said Mr. Fortescue. "I thought I might as well do it myself. Since you both arrived here within five minutes of me, I gather it was effective."

He put his hand into the side pocket of his coat, pulled out what seemed to be an ordinary cigarette lighter and placed it on the table.

"Extremely effective," said Mr. Behrens. "How does it work?"

"It's a transmitting set, which sends out a single VHF note. It's battery-powered, and will transmit for two hundred hours. It's tuned into the receiving sets in your cars, which incorporate a direction finder. The whole thing's a development of the device which the Germans used for locating transmitting sets in Occupied France—only it's much more accurate, and it works over a much longer range."

"What sort of fix does it give you?"

"The makers say one mile at a hundred miles. That's under laboratory conditions. But you can't rely on that in practice."

"I'll say you can't," said Mr. Calder. "Every time your car passed under a power line, the beam jumped about like a performing flea. And another thing. You were doubling about—changing direction—going back on your tracks. If we were really after someone, and he didn't know we were there, presumably he'd get on to some route nationale, or autobahn, and go down it damned fast. Every time we stopped to plot his position, he'd get ten miles farther away from us."

"There's quite a simple solution to that," said Mr. Fortescue. "You must be given very fast cars. Anything else?"

"Can't they fit a cut-out to eliminate interference from power lines?"

"They're working on it now. It's the one big snag in the apparatus. But it's difficult technical problem."

"Well, here's an easy one," said Mr. Calder. "I want a map-board with an electric light built into it, so that I don't have to waste time messing about with a torch every time I plot."

"A good idea," said Mr. Fortescue. "What about you, Behrens?"

"I didn't experience any real snags," said Mr. Behrens. "We were helped by the fact that we were operating on a stretch of moor with very few roads. So, however roughly we plotted, there was never any real doubt where you were and which direction you were going. If there were a lot of little roads, it might be trickier. But I think it's a perfectly sound method of following a car without haveing to get within miles of it."

"Yes," said Mr. Fortescue. "I think the experiment can be said to have been successful."

"Was it just an experiment?" said Mr. Calder. "Or had you something practical in mind. Something you intended to use us on."

Mr. Fortescue said, "I've got something very practical in mind. We're going to use this device to uncover Route M."

For a long moment nobody spoke, and the only sound was the battering of the rain against the windows. Then Mr. Behrens said, "That's a very interesting idea. Which of us is going to be the hare on *that* run?"

"I'm afraid," said Mr. Fortescue, with a smile, "that you're both too well known to our friends on the other side to make convincing hares. You'll be acting as hounds, just as you did today. The hare's going to be Nichol. Do either of you know him?"

"David Nichol. Early thirties."

"That's right."

"I taught him German—that would have been just after the war. he must have been about fifteen. He was a good linguist, even then."

"He started learning European languages when he was eight. He speaks half a dozen, and is completely fluent in German and Russian."

"Unusual application for a boy of eight," said Mr. Calder.

"He was an unusual boy," said Mr. Fortescue. "With an unusual background. His father, John Nichol, was an ardent Communist. He was one of the first to join the anti-Franco forces in the field. He was very lucky. He survived for nearly a year."

"With that background," said Mr. Calder, "David should be a thorough-going Communist himself."

"And so he might have been. But some very odd stories got back to his mother, about the circumstances of his father's death. Very odd, indeed. According to his comrades, some of whom ultimately got back to England from internment, or prison camp, John Nichol wasn't an ordinary battle casualty. There was a mystery about his death. One story, which was widely believed, was that he had been betrayed to a Franco patrol by the orders of the commissar of his battalion. The Russians were becoming alarmed by his growing influence in the group, and came to the conclusion that he ought to be liquidated before he became canonized."

"There's a ring of probability about that," agreed Mr. Calder.

"It was probable enough to convince his mother. She decided to dedicate David—then aged eight, mind you—to the anti-Communist front. She was a woman of considerable imagination, and great persistence. She had her son trained in such a way that he was bound to go into Intelligence, which he did. Of course, we realized as soon as we set eyes on him that we'd got a man in a milion. Single-minded, dedicated, with all the basic skills already learned. The difficulty was to know how to use him best."

Mr. Fortescue stopped to tap out his pipe, and said, "In the end, we sold him to the Russians."

"With a return ticket, I presume."

"We hoped so. We sent him to Korea, and arranged for him to be captured. He was an exceptionally intelligent and docile prisoner. They sent him to the Hwei Pé Camp School where he was thoroughly indoctrinated. When Soviet Intelligence were completely happy about him, they arranged for him to be returned to this country on exchange."

"Nice," said Mr. Behrens.

"He's been invaluable," agreed Mr. Fortescue. "But he can't keep it up forever. That's why we're going to use him to uncover Route M. A final fling."

"It seems almost a waste," said Mr. Calder. "I don't mean that as a criticism," he added hastily. "You'd be able to judge best. But a well-placed double agent—"

"Discovering how Route M works—where it starts—what the stations are en route—is becoming more important than anything else in our program. In the last ten years they've taken a constant stream of people out by it. Their agents, our agents, scientists, diplomats, all sorts. It's got to be shut down."

"If we shut it down, won't they simply open another route?"

"Oh, certainly. But it'll take time. It's the next six months that are important."

"Who do we think we're going to lose in the next six months?" said Mr. Calder. "Or is that an indiscreet question?"

"Extremely indiscreet," said Mr. Fortescue. "But I think I'd better tell you."

And he did.

When he had finished, Mr. Calder said, "If that's even on the cards, sir, I agree, of course. It's worth three of Nichol to put the ROAD CLOSED signs up. How soon will things start moving?"

"The first steps have been taken. Nichol has let his Russian masters know that he is under suspicion. He has asked for asylum in the USSR and they've promised to get him out. If we suspect him, it follows we won't allow him out of England by any normal route. He'd be stopped at the port or the airfield. Therefore he's got to go unofficially. And that means Route M. As soon as he gets his marching order he'll tip us off, and we'll let you know. After that, I can give you very few instructions. You'll have to deal with each situation as it arises. If you can locate the route without the other side realizing what you're doing, so much the better. If you have to get rough and close it permanently it can't be helped."

"It seems to me," said Mr. Calder thoughtfully, "that there's one point where things are bound to get a mite complicated. And that's when we come to the actual cross-over. A lot's going to depend on Nichol, then."

"I recall him quite clearly, now," said Mr. Behrens. "A shock of thick black hair. A white, rather serious face. Very solemn and self-contained. A person who had elevated self-control to a moral principle."

"He has never touched alcohol in his life," said Mr. Fortescue, "and has never had other than a brotherly regard for a woman. Although," he added, "to judge from modern trends in fiction, even that is not an entirely safe simile these days."

"He sounds a bit of a prig," said Mr. Calder.

"Not a prig," said Mr. Behrens. "A puritan."

On a day in late April, David Nichol walked along the west bank of Hamble River and out onto the jetty. Ahead of him stretched the estuary, flat and placid. He looked very different from the smart young man in conventional clothes who had caught the train from Waterloo.

His journey had taken him to a room in a small hotel in a back street in Southampton, where he had stripped to the skin and put on the seaman's rig carefully laid out for him on the bed: corduroy trousers, rubber-soled shoes, and thick gray stockings into which the trousers ends were tucked; a string vest, a collarless shirt, a thick, blue, roll-necked jersey and a duffle coat.

Most of his own clothes went into the wall cupboard. A few personal belongings went into pockets or were squeezed into the top of an already bulging kit bag. Twenty minutes after entering the hotel, he had left it by the back door. From beginning to end he had spoken no word to anyone in the hotel.

His next stop was at a small bicycle shop. Here also he was expected. The owner of the shop—a long man with a squint—had a bicycle ready for him, and helped him to lash the kit bag onto the carrier. He also was a man of few words.

Nichol had stopped at a pull-in for motorists at Botley, and had eaten a meal of eggs and chips, with two mugs of teak-colored tea and several wedges of bread and butter, after which he had pedaled slowly on his way.

Just short of the jetty which he was making for stood a bungalow with a derelict strip of garden in front, and an overgrown lawn running down to the river behind. After examining the name on the gate, Nichol had wheeled his bicycle boldly into the garden, propped it against the wall, unwrapped the kit bag, shouldered it and walked away up the path to the gate. As he did so he saw, out of the corner of his eye, a curtain in one of the front windows of the bungalow twitch apart and close again.

At the far end of the jetty a thickset man with a beard was sitting on one of the iron mooring-bollards smoking a pipe, and watching the herring gulls fighting for galley scraps. He turned his head as Nichol approached.

"Nichol?"

That's right, sir."

"You made good time. No hitches?"

"Smooth as clockwork."

"We shall be sailing in an hour. Can you handle a dinghy?"

"I've done most of my rowing at Windsor," said Nichol, "but as long as it's calm I shall make out all right."

"I could easily row you myself," said the man. "But it might look a bit odd if the owner took the sculls and the latest-joined member of the crew sat in the stern. I don't think we're being watched. But I don't believe in taking any chances."

"I'll manage," said Nichol.

In fact, he rowed very competently, and they were soon tying up under the stem of the ten-ton Hillyard Bermuda fore-and-aft-rigged sloop which was swinging in the tideway.

"You get below and lie down," said the owner. "I've declared a crew of two. One's ashore now. the other's below. They're both dressed exactly like you. All we've got to be careful not to do is to let the three of you appear on deck at the same time."

Nichol nodded, and disappeared down the orlop ladder. The owner cast a slow glance up the Middle Reach of Hamble River. No one appeared to be the least interested in him or his boat. He extracted a cigar from a case in his breast pocket, and lit it.

Almost exactly fourteen hours later, he said, "Slow ahead. Dead slow. Cut the engine."

It was an hour before daylight, and the sloop lay a quarter of a mile southwest of the Nez de Jobourg, rising and falling on a gentle swell. A thick white blanket of early morning mist lay over the water.

"Couldn't have had better weather if we'd booked it in advance," said the owner. He had been up all night, his eyes were red-rimmed and his voice was hoarse, but he sounded happy.

"Looks all right to me," said Nichol. "What next?"

"Bertrand will row you ashore in the dinghy. I'm not sure, to within a mile, exactly where you are. But it's not important. All you have to do it to scramble up the cliff—there are half a dozen paths—and you'll find yourself on quite a good road. It runs parallel to the top of the cliff, about half a mile inland. It's got kilometer stones marked Auderville on one side and Beaumont-Hague on the other. You want the stone which shows Auderville—four and Beaumont—six. That's where the car will be waiting. Clear?"

"Quite clear," said Nichol. "As I don't even know your name, I'm afraid I can't write you a bread and butter letter—but thanks for a lovely trip."

"Don't mention it," said the bearded man. "Your kit bag is already in the boat, I see. Goodbye."

An hour later the sun was rising, red and glorious, out of the mist. The cutter had rounded the Nez de Jobourg and was out of sight, and

Nichol was walking along the grass verge of the road, counting the little white hundred-meter stones—seven, eight, nine. The next kilometer stone must be in the dip ahead. No sign of a car.

Nichol perched on the stone and lowered his kit bag to the ground. It was a quarter to seven. Soon farm traffic would be passing. He would have to make a plan.

Someone came through a gap in the hedge and walked slowly toward him. It was a girl.

His first impressions were of size and color. She was big and she was blonde. As she came closer, he took in other details. She had a peasant's nose with no bridge to it, eyes which were pulled fractionally upward at the outer corners, and a generous mouth. She was wearing trousers which looked like jodhpurs but were more generously cut, a polo-necked sweater, and a windcheater. She had a businesslike look about her, Nichol thought. The sort of girl who could ride a horse, drive a car or plough a field.

She said, "Mr. Nichol? Put out your right hand. Press the tip of your index finger onto this black stuff. It'll wash off, I assure you. Now onto this pad. Fine."

She had taken out a small card which she compared carefully with the fingerprint which Nichol had made on her pad. Then she said, "The car is in a field, two hundred meters down the road. Give me your bag."

"It's a bit heavy," said Nichol. "I'd better take it—"

Before he could say any more she had swung the kit bag onto her shoulder and was walking off down the road.

The car, a dark green Citroën covertible tourer, had been skillfully tucked away in a dip among bushes.

"It is time that you ceased to be a sailor," said the girl. She spoke in the clear unaccented English of a foreigner who has been very carefully coached in a language, but mostly out of books. "Your traveling clothes are in the kit bag. You had better take off everything you are wearing. Even the underclothes are English."

"All right," said Nichol. The new clothes fitted him well. Gray worsted sports trousers, a heavy silk shirt with open neck and a silk scarf; a gray sports jacket, tighter at the waist than an English tailor would have cut it, and with padded shoulders.

As he took his old clothes off, the girl rolled them up and stowed them in the empty kit bag. Since the girl herself seemed to regard the operation as a matter of routine, Nichol tried to convey the impression that, so far as he was concerned, there was nothing out of the ordinary in stripping to the skin in front of a girl.

When he was dressed, she said, almost as though the operation they had just concluded had effected an introduction between them, "My name, by the way, is Shura."

"I had better know your second name, too."

She looked surprised. "The same as yours, of course," she said. "Shura Nichol. We are man and wife. That is how our papers are made out."

Nichol said, "Oh, I see. Yes. I suppose that's a sensible sort of arrangement."

"We are on a camping holiday. The kit is all in the back of the car. There are many camp sites in France and Germany. If we went to hotels, there would be registration forms to fill in—"

"An excellent idea," said Nichol. "Do I drive the car, or do you?"

"We take it in turns. It will be a long day's run. More than three hundred miles. We had better get started."

She threw the kit bag into the bushes.

"Isn't that a bit risky?"

"In England, perhaps. In France, no. The peasant who finds it will not report it. He will think it good luck."

The tip of Nichol's fingers touched the cigarette lighter, which he had transferred to his new clothes along with his personal possessions. Luck, he said to himself, that's what I'm going to need, too. Any goddamned amount of it.

Eighty miles away, in a wood south of Bolbec, the sensitive needle on the dial of Mr. Calder's car began to quiver. He picked up the microphone.

"He's off, I think," he said.

"Moving southeast," agreed the voice of Mr. Behrens.

The thing which David Nichol admired most in that long day's run was his companion's driving. He himself was a good driver. A part of his training had been the proper handling of cars, and a course at the Police Driving School had added technique to a natural aptitude. But he was not as good as Shura. She drove as safely as he did, and nearly five miles an hour faster.

There were other things to admire about her. Every move she made had the unconscious economy and control which is only achieved by an athlete at the height of training. Muscle was there under the flesh, but it was in the right place and was not obtrusive. A ballet dancer at the peak of her career, an Olympic runner or jumper would have carried her subjugated body and limbs in just such a fashion.

As she drove down the long straight road from Bayeux to Caen, he

looked at her out of the corner of his eye and found himself wondering
about her past. She was clearly a Slav; a South Russian, he thought.
Perhaps a Georgian. She could not have attained her perfection in English—which was matched, as he soon noted, by a nearly equal perfection
in French—without at least twelve years' training. Yet she did not look
more than twenty-four.

Could a totalitarian regime select boys and girls at twelve, as a breeder
might select promising foals, and train them solely for its purposes?
Teach them the requisite languages, train them in judo, and the use of
poisons, teach them how to shoot, how to drive a car, how to operate a
wireless set? There was nothing impossible about it. Sparta had selected
her soldiers at the age of seven.

It would dehumanize them, of course. The only thing that Shura had
not learned to do was to smile. Or could she do that too? Or make love?
If the job demanded it, she could probably do that just as efficiently as
she drove a car.

They had a picnic lunch in a wood south of Montargis. There was hot
soup in a vacuum flask, and pâté and fruit. Shura served him first and
then herself. She produced a bottle of wine and when he shook his head
put it away, unopened, and substituted citronate.

*"I fancy they've stopped for lunch," said Mr. Behrens. "We'll have time to
work out an accurate fix on them now."*
"We might have time for lunch ourselves," said Mr. Calder, sourly.

All that afternoon they drove on, east and south. Sometimes they
talked. Nichol knew very well that if he asked her questions about herself
they would be politely blocked, and she seemed as disinterested in him
as an air hostess in a passenger.

There were maps in the glove compartment, but she seemed to know
the route and never asked for directions. He tried to estimate where they
would be likely to spend the night. If they kept up their present speed
and general direction they would be somewhere south of Dijon. He had
talked about camping. He knew that France was well ahead of other
countries in this respect and had numerous camps, some of them run by
national motoring and cycling organizations, others by the local syndicat
d'initiative.

They were well organized places with numbered tent sites, running
water on tap and good sanitary arrangements. During the summer months
a camp superintendent would live permanently on the site, in his own
caravan.

They had crossed the Saône a few kilometers south of Beaune and were now running up the heavily wooded valley of one of its tributaries. Nichol, who was driving, glimpsed the giant pylons of the recently completed Saône-et-Loire hydro-electric project, striding up the hillside on the right of the road. It was half-past seven. There was perhaps an hour of daylight left.

"Not far now," said Shura. "The camp lies up this side road. It is a beautiful site."

"You have been there before."

"Once or twice. We turn left here. The road leads only to the camp site. We shall see it in a moment."

The road climbed gently round the contours of the hill. They swung round the final bend, under a wooden arch which said CAMP DE LOUVATANGE, and came to rest in the graveled space which formed the car park.

Despite the earliness of the season, three or four caravans were parked round the opening, and the flysheets of more than one tent could be seen among the trees beyond.

The door of the nearest caravan opened, and a man came out. He had a gingery mustache, thin gingery hair and a face the color of smoked salmon. He said, in very bad French, "Welcome to the camp. My name's Horton. Major Horton. I'm in charge here. If there's anything I can do for you, you must let me know."

His bulbous eyes frankly appraised the girl's face and figure, and he said with increased warmth, "Anything at all. As soon as you've settled down, come and have a drink and a chat in my caravan, and I'll put you wise to the camp routine."

Ex-public school, ex-Army, thought Nichol. Ex-Kenya, pro-segregation and anti- any sort of hard work as long as someone would pay him gin money.

"It would give us great pleasure to do that," he said in formal French.

"Hullo," said the major. "Here comes another of 'em. Wonder who *he* is? Wasn't told about this one. Unusual rush of business for the time of year."

"These damned power lines are playing Old Harry with my set," said Mr. Calder. "Over."

"Not much better here," said Mr. Behrens. "I think he's crossed the river. We shall have to keep pretty close behind him if we don't want to lose him."

"Why not let him settle down for the night? Then we can fix him accurately."

"Suppose he doesn't stop?"

"Drive all night, you mean?"

"Why not? There must be at least two of them."

"If they drive all night," said Mr. Calder, "we shall have to do the same. I'll take the Besançon road, you cross the river lower down and keep on his tail. I'll be able to give you some sort of cross-bearing when I get to the top."

Mr. Behrens said nothing. He was beginning to feel the strain. He could, if necessary, go on all night. But what he wanted at that moment, more than anything else in the world, was a hot bath and a good dinner.

He swung the car round the bend, saw too late the notice ahead of him, braked and came to a halt in a graveled forecourt.

Three people were walking toward him. One was a girl, the second a man in a bush jacket, with a reddish mustache. The third was David Nichol . . . .

He had time to drop the earphones onto the floor and slide the seat cushion back over the set before the man caught up with him. He glanced at Mr. Behrens' GB plate.

"My name's Horton," he said. "Major Horton. You wouldn't be a Modern Romany, I suppose?"

"That's right," said Mr. Behrens.

Nichol and the girl were moving off toward their own car.

"Your organizing secretary was here last week. He told me I should be seeing some of you chaps soon. I must say, I take my hat off to you. Straight out from your desks and offices. You won't have had much experience of this sort of thing, I take it?"

Nichol and the girl had got into the car, and were bumping off up one of the paths into the wood.

"I'm an accountant," said Mr. Behrens boldly. "I spend my life among balance sheets, and profit and loss accounts. It was only last week that I decided I *must* revert to a simpler method of existence. I haven't got much kit with me. A ground sheet, a couple of blankets."

"You're a real Romany," said the major admiringly. "I can see that. Prepared to rough it." Mr. Behrens shuddered. "I'm and old campaigner myself. I can probably give you a few tips. Let's find a nice sheltered place for you."

The major pointed at the taillight of the green Citröen.

"Better give them a bit of elbow room," he said with a chuckle. "They look to me like a honeymoon couple. Don't want to intrude on their privacy, eh?"

"Certainly not," agreed Mr. Behrens.

"Now you'll find quite a snug little berth here, under the roots of this tree. Spread the ground sheet over you, and peg it down each side. What about grub?"

"I've got some cold food with me, and a flask of coffee. I wasn't thinking of doing any actual cooking. Not yet."

"We could have a twig fire going in no time," said the major. "And I've got a few old safari pots and pans I could lend you."

"Thank you, no," said Mr. Behrens. "I've had a long and tiring day. I'll just rig up my—er—bivvy." The bitter thought was of Mr. Calder, at that very moment drawing up before some snug hostelry. "I'll be quite happy with a packet of sandwiches and a hot drink."

"The great thing," said the major, "when you're sleeping on mother earth is to dig a hole for your hip."

A hundred yards away, Shura had finished erecting the safari-model combined dwelling and sleeping tent and had plugged in the electric light from a spare battery in the car. It looked, Nichol thought, extremely inviting, a tiny refuge of light and shelter in a darkening world.

"Can I help?" he asked.

"It is really easier for me to do it. I know where everything is. Perhaps you cold unroll the beds, while I set the table."

There were, Nichol saw, two sleeping bags, each with an inflatable mattress and pillow.

"All you have to do," said the girl, "is to blow them up. You will have to find what degree of inflation suits you best. I like mine quite soft. Just enough to keep my body off the ground. Will you have an apértif before we eat?"

"Thank you," said Nichol. "I think I should enjoy that."

"Tournedos Rossini will do very nicely," said Mr. Calder. "Followed, I think, by a Sorbet, and a bottle of Clos des Lambrays, 1955."
Outside, it had started to rain.

David Nichol heard the rain pattering on the flysheet of the tent, and turned over in his sleeping bag. He was tired, but sleep seemed far away. There was something wrong with his mattress. He had inflated it too hard, and was rolling and bouncing like a small boat on a choppy sea. Also he was too hot.

He threw back the down-lined coverlet, and lay for a moment with his arms outside. A warm hand came out from the sleeping bag beside him. It touched his hand, then moved down to the mattress. There was a hiss of escaping air. Nichol felt himself sinking.

"Better?" asked Shura.

"Much better," he said.

Mr. Behrens was first up. He shaved under a cold tap, repacked his belongings, and ten minutes later was freewheeling out of the car park and down the hill. He felt it wiser not to disturb Major Horton. If there was indeed a fee to pay for one of the most excruciating nights he had ever spent, it could be collected, in due course, from the Modern Romanies.

In fact, he had not been unobserved. A pair of cold and protuberant eyes under projecting ginger eyebrows had watched his unobtrusive departure.

There was a telephone in Major Horton's caravan, connected to the exchange at Besançon. He asked for a number and when connected spoke rapidly. His French seemed to have improved.

Mr. Behrens stopped at the first café which he found open, and had breakfast and a more satisfactory wash and shave. He then drove his car into a side turning and switched on his set.

It was still only seven o'clock.

Mr. Calder answered at once.

"I hope you had a good night," said Mr. Behrens.

"Excellent," said Mr. Calder. "And you—?"

"Unspeakable."

"When you went off the air so suddenly, I assumed you'd run into our friend."

"You assumed correctly. My right hip is still paralyzed. I'll tell you all about it one day. I think he's off again."

It was a false alarm. it was after eight before the needle flickered, and started to creep across the dial.

"Due east," said Mr. Behrens.

"There are only two roads to Belfort," said Mr. Calder, who had been devoting his attention to the map. "The southern looks the natural one for them. I'll take it myself, and keep ahead. You can take the northern route through Vesoul. And keep out of trouble."

"I'll do my best," snapped Mr. Behrens. "Out."

It was at eleven o'clock, on the long climb up to Altkirch, that he ran into the road block. It was a single whitewashed pole on trestles across the road. In the split second when he spotted it as he came round the corner, he wondered if his car was heavy enough to crash it. The German frontier was about twenty miles ahead. He braked and came to a halt.

One of the policemen advanced toward the car. The other remained seated on his chair beside the road. They were oldish men, police reservists, Mr. Behrens thought. He was uncomfortably aware that he had had no time to cover up the apparatus on the seat beside him.

"What's all this about?" he said.

"Routine check," said the man. But he had seen the wireless set. His eyes jerked down to the number plate on the car, and Mr. Behrens saw him glance back at his companion, who got quickly off his chair.

Mr. Behrens opened the door of the car and slid out. They were on an upland plateau, with a long view of the road in both directions. There was no other car in sight.

On his left, twenty yards down the track, was a small hay barn. He could see the policemen's bicycles propped up against it.

"This apparatus—you have a license for it?"

Mr. Behrens sighed deeply.

"Of course," he said. He dipped his hand inside his coat and pulled out an automatic pistol. "If you do not do what I say, I shall be forced to shoot you both. I have already killed three men. I should not advise you to touch your own guns."

The two men backed away. there was no fight in them.

"Into that barn," he said.

The windows of the barn were mere slits, and the bar across the double doors looked stout. They would break out, but it would take them time.

He wheeled the two bicycles back to the road, and threw them down the ravine on the other side. Then he drove off.

Forty minutes later he was in Germany. There was no trouble at the frontier, where he joined a stream of cars passing the checkpost. His English passport and GB plate took him through without a hitch.

As soon as he had got clear of the traffic, he switched on his set again.

The earphones crackled angrily.

"Where the devil have you been?" said Mr. Calder.

"A bit of a holdup," said Mr. Behrens. "The police."

"You've been held up by the police?"

"On the contrary," said Mr. Behrens, pleased by his own wit.

"What are you talking about?"

"I'll tell you later. Where's our friend?"

"Ahead of us," said Mr. Calder. "East by northeast. I hope he stops for lunch soon."

The afternoon run was uneventful. Shura drove and Nichol kept his eyes on the map. They were turning slowly north, and he saw now that their long detour had been designed to avoid the barrier of Cologne, the

Ruhr and the Lower Rhine where the NATO and West German defenses were thickest.

By teatime they were running into the southern part of the Black Forest, a region of dumpy hills, thick woodland and occasional lakes. They passed through empty holiday resorts. By August they would be packed with stout fathers in Lederhosen, white-faced Haus-fraus, and a Pied Piper's horde of flaxen-haired children.

At six o'clock they stopped at one of those lakeside villages and found a cafe open. They were the only customers.

"Where do you plan to spend the night?" asked Nichol.

"It is a Gast-haus in the forest, near Adelsheim. We shall have no company. It is not yet open for the season."

Now that they had left France behind, she seemed more relaxed, a little more sure of herself, a little readier to talk.

"You know the proprietor then? He allows you to stay there out of season?"

"Certainly. His name is Bauer. He was a member of Goëring's personal bodyguard. The Reichsmarschall was an interesting man. Did you know that he was fond of birds?"

"Yes," said Nichol, cautiously. "So I had heard."

"Each of his country retreats was named after a different bird."

"A romantic idea."

"He was hightly romantic," agreed Shura. "This one was the retreat of the nightingale. Die Nachtigall."

It took them two hours, by tortuous roads which zigzagged up hills, twisted into hidden valleys, crossed streams brown with the local iron-ore and climbed again through pine forest cut into geometrical patterns. It was too dark to read the map and some of the roads they used would not, he felt certain, have been marked on any map at all. The last fifteen minutes were spent bumping along a sandy track.

"It is a private road," said Shura.

"It feels like one," agreed Nichol.

The Gast-haus der Nachtigall was a three-story, shingle-roofed building, with a deep balcony along the second-floor frontage, and a wide door leading under the balcony into an interior courtyard. There were no lights in the windows, but Shura drove confidently into the courtyard and sounded her horn.

A door serving the kitchen quarters opened and a man came out.

"Good evening, Herr Bauer," said Shura, in German.

"Good evening, Fraulein. You have made good time."

Horn-rimmed glasses set on a long, thin nose. The hair gray, running back from the brown, seamed expanse of the forehead. The mouth prim.

He said, "My boy will take your things up to your room. A fire has been lit in the Gast-zimmer. Come."

He led the way into the front room. It was paneled in pitch pine, and from the walls the creatures of the Schwartzwald looked down at them: squirrels, badgers, roebuck, blue hare, and ruffed capercaillie.

Herr Bauer had brought them, unasked, a tall bottle of white wine and a squat bottle of brandy. He filled two large glasses with wine and two small ones with brandy.

"After a journey," he said, "it is kinder to the stomach to take a small amount of fortified spirits before you drink a natural wine."

Nichol swallowed the brandy. It was aromatic. The glass of wine followed it more slowly. Herr Bauer refilled the wine glasses, said, "Dinner in half an hour," and withdrew.

Nichol said, "He doesn't look much like an S.S. man, does he?"

Shura said shortly, "I imagine that even in S.S. units there must have been administrative people—clerks, and quartermasters." She seemed to be regretting her earlier confidence.

Nichol nodded. The warmth from the tiled stove was welcome. Being locked away alone with Shura in this house in the middle of a forest gave him a delusive feeling of security. Tomorrow there would be trouble. Tonight was tonight.

"The luggage will be in our room by now," she said. "I will go and change. Give me a quarter of an hour."

Nichol sipped the second glass of wine. Somewhere at the back of his consciousness a very faint alarm had sounded. He took a moment to track it down. Two days before, when they had first met, the girl had shown no embarrassment when he had stripped to the skin in front of her. Why should she mind taking off all *her* clothes in front of him. And above all, why had she said something so entirely out of character, so miss-ish, as "I'll go and change. Give me a quarter of an hour." It made no sense.

Nichol put down his wine glass, got up and went across to the door. The place was quiet as a tomb.

He went out. There was a staircase ahead of him, leading to a landing running the length of the buildings. He guessed that the main bedrooms would face south.

There was a light under the door of one of them, and after a moment's hesitation he turned the handle and went in.

It was their room. Shura's suitcase was on one side of the double bed, open, and her windcheater, sweater and trousers were lying beside it. Evidently she had changed, but she had done so very quickly.

There was a newish suitcase on the other side of the bed. Nichol opened it and found shirts and underclothes, a pair of flannel trousers, a dark blue pullover and a jacket, all new and neatly packed. He took off his shirt and tie, ran some hot water into the basin and started to clean himself up.

Herr Bauer said, "A car has just come into the southwest driveway. It has pulled off the road."

He and Shura were in a basement room. They were watching a map of the estate on the wall, covered by glass. In the bottom left-hand corner two pinpoints of light glared red. "It could be a casual trespasser, a pair of lovers in a car. But if you are being followed—"

"I think we are being followed," said Shura. "There was a man in a dark blue Saab who came into camp after us last night. He left before we got up, and I have not seen him at all today."

. . ."Martin is patroling now. If there is a dark blue Saab, we should take no risks. The driver will have to be attended to."

As he spoke, the lights on the panel flicked and changed pattern.

"Possibly I was wrong," said Herr Bauer. "The car is going. Nevertheless, I think we will take all precautions tonight. If there should be trouble—I hope your passenger is a sound sleeper?"

"I will make certain," said Shura seriously, "that he sleeps very well indeed."

It was, in fact, Mr. Behrens who had driven his car into the edge of the Nachtigall domain. He had backed out again in answer to a call on the wireless from Mr. Calder, who had come to a halt half a mile farther down the road. It was the first time they had set eyes on each other since leaving England.

Mr. Behrens pulled up, walked across and climbed into the back of Mr. Calder's car. In the darkness beside him something stirred.

He put out his hand and a cold nose was pushed into it.

"I didn't know you were bringing Rasselas with you," he said.

"He refused to be left behind." When Mr. Calder spoke, the great dog turned his head, and his amber eyes reflected the light from the dashboard.

"How are you going to get him back again?"

"We'll think about that when the time comes," said Mr. Calder. "I want to hear about your adventures last night. Tell me more about that chap at the camp."

"He called himself Major Horton. Leathery skin, baldish, with a halo of reddish hair, thick gingery eyebrows, poached egg eyes."

"Sounds an unpleasant character. Do you think he rumbled you?"

"I wondered" said Mr. Behrens. "He did seem to accept me rather easily. If I really had been a Modern Romany, or whatever it was he called me, presumably I'd have had some sort of card or papers. And if he did suspect me, that would account for the trouble I had near Altkirch." He told Mr. Calder about it.

Mr. Calder said, "We shall have to sort that out with the Department when we get back. The important point at the moment is, *were you followed?*"

"I'm quite certain I wasn't."

"Did it occur to you that they might have put a midget transmitter in your car, during the night?"

"Certainly it occurred to me," said Mr. Behrens coldly. "I spent half an hour after breakfast turning my car out. Nothing had been tampered with."

"In that case," said Mr. Calder, "I wonder why we have already aroused such interest."

"Interest?"

"Before you arrived, a man walked up to the edge of the trees over there and kept me under observation for several minutes. He has gone now."

"You saw him?"

"No. But Rasselas told me about him. Never mind. The first thing is to find somewhere to eat. I passed a nice little place in the outskirts of Ringheim."

They were finishing dinner when Mr. Calder suddenly said, "Got it?"

"Got what?"

"Nachtigall—the nightingale. It was one of Goëring's hideouts. He had five or six of them, all in remote areas, all top secret. When life at the center got too much for him he used to lie up in one of them. He called them his 'nests.' They were all named after birds, you see. The lark's nest, the heron's nest, the nightingale's nest."

"I wonder if he had one called the cuckoo's nest."

"I remember being shown round one of them by an American Intelligence officer in 1945. It had a very elaborate approach warning system, operated by crossing beams of infrared light. And one or two rather nasty booby traps for the benefit of unwanted visitors."

"A highly suitable staging point for our friends."

"Just what I thought," said Mr. Calder. "A bit later on I'll go and take a look at it. You'd better stop here and catch up on the sleep you didn't have last night."

"Are you sure you'll be all right by yourself?"

"I shan't be by myself," said Mr. Calder.

A tail thumped against the floorboards.

It was past midnight when Mr. Calder switched off the engine of his car, let it coast quietly down the last hundred yards of road and came to a halt under a clump of trees. It was a clear night, with a full moon marbling the sky. He had been driving without lights.

Now he climbed out of the car and stood for a moment. Rasselas sat beside him, head cocked, the tip of his right ear an inch from Mr. Calder's left shoulder. His nose gave a thrust, as if to say, "Go on—what are we waiting for?" Mr. Calder crossed the road and climbed through the boundary wire.

It was tidy woodland with most of the undergrowth cleared, and man and dog advanced steadily on a long slant toward the house.

They were halfway across one of the open glades when Rasselas stopped. He had heard something, away to the right. There was a thick patch of bushes on the far side of the glade, with a slight depression in the middle, which made an admirable hiding place.

From watching Rasselas, Mr. Calder could chart, with great exactness, the progress of his enemies. He saw the ears prick, the amber eyes swivel slowly as they followed something invisible to him. The the lip lifted in a silent snarl as two men stepped out into the glade.

They were dressed in foresters' uniform with leather leggings, and both carried, slung across their backs, short, double-barreled rifles. Mr. Calder recognized them as the weapons issued during the war to guards in charge of working parties. They threw a spread of heavy buckshot, and were weapons for stopping and crippling, rather than for killing. One of the men carried a stick, which seemed to have some sort of spike on the end of it. The other had a heavy leather whip.

Mr. Calder slid his right hand gently inside his coat, until his fingers rested on the warm butt of his automatic.

The men walked slowly across the glade, heads turning to right and left, passed within six paces of where Mr. Calder was lying, seemed to hesitate for an instant and then were gone.

It was fully ten minutes before Rasselas stirred. Then he edged his way, silently, out of the thicket. Mr. Calder followed even more slowly. He was a professional himself and he recognized professional opposition when he saw it.

He moved slowly forward, Rasselas drifting beside him like a gray shadow. Now there was only a single line of trees between him and the house, since he was approaching it from the southwest corner and had a clear view of the long southern frontage. He noticed that a light still showed in one of the bedroom windows.

The space between the treeline and the house was dotted with bushes and shrubs, and Mr. Calder reckoned that if he went on his stomach, commando-fashion, it would be an easy matter to keep out of sight until he reached the house. If he could find a window open, he had a mind to explore further. As he started to move forward, Rasselas gave out a very soft, rumbling growl. Mr. Calder paused. When nothing happened, he moved again. Rasselas caught his ankle in his teeth.

At that moment the ground under Mr. Calder's hands gave way. At one moment he had his palms on solid earth. The next, his fingers were slithering over the lip of a cavity which had opened in front of him. If he had been moving forward, nothing could have stopped him falling into it.

It was a deep trench, with sheer walls cut into the chalk soil. It had been masked by a thin net of Hessian, on which sand and leaves had been sprinkled.

Mr. Calder extracted the pencil torch from his pocket, and directed its pinhead of light downward. Set into balks of timber at the bottom of the trench was a treble row of steel spikes, needle-thin, needle-sharp and fully twelve inches long.

He thought about an intruder, animal or human, falling on to them. The weight of his fall would drive the spikes through an arm or a leg.

He drew back slowly from the lip of the trench. It extended, so far as he could see, right along the front edge of the tree belt. As he was looking, the single light in the Gast-haus went out.

"There might have been some way round," he said to Mr. Behrens next morning. "But quite frankly, I didn't try. I could *feel* those spikes, all the way home."

"They were expecting you?"

"I think they must have been," said Mr. Calder. "It would take some time to uncover that trench. They daren't leave it open. I could feel a sort of ledge cut inside the lip, so I imagine it's boarded over by day and covered with loose sand. It's the sort of job that'd take a couple of hours to do properly. And whatever the size of the staff, I don't see that they could afford to keep two men patroling all night, and every night."

Mr. Behrens considered the matter.

"The girl might have been suspicious," he said, "when I practically bumped into her at the camp site. But surely—after a full day's drive—with no glimpse of a pursuer—"

"What about the trouble you had near Altkirch? It must have been a pretty definite tip-off to get the French police moving so quickly."

"I had the impression it was my car they were looking for," agreed Mr. Behrens. "The first thing the man spotted was the wireless. But it was only when he saw the number plate that he started to get excited. But if they were tipped off, who do you suggest did it? That man at the camp? Or the girl?"

"Or Nichol," said Mr. Calder.

Mr. Behrens did not sound surprised or horrified at the suggestion. He said, "It's a possibility that has to be borne in mind, of course. I hope it's not true. It suggests one precaution to me, however. The only car they know about is mine. The sensible thing now will be for me to keep close behind him. You keep right out on the wing."

Mr. Calder thought about this for a bit, and then grunted. "Yes," he said. "That seems right."

It was half past six that morning when Shura slipped quietly out of bed. She put a raincoat over her pajamas, and tiptoed from the room.

Herr Bauer was in the control room talking to two men. He looked up as she came in. He said, "We had a visitor last night."

"What have you done with him?"

"We have done nothing with him. He came, looked at us and went away." Herr Bauer glanced sourly at the two men, who shuffled and look at their feet.

"There are traces, too, of a car having driven in. It might all be nothing. It might be something."

Shura said, "If the car was a dark blue Saab, then we have been followed across Europe. And I have not the least idea how."

Herr Bauer said, "There are not more than four ways out of the Odenwald. I can have them watched. When you stop for your midday meal, telephone back to me here. I shall be able to tell you then . . . ."

Nichol woke up at eight o'clock. He stretched out an arm, found the bed empty and sat up.

Shura was outside, on the balcony.

"I overslept," he said. "Are we late?"

"No hurry this morning. We need not start before eleven. Breakfast is being brought up to us here."

They took the morning's run at a much slower pace. Nichol had the impression that the clock had become more important than the map. They skirted Wurzburg and Bamberg to the south and stopped for their lunch in a tiny village called Plankenfels, ten miles short of Bayreuth.

Shura slipped away while the food was being cooked. When she came back Nichol thought he detected a change in her manner. It was very slight, and if he had not got to know her so well in the three days he had been with her, he might not have noticed it. Something seemed to have put her on her mettle.

During the afternoon Shura did the driving, while Nichol kept his eye on the map. They avoided Bayreuth, making a detour to the south, and climbed into the Fichtelgebirge. Gradually the country became more desolate, the farms fewer, the houses farther apart. Ahead of them, on the map, right across their track and slowly drawing nearer, sprawled the irregular green line which marked the farthest advance of the Russian Army in 1945 and now formed the boundary between the eastern and western worlds.

At this particular point the line joined the national boundary of Czechoslovakia, and ran almost due west, forming a right angle with it. It was into the neck of this sack that they were driving. They had been avoiding main roads for some time and Nichol was hard put to it to map their twisting progress, but in the fading light he glimpsed a board with the name QUELLENREUTH, and knew they were not more than ten kilometers from the frontier.

In the next village they turned left. A moment later, right again. They were now heading straight up into the angle itself, an area where his map was blank. He soon saw the reason. It was thick woodland. As they dived in among the trees, they switched on their headlights.

They were running north, and climbing. After about three miles, Shura seemed to hesitate for the first time. She slowed to a crawl, her eyes on the roadside. She saw what she was looking for, swung the wheel and put the car down a sandy track.

The track seemed to go on interminably, diving into the very heart of the forest, a tunnel of darkness among the trees. Then they were in a clearing. Nichol caught a glimpse of a log hut as Shura swung the car round, brought it to a halt and switched off all the lights.

Nichol stirred, but the girl put a hand on his arm. They sat in the darkness and waited. Then the car door was opened from outside, and a man gestured them out. They stumbled across the clearing to the hut; the door was opened and they went into darkness.

A torch came on. By its reflected light Nichol saw the face of its holder. He had never met him, but he recognized him at once from many photographs carefully studied. Colonel Tyschenko had been military attaché in Ottawa and Washington and in neither case had his hosts been under any illusions as to his real interests.

"I am sorry," he said speaking Russian, "to receive you in this melo-dramatic way. But we are waiting for the man who has been following you."

"The man in the Saab?" said the girl.

"Yes. He should be here any moment now. We will keep silent, if you please."

It seemed to Nichol like an hour, but was in fact only twelve minutes by the illuminated hand on his watch before there were footsteps outside. The door opened, and three men came in. As soon as the door was shut, Colonel Tyschenko snapped on the light, and the six occupants of the hut blinked at each other.

Two of the newcomers were Russian Security men, soldiers in plain clothes. They both carried machine pistols. The third was Mr. Behrens, his hands in his pockets, and a look of distaste on his leathery face.

"He parked his car a quarter of a mile down the track," said one of the men, "and was walking toward the hut when we stopped him. He had a gun. We have taken it."

Colonel Tyschenko had been staring in some surprise at the scholarly figure in the raincoat. Then his face broke into a smile. "Why," he said, "it is Mr. Behrens. This *is* an unexpected pleasure. Where is your friend—the fat little man—Calder?"

"He'll be here in a moment," said Mr. Behrens. "And he's got six men with him."

The colonel chuckled. "No doubt," he said. "No doubt. The six invis-ible men. It would be a good title for a film. I should be interested to know how you followed our car."

"It's Nichol's suit," said Mr. Behrens. "It has been impregnated with a particularly potent smell. When in doubt as to which way he had gone, I had only to get out of the car and sniff."

"Remarkable," said the colonel. "Particularly since he will have changed his clothes at least three times since leaving London."

"We found a wireless set in the car," said one of the men.

"I see," said the colonel. "That opens up an interesting field of specu-lation." He turned to Nichol. "*What* are you carrying that you had on you, *when you left London?*"

Nichol said slowly, "Fountain pen, silver pencil, notecase, wristwatch, and signet ring."

He hoped that the cigarette lighter, which he dropped as they got out of the car, had fallen into an inconspicuous place.

"The details are not important," said the colonel. "We shall be able to work them all out when we get you and Mr. Behrens, and the contents of his car, safely into our own territory."

He turned to the security men and said, "One stays here. One to go and check the arrangements for the crossing. We are using the normal route. Hurry."

The man nearest the door turned and went out.

Shura spoke for the first time, "I hope, Colonel, that you do not blame me for this. I should, perhaps, have thought that some electrical device might be used."

There was a pleading note in her voice that Nichol had never heard before; he had not imagined that such a girl could ever be humble.

The colonel said, "No, Shura. I don't think anyone could blame you too much. Indeed, you did well to take notice of the Saab and call Herr Bauer's attention to it.'

The girl actually blushed.

"Thank you," she said . . . .

Mr. Behrens, standing against the far wall of the hut where the guard had left him, considered the position. Even now that one of the guards had departed it was almost entirely unsatisfactory. Colonel Tyschenko was carrying a Vostok MU-2 pistol in a shoulder holster. He could see the light wooden butt as the colonel leaned forward to speak to Shura. The guard had a German-type Schmeisser machine pistol across his shoulders, carried in such a way that he could swing it round to the front and fire without unslinging it. The girl had a gun, but it was probably in her shoulder satchel on the table. He and Nichol were unarmed.

The door handle turned very gently, round, and back again.

Mr. Behrens took a deep breath, and let it out slowly. He was not fond of violence.

He said, "If you don't mind, I have to go outside for a moment."

Colonel Tyschenko looked at him, then said, "Of course. But I should warn you that this man can put a burst of six shots into a moving target at fifty yards."

"I wasn't thinking of making a dash for it," said Mr. Behrens, sourly. He started toward the door. The colonel signaled to the guard, who slipped back the bolt of the door and swung his gun round to the ready.

Mr. Behrens did not hurry. He wanted to be in one particular spot, next to the girl. The guard put a hand on the handle of the door and turned it. The door came open fast, as if kicked, and Rasselas came through in a smooth golden curve, his teeth bared, making straight for Colonel Tyschenko's throat.

Behind the dog waddled the squat figure of Mr. Calder. He shot the guard twice, at close quarters, through the chest, before he could get his hand to the trigger of his machine pistol.

The colonel twisted as Rasselas struck him, and the dog catapulted over his shoulder, onto the floor. In the same moment, the colonel pulled out his Vostok and shot Nichol, who was jumping at him, through the right side of the body.

Rasselas buried his teeth in the colonel's leg.

Mr. Behrens had wrapped his arms round Shura from behind. It was a temporary advantage only. She was twice as strong as he, and better trained. She pried apart his fingers, grabbed his forearm and threw him across her outstretched leg. Then she stooped to grab her satchel, which Mr. Behrens had managed to knock onto the floor.

Mr. Calder crouched, steadied himself and shot Colonel Tyschenko. The bullet went through the colonel's mouth and out at the back of his head. As he fell, his Vostok dropped within a few inches of Nichol's hand. He rolled over and picked it up.

Shura's hand was already inside her satchel when Nichol shot her. He was lying on the ground, and the bullet went upward, through her chest and into the top of her spine. The impact lifted her onto her toes. For a moment she looked as though she were poised for a dive. Then her knees buckled. As she fell, she struck the edge of the table, and slid off it. She was dead before she hit the floor beside Nichol.

After the last shot, there was a moment of complete silence.

Rasselas crouched over the colonel's body, motionless except for the angry twitching of his tail. The smell of the blood had excited him. His ancestors had hunted wolves and had fed on their entrails.

Mr. Behrens was the first to move. He groped for his glasses, put them on and climbed to his feet. He said, "We've got precious little time. That other guard will be here any moment."

"He won't be coming back," said Mr. Calder. He was breathing heavily, as though the death he had dealt out had been a physical exertion. "I can promise you that."

"In that case—" said Mr. Behrens.

"In that case," said Mr. Calder, "we've still got a hell of a lot to do. And the fact that we've now got all night to do it in doesn't make it any easier. I think the bodies will have to be buried."

"Yes," said Mr. Behrens.

"It's sandy soil, and we've got spades in the car. We shall have to put them four feet down."

"Yes," said Mr. Behrens again. It would mean hours of digging. But he could see the sense in it. It was the rule. If you made a mess, you cleared it up. But there was more to it than that. If Colonel Tyschenko, his courier and his two personal bodyguards disappeared, the first idea would be that they had defected. And the mere suspicion of this would cause their opponents the maximum of trouble and uncertainty.

"Any blood there is, is on the matting. We'll bury that with them. We can use the girl's car for transport. After that I'll drive it off and leave it in the thickest part of the forest. This isn't a part of the world where intruders are encouraged. It could stand there until it falls to pieces."

"There's one other thing," said Mr. Behrens. "We ought to get Nichol to a doctor before morning. The nearest one I know of, who won't ask a lot of questions, is a hundred miles away."

Mr. Calder considered the problem.

He said, "Give me a hand with the first part, getting the bodies moved. Then leave me to do the rest."

"Will you be able to finish before the morning?"

"Almost certainly not. But I can lie up by day, and finish the job tomorrow night. I'll see you in Cologne, at our usual place, the day after tomorrow."

And so at four o'clock that morning Mr. Behrens was driving his car once more. His head was singing with the Benzedrine he had inhaled to keep himself awake. Beside him, Nichol was propped in the passenger seat. He had been delirious for some time and was now dozing. Mr. Behrens could only pray that they were not stopped. They would neither of them stand up to much inspection. And unless he could get Nichol into a doctor's hands in time to save his life, they were going to lose half the results of their efforts.

The continental side of Route M they now knew about and could deal with. But the English side—how it worked, who operated it—that was all locked away inside the white face and under the tangled head of black hair that lolled on the seat beside him.

A red light sprang out of the night. Mr. Behrens cursed, and slowed. But it was only the warning light for a level-crossing gate on the main line from Cologne to Basel.

Mr. Behrens coasted up to the barrier and switched off the engine. Nichol turned his head, and looked at him. The sudden silence and cessation of movement had wakened him.

"Where are we?" he said.

"Nearly there," said Mr. Behrens.

"There's something," said Nichol, "that I ought to tell you."

"Don't talk more than you must," said Mr. Behrens.

Nichol hardly seemed to hear him. His body was in the present, but his mind was in the past. He went on in a conversational voice.

"Last night, at that hotel, I made love to Shura. She seemed to want it. It was the most wonderful thing I have ever done. It was the first time in my life. I've been rather strictly brought up. You appreciate that. I'd never imagined it could be such a perfect thing. And then I shot her. I had to shoot her." He sounded serious, and puzzled. "That can't be right, you know."

"In this job," said Mr. Behrens, "there is neither right nor wrong. Only expediency."

The night express thundered past, and the gates rose and Mr. Behrens engaged gear and drove on.

TO SLAY AN EAGLE

Stephen Dentinger

AUGSHEIM IN THE AUTUMN was still a place only beginning to recover from the destructions of war. Coming in low on the airport approach, Emerson gazed out over the ruins and remembered how it had been. He remembered his first sight of the city, flare-lit at midnight as he streaked in over it in the lead bomber. He remembered especially the blaze from the fire bombs, destroying everything in its path. Circling that night and heading back for home, over the burning city, he never imagined he'd see it again, never imagined he'd want to return there to the wounded land whose scars he'd caused.

He didn't want to return now, but he had a job to do. A dirty job.

"November is a bad month anywhere," the girl said.

"Especially in Germany. Drizzle and fog and mist." Emerson lit an American cigarette and settled back in his chair.

"You've been here before?"

"To Augsheim? Only once, from the air. But I've seen Berlin and Munich. And Bonn, of course."

She was young and almost beautiful and her name was Mona Kirst. They'd met by careful prearrangement in a back street bar that catered to prostitutes.

"Augsheim used to be beautiful," she said, "before the war. I remember when I was only a child how I used to play in the park. Now it's only a mud hole, without flowers or even grass."

"It'll come back," he assured her. Then, glancing at his watch, he said, "Hadn't we better . . . ?"

"Yes." She finished her drink and rose to leave. Emerson followed. It was the most natural thing in the world in that place, at that time. Nobody even looked up.

Mona Kirst lived on the third floor of a sagging apartment house overlooking the mud hole she'd mentioned. Further down the block the steel skeleton of a new building was rising—the first visible sign of the phoenix which would come from this fire. "You were lucky," he remarked, following her up the stairs. "Not many buildings survived."

"Were any of us lucky? Really?"

They passed an old woman on the stairs, and a British soldier who seemed embarrassed. Both of them looked away as they passed. Then Mona unlocked the door at the top of the landing and they entered a dingy, dank room with a double bed and a battered kitchen set as its only furniture.

There was a man stretched out on the bed, fully clothed. His name was Visor, and Emerson had journeyed four thousand miles to meet him.

"Ah! You must be Emerson!" He rose to shake hands. "Do you have a word from Washington?"

Emerson had always thought passwords were foolish, but he said it anyway. *"The Sphinx is drowsy, her wings are furled."*

Visor nodded. *"Her ear is heavy, she broods on the world."* He motioned Emerson to sit on the bed. "A fitting quotation for someone with your name. How much did they tell you of the mission?"

Emerson looked at the girl. "What about her?"

Visor shrugged. He was a big man, and he did it well. "She was necessary for the meeting. In this neighborhood, no one pays any attention to a prostitute's customers. Not even if there are two at a time."

"I mean, can she be trusted?"

"She is my sister," Visor replied.

Emerson stared at the two of them, not knowing whether to believe it. Finally Visor motioned her into the bathroom. Emerson nodded to show his approval and started talking. "I was sent because of Eagle. That's all I know."

The big man nodded. He was close to fifty, more likely the girl's father than her brother. But it was obvious he'd been in the business a long time, and when he spoke he chose his words carefully. "As you may know, Eagle is the code name for an American army colonel. His name is Roger China, and he must be dead within forty-eight hours."

"Alright."

"Washington tells me you're a good man, a killer. Have you ever worked in this area before?"

Emerson gazed out the window at the mud hole. "Yes. Once."

"Have you ever killed a fellow countryman before?"

"No."

"Then perhaps I should tell you something about Colonel China. Since the beginning of the occupation, he has looted German art treasures valued at something like two million dollars. The proceeds from this looting have gone to set up a neo-Nazi movement of highly dangerous potential. Unfortunately, and ironically, his fame as a war hero and his influence in Congress make his removal and court-martial extremely difficult. For urgent reasons of national security which even I do not fully understand, the verdict of Washington is that Colonel China must be removed."

Emerson nodded. "You don't need to tell me any more."

They shook hands. Then Visor added, "There's one other thing."

"Yes?"

"It must look like an accident."

Emerson was staying at a small hotel a mile across town from Mona Kirst's room. When he returned there, the sky to the west had taken on a sort of glow, diffusing the pale light of the full moon through a layer of mist. He'd flown many missions under a moon like that, skimming over the ice-blue clouds with a sense of power he couldn't put into words. All was silent in his world above the clouds, with even the bomber's roar muffled by the sands of night. It was a world he hoped to recapture someday, somewhere.

"This is a man to see you," the balding little desk clerk told him. "Over there."

Emerson turned to see a stocky, middle-aged German standing by the side of the desk. He had a folded newspaper stuffed into one pocket of his topcoat. "Mister Emerson? I've been waiting for you." He spoke English well, but with a strong accent.

"Yes?" Emerson's muscles tensed. Had Colonel China somehow heard of his mission?

"My name is Burkherdt, and I'm with the *Augsheim Zeitung*. I would like an interview."

Emerson raised an eyebrow. "Do all American businessmen rate newspaper interviews?"

The stocky man squinted and shook his head. He needed a shave. "All, no. But you are something special, are you not? You led the bombing raid in Augsheim in the final days of the war."

"Oh?"

"Now can we talk in private?"

Emerson glanced at the room clerk still hovering behind his desk and motioned toward a little bar off the lobby. "How about in there?"

The bartender frowned as they entered. "It's late," he said. "We close in ten minutes."

Emerson laid a bill on the bar. "That's all right. One drink and then leave us alone. We just want to talk."

The reporter slipped off his topcoat and tossed it over a chair. Underneath, his suit was rumpled and stained. He gave the appearance of a man without a woman's care, a man no longer interested in his appearance. "So you came back to see the city, Mr. Emerson."

"The reporters on the *Augsheim Zeitung* are very alert. How did you know about mè?" There was no sense denying it at this point, and the web of a plan was beginning to form in Emerson's mind. Perhaps he could use this reporter's story to reach Colonel China.

"I researched an article on the bombing raid last year. Your name appears in the Air Force's official history. I was checking airport arrivals this morning and I recognized your name on the passenger list. Simple, no?"

"I suppose so. What do you want, Burkherdt?"

"A story. What does any newspaperman ever want? Why did you come back—to see the place?"

"Perhaps you might say that, I suppose. I had an interest in it, and I heard they were rebuilding here."

"Rebuilding, yes. All Europe is rebuilding this November. Have you seen the ruins?"

"I've seen them."

"Like Rome, no? Or ancient Greece?"

"Not exactly."

"You are out of the Air Force now?"

Emerson nodded. "I've been out for almost two years."

The stocky man was making notes on the back of an old envelope. "I was in it, you know—in the bombing. My wife, too. She was horribly burned."

"I'm sorry."

"She was a Catholic. Religion never meant much to me, but that night she died. . . . She was begging me to kill her at the end, to put her out of her pain. I knew it was against her religion. I sat there for two hours holding her hand, just talking to her, making her want to live again. When finally she overcame the pain enough to say she still wanted to live, only then did I give her the release of death. The sin, if there was a sin, would be on my soul, not hers."

Emerson looked at his hands. "A lot of innocent people died in the war."

Burkherdt nodded sadly. "But you helped to end the war. They say Hitler himself flew over the city on the morning after the bombing, looking down at the fires that still were burning. Perhaps it was then that he knew it was hopeless."

"Look, what do you want of me?"

"Only your observations on the city, Mr. Emerson. What do you see of Augsheim now, three years after you destroyed it?"

"I see a city trying to rebuild itself, trying and seeming to succeed. I see a city far from dead. I see. . . hell, what do you want me to see? If I hadn't led that bombing raid, someone else would have!"

Burkherdt scratched his bristled face. "Of course, of course. Tell me, do you ever dream about them? About the people who burned to death in Augsheim?"

"No. I never dream."

"They say that killing people from ten thousand feet is different from killing them face-to-face. They say it's an impersonal thing, with no feeling afterward. Did you find it so?"

"There are feelings," Emerson said, aware that his palms were sweating. "There were for me, anyway."

"Feelings, but no dreams."

"I think you've got enough," Emerson said, getting to his feet. "They're closing now."

"You haven't finished your drink. Just one or two more questions, please. Are you married?"

"No."

"What is your job?"

"I'm a buyer for a chain of specialty shops. I'm looking for possible gift items to import."

"There is nothing for you in Augsheim."

Emerson got to his feet. "Nothing but memories. Thank you, Mr. Burkherdt, but I really must be going now. I've had a long day."

"Certainly." The German studied him through drooping eyes. "I appreciate the interview."

Emerson went upstairs to his room and undressed for bed. He fell asleep almost immediately. It was a trick he'd learned during the war.

Burkherdt's interview was not in the morning paper, and so he waited till afternoon. He found it on page one of the *Zeitung*, complete with a candid photograph of himself emerging from the hotel on the previous day. He wondered if Burkherdt had followed him on his journey to Mona's room, but then decided against it. The reporter surely would have mentioned something.

Toward evening he went again to the bar where he'd met Mona. This time they dispensed with the preliminaries and went at once to her room. Visor was not there.

"He didn't think it would be safe two nights in a row," she explained. "But here is the information you wanted. China's picture and a schedule of his usual movements."

Emerson studied the face in the photograph, an ordinary enough face, set between officer's cap and eagled shoulders.

"All right," he told her.

"Stay a bit," she cautioned, "in case someone is watching. My customers are always good for at least a half hour."

He sat down on the bed. "Why do you do this, anyway?" She smiled sadly, staring at the darkened square of window. "An odd question for you to ask. Why do you do it? Why do you kill?"

"You know about it?"

"Enough. He tells me. He trusts me. You should, too."

"Did you see the story about me in the *Zeitung?*"

"Yes."

"I destroyed your park, your building, your lives."

"Yes."

"And this was only one of the cities. There were many others. It's no different up there. It's exactly the same as killing a man with your bare hands—or at least it was for me. When the war ended, I had to go on. Now I work unofficially for a government agency that would throw me to the wolves in a minute. Why do I do it? Because if I didn't I think I'd go mad."

"Are you so sure of your sanity now?" she asked.

"Is anybody?"

She lit a cigarette, waving the wooden match afterwards to put it out. It might have been a signal to some watcher outside the window, but he knew it wasn't. He trusted her, just as Visor did. "Do you want to make love to me?" she asked casually.

His mouth seemed suddenly dry. "I'm sorry. I have to be going."

"It's the killing, isn't it? It's that instead of sex."

"I have a job to do."

"Get out of it," she said. "Get out of it before it destroys you."

He paused at the door. "I guess it destroyed me the first time I flew over a burning city."

Then, more serious than he'd seen her before, she came to him at the door. "Emerson," she whispered, "be careful. You came back too soon."

He left her in the doorway and hurried down to the street.

Emerson waited in the shadow of a ruined building until he saw Colonel Roger China enter the Allied Officers' Club on schedule. Then he walked several blocks until he found a telephone. It took them several minutes to page Colonel China and get him to the phone, but finally his voice came on the other end of the line.

"China here."

"Colonel, you don't know me, but as a fellow officer I thought I might appeal to you. My name is Emerson. You may have read about me in the newspaper."

"Emerson. Yes, you're the one who led the bombing raid."

"I must talk to somebody. Could I come to see you?"

"When?"

"Tonight. Now."

A snort from the other end. "I'm afraid that's impossible."

"Please, sir. It's an important matter."

There was a moment's hesitation, and then China said, "Very well. I can give you ten minutes. No more. Ask for me at the desk."

"Thank you, sir."

Emerson waited a half hour before putting in his appearance. He saw Colonel China at once, standing with a group of English and French officers near the entrance to the club dining room. Playing out the charade, he asked at the desk, and waited while the colonel was summoned.

"You're Emerson?"

"That's right, sir. Pleased to meet you." The harsh lights of the club anteroom played down on China's balding head, giving it momentarily the appearance of a grinning skull. His eyes were dark and deep-set, and the weathered skin of his slim face was stretched taut. He was an ugly man, but he had the bearing of a leader.

"We can talk in here," China said, leading him into a smoking room hung heavily with the male trappings of the military.

"You have a nice club here."

The colonel nodded. "It's a nice retreat from the rest of Augsheim. If I may say so, you did a thorough job with your bombs, Emerson."

"I'd like to forget about that, sir. It's one of the reasons I came to you."

"And why me?"

"You're the ranking officer in Augsheim. After that newspaper interview, I felt I had to talk to someone—a countryman."

"What's your trouble, man?"

"I . . . I feel I did the wrong thing. I feel that the whole war was wrong and I was wrong to kill all those people. I suppose that's really why I came back here. I need somebody like you to tell me, sir."

Colonel China regarded him with something like distaste. "War is never wrong to a soldier. If you think so, it's just as well you're out. I won't say I agree with every aspect of our goverment's policy, but I fought for it. Now, after the war, is the time to work for changes in that policy."

"I do want to change it, though!" Emerson insisted. "War is nothing but burning and looting and killing!"

China smiled slightly. "But you see, even to change it, to achieve an end to war, would necessitate more of the same. This old world will never be free of war until the Russians and the English—and, yes, the Americans too—are as defeated as Germany is today. Perhaps that will be the only true communism this planet will ever know—the communism of destruction and defeat."

"Who would rule a world like that?"

"The strong will survive. There are always rulers. Hitler was one, until he went mad." Then suddenly he got to his feet, ending the conversation. "I've given you more than ten minutes already. Come see me tomorrow at my office."

"Thank you, sir. You've helped me."

Colonel China paused. "I did it for a fellow officer. Have all the doubts you want, but remember one thing. Don't ever forget how to kill."

Emerson found a nearby bar from which he could observe the club parking lot. He kept his eye on the big black car in which China had arrived. The Allied Officers' Club had been carefully chosen as the one place where China would probably drive himself. An enlisted man who might be his regular driver would not be allowed inside, and colonels weren't usually important enough to keep drivers waiting outside a bar all night. No, China had arrived alone and would leave alone—unless he decided to drive another officer home. In that event, Emerson had two alternate plans.

It was two in the morning before China appeared, but he was alone. Though he'd obviously been drinking, he walked hurriedly to his car and got in. Emerson stepped out of his hiding place and ran across the street.

"Please, sir," he said, pulling open the door on the passenger side. "I've been drinking. Could you drop me at my hotel?"

Colonel China stared at him with surprised distaste. "What's the matter with you, Emerson? Get out of this car!"

Emerson gave a last glance to make sure the parking lot was empty.

Then he leaned over and delivered a short judo blow to the colonel's throat. The man coughed once and started to sag, and Emerson broke his neck with a second blow.

He slid over the body into the driver's seat and edged the car quickly out of the lot. The highway to Colonel China's rented house had been carefully covered, and Emerson knew exactly the right place for the accident. He aimed the car for the guard rail and jumped.

It started burning at the bottom of the gully, and he had to keep low to avoid being silhouetted by the flames.

Emerson had killed a great many men in the brief years since the war. It didn't bother him any more, if it ever had. He reported to a quiet man behind a desk in Washington and went where he was sent, to contact people like Visor and Mona in dingy back rooms. Sometimes he wondered how much official Washington ever knew of his activities, if they knew anything. Perhaps, in the bureaucratic confusion of the postwar world, he was a lost segment simply serving the whims of some minor department head. But the truth of Emerson was that he didn't really care.

He walked back into town, thinking abstractedly that he would like to see Mona again before he left Augsheim. The city was sleeping, and he strolled for a long while among the ruins, seeing them for the first time bathed in a silvery moonglow. The mists of the previous night had dissipated, and the air was clear with November coolness.

Piles of brick, blackened timbers. Still, after all this time. Perhaps some bodies, too, undiscovered yet in their unmarked tombs. The city would come back, but not the same. Not ever the same.

He paused on the street where Mona Kirst had her apartment, and pressed his face against the damp bark of a tree to stare up at the rectangle of curtained light that was her window. She would not be alone, not even at three in the morning. He wondered vaguely where Visor was that night, and turning to walk back to his hotel caught the distant shrill pitch of sirens heading out of town. Perhaps the burning car had only now been discovered, and Roger China had spent this hour alone in his death.

Ahead, finally, the hotel glowed like a beacon on the dim street. He hurried toward it, suddenly tired, not hearing the voices until they were almost upon him.

"Emerson!"

"That's him. Get him!" The words were German, but he understood. He turned to see a half dozen men emerging from the shadows. Some carried clubs, and at least one had a knife.

"We've been waiting for you, Emerson. This is for the city. For

Augsheim. And for our families."

He thought he saw the reporter, Burkherdt, watching from across the street. Then he closed his eyes against their hatred as the first blows fell. In that final moment he was once more skimming over the ice-blue clouds in the lead bomber, free and powerful as an eagle.

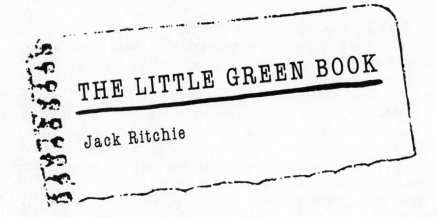

THE LITTLE GREEN BOOK

Jack Ritchie

THE OLD MAN sighed. "Amador is dead, too?"

"Yes," I said. "And yet he almost succeeded. He killed two of the General's guards before he was shot down."

The old man sat down on the bench beside the mountain hut. "Tell me how it went."

"I took the motor bus to the capitol and went to where Amador lives with his parents," I said.

"When I arrived we had several glasses of wine, for there was still an hour before the General's ceremony."

The old man frowned slightly, for he does not drink.

"Amador needed some courage," I said. "I thought it was for the best that he drink a little. I do not think that a little wine did harm. He did not fail because of that."

The old man waved a hand slightly. "Go on."

"I gave him the revolver," I said. "And then I went alone to the church which overlooks the Presidential Square. I climbed to the tower where I could watch what would happen. There were many people in the square and on the platform with the General there were foreigners who people say advise the General."

The old man nodded. "It has happened in other countries."

"There were speeches to mark the opening of the new military road," I said. "From the tower I could not see Amador in the crowd. I did not see him at all until it happened." I paused for a moment and then went on. "When the General rose to say his words, I heard the gunshots and saw the two guards fall. And then I saw Amador—for just one moment. He had almost reached the top of the platform when the machine guns fired. And then it was over. Amador was dead."

The old man rubbed his eyes.

"How many have we lost? Cajal, Molinos, Gondomar?"

"And Evariste," I said. He spoke tiredly. "I had almost forgotten. I am an old man and I forget."

"It does not matter," I said.

"They were not patriots. They did what they did for money."

The old man shook his head. "You are too harsh. The money I gave them does not replace their lives."

We looked silently down the mountain. Below us lay the border and beyond that the north and freedom. There were wire fences and guards, but one could get through if one knew the way.

Once again I asked, though I knew what his answer would be. "Why do you not leave? Why do you not go where you are safe?"

The old man smiled faintly. "So many of my kind have fled across the border vowing that they would remember the homeland. But once they were gone and safe, they were content to live and forget. No, I cannot leave my country's soil. My place is here."

In the days before the General came to power, the old man had been one of the great land owners. In the mornings he would ride his horse among the fields and the workers, and when he returned in the evening he would not have seen one-tenth of what he owned.

The estates are broken up now and each family has been allotted 20 acres. The peasants seem content, though there are shortages and there is talk that soon each man's 20 acres will be taken away again to create a commune such as they have in many parts of the country. But that is talk which no one chooses to believe.

The old man stared at his folded hands. "We must find someone else."

I looked to where the sun had almost set. "I think that the time has now come for me to do what we know is necessary."

The old man looked up. "No. I cannot allow you to go. If there were some guarantee that you would succeed, then perhaps I might. But if you failed, then I would be alone. I could do nothing anymore." He rose and patted my shoulder. "You are my eyes and my ears. I cannot leave this hut. I must hide here. If my face were seen, it would be the end. Many people still believe in the General."

It had been six months since I had turned the mountain path and seen the old man for the first time. I had been hunting for the small deer of this region, for since the General has come there is little meat in my village.

He had been ragged and bearded and yet I had known who he was, for he had once been president of the Republic and his picture had been on the walls of every schoolroom.

He had raised his hands when I pointed the gun and had waited. Perhaps to be shot.

I had stood there and wondered what to do, for in times such as these one must protect oneself. To allow a man such as he to go free—to escape—could be dangerous if it were ever known.

I do not know what I might have done, but then the rains came—swiftly and heavily as they do in the season—and we had taken refuge in the hut.

And I had let him talk, for there was nothing else to do until the rains ceased, and he had spoken of freedom and country and what must be done by patriots.

When the rains stopped, I had shared my food with him, for he was hungry, and we came to an agreement.

Now the old man's eyes were tired. "We must go on. We must not fail again."

"No," I said. "The General must die."

For a moment doubt seemed to cross his face. "Does it do any good to kill this one man?"

"He is the General," I said.

He smiled sadly. "You are simple and direct. But if we kill this one man, will it change things? Is this new movement more than just one man? Will the General be replaced by someone who is worse?"   "I do not know," I said. "But we must hope that what we do is right."

He nodded slowly. "Yes. We must do something. Whatever we can." He took several weary breaths. "I sit here and know nothing of what occurs in our country. Without a radio or even newspapers it is difficult to know what the people really want."

I spat upon the ground. "The newspapers are not worth reading. They are all about the General and how much his people love him."

We were silent and then the old man said again, "Now we must find someone else. Someone who will be more successful than Amador."

"Yes," I said. "I will go to the capital tomorrow."

It was almost dark now. I bade the old man goodbye and went down the path to the village where I sleep.

I returned to the hut on the mountain three days later.

The old man had been hiding in the brush, but he came out when he saw that it was only me.

"You have found someone?" he asked.

"Yes," I said. "Guerrero is his name. He is a man who drinks. Who brawls. But he is a man of great physical courage and will do much for money."

The old man frowned. "Can we trust such a one as that? Will he risk death?"

"He does not plan to die," I said. "He is very expert with a rifle."

The old man gave that thought. "Do you think he will succeed?"

"Yes," I said. "I think he will succeed."

The old man took the little green book from his pocket and wrote. He tore the paper from the book along the dotted lines. "Ten thousand," he said. "You will remind Guerrero that this check is good. Not in this country, of course, but across the border where I still have lands and money. Will he know how he can get the money?"

"He will know," I said. "Like the others."

Down the mountainside, at the turn in the path, I waved to the old man and then continued on my way.

Cajal. Molinos. Gondomar. Evariste. Amador. And now Guerrero.

I smiled.

They were but names and I had taken them from the air. The men did not exist and never had.

How much money did the old man still have?

But perhaps I should not be greedy.

This time when I crossed the border to cash the check, I thought I would remain there.

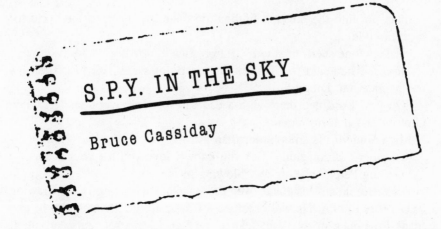

S.P.Y. IN THE SKY

Bruce Cassiday

IN HIS LIFETIME, Peter Baron had made love to any number of girls under many strange and exotic conditions. Never before, however, had he made love to a girl in a lifeboat. Particularly a girl as delectable in appearance and as rich in pocketbook as Mara Gibson. What redblooded American male would not give his right arm to make love to Gibson Aircraft, Gibson Steel, Gibson Soap, Gibson Trust?—all in such a lush, ecstatic package?

"Where are the rest of them?" the lovely girl whispered in his arms, teasing Baron's nose with the tip of her tongue.

He cocked his head and listened to the telltale splashing in the ocean beside the yacht. "Still in the sea, Mara."

She giggled. "Bathing in the nude. Isn't it frighteningly decadent, Peter?"

"Terrifyingly," he agreed.

"And in the Pacific Ocean!" Mara went on, ecstatic.

"Something to write your congressman about," Baron vowed.

"Under the shadow of Kilauea Volcano!" sighed Mara. "Doesn't Wayne Franklyn give you goose bumps, the way he thinks them up?"

Wayne Franklyn did indeed give Peter Baron goose bumps, but not in the way Mara meant. Franklyn was *the* top box office attraction in the motion picture business. He was *the* top draw in the international jet set, of whom Mara Gibson was among the first dozen. To bathe in the moonlit waters off the Island of Hawaii, outside Wayne Franklyn's chartered 168-foot pleasure yacht *Bird of Paradise* was, of course, to *live* in This Year of Our Lord 1965.

Mara Gibson and Peter Baron had been *living* in the prescribed fashion—swimming naked in the sea—before they had tired of the sport and

climbed up into the covered lifeboat on board the deck of the yacht for
a quick cuddle.

"Has anyone seen Franklyn?" Baron asked curiously.

"Idiot," Mara said fondly, nibbling on Baron's ear. "He hasn't left his
cabin since San Diego."

"Oh yes. Confined there with a bad case of Hollywood starlet. Gilda
Glowe, isn't that her name?"

Mara pouted. "Is she prettier than I am?"

"Possibly," Baron said. "But you know I love you for your brains."

"Darling Peter," she sighed, blowing in his ear.

Peter Baron ran his hand over her naked, water-slick body, drawing
her closely to him. He was cramped for room in the lifeboat. But he had
made love once in the front seat of the Lancia, bucket seats and all. It
had been an affair his Lancia would never forget. A chiropractor named
Larghini would never forget, either. He had made 200,000-*lire* profit
unkinking Baron's backbone.

Mara kissed energetically, plunging into the game, snuggling in his
arms and pressing every inch of her to him. They made quite beautiful,
idyllic love together, considering the weight of the canvas over them.

It was altogether fitting that it should be culminated by an enormous,
earth-shaking explosion. Peter Baron lifted his head and drew aside the
canvas top to look out. He saw the profile of Kilauea Volcano in the
night, its top belching smoke and ash and glowing as red as the tip end
of an expensive perfecto. The night sky was the color of underexposed
Ektachrome. Beneath the yacht the sea curled giddily, dotted still with
the gleaming white bodies of naked tycoons and sportive courtesans.

"Kilauea," he explained to Mara. "She's blown her top."

Mara rose beside him, a nymph emerging from the deep, minus sea-
weed—minus everything, in fact. "Do you think she knows about us?"
She turned his chin and pressed her breasts against him.

"If she didn't, she does now," Peter Baron observed. "Others, too," he
added, suddenly realizing what a dazzling picture of depravity they presented to those still aboard the yacht, fully clothed, and now goggling at
them rather than the volcano.

"Oh, dear," said Mara, clasping her hands modestly to her bosom.

Baron rose to the occasion with dignity. "What's the matter? Haven't
any of you Peeping Toms ever seen a volcano erupt before?"

He pulled Mara down with him beneath the canvas cover and soon
they were giggling and kissing each other again.

"Peter!" A voice whispered urgently at the edge of the lifeboat. Baron
put his finger across Mara Gibson's rich lips and poked his head through

the canvas cover. He saw Il Duca Francesco di Farinese, his associate in freelance espionage, silhouetted in the darkness.

"What is it?" Baron asked a bit ungently.

"It's something rather special. Come on out."

"Quite impossible," Baron said. "You see, I have no clothes."

"I've brought them." Duke shoved a bundle into Baron's protecting hands. "Hurry up!"

Baron shrugged at Mara's angry pout and slowly writhed into his trousers and shirt. It was not easy in the cramped confines of the boat, especially when Mara kept tickling him and trying to pull them off again. But soon he was clothed and relatively decent.

He lifted the hood of the lifeboat and stepped onto the deck of the yacht. Duke was peering over the rail toward the shore of Hawaii.

"This had better be good," Baron grumbled.

Duke merely lifted his hand languidly.

Baron's eyes traveled quickly over the cavorting jet-setters shoreward. Flames were shooting into the sky at the top of the volcano. Massive clouds of ash and rock showered the ocean. Molten streams of red-hot lava slid ponderously down the steep slopes into the water. Steam hissed up where hot rock met water.

And then he made out a tiny figure in a dinghy almost 200 yards away, rowing weakly against the current. The man was scorched; his shirt hung in black tatters. The dinghy had been burnt by falling ash.

"Get the Skipper!" whispered Baron.

Duke pointed down to the side of the yacht. In the 20-foot shore launch which brought passengers to and from the yacht sat the Skipper, a big curly-haired giant named Nils Gustavson, steering the craft quickly toward the man in the dinghy.

"He was caught by that volcano eruption," Baron mused. "I wonder what he was doing in the lava cliffs?"

"Fishing?" Duke suggested. "Diving? Swimming?"

"Go on," Baron scoffed. "How could he be swimming? He has all his clothes on."

Others clustered to the railing to watch the rescue of the man in the rowboat. Captain Gustavson did not waste a motion pulling the exhausted rower from the dinghy and turning the launch back to the yacht. Within minutes, Gustavson's first mate and a member of the crew were laying the man out on a stretcher.

Baron could see that the rower had lapsed into unconsciousness. Great blisters had erupted on the man's face and neck. Gustavson tore off the ruined shirt. Someone gasped. The man's body was bright red, as if it had been boiled in water.

"Volcanic ash, and boiling seawater," said Gustavson. "Poor devil."

Baron leaned down close to the man's face. There was a flicker of one eyelid. "He's coming to."

The man opened his eyes and stared at the sky through a veil of pain. Then they shifted to Gustavson's face. Recognition flickered in them for an instant, and then the blistered lips trembled.

"I couldn't remove the—" he stammered.

Baron leaned closer. "You couldn't remove the what?"

"The cassette," gasped the dying man. "For God's sake, get it out before the whole world—"

The man's eyes closed. Then he blinked them several times and sat bolt upright. "Before the whole world goes up in flames!" His breath rushed out of his lungs in a terrible spasm of agony.

Instantly his eyes rolled, his mouth fell open, and he slumped to the deck. His eyes opened wide and he lay there dead.

A cluster of a dozen people stood around staring helplessly. The Skipper slowly unfolded a blanket and laid it over the man's body. Baron stood, signaling Duke to join him at the rail out of earshot of the others.

"Do you recognize him?" Baron whispered.

Duke shook his head. "Should I?"

"He's Hans van Harten, the Dutch expert in moon photography analysis."

"Moon photography!" echoed Duke, startled.

"What could he have found out that threatens the world?" Baron leaned over the rail and stared at the black mass of smoke and fire swirling out of the crater of Kilauea.

From the bow of the moving launch, Peter Baron watched the smoke and ash drifting over the Island. After the main eruption of Kilauea, smaller recurrences had continued spasmodically through the night. Now it was morning. Behind the launch the *Bird of Paradise* rose at anchor in Hilo Bay. Captain Gustavson, his executive officer, and Baron and Duke were going into Hilo now, with van Harten's body, wrapped and tagged, on the launch deck.

"Some vacation," Duke observed glumly to Baron as they hung over the rail, watching the famous Hawaiian fishing fleet going out to sea amidst a swarm of breakfasting sea gulls.

"I'm not going to get involved in anything," Baron said lightly. "I've already made that clear, haven't I, Captain?"

Gustavson turned a haggard face to Baron and nodded. "Don't worry.

I'll take care of the body. I know Chief Kai of the Hilo Police Department."

"Didn't you know van Harten, too?" Baron asked innocently.

Gustavson sent him a quick glance which might have contained a flash of fear. "I never saw him before in my life."

Baron shrugged. Gustavson was lying. But it didn't much matter.

"Why are we coming ashore?" Duke wanted to know.

"I'm sick of that crowd on the yacht," Baron said. "I'd like a breath of fresh air among honest people."

"This was your idea of a vacation," Duke scoffed.

"I made a mistake."

"With Mara Gibson? Don't be a hypocrite, Peter!"

During the rescue operations last night Mara had retired to her cabin in a deep sulk. Baron had made no attempt to cheer her up. She was angry with him. He knew that he had made a mistake accepting her invitation to join the jet-setters. A spoiled bunch of rich bitches and heavy-handed tycoons disporting themselves: Baron should never have let himself be talked into the orgy.

Gustavson tied the launch up at the dock and his men loaded the body ashore. An escort from the Police Department waited at dockside to receive the body, having been informed of the arrival of the corpse by R/T from the yacht.

Baron and Duke followed Gustavson along the street to Police Headquarters. "I want to find out what van Harten was doing on the island," Baron explained to Duke. "But I don't want to be involved."

"How would the police know about the Dutchman?" Duke wondered.

"Van Harten is a foreigner and would need a passport. His passport would say wheter or not he was here on business or pleasure."

At the Station Gustavson disappeared with a hard-faced police secretary. Baron and Duke amused themselves by reading the notices on the bulletin board while the Skipper was closeted with Chief Kai.

When Gustavson reappeared, he was blank-faced and tight-lipped.

"What happened?"

"Nothing. Dead of burns. That's what the preliminary investigation shows."

"Why was van Harten here in the Islands?"

Gustavson licked his lips. "Nobody knows. It wasn't official. He hadn't checked in with his passport. That means he was here illegally. You know he's an internationally recognized pacifist, don't you? Chief Kai is looking into that, fishing for Red angles. This is going to boil up into a flap. My client won't like it."

Baron grinned. "Are you going to tell Wayne Franklyn?"

"Tell him? How can I?" Gustavson looked annoyed. "I couldn't even contact him if the ship was sinking!" He sighed. "The Hilo police promise to keep it quiet." He walked off, shaking his head.

Baron turned to Duke. "Well, well, well."

"What does that cryptic statement mean?"

"There's something doing here." Baron straightened, as if shedding a weight from his shoulders. "But yours truly isn't going to be in on it. I'm on vacation."

"Amen," Duke said.

The two of them made their way across the room crowded with Islanders in sport shirts and bright colored hats, and tourists hung with camera cases and guide books. As they approached the doorway, a big man in uniform bustled through, shouldering aside a Hawaiian woman festooned with a heap of orchid leis.

The big man's eyes fell on Baron. His face lit up. "Peter Baron!" He came over and slapped Baron on the back. "Long time no see!"

Gene Stratford was a chicken colonel now, big and jaunty and glib as ever. Baron shook his hand and tried to remember where he had seen Stratford.

"Paris, France," Stratford said, filling in the gaps. "Remember that little bistro and that mademoiselle from the Left Bank? *Beaucoup bonbons* there, Peter!"

Baron remembered. Stratford was Army G-2. Intelligence. He was a tough, hard-working man, an expert in Security, in spite of his bluff, outgoing appearance.

Duke drifted casually out of hearing and wandered out into the palm-shaded street.

Stratford glanced around and leaned close to Baron. "I didn't know you were on this hardware case."

Baron opened his mouth to speak, but Stratford barged right on.

"It certainly looks like nuclear holocaust, doesn't it?"

Baron blinked. Gene Stratford's face was actually bright with excitement. There was glee in his blue eyes—the typical military man's response to the prospect of debacle. Baron felt a chill in his spine.

"Sorry Gene," he said. "I'm not in on it. I'm here strictly on vacation."

Stratford's face stiffened and he went pale. Then he straightened quickly, and became self-possessed and distant.

"I see. Peter, it's been good to see you, and I'm only sorry I've got to push on. *Aloha*, as we say in the Islands."

Baron nodded. The big man stepped lightly across the room, trying to appear unconcerned at his inadvertent breach of security. Baron watched him weave his way in through the crowd of people toward a door down the hall marked MORGUE.

G-2, Island Security, was obviously interested in the death of Hans van Harten.

Baron saw Duke standing in the sunny street, waiting for him. A pale man wearing sunglasses with enormous ear frames faced Baron; he looked away as Baron's eyes fell on him. He wore an aloha shirt and tight white jeans. His hair was black and oily, and he did not seem to be a native any more than he seemed to be a tourist. The man had been watching Baron while he was talking to Stratford.

Moving quickly, Baron passed by the man. The man lifted his right hand to his sunglasses, as if he were going to adjust them.

Instinct told Baron that if this man had been interested in Baron's conversation with G-2, the man could be dangerous.

The pale fingers squeezed the rims of the sunglasses. There was a whirring sound. Something zipped out of the front of the ear frame, emerging beside the right lens.

Forewarned, Baron had instantly flung himself through the air at the pale man, taking him backwards in a smoothly executed football block.

Behind Baron, a man gasped and collapsed to the floor. He was a short, fat man with a tourist camera strung from his neck.

The pale man writhed out from under Baron and leaped to his feet. He ran out into the street.

"Duke! Stop him!"   The pale man was racing down the palm-shaded sidewalk. Duke leaped toward him, but failed to catch him. The fugitive mounted a Honda motorcycle parked at the curb in a quick, flowing motion. He switched it on and kicked the starter. The engine coughed and caught. Smoke gushed out.

Duke jumped up and grasped the man around the shoulders, pulling him to the sidewalk. They struggled violently. One hand fumbling in his pockets Baron ran forward to grab the idling Honda. Slipping a magnetized homing device out of his pocket, he clapped it to the underside of the license plate.

Duke smashed a fist into the pale man's chest, and he fell back. Baron signaled Duke not to move. Puzzled, Duke waited obediently on the sidewalk.

The pale man leaped on the Honda and gunned it, turning into the flow of traffic and vanishing in the direction of the mountains behind Hilo.

"You let him escape!" Duke said indignantly.

"I want to know who he's working for," Baron explained. "Besides, he didn't really do anything."

"Didn't he?" Duke asked dubiously as they walked back into the police station. "He shot something out of those sunglasses. I saw him. He aimed at you, and hit a man standing behind you."

A policeman was feeling the fallen man's pulse. "He's dead," he announced grimly, looking up. "His wallet says he's Ted Anderson, a tourist from Milwaukee."

Duke leaned down to sniff the needle which had penetrated a good eighth of an inch into the man's forehead.

"Instantaneous poison," he whispered to Baron. "Some kind of curare, or a derivative, if I'm not mistaken. Just like a poisoned dart. Interesting device. Lethal lens." He smiled flatly at Baron.

Baron looked down at the corpse, which, but for the grace of God, would have been Peter Baron.

In a small cocktail lounge on Kilauea Boulevard Baron and Duke ate a belated lunch and sat back to relax over coffee.

"I didn't much like Chief Kai's attitude," Duke confessed. "I rather think he overstressed your part in the incident."

Baron frowned. "He's a rugged individualist right out of Hawaiian history—blood of King Kamehameha and all that. He doesn't convince easily."

"Obviously he sensed a connection between van Harten's death and that of that fellow Anderson from Milwaukee."

Baron sipped his Kona coffee. "Of course, Chief Kai's instincts are right. But I couldn't give him the satisfaction of being sure."

"Naturally not."

"And what he doesn't know won't hurt us. What I want you to do is to make a personal investigation of Captain Nils Gustavson, our smiling host."

"Including his dealings with Wayne Franklyn?"

"Excluding Franklyn. Franklyn just supplied the money for the cruise, not the intrigue. Find out if Gustavson has a record of any kind. Ask about the history of *Bird of Paradise*, where she sailed last, and all that."

Duke nodded. "What are you planning."

"I intend to trace our friend with the lethal sunglasses. You saw me attach that limpet homer to his license plate. I'll simply rent a car and find him with the RDF." Baron patted a leather carrying case by his chair. "That's why I sent the beach boy out to the yacht at noon to pick this up."

Baron left Duke at Hilo and within 40 minutes was driving a rented

Mustang along Highway H 11, the road to Mauna Loa Volcano, the parent of Kilauea. The RDF indicated the Honda's position to be exactly to the southeast. On the map the line extended to Kumukahi Point, the easternmost tip of the Island of Hawaii.

The road was stunning in its tropical beauty. Baron drove by enormous palm trees, slender blossoming palms, red lehua flowers, giant tree ferns, fields of sugar cane, fragrant ginger, and purple tibouchina. A macadamia nut orchard zoomed past just outside Hilo.

A road turned off right going to Mountain View, Glenwood, and Kilauea Crater. Baron checked his direction finder and drove toward a village called Pahoa on H 13.

Five miles further on he was distressed to find that a RDF check showed his quarry in an easterly position, although the road continued southeast. He would have to go to Pahoa first, and then make a left turn on H 132 toward Kapoho, a one-time village which had been covered by a recent lava flow. The road continued past Kapoho, curving toward the shore.

The sun dropped past the top of the volcano as he drove through Pahoa and turned left toward Kumukahi Point. The jungle road degenerated, passing through a wonderland of volcanic upthrusts and pockmarked slopes of ebony lava, now creating exotic shadows in the twilight.

The road ended abruptly at a village which was not shown on the map. It was simply a collection of shacks, a tin building, and a jetty extending out into the Pacific. Angry little waves boiled in the surf around the jetty. An ancient fishing boat bobbed up and down in the water. It was similar to those he had seen in the Hilo Bay fishing fleet.

As Baron stood there, debating what to do, he saw the Honda. It was parked on the end of the sagging jetty, half-concealed behind a crate. Baron touched its license plate: the magnetic homing device was there. He pulled it off and thrust it in his pocket.

There was a sudden rumble from the volcano, which towered behind him. He turned and glanced up apprehensively. Clouds were forming now; ash was showering down the slope. A red glow sputtered for a moment at the apex of the volcano, and then went out like a fizzling punk. As Baron turned back to the jetty, he thought he saw the shadow of someone crouching inside the boat.

Baron jumped down onto the deck and moved into the sheltered portion of the craft. He ducked aside, expecting an attack. He was not disappointed.

A figure darted out of the shadows and pounced on him, sprawling when he missed Baron. Baron crouched, waiting.

The man jumped up, circling Baron. It was the killer with the sunglasses. They had dropped and lay on the deck of the sampan. His pale face had beady eyes and ferret teeth.

The killer leaped, looping a knotted rope over Baron's head. Quickly crossing the ends and pulling, the man garotted Baron. Baron kicked him in the groin.

The would-be killer slumped to the deck, cursing.

Baron grabbed the rope, and twisted it around the man's wrists to subdue him. The man pulled back suddenly, yanking Baron off balance. Then he rose and jumped feet first over the side of the sampan.

Peter Baron followed. He splashed into the warm, waist-deep surf, and swung a fist at his assailant. The man swung back. Something glinted in the darkness. The man had slipped brass knuckles on his hand—brass knuckles with a razor-sharp curved blade which fitted around the fingers like a scimitar.

The man slashed at Baron, driving him back in the waist-deep water. Baron grabbed at the man's wrist, twisting the razor away. The man grunted desperately, pushing the razor-sharp edge closer to Baron's throat.

Baron's back slammed against one of the jetty's pilings. The waves slapped against him, threatening his balance. The razor came closer; the man's breath was hot on Baron's face.

Baron let his feet fly out from under him and slipped down against the piling. The man fell forward toward the piling. The razor, which Baron held twisted away from him, was turned toward the killer's throat. When he fell, it severed his jugular vein.

In a moment it was all over. Blood flowed down the man's neck. Slowly he sank into the choppy waist-deep waters. Crimson tinted the surf, spreading out from the body.

Baron hoisted the corpse onto the jetty. Inside the sampan he lit a match and found what he was looking for: the lethal sunglasses.

Once before, in Pakistan, he had run across a pair such as these. Duke Farinese had recently reported a fight involving a Russian agent wearing brass knuckles with a curved scimitar blade.

Could it be possible? Were these from the same arsenal of evil?

He had driven less than a mile from the deserted village when the road wound suddenly across an outcrop of lava. From this eminence, Baron could see down across the thick jungle to the shore. Coming up to the jetty of the deserted fishing village was a small boat. Part of the craft was smouldering. It had been set on fire by falling ash from the recent eruption.

Baron picked up his carrying bag and removed his black-light binoculars. When Duke had outfitted him with these night lenses, he had explained that black-light projection could pick out objects clearly in the darkness.

With the black-light glasses, commonly called a "snooperscope," Baron focused on the boat as it neared the jetty. There were two men aboard—an enormous blond man who must have been six feet four at least, and a husky oriental, stripped to the waist. The Oriental was completely bald and muscular.

The two men were shouting at one another, engaged in a violent argument. As they came up to the deserted jetty, one of them spotted the body of the dead man. They both leaped onto the planking and bent excitedly over the corpse. Baron would have given a lot to know what they were saying.

Quickly they lifted the corpse and vanished with it behind the corrugated sheet metal shed near the wharf.

Baron climbed into the Mustang and drove quickly back to the settlement, parking behind a clump of palms and giant ferns. He walked quietly toward the jetty, keeping to the shadows.

The two men had vanished. Their boat, still smouldering, was tied up. Baron boarded her. By darting his pencil flashlight over the equipment on the deck, he found that the men had carried with them scuba gear, grappling hooks, long chains, and underwater flashlights. The scuba gear had been used. It was wet.

The sullen remnants of fire aboard proved that the boat had been sailed in very close to the fall of ash at the lava flow. Baron touched the wet suit. It was very hot. The waters next to red-hot lava must have been boiling. Was that why the boat had returned?

Darkness was settling quickly. The jungle came alive with night sounds: birds whacking away, small animals howling and screeching. Waves lapped against the black sands of the beach.

And Baron was aware of another noise, a foreign metallic sound. He looked up into the sky. It seemed almost as if some giant bird were winging across the heavens. Then, from above the coconut palms, the shape of a helicopter appeared dramatically, its big overhead blades rotating noisily.

Baron ran to the Mustang for his black-light binoculars. The helicopter was flying so low he could see the inside clearly. In the red glow of the dash light the faces of her two passengers were clearly defined: the Oriental and the blond man. The blond man was hard-eyed and scar-faced, with Scandinavian features. The Oriental was definitely Chinese, with a round face and heavy-lidded eyes.

The helicopter flew in a broad curve over the steep lava cliffs dropping into the ocean. She vanished in a southerly direction, following the coast line. Smoke and steam whirled up around her as she passed over the new flow of lava.

She hovered like a hummingbird, and then tried to descend to the lava rocks. She dropped out of sight suddenly. Then, a moment later, she appeared again, scooting out to sea, her fuselage quivering, her rotor chopping desperately at the air.

Air currents caused by steam sizzling up from the boiling water had almost capsized her. She approached again, coming in easily, lowering toward the danger spot. Just before she seemed to settle like a feeding butterfly, she zoomed up panic-stricken, and hung there in the air.

A rumble sounded from Kilauea's crater. Flames shot high into the air, painting the sky and the land blood-red. Ash and molten rock flew up. Smoke followed.

The helicopter sped back toward the deserted fishing village. She lowered quickly into the jungle.

Baron plunged into the tangled tropical undergrowth.

An hour later he returned to his car. He had been unable to find a trace of the mysterious helicopter.

In her plush suite aboard *Bird of Paradise*, an angry Mara Gibson eyed Peter Baron over the top of her vodka Martini. "Little men with poison darts, boats on fire, helicopters in the jungle! Really, Peter, what a moron you must think me to swallow that tale. I smell female!"

"Angel," murmured Peter Baron over his stinger on the rocks, "I assure you, it *was* a business trip."

Outside, the lights of Hilo glittered against the dramatic backdrop of Mauna Kea, the big, extinct volcano, towering in the distance. The scent of frangi pani blossoms and wild ginger drifted across the sparkling waters of Hilo Bay.

"It's a woman," Mara said with assurance. "Or perhaps a dozen of them, all sitting cross-legged in *muu-muus* in one of those filthy grass shacks, weaving baskets and grinding *poi*—"

"No. It was business." Baron slipped his arm around her shoulders. She was wearing a low-cut strapless dress.

"Washing your feet, probably, bathing your body in *okolehau*, chanting those saccharine Hawaiian songs, strumming an obscene ukelele—"

Baron put his drink down and lifted hers out of her hand. He kissed her. She drew back stiffly.

"Bedding you down in some dusty banana-leaf pallet, stroking your hair and squeezing coconut juice into your mouth—"

Baron's hand slid into the top of Mara Gibson's dress. He pulled it downward. She had nothing on underneath.

"Tempting you with pineapple juice out of coconut shells, stuffing you with enormous luaus of roast pig and fish—"

Baron leaned over and kissed her and she sighed deeply, sliding down on to the seat, her legs twisting convulsively alongside his.

"Anointing your fevered temples with coconut oil, waving palm fronds to keep the flies off and the breeze circulating through the hut—"

Her dress was down to her waist now, and her arms were around his neck.

"Stripping their sarongs off in seductive gestures and lifting their—"

Mara Gibson's $250 summer casual dress by Hattie Carnegie slid to the deck of the suite. Baron turned and snapped off the lamp. The room glowed in the faint blue night light. The sultry strains of guitar music drifted across the waters of Hilo Bay. Lovely Hula Hands.

Baron reached out for Mara Gibson's warm flesh.

The beep-beep sound shattered the silence like some ghastly piping from hell.

"What's that?" Mara murmured sleepily.

Baron reached reluctantly over to his clothes and removed his cigarette-case R/T.

"Duke," said a tinny voice.

"Yes?"

"I'm onto something interesting. Come quickly."

"Where?"

"A dive called the Mahimahi on the waterfront. I'm in the back room. Observe security precautions."

Baron rose, slowly slipping on his clothes.

"You filthy sadist," Mara Gibson muttered between clenched teeth. "I could spit."

"You're doing quite nicely," Baron said, kissing her deeply. "Duty calls."

Five minutes later he was on deck untying one of the ship-to-shore outboards. He gave the starter rope a twist just as a shadowy form loomed beside him.

"I'm coming with you," Mara Gibson said, and jumped down into the dinghy. It rocked dangerously.

"No, you're not," Baron protested. "Do you want to sink this boat?"

"If I have to, I will."

Baron grasped her around the waist and lifted her up to the deck of the yacht.

"Let me down, you oaf!" she cried. "What do you think I am, more of your cheap female merchandise?"

"No. Expensive." Baron snapped the rope and started the outboard. "I love you." He waved cheerfully as the outboard sped into the night.

"I hate you!" Mara's voice cried across the water.

"Ambivalence," Baron said. "You ought to tell your analyst."

The back room of the Mahimahi was a classic site for a surveillance. The actual bar was well-lighted and quiet. No one sat inside but a trio of men at a table. The bar was located on the bay, facing a narrow and quiet street.

Baron found Duke in a stuffy back room, seated at a square table, with a miniature TV receiver operating in front of him. Baron glanced over Duke's shoulder. The TV showed the round table with the three men seated at it. One of them was the Skipper of *Bird of Paradise*, Captain Nils Gustavson; the second was the Chinese with the Yul Brynner head; and the third was the tall Swede with the battered face.

"Where is the camera?" Baron asked.

Duke chuckled. "Inside a bottle of brandy on a shelf in the bar. Neat, eh?"

"How'd you plant it there?"

"When I followed Gustavson to the dive, I entered the kitchen. It took a twenty-dollar bill to make friends with the chef. I put the mini-camera and listener in a bottle of brandy, scraped a hole in the label, and had the chef place it where I wanted it. The other two just came in."

"Did you investigate the Skipper's background?"

"Yes. The report is negative. He's clean. So is *Bird of Paradise*."

"What's going on out there?"

"There's some kind of argument. The two men want the Skipper to rent them the yacht's launch. Something about 'going in closer.' I gather they're trying to get in close to shore near the spot we found van Harten in the rowboat. They want the launch: it's got a fast engine and can go in and get out safely."

"And the Skipper?"

"He's afraid of his client, Wayne Franklyn."

Baron peered at the miniature TV. The Chinese was speaking in perfect, almost scholarly English. He wore a large jade ring on his left hand.

"It's that treacherous falling ash, Gustavson," he said reasonably. "Otherwise, we could use a catamaran to get in."

"I can't endanger the launch," Gustavson protested. "If Kilauea blows again, the lava might bury the boat."

The Swede snorted. "The launch is fast. With it we could get out."

"No."

"We've got to get into the tube!" snapped the Swede. He leaned toward Gustavson threateningly, his fist clutching a bottle. "Look, the American liquidator The Boss hired for protection, is dead already. Someone is on to us. If you don't cooperate—and quick—we can always dispose of you!"

"That doesn't scare me!"

The Chinese peered into Gustavson's eyes, his pudgy round face glistening with perspiration. "The Boss is plenty irritated about the parcel. He went out himself to the buoy. When it wasn't there, you could hear the atmospheric disturbances in Bombay!"

The Skipper was shaken, but tried to appear unconcerned. "Tell the Boss he doesn't own me. And he can keep his filthy ten thousand."

The Chinese's eyes gleamed. "The Boss may not own you, Gustavson, but he can make your life miserable. Do you know what he thinks? He thinks you've sold him out. He thinks you've taken the package to the opposition! He thinks you really made the exchange!"

"I didn't! The man was dying!" Gustavson whispered, haggard. "He didn't have it."

"Forget all that!" said the Chinese impatiently. "We need the launch. Well?"

Baron's eyes focused suddenly on someone standing beyond the three men at the table. It was a woman, in the entrance to The Mahimahi. Duke gasped.

"Mara!" groaned Baron.

"What's she doing here?" Duke wondered.

"She followed me!"

The Skipper had looked up and had seen her. Quickly he gestured the Chinese and Swede for silence.

"Miss Gibson," Gustavson said politely, standing up at the table. "Can I help you?"

"Perhaps you can, Captain Gustavson. I'm looking for Peter Baron."

Gustavson's face was expressionless. The Chinese's face tightened and the eyes glittered. The Swede half rose from his chair.

"I'm afraid he isn't here," said the Skipper politely.

"But I followed him."

There was a thick silence. Mara Gibson walked over to the table. "It's a joke, isn't it? He's hiding from me."

The Chinese pushed his chair back and removed something from his pocket. Duke gripped Baron's arm in front of the mini-TV. "Geiger counter. Radio-wave detector. We're unfrocked!"

Already the Chinese was waving a small wand about in the air, pointing it at all corners of the bar. The counter began clicking suggestively. Like a cat the Chinese stalked the clicking sound.

Mara Gibson looked at him curiously. "What's that silly man doing?"

The bald Chinese had the wand pointed at the brandy bottle on the shelf. He pocketed the device and grabbed the bottle. Shaking it, he dropped the miniature camera and bug out onto the table. His eyes roved the bar quickly.

"Grab the girl," he snapped.

The Swede jumped up and grasped Mara Gibson from behind, pulling her elbows painfully in back of her. She screamed loudly. The tall man put a hand the size of a dictionary over her mouth.

Baron burst through the door, with Duke behind him. Baron swung at Gustavson, who was too startled to react. Gustavson went down. Baron turned and slammed a fist against the Swede. He turned and kicked Baron onto the table, which went over.

Duke dove through the air at the Chinese, who neatly sidestepped him.

"Olson!" the Chinese cried warningly.

The Swede looked up and nodded. The Chinese took an enormous gulp of air into his chest and held it. Then, with a quick motion, he flipped the cap off the enormous jade ring he wore on his left hand.

A mist sprayed up.

Baron shouted: "Hold your breath! Paralysis vapor!"

It was too late, however. He could feel the iron band clamp around his throat. The muscles contracted and no air could enter his tortured throat.

Olson, holding his breath, ran out the doorway with Mara Gibson. The Chinese turned once to survey the room with an inscrutable smile, and followed.

Duke staggered, clutching his throat. Gustavson opened his mouth to speak, and sank to his knees. The blackness flowed up and around Baron.

In the bright beam of the flashlight, Captain Nils Gustavson blinked and held up a hand to shield his eyes. Peter Baron and Duke Farinese faced him in the ship-to-shore launch.

"Get that light out my eyes," Gustavson croaked.

"Count your blessings that we're interrogating you and not the Hilo police," Baron said succinctly.

Duke lowered the beam from the Skipper's eyes. "He isn't joking, you know. You're on a tight rope."

Gustavson groaned.

"Who were those two men?" Baron wanted to know.

"I haven't the vaguest idea. Never saw them before in my life."

"But you did meet them. Would you feel like telling us about it?"

"I don't know why I should." Gustavson lifted his chin a bit.

"I do," Baron said, taking the flashlight and pointing it directly into Gustavson's eyes. "Because we would like to hear. And if we don't, we shall turn you over to Chief Kai."

Gustavson waved away the light, shuddering. "I'll talk."

"Good. First begin with the ten thousand dollars."

"It was an honest assignment. I was simply to pick up a package from a certain man who would appear in a rowboat near the shore of the Island of Hawaii."

"Van Harten," murmured Baron. "And then?"

"Then I was to deliver the package to a buoy some miles outside Hilo Bay. I was simply a courier."

"And inside the package?" Baron persisted.

"I have absolutely no idea." Gustavson looked into Baron's eyes. The Skipper was telling the truth.

"How do you know van Harten was the right man?"

Gustavson held out a folded letter on ornate writing paper, and a small black and white photograph.

The photograph was Hans van Harten. The letter, carefully written in a controlled and Spenserian hand, reminded Baron of the 1900's.

Baron passed the letter to Duke Farinese. "Look at the handwriting, not the message. The message simply instructs our host as he has explained."

Duke studied the handwriting. "Ahah!"

"I'll keep these," Baron told Gustavson. "Captain, I strongly recommend that you take the launch back to the *Bird of Paradise* and stay there."

"Agreed," muttered Gustavson.

"*Au revoir*, Baron said, and he and Duke jumped to the dock. They watched the launch putt-putt across the smooth waters toward the *Bird of Paradise*.

Baron and Duke strolled up the dock to Kilauea Boulevard. A soft, warm wind, scented with wild ginger, blew in the palms, rustling the fronds overhead. A woman's voice singing an enchanting love song drifted on the night air.

"The calligraphy?"

"Obviously his," said Duke.

"The volatile paralysis vapor, the razor knuckles, the Geiger counter, the lethal sunglasses?" Baron murmured.

"Unmistakable."

"The Chinese with the basketball head, and the scarred Swede?"

"Typical. It all adds up."

"What is Mr. Satin doing here in the Hawaiian Islands?" Baron wondered.

Duke shrugged. "Nothing innocent, I'm sure. Not with I.C.E. in the picture."

The last time Peter Baron had battled I.C.E., the International Combine of Endeavor, commonly called the International Combine of Evil, he had dealt directly with its mastermind, a cold-blooded fat man named Mr. Satin. He and Duke had beaten Mr. Satin in the Deep Sleep affair, involving a secret nerve gas which could have put the supreme war weapon of the world in the hands of I.C.E., making them rulers of the globe.

"With I.C.E. in the picture," Baron said, "I've got to lay my cards on the table. We go to G-2, Colonel Gene Stratford. There is something out there which I.C.E. needs desperately. I've got to know what it is."

"And what about Mara Gibson?"

Baron sighed. "I hope that when we find out what's out there, we may be able to trace her more easily."

Colonel Gene Stratford, bleary-eyed and sleepy, sat in a smoking jacket hastily thrown over his pajamas and listened to Baron's story in the army man's suite at the Hilo Hotel.

"It must be a horse trade," Baron insisted. "I know things you have to know. And you know things I have to know."

Stratford frowned. "Alright."

"First of all, I know this is a top-priority flap, or Island G-2 wouldn't be involved. Second, I know it has to do with 'hardware,' and hardware means satellites and ballistic missiles. Third, I know that a 'nuclear holocaust' can happen if the matter is not buttoned up tightly. Fourth, I know that van Harten was a Dutch moon photography expert, so the thing must have to do with photographs. Fifth, I know that the peace and welfare of the world is at stake; van Harten believed his mission will save the world from going 'up in flames'—his dying words. Well, would you care to put us in the picture?"

Colonel Stratford rubbed his face wearily, and then thrust his hands into the pockets of his smoking jacket.

"Forty-eight hours ago, the U.S. Army's most important satellite was scheduled to land near Hawaii in our regular recovery area south of the

Islands. It's a top, top secret flight. This piece of hardware is called S.P.Y. That's gobbledygook for 'Satellite for Photographic Intelligence.' S.P.I., actually, but we call it S.P.Y. From that, you may be able to deduce what the satellite is doing. We've been aware for some time that the Chinese Communists have been planting missile launching centers in North Vietnam, close to Russia and close to Formosa. Inside S.P.Y. is one of the newest of modern cameras, loaded with our most sensitive film—hundreds of times as sensitive as microfilm. From the height at which S.P.Y. orbits the earth, the film is capable of picking out a soda cracker."

Stratford started pacing his hotel suite.

"We sent the camera over Russia, China, Vietnam, and so on, to photograph everything. A continuous strip of film, showing not only enemy terrain, but also that of the United States, South America and Canada, has been photographed, according to information from the satellite. We cannot transmit the pictures to earth. The film is so tiny that the actual negative itself is needed for proper enlargement.

"After performing its mission, the satellite received its signals to land. Suddenly, as it approached the recovery zone, it vanished from the radar screen. It hasn't been found since.

"You can imagine the flap in the Pentagon. If those pictures fall into the hands of the Russians, the Chinese Reds, or anyone else who hates America . . . well, nobody wants to think about it."

Baron did not say it. If I.C.E. had those pictures, it could pinpoint the missile sites, blow them *all* up, and have the whole world literally at its mercy!

Baron recapitulated: "Then someone else sent out interference signals which interrupted the satellite. Is that it?"

Stratford nodded glumly. "For forty-eight hours, we've combed the entire recovery area, mile by mile. S.P.Y. isn't there."

In the heavy silence Baron gazed at Stratford. "What do you know about volcano tubes, Gene?"

Stratford blinked. He pulled out a pipe and began tamping it with tobacco from a plastic pouch. "Tubes are simply air holes—vents, I suppose you'd call them—formed when lava cools. Volcanoes are sometimes honeycombed with tubes, which form a complicated network of tunnels. The Blow Hole on Oahu near Diamond Head is a good example."

"Then a tube could extend down below the surface of the sea?"

"Certainly." Stratford fought with three matches before he got his mixture going. Smoke billowed up, equivalent to Kilauea's best. A thought occurred to him. "Van Harten was burned and boiled. It's a wild idea, but are you suggesting he was fatally hurt escaping from an underwater volcano tube?"

"The Swede's statement about the tube; the scuba gear in the boat; the chopper." Baron smiled. "It adds up. I'll wager that's where the satellite is—inside a tube. Who would ever think to look there?"

"Van Harten is a noted Dutch scientist, *and* a pacifist. He wouldn't work for the Russians or the Chinese!"

Baron did not want to mention I.C.E. "He might if they tricked him into developing, enlarging and analyzing the films to help promote world peace by exposing the missile buildup!"

Stratford puffed at his pipe excitedly.

"The satellite was intercepted and delivered to the tube, where van Harten was brought to work on it undisturbed," Baron theorized. "He was interrupted by Kilauea and had to flee for his life. His dying words were, 'I couldn't remove the cassette.' The films are presumably still in the satellite."

Duke said: "And the Chinese and Olson are trying to get into the tube to deliver the films from the satellite."

Baron nodded. "It's obvious that the boiling sea has been impossible to negotiate. Is there any way to get inside a volcano tube from land?"

"It's extremely dangerous. If you should get lost inside that maze of tunnels, you could wander for months and then starve. Without a guide or a map, it's suicide."

"Is there a map of Kilauea's tubes available?"

"Professor Swinburn of the University of Hawaii knows the network intimately." Stratford was already reaching for the phone. "I'll get him over here!"

Ten minutes later Stratford grimly hung up the phone. "Swinburn is in the wilds of Peru, writing and photographing an article for the *National Geographic*. He is trekking into the Andes with hired porters and burros. It will take two days to reach him." Stratford blinked. "And you want to know something else? We aren't the first to call Swinburn about the tubes. Two days ago a man named Albert Smithsonian wanted the same information."

Peter Baron shivered. "A pseudonym for I.C.E.," he whispered. "They're ahead of us!" Instantly he made his decision. "We go in from the sea. Or rather, I go in."

Stratford looked at him as if he were mad. "Do you prefer to be roasted or boiled?"

"Hasn't the Navy developed a two-man submarine called a mini-sub?"

"The Navy?" Stratford echoed distantly.

"Yes. That rival department that deals with rafts and kayaks and that kind of thing?"

"I have heard vaguely of them," Stratford admitted. "We could possibly obtain a mini-sub."

"That won't help," Duke interrupted harshly. "You've got to swim through that boiling water to the tube's entrance! You'll be cooked alive— like van Harten!"

"Not in the special wet suit you're going to make for me, Duke."

Lieutenant (jg) James Battles was a no-nonsense, crew-cut, incredibly young man with cold blue eyes and a contemptuous smile. For the last time he went over his instructions to Peter Baron preparatory to climbing into the two-man submarine lashed to the side of the rocking Navy launch. Surveying the scene aloofly stood G-2's Colonel Stratford. Duke Farinese's face was green; the sea was choppy and hostile to the young Italian's vital organs.

Several hundred yards off the bleak volcanic cliffs of Hawaii's southeast shore, the Navy launch rocked and rolled in the morning tide. The sun had just risen, pale and red through the streamers of smoke which still cast a pall over the sea. Kilauea had erupted once during the night, and even now was rumbling disagreeably. Steam from the cooling lava churned up near the rocky shore.

"I handle the sub," Battles said sternly. "We go in as close to the deck as we can." The "deck" meant the bottom of the sea, Baron presumed. "I'll find that tube opening, if it's there. I've got the best record in the Islands for underwater reconaissance in these minis. That's why I'm here."

Baron said nothing.

"All right, when we find the entrance, I'll surface. You climb out, Mr. Baron, and dive in."

"I'm ready, sonny," Baron said.

Duke stepped forward, trying to look hearty in spite of his color. "The asbestos underwear should keep the heat from boiling you," he said. "I've tried to model it to give you freedom of movement. Can you lift your arm?"

Baron turned around in the asbestos-lined wet-suit, did a deep-knee bend, and then lifted both arms above his head like a model. "Am I beautiful?"

Stratford growled, "Let's get this show on the road. Kilauea looks like she's going to blow again."

"When I get inside I'll call you on R/T," Baron told Duke. "Let's go, Lieutenant."

Baron stepped dutifully down from the deck of the launch into the submarine.

Battles helped him in and then crawled in beside him. He closed the hatch from inside. Then the sub moved.

Through the thick glass porthole, Baron saw the water close over them: light green, dark green, black. Down they went, diving like a fish. A light beam flashed on, illuminating an enormous clump of kelp floating off the portside.

Baron watched, fascinated. The water was devoid of fish: most had moved out when the first lava flow warmed the sea. They passed over rocks and caverns. An occasional plant weaved about in front of the sub, like a hula-skirted Hawaiian girl. Lava formations appeared.

The sub's spotlight showed a gaping hole. From the bed of the ocean a rope line extended above them, attached to a buoy.

"I think we've found it," Baron said. I.C.E. would need a buoy to guide in small craft. "Let's surface."

They went up. The waves sloshed them about. Battles flipped some handles. "Ready?"

"Ready."

"Good luck."

The hatch opened. Steam hissed up around the sub. At sea Baron saw the Navy launch, rocking in the water. Behind him a scoriac cliff of ancient lava rose from the water, into smoke. Kilauea had spared a small segment of cliffside here; it was the only reason van Harten had escaped.

As Baron fastened his face mask he could hear an ominous rumble from the mountain. In a moment ash would be falling.

"You'd better get out of here," he told Battles. Then he fell backward into the water and dove downward. The water was hot, but Duke's asbestos rig kept him from boiling. Sweat leaked out on his skin. He finned downward. The gaping hole appeared. He saw the buoy line.

Blackness closed around him as he finned into the hole. After a dozen yards he was in calm water. He probed upward, swimming along the ceiling. Suddenly he was out of the water in an enormous cavern.

He flipped back his face mask and gazed about. With his waterproof flashlight,he explored the cavern and climbed out.

Then he saw the satellite, with its familiar cone-like shape, lying in black sand in the middle of the chamber.

"Good morning, Mr. Baron," said a voice softly. "If you do not move, perhaps you have remaining a few more precious minutes of life."

The Chinese was speaking. Beside him Olson held a machine pistol aimed at Baron's chest. Mara Gibson was lying on a rock beside them, tied and gagged, her dress pasted to her sweaty body.

"So you did get a map of the tubes from Professor Swinburn," Baron said softly.

"Just this morning." The Chinese opened a paper and smiled at it. "I congratulate you on your own entry. Asbestos?" He admired Baron's rig.

Without answering, Baron glanced at the machine pistol in Olson's hands. Then he indicated Mara. "Why don't you loosen her gag?"

The Chinese reached over and removed the handkerchief. "Is that better?"

She glared at him. "Much, Mr. Chang. Peter," she said, "I'm so dreadfully sorry."

"Couldn't you have left her outside?" Baron asked Chang.

"She kept trying to escape," Chang shrugged. He smiled lewdly. "Mr. Satin did not want her. He is not so inclined."

The cave echoed with the rumbling of a sudden underground disturbance. Baron glanced around apprehensively. A muffled explosion followed.

"I'll never understand why Mr. Satin bothered with Captain Gustavson," Baron murmured. "Van Harten could simply have developed and printed the pictures, and handed them directly to I.C.E."

"That was your fault, my dear Baron. Mr. Satin had hired Gustavson because he was a reliable freelance courier. I.C.E. had used him before. The original plan was that Mr. Satin would be a guest among the jet-setters aboard the pleasure yacht."

Baron's eyes widened. "Gustavson would pick up the pictures from van Harten, and Mr. Satin would debark the yacht at Hilo."

"When you were invited aboard by Miss Gibson here, Mr. Satin had to change his plans."

"Why didn't he drop Gustavson completely?"

"Gustavson knew too much about I.C.E. If he didn't get his money, he might blackmail I.C.E. Also, Gustavson might become curious about the switch in plans. Mr. Satin decided to keep Gustavson in as a link to forestall a leak in security.

"Why the underwater entry into the tube?" Baron asked. "Why not come in from the land side?"

"Secrecy," the Chinese answered. "From the sea, no one would notice."

Chang removed a velvet bag from his pocket and took out several intricate hand tools. He sat down in front of the satellite, and studied it for a moment. Then, referring to a piece of paper, he began twisting one of the screws in the framework. In a moment he had a port open, and the cassette of film in his hand.

"Stupid van Harten," Chang murmured. "He had no idea how to open this. And then the volcano undid him."

Baron caught Mara Gibson's eye to warn her of a diversion. She winked at him. There came another ominous rumbling, and the cave rocked.

Baron let his hand drop.

Mara screamed at the top of her voice. Olson jumped and whirled on her. The moment the barrel of the machine pistol was off him, Baron made his move. In one motion, he chopped Olson with a blow to the neck.

Chang spun and leaped at Baron. The Chinese was strong and heavy, an expert karate fighter. Baron used every karate trick he had ever learned, but Chang kept backing him around the cave.

In desperation, Baron lunged at the huge man, hitting at his head and neck, and kneeing him in the groin. Chang grunted and wrapped his arms around Baron, throwing him to the floor of the cave.

He lay under the enormous Chinese, feeling the man's fingers seeking out the pressure points in his neck which would kill him in a matter of seconds.

Baron grabbed the jade ring on Chang's left hand and sucked in a deep breath of air. Then he forced the top of the ring open. Volatile paralysis vapor spread through the cave in a quick mist.

Baron held his breath. Chang's grip relaxed slowly. Unconsciousness was a black pool waiting to claim Baron. Staggering across the chamber for his face mask, he almost went down. But he found the mask and slipped it on quickly. Breathing the pure air from the scuba tanks, he waited for his strength to return.

He grabbed the cassette of film, and lifted Mara Gibson. Using the buddy system, he gave her a breath of the fresh uncontaminated air. He untied her hands and feet as she revived. Soon she was alert enough to walk. He found Dr. Swinburn's map on Chang, and following its directions, he led her through the complicated system of tubes.

"Listen," cried Mara.

Baron could hear the rumbling again, as if Kilauea were ready to spew forth fire and ash. The mountain shook. Baron almost lost his footing.

They ran through the tube, upward and outward. The ground trembled and jumped beneath their feet. An enormous cloud of steam and sulphuric smoke rushed up out of the bowels of the earth, enveloping them in its yellowish, noxious cloud.

"Lava," said Baron. "It must have flowed into the chamber below."

Mara shuddered.

Five minutes later they were out in the deep jungle, breathing fresh air thankfully. Baron flicked on his cigarette case R/T.

"Duke," a voice answered.

"We're out safely," Baron gasped. "In the jungle. Get back to Hilo. We'll rendezvous there. The bundle is intact."

Duke breathed in relief. "I'll tell Stratford."

Mara Gibson looked up into Baron's eyes. "This whole thing is like a dream, isn't it."

"If you like nightmares."

"Someday maybe you can tell me what's been happening," she suggested softly.

"Someday when there's nothing better to do." He leaned down to kiss her, and she knew what he meant.

THE CASE OF XX2

Julian Symons

"PREPOSTEROUS," SAID QUARLES, as he allowed himself to be hustled out of his office by young Mr. Hurley. The office overlooked Leicester Square, and its window proclaimed *Francis Quarles, Investigator.* "Ridiculous," said Quarles, as he lowered his bulky body into the back seat of an unobtrusive but luxurious car. Young Mr. Hurley murmured something to the driver and then got into a seat opposite Quarles.

"I do assure you, sir," he said, "that I would explain the position if I were allowed to. It really is an exceptional case, and important people are involved in it. I was given instructions to kidnap you if necessary." He was a fair-haired, open-faced young man who seemed to maintain an appearance of gravity only by an effort. "That will probably sound absurd," he added.

"I am in no doubt as to your energy," Quarles assured him. "And I am sure you would regard a kidnaping merely as something in the run of the day's work. But I should be happy to know some details of the matter of life and death on which you wish to consult me."

"I'm sorry, sir. It's not my story." Young Mr. Hurley blushed. "Though in a sense it's only too much my story."

"And the important people involved?"

Young Mr. Hurley mentioned a name, and it was the name of a very important person indeed. After that there was silence, until they reached their destination in Pall Mall. Here Mr. Hurley hustled and bustled Quarles up marble steps, through an entrance hall and into an elevator. He asked Quarles to wait and rushed away down a corridor. A few moments later he was back and shepherding Quarles into a room where a man sat behind a large desk. Quarles had never met the man, but he had seen his photograph many times in the newspapers. He was the very important person—one of the most important Ministers of the day—mentioned by Hurley in the car. The Minister, when he stood up to shake hands, was revealed as an even bigger man than the detective. He spoke in the homely voice, with just a touch of Lancashire accent, that was one of his two claims to popular fame. The other was his irascibility.

"Mr. Quarles, I owe you a personal apology for bringing you here in this unorthodox way. But the situation didn't allow for ordinary conventions. I'm calling on your help as a citizen, Mr. Quarles, in a national emergency."

The Minister's gaze was direct and compelling. The answering stare of Quarles's small black eyes was equally direct. "Tell me what you want."

"Three days ago," the Minister said, "a document of vital importance to the national safety was stolen from Hurley." He made a gesture towards the young man who stood like a watchdog by the door.

"What document?"

"It was typed on four large sheets of foolscap paper and folded into a foolscap envelope."

"Its nature?"

"It was a confidential report sent to me by a certain department. It gave details of the steps that are being taken in this country for the manufacture, should it be necessary, of a certain weapon of warfare. The weapon is at present secret. It is known as XX-2."

"And you want me to discover the thief?"

"No, no, Mr. Quarles!" The Minister was almost impatient. "I thought Hurley might have told you that much. We know the thief—he is a man named Zelbec. We want you to recover the document." The Minister's gaze was straight at Quarles as he added, "Illegally, if necessary."

Quarles sat back in his chair. "You had better tell me about it."

Three days before, on Monday of that week, the Minister had instructed Hurley to bring the XX-2 report down to Watermead in Norfolk, where he was taking a holiday which included a conference with certain allied diplomats and military men. Hurley had received a telephone call just after he had taken the report, in its sealed envelope, out of the safe in the Minister's room. The call purported to come from the staff of one of the allies with whom the Minister was conferring, and the caller mentioned the XX-2 report by name. The caller said that his name was Robins, and that he was speaking from the Minister's residence. He and Hurley talked amiably for a minute or two, but Hurley became suspicious when Robins asked casually about the train on which Hurley was traveling, so that he could be met at Watermead Station. Hurley asked to speak to the Minister, and the line went dead.

"Just a moment," Quarles said. "Exactly how many people know about the XX-2 report?"

The Minister shook his head. "Too many for us to make any check-up by that means."

"And where was it while you were telephoning?" Quarles asked Hurley.

The young man flushed. "In the Minister's room next door. But it was on the desk, in exactly the same place, when I returned."

The Minister was tapping his desk with a broad, flat fingernail. "I told you, Mr. Quarles, that we know the name of the thief. We also know how and where the theft was committed. If you would kindly listen," and the Minister continued to relate the facts.

Hurley, his suspicions roused, tried to ring the Minister at Watermead, but failed to reach him. (It was discovered later that the wires had been cut.) He took an earlier train instead of the one he had planned, telling the Minister's assistant-secretary, Macpherson, to get this information through as soon as possible. A few minutes later Macpherson, still unable to get through, sent a wire in code for urgent delivery. Hurley then boarded the train—

"Tell him about Macpherson," said the irrepressible Hurley. The Minister frowned.

"That has nothing to do with it."

"It was an extremely odd thing to happen, sir." Hurley said to Quarles: "Macpherson left after sending that code message and was knocked over by a hit-and-run driver almost as soon as he was out of the door. Nearly killed — they brought him in here and he's been unconscious ever since. Chap didn't stop and nobody got his number."

"Hurley," said the Minister, and young Hurley, unabashed, said, "Sorry, sir."

Hurley boarded the train, the Minister resumed, carrying the XX-2 report in his brown briefcase. There was nobody in his carriage, but an amiable foreign gentleman sat opposite him at lunch. This gentleman must have managed to drop something potent into Hurley's coffee, for on his return to the carriage Hurley felt extraordinarily sleepy. He fell asleep and by the time he woke, he had traveled some distance beyond Watermead. On the rack above him was a brown briefcase—but it was not Hurley's briefcase, and it contained only wads of newspaper. His briefcase, with the XX-2 report in it, was gone.

The Minister told the end of this story almost with a grim relish, his eye firmly fixed on Hurley, who wriggled with embarrassment. When Hurley was shown a number of photographs of well-known agents he unhesitatingly picked out the picture of a man named Zelbec as that of the man who had sat opposite him at lunch.

"And Zelbec is a foreign agent?" The Minister nodded. "For what power?"

"My dear Mr. Quarles," the Minister said in a tone of some superiority, "Zelbec has no national patriotism of any kind. He simply works for those who pay him. He has even worked for us."

"Why don't you arrest him?"

"On what charge? Drinking coffee with Hurley?" The Minister leaned his large body forward. "But there is another reason. You understand that I can name no names, but we believe we know the power that most likely is employing Zelbec. Now, here is the interesting thing: we also have means of knowing—positive knowledge, mind you—that the XX-2 report has not yet reached them. Even more: Zelbec has not been in touch with them, nor with anyone else likely to be interested. For some reason of his own, he is playing a waiting game. That gives us a chance to send somebody to see him. Since the prime purpose of such a visit would be to regain the document—by any means that seem suitable, Mr. Quarles— obviously the emissary cannot be official." He coughed. "The responsible authorities have advised me that I could have no better unofficial agent than yourself." Quarles nodded agreement with the remark. "But you must understand that you will have no status and that you can be given no protection. I can assure you, however, that your services will not be forgotten."

"One thing strikes me," said Quarles. "Why doesn't Zelbec make half a dozen copies of the XX-2 report and sell them in half a dozen places?"

"Because he wants to stay alive," the Minister said grimly. "Well, Mr. Quarles—"

Again young Hurley was unable to repress himself.

"The burglary, sir. You haven't told him about the burglary."

"Nothing to do with it," the Minister said impatiently.

Quarles asked, "What burglary?"—and it was Hurley who replied.

"Last night—just after midnight—somebody tried to get in here— not into the offices, but into the living quarters. Cut a pane of glass and came in through the window. Fortunately the night watchman was alert and spotted the chap before he could do any damage. Didn't catch him, though."

The Minister looked rather ostentatiously at his watch, and shot out a hand. "Good luck, Mr. Quarles."

The agent Zelbec, a squat man with powerful shoulders, a completely bald head and an almost perpetual smile, lived in a neat semi-detached house at Worcester park. He was in the garden pruning rose bushes when Quarles pushed open the little wooden gate. Quarles had decided that the element of surprise was not important. He had telephoned for an appointment, mentioning "a certain document," and Zelbec led him inside the house where a pretty girl, introduced as the foreign agent's daughter, gave them iced coffee. Quite bluntly Quarles stated his case: Zelbec was in possession of a document; what was he prepared to accept for it?

"Permit me to ask, Mr. Quarles, for whom are you acting?"

Quarles sipped his iced coffee. "There is no reason why I should conceal from you that I am representing the British Government."

"And supposing I am in possession of this document—which I do not admit for a moment, you understand—what can you offer for it?"

"What would you say to a hundred thousand pounds?"

Behind the smile Zelbec seemed disturbed. "You mean that?"

"Certainly. You don't suppose," Quarles chuckled, "that I have brought the money with me. But I can obtain it in two hours. Of course, you have the document?"

There was the faintest possible hesitation before Zelbec replied, "Of course."

"And you will let me see it?" Zelbec shook his bald head. "My dear Mr. Zelbec, you can satisfy yourself that I am unarmed. I will then stand with my hands above my head and you can cover me with the revolver which I see is unsettling the fit of your jacket. All I ask is that you let me see the document in question."

Zelbec wiped perspiration away from his forehead: "No," he said. And then: "Is it that important to you?"

"You should know the importance of the document, Mr. Zelbec. Or don't you know?" Quarles said tauntingly, "Are you *unable* to show it?"

The smile on Zelbec's face was suddenly wiped out. The revolver Quarles had mentioned was in his hand. "Get out," he said.

"Thank you." Quarles stood up. "You have been most helpful."

He got out.

The Minister contemplated Quarles with no particular friendliness. "You have not got the report?" Quarles shook his head. "You have failed?" Quarles shook his head again, and said to young Hurley, "Why are you wearing a black tie?"

"Poor old Macpherson—remember I told you he was knocked over by a hit-and-run driver—he died this morning."

"Died!" Quarles said. "What have you done with his clothes? The ones he was wearing at the time of the accident?"

"Why, I don't know —"

"Where's his room?"

A bewildered Hurley led Quarles up two flights of stairs and into a room where something lay on a bed covered with a sheet. On a chair was a blood-stained, gray suit. Quarles felt in it rapidly. "There should be — ah, yes, here it is. A secret pocket in the lining." He took a knife from his pocket. "And here—" he slit the lining and produced a long envelope, "—is the XX-2 report."

Hurley gasped and looked at the thing on the bed. "But *Macpherson*—"

"Yes," said Quarles. "Macpherson."

"It was a simple but ingenious plot," Quarles said to a remarkably subdued Hurley and an attentive Minister, "with two strings to it. First of all, there was Macpherson, prepared with an envelope, all ready to make the substitution here if possible; then there was Zelbec, if Macpherson failed.

"But Macpherson didn't fail. The XX-2 report was stolen by him, and the other envelope substituted, while Hurley was occupied with that telephone call. Then to remove suspicion from Macpherson, Zelbec went solemnly through the farce of doping Hurley's coffee and stealing his briefcase—thereby identifying himself as the thief. In the meantime, Macpherson went out to deliver the report — and the totally unexpected happened. He was knocked down by a car."

"But I don't see how you worked it out," Hurley said.

"Two deductions. First: if Zelbec had the report, why hadn't it already reached the power for whom he was acting? Could it be because he *didn't* have it? That something had gone wrong? To test this, I offered Zelbec a fantastic sum of money for the document — *providing he could produce it*! If he were really holding it to sell to the highest bidder, as you suggested, my offer of a hundred thousand pounds must tempt him. But he could not produce the report. And, as you knew positively, he hadn't passed it on. Now to the basis for the second deduction. I asked myself: who else could have stolen it? It could have been Hurley." Hurley started. "But if Hurley had stolen the report and faked being drugged, there was no reason why he shouldn't have already passed it on by the time I was called in. So I was left with only one answer to my questions: who could (a) have stolen the report, and (b) have been unable, through some unforeseen event, to pass it on? I remembered Macpherson's accident, I remembered the attempt at burglary—and I knew that logically the report must be somewhere in Macpherson's clothing. And there it was."

"One thing you haven't explained, Mr. Quarles," the Minister said. "Who was the hit-and-run driver?"

"Considering the circumstances," Quarles said, "I think we might say his name was Providence."

THE SPY AND THE BERMUDA CIPHER

Edward D. Hoch

RAND WAS AWAKENED at four in the morning by a disheveled Frank Malley, who stood above his cot like some dark angel of judgment. "Telephone, Rand. It's Inspector Stephens of Scotland Yard. He says he has to talk with you and nobody else."

Rand groaned and rolled over. "In the middle of the night?" He'd known Stephens casually for years, but the man had never phoned him in the dead of night.

Rand roused himself with a sigh and felt his way across the darkened office to the telephone, then waited while the call was switched to his line. Outside, fog was rising from the Thames.

"Hello?"

"Rand?"

"Yes." He recognized the familiar harshness of the Inspector's voice. "What is it, Stephens?"

"I tried to reach you at your flat."

"I've been sleeping in the office this week. Busy time. What's so urgent?"

"A mess, Rand. You'd better come down."

"Down where? What is it?"

"We have a dead man here. He may be Jimmy King from your department."

"My God!" Rand steadied himself against the desk, wide-awake now. "How did it happen?"

"It would be better if you saw for yourself. I can have a car pick you up in five minutes."

"Very well." He hung up and dressed quickly. Then he hurried down to the central decoding room where Malley and the others were working

417

through the night. "How's it going?" he asked.

Malley shrugged. He was a big Irishman who liked his work. "Nothing yet. We're trying some transpositions now."

Rand glanced up at the blackboards with their solid rows of meaningless letters. "What time did King go off duty?"

"A little before midnight, I think. What's wrong?"

"I'll tell you later," Rand said. He went downstairs to wait for the police car.

The ride through the dim, nearly deserted city was something of a nightmare. They followed the river east toward Greenwich, and here the fog was thickest, obscuring even the outline of the road ahead.

"What's the trouble?" Rand asked the uniformed driver. "What happened?"

"I wouldn't know, sir."

"Was it an automobile accident?"

"I don't think so, sir."

Finally they stopped behind two other police cars at a dark blur of a house, almost hidden from the road by a small forest of brambles and bushes. Rand knew they were somewhere in Greenwich, and the sound of groaning foghorns told him the river was not far away.

He followed a constable up the steps and into a dimly lit hallway. They walked down it to the very last door, where a group of silent men stood waiting in front of it. Rand recognized Stephens at once and shook his hand. "Sorry to get you here like this, Rand."

"That's all right, Inspector."

Stephens reached out a gloved hand and pushed open the door. Jimmy King's body was crumpled near the center of the room, his dead eyes staring at the ceiling. There was a bloody wound in his left side, near the heart. But as Rand's eyes left the body they took in the room itself, and he felt his breathing quicken. The room was lined with bookcases that held a large assortment of encyclopedias and atlases and leather-bound textbooks. And on top of the bookcases, spaced evenly around the room some six feet above the floor, were 24 clocks.

"Clocks?" Rand asked.

The Scotland Yard man nodded glumly. "It looks as if his time ran out."

Hastings was at his desk in Security by nine o'clock, eyeing Rand distastefully across a desk already littered with the raw materials of a day's work. "What is this business with King?" he asked. "He was one of your people, wasn't he?"

Rand nodded. King had joined the Department of Concealed Communications two years earlier, when he was fresh out of college. He was bright and quick to learn, and had proved especially good with transposition ciphers.

"What was he working on?" Hastings wanted to know.

"The same thing as everyone else in Double-C, the Bermuda Cipher."

"You haven't cracked that one yet?"

Rand shook his head. "Day and night for a week. I've even been sleeping in the office." The Bermuda Cipher had been picked ten days earlier by a joint U.S.-British listening post near the Russian border. It was a long message, apparently destined for certain Russian agents operating in the London area. The first word of the message, in Russian plaintext, had been *Bermuda*. It was followed by 346 letter-groups of five characters each. They had been sent over standard teletype lines from Moscow to Paris, then hand-delivered to someone in London. It was not the first such message. A previous one, from London to Moscow, had been headed with the Russian word for *Hong Kong*. They'd had no luck deciphering that one, either.

"All right," Hastings said, "he was working on the Bermuda Cipher. Anything else? Anything that might have taken him to that house in Greenwich?"

"Nothing," Rand told him. "What have you learned about the owner?"

"The property is owned by the estate of a deceased manufacturer. It was rented eighteen months ago by a man named John April. The neighbors describe him as something of an eccentric. He's tall and middle-aged, with bushy hair and a little beard."

"He's an eccentric, all right," Rand agreed. "He had twenty-four clocks in the room where Jimmy's body was found."

"Clocks?"

Rand nodded. "One for each of the twenty-four time zones of the world. They were set an hour apart, to show the time anywhere on the planet. I suppose the location of the house in Greenwich must have given him the idea. Greenwich Mean Time is the standard for the world, of course."

Hastings pursed his lips distastefully. "Did Stephens tell you how they happened to find the body?"

"They had a phone call from a girl at three o'clock this morning. She said only that there'd been a killing at the Greenwich address and then hung up."

"The neighbors saw nothing?"

"In the middle of the night, with that fog? Not a thing."

"Find anything interesting in the house?"

"I'm going back for another look this afternoon, " Rand said. "What I saw wasn't much. Cheap furnishings, probably left by the owner. The murder room was the only one of interest. Apparently it was used as a study of some sort. Stephens' people are searching it, of course."

"What about the twenty-four clocks? Did they all have the correct time?"

Rand allowed himself a slight smile. "Right to the minute. The clocks are numbered from One to Twenty-four. Clock Number One has the correct time for London, Paris and Berlin, which is the same since we adopted British Standard Time in '68. Clock Number Two is an hour later and shows the time in Athens, Jerusalem, and Cairo."

Hastings leaned back in his chair, looking unhappy. "Why should your man King be murdered in a room with twenty-four clocks?"

"I don't even know what he was doing in the house. When we discover that, we'll be a long way toward an answer."

"I want you to get to the bottom of this thing, Rand. If King was involved in anything subversive, it might endanger your whole department."

Rand rose to leave. He'd had enough of Hastings for one morning. "What's subversive about getting killed?"

"You at least must admit that the manner of his death was in extremely bad taste."

Rand turned and left the office without further comment.

He went down to the decoding room where Frank Malley was working at the blackboards. "Time to go home, Frank. The day crew can take over."

The Irishman sighed. "Not a thing yet. And I feel I'm so near!"

"What have you done so far?"

"I keep thinking it should be a modified Vigenere. That's always been a favorite with the Russians. The message uses letters instead of numbers, but I think I've figured that part of it. Only the first ten letters of the Russian alphabet are used. They easily transpose into the numbers one through zero. The trouble with a Vigenere, though, is that a key word or key number is needed for the solution."

Rand scanned the blackboard quickly. "What about Bermuda as the key word?"

"Tried it first thing. Nothing."

Rand had been doing Vigeneres and Nihilist ciphers while Malley was still in grade school. Somehow the look of this was different. "I think you're on the wrong track," he said. "But keep at it if you want to. I'll be back to help out the day men as soon as I can."

He went up to his office and glanced quickly through the morning's mail. But he was unable to concentrate on it, unable to think of anything but Jimmy King's outstretched body. He stood for a time at the window, watching the almost imperceptible movement of Big Ben's minute hand across the river. The fog had lifted, and was now replaced by bright May sunshine.

He phoned Inspector Stephens and learned they had just completed the autopsy on King. "As we thought, a knife wound in the side. A long slender blade that went through the heart. Perhaps something like a sword cane."

"Time of death?"

"Between two and three, as near as we can figure."

Rand hung up and pondered some more. King had left Double-C just before midnight, and two or three hours later he'd been killed in a house in Greenwich. Why had he gone there? To meet the girl who had phoned Scotland Yard?

He went out to the dead man's desk in the main office, ignoring the stares of the secretaries, and began to go through King's drawers. There were few personal items—a packet of matches from a gambling club, a few small coins, a notebook of telephone numbers. Rand paused at this last and leafed through the pages.

Several girls' names were listed, with phone numbers. He was sorry he hadn't known King better outside of office hours. As it was, the names meant nothing to him.

He dropped the address book into his pocket and went back to the decoding room. "Frank, did Jimmy King ever mention any girls to you?"

"Not to me. He was all business."

Rand grunted and went over to the blackboard. "A number cipher of some sort," he decided, studying the number-groups which had now replaced the previous letter-groups. "But not necessarily a Vigenere."

"Any ideas?"

Rand smiled. "Lots of them." He reached for the chalk.

But two hours later he gave up in disgust and left the building.

Inspector Stephens led Rand down the Greenwich hallway to the room at the end. "And this is where we found the body."

"I remember," Rand said. He gazed again over the faces of the 24 clocks, each with its own number and identifying card. "What do you think this room was used for?"

The Scotland Yard man shrugged. "A study, I suppose."

Rand glanced over the shelves of books. There was a complete set of the Encyclopaedia Britannica, a number of atlases, some textbooks in forensic medicine, and even a leather-bound edition of Dickens. "What do you make of the books?" he asked Stephens.

"We've been through them. Everything but the Britannica apparently came from the sale of an estate. There's a bookplate in each one—the same bookplate. We checked out—the name's meaningless."

Rand opened a couple of books at random, studying the faded bookplate of some long-dead collector. "Odd. They don't even seem read."

"Just for show."

"Are the clocks for show too?" He replaced the books and turned back to Stephens. "Any lead on the girl who phoned?"

"None," Stephens replied.

"Or the missing Mr. April?"

"Not really. The neighbors confirm that he carried a cane. Could have been the murder weapon."

Rand nodded. "Jimmy confronted April in this room and April killed him. The girl with Jimmy called Scotland Yard. Simple. If only we had April."

"He left some clothing in an upstairs closet, but nothing that can be traced. We know he was about the same size and weight as the dead man, and the neighbors put April's age at around fifty. But that's all we've got. The beard could be a fake."

Rand looked again at the 24 clocks surrounding them. "I wonder why anyone would want to know the time in every major city of the world?"

"The man was an eccentric. He lived in Greenwich, so he had twenty-four clocks."

"Perhaps," Rand said. Once more he studied the numbered cards below each clock. Some cards listed only one city, while others carried the names of several. Clock Number 5 was tagged *Karachi*, while Clock Number 8 had *Canton, Hong Kong, Manila*. On Clock Number 20 he found the names of *Bermuda, Caracas, Halifax*. The final clock, Number 24, said *Dakar, Dublin*.

He looked again at the card for Clock Number 20, remembering the Bermuda Cipher. But after a time he could only sigh and walk away.

At eight o'clock that evening the girl phoned his apartment. Her voice was low and husky, and he knew at once that this was the one. "Mr. Rand?"

"Speaking"

"I was a friend of Jimmy's."

"Oh?"

"I must talk to you. I have some information about his death."

"All right."

"Where can we meet?"

"You're welcome to come up here."

"No. Your place might be watched."

"My phone might be tapped too. Did you think of that?"

"I had to take the chance. Can you meet me at Battersea Park? At the entrance to the amusement area?"

"When?"

"Is nine too soon?"

"I'll be there. How will I know you?"

She hesitated. "You'll know me."

The pleasant May weather had brought out the children and the lovers, and somehow Rand felt a bit out of place lounging against the wall of a candy-stripped pavilion waiting for a girl he had never seen. Then, quite suddenly, she was there before him—and he did know her. The mouth, nose, eyes—they all belonged to Jimmy King.

"You're his sister," he said, giving words to the obvious.

She nodded. "I'm Rita. He never mentioned me?"

"Not that I remember. I'm afraid I wasn't as close to Jimmy as I might have been."

"I don't think he would have permitted it." She glanced around at the crowd of evening funseekers. "Is there some place we could go?"

Rand steered her up the walk to a little tea-and-sandwich shop beneath the trees. They took a table in the rear and waited until the elderly woman proprietor had served them.

"Now then, Miss King, what do you know about your brother's death?"

"Everything, I'm afraid. In a way I was the cause of it."

"You'd better tell me about it," Rand said grimly.

"Well, in the first place I'm twenty-seven—two years older than Jimmy was. Ever since college I've been pretty much on my own. Our parents died a few years back, leaving me enough money to get by on." She tossed her blonde hair as she spoke, in a gesture Rand found a bit too youthful for a woman of 27.

"Go on."

"In college I drifted into the wrong sort of crowd. My politics had always been liberal, and before I realized it I was involved with a Communist cell."

"No wonder Jimmy never mentioned you."

She tossed her hair again. "It could have meant his job, I suppose. But

I wasn't thinking about that. I fell in love with a man named Pete Jentor, and that was the beginning of it. He was thirty-three, married, and a member of the Party. I thought it all very worldly and daring."

"You became a Communist too?"

"Not entirely, but close enough. Until I got my senses back." She sipped her tea. "I'd been seeing Peter regularly, and I soon learned that he and a man named John April were actually Russian agents, operating a spy network in London. It was something out of a thriller!"

Rand was alert now, sensing the break he'd been hoping for. "Did you ever meet John April?"

She shook her head. "I only saw him once, at a distance, with Peter. An older man, with gray hair and a little beard. He walked with a cane."

"Yes," Rand said quietly. Then, "How did you know my name?"

"Jimmy mentioned you once when we had dinner. He said he worked on codes and things, but of course he never told me any details. Then when Peter told me that the house in Greenwich was a message center for Communist agents, I realized that my lover and my brother were working directly against each other."

"This Jentor told you it was a message center? When?"

"A month or so ago. I did nothing at first, until he told me something else. Then I decided I should tell Jimmy what I knew."

"You told your brother about the house in Greenwich? When?"

"Last night. He finished work at midnight, and I was waiting for him. I drove him there, telling him what I knew on the way. He told me to wait in the car and went in alone, through the back door."

"Then what happened?"

"We both thought the place was empty, but after about fifteen minutes I heard him scream. I was terrified, but I had to find out what happened to him. I—I found him like that. Dead."

"Who else was there?" She didn't answer and he asked the question again. "It was Jentor, wasn't it? He killed your brother."

"*No!* It was John April who did it!"

"All right. Tell me the rest."

"Peter was there, but he couldn't stop April. Before he could do anything, Jimmy was dead, stabbed with April's sword cane. April ran out. He was gone before I got inside."

"What about all those clocks? What do they mean?"

"I don't know. Peter said April was a strange man."

"So then you let Jentor escape too, before you called Scotland Yard."

"Yes," she said quietly. "I know he didn't kill my brother."

Rand reached out to grab her arm. He was afraid she would run away.

"You phoned me because you felt responsible for your brother's death." Tears were forming in the corners of her eyes.

"I took him there, to that house. And now he's dead."

"If you really want to help, you'll take me to Jentor."

"No! He'd kill me."

"Not if he loves you."

"I can't!"

"Think about it." Rand studied her tear-streaked face. "Do you have any other brothers?"

"Jimmy was the youngest of four. I guess he was always my favorite."

"Where is Jentor? What else did he say to you that suddenly made you go to Jimmy?"

"I can't tell you."

"Think about it," he said. "Think about your brother's dead body." He released her arm and watched her hurry away from the table.

Frank Malley was still at the blackboards the following morning. "I thought we had something," he told Rand. "But it was a false alarm. Fool with enough combinations and you can make words out of anything."

Rand grunted and inspected the night's work with a sinking feeling. They were no closer to cracking the Bermuda Cipher than they'd been a week earlier. "Look," he said, "we always assume that five-number groups are just that length out of custom, to aid in transmission and to disguise the real length of the individual words. But suppose the five-number groups are just that—with each group standing for one word."

"You mean a code instead of a cipher?"

"It's a possibility."

"But no group is ever repeated, even in this lengthy message. Doesn't that rule out a code?"

Rand gazed at the blackboard and thought about it. "A book code," he answered finally. "A dictionary or Bible code—one using different page numbers even when it was the same word. Look—the first two numbers are the page, the next two the line, and the last is the word in that line. You'll notice none of the groups ends in a "Could be," Malley admitted. "I considered a book code early on, but Jimmy tossed it out. Said the Russians wouldn't trust their whole message system between London and Moscow to a single book that could fall into British hands."

"Still," Rand mused, "it's worth thinking about." He was remembering the room where Jimmy had died—the room his sister described as a message center. He was especially remembering the books in it. But which one? Which one out of all those hundreds? And he thought again about the 24 clocks, each showing a different hour of the day and night.

Rand went back to his office and sorted through the morning's mail. There was a message to call Hastings with a progress report, but just then there was no progress to report—nothing but the meeting with Jimmy's sister. He sat there instead and brooded about her. Peter Jentor had told her something—something other than the fact that the Greenwich house was a Russian message center. Whatever he'd told her had caused her to phone Jimmy almost at once.

He stared gloomily out the window. Somehow the 24 clocks were a key to the Bermuda Cipher. Jimmy had seen it right away, and had been killed. The clocks and the books, the books and the clocks. But which books? If *Bermuda* referred to Clock Number 20, what then? Could the book he sought be on the shelf beneath the clock! He remembered that the books were mostly from an old estate library, mostly unread. Window dressing, Stephens had said—except for the set of Encyclopaedia Britannica.

He stared across his office at the department's own set. A to Anno, Anno to Baltic . . . .

All 24 volumes.

24.

It just might be worth one more drive out to Greenwich.

The house behind the shrubbery was as he'd left it, and he used the key that Inspector Stephens had given him. Somewhere above him a bird chirped, but otherwise the street was quiet in the May sunshine. The 24 clocks were still there, still humming their messages, but this time he barely glanced at them. He went at once to the set of the Britannica and pulled out Volume 20. He remembered the numbers in the first five-digit group: 46093. Page 46, ninth line, third word.

Chinese.

He stared at it, holding his breath.

Maybe. Just maybe.

He got on the phone and called Frank Malley at Double-C. "Frank, I'm out at the house where Jimmy King was killed. I think the book we're looking for might be an edition of the Encyclopaedia Britannica. Can you read me a few number-groups? From the beginning?"

"Sure. 46093."

"I remembered that. What's next?"

"14871."

"Page fourteen, line eighty-seven—that'll be in the second column on the page—first word."

"Got it?"

"Yes. So far it's *Chinese agents*. Keep going."

Five minutes later they had enough to be sure: *Chinese agents arriving London to establish power base for action in Middle East.* "All right," Rand said. "That's enough. Jump in a car and bring the rest of the message out here with you—I know our office Britannica is a different edition. We'll have to work here."

"I'm on my way," Malley said.

Rand hung up and lit a cigarette. The Russians, he decided, must have a great deal of patience these days to go back to using a book code. Even with the Britannica, their choice of words was limited. But the method did have the advantage of defying solution unless the precise code book was known. With 24 volumes of the encyclopedia from which to choose, detection was almost impossible.

And the clocks were merely that;—24 clocks. The secret of the code was on the cards tacked beneath each clock. If the first word of the message, in Russian plain text, was *Hong Kong*, Clock Number 8, that meant Volume 8 of the Britannica was to be used. *Bermuda* meant Clock Number 20, and therefore Volume 20. Of course they were limited to the first 99 pages of each volume, but with 24 volumes from which to choose, almost any message could be sent.

There was just one thing he needed now. Peter Jentor and the final key to Jimmy's killing. He picked up the phone and dialed Rita King's number, hoping she was there.

"Hello?"

"This is Rand, Miss King. It's very important. Do you think you could meet me at the house in Greenwich, and bring Jentor along?"

"He'd never come!"

"I think he would, if you talk to him. Tell him we just want April. If he turns April in, we'll see that he gets a break."

"Rand—"

"What is it?"

"I'm afraid for you. I've already caused Jimmy's death."

"How? What did you tell him?"

"I—"

"Tell me!" he insisted.

"Peter said—" She stopped, and he could hear her heavy breathing. "What did he say? What?"

Then the words came out in a flood. "He was drunk one night and he told me there was a spy in Jimmy's department. He told me that John April was really someone from Double-C."

There was a noise behind him at the door and Rand whirled to face the intruder. Frank Malley stood in the doorway with his briefcase. "Well," he announced, "here I am!"

Seated opposite each other at the little desk, Rand and Malley decoded the entire message. Working together it took just under an hour, and when they finished, Rand read through the lengthy message. *"Chinese agents arriving London to establish power base for action in Middle East. Chinese freighter bound for Mediterranean with cargo of rockets. Agents met Arab government officials in Aden two weeks ago. Contact regular sources for . . ."*

Rand read on to the end of the message, then tossed it to Malley. "Hastings should be happy to see this one."

"Damn right!" the Irishman replied.

Rand leaned back in his chair. "Frank, how many people are there in the department now?"

"In Double-C? Around fifty, I guess. You certainly know better than I do."

"Any problems? Any security risks?"

"How would I know? You're sure edgy today. What's up? With the message solved, you should be happy."

"It's Jimmy's murder. I was talking to his sister when you came in."

"You sure jumped a mile! Bad nerves."

Rand nodded. "She's coming over here. Maybe with a man named Peter Jentor." He watched Malley's face, but there was no change in expression.

A few moments later they heard a car stop in the street outside. "Someone's coming now," Malley said.

Rand nodded and slipped the small pistol from his pocket. After a moment the front door opened and two sets of footsteps approached down the hallway. A handsome dark-haired young man of about 30 entered, closely followed by Rita King. "I brought him," she said. "Who's this?"

Rand kept the pistol out of sight below the desk top. "Frank Malley from my office. He worked closely with your brother." He shifted his gaze to the dark-haired young man. "And you would be Peter Jentor."

"That's right." Jentor brought his hands into view, and Rand saw the slender bamboo cane for the first time. His grip tightened on the pistol. "Rita said you wanted to make a deal."

"Not exactly a deal. I want John April."

"April's gone. Out of the country."

"Is he the one who killed Jimmy King?"

Jentor hesitated only an instant. "Yes. April killed him."

"Who is John April?" Rand asked.

"A Russian agent. I don't know any more."

"Why did he kill Jimmy King?"

"King came here with Rita. He found this place, and April had to kill him."

"Why didn't you take the volumes of the encyclopedia with you?"

"The neighbors would have seen us."

Rand pressed his advantage. "In the middle of the night, in that fog? No, Jentor, the books had to be left here because there was only you to carry them away. No April, only you."

"It was April," Jentor insisted again. "He's one of your own people, Rand. One of the Double-C people."

"You told Rita that, and she brought Jimmy out here. She had a loyalty to him that she didn't have to her country."

Rita let out a soft sob, and Jentor moved forward a step to comfort her. "April killed him," Jentor repeated.

But Rand was shaking his head. "No, you did, Jentor. Only you. April couldn't have killed him because Jimmy King and John April were the same person. King was the spy in my department, but his sister never knew it."

It was then that Jentor bared his sword cane and lunged forward.

Rand's shot clipped him in the shoulder, but Jentor might have found his target with the sword cane if Inspector Stephens had not appeared in the doorway and tackled the lunging man with a flying leap. After that it was over in moments, and Jentor was handcuffed by one of Stephens' men.

"A timely arrival," Rand told the Inspector. "Thanks."

"My man watching the house called me. He said there was a lot of traffic going in."

It was Frank Malley who spoke then. "Good Lord, Rand, were you serious about Jimmy being a Red spy?"

"All too serious, I'm afraid." Rand put the pistol away as one of the detectives bandaged the flesh wound in Jentor's shoulder. "Rita was told they had a spy in my department. We have a lot of people there, but consider the evidence. April's clothes showed he was the same size as Jimmy. You told me yourself, Frank, that it was Jimmy who discouraged the idea of a book code as a solution to the Bermuda Cipher. April's grey hair and beard were an easy disguise, and no one ever saw him close up, including his sister. And consider the name—April. Jimmy King was the youngest of four brothers. With his interest in numbers and such, April—the fourth month—is exactly the kind of pseudonym he'd pick."

Rita spoke up from the sidelines. "I can't believe it. If Jimmy was working with them all the time, why would Peter kill him?"

Rand turned to the handcuffed man. "Want to tell us now?"

The dark-haired man touched his bandaged shoulder. "Why not? You know it all anyway. Rita told him about the place and brought him out here, not realizing that Jimmy was April. He went along with it, not wanting her to know the truth, but when he came in here he got the crazy idea of selling us out to the British. He was going to kill me with his sword cane, expose the message center, and become a hero. From the beginning he was only in it for the money, and suddenly the money on the other side looked better. We struggled and I killed him in self-defense."

"We'll let the courts decide that," Stephens said. "Let's go."

Rita paused at the door and turned to Rand. "Did you know it all the time?" she asked.

Not all the time, no. But ever since I talked to you I was wondering what Jimmy was doing in here for fifteen minutes before you heard his scream. The facts didn't quite fit together the way you told it, but they did fit nicely if Jimmy was the spy, having a final confrontation with Jentor."

"I lost them all, didn't I?" she said. "Jimmy and Peter both."

Rand took a final look at the clocks. "Come on," be said, taking her arm. "It's time we were going."

THE SPORTS PAGE

Isaac Asimov

"Is 'BLAIN' AN English word?" asked Mario Gonzalo, as the company of the Black Widowers sat down to their monthly banquet.

"Brain?" asked James Drake, scraping his chair toward the table and looking over the selection of bread and rolls.

"Blain," said Gonzalo sharply.

"How do you spell it?" asked Roger Halsted, who had no difficulty in deciding to take two slices of pumpernickel. He was buttering them.

"What's the difference how it's spelled?" said Gonzalo in annoyance. He placed his napkin carefully over his lightly striped and definitely pink trousers. "Spell it any way you want. Is it an English word?"

Thomas Trumbull, host for the evening, furrowed his bronzed forehead, and said, "Damn it, Mario, we've had a pretty sensible session so far. What's all this about 'blain'?"

"I'm asking you a question. Why don't you answer it?"

"All right. It's not an English word."

Gonzalo looked about the table, "Everyone agree 'blain' isn't English?"

There was a hesitant chorus of agreement. Even Emmanuel Rubin, his eyes magnified by his glasses and his straggly beard a bit shorter than usual, as though it had recently been absent-mindedly trimmed, finally muttered, "No such word."

Lawrence Pentili, who had arrived as Trumbull's guest, and who was an elderly man with sparse white hair, and with muttonchop side-whiskers grown long, as though they were announcing that hair could still be produced, smiled and said, "Never heard that word."

Only Geoffrey Avalon held his peace. Sitting bolt upright as always, he frowned and with his middle finger stirred the ice in the unfinished half of his second drink.

"All right," said Gonzalo, "we all agree it's not an English word. You can see that in a second. But *how* do you see it? Do you go through a list of all the English words you know and see that 'blain' isn't on it? Do you check the sound for familiarity? Do you . . ."

Halsted's soft voice interrupted. "No one knows how human recall works, so why ask? Even people who have theories about how the mechanism of memory works don't understand how information can be fished out once it has been inserted. Every word I use has to be recalled from my vocabulary, and each is there when I need it."

Trumbull said, "There are lots of times when you can't think of the word you want."

Halsted had just turned with satisfaction to the turtle soup that Henry, the incomparable waiter of the Black Widowers, had placed before him. He said, stuttering slightly as he often did under stress, "Yes, and that upsets you. Most people take it hard when they can't think of a word, get very upset, as though something has gone wrong that shouldn't have gone wrong. Me, I tend to stutter when I can't think of a word."

Now at last Avalon's deep baritone sounded, and dominated the table. "Well, wait now. As a matter of fact, there *is* such a word as 'blain.' It's archaic, but it's English. It's some sort of animal ailment, or blister."

"Right," said Gonzalo with satisfaction. "The word is used in the Bible in connection with the plagues of Egypt in the Book of Exodus. I knew someone here would get it. I thought it would be Manny."

Rubin said indignantly, "I thought you meant *current* English."

"I didn't say so," said Gonzalo. "Besides, it's part of the word 'chilblains,' and that's current English.

"No, it's *not*," said Rubin, heating up further, "and besides . . ."

Trumbull said, loudly, "Don't get defensive, Manny. What I want to know is how Mario knows all this. And, incidentally, we're having finnan haddie today at my request, and if anyone here doesn't like it, he can negotiate with Henry for substitutes. Well, Mario?"

Gonzalo said, "I read it in a psychology book. There's nothing that says I have to be born knowing everything, the way Manny claims he's been. I pick up knowledge by keeping my eyes and ears open. And what I want to do now is make a point. Remembering too well is dangerous."

"It's a danger you'll never face," muttered Rubin.

"I don't care," said Gonzalo. "Look, I asked a question and I got a quick and certain response from everyone here but Jeff. He was uncertain and hesitated because he remembered too much. He remembered the use of 'blain' in the Bible. Well, human beings are faced with choices every minute. There has to be a decision and the decision has to be based on what he knows. And if he knows too much, he'll hesitate."

"And so," asked Drake who, having speared some of the finnan haddie on his fork and placed it in his mouth, looked first thoughtful and then satisfied.

"So that's bad," said Gonzalo. "In the long run, what counts is a quick response and action. Even a less than good decision is better than indecision, most times. That's why human beings have evolved an imperfect memory. Forgetting has survival value."

Avalon smiled and nodded. "That's not a bad notion, Mario," he said, with, perhaps, a trace of condescension. "Have I ever told you my theory of the evolutionary value of contentiousness? In a hunting society. . . "

But Gonzalo held up both arms. "I'm not finished, Jeff. Don't you all see that's why Henry here does so much better than we do in solving the puzzles that arise from time to time? Every one of us here at the table practices being deep. . . "

"Not everybody, Mario," said Rubin, "unless you're about to start."

Gonzalo ignored him. "Henry doesn't. He doesn't gunk his mind up with irrelevant information, so he can see clearly."

Henry, who was clearing some of the excess dishes, said gently, "If I may interpose, Mr. Gonzalo, I'm afraid that whatever I do could not be done, were it not that you gentlemen usually eliminate all that would otherwise confuse me." His unlined, sixtyish face showed only imperturbable efficiency, as he next poured several refills of the white wine.

Trumbull said, "Mario, your theory is junk and, Henry, that false modesty is unbecoming to you. You have more brains than any of us do, Henry, and you know it."

"No, sir," said Henry. "With respect, the most I'll admit is that I have a faculty for seeing the obvious."

"*Because*," said Gonzalo, "you don't have the difficulty of trying to look at the obvious through layers of crud, as Manny does."

Henry bowed his head slightly and seemed almost relieved when the infuriated Rubin launched into an analysis of the value of miscellaneous knowledge to the writer, and of the fact—which he announced as such with fervor—of the equation of general intelligence with the ability to remember, recall, analyze, and synthesize.

But Pentili, the guest, seemed to have lost interest in the conversation. His eyes followed Henry thoughtfully.

Waiting for the precise moment when the desserts had been eaten and when several of the coffees were about ready for the refill, Trumbull tapped his water glass with his spoon and announced it was time for the grilling.

"Since I am host," he growled, "I am delighted to be disqualified as griller. Mario, you did all that preaching over the soup. Why don't you grill our guest?"

Gonzalo said, "Dee-lighted," and cleared his throat ostentatiously. "Mr. Pentili, how do you justify your existence?"

Pentili smiled broadly so that a round little ball of flesh bunched up over each cheekbone, giving him the look of a beardless Santa Claus in mufti. "Thank heaven, I no longer have to. I am retired and I have either already justified my existence or have already failed."

"And in the days when you might have been justifying it, what were you doing to make your existence possible?"

"Breathing. But if you mean, how did I make my living, I served Uncle Sam in the same fashion, more or less, that Tom does."

"You were a cipher expert?"

"No, but I was involved in intelligence."

"And *that* justifies your existence?" put in Rubin.

"Shall we argue the point?" said Pentili agreeably.

"No," said Trumbull. "It's been argued fifty times. Go ahead, Mario."

Gonzalo looked eager. "The last time Tom had a guest here, he had a problem. Do you have one?"

"At the present time, certainly not. I leave problems to Tom and the others these days. I'm a more or less happy observer. But I have a question, if I may ask one?"

"Go ahead."

Pentili said, "You had said that Henry—who, I take it, is our waiter . . ."

Trumbull said, "Henry is a valued member of the Black Widowers and the best of us all."

"I see. But I take it that Henry solves puzzles. What kind?"

A shade of uneasiness crossed Henry's face but disappeared almost at once. He said, "Some questions arise at one time or another on the occasion of these banquets, sir, and the members have been able to propose answers."

"*You* have proposed them," said Gonzalo energetically.

Avalon raised his hand. "I protest. This is not a fit subject for discussion. Everything said here is entirely confidential, and we ought not to talk about previous sessions in front of our guest."

"No, no," said Pentili, shaking his head. "I ask for no confidences. It just occurred to me that, if it were appropriate to do so, I could pose a problem for Henry."

Gonzalo said, "I thought you said you didn't have a problem."

"I don't," said Pentili, twinkling, "but I once had a problem, many years ago, and it was never solved to my satisfaction. It is of no importance any longer, you understand, except as an irritating grain of sand inside the tissues of my curiosity."

"What was that, Larry?" asked Trumbull with sudden interest.

"You had just entered the department, Tom. It didn't involve you—or almost anyone, but me."

"May we hear it?" said Gonzalo.

"As I said," said Pentili, "it's entirely unimportant and I assure you I had not meant to bring it up. It was just that when mention was made specifically of Henry's facility with . . . ."

Henry said softly, "If I may be allowed a word, sir. I am not the expert at solving puzzles that Mr. Gonzalo is kind enough to think me. There have been occasions when, indeed, I have been helpful in that direction but that has only been when the membership has considered the problem and eliminated much of what is not essential. If, in that case, some simple thread is left exposed, I can pick it up as well as another, but I can do no more than that."

"Oh." Pentili looked abashed. "Well, I'm perfectly willing to present the problem to the membership generally."

"In that case, sir," said Avalon, "we are all ears."

Pentili, having finished his brandy and having declined a refill, said, "I will ask you, gentlemen, to cast your mind back to 1961. John F. Kennedy was in the first months of his tragically abbreviated Administration, and an invasion of Cuba by Cuban exiles was being planned. Kennedy had inherited those plans and had refused to chance the repercussions of having the invaders granted American air support. He was assured by intelligence reports that it was quite certain the Cuban populace would rise in support of the invaders. A free Cuban Government would quickly be formed, and at *its* request the United States might move.

"It is easy, in hindsight, to realize how wretchedly we had underestimated Castro's hold on his army and his people, but at the time we saw everything through a pinkly optimistic haze. You all know what happened. The invaders landed at the Bay of Pigs and were met at once by well-organized Castroites. The Cuban people did *not* rise, and in the absence of effective air support, the invaders were all either killed or taken. It was a tragic affair for them and an embarrassing fiasco for the United States. Kennedy accepted the responsibility since he was President and had given the final kickoff signal. Although others were clearly more to blame, no one stepped forward to take his medicine. As Kennedy said, 'Victory has a thousand fathers, but defeat is an orphan.'"

Rubin, who had been staring at his coffee cup, said suddenly, "I remember that. At the time, Kennedy said it was an old saying, but no one, to my knowledge, has ever discovered the source. It will have to go into the quotation books with Kennedy's name under it."

Avalon cleared his throat. "A defeat or even a humiliation does not stand alone in time. Smarting from the Bay of Pigs, Kennedy was determined not to submit again, so the next year he faced down the Soviets on the Cuban missiles affair and won for us our greatest victory of the Cold War."

Rubin said, with vehemence, "And victories don't stand alone, either. President Johnson, determined not to appear less *macho* than his predecessor, led us step by step into the quagmire of Vietnam, and this led to our. . . "

"Come on, you idiots," shouted Trumbull. "This isn't a contemporary history class. We're listening to Larry Pentili."

In the sudden silence that followed, Pentili said, with a bit of gloominess flitting over his face, "Actually, it is all pertinent. You see, the real villain of the Bay of Pigs affair was faulty intelligence. Had we known quite accurately what the situation was in Cuba, Kennedy would have canceled the invasion or given it effective air support. In that case, there would have been no fiasco to give either Castro or Khrushchev the false notion that they could get away with establishing missile sites ninety miles off Florida and then, if we accept Rubin's psychohistorical interpretation, there would have been no Vietnam.

"And in my opinion, information need *not* have been faulty. We had one operative who had been planted in Cuba and who was back in Washington some half a year before the Bay of Pigs with reports he had been unable to radio out. . . . "

"Why not?" said Gonzalo, at once.

"Because he was playing a difficult role that he dared not risk. He was a Soviet agent, you see, and his whole value to us was that the Soviets allowed him to travel to the United States freely and to circulate in Washington freely because they thought he was spying on us for them."

"Maybe he was," said Drake, peering through his cigarette smoke."How can you tell which side a double agent is fooling?"

"Maybe both sides," said Halsted.

"Maybe," conceded Pentili, "but the Soviets never discovered anything more than we deliberately had this Russian of ours reveal. On the other hand, through him we learned a great many useful things that the Soviets could not conceivably have wanted us to know."

"I wonder," said Rubin, with something more than a trace of sarcasm in his voice, "if the Soviets might not have reasoned in precisely the same way."

"I don't think so," said Pentili, "for in the end it was the Soviets who eliminated him and not we. How they caught on to him, how he had given himself away, we never discovered, but it was clear that the Soviets finally came around to agreeing with us that he was essentially our Russian and not theirs. Too bad, but, of course, from their standpoint he was a traitor. In reverse, we'd have done the same thing."

Avalon said, "Frankly, I would hesitate to trust a traitor. A man who betrays once can betray again."

"Yes," said Pentili, "and for that reason he never knew anything more than it was considered safe for him to know. Yet I, for one, *did* trust him. It was always my opinion that he chose us because he came to believe in the American ideal. During the three years he worked with us, he never gave us any ground for concern.

"His name was Stepan and he was an earnest man, rather humorless, who went about his task with a conscious dedication. He was determined to learn idiomatic English and to speak it with a general American accent. He was therefore a faithful listener to news programs not for their contents but for the sanitized pronunciations of men like Walter Cronkite. To develop his vocabulary, Stepan worked at crossword puzzles, with indifferent success, and was very fond of the word game Scrabble, at which he usually lost."

Avalon said, "Scrabble is that game that involves small wooden tiles with letters on them out of which you form words on a board?"

"It has its complications. . . . " began Rubin.

Pentili overrode him. "You have the essentials, Mr. Avalon. I mention the game because it has something to do with the problem. Stepan never achieved his aim fully. He retained his Russian accent, and his vocabulary was never as unlimited as he would have liked it to be, but we encouraged him because we felt it to be a sign of increasing dedication to us. The Soviets probably supported it because they felt it would make him a more efficient spy on us and for them."

"They may have been right," said Rubin dryly.

"*They* killed him, remember," said Pentili. "In September 1960, Stepan arrived from Cuba. We had only the most indirect notion of his activities in that country, but his initial guarded contact with us gave us every reason to think he had information of the most vital importance. It remained only to get that information in such a way as not to blow his cover.

"In very indirect fashion, we arranged to make contact with him in a hotel room. The trouble was that, although neither he nor we knew it at the time, his cover was already blown. Someone got to him before we did, and when our man finally arrived, Stepan was dead; knifed. What it was he meant to tell us, we never learned."

Avalon ran his finger thoughtfully around the rim of his long-empty coffee cup. "Are you certain, sir, that he was killed by the Soviets? We live in a violent society and people are killed every day for a variety of reasons."

Pentili sighed. "To have an agent killed just at the point of delivery of a vital message, and to have that killing come about through some unrelated cause, is asking too much of coincidence. Besides, the Washington police were bound to treat it as an ordinary killing, and we helped them since the man was a Soviet national. Nothing was turned up, no theft, no plausible motive arising out of his private life. There were no traces left behind of any kind; an ordinary culprit would have left some.

"Second, there was some interest in the murder on the part of the Soviet embassy, but not enough. They were just a shade too easily satisfied. Third, certain avenues of information, which would have remained open had Stepan been in the clear and had he died for reasons not connected with his work, were closed. No, Mr. Avalon, there was no doubt in my mind that he died the death of an agent."

Gonzalo, suddenly aware of crumbs defacing the fine cut of his lapel, brushed at himself delicately and said, "Where's the puzzle, though, Mr. Pentili? You mean who, killed him? Now? After all these years?"

"No, it doesn't matter a hippie's curse who killed him. Even after he was knifed, though, Stepan must have tried to get across *something*, perhaps enough to give us the essential core of what we needed, but if so, he failed. I have been wondering frequently, and painfully, in the years since my retirement whether a greater shrewdness or persistence on our part might not have saved our country some of its losses in the years since that murder."

Halsted said, "I'm sorry if this question is embarrassing, Mr. Pentili, but was your retirement forced on you because of Stepan's death?"

"You mean that I might have been fired as punishment for not having kept him alive? No. The episode did not reflect any discredit on me and I retired only a few years ago, in the ordinary course of events, with a generous pension, the expressed esteem of my confreres, and an award handed me by President Nixon. In fact, danger came to me not through Stepan's death but through my insistence that he was trying to tell us something significant. The department dismissed the matter; erroneously, in my opinion; and I was more or less forced to dismiss it, too. But I have wondered about it since; all the more so, since my retirement."

Gonzalo said, "What was Stepan's way of getting across the information?"

Pentili said, "We are quite certain that Stepan had no documents on him, no letters, no written message. He didn't work that way. He had what any traveler might be expected to have in a hotel room. He had clothes, toiletries, and so on, in a single suitcase, and an extra suit in a garment bag. There were signs of a search, but it was a skillful one that left a minimum of disarray. Something may have been taken away, of course, but if so, we cannot tell what it was, and that has nothing to do with the problem.

"The only items that might not be considered perfectly routine were a crossword puzzle book, with approximately half the puzzles worked out completely or nearly completely in Stepan's own handwriting, the Scrabble set he always carried with him . . ."

Rubin interrupted. "So he could strike up games with occasional strangers?"

Pentili said, "No. He had the habit of playing four-handed games with himself when he had nothing to do and using a pocket dictionary to help. He said there was nothing better for developing a vocabulary. The dictionary was there, in his jacket pocket, with the jacket hanging in the closet.

"He was knifed while standing, apparently, and that was the one flaw in an otherwise flawless performance, for he was not killed outright. The killer or killers had to leave rapidly, and they left a spark of life behind. Stepan had collapsed just next to the desk and, when they were gone, he managed to pull himself upright. On the desk was a newspaper—the *Washington Post*, by the way—and the Scrabble set.

"He opened the top desk drawer and pawed about for the pen. He found it and tried to write with it but it was dry—a common situation in hotel rooms—so he dropped it to the floor. His own pen was in his inner jacket pocket at the other end of the room, and he knew he couldn't make it there. He had a couple of minutes to live and he had to make use of whatever objects were on the desk.

"The newspaper, at the time of the knifing, was folded as it had been when he had bought it a hour earlier, but he . . ."

Halsted said, "How did you find out all this?"

"Circumstantial. I assure you we are expert at this. The desk drawer was open; the pen, quite dry, was on the floor. Most of all, Stepan was bleeding, partly from his right hand, which he had instinctively used to try to ward off the weapon, and his own blood marked his every movement and everything he had touched.

"As I say, he unfolded the newspaper to the sports page. He then lifted the top of the box of the Scrabble set, removed the board, and managed to take out five letters, which he put in the wooden holder used for the purpose. Then he died. The letters were 'e,' 'p,' 'o,' 'c,' and 'k.'

"In that order?" asked Drake.

"In that order, left to right."

"Epock is a period of time in history, isn't it?" said Gonzalo.

"It's a point in time," said Rubin, "marked by some significant historical event and later used as a reference, but it's spelled e-p-o-c-h. It ends with an 'h.'

"Making a mistake in spelling under the conditions isn't surprising," said Gonzalo defensively. "The man was dying and maybe he could hardly see. Maybe the 'k' looked like an 'h' to him. Besides, he was a Russian, and he might not have known how to spell the word."

Pentili said, with a trace of impatience, "That is not really the point. 'Epock' or 'epoch,' 'k' or 'h,' what does it mean?"

Avalon said, "Actually, Tom is the code expert. . . . "

Trumbull shrugged. "Larry has come to *you* men. You work at it. If anything occurs to me, I'll interrupt."

Avalon said, "Would you have a code book, Mr. Pentili, in which 'epoch' stands for some phrase or sentence? Is it a recognized code?"

"I assure you that neither 'epock' nor 'epoch' means anything in any code of which Stepan had knowledge. No, the answer had to be in the sports page, and if the letters had any meaning it was in connection with the sports page."

"Why do you say that?" asked Halsted.

"Let me explain further," said Pentili—then interrupted himself to say, "I *will* have a little more brandy, Henry, if you don't mind. You're listening to all this, I hope."

"Yes, sir," said Henry.

"Good!" said Pentili. "Now in the ordinary course of events, Stepan might have, in an emergency, transmitted information more densely—that is, with the greatest information per symbol—by transmitting a number. Each number could represent a given phrase. That's an inflexible message, of course, since the proper phrase might not exist, but a number might give a fair approximation, and in the extremity of approaching death, he could do no more. He opened the paper to a page on which there were numbers and where one number might be significant."

Halsted said, "He might merely have wanted a sheet of paper to write on."

"He had nothing to write with," said Pentili.

"His blood."

Pentili twisted his mouth distastefully. "He might have done that but he didn't. He might not even have been aware he was bleeding. And if he wanted to do that, why open the paper? The front page would have been enough."

"He might have opened it at random," said Halsted stubbornly.

"Why? He was a professional. He had lived with death for years and he knew that the information he carried was more important than his life. What he did would have to be to pass on that information."

Trumbull said, "Come on, Roger, you're being trivial."

Pentili said, "It's all right, Tom. As a matter of fact, the general opinion in the department was that there was no puzzle; that Gregory's attempt at the point of death meant nothing; that whatever he tried to do had failed. I was the only one who wanted to follow it up, and I must admit I never succeeded in translating the message."

"The trouble was, you see, that he had opened to the sports page. About the only page in the paper that could have been more littered with numbers was the financial page. How can we look at all the numbers on the sports page and select the one that was significant?"

Avalon said, "If we assume that Gregory knew what he was doing, then despite all the numbers, the particular significant number must have been obvious, or should have been. For instance, all the numbers on the page may have had no meaning at all. It may have been the number of the page that counted."

"First thought! However, it was page 32, and 32 stood for 'Cancel previous message.' There was no previous message, and that was not it."

Avalon said, "What was on the sports page?"

"I can't reproduce it from memory, of course, and I don't have a Xerox copy to show you. That page dealt with baseball almost entirely, for the baseball season was in its last few weeks. It had baseball standings on it, the box scores of particular games, some pitching statistics."

"And was Stepan knowledgeable about baseball?"

"To a limited extent," said Pentili. "He was professionally interested in America, reading American history avidly, for instance, so he would be interested in the national game. You remember World War II movies with their cliché that any Nazi spy, no matter how cleverly schooled, would always give himself away by his ignorance of last year's World Series? Stepan intended not to be caught in this fashion, but he could scarcely make himself an expert."

"Well," said Avalon stiffly, "if ignorance of baseball is the hallmark of the Nazi spy, I had better turn myself in. I know nothing of the game."

"Nor I," said Drake, shrugging.

Gonzalo said, "Come on, nobody can read the papers, watch television, or talk to people without knowing something about the game. You guys are just indulging in snobbery. Why don't we figure this out? What kind of a number ought it to be? How many digits?"

Pentili said, "At least two digits, possibly three. Not more than three."

"All right. If Gregory was no baseball expert, he would have to pick something simple and obvious. Batting averages are in three digits. Maybe there was some batting average that made the headlines."

Pentili shook his head. "There were no numbers in the headlines. We would have been on to that like a shot. I assure you that nowhere on the page, *nowhere*, was there any one number that stood out from the rest. No, gentlemen, I am quite convinced that the sports page by itself was insufficient, that Gregory in his last moments used it only because there was nothing else he could do. The number was there but there was no way of picking it out without a hint—so he prepared one."

Rubin said, "You mean the Scrabble letters? 'Epock'?"

"Yes."

"I don't see what kind of hint that might be."

Gonzalo said, "He might not have finished, you know. He managed to get five letters out and then died. Maybe he gave up on the sports page and was trying to spell out the number, only he didn't finish. If he wanted to write 'one hundred twenty-two,' for instance, that would take a lot more than five letters."

Rubin said, "Are you telling us there's a number that begins with 'epock?" He rolled his eyes upward in exasperation.

Gonzalo said, "The letters don't have to be in order. In Scrabble, you're always arranging and rearranging your letters—like in anagrams. After he had all the letters he wanted, he'd have rearranged them into the number he was spelling. He died too soon."

Halsted said, "Sorry, Mario, that's not possible. The written forms of the numbers have an odd distribution of letters. For instance" (his mathematician's eyes gleamed), "do you know that you can write all the numbers from zero to nine hundred ninety-nine without using the letter 'a'?"

"So?" said Gonzalo. "There's no 'a' in 'epock.'"

"No, but there's a 'p' and a 'c'. Write out the numbers in order and you won't come to a 'p' till you reach—uh—one heptillion, which has twenty-four digits. And you won't reach a 'c' till one octillion, which has twenty-seven. Of course, that's in the American system of numeration. In the British system . . ."

"You made your point," growled Trumbull.

Rubin said, "He could still have been incomplete, though. He may have given up on the sports page altogether, fresh, and intended to take out those five letters plus a 't,' rearranging the whole to spell 'pocket.' There may have been something in his pocket that carried the message. . . ."

"There wasn't," interposed Pentili curtly.

"It may have been removed after the knifing and he was too far gone to realize it."

"That's a second-order conjecture. You assume an additional 't' and then a pocket-picking as well to account for it. Unlikely!"

"Might 'pocket' have been a code word?" said Rubin.

"No!" Pentili waved his hand left and right, palm outward, in a gesture of impatience. "Gentlemen, it is amusing to listen to your conjectures but you are moving in the wrong direction. Habit has a firm hold even at the moment of death. Stepan was a neat person, and when death came he had his hand on the top of the Scrabble box and was clearly making an effort to replace it. There is no question in my mind that he had taken out all the tiles he was going to. We have these five letters, no more."

Halsted said, "He would not have had time to rearrange the letters."

Pentili sighed. "There are exactly 120 different ways in which 5 different letters can be arranged. Not one of the rearrangements is an English word, any more than 'blain' is," he smiled briefly: "One arrangement is 'kopec,' which is a small Russian coin usually spelled 'kopek,' but that has no significance that any of us could see. No, there must be a reference to a number."

Avalon said suddenly, "Was there anything on the sports page besides sports? I mean, were there advertisements, for instance?"

Pentili looked with concentration into the middle distance as though he were concentrating on an invisible sheet of paper. He said, thoughtfully, "No advertisements. There was, however, a bridge column."

"Ah, could the letters have referred to that? See here, Mr. Pentili, I am not a bridge buff in the real sense, but I play the game and sometimes read a bridge column. They invariably have a hand shown under the heads, 'north,' 'south,' 'east' and 'west.' Each hand has its cards listed according to suit, 'spades,' 'hearts,' 'diamonds,' 'clubs,' and under each suit the cards are listed in descending order of value."

"Well?" said Pentili stonily.

"So consider 'epock.' The 'e' may stand for 'east,' the 'c' for 'clubs.' East's hand may have five clubs, which may, as an example, be J, 8, 4,

3, 2. The Jack and the 3 are excluded because they are occupied by letters that do not stand for digits. That leaves 842 as your code."

Pentili looked at him with some surprise. He said, "I must admit that I've never thought of this. When I am back in my office I will look at the bridge hand. Amazing, Mr. Avalon, I would not have thought a new notion could have been advanced at this stage of the game."

Avalon said, flushing a little, "I can but do my poor best, sir."

"However," said Pentili, "I don't believe your suggestion can be useful. Poor Stepan was not, to my knowledge, a bridge player, and it seems to me only a monomaniac on the subject would have tried to use bridge for a code like that at the point of death. It has to be very simple. He might have used the page number as the code, but I suspect he could no longer see the tiny symbols on the newspaper page. He recognized the sports page as a whole and he could still see the large letters of the Scrabble set. And we can find nothing simple there."

Gonzalo said, "Unless Henry has a suggestion."

"Ah," said Pentili, "then it comes to Henry in the end. What does all this mean, Henry?"

Henry, who had been remaining silently at the sideboard throughout the discussion, said, "I cannot say, sir, unless the number 20 would be of signifi—"

He was interrupted by a suddenly frowning Pentili. "Twenty! Is that a guess, Henry?"

"Not entirely, sir. Is it significant, then?"

"Significant? I've spent years gloomily suspecting he was trying to tell us twenty. Twenty meant 'Government is firm control.' I haven't mentioned twenty in the course of the story, have I?"

There was a chorused negative.

"If I could have shown," said Pentili, "that Stepan was trying to tell us twenty, I might have been able to stop the Bay of Pigs. At least I would have tried; God, I would have tried. But I don't see how you get twenty out of this, Henry."

"Why, sir, if it is true that Mr. Stepan was only moderately knowledgeable in baseball, then he would see on the sports page only what other moderately knowledgeable people would see—like myself, for instance. As Mr. Gonzalo would say, I speak from ignorance when I say that all I see on the sports page is the result of the games—the *score* in other words—and that brings 'twenty' rather forcibly to mind."

Avalon, possibly smarting at the failure of his own suggestion, said, "I don't think much of that, Henry. 'Score' is rather an archaic word. Would Stepan have known it?"

"I imagine he would, Mr. Avalon," said Henry. "Mr. Pentili has said that Stepan was an avid reader of American history, and one of the best known historical phrases is 'Fourscore and seven years ago . . . .' "

Pentili looked disappointed. "It's a clever notion, Henry, but not convincing. Too bad."

"It becomes convincing, sir, when you realize that the Scrabble letters also signify twenty."

"In what way?"

"When Mr. Gonzalo asked his question about 'blain' he specifically asked if it were an *English* word. No one has specified that 'epock' must be English."

Gonzalo said delightedly, "You mean it's Russian for twenty?"

Pentili said, "No, it is *not* Russian for twenty. I've already mentioned the 'kopec' 'kopek' possibility, but that has nothing to do with twenty, surely."

"I'm not thinking of Russian words," said Henry. "As you have said, habits are hard to break even at the point of death, and Mr. Stepan must have found himself using Russian letters. . . ."

"The Cyrillic alphabet," said Rubin.

"Yes, Mr. Rubin. Now I have seen the USSR written in Russian in letters that look like CCCP. I suspect therefore that the Russian 'c' is equivalent to our 's' and the Russian 'p' is equivalent to our 'r.' "

"Quite so," said Pentili, looking dumbfounded.

"And the Russian 'k' is equivalent to our hard 'c' so that in *our* letters, 'epock' becomes 'erosc,' and that can be rearranged to read 'score.' "

Pentili seemed overcome by a deep depression. "You win, Henry. Why couldn't you have told me all this in 1960?"

"Had I but known, sir," said Henry.

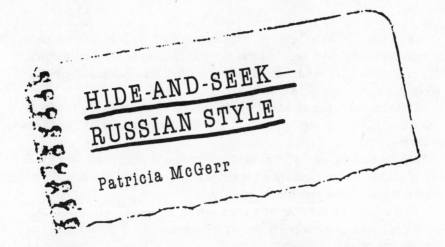

HIDE-AND-SEEK— RUSSIAN STYLE

Patricia McGerr

IT WAS ALMOST time to leave for the airport. Hugh stowed her suitcase in the trunk of the car, slammed down the lid. He was waiting on the sidewalk when Selena came out of the house. She closed the door, made sure the lock was engaged, and turned back to her husband. His artist's eye took in the belted black coat, soft leather boots, black handbag, black gloves. She was a study in quiet chic—from the neck down. But on her head, incongruously garish, was a stocking cap bordered with wide orange, green, and purple stripes.

"What—" His brows drew together in a scowl. "What's that on your head?"

"Moscow in January," she said demurely, "is very cold. This will keep my ears warm."

"And make you visible from a block away. That chewing gum you bought aroused my suspicions. The signal flag on your head confirms them. You're up to something, Selena. Why are you taking this trip?"

"I told you that two weeks ago." She moved past him, got in the car. He walked round to the driver's side and settled himself behind the wheel.

"Two weeks ago," he resumed, "you told me that a heart attack had forced an old school chum of yours to drop out of an alumni association tour and you'd decided to take her place. It had a false ring then and the longer I think about it, the more preposterous it gets." He started the engine, eased the car out of the parking space.

"Funny coincidence," she said. "That's exactly how I reasoned last month when you suddenly took off for the Middle East to paint the portrait of an Arab prince. It lacked credibility."

"Of course it did. I was on a job for Section Q and the portrait commission was my cover story. So you were right not to believe me. Am I right

447

too? Are you hiding a secret mission?"

"How could I be? The only Intelligence work I've ever done were assignments you gave me. And that stopped as soon as we were married. Do you think I got bored after eight years and found employment with some competing spy network?"

"I don't know what to think." He looked again at her gaudy headgear. "But I've a feeling you're involved in something and I'd like to know what it is."

"Maybe that's good," she retorted. "Now you'll understand how I feel when you go off to God-knows-where to do God-knows-what and I lie awake wondering if you'll ever come back."

"That's how it has to be. You know—wait a minute!" His voice sharpened in alarm. "This trip—whatever it's about—you're not walking into danger, are you?"

"Of course not."

"How can I be sure of that?"

"I'll make a bargain with you. I'll give you an honest answer if you give your word that in the future you'll always answer truthfully when I ask the same question."

"That's blackmail!"

"I call it a fair exchange. Oh, I know you think you're saving me worry by hiding the risks you run. The opposite is true. When I'm in the dark I imagine the worst. But if I can believe you when you say a job is routine, without physical danger, then I'll worry only when there's real cause. Agreed?"

"I'm beginning to suspect," he said, "that you planned the whole thing—including that crazy hat—just to make me trade off my right to lie to you."

"It's possible," she returned. "It's also possible that you've been a spymaster so long that you see agents behind every bush. If I choose to defy fashion when I'm thousands of miles from home, why should that upset you?"

"Why indeed?" He was silent while they crossed Key Bridge from Georgetown to the Virginia side of the Potomac. "You're right," he said at last. "When the shoe is on the other foot it rubs blisters. Okay, it's a deal."

"Then I'll tell you as much as I can without betraying a confidence. I'm going to Moscow to do an errand for a friend. It's a private family matter and doesn't involve any government agencies. The only danger is from one of those viruses that lie in wait for tourists. To put your mind at rest I promise not to drink the water."

"All right," he conceded, "it appears I'll have to be content with that."

"I'll be home in eight days," she assured him, "and tell you all about it."

The Moscow-bound 707 took off from Dulles Airport at eight p.m. It was a charter fight packed to the limit with the alumni of two colleges. Selena, buckled into an aisle seat, pulled the cap from her head and stared at the clashing colors.

That was careless, she thought, to put it on before I left home. Hugh's been in the business too long not to recognize an identification device when he sees one. But I couldn't pack it in my suitcase. I've no idea when contact will be made. It may happen at the airport. So I must wear the cap when I step off the plane.

I wish, though, I could have told Hugh the whole story. If only I hadn't let Trinka swear me to secrecy. But in view of the precarious state of her health what choice did I have?

Two weeks earlier the husband of a college classmate had phoned Selena to say that his wife was in the hospital recovering from a coronary and urgently wanted Selena to visit her. The request was puzzling but one she could not refuse. Driving that same afternoon to the hospital in a Washington suburb, she pieced together memories of the woman she was going to see.

Caterina Rodinova, class of '55. They had not been special friends in school, but she remembered well the shy girl whose Russian birth and illustrious ancestry had made her a campus celebrity. Something to do with her grandfather. A novelist? No, a poet. Yes, of course. It came back in a rush. Leonid Korodin, known as the Poet of the Revolution. His verses had been a rallying cry for Communists round the world. There was a square named after him in Moscow. And Trinka's mother had been his only child.

Trinka's mother escaped from Russia with the little girl a few days before the Nazis attacked. They spent the war years in England, then came to the United States. Trinka had married Robert Hudson soon after graduation and they'd moved to the West Coast where they'd lived until a few months ago when, as Robert explained briefly on the phone, his company transferred him to Washington. And now, after being out of touch for nearly twenty years, Trinka wanted to see Selena. Why?

She was no closer to an answer when she walked into the yellow-walled hospital room and stood beside the narrow bed. Long, softly waved flaxen hair spread over the pillow, framing a pale face whose delicate features were nearly eclipsed by a pair of enormous brown eyes.

"Selena?" The eyes were questioning, then the lips curved in a tremulous smile. "Yes, it is you. Oh, thank you! Thank you for coming."

"I was surprised when your husband called. I didn't know you'd moved back east."

"Yes." The woman in the bed shook her head, impatient with small talk. "I need help desperately and I didn't know where to turn. Then I remembered that you lived in Washington. In school you were always so resourceful, someone to trust and rely on. You will help me, won't you?"

"Of course." Selena moved a chair close to the bed and sat down. "I'll do whatever I can."

"It's terribly important. But first you must promise that what I say will be just between the two of us. Even Robert doesn't know. I must be sure you will not give away my secret."

"You know I won't."

"Will you swear?"

"On my word of honor," Selena said solemnly. "But Trinka dear, you must not become so agitated. You'd better rest now. I'll come back tomorrow and we'll talk again."

"No!" She tried to raise herself from the pillow. "I can't rest until I know you'll help me."

"Very well." Selena held the other woman's hand in both of hers—the hand felt like a small bird that needed quieting. "Talk slowly, without excitement. You must not strain your heart."

"You're right." She lay back and was silent for almost a minute while her breath grew smooth and even. Then she smiled faintly. "I can be calm now, since you'll solve my problem. Did you know our alumni association is sponsoring a tour of Moscow and Leningrad?"

"I probably received a notice. Why? Did you sign on?"

"Yes, but it goes in the middle of January, so I have to cancel. The doctor says it will be many weeks before I can do anything strenuous."

"What a shame! Have you not been back in all these years?"

"No, my father was killed defending Leningrad and my mother was not in sympathy with the régime, which made a coldness between her and her father. So she never wanted to return."

"But you still have relatives there?"

"Only a great-aunt, the sister of my grandfather. He died three years ago."

"Yes, I remember reading the obituaries. He was a great poet."

"Very great." The words were emphatic. "I wish I had known him. But now he is dead and my great-aunt, with whom he lived in Moscow, is old and far from well. So I seized the chance to join the alumni tour.

In a large group it is easier to be inconspicuous."

"There'll be other tours," Selena comforted. "Since Soviet-American relations have improved, it seems almost every organization is taking its members to Russia. As soon as you've recovered—"

"That may be too late. You must go now, in my place."

"To Russia?" She was startled. "Oh, Trinka, I don't see how—"

"It is for my grandfather. You know of him what the world knows. When he was young he wrote against the tyranny of the Czar and in favor of the people. His poetry inspired the men who made the Revolution. Afterwards he wrote many poems to celebrate the victory and the new world that was being made. Every schoolboy learned by heart the major works of Leonid Korodin. During his life he was greatly honored and when he died he was given a state funeral. The President of the Supreme Soviet gave the eulogy and the Party Chairman laid a wreath on the ·grave. Those are the public facts. What I tell you now you must keep secret until after you have returned. You understand?"

"Yes," Selena said. "I've given you my word."

"For some years before his death he was silent. There were new editions of his old work, but not one new poem. Well, he was old, perhaps his mind was failing. That's what everyone believed. Then, soon after we moved to Washington, there came to see me a man who had been my grandfather's close friend—or I should say his protégé, for Mikhail is much younger and also a poet, though not famous.

"He told me that my grandfather had, little by little, year after year, lost his illusions, begun to see in the new government many of the evils he had denounced in the old. He wrote poems of criticism that the Committee disapproved of and, when nothing he wrote could be published, he finally lost the will to write. Of course, none of this was made public. He was a hero of the Soviet and the authorities did not wish to label him a dissident.

"So he remained in seclusion and few people learned of his changed opinions. Even Mikhail was not allowed to see him—he thought it was because he himself held unorthodox views. But before Mikhail got out of the country he visited my great-aunt. She showed him a poem my grandfather wrote before his final illness. All the others, the ones the Committee rejected, had been destroyed, but this one he wrote in secret. It is a kind of last testament, and Mikhail said it is his greatest work. His sister has kept it hidden, but she fears that when she dies—which may be soon—it will be lost forever."

"And that's why you planned to go to Moscow," Selena concluded. "To save your grandfather's poem. Is it so important?"

"A work of art," Trinka answered, "is always important. And truth is more important still. But for me there is a stronger personal reason. I have two sons. I want them to be proud of their great-grandfather, to honor his memory. Now they know only what my mother, in her bitterness, taught them—that he helped to overthrow one oppressor to put a worse one in its place. Publication of his last poem will show them, show all the world, that he was, in the end as in the beginning, a defender of freedom. You will get it for me, Selena? You are my only hope."

The large eyes were fixed on Selena's in anguished entreaty. Selena hesitated only an instant before saying, "Yes, Trinka. I will bring back your grandfather's poem."

She phoned the travel agency at once and was told she was in luck. The Soviet tour was fully booked, but there had been a single cancellation, due to illness. Since time was so short, she could bring her check to the office and fill out the necessary forms. When she had done so, the agency head examined her visa application and nodded approval.

"It all seems in order," he said. "We'll have to press a bit to get it through in time, but we'll manage. Maybe you'll do us a favor in return."

"A favor?"

"Nothing big." He smiled genially. "This group will make up seven busloads and we need one person on each bus to act as leader. Will you be responsible for bus Number One?"

"Oh, I don't think—"

"It's no work," he assured her. "You merely check the list of names each day to make sure nobody is left behind. Since you're traveling alone, it will help you get acquainted. Then that's settled." He was out of his chair, ushering her to the door before she could demur further. "Thank you for coming in, Mrs. Pierce. I'm sure you'll enjoy the trip."

She saw Trinka again on the day before departure. Home from the hospital, though still in bed, she looked much better.

"I told Mikhail you were taking my place," she explained. "But he doesn't think you should go to see my great-aunt. For me, as a member of the family, it would have been natural. But if a strange American visits her, the powers will become suspicious."

"Then I can't get the poem? In that case there's no point in my going."

"Yes, you must go. Mikhail has made arrangements. The writers and artists who are out of favor have an underground organization. The poem speaks for all of them and they are determined that it reach the outside world. Many will work together to put it into your hands. Mikhail told me to give you this."

From the drawer of her bedside table she pulled out the orange, green, and purple cap. "You must wear it at all times and they will know you are my friend. And you must take with you many packs of chewing gum."

"Chewing gum?"

"It is not made in the Soviet Union. So always, Mikhail says, wherever American tourists go, there are youngsters asking for it. The one who recognizes your cap will come close and say 'gum chew' instead of 'chewing gum.' You will give him a package and he will give you a pin or medal. They are not beggars, these boys—they exchange some small souvenir for the gum, though, of course, the gum can be sold for a much higher price.

"In each tour city the daily schedule is posted in the hotel, so they will know where to look for you, but other information—like your room number—you should write on the gum wrapper. And their instructions will come to you with the pin. It sounds complicated, I know, but Mikhail said his friends must always be on guard against spies. Can you handle it, Selena?"

"I'll do my best," she promised. "Don't worry. Next week I'll bring you your grandfather's poem."

The Washington-to-Moscow flight, with a stopover at Shannon to change crews, took nearly twelve hours. With clocks turned forward eight hours, it was mid-afternoon when Selena's plane landed. Buses carried the tourists to the main airport building where they lined up to walk past solemn young men in uniform who stared hard at each passenger's face while checking passports and visa photos. They filled out forms listing currency and valuables and then, having claimed their luggage, carried it through customs.

The formalities over, Selena stood near the door with one hand in her coat pocket clutching a package of chewing gum. From now on, she thought, I must be constantly alert, ready to make contact. She stiffened as a high-booted young woman in a fox fur hat came close and spoke her name.

"You are Mrs. Pierce, yes?"

"Yes." The hand that held the gum relaxed. That was not the password.

"I am your Intourist representative." Her English was precise, only slightly accented. "You are leader of bus Number One, yes?"

"Yes, I am."

"Here is the list." She gave Selena a paper with two columns of typed names. "You can all go to your buses. Please check the names and do not let the driver leave until everyone is aboard. Also please collect from each person his passport to have ready when you arrive at the hotel."

It was the first hint that the job of bus leader was not the sinecure the American agent had made it seem. Selena accepted the list and promised to follow orders. The buses, seven of them, were lined up outside the door. Each had in its left front window a two-foot square card on which was printed in bright blue letters: INTOURIST-MOSCOW—and the name of the travel agency. Beneath the printing, the bus numbers—from 1 to 7—had been added in heavy crayon.

Soon, with 28 passengers and a plump rosy-cheeked guide named Olga, bus Number 1 left the airport for the 35-kilometer ride to the center of the city where it deposited them at the huge modern Hotel Rossia. There Selena turned over the passports to the Intourist representative and waited with the others for their luggage and room assignments.

It was six o'clock when she was at last alone in her room where the single bed with its linen-encased blanket was almost irresistibly inviting. Flying into the sun had cut short the night and telescoped mealtimes, so there had been a surfeit of food and little sleep. She would gladly have skipped supper to take a long hot bath and sleep the clock round. But she could not depart from the formal program. Only by following it exactly could she be sure to be in place when Trinka's allies came to seek her.

So she left her coat in the room but still wore the stocking cap when she descended to the below-lobby restaurant where her group was scheduled to eat all its Moscow meals. Ready in her handbag was a package of chewing gum with her room number on the wrapper. But no one accosted her on the way to the dining room and the meal proved uneventful. Before returning to her room she stopped to copy the tour schedule which was posted at the restaurant entrance:

FRIDAY

8:30 Breakfast
9:30 Kremlin Museum and Armory
1:00 Lunch
2:30 Qs & As
5:30 Dinner
6:15 Bolshoi Ballet

SATURDAY

9:00 Breakfast
10:00 City Tour
1:00 Lunch
2:00 National Fair & Space Museum
5:30 Dinner
6:15 Siberian Folk Dance

SUNDAY

9:00 Breakfast
10:00 Troika Rides
1:30 Lunch
2:30 Subway Tour
9:30 Lv for Railway Station
10:40 Train to Leningrad

"What's that mean?"

A fellow tourist, also studying the poster, pointed to the fourth item under Friday.

"Questions and answers, I imagine," Selena said.

"Well, of course I figured that out," the woman said irritably. "But what does it mean? You're our bus leader. Aren't you supposed to know these things?"

"It's a propaganda session." A tall man from another bus came to her rescue. "They bring in experts in various fields. We ask the questions and they give the party-line answers."

"Sounds dull. I think I'll go shopping instead." The woman looked again at Selena. "Don't hold the bus for me."

She moved away and the man gave Selena a companionable wink. "It begins to appear," he said, "that leading a bus isn't all prestige and perquisites, the way they made it sound back in Washington."

"You're a bus leader too?"

"Number Four. Bill Parsons." He offered his hand. "When the going gets rough, maybe we can swap miseries over a vodka or two."

In her own room again she studied the schedule, trying to guess where and when contact would be made. Soon, she hoped. Once the poet's papers were passed over and packed safely away, she could begin to enjoy the sights like an ordinary tourist. Except for her responsibilities as bus leader.

She smiled, remembering the exchange at the dining-room door. Qs and As. "Questions and Answers." Like the chicken-egg enigma, she'd never known—perhaps no one did—which came first? Did Section Q get its name from the fact that its agents established identity with sentences beginning with the letter Q? Or did the name of the section give rise to the device? If I were on an agency assignment instead of a private errand, that conversation would have been loaded with significance. And the woman would be my contact. She put the schedule away and got ready for bed.

How do our Russian-speaking agents meet, she wondered drowsily. The Cyrillic alphabet has no letter Q. But it had been a long day—two days, in fact, with Wednesday running unseparated into Thursday—and sleep put an effective end to her curiosity.

The first onslaught of chewing-gum seekers came the next morning as they waited in the icy wind outside the Kremlin Museum. About a dozen neatly dressed boys paced the lines and many of the Americans exchanged packages for square pins decorated with pictures of the Kremlin tower, the Soviet flag, and other emblems. None of them singled out Selena or spoke the magic phrase, "gum chew."

Another group met them when they left the Museum, and a third pounced as they entered a church. By the time the bus returned to the hotel the tourists had begun to be selective about the souvenirs for which they would trade the coveted merchandise. But the orange, green, and purple headcovering remained unremarked except by their guide, who called it a useful beacon to help straying Number 1 bus riders find their way back to the fold.

During the lunch break Selena was given 28 ballet tickets to distribute. Keeping one for herself, she added the theater-seat location to the hotel-room number on the chewing-gum wrapper. But, though many teenagers asked for gum outside the Hall of Friendship where the question-and-answer session was held, none said "gum chew" and the marked package stayed in her pocket.

That night the Bolshoi troupe danced *Giselle* and Selena almost forgot her anxiety in the beauty of the performance. Trinka didn't say contact would be made the first day, she reminded herself. It could happen tomorrow. Or even on Sunday. The transfer of a few sheets of paper would take only an instant. There was no reason to assume that delay meant something had gone wrong.

It was about 10:30 when the ballet ended. They reclaimed their coats and came out of the theater to see a large segment of the audience moving rapidly on foot in one direction. When they asked their bus driver for an explanation, he tapped his watch, summoned his small store of English to say, "On the hour. The tomb of Lenin."

"The changing of the guard?" Selena asked.

"Yes," he said. "Guard change."

"The hotel's just across Red Square," someone said. "We can walk."

So bus Number 1 returned to the hotel half empty. Selena joined the hardier travelers to follow the swarm who, like lemmings, were moving toward Lenin's tomb.

A crowd of several hundred, mostly Russians, were standing in the Square. They waited with almost breathless anticipation, their eyes fixed on the two soldiers who stood motionless guarding the tomb. Then the clock began to strike and an officer, leading two other soldiers, marched smartly past the crowd. Like Arlington, Selena thought with an odd sense of recognition. It's almost the same ceremony as at the Tomb of the Unknowns.

Then, when she had stopped expecting it, a voice close to her ear said softly, "Gum chew." She almost jumped, almost exclaimed. The words were so out of keeping with the moment's solemnity. But her control held and she made no sound, did not even look round to see the speaker. Instead, moving slowly, she put her hand in her pocket, drew out the gum, and held it in half-open palm behind her back.

A hand took it from her, then slid a folded paper inside her glove. That's not how it was planned, she thought. And he's a man, not a boy.

She waited impatiently for the ceremony to end so that she could get back to the hotel. Some of her group went on to the bar for a warm-up drink, but she declined the invitation and hurried instead to her room to pull the slip of paper from her glove. It had written on it in block letters a single word: QUIT.

She stared at it, unbelieving. That was not a message from the friends of Trinka's grandfather. The word, with its revealing initial letter, could have had only one source. It was an order from Section Q. An order, more specifically, from her husband. But how — why?

Her mind was aswirl with questions. How did Hugh learn about her mission, about the "gum-chew" code? And why had he sent an emissary to warn her off? That Section Q had operatives in Moscow did not surprise her. But surely they had more important things to do than meddle in minor domestic matters. Yet one of them must have trailed her from the theater to Red Square and there traded his note for her gum. You sent a man to do a boy's work, Hugh, she mentally accused him. Why?

There was only one way to get an answer. She looked at her watch as she started toward the phone. Midnight in Moscow was four p.m. in Washington. He was probably in his studio and—her lips curved in a wry smile—probably expecting her call.

It would take, the operator told her, about half an hour to complete the call. Waiting, Selena sorted out her thoughts. She must accept the possibility of a listener on the line, but that would present no real problem. Hugh would know why she was calling and they were both skilled at conveying information in veiled terms. So when the connection was made they hurried through the conventional remarks expected of a tourist calling home and she waited for him to answer the questions she didn't ask.

"I visited your sick friend," he said. "We had an interesting talk."

"Really? I hope it didn't overtire her."

"Not at all. I think she was glad to see me. But you'd better stay clear of her. Her disease may be contagious and dangerous."

"You're exaggerating."

"No, I'm not. I've gotten an expert diagnosis. You'll be sorry to hear, too, about your cousin. She was caught smuggling drugs into Turkey and is likely to get ten years in jail. There's not a thing the family can do to help her."

"How dreadful!"

"She should have had better sense. Well, that's enough bad news. I miss you, darling. Please take care of yourself and hurry home."

She rang off and made translation. The sick friend was, of course, Trinka. I might have guessed his suspicions would lead him to the classmate I replaced on the tour. And when he told Trinka he was worried about me, she felt obliged to set his mind at rest by telling him all the facts—about the poem, the chewing gum, everything.

And the talk about my non-existent cousin in Turkey was meant to scare me off. He was saying that if I'm caught and put in a Russian prison, no one at home can get me out. But that's nonsense. I'm not smuggling drugs or valuables or military secrets. All I plan to carry out are a few sheets of paper that the authorities don't even know exist.

Hugh is being overprotective, that's all. He's so determined to keep me away from the kind of fire he plays with daily that he doesn't even want me to do a small favor for a friend. It's sweet of him to be solicitous, but this time he's frightened by shadows. I wonder, though, what he meant by "an expert diagnosis"?

On Sunday morning bus leaders were given two items to distribute —
tickets for the folk dance and car-and-compartment numbers for the train.
Selena took out a fresh pack of gum and wrote her new locations on the
wrapper. The morning was, from her point of view, uneventful. But that
afternoon, on the way into the huge barnlike building that houses the
Soviet Space Exhibit, a chewing gum squad approached. One of the boys
zeroed in on Selena with the query, "Gum chew? You trade?"

He held out a pin bearing a likeness of Lenin. She accepted it and gave
him the marked package.

"You shouldn't encourage them," the woman beside her said disapprov-
ingly. "The ban on gum is the only good thing about Communism. My
dentist says —"

Selena listened absently to the lecture as she dropped the souvenir into
her purse. There was a small piece of paper on the back of the pin, but
she would have to wait until she was alone to read it. Did it set time and
place for a rendezvous, explain how the poem was to be handed over?
Trying to guess what the message said blinded her eyes to the rocket
display, deafened her ears to the glories of the Soyuz program.

When the space tour ended, she hurried to board the bus ahead of the
others and, taking out the pin, slid the note free. It read: *Be patient. There
are difficulties.* Be patient! She crumpled the paper. I could find better
advice in a fortune cookie. Don't they realize tomorrow is my last day in
Moscow?

For nearly 24 hours nothing happened. She concluded that the difficulties, whatever they were, had proved insurmountable. She must return
home empty-handed. The final event was a tour of the Moscow Metro.
En route to the entrance Olga, the Intourist representative, emphasized
the problem of remaining together and insisted that all write down the
name of the square where their bus would be parked. If any of them
became separated, they should return to that square and wait for the
others. Thus prepared, they went underground.

On the platform, interrupted by the noise of arriving and departing
trains, Olga described the workings of the system, provided statistics,
and explained the symbolism of the art on walls and ceiling. Then they
were ready to ride. Since they could not all crowd into one car, they
spread out along the platform with instructions to ride to the second stop,
get off there, then regroup. A train stopped, the doors opened, people
poured out, and others, including Selena's group, raced aboard. A
stranger, following closely, nearly knocked her down.

"Quiet," he whispered. "Get off at the next stop."

He moved swiftly away from her to the other end of the car. While

most of her companions found seats, she stayed near the door. Section
Q again. Another message from Hugh.

The train hurtled through a tunnel, emerged again into light, and the
doors opened. Selena let herself be swept onto the platform. Several
people tried to call her back, but she pretended not to hear until the doors
began to close. Then she looked through the windows at her fellow
tourists and pantomimed dismay.

The Q-man, having left the car by the farthest door, walked past her
to the escalator. She followed him up and out of the station. On the
sidewalk, a few paces from the exit, he slowed down and she fell into
step beside him.

"Our mutual friend," he began without introduction, "thinks he failed
to make his point on the phone. He's afraid you may be going ahead with
a high-risk enterprise."

"I understood what he was trying to tell me."

"Understood?" he challenged. "Or accepted?"

"It doesn't matter, since the enterprise appears to be canceled." She
quoted yesterday's pinned message, adding, "In a few hours I'll be leaving town, so you can tell our friend to stop worrying."

"Mmm. Maybe. But he wants me to put you in the picture, so you'll
know the threat is real. I gather this mission of yours is freelance, not
for Section Q. Right?"

"That's right."

"As soon as our friend found out what you were doing, he asked me
to sniff out the facts."

"An expert diagnosis?" she murmured.

"You could call it that. Here's what I found. Your classmate was naive
to think she could hide inside a tour group. When her name turned up
on the visa list, it triggered questions about why, after so many years,
she was returning to her native land. The query was bucked to the KGB
and a couple of agents visited the great-aunt.

"Communist bureaucracies move just as slowly as democratic ones, so
by the time they got to her the plan had been changed. Somebody from
the literary group had already picked up the poem in order to pass it on
to you. The agents put pressure on the aunt to make her talk and she told
them everything she knew—including the fact that the poem is pure
dynamite. The invasion of Czechoslovakia touched off Korodin's outrage
and it all poured out—the suppression of freedom, the silencing of artists,
the enslavement of the people.

"It's a rather long narrative that starts with 1918 and, verse after verse,
traces the betrayal of the Revolution. Taken alone, the words wouldn't do

much harm, but in the handwriting of Communism's great prophet—well, you can see why they'd go to any length to stop the original manuscript from being taken out of the country."

"Do they know who has it now?"

"No, all the old lady knew was that a messenger came for it and said it would be delivered to the poet's granddaughter in America. You can be sure your tour was under surveillance from the moment the plane landed."

"There are one hundred and seventy-six of us," she point out. "in seven buses. Even the KGB can't watch all of us all the time."

"True. That's why I took a chance on cutting you out from the herd on the subway. I'm glad you don't have the poem, but you may still receive it before you leave Moscow. If you do, destroy it. Tear up the pages, burn the scraps, and dispose of the ashes in a way that can't be traced back to you."

"I can't do that. If the poem is all you say it is, it must be saved."

"It can't be saved. As you say, they can't watch all of you every minute. But there's one place where everybody can be thoroughly searched. That's at the Leningrad airport before you take off for the United States. If you're carrying the document, it will be found. You'll be arrested and they can convict you of stealing a priceless Korodin manuscript without revealing its contents. There's no power in Washington that can set you free, not even the President. Do I make myself clear?"

"Very."

And you'll destroy the poem?"

"I'll probably never see it," she evaded. "Time is running out."

"A lot can happen in six hours. In six minutes even. I'll make a deal with you. My instructions are to get you safely out of the country and avoid an international incident. Section Q isn't concerned with the poem. Until three days ago no one on our side had even heard of it. But it's valuable propaganda and I hate to see it go down the drain."

"Then I shouldn't burn it?"

"Not right away. You'll receive it before you leave Moscow or not at all. There's no way they can get it to Leningrad. So I'll wait tonight at the railway station. In the dark and confusion I'll be able to get close to you. If you have the poem, give it to me. I'll keep it safe until the hunt dies down. Then we'll figure a way to get it to the poet's granddaughter. How does that sound?"

"Fine. Your facilities are certainly better than mine."

"And you'll give me the poem this evening?"

"I will," she agreed, "if I get it."

They separated and she took a taxi back to the parked bus. When the others emerged from the Metro there was much merriment over the leader's being the one who got lost and Selena expressed embarrassment at having thought they were to leave the train at the first stop instead of the second.

After returning to the hotel some tourists used the few remaining hours to buy gifts in the hotel's "hard currency" shop and others wrote and mailed postcards. For Selena it was simply a time of waiting, with each minute that passed bringing her closer to failure of her mission.

At last, when dinner was over, they boarded the bus for the station. Their luggage, unloaded from another bus, lay on the platform and the confusion the Q-man had forecast was compounded as they milled about, each traveler obliged to identify his own suitcase and either carry it to his assigned compartment or find a porter to do it for him.

A man bumped against Selena, muttered, "Quickly," and held out his hand.

"Nothing," she responded and he faded away. She found her car and compartment and carried her own bag aboard.

The compartments, composed of two upper and lower berths with a narrow aisle between them, were already made up for the night. In the one with Selena's number, three people from her bus were sitting on the lower berths—a husband, wife, and 15-year-old boy. They looked with dismay at Selena and her suitcase.

"There's no space." The wife spread her hands helplessly. "My husband put his bag and mine under the beds, but there's no room for Buddy's." She patted the one beside her. "And now one more!"

Selena, standing in the doorway as other people carrying luggage brushed past her, agreed with the assessment. While the husband poked futilely beneath the bunks as if be might magically make more room, a porter tapped Selena's arm.

"*Spassibo*,'" he said. "I help."

She stepped aside. He sidled into the room and hoisted her bag into an open area above the door.

"Hey," Buddy said, "there's a big luggage section up there. We didn't even see it."

The Russian took the boy's bag from the bunk and shoved it in next to Selena's.

"Thanks a lot." The husband pulled a handful of kopeks from his pocket.

"*Nyet*." The man waved the coins away, edged past Selena, and hurried down the corridor.

It was a long and uncomfortable night. The only way four people could occupy such cramped quarters was to go to bed at once. Selena slept fitfully, burdened with thoughts of the failure of her mission. The difficulties had evidently proved insoluble. She must return to Trinka without the poem.

The train pulled into Leningrad at seven a.m. Buddy brought down his own bag, then reached for Selena's.

"Hey!" he exclaimed. "There's something else up here. Some paper."

He held an envelope toward Selena. "Is that yours?"

"What—oh, yes, it is mine." She took it from him and stuffed it in her handbag. "I almost forgot I put it up there. Thank you."

The next quarter hour was chaos as passengers and luggage debarked from the train and the tourists were once more shepherded to seven waiting buses. The envelope was like a burning brand in her handbag all the way to the hotel. Another message from Section Q? No, that connection was broken on the station platform. The number of her compartment was known, of course, to Russian underground. One of them, posing as a porter, had delivered the envelope when he lifted up her suitcase. So it must be the poem. They had, after all, found a way to get it to Leningrad.

The most beautiful city in the Soviet Union, that's what they call Leningrad—formerly St. Petersburg, home of the Czars, capital of old Russia, a treasurehouse of art and architecture. But for Selena, moving from one historic scene to another, the vision was blurred by internal debate.

As soon as she reached her hotel room she had opened the envelope and found four sheets of paper covered with closely written Russian script—the last Korodin poem. Four sticks, to follow the Q-man's metaphor, of pure dynamite. In the Hermitage she looked at Rembrandts and Goyas and Renoirs and thought, It's only four pieces of paper. There must be a way to hide them long enough to get them past customs.

In the summer palace at Pushkin she listened to the account of how artisans had recreated, down to the most intricate detail, silk screen destroyed in the war and thought, If I had their skill I'd be able to camouflage the poem and carry it away. What she needed was lab equipment that could photograph the pages, reduce them to microdots, copy them in invisible ink. But she was out of touch with Section Q. Their interest in her had ended in Moscow.

She considered phoning Hugh again to ask for help. But his order had been given—destroy the poem. And it was unlikely she could persuade him to a different view, or even explain the problem, on a line that was sure to be monitored. The decision was hers alone to make—to burn the pages and drop the ashes in the River Neva or risk her own freedom by trying to smuggle them out.

Her most vivid recollection of Leningrad was the Tuesday-afternoon tour of the St. Peter and Paul Fortress. In Czarist times it had been a prison, and after they had crowded into a bare cell the guide clanged shut the door and turned out the light. It was a moment of theatrics designed to dramatize the sufferings of the early revolutionaries, but for Selena it seemed a foretaste of her future.

That evening, as she dressed for the opera, she was aware that the articles in her suitcase had been taken out and repacked in slightly different order. Her room had been searched. Was everyone on the tour given the same attention? Or had they drawn the accurate conclusion that the person whose name was added to the visa list after the poet's granddaughter dropped out was the most likely suspect?

They'd found nothing, of course, since she carried the poem at all times in a zippered compartment of her handbag. But that would do no good at the airport where her handbag and even her person could be, and probably would be, searched.

I can't do it, Trinka, she mentally addressed her friend. I'd try, I'd take the risk if there was even a slim chance of getting through. You thought that no one else knew about the poem, that bringing it back would be easy. But now, with the authorities on the alert, I'd be bucking hopeless odds. To sacrifice myself in an effort sure to fail would be the worst kind of folly.

But even as her mind formed the argument, she saw again Trinka's ashen face and trustful eyes, heard her plead her sons' right to take pride in their ancestry. I can't let that go up in smoke. There must be a way. I've got to find it.

Wednesday was the last full day of the tour and as the time of decision narrowed she grew more desperate. In the afternoon they visited a museum where native arts and crafts were on display and she stood before a case containing a gaily painted wooden doll. It was large and bulb-shaped, and inside the doll, according to the guide, there were twelve other dolls, successively smaller in size, one within the other. It was typically Russian and souvenir shops were filled with small-scale replicas.

I'll buy one of those, Selena thought, fold the manuscript tightly, and put it inside the middle doll. Since they're bound to find it anyway, I might as well make it easy by choosing the most obvious hiding place.

That night they celebrated the trip's end with a gala dinner at the Sadok Restaurant. The tables were laden with vodka and champagne. A six-piece orchestra accompanied two singers and an acrobatic dancer. Toasts were effusive and spirits high. As a memento of the occasion the leader of each bus was presented with the window card bearing the bus's identifying number.

"Now you can show everyone that we were Number One," Buddy said while the large white cardboard was passed round the table for autographs. She caught the envious note in the boy's voice and started to say, "Perhaps you'd like . . ." when an idea struck her. Instead of offering him the sign as she'd intended, she finished lamely, "to be a bus leader yourself some day."

The most obvious hiding place. The concept triggered by the Russian doll summoned memory of Edgar Allan Poe's tale of the purloined letter which had been successfully hidden by leaving it in plain sight. Perhaps, just perhaps, she had the answer.

It was after eleven when the party ended. Selena pushed through the throng waiting at the coat-check counter to reach the side of Bill Parsons, leader of bus No. 4. The sign tucked under his arm was, she noted, auspiciously free of autographs.

"Hello, fellow sufferer," he hailed her. "I guess neither of us will let ourselves be conned into this job again. Rounding up stray sheep, getting blamed when they don't like their theater seats, making sure everybody gets back the right passport. It's a real headache."

"At least we've been rewarded." She waved her sign.

"Some reward! Believe me, I don't need any reminders."

"Aren't you going to take yours home?"

"Carry that back to the States? You've got to be kidding."

"In that case—" She moved closer, dropped her voice. "I have two nephews who have their bedroom walls covered with strange signs."

"Sure, I did the same thing when I was a kid. *Keep Off the Grass, Beware of the Dog*—that sort of thing. One saying INTOURIST—LENINGRAD should be a real collector's item."

"That's the problem," she said "If I give it to one and not the other—"

"There'll be jealousy." He nodded, understanding. "But it's no problem. Take mine and make both boys happy."

"Well, if you're sure—"

"It will save the chambermaid from carrying it out with the trash tomorrow."

"That's very kind of you." She accepted the second sign. "I'm really grateful."

That night she slept peacefully for the first time since leaving Washington. Her plan was made. It might succeed, it might fail. But the time for vacillation was over.

After breakfast she used her nail scissors to loosen the lining of the top of her suitcase and pulled it free till half of the paper-backed cloth hung limp. Then she carried it to the counter near the elevators where a lady was in attendance day and night to hand out keys, serve tea, and solve minor problems. She spoke little English, but Selena's problem was clearly visible, her need for an adhesive substance apparent. The lady nodded and smiled assurance that the need would soon be filled.

Selena took the suitcase back to her room and began to copy the signatures and good wishes that the other riders had penned on the back of the bus Number 1 sign on the blank surface of the sign from bus Number 4. She was just finishing when a knock on the door signaled the arrival of a chambermaid with a tube of glue. Accepting it with thanks, Selena shut the door and placed a chair in front of it to guard against surprise interruption.

Then she took from the envelope the four pages of the Korodin poem. Placing the Number 1 sign face down on her dressing table, she separated the pages into two pairs and laid them side by side on the back of the card. They fitted easily, with a wide margin all around. Applying glue to that margin, she then put the other bus sign, with the number 4 inside, on top of the flattened pages, evened the edges, and pressed them firmly together. The result was, to all appearances, a single sign—that for bus Number 1—covered front and back with autographs. Only close inspection would reveal its double thickness.

That done, she used the glue to repair the damage she'd done to her suitcase. Then she made another trip to the service counter to return the tube. She finished her packing well in advance of the eleven a.m. deadline and went down to the lobby with suitcase and sign. Soon the buses, now minus number cards in the windows, began loading and they were on their way to the airport. And if the KGB is half as efficient as people think, she told herself, they know by now that the tourist in Room 451 ripped the lining off her suitcase and glued it back again. Let them deduce from that a belief that they've pinpointed the location of the missing document.

At the airport she held her sign with its secret pocket conspicuously in front of her and was glad to see that most of the other bus leaders were also carrying theirs. Those who still had rubles were directed to the exchange window, while the rest were channeled to customs officials who inspected luggage and packages, women's handbags, men's wallets, even clothing pockets. The search was slow and painstaking but the Intourist representative shrugged off questions and complaints, professing ignorance of the cause.

"They must have been tipped off that one of us is trying to smuggle out Russian currency," someone suggested. The rumor circulated swiftly and gained wide acceptance since it accounted for the thoroughness of the search. A few people who had planned, in spite of the taboo, to take home one or two rubles as contraband souvenirs, flushed guiltily and scurried back to the exchange window.

When Selena's turn came she laid the Number 1 bus sign on a bench, took off her coat, and gave it with her handbag to the customs man. She stood stoically while her body was patted by a woman official with head cocked and narrowed eyes—listening, Selena knew, for the telltale crackle of paper. Then she put her coat back on, slung her purse over her arm, and picked up the sign. She was starting to move on when the woman said sharply, "Wait!"

Oh, no! Selena froze, felt the blood pounding in her temples. This is it. I've been caught. Maybe the woman official is an Edgar Allan Poe fan. Selena turned slowly back, forcing an expression of polite inquiry.

"The hat." The woman pointed to her head. Trying not to show relief, Selena pulled off the knitted cap and gave it to the man to inspect while the woman ruffled her hair. In a few seconds she was dismissed. She put the cap back on, again picked up her sign, and went on to passport control. The man in the booth glanced without interest at the sign, then fixed his eyes unblinkingly first on her face, then on the pictures in passport and visa. Finding them to be likenesses he tore off two-thirds of the visa and returned the remnant with her passport.

On the other side of the barrier the tension drained away. She sank exhausted onto a bench to await the call to board the plane. Around her people chattered angrily about the delay and promised that their first act on arriving home would be a call to the White House, the State Department, or their congressman. Selena hardly heard them. Her entire attention was focused on the journey's end.

When the boarding announcement came she was among the first out the door. And when they neared the huge Pan American jet she had to hold herself back from breaking into a run. But a few paces from the plane her exhilaration faded. Two soldiers stood at the foot of the steps checking everyone who boarded. One more hurdle.

She steeled herself and moved slowly forward. But those men, like the one in the booth, were interested only in faces. One took the final portion of her visa sheet, made sure of her identity, and let her pass.

Her seat was again on the aisle beside an elderly couple who were grumbling about the airport search.

"Such a mess," the woman said, "having everything opened and pawed through. I'll be very surprised if all the suitcases get on the plane."

"You don't have to come to Russia to lose your baggage." Her husband was more philosophical. "It's part of the flying experience."

At least, Selena mused, I can be the first one through U.S. customs since I'm certain my suitcase won't be put on board. After they tear out the lining and take it all apart, will they put it back together and send it on a later plane? Or is it lost forever?

She didn't really care. The suitcase and its contents were expendable. The valuable cargo was now on her lap. Soon they were airborne and when, a little later, the captain announced that they had just flown out of Soviet air space, Selena joined in the applause, then rested her hands lightly on the twinned cards. After I deliver the poem to Trinka, she decided, I'll look up young Buddy and give him the sign for bus Number 1.

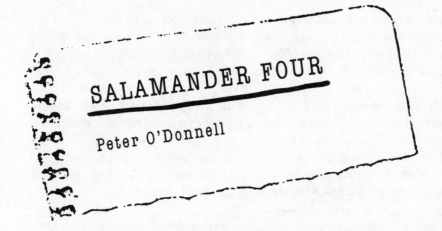

SALAMANDER FOUR

Peter O'Donnell

THE LONG TWILIGHT came at three in the afternoon, laying its soft purple mantle over pine and spruce forests which the first snows of winter had already dressed in thin white undershift.

The house stood in a wide clearing between a narrow dirt road and a small lake dotted with tiny green and white skerries. Beside the house stood a sauna bath-house, set closer to the lake for the ritual icy plunge of the steam-broiled body.

The timber-built house was on one level, most of the space within was taken up by one very large room. It was warm in the room. An open log-fire in a big stone fireplace at one end supplemented the central heating. In the cellar below the thick pine floor, a small diesel generator supplied power for the boiler-pump and for the well-planned fluorescent lighting which produced a daylight effect over the solid bench where a man stood working.

He held a mallet and a half-inch gouge of shallow sweep, but he had not set blade to wood for thirty minutes now. He was working only with his rather deep-set eyes, looking from the clay model on his right to the mahogany statue in front of him, twenty-four inches high, and then to the living original from which the preliminary clay sketch had been modelled three weeks earlier.

Modesty Blaise said, "Can we take a break, Alex? Coffee and a cigarette?"

The man did not answer, seemed unaware that she had spoken. He was of medium build, dark, with big clumsy-looking hands. Usually his manner was slow and patient. Now he was a little tense, chewing his lower lip as he stared at the statue, assessing the values of the planes and hollows in the rich dark wood feeling in his mind the sweep of the grain, the curve of limb and breast, the soft subtle column of the neck.

Modesty Blaise sat on a round, blanket-covered table with a revolving top. Her legs and feet were drawn up together on one side, a hand resting loosely just below the knee. She was leaning sideways a little, supporting herself on one straight arm. Highlights gleamed on her naked body. Her hair was drawn back and tied at the nape of her neck. It was an easy, natural pose. Alex Hemmer had caught it exactly in the clay model; and now, after three weeks of work, the pose had been captured in wood. But both on the model and on the carving, the face was still undefined.

Modesty closed her mind to the ache that had crept into her supporting arm, and watched as Alex Hemmer put down his tools neatly beside the long row of chisels and gouges, moved to the clay model and began once again to work on the face. He had modelled and destroyed a dozen faces in the clay during the past two days, but this was nothing compared with the agonies and frustrations she had watched him suffer in the beginning.

She wondered if John Dall would be pleased with the final result—if Alex ever made it.

The thing had all begun with John Dall. As one of the richest men in America, he could afford to indulge an expensive whim. And so, on a day three months ago now, one of his minions had escorted Alex Hemmer from his remote house in northern Finland to Dall's ranch near Amarillo, Texas, where Modesty Blaise was ending a six-week visit.

Hemmer was not a world-famous sculptor, though he might yet become one. But he was a first-class representational sculptor whose technique was admired even by the abstract school.

"I don't want a Moore or a Hepworth," Dall said. He was a lean, fit man nearing forty, with thick black hair cropped short and a face that betrayed a touch of redskin ancestry. "I want a statue that looks like her, Mr. Hemmer. Not life-size. About this high." He held a hand at about table height. "And I'd like this sort of pose, it's the way she often sits." He sat down on the great Persian carpet and leaned sideways on one arm.

Modesty laughed and said, "You look cute, Johnnie."

Dall got to his feet, grinning a little. "That's more than you ever will, honey. If the statue looks cute, our friend here will have failed pretty badly." He turned to the sculptor. "How about it, Mr. Hemmer?"

Alex Hemmer put down his untouched drink and stared at Modesty. She sat at one end of a big couch, looking back at him without embarrassment. The silence went on, and Alex Hemmer's patient gaze was so concentrated that it was as if he had fallen into a trance. Once Dall started to speak, but Modesty stopped him with a little movement of her hand.

At last Hemmer said, "Marble or bronze?" He spoke good English and with care.

"Neither," Dall said tersely. "Wood. I know wood tends to hide itself, but good lighting can fix that. My choice would be mahogany—I'll listen to argument about that, but not about wood. It's warmer than marble or stone or bronze, and it's a living thing." He looked at Modesty. "It's right for you."

Hemmer nodded slowly. "Thank you. If you had said marble or bronze, I would go away. The material must be in harmony with the subject. As you say, wood is warm and alive. Also, with wood a sculptor can be more adventurous. It is the only material for a statue of this lady."

"You have a pretty good instinct," Dall said, and smiled. "Mahogany?"

"Yes. The color grows better with time. But it must be unpolished."

"Fine. When can you start?"

Hemmer would work only in his own workshop, and before all else there was the matter of finding the right block of wood. It must not be green wood; kiln-dried might do, but best of all would be seasoned wood.

Dall could arrange that. He owned a number of mills and two hundred thousand acres of timber, including forests in Central America where mahogany was cut.

Next day Dall flew with Hemmer down into the timber country. Modesty went home. Some weeks later she received a polite cable from Hemmer, in Finland, saying that the selected block of mahogany had arrived and he was ready to begin.

For the first week she stayed in a small hotel near Tepasto. Daily she drove her hired Volvo 144S fifteen miles out into the pine forest where Hemmer's lonely house stood. He began the clay model with quiet enthusiasm, but by the third day she saw that he was close to despair. There were no dramatics about it. He began to pull chunks of clay off the armature on which it was built and said, "I am very sorry. I think I am not able to do this. It will not come right."

She had little creative ability herself, but deep intuition, and this allowed her to sense how shattering it must be for the artist who strikes a creative block. She made him stop work, then got dressed and busied herself making fresh coffee and a good meal.

For the next three days she would not let him work. They talked, took long walks in the forest, sawed logs for the fire with a big double-handed saw, and when dusk came they played bezique until it was time for her to go. She had to teach him the game, and he had no card sense, but though he played badly he seemed to enjoy it.

There was a telephone in the house, because by good fortune the cable between Muonio and Ivalo ran close by. She had never heard it ring, and had seen him use it only once to order supplies, but he always called the hotel an hour after she left him, to make sure she had got home safely.

During this time she came to know him well, and developed a gentle affection for him. To her surprise she learned that he was not Finnish, but Hungarian. As a young man he had taken part in the abortive revolution of '56. In those days he had seen horrors which had destroyed all the romantic fires of youth in him. The girl he was to marry had been crushed under a tank, and in the dying hours of the fighting he had fled across the Austrian border.

He had settled in Finland, partly because there was a strange similarity of language but mainly because it was remote, a land of quietness. Alex Hemmer had opted out. He would never again allow himself to be involved in the clash of nations or ideologies or commerce or even personalities. He did the work he loved and had learned to do well, and he was content.

But now his contentment was undermined and she knew he was beginning to feel afraid. She believed she knew the cause of his creative power drying up. After three full days of idle leisure they agreed that he should start work again the following morning.

That day she checked out of the hotel and arrived at his house with her luggage in the boot of the car. He was waiting nervously, gazing at the shapeless mass of clay on the armature, bracing himself, his face a little drawn. But when she had undressed and put on the wrap she wore between sessions, she did not take up her pose on the table. She went to him and took his anxious face between her hands and kissed him long and hard on the lips. She knew it was only then he realized that desire for her had been sleeping within him.

Throughout that day they made love. He was not deeply versed in the art, but neither was he completely without experience, and it was made joyful for her by his total absorption in her, an absorption that sprang from the feeling of a sculptor for his material. When they lay together in the small warm bedroom he would feed upon her with the senses of sight and touch, dwelling upon every plane and muscle and subtly differing texture of her body.

He was slow and gentle, sometimes lost in wonderment at the sight or touch of some quality in a curve of flesh, sometimes studying her face with an intent, slightly baffled smile. Then would come the warm joining and the long smooth ascent, growing swifter to the final happening and the great sigh.

That day, as the early twilight came, they broiled themselves in the steam of the sauna bathhouse and afterwards broke the mushy skin of ice at the lake's edge for the breathless plunge. They dried, glowing, in front of the fire, and she made a meal.

At last, when they had eaten, she posed for him once again. He began to shape the clay on the armature, working with easy confidence. By midnight the model was finished—all but the face, which he intended to leave until after the carving of the body in wood had been completed.

That night he had taken her into his arms and fallen instantly into a deep sleep of utter contentment. Now, three weeks later, the mahogany sculpture was almost finished. He was having difficulty with the face, but there was no return of anxiety. He was enjoying the challenge, as a man might enjoy the challenge of a high mountain.

He put down the wooden spatula he had been using and said, "Yes, of course."

"Of course what, Alex?"

"You said you would like coffee and a cigarette."

"That was fifteen minutes ago."

He stared. "Truly?"

"Truly. But that's not a record." She picked up the wrap that lay behind her and drew it on as she got down from the table. "Last night I asked you to stop working and come to bed. Forty minutes later you said, 'Yes, by God!' "

He rubbed a hand ruefully across his brow, leaving an oily smear. "It is your own fault, Modesty. You have a maddening face."

"Thank you." She lifted the coffee pot which stood on a hob by the fire, and poured coffee into two big china mugs. He gave her a cigarette and lit it for her, then took her chin in one hand and turned her head first one way and then the other.

"At one moment it is a very young face, the face of a rather wicked child. The next moment it is older than the face of Eve."

She smiled. "You'd better capture the old one, Alex. I missed out on being a child."

"No. You are sometimes that now." He looked at the sculpture. "I must capture both in the wood. And many other things also. I know I can do it."

"Good." She sat down, sipping the hot, sweet coffee. There was a comfortable silence. Alex Hemmer gazed absently at the statue. After a while he said, "You have no vanity. You do not particularly want to have this sculpture made. Why did you agree?"

"John Dall asked me, and I owe him a debt."

"What kind of debt?"

"He once came halfway across the world to help me when I needed it."

Alex Hemmer nodded thoughtfully. "He told me a little about you. I know that you have known much danger. And that you saved Dall's life, you and a strange man called Willie Garvin."

"There's nothing strange about Willie. Rare, perhaps. Not strange. And preventing John Dall being murdered was just a spin-off that came about because he helped us."

"Will you tell me the story?"

"No, Alex. It's past. And anyway, it would offend your principles. You don't believe in people getting involved."

"That is only for me. I do not try to persuade anybody else."

She smiled. "Good. But you haven't much chance, living like a hermit."

After a moment or two, still gazing at the statue, he said, "Will you tell John Dall that we made love?"

"I'd tell him if he asked me, Alex, but he'll never ask."

"He will know, though," Alex Hemmer said quietly. "When he sees that statue, he will know."

She looked at the carving, then at Hemmer, and grinned suddenly. It was a sparkling grin, full of wicked humor, that lit up her face as if by a bright light from within. "I expect he will," she said.

"And so?"

"So it doesn't matter. He's not under the impression that he owns me or has any exclusive rights."

Hemmer said, a little wryly, "I do not think any man would have that impression." He paused. "I am curious about Willie Garvin. Tell me something of him."

"No. You'll only get confused, Alex. Everybody does. But I expect you'll be seeing him."

Hemmer looked surprised. "He is coming to Finland?"

"He's already here. We traveled over together. He's spending a month working in a lumber camp near Rytinki."

"Working? I understood he was a rich man."

"He is. But he likes a change and he likes logging."

"Logging is a very tough change."

"That's probably the point. You see? You're getting confused already. Anyway, I expect he's finished his stint by now and moved up to that little hotel where I was staying. I left a message there to tell him I'd moved in with you. I expect he'll call, If he doesn't get too tangled up with that lovely Finnish girl who runs the bakery."

Hemmer pushed a hand slowly through his hair and shook his head. Vaguely he could think of a number of questions he wanted to ask, but he had a suspicion that they would only lead to still more questions and that in the end his curiosity would remain unsatisfied.

As he put down his empty mug there came a faint sound from the heavy door between the big main room and the outer porch. It was an odd sound, as if someone were slapping at the timber with an open hand.

Modesty said, "A visitor?" She threw her cigarette in the fire and belted the wrap more firmly about her.

Alex Hemmer said, "I did not hear a car, and who would come on foot?" He moved to the door and opened it. A man who had been kneeling slumped against the door fell across the threshold. He wore heavy cord trousers tucked into stout boots, and a windcheater that had once been white but was now wet and caked with dirt. The hood had fallen back from his head. His ungloved hands and his face were very white with cold.

Modesty came past Hemmer, bent down and put her hands under the man's shoulders. She said, "Take his feet and help me get him in front of the fire, Alex. Then close the door, bring some brandy, and put hot-water-bottles in the bed."

Hemmer opened his mouth to voice a useless question, then closed it again. Together they lifted the unconscious man on to the rug in front of the fire. Hemmer brought a bottle of brandy and a glass from the cupboard, then went into the kitchen to fill hot-water-bottles.

When he returned he saw that Modesty had dragged off the man's boots and icy wet trousers. She had also partly taken off the windcheater, but his right arm was still in the stained and blackened sleeve.

The man had thinning brown hair and was perhaps in his middle forties, not a big man, but wiry. He had a lean face with a long jaw that bore a day's stubble of beard. His eyes were closed and he was muttering in a foreign language.

Hemmer said, "It sounds like German."

"Yes." Modesty looked up. "Pass me the scissors, Alex."

He gave them to her wonderingly, and watched as she began to cut away the sleeve of the windcheater and the thick sweater beneath. Then he realized that the black stains were dried blood.

"He is hurt?"

"Yes. Will you get your first-aid box from the bedroom, Alex? And a bowl of hot water, please."

He brought them for her, knelt down and began to massage one of the frozen hands, watching Modesty. She worked quickly and competently, as if no stranger to this kind of thing. The man still muttered occasionally, a rather desperate note in his voice.

"What is he saying?" Hemmer asked.

"He's saying, '*Don't let them find me, please. They're not far behind.*' "

She had soaked the clothing away from the wound and was washing the long deep gouge torn in the flesh of his upper arm. It was an ugly wound, raw and oozing. Hemmer had seen far worse during the bad days in Budapest, but even so he had to swallow a wave of nausea as he said, "What do you think he means, Modesty?"

"I think he means that the men who shot him are close behind."

"*Shot* him?"

"It's a bullet wound. You can see the two holes in the arm of his windcheater. In and out. It missed the bone, but it's taken a lot of flesh." She laid a strip of lint over the wound, spread a pad of cottonwool on top and began to bandage the arm. "We'll make a better dressing of it later. And we'll save the brandy for then too. The main thing now is to get him out of sight in the bedroom before his friends arrive."

Hemmer stood up, his big hands opening and shutting nervously. "If we hide him, we are involved," he said.

She finished the bandage before she answered. Her face was quiet and without anger. She said, "All right. I know how you feel. But he's a hurt man. Just help me get him to the bedroom."

"I will not help to hide him," Hemmer said stubbornly. "For God's sake, he may be a criminal! The people he fears may be the police. We do not know *anything* yet."

"That's right, Alex. We don't know yet. So let's find out before we throw him to the wolves."

He paced away across the room, pounding one fist gently into the palm of the other hand, dismayed and uncertain. As he swung round he saw that she had managed to lift the limp figure into a hunched kneeling position. Suddenly, with astonishing strength, she heaved the man upright, ducked so that he folded forward across her shoulder, then straightened up slowly.

Hemmer swore in Hungarian and started towards her. "All right! I'll carry him!"

She looked at him, slightly bent under her burden. The wrap had fallen open and he could see the flat plane of her taut stomach-muscles. She said, "Alex, we were involved from the moment he fell into this room, whether you like it or not. Leaving him on the floor here for his enemies to find, whoever they are, is just as much an act of involvement as hiding him from them. I'm not asking you to make a choice, I'm just telling you that I've made my own for the moment. Either I hide him now or I take him to the car and start driving. I'm not pressing you one way or the other, but just say which."

Hemmer swore again and said, "The bedroom! Don't just stand there with that weight on your back!"

She turned and moved slowly through the doorway. Hemmer followed, and helped her lower him to the bed. She stripped off his damp underclothes, put the hot-water-bottle around him, and piled on blankets and eiderdown.

The man stopped muttering. It seemed that the warmth had induced a sleep of exhaustion. Hemmer stood looking down at him, feeling a muddled blend of compassion and anger. Modesty was bending over her open suitcase. She straightened up, went to the door, beckoned Hemmer out and switched off the light.

"Get his clothes and all that first-aid stuff out of sight, Alex," she said softly, closing the door. Hemmer obeyed with dull resignation. He had to admit to himself that she had not used any wiles to secure his help. Her alternative of driving the wounded man away in her car had not been a threat, simply a statement of intent.

She had brought out a mop and was drying the floor, working with her head cocked slightly, listening. "Soon now," she said, and put the mop away. Hemmer held his breath to listen, and after a moment could just make out the faint drone of a car moving in low gear down the slight slope of the dirt road.

Modesty ran her eye over the area in front of the fire where the wounded man had lain. Satisfied, she sat on the edge of the big round table, swung her legs up to take the familiar pose, then slipped the wrap off and let it fall behind her. She said, "Start modeling, Alex. And don't answer when they knock. I've left the door on the latch so they can walk in."

"But you *can't—*" he began incredulously.

"It couldn't be better," she said with a touch of impatience. "Could anything look less likely than that we have something to hide? Oh, come *on*, Alex. Forget about our new guest and just be yourself. If you can go into one of your creative trances, so much the better."

With sudden angry energy he snatched up the mallet and a fishtail gouge, swivelled the table an inch or two, then moved to the statue and began to carve the line of the brow, ignoring the clay model, carving direct. His lips were tight and he was breathing hard through his nose.

Three minutes later, when a hand knocked sharply on the door, he merely glanced at her briefly from under lowered brows and went on with his work. The knock was repeated. After a long pause there came the sound of the heavy iron latch lifting. The door opened tentatively. A voice said, "Excuse me, please."

Modesty did not move. Her back was half turned to the door and she could see it only from the corner of her eye. Hemmer put down the mallet and began to use the palm of his hand on the handle of the gouge, tapping delicately.

Three men moved uncertainly over the threshold, then stopped short, staring. One said, "Please. I am sorry we intrude but it is urgent." He did not speak in Finnish, but in the widely understood Swedish tongue, and with an accent. An icy wind stirred in the room, and one of the men closed the door.

The first man spoke again. "I am sorry. It seems very bad to intrude, but—"

Modesty said without moving, very coldly. "Alex, there are people here." She spoke in Swedish. Hemmer might not have heard. His face was feverishly intent as he changed to a skew chisel and picked up the mallet again. The men shuffled uneasily, perplexed. Modesty lifted her voice and said, "Do you know whose house this is?"

"No. I regret, *Fröken*. A friend of ours is lost. He was hurt in an accident. We thought he might have found his way here."

Modesty said, "This is the house of Alex Hemmer, the most famous sculptor of this country. He is engaged in important work. It is bad enough that you enter unasked and stare when I am posing in this way. But to disturb Herr Hemmer at work is an outrage. Have you understood me?" On the last words she turned her head suddenly to glare with angry indignation.

Three men. Well dressed in expensive winter clothing and boots, with fur hats. Different faces but the same eyes. No, the same gaze. The familiar cold flat gaze, usually empty and incurious but now hazed by confusion and unease.

She had barely turned her head and sighted them when Hemmer let out an explosive oath. "Keep still!" he cried. "Dear God, you sit still for weeks and at this moment you move! *This* moment!" He flung down the chisel and pressed his hands to his eyes as if trying to retain an inner vision.

Modesty said in a low, furious voice, "Get out, you fools—see what you have done!"

"But . . .our friend," the spokesman persisted doggedly.

"You think Herr Hemmer entertains lost strangers tonight?" she said with fierce contempt. "Get *out!*"

She turned her head back into position. There came a muttered apology, a scuffling of feet. The door opened and closed. She listened for the sound of the car starting up, then for the fading sound as it moved away.

Hemmer dropped his hands from his eyes and drew in a deep breath. "Do not move again!" he said urgently. "What the devil got into you? Now hold it just like that. Hold it!" He picked up the chisel.

Dumbfounded, trying to keep her eyes from widening in astonishment, trying to suppress a sudden huge urge to laugh, Modesty Blaise said dazedly to herself, "My God! . . . ." And held it.

Half an hour later Hemmer put down a spoon gouge, stepped back from the bench and eased his cramped fingers. "I have got you," he said with quiet but intense triumph. "Not finished. Barely sketched in. But it is there, Modesty. I can see it there in the wood."

"I'm very glad for you." She got down from the table and put on the wrap. He was rubbing his eyes, but suddenly he snatched his hands away, stared at the bedroom door and then at Modesty. "That man!" he exclaimed.

"Yes." She tied the belt. "I don't think you noticed much about his friends when they came for him. They weren't policemen. And they weren't at all nice."

He sank down on a heavy teak chair and gestured vaguely towards the statue. "I suddenly found what I wanted . . ."

She smiled. "So I gathered. And very convincing it made you."

He drew in a long breath, frowning, reaching back into memory. "Yes. I remember now. But suppose they had searched? Suppose the man had called out in his sleep?"

She took a small automatic from the pocket of her wrap, drew the magazine out and worked the slide to eject the cartridge in the breech. "Then there would have been an argument, Alex. We might well have disturbed even your concentration."

"A gun," he said with weary distaste. "I hate guns."

"Guns are neutral. It's more logical to hate me." She looked at the big clock on the mantelpiece. "Time we had something to eat. Do you mind if I make a phone call first? I want to see if Willie Garvin's at the hotel."

He gripped his big hands between his knees and said slowly, "I will not be involved any further, Modesty."

"I know."

He got up. "I will start preparing the meal while you make the call." He went into the kitchen and closed the door.

It was ten minutes later when she joined him. He saw that she had dressed now, in a shirt and dark slacks with calf-length leather boots. She said, "Thanks, Alex. I got through. Willie arrived this morning. And our guest is still sleeping. I sat him up and got a little brandy down him. He said, '*Danke*,' and went to sleep again without even opening his eyes. But I'll have to rouse him later. I've got to find out what it's all about."

Hemmer looked at the automatic which now rested in a little holster on her belt. He said, "Why are you wearing that?"

"Those men may come back. We convinced them just now, but they could have second thoughts. I'd rather be safe than sorry."

The meal was a silent one. Hemmer brooded, a little sulky. Modesty was not unfriendly but seemed busy with her own thoughts. When they had cleared away she carried a big bowl of hot water into the bedroom. The man in the bed had thawed out now, and there was color in his face and hands.

Hemmer sat watching as she gave him a blanket bath, washing the sweat and grime from his body. When she had dried him she drew the covers over him again and took the rough dressing from his arm. She examined the wound closely, nodded her satisfaction, then brought a little bottle of clear liquid from her suitcase. It was after she had swabbed the wound and was re-bandaging the arm that the man's breathing changed.

He stirred, opened his eyes, went rigid for a moment, then slowly relaxed. The eyes were blue and wary. They focused on Modesty as she bent over him. He gave a feeble laugh of disbelief and murmured, "*Lieber Gott* . . ." A pause, and the next words were in English, the voice stronger. "You have changed very little, Mam'selle . . . except that your hair was up when I last saw you."

One of Modesty's eyebrows lifted sharply. "You know me?"

"We have not met. But I saw you in Vienna, five years ago. You are Modesty Blaise. Your people called you Mam'selle, I remember. You were there on business . . . and I was on the same business." Humor touched the intelligent blue eyes. "To your cost, I now regret. I am Waldo."

Modesty said, "My God." She sat down on the edge of the bed and began to laugh. "Fifty thousand you cost me, wasn't it?"

"A little more, I am sorry to say."

"Thank you for the flowers you sent afterwards. I'd have liked to meet you at the time."

"I have always been a very retiring man."

"Yours is that kind of business, Waldo."

"It was. And perhaps even a gentlemanly business. But no longer." He looked down at his bandaged arm. "The game has changed, Mam'selle.

You did well to retire. I am taking the same road myself."

Alex Hemmer stood up and moved to the bedside. Modesty said, "Waldo, this is Alex Hemmer, your host."

"I am in your debt, Herr Hemmer."

"Not mine." Hemmer looked at Modesty. "Will you explain to me what you have been speaking of?"

She nodded and took out a packet of cigarettes. Hemmer shook his head. She lit two, and placed one between Waldo's lips.

"For the last fifteen years," she said, "Waldo has been the top industrial spy in the business. The top solo man, anyway, and a founder-member of the profession. Quite a lot of what he does is legal. Some of it isn't. And the whole business works only because some of the biggest corporations in the world are ready to hand out a lot of money for details of new processes and inventions their rivals are developing."

"This I know," Hemmer said with a shade of impatience. "I have read of it."

"No doubt," Modesty said. "But you won't have read of Waldo. He's known only in special circles. Quite a big section of my own organization was devoted to industrial espionage, and very rewarding it was. In Vienna, five years ago, Waldo and I were both after something the Farbstein Corporation had come up with, and he snatched it from under my nose." She smiled. "Afterwards Waldo sent me a beautiful bouquet with a very witty and charming note of apology."

"I hoped you would know it was an act of courtesy and not of vanity," Waldo said.

"I knew." She studied his tired, aging face. "It showed style, Waldo. I've always liked style."

Somehow Waldo contrived to bow while lying in bed. "Your own great quality, Mam'selle. But a dying thing. The game has changed."

"So you said. Your three friends called and went away satisfied, but I don't know whether they'll remain so. Who are they?"

"Salamander Four."

She stared. Hemmer said, "What is Salamander Four?"

Still looking at Waldo she answered, "International group based in Amsterdam. The big boys of industrial espionage. Very businesslike. Very high-powered men at the top. There are names in Salamander Four that you can read in the city and society and even political columns of newspapers in a dozen different countries. But they've always worked clean. I've never known them to hire killers."

Waldo gave a little shrug, and winced. "That also has changed. Mam'selle. I did not believe it myself until now."

"What happened?"

"The Kellgren Laboratories in Sweden have developed a new color film. Salamander Four were after the process. So was I, for a client of my own in West Germany. Well . . . I won, and Salamander Four lost. That should be the end of it. But they do not have your appreciation of style, Mam'selle. They want me dead, and I have been running hard for two weeks now."

He stubbed out the cigarette in the ashtray she held for him, and smiled resignedly. "But Europe has become too small. They caught up with me about seven kilometers from here, I think. They rammed my car. I went into a ditch, but was able to get out and run into the forest. They followed, shooting at me. I was hit in the arm, but in the end I lost them." He grimaced. "I lost myself, also. I don't remember very well how I came to this house."

Modesty got up and paced the little room, holding her elbows. After a while she said, "What were your plans, Waldo?"

"Australia." His gaze was rueful. "I can afford to retire, and the work has no pleasure for me now. Salamander Four will not reach out to Australia for me. It will be enough for them that I have been driven from the scene."

"What route?"

"By air. Each night for the next three nights there will be a private aircraft waiting at Ivalo to fly me across the border and down to Leningrad."

"Will you be safe in transit across Russia?"

"By air, yes. I have industrial contacts there. They are very different from the politicians. All arrangements have been expensively made. It is only the journey between here and Ivalo that is dangerous for me." He hesitated, then went on apologetically. "Is it possible to borrow or to hire a car, Mam'selle?"

Hemmer grunted. Modesty said, "You can't drive with that arm. I'll take you to Ivalo myself." She looked at Hemmer. "Tomorrow morning, if that's all right with you, Alex. Otherwise we'll leave tonight."

Hemmer got to his feet. "You must do what you think best," he said, and went out of the room.

After a moment Waldo said, "I have caused trouble. I am sorry."

"It's nothing. Artists are difficult people. They dream up a nice world to live in, and it makes the real world very hard for them to cope with." She smiled at him. "I've got some hot soup ready. You're going to eat, Waldo, then sleep until I wake you tomorrow."

He sighed. "I wish I had the words to thank you. In a way I am like your friend. All these years I have evaded physical conflict, and now that it comes upon me I am lost. I have never swum in these waters." He thought for a moment. "It is possible Salamander Four will keep watch on this house, I think."

"They may. I'll wake you early, so you can be tucked down out of sight in the back of the car before first light. An hour later they can watch me come out and drive off on my own, if they're interested."

He nodded, and looked about him. "This is the only bed. Where will you sleep?"

"Alex can sleep in the other room, on the rug in front of the fire."

"And you?"

She touched the gun at her wrist. "I'll be sitting up, Waldo. Just in case our Salamander Four friends come back tonight. You can sleep soundly. I've swum in these waters quite a lot."

An hour before dawn, heavy smoke began to belch from the chimney, rolling and billowing around the house. Under cover of the smoke and the darkness, Modesty took Waldo out to the Volvo. He lay down on the back seat with a thick rug over him and three hot water bottles. He wore a sweater and a warm jacket provided by Hemmer. The rest of his clothes had been dried overnight. He had eaten and slept well, and his hurt arm was strapped comfortably in a sling under the jacket.

Modesty went back into the house and raked aside the oily rags she had put on the fire to make smoke. Hemmer stood gazing absently at the statue, running a hand over the chiselled curves of the close-grained wood.

She said, "Will you be able to finish it without me, Alex? You said you could see what you wanted in the wood now."

He shook his head. "I can see it. But I cannot carve it without also being able to see your face."

"Would you like me to fix breakfast for you? I've got an hour, and it won't take me long to pack."

"Thank you."

There was little conversation, but she seemed to feel no sense of strain, and her manner was amiably relaxed. Hemmer felt confused. Once he said, "Do you think I am a coward because I will not let myself be involved?"

She said, "No, I don't think that, Alex. I've no criticism at all. Will you have some more coffee?"

Later, after the sun had risen, she came out of the bedroom wearing a tartan lumberjacket and black slacks tucked into her boots, a little white fur cap on her head, suitcase in her hand. She put a hand to his cheek, kissed him lightly on the lips and said, "Goodbye, Alex. Take care of yourself."

He took the case and walked with her to the car to put it in the boot. The cold made her tanned cheeks glow, and he found her heart-achingly lovely.

He said, "Will you come back?"

"What do *you* think, Alex?"

"I don't know." He managed to smile. "I just hope that if you come back it will not be simply for Dall's sake."

She said nothing, and he could read nothing in her eyes. After a moment she turned and got into the car. He closed the door and stepped back. The engine fired and revved. She waved, and eased the car smoothly away over the rutted snow, its studded tires biting firmly.

The dirt road curved gently up through the forest to join a road which led on to Highway Four, the arctic highway running north to Ivalo. But she had decided to branch off and take the lesser road, through Pokka and Inari, since it was more direct. With winter only just begun, the road would still be clear of heavy snow.

She said, "Are you comfortable, Waldo?"

His voice behind her answered. "So comfortable I could sleep, Mam'selle. It was beginning to grow cold, but now the car-heater has taken effect."

"Sleep if you can. There's a long drive ahead. And there may be a lot of hanging around at Ivalo if the weather isn't clear for takeoff. We could wait all night."

"But there is no need for you to wait with me, Mam'selle."

"Don't argue. With Salamander Four in the field, I'm going to see you off. You can thank the flowers for that."

She heard his soft, pleasant laugh, and said, "Whether you sleep or not, stay tucked down. If Salamander Four didn't take careful note of this car last night, they're not the men they ought to be. And if they know you were heading north, they'll be watching out. I hope they'll watch Highway Four, but I won't bank on it. If they see me alone at the wheel it's one thing, but seeing me with a passenger is something else."

It was an hour later, after they had passed a small village north of Hanhimaa, that the grey Mercedes came on their tail. Here the road wound round a long low hill, with tall spruce on one side and a shallow drop on the other. All along the edge of the drop were set big stones to mark the limit of the road. A thin layer of unfrozen snow covered the surface.

Modesty roused Waldo, who was dozing. "I think they picked us up going through the last village," she said. "Don't quite know what they'll try, but nothing drastic to begin with, I imagine. They're only working on suspicion so far."

"Can you leave them behind?" Waldo asked quietly.

"I don't fancy trying to run away from a Merc, and I don't want to drive rally-style for the next few hours." She studied the mirror. "Only one man in the car, I think. We'll aim at settling things as soon as he shows his hand."

She took the automatic, an MAB .25, from her pocket and passed it back to him between the bucket seats. "I don't want any shooting, Waldo, but if things go wrong you can look after yourself with this. Stay down when we stop, and don't show yourself. If anyone opens the back door to look in, you can take it something's gone wrong and I'm out of action. Then it's up to you."

He hesitated, and she knew he wanted to protest, but after a moment he said, "Understood." She allowed herself a brief smile. Waldo was a professional, not the man to jog your arm when you were calling the shots.

Behind her the Mercedes drew closer, flashed its lights and peeped its horn. She slowed a little, turned and looked over her shoulder. There was only one man in the car. Evidently he was intending to make a soft approach . . . anxiety about a slight rear-wheel wobble on the Volvo, or a suspect tire. Any excuse to stop her and take a look in the car.

She had switched the heater to "screen" two minutes ago. Already the side windows were heavily misted, and only the electrically heated section of the rear window was clear.

Flash of headlights from behind, and a more urgent peep of the horn. Ahead the road swelled to form a short lay-by. Here, by some freak of trapped warmth from the sun, the thin snow had melted. The surface was smooth dry tarmac, in contrast to the dirt and gravel surface of the road.

She drew into the lay-by and halted. The Mercedes cut in ahead and stopped sharply. The man who emerged was the spokesman of the night before. She was out in the road, had closed the door and was moving to meet him as he came towards her. He smiled, but his eyes remained very cold.

"Excuse me, Fröken. There is something hanging loose under your car—" He stopped short with assumed surprise. "Surely it is the lady we met last night?"

"Did you find your friend?" Modesty said. His right hand was in the pocket of the thick thigh-length jacket he wore. He stopped three paces from her.

"No, we did not find him, Fröken," he said, watching her. "Did *you*?" The smile had vanished. She knew that her quick exit from the car and the closing of the door had sharpened his suspicions. When she made no reply he said, "I wish to look in your car, please."

She said, "No. Go back to Salamander Four and tell them—"

That was as far as she got. The use of the name was calculated to freeze him for an instant, long enough for her to take one stride and strike with the kongo, the little double mushroom of hard, polished sandalwood that was gripped in her right hand, the two knobs protruding from her fist as it rested in the slanting pocket of her lumberjacket.

But her calculation was wrong. Almost as the words "Salamander Four" left her lips, he jerked a revolver from his pocket and fired at her head.

It was her own speed of reaction, far faster than thought, which saved her; and perhaps also the long experience which had taught her that to duck or dodge away from a gun at short range is foolish. A bullet kills as readily at ten feet as at two feet, and moving back allows a gunman more shots.

She had ducked sideways and was lunging towards the gun. The bullet cracked past her head, missing by a finger's width. Then her left hand closed over the cylinder and breech, squeezing with all her strength, holding the hammer back and forcing a pinch of her flesh between hammer and cartridge.

She made no attempt to force the gun sideways or to wrench it from him, but went with the movement of his arm as he jerked back hard, and in the same moment struck with the kongo in her right hand, aiming for the temple.

As he staggered back across the front of the Volvo the gun came free of his grasp and was left reversed in her hand. The blow with the kongo had been awkwardly struck and was slightly off target. He did not fall, but recovered his balance and thrust towards her again, his face twisted with shock and fury. She went to meet him, and took him with a drop-kick, her booted feet smashing home just over the heart.

As she landed in a crouch he went back three tottering paces and fell. She heard the soft thump as his head struck one of the big stones bordering the edge of the road. His legs twitched, and he lay still.

Carefully she detached the gun from her left hand. It was a Smith & Wesson Chief's Special .38. She eased the hammer down, grimly thankful that it had not been the Centennial Model with the enclosed hammer, and sucked her hand where the pinched flesh oozed a bead of blood. As she put on the safety she went to the Volvo and called, "Relax on that trigger, Waldo. It's me." Her voice was taut with fury.

When she opened the rear door his pale face stared up at her and she saw the MAB in his hand. He sat up slowly and said, "When I heard the shot, I thought . . ."

"You very nearly thought right." He saw her lips compress in a thin hard line, saw that her blue-black eyes were stormy. She was breathing hard, not from exertion but from anger.

"The bastard!" she said, seething. "If he'd *known* who I was, if he'd even *known* you were in the car, I wouldn't mind. But he didn't know a damn thing. As far as he knew I was just a girl who stood here and said 'Salamander Four'. So he tried to blow my brains out." She reached over to put the Special on the front seat, and picked up her gloves. "No questions. Just out with the gun, and bang!"

Waldo made a sympathetic noise, then watched as she walked to the unconscious man and knelt over him. He felt an inward chill, knowing that if he had been in her place he would have been dead by now. He saw her take off a glove and rest her fingers on the man's neck. Ten seconds later she stood up and walked back to the car.

"How is he?" Waldo asked.

She shrugged, frowning a little with annoyance. "He hit his head on that stone, and he's what might best be described as dead."

Waldo laughed shortly. "I shall try to remember him as he was when he was alive. It will help to ease my sorrow." He looked past her at the body. "But it makes a bad situation. Will you arrange a car accident?"

"No." She looked up and down the empty road, pulling on her glove. "It would take too long to make it convincing. Better to keep things simple and just bend the truth a little. Stay there."

She walked to the Mercedes, backed it to within a few feet of the body, then switched off and got out. He saw her unlock the boot, take out the jack, toolbox and spare wheel. She spread them around on the ground, returned to the Volvo, and took a quart can of oil from the boot.

Unscrewing the cap of the can, she poured a little oil on the dry tarmac close to the dead man's feet, then smeared some on the soles of his boots. She scraped her foot through the puddle of oil once or twice, put the cap on, but did not screw it up tightly. When she laid the can down on its side, oil dripped from it very slowly.

Crouching by the offside rear wheel, she took a thin screwdriver from the toolbox and jabbed it between the treads of the tire, pressing hard. The tire deflated. She returned the screwdriver and used her gloved hands to brush a little dirt from the breast of the man's jacket, where her drop-

PETER O'DONNELL

kick had landed.

After a final study of the scene she walked back to the Volvo and got in behind the wheel.

Waldo said, "He was preparing to change the wheel. The oil leaked a little from the can. He stepped on the oil-patch and his feet went from under him. His head hit the stone when he fell. A matter of simple deduction."

"It's better than anything fancy," Modesty said, and started the engine. "Next village or garage we come to I'll report it, to account for our tracks. I'll be very upset and rather shaky, not quite sure that he's dead, but I think so, and anyway I was too scared to move him. You stay under the rug, Waldo."

As she drove out of the lay-by, Waldo leaned back in his seat. "I wonder where his two colleagues are?" he said thoughtfully.

Modesty changed up and the car gathered speed. "I think we could both make a good guess," she said.

They came on foot, two hours after sunrise. When the door opened and they walked in, Alex Hemmer was sitting staring into the fire, as he had been sitting ever since Modesty Blaise drove away.

He recognized them from the night before, though he had not been consciously aware of them then. One had a gingery growth of beard. The other, a little taller, had a pasty face and a thin nose. Hemmer got to his feet, feeling sudden unease as the door closed behind them.

The thin-nosed one walked forward and said, "You lied last night. He was here. There is a trail in the snow, and spots of blood. Impossible to see in the dark, but clear enough now."

He hit Hemmer across the face with sudden ferocity. It was a back-handed blow, and the shock of it seemed to scramble Hemmer's brains. He reeled back and toppled over a chair. The man with the beard kicked him and said, "Where is he?"

"Gone . . ." Hemmer wheezed, fighting down the sickness that threatened to overwhelm him. Through the sound of his own harsh breathing he heard footsteps move across the room, heard the bedroom door thrown open, then the kitchen door.

"The woman took him when she left in the car?" said a voice. Hemmer's vision cleared a little. The two men were standing over him. He shook his head.

"Gone where?" said the thin-nosed man.

"I . . . don't know." Hemmer felt completely helpless before the casual ruthlessness of these two men, but fear had not touched him yet, only a slow and impotent anger. Stolidly he began to get to his feet. A knee hit him under the chin and he sprawled again.

Vaguely he was aware of being hauled to a kneeling position, of rough hands doing something to his right arm, forcing it into a gap with smooth wood on each side. When his head cleared a little he found that he was crouched against the back of the heavy fireside chair. His hand had been thrust between the vertical wooden rails and his hand rested on the broad seat. The thin-nosed man stood on one side of the chair, bending a little to grip the imprisoned forearm. The man with the beard had picked up the beechwood mallet that lay on the table by the statue.

"Where did they go?" the thin-nosed man said with cold anger.

Hemmer shook his head again. "I don't know."

The man nodded to his companion. "All right. Break his hand."

It was then that fear struck into Hemmer, piercing and incredulous fear. He tried to rise, but his legs had lost their strength. The bearded man moved forward and lifted the mallet high. Staring up at him through the wooden rails, Hemmer screamed soundlessly within himself.

He felt a gust of cold air on his back, and saw something glitter as it flashed three feet over his head from behind. The bearded man jumped as if stung. The mallet jerked in his grasp. In the moment before it fell, Hemmer saw that the five-inch blade of a small throwing-knife with a dimpled bone haft had driven through the handle of the mallet just above the point of grip, so that the edge of the blade had nicked the bearded man's fingers. Spots of blood fell as the mallet clattered to the floor.

The thin-nosed man jerked upright, a hand streaking to the pocket of his fur jacket.

A voice said, "Garvin". It was a deep, relaxed voice, and its effect was astonishing. As if the single word held some potent magic, both men froze instantly in mid-action, their postures slightly grotesque. Into Hemmer's dazed mind flickered the memory of the ancient Nordic legend which held that a troll overtaken by sunrise is turned instantly to stone.

He twisted his head round slowly. A man stood in the open doorway, a man in his middle thirties perhaps, with thick fair hair and a brown face that was pleasantly unhandsome and a little rough-hewn. He was hatless, and wore a lumberjacket of dull green and brown, with dark trousers tucked into leather boots. In his left hand was a knife, a twin of the other, held by the blade between two fingers and a thumb.

Hemmer's first impression was one of hugeness. Then he realized that though the man was big, well over six feet, it was the impact of his personality that made the room seem to shrink. It extended beyond his physical body like an aura. In it there was an immense vitality combined with a quiet, vast assurance that contained no element of conceit.

"Willie Garvin," said the man, though clearly the knife and the single word had been sufficient introduction for the two intruders. Then, as Hemmer drew his arm free and made to rise—"Stay down a minute, Mr. 'emmer. You might get in the way."

Hemmer stayed down. The two men were still frozen and there was a glaze of fear in their eyes. Willie Garvin pushed the door shut behind him and moved forward unhurriedly, the knife-hilt resting lightly on his shoulder now.

"Better get to know each other," he said as he passed the thin-nosed man. "Who're you?" On the last word his right arm lifted and swung in a backward jab, so fast that to Hemmer it was a blur. The elbow struck just under the man's ear. His knees folded and he melted to the floor without a sound.

Now Hemmer saw that the knife had been reversed and was held by the hilt. Willie Garvin made a quick jab towards the stomach of the bearded man. It was a feint that compelled instinctive reaction. The man's hands dropped to ward off the thrust, and as they did so Willie Garvin took another half-pace forward and struck upwards under the side of the jaw, hitting with the inside edge of his empty right hand.

The bearded man seemed to grow taller for a moment, then crumpled in a heap.

"I wonder if you could find me a bit of cord, Mr. 'emmer?" Willie Garvin said politely. "We'll get 'em tied up, and then p'raps we could 'ave a nice cup of coffee."

Hemmer got slowly to his feet. He tried to frame a question, but his mind was too confused. "Cord," he repeated at last, and nodded. "Yes." He went through into the kitchen.

When he returned with a length of picture cord, Willie Garvin's knives had disappeared and the mallet with the split handle lay on the table. "Sorry about the damage," said Willie. "The Princess told me not to play rougher than I 'ad to, so I figured a nice fancy throw might keep 'em quiet."

"And your name, also, I think."

"It rings a bell with some people," Willie acknowledged.

Hemmer rubbed his brow. "You said . . . the Princess?"

"Modesty." Willie took the cord from Hemmer and knelt over the thin-nosed man. "She rang me again last night, after you'd gone to sleep. I left the Land-Rover the other side of the lake and came the rest of the way on foot. Been waiting in the bath-'ouse since a couple of hours before dawn."

"But . . . that was before she left!"

"Well, we 'ad to overlap, and she didn't want me on show. These two might 'ave been watching, and she reckoned you might get upset and start a lot of argument. Any chance of that coffee, Mr. 'emmer?"

Hemmer went into the kitchen and began to make coffee. He found that his hands were shaking with the reaction from that moment of piercing terror. When he returned five minutes later the two men had come to their senses. They lay with their hands bound behind them, and their faces were pallid with fear. Willie Garvin was smoking a cigarette, studying the statue with great concentration.

"You've really got something 'ere," he said slowly. "John Dall's going to love it. The body's perfect. It lives. You can pretty well see the 'eart beating. Only got the face to finish now, eh?"

Hemmer put down the coffee pot and the mugs. He said, "She brought you here to guard me. How did she know what would happen?"

"It stuck out a mile that Waldo must've left quite a trail," Willie said gently. "And it was an odds-on chance that Salamander Four would double-check and pick it up in daylight. This is the only 'ouse for miles. So Modesty fixed for me to cover you."

"I did not realize they would come back," Hemmer said simply. "It just did not occur to me."

"She said it wouldn't." Willie took the mug of coffee offered him, and stirred in several spoonfuls of sugar. "She told me about you not liking to get involved, and all that. It's a nice idea, but it makes things rough when you run up against a couple of villains like we got 'ere."

Hemmer gave a little start and put down his coffee. "There were three of them," he said. "There is another!"

"That's right. We figured they'd split, so that one or two could cover the road while the other one or two checked this 'ouse."

"Then . . . the third one will he waiting for Modesty on the road." Hemmer's big hands worked anxiously.

Willie nodded. "That's 'is bad luck," he said cheerfully, and drained the mug. "I'll go an' fetch the Land-Rover. Be back in about twenty minutes." He went out, whistling a Chopin mazurka with remarkable accuracy.

In the time of waiting, Alex Hemmer found much to occupy his thoughts. The two men made no move, and spoke only once, when the thin-nosed one lifted his head and said listlessly, "The woman, she is Modesty Blaise?" Hemmer nodded, and the man slumped down again, dull-eyed.

When Willie Garvin returned Hemmer said, "What will you do with them?"

"I was thinking about that, Mr. 'emmer. Just dropping 'em in the lake would suit me allright, but the Princess wouldn't like it. She'd say it was the lazy way out. So I'm taking 'em down to that lumber camp where I've been working. I can make it in six hours."

"The lumber camp?"

"That's right." Willie looked at Hemmer. "I like working with Finns. You got the most literate country in the world 'ere. Even the jacks, now, they're 'ard as nails but they've got a bit of culture. So they're quite proud of people like you, Mr. 'emmer. And when I tell 'em these two were going to smash your 'ands with a mallet, they won't like it much."

Willie turned and squatted in front of the bound men, staring at them with frosty blue eyes. "It's going to be the longest winter you ever lived through," he said slowly. "Those jacks'll keep you 'auling on ropes and 'eaving on saws till you feel like one big raw blister."

The bearded man said with a flash of defiance, "Salamander Four will get you."

Willie Garvin smiled. Not a warm smile. "It'll be a long time before you can tell them anything." He held up a hand with the finger and thumb half an inch apart. "There's a dossier that thick, a blue-print of Salamander Four, pretty well the whole structure, with names an' facts an' figures. Especially names. It's a souvenir from when Modesty Blaise ran The Network. We spent three years compiling it."

He stood up. "In a couple of days that dossier will be with a man called Tarrant. He'll open it if anything nasty 'appens to Modesty Blaise or me. Then the roof falls in on Salamander Four. So when you get back, tell 'em that. I don't know who your immediate boss is, but at a guess I'd say it's Walburn or Geiss or Sarmiento. Maybe de Chardin, going further up the scale. Whoever it is, just tell 'im."

For a moment the two men were startled out of their apathy by the list of names. They exchanged a shaken look. Willie Garvin turned and said, "Excuse me while I get 'em in the truck, Mr. 'emmer."

He herded the bound men out of the house and spent several minutes securing them in the back of the Land-Rover to his satisfaction. Hemmer watched from the doorway. Everything had happened so quickly that his mind seemed to have seized up. He felt drained.

Willie Garvin came back into the house. "Just wanted another look at that statue before I go, if it's all right with you."

For long minutes he studied the work, absorbed, moving round to gaze from all sides. "It's great," he said at last, very softly, and touched a big hand to the column of the neck. "That's what always gets me, Mr. 'emmer. I could look at 'er throat for hours."

Hemmer stared. That this rough, dangerous man with the strange Cockney accent should have reflected Hemmer's own inmost visual pleasure so exactly was astounding.

"That is my feeling also, Mr Garvin," he said. "Yet the throat, the neck, came easily. It is the face that is difficult."

Willie Garvin laughed. "I can imagine. You 'ave to choose one look, and you want 'em all."

"I can get them," Hemmer said. "I can do it, if she comes back. But I think she despises me now, Mr. Garvin, because I would not be involved. Or tried not to be."

"That's your privilege," Willie Garvin said simply. "She wouldn't think any less of you for it."

"You think she may come back, then?"

Willie Garvin shrugged, and when he spoke his face was as neutral as Modesty's had been when she spoke the same words. "What do *you* think?" He did not wait for a reply, but held out his hand. "Well, so long, Mr. 'emmer. Been nice meeting you."

It was not until five minutes after the Land-Rover had moved off that Hemmer realized he had not spoken a word of thanks to the man who had saved him from a maimed hand.

Five days passed before he finally gave up hope that she would return. It was only then that he went to the clay model and began patiently, stubbornly, to seek the face that he wanted.

Throughout the day he worked without success. At nightfall he took up his chisel and turned to the wood, deciding that he must take the final gamble. By working direct on the carving, some miracle of imagination might guide his hands to find what he wanted.

It was then that he heard a car turn off the dirt road and stop outside the house. He stood watching the door, telling himself it was foolish to hope. If she had intended to return she would have done so days ago.

He had left the door on the latch. It opened and she came in, taking off her gloves, saying, "Hallo, Alex." She looked at the statue, then sat down in the chair by the fire and pulled off her boots and socks.

Hemmer said, "I thought you would not come back."

"I've been over to London." She stood up and took off her jacket and sweater. "I had to see about some papers there."

"A dossier? For a man called Tarrant?"

"That's right." She walked across the room and kissed him. "How have you been, Alex?"

"I have been thinking a lot." He gave a little sigh. "It has not changed what I believe, Modesty."

She smiled, and said gently, "Alex, I don't care a damn about what you believe."

He put down the chisel and rubbed his brow. "Tell me something. You did not just hide Waldo from the men who wanted to kill him. You went to much trouble to help him, to get him safely out of danger. It seemed that you liked him, *wanted* to help him. Why was that?"

She took off her shirt and slacks, and stood up, reaching behind to unclip her bra. "I haven't thought about it. But . . . I suppose because Waldo has style. Yes. Maybe I'll start a society for the Preservation of Style."

He nodded soberly. "It is something hard to define. How does a man acquire style, Modesty?"

Naked now, she sat on the edge of the table and swung her legs up on to it. "God knows, Alex. You could start by learning to laugh a little. At yourself, at me if you like, or at a situation. Waldo laughed when he first opened his eyes and saw me, remember?"

"Do you think you can teach me to laugh a little?"

"I can try. A good time to start is when we're making love." She took up the familiar pose. Her eyes held a smile, natural and unforced, a smile both young and old, innocent and experienced, candid yet concealing.

Hemmer gazed for a full two minutes before he said, "Making love is something to laugh about?"

"It ought to be all things, Alex. Even hilarious sometimes. How long have I got for teaching you? I mean, how long before you finish the statue?"

"I could finish it in a day and a half." A little glint of amusement came into his eyes, and he gave a slow smile. "But I am a slow learner, so I will make it last at least two weeks."

Her face lit up. "There! That had a touch of style."

He was still smiling as he turned to the statue and took up his chisel and mallet. He could see the contours of the face clearly beneath the surface of the wood now. The image filled his mind, and his hands almost stung with the sudden tingling of blood in them.

The grain . . . so. The curve . . . so. A small slanting plane here, and the imperceptible rounding to give the highlight there . . .

With a long inhalation of pleasure he set the blade to the wood and began to tap.

NON-INTERFERENCE

Janwillem van de Wettering

"TO DINGJUM?" ADJUTANT Grijpstra of the Amsterdam Municipal Police asked. "That's a long way off, Sergeant. That's in the North. You sure?" He looked at Sergeant De Gier suspiciously. De Gier's tall, wide-shouldered body sprawled behind his dented desk with his feet propped up on its top, between files not arranged neatly. Sunlight glinted off his pistol's butt and barrel, protruding from a well-worn shoulder holster that contrasted crudely with the sergeant's spotless, tailored blue shirt. De Gier smiled innocently, showing strong white teeth and sparkling, oversized, soft brown eyes. His moustache, model cavalry officer, previous century, was swept up neatly under his long straight nose and high cheekbones supporting a noble brow, supporting thick brown curls in turn.

"Sure," the sergeant said. "I think we should go to Dingjum. It'll be a nice day today, we have just been supplied with a new car, Dingjum is a pleasant little town, set in unspoiled country, we'll drive along Holland's longest and neatest dike, with the sea on one side and a lake on the other, we'll watch birds, sails on the horizon, interesting cloud formations—the car has a sunroof, we can drive and watch the sky in turns—I think I'm sure it's a lovely idea."

Adjutant Grijpstra sighed. His hands, clasped on a steadily rising and receding round belly, covered by a pinstriped blue waistcoat, gently unhooked their fingers and rose in feeble protest. "Dingjum is some sixty miles outside of our territory, Sergeant. We're specialists, members of the celebrated Murder Brigade, we only move for specific and urgent reasons. Whatever could demand our presence in the little rural town of Dingjum?"

Sergeant De Gier withdrew his feet and jumped up in one extended, graceful and lithe, powerful movement. He found a newspaper on a filing cabinet and handed it to the gray-haired solid adjutant, still at ease in his swivel-chair on the other side of the small gray-painted room. "Front page news. Absorb its contents. *Fresh contents*. This happened less than a week ago."

Grijpstra read. He mumbled. "A *Chinese* businessman? In *Dingjum*? An *arrow* into his throat? While watering exotic plants in a *greenhouse*?"

The sergeant poured coffee from a thermos-flask into paper cups. "Exotic is right."

Adjutant Grijpstra put the newspaper down and reached for the coffee. "Thanks. I still fail to see what we could do in Dingjum. There's State Police out there. We would interfere. They might not like that."

"We're never liked," Sergeant De Gier said, contentedly slipping behind his desk again. "However, there might be an exception. Lieutenant Sudema is in charge of the local station; you remember the lieutenant?"

"Yes," Grijpstra said. "That was a while ago. I didn't care for all the tomato salad he made us eat."

"And we gave Lieutenant Sudema the credit for our solution," De Gier said gently. "We always do when we can. We're not so bad, Adjutant."

"Oh, but we are," Grijpstra said. "We disturb the peace of our esteemed colleagues. We did that time. The lieutenant didn't exactly welcome us. And we had a legal excuse then; we don't have one now. We found a corpse in Amsterdam that lived, when still alive, in Dingjum. We pursued a hot trail. We're pursuing nothing now."

"I sort of like going after nothing," the sergeant said softly. "Oh, come on now, Grijpstra. An arrow in a millionaire's throat, and the millionaire is a Chinese who officially resides in the Fiji Islands but who somehow owns a capital villa here, and who originated in Taiwan, and who has married one of our former beauty queens, and who owns a factory of computer parts that he doesn't manage; it's all in the article; that's a lot of nothing that adds up nicely."

"Where?" Grijpstra said, looking at the paper again. "Ah. The tale continues on page three. Let's see." He turned pages, holding the paper up to get a better look at the dead man's wife. "Why does she wear a tiny two-piece bathing suit? Ah, that was her prize-winning outfit. Some years ago. Still a bit of a girl then, though definitely sexy. A woman now, eh what? A most attractive woman?"

"You bet," De Gier said. "You'd meet her, if we would go to Dingjum. Don't you want to meet with a mature beauty queen?"

"Nah," Grijpstra said.

"You do" De Gier said. "And more than I. You've repressed your lusts; there's an evil power in you, pushing its tentacles through your flimsy defenses. You'd go a long way to be able to meet a sex symbol in her dainty flesh. Maybe *she* shot that arrow? If the Chinese dead man was a millionaire? The couple has no children. Wouldn't the lady make a first class suspect? You could manipulate her, ask her tricky questions, prod her luscious soul, wiggle, finger, feel. . . ."

"What's with you?" Grijpstra asked furiously.

"Spring," De Gier whispered. "Spring brings out romantic desire in me. It's a good spring now and we could go for a drive."

Grijpstra pulled himself free of his desk and swiveled his chair. His short legs, in trouserpipes that were rather badly rumpled, and sagging socks and shoes that hadn't been recently polished, scissored slowly. "Yeh," Grijpstra said. "Never mind your romantic needs for now. A *Chinese* multimillionaire living off the fat of our land, and officially residing in the Fiji Islands, what does that lead to?"

"Non-payment of taxes," De Gier said. "Easy question, easy answer. It also points to extreme cleverness."

The adjutant's heavy body made another complete turn, while a steady sun ray highlighted his short silver hair. "How so?"

"Our corpse," De Gier said, "the former Lee Dzung, married one of this country's certified beautiful women. Why? To kill a whole flock of fat ducks with one broadside of his foreign gun. He doesn't pay taxes in Holland, right?"

"Right," Grijpstra said. "In Fiji, tax would be nominal. But Dzung is active in business here. His factory produces high priced products."

"Now then, Adjutant. Dzung is our guest, he flies in and out, and when he's here he has a beautiful villa, it says so in the article, surrounded by a park, which is owned by his wife, and he owns his wife."

"Yes," Grijpstra said. "If Dzung owned property here he would have to become a resident and pay Dutch income taxes. A diabolic way out that would satisfy human greed, and Dzung picked the best looking wife the country could provide, doubly attractive to him for she is of another race. Long-legged, full-bosomed, golden-haired." Grijpstra studied the photograph again, grunting with pleasure. "A dirty boy's dream. The answer to all his hidden filthy desires."

"You're so Calvinistic," De Gier mused. "Maybe you become over-excited when you contemplate that perfect and inviting shape, but why should Dzung?"

"It's natural," Grijpstra said. "Aren't Chinese Confucianists? Confucianism preaches a strict code of morals, an impossible system that automatically produces pleasurable guilt." Grijpstra grinned. "Show me a Chinese beauty queen and my feelings of forbidden lust will be doubled, too. Now suppose I could marry her, and put her in a pagoda, and spend a few months a year with her in a, to me, exotic setting, and have expert foreigners produce my pricy gadgets, and make tax-free profits . . . for that's another point here . . ." the adjutant's blunt forefinger poked in the direction of De Gier's immaculate shirt—". . . if the Dingjum factory is owned by a mother company in far-off Fiji, full profits can be channeled there."

De Gier got up, reaching for a silk scarf of a delicate baby-blue color that went well with his indigo shirt. "Shall we go?"

"Whoa," Grijpstra said.

De Gier knotted his scarf, tucking it neatly into his collar.

"An excuse, Sergeant?" Grijpstra pleaded. "We do need an excuse."

De Gier scratched his strong chin. "Yep. Let's see now. About a month ago a bum fell into the Emperor's Canal. The water police fished him out last week. Remember?"

"Yagh." The adjutant grimaced.

"You're telling me," De Gier said. "I almost fainted when they brought that mess in."

Grijpstra looked stern. "You fell into my arms. Was the bum connected to the North?"

"If he wasn't he is now," De Gier said. He opened a drawer and found a disheveled file. "No, right. He *was* from the North. We haven't checked the death properly yet. An accident probably, the man was an alcoholic, but he could have been pushed. He will have relatives in the North and we can check with the register of his place of birth, which is, let's see now, the town of Dokkum."

"Close enough to Dingjum," Grijpstra said. "Then on the way back, remembering all that tomato salad Lieutenant Sudema made us eat, when we consulted him on that other case . . . "

" . . . we sort of casually drop in and ask how the lieutenant has been doing of late."

"Adjutant Grijpstra," Lieutenant Sudema said. "How nice to see you. And Sergeant De Gier. What a pleasant surprise." The lieutenant, splendidly uniformed, saluted his colleagues. He stood between two plane trees, artfully cut so that their branches framed his station, housed in a medieval brick cottage with a pointed gable that carried a stone angel, grasping for a trumpet that had been missing for a century or so. "Amazing. I haven't seen you for a year, a Chinese businessman is most mysteriously murdered here, and you pop up, on a lovely day like this. Out of the blue." The lieutenant pointed at the sky. "It *is* a nice day, today, don't you think?"

"Happened to pass by," Adjutant Grijpstra said. "We were checking the register in Dokkum regarding a dead drunk at our end and . . ."

"Dokkum is south of here, of course," the lieutenant said. "Close to the highway. But you came up another ten miles just to say hello."

"How's your wife?" De Gier asked.

"You came to see my wife?" Lieutenant Sudema asked. "I see. You're a bachelor, and from Amsterdam, of course; a wicked city, in our provincial eyes that is. Free sex hasn't exactly penetrated here. My wife is well, Sergeant. You did make quite an impression on her the last time you darkened our doorstep. Would you like to meet her again? She's at work now but she'll be back later today. You could wait."

De Gier scratched his right buttock. "You're making him nervous," Grijpstra said. "I've known the sergeant some ten years by now and he's quite shy with women. They'll have to attack him to get anywhere and they'll have to be single."

"My wife isn't single," Lieutenant Sudema said.

"I know," De Gier said. "I was merely inquiring whether Gyske is in good health."

"You're not interested in my murder?"

"He is," Adjutant Grijpstra said, "and so am I. Any progress?"

The lieutenant asked his guests in and found comfortable chairs. A constable brought coffee. He was sent out again to bring in two bags of large fresh tomatoes from the lieutenant's private crop. Sudema discussed tomatoes for a while, and their diseases. The lieutenant's tomatoes were disease-free but that was only because . . .

"Right," Grijpstra mumbled from time to time. "You don't say," Sergeant De Gier murmured once in a while.

"So Mr. Lee Dzung was shot dead with an arrow was he?" Grijpstra asked.

"So we thought," Sudema said.

"He wasn't?" De Gier asked.

"No," Lieutenant Sudema said. "If it had been an arrow, the case might have been hard to crack. There are these newfangled crossbows now, with telescopes; horrible weapons I'll have you know, and all over the place. I thought it had to be one of those. There was an article about crossbows in the Police Gazette that I had happened to read, and some of the weapons make use of small darts. When I saw the corpse, some metal protruded from the wound, sharp and gleaming, so I thought it was a dart. But you know what it really was?"

"Do tell." The sergeant sat forward in his chair.

"A. . . " the lieutenant opened a drawer in his desk and checked with his notebook, " . . .what was it called now; right, here, a *shuriken*."

"A what?" Grijpstra asked.

"Metal disc," De Gier said. "Shaped like a star with a hole in the middle. A *shuriken* isn't shot but thrown. A very deadly weapon, Adjutant, when it flies from the hand of a trained assassin."

The lieutenant pushed his chair back. "So, you see, the case is out of my hands. Are you ready for lunch? The local pub still serves its famous lambchops with the local tomato salad, made out of my tomatoes, of course. I trust you'll be my guests?"

They walked along a country lane, shaded by tall elms. The lieutenant and the sergeant strode along and the adjutant panted, bringing up the rear.

"Why is the case out of your hands?" Grijpstra asked, wheezing between words.

The lieutenant waved airily. "State Security took over. As soon as the pathologist dug up that, what was it now?"

"*Shuriken*?" De Gier asked.

"Right, as soon as we found that a bizarre Far Eastern weapon had been used, we drew our conclusion. Mr. Dzung manufactures a new type of computer chip, that holds more information better, and is capable of programming computers in a most superb way. He makes them in Taiwan. Now he also makes them here. Why? Eh?"

"Why?" De Gier asked.

"You don't know?" Lieutenant Sudema stopped in his tracks. The adjutant bumped into him. De Gier caught them both. "No," De Gier said.

"Is Taiwan close to Russia?" Sudema asked. "Listen, Sergeant, that part wasn't clear to me, either; all I knew was that some outlandish weapon was used, so the killer wasn't Dutch. Mr. Dzung is Chinese. The killer probably, too. Two Chinese visited here last week. I enquired at Mr. Dzung's factory and the manager, a Dr. Haas, tells me that the other Chinese had argued with Mr. Dzung, in Chinese, of course, so he didn't know what about. He assumed that the other Chinese wanted something that Mr. Dzung wouldn't give. An assurance perhaps. That's what the conversation sounded like. Much shouting back and forth."

"Taiwan is friendly with America" Grijpstra said.

Lieutenant Sudema clapped his hands. "Right, you're so right. The State Security chaps, called in by me, working overtime, in the weekend and all, telexed with the CIA. It was all clear at once. Dzung manufactures special computer chips in Taipeh—that's the capital of Taiwan—with American know-how, and with his own, too, for Dzung was a genius and came up with considerable improvements that he patented at once. Those chips may not be sent to Russia, though it's easier to send stuff to Russia from here than from Taiwan."

"And the two Chinese that came to yell at Dzung?" the sergeant asked.

"Assassins," the lieutenant whispered. "*Ninjas*. Ever heard of them? The most dangerous killers on Earth. They could have killed Dzung straight off but they were good enough to warn him first. Dzung didn't listen. So?" The lieutenant stood on one leg, produced a transparent object from his trouser pocket, swung his body from the hip and let go of the object. "*Zip!*"

"*Wow,*" De Gier said, "Ninjas in Dingjum. Throwing a *shuriken*, Tsssshhh!"

"Nah," Grijpstra said.

"You don't believe it?" Lieutenant Sudema asked. "I'm sorry to hear that. I wouldn't believe it at first, either, because, let's face it, Adjutant, we're staunch Dutchmen here, very limited in our outlook and ways. We don't throw exotic razor-sharp steel stars at each other. The very idea. But why wouldn't some nasty outside fellow throw a whatdoyoucallit on Dutch territory? It's a big bad world out there and it does interfere with us at times. We may as well face that."

"You really don't believe in the lieutenant's theory?" De Gier asked Grijpstra. "If a *shuriken* was found in Mr. Dzung's throat, then somebody threw it."

"Not a ninja," Grijpstra said. "Ninja, indeed. Ridiculous. One of these black hooded chaps that slither about on slippers? A ninja in Dingjum would be as conspicuous as a man from Mars."

"I didn't see the Chinese," the lieutenant said. "State Security is making an effort, but they won't catch them; so much is sure. Those ninjas got out of the country immediately after they had fulfilled their contract. Slipped across the border to Germany, flew out of Frankfurt—so State Security presumes."

"Crazy," Grijpstra said.

Lieutenant Sudema towered over the adjutant and glared down from under the visor of his immaculate cap. "So what else, colleague?"

Grijpstra looked up. "His wife, maybe? Did you interrogate his wife?"

Sudema marched on. De Gier loped along next to him. Grijpstra hobbled behind. The lieutenant turned. "That poor girl had a bad deal; she's better off now. Dzung didn't turn out to be a nice man. Do you know that he wouldn't even let her out of his grounds? He treated her something terrible, like a slave almost, as his sex object; she was just another possession. Everything was in her name, the car, the house, but he kept her short. Wouldn't even pay for driving lessons."

"So the pathetic doll did pretty good out of that murder," De Gier said brightly.

Sudema flapped a hand. "Makes her a suspect, sure. You don't think I didn't see that? Listen, Sergeant. Mr. Dzung got killed at 11:05 AM; a gardener saw him fall. At that moment, Mrs. Dzung was in the basement, operating a laundry machine, being assisted by a maid. She's not good at sports. She was nowhere near."

"I would like to see the location," Grijpstra said. "After lunch of course. I wouldn't miss your tomato salad. Eh, De Gier? Remember that tomato salad? With that delicious dressing? Made with herbs from the lieutenant's lovely wife's very own garden?"

Mrs. Dzung stood in the open doorway. De Gier gaped. Grijpstra stepped back in abject wonder. Mrs. Dzung looked even better than in the photograph they had studied. She was tall, very tall, but perfectly proportioned. She was also well-dressed, in tight leather dark trousers and a flowing white blouse. Her long hair wasn't blond but gold, and as fine as the rays in a spider's web, and luxurious, cascading down her supple shoulders. Her large eyes were sparkling blue and seemed semi-transparent, with the pure color reaching inward, attracting the observer into their unfathomable depths. Her nose was finely chiseled and her lips full, though tight in contour. They parted to smile down at her audience. "Hello Lieutenant."

Sudema introduced his companions. Mrs. Dzung was called Emily, she said in a voice that vibrated pleasantly, soothingly, De Gier thought; there was a motherly quality to the woman though she still had to be quite young, in her early twenties, no more. De Gier felt that he wanted to be lifted up and pressed into those giant breasts, turned upside down like a cat that is cuddled, a large tomcat that will purr and meanwhile reach out with a sly paw, pushing gently, kneading firmly, begging for a kiss from those supple and moist lips.

"Minny to my friends," the vibrating voice murmured.

"I'm your friend," De Gier said. He felt very friendly. He would hold her hand and they would jog along friendly beaches, past a friendly sea, and then run up a dune and be really pally between the wildflowers and the waving grass.

"My colleagues," Lieutenant Sudema said, "would like me to show them around your garden. This must be painful to you, Minny, you don't have to come along."

"Come back for tea," Mrs. Dzung said. "I'll have it ready on the rear terrace." Her eyes met De Gier's, expressing a special invitation. "Yes," De Gier said, "oh, yes, for sure!"

"She likes you," Sudema said as he took them to the greenhouse. "She likes me, too. We're as tall as she. She told me she doesn't like looking down on men. I'm married."

"Dzung was small-sized?" Grijpstra asked.

"Fat, too." Sudema's face showed some degree of well-meant pity. "She told me pudgy men turn her off completely."

De Gier nodded. "Fat men have a hard time. Drag all that weight around while available women turn away. Lonely, heavy. . . "

"Who's fat?" Grijpstra asked. "Tell me, is the factory's director, this Dr. Haas you mentioned, fat? Dzung didn't run his company, right? He couldn't because he isn't a resident here. There must be somebody else in charge. Is that fellow fat?"

"Dr. Haas?" Sudema thought. "He's sort of regular."

"Tall?"

"Regular," the lieutenant said again. "Ordinary looking, even though he's got all these PhDs in science and all, but likable nevertheless, I thought. The State Security fellows had a long talk with him, they were rather impressed."

"Why?" De Gier asked. "You just described him as regular. Regularity is hardly impressive."

"Looks don't always matter, Sergeant."

Grijpstra patted Sudema's shoulder. "I'm glad you say that. That's the sergeant's trouble, he doesn't penetrate beyond the outside layer. Like with that lady just now. Did you see him gape? Biased De Gier could never consider her as a suspect. She immediately, because she happens to look fertile and warm, changes into some sort of goddess in his immature mind. When there are beautiful people around, I may as well forget about De Gier. He becomes a dead weight that I have to drag around. Disgusting. Quite."

"That lady is no suspect," the lieutenant said sternly.

"Why are we standing here?" De Gier asked. "That's the greenhouse over there. This is some garden by the way." He looked around. "Just look at the placement of these rocks. Makes you think you're surrounded by mountains. Very foreign."

"Exactly," the lieutenant said. "The ninja feller was hiding here, behind this little artificial hill. He crouched down, waiting for Dzung to move about in the greenhouse over there. Because of the warm weather, the windows were open, but as you can see the view is somewhat obstructed by all those flowering plants in there. The killer waited patiently, right here."

"Orchids," De Gier said. "Lee Dzung was growing beautiful orchids. This is an elegant place. Maybe Chinese heaven looks like this. Wasn't he smart, this Mr. Dzung?"

"Okay," Sudema said. "Dzung was moving about inside the greenhouse. The killer is waiting for his chance. He throws the. . . hmmm. . . well, he threw it, jumped over that outside wall and was gone. Nobody saw him. The gardener was on the other side of the greenhouse. He heard Dzung fall."

"Yeh," Grijpstra said. "Smart is the word. But Dzung got killed. He got outsmarted. Pity, really. I like a man to get away with the whole thing. Just think: No taxes. Immense profits. Flies in and out in first class airplanes. Has this wonderful woman in what he considers an exotic foreign country. Plays about in surroundings that must be ideal to Chinese taste."

"As you say," Sudema said. "Dzung flew in and out. There's a Lear Jet in Amsterdam Airport, now, registered in Fiji."

"I wonder if Dzung made a will," Grijpstra said.

"Who cares?" De Gier asked. "He's subject to Dutch law. Minny is legally married to the deceased so she inherits the house and whatever else he owns in Holland."

"Dzung would have known that, wouldn't he?" Grijpstra asked. "He probably has other wives."

"Mistresses more likely," De Gier said. "He had to marry here so that he could have this heaven in Minny's name. If he was smart, he wouldn't marry unless he had to." De Gier turned around. "What's the place worth? Just check that palace. Terraces, spires, three stories. Well-furnished, I'm sure."

"Nothing but the best," the lieutenant said. "There's a Chinese wing, toward the other side, stocked with treasures. Screens and paintings and sculptures and what not. Most outlandish. Minny took me on a tour."

"A tour. . . " De Gier said, "maybe I could ask her. . . "

"None of that." Grijpstra's heavy finger poked at the sergeant's stomach. "There will be no flirtation with a suspect."

"Ah." Sudema smiled benignly. "No interference, of course. I'm taking you around, showing you this and that, discussing theories, analyzing suspicions, but this case is closed; to you, and to me, too. State Security took over."

Minny called from the terrace. "Tea is ready."

De Gier noticed that his hostess had changed into a modest dress, and that her long hair was done up in a simple bun. There was faint makeup accentuating her large eyes, that threw him a penetrating glance from behind darkened lashes. "Poor Lee," Minny said. "He always enjoyed himself so much, wandering about in his gown, fussing with the plants, creating the illusion of a river by spreading all those pebbles. Do you know that he brought a truckload of oval pebbles in and then put them down parallel, one by one? See it there? It's coming out between those two little hills, like a stream rushing out of mountains? He explained it to me; he was such an artist."

"In Chinese?" Grijpstra asked.

"In English," Minny said.

"You speak good English?"

"Some," Minny said. "I was learning."

"Did your husband often go to his factory in Dingjum?" Grijpstra asked.

Minny arranged her long slender legs, pulling up her skirt a little, then dropping it again. De Gier shivered.

"Are you cold?" Minny asked, her soft eyes expressing concern about the sergeant's involuntary shudder.

"Just impressed by your beauty," De Gier said kindly. "Did your husband take an interest in his product? Computer chips was it? Some advanced line of specialized mint goods?"

"You should see that factory," Minny said. "Everything is automated. The chips manufacture chips. The machines hum day and night and Dr. Haas watches them from a glass cage stuck to the ceiling. Dr. Haas used to visit here from time to time and they'd work with a computer that Lee rigged up on the third floor. It was linked to the factory. Lee hardly ever went out."

"You know Dr. Haas well?"

"He'd come over for dinner."

"Often?"

"Yes," Minny said. "Too often, and always so late. I like to have dinner early but Haas worked until eight o'clock at night. I got bored. Chips and computers, that's what my husband and Haas always talked about. It's another language. Other languages bore me, too."

"Would you show me that stone river?" De Gier asked. "I'm fascinated. So Mr. Dzung personally arranged a million pebbles so they would look like wavelets; how poetic."

"There's a real stream on the other side of the house," Minny said, "and quite a large pond. Lee was breeding goldfish. Some are so beautiful, with all sorts of blended colors and many-finned tails."

De Gier saw the stone river first, and picked up some pebbles. He

followed his hostess down a path around the main building of the estate
and squatted at the side of a pond. Minny sat next to him on an ornamen-
tal rock. "Can you make pebbles bounce off water?" De Gier asked. "I
used to be good at that when I was a kid. Maybe I can still do it." He
threw a pebble with a clumsy twist of his wrist. It ricocheted once and
sank.

"That wasn't so good," Minny said. "Let me try, too."

All Minny's pebbles splashed and disappeared. "Maybe they aren't the
right pebbles," De Gier said, staring discreetly at Minny's slim ankles.
"Were you really happy with Lee?"

He thought she moved closer, for her hand almost touched his. "Yes,"
Minny said. "I like older men. My father left my mother when I was
small so I'm probably frustrated. Lee was over forty."

"I'm thirty-nine," De Gier said.

She straightened her dress down her legs. "You look younger."

"I'll be forty next month." The sergeant got up and extended a hand.
She held on to him and allowed herself to be lifted. They walked along
and reached a lawn that stretched to the far fence. A tennis ball had been
left on the path. "That's Poopy's ball," Minny said. "Poopy is my terrier.
Lee didn't like the dog; it would dig holes in all his funny gardens. Poopy
is staying with my sister now."

De Gier picked up the ball and ran out to the lawn. "Catch." She
jumped but the ball whizzed by her and hit the house. It came bouncing
back. De Gier put up a slow hand and missed it, too.

Grijpstra and Sudema appeared. "Come and see me sometime," Minny
said into the sergeant's ear. "It gets lonely here. But please, phone me
first."

"Sure," De Gier smiled, "Thank you for the tea," he said loudly. "And
for letting us see the gardens. I envy you."

A maid came out of the mansion to tell Minny that the laundry machinery in the cellar wasn't working properly again. Minny said goodbye and
disappeared into the house.

"Let's go, Sergeant" Grijpstra ordered briskly. De Gier glanced over
his shoulder. "Just a minute." He ran back to the side-garden and picked
up Poopy's ball. Released from a swing of De Gier's long arm, it hit a
wall and came shooting back. He caught it without effort.

"Are you coming?" Grijpstra bellowed.

De Gier dug in his pocket and produced a pebble. The pebble was
flung at the pond's surface and bounced off, and again, and again, in
long graceful curves.

The sergeant came running back.

Grijpstra frowned. "Childish!"

"Heh, heh," said De Gier.

"Tell me everything," Sergeant Grijpstra said, as he waved at Sudema who was saluting them from under the plane trees that guarded his station. The lieutenant had begged to be excused for a while. His tomatoes needed their daily attention. He would be available again a little later in the day. De Gier drove around the corner, parked the VW, lit a cigarette and reported on his recent adventure.

"Okay," Grijpstra said. "You've got something there, but that business about phoning her first means nothing. Maybe there's no lover as yet in Minny's life. Women hate being surprised by an erotic enthusiast suddenly appearing at the door. Minny is attractive but a quarter of her beauty is clothes, make-up, perfume and what not. She wants to smack you with the full hundred percent of her oversized dazzle; and to work that up may take her an hour."

"Wow," De Gier said.

"Beg pardon, Sergeant?"

"She's beautiful," De Gier said. "A Viking Queen. You know, you meet this absolutely stunning woman and you somehow manage to wake up next to her in the morning, and you kiss her awake and you wait for the heavenly wisdom flowing out of that lovely shape, and it isn't there?"

"I have no idea what you're talking about," Grijpstra said. "I live a quiet life. I paint tasteless pictures on my days off. Now, what are you saying?"

"That," De Gier said, "I don't think Minny will be disappointing."

Grijpstra withdrew into a disagreeable silence.

"I'm," De Gier said dreamily, "telling you that Minny is capable of murder. She inspires me." He grinned at the adjutant. "To do good things, of course. But then I'm a good guy. Now, what if she was involved with a bad guy, a ninja? Wouldn't she inspire him to do evil?"

Grijpstra moved his back against his seat, grunting softly. "Yeh. Maybe. So she can't throw pebbles and she can't catch balls. Why? She must have tried some sports. All schools have games. She looks athletic."

"Did you notice that her left eye tends to drift somewhat?" De Gier asked. "She may have trouble focusing, especially when she's tired. These last days must have been a strain."

"Let's go," Grijpstra said. "We stayed in a hotel in Dingjum once, that time we were here before. An old-fashioned inn. Think you can find it again?"

The innkeeper remembered the two Chinese visitors who came for Mr.

Dzung. "Mr. Wang and Mr. Tzu. Their full names and addresses are in the register; let me look them up."

"You checked their passports?" Grijpstra asked.

The innkeeper nodded. "I always do."

De Gier noted the names and addresses on his pad. Both Chinese originated in Taipeh.

"They were older men," the innkeeper said. "Quite pleasant."

"Athletic?" De Gier asked.

The innkeeper laughed. "Not really. I have a mini golf course in the back and they puttered about; they weren't too good."

"And where did they go from here?"

"Let's see now," the innkeeper said. "Wait a minute. Maybe I do know. They phoned Philips Electronics; I remember because they couldn't find the right number and there was some trouble with the operator, it seemed. I helped them out. They were supposed to meet someone there and we couldn't locate the fellow, but they did talk to him in the end."

"So you think they left for Philips Headquarters from here?"

"Yes," the innkeeper said. "I remember now. They had a rented car and my wife helped them to trace a route on the map."

"Can we use the phone?" De Gier asked. "It would help if you remembered the name of the man at Philips."

De Gier dialed. "Sir? A Mr. Wang and a Mr. Tzu, are they still around?"

He listened. "They're in Amsterdam now?" He thanked his informant and replaced the phone.

"Back again?" Sudema asked. "I thought I was rid of you. I beg your pardon. Always happy to entertain colleagues, of course. Especially when they don't interfere. You wouldn't be interfering, would you now?"

"You know, lieutenant," Grijpstra said, "I do admire you. You said that Minny wasn't a suspect and, by jove, she isn't."

"Not a direct murder suspect," De Gier said. "No, sir!"

"And you did express doubts about those two Chinese," Grijpstra said. "You and I both know what State Security is like. A bunch of old dodderers wandering about their Victorian offices looking for a lost slipper. They actually managed to come out here?"

"Briefly," Sudema said. "They talked to Dr. Haas and wrote their report. They also checked out some shipments of chips that were sent to Germany and probably reached Moscow."

"And what is Dr. Haas going to do, now that his boss is dead?"

Sudema rolled a cigarette and studied its ends. He tapped the cigarette on his desk. "Yes, Adjutant, I know. I'm perhaps not quite as foolish as you city slicker chaps may be thinking. There could be a possible connection there. Minny has talked to her lawyer and it seems pretty clear that the factory is now hers. It may be an affiliated company to the Fiji tax-free head office, and linked to Taipeh, but according to Dr. Haas, all the patents are in Lee Dzung's name and Minny will probably inherit them outright, too."

De Gier rolled a cigarette, too, and imitated Sudema's careful treatment of the ends. "If that lawyer knows his job, Minny stands a chance of getting hold of all Dzung's assets."

Sudema blew a little smoke to the station's rustic ceiling and admired its age-old beams. "Minny didn't kill Dzung."

Grijpstra peeled a cigar out of plastic. "You know, Lieutenant, I would just love to watch you while you make monkeys out of State Security. I could never stand seeing those nincompoops waste the taxpayers' money. Do you have any idea about the size of their budget?"

"I saw the Mercedes limousine they parked in front of this station," Sudema said. He hit the desk. "Do you know that they wouldn't eat at our restaurant here? They said they didn't care for tomato salad. They actually preferred to go back to Amsterdam and some fancy bodega. It took them three and a half hours to get back here again."

"I think we should go and see Dr. Haas sometime," De Gier said, "and perhaps you can come along, Lieutenant. I know how busy you are but this might be worth it. As an officer you don't need us to sign the final report with you. We weren't really here, anyway; we were just passing through as we happened to be in the neighborhood."

"I do," Sudema said, "sometimes read the weekly magazines. We're dealing with Taiwan Chinese. You mentioned that Dzung was a smart guy. I agree. The Taiwan authorities probably squeezed Dzung in Taipeh. Imagine—here's a genius who comes up with a superb product and he makes an immense profit. Who runs Taiwan? Generals and so forth, corrupt warlords who escaped from the communist mainland. So Dzung thinks of a way in which he can have his noodles with sauce and eat them, too. Maybe he sold his stuff from here to Russia out of spite."

"How did he get Minny?" Grijpstra asked.

"My guess is as good as yours, Adjutant."

"Let the sergeant guess." Grijpstra pushed De Gier's shoulder. "Share your knowledge of the world, De Gier."

"Me?" De Gier looked up. "Escort service, I would imagine. Dzung came here, he set up his operation with Dr. Haas. He probably found Haas through some technical paper. All these top-notch scientists correspond, meet at congresses, get together on schemes. Haas introduced

Dzung to an organization that rents out attractive females. Dzung selected the very best. Haas suggested marriage and Minny was willing. She preferred to be legal."

Sudema rolled another perfect cigarette. "Yes, I think so, too, and there may be some risk there: Minny obviously benefits by her husband's death. Dr. Haas does not. For one thing, he's married and has some kids. He strikes me as a scientist, not as a businessman. Dzung is the genius, not Haas. And. . ." Sudema was admiring the beams of his ceiling again, "let's face it, Dutchmen aren't killers. The Taiwanese are. If Dzung was selling superchips to the Russians, the Americans would lean on the generals of Taipeh. . . . "

"Who would send thugs, ninjas, lithe louts trained in bizarre murderous methods," Grijpstra said, sucking his cigar contently. "The CIA must be pleased that Dzung caught that steel star in his neck. But I still think all this is very far-fetched. Now what if there were no assassins? Not from Taipeh anyway? Now suppose you could prove that? Wouldn't that be great? A feather in your hat?"

"I think I could help," De Gier said.

"Please do," the lieutenant said, "I'm very fond of feathers." Grijpstra got up. "I could save you some time. You drive to Amsterdam with my sergeant and I'll visit this Dr. Haas. When you come back you can tie things up."

"You wouldn't interfere now?" Sudema asked. "Right, Adjutant?"

"Never," Grijpstra said. "Just tell me where I can find the good doctor."

"You're not coming through very clearly," the operator at the radio room of Amsterdam Municipal Headquarters said.

De Gier frowned at the small microphone in his hand. "As long as you can hear me. I'm looking for a Mr. Tzu and a Mr. Wang, staying in a hotel in Amsterdam; could you check which hotel I should go to and let me know within the next half hour?"

"Will try. Over and out."

The VW was speeding along the Great Dike and approaching the capital. Sudema had been watching swans on the lake. He glanced at De Gier's handsome profile. "Shouldn't we call for an arrest team? I'm a fairly good shot but my book on martial arts says that a good thrower of . . . what the hell, what do you call those things again?"

"*Shuriken*, Lieutenant?"

"Right. That a good thrower of those damned things can fling a dozen in no time at all. It'll be like a barrage from an automatic rifle."

"Nah," De Gier said.

"Suit yourself," Sudema said. "I hear you won the prizes at the national police unarmed combat contest this year. Can you catch those what-doyoucallums?"

"Forget unarmed combat," De Gier said. "Nothing beats a gun. Make sure that they can't reach you with any part of their bodies and shoot to kill in case of doubt. Don't complain and explain later. Self-defense is still a good excuse." He grinned at the lieutenant. "Don't worry about the present situation, though."

"You're pretty sure, eh, Sergeant?"

"I don't think Wang and Tzu are assassins," De Gier said. "If I did, I would probably ask for assistance. I'm not really a hero, you know. I have to go home and feed my cat. There're some books I'd still like to read, and perhaps I'll meet a lady sometime who'll look like Minny."

"Not Minny herself? I think you'd be welcome."

"Wouldn't that be nice?" De Gier asked. "And wander about in that exotic abode the morning after? Breakfast on the terrace? If she really baked those cookies that came with the tea herself, she'll be a good cook, too."

The lieutenant smiled happily. "And she isn't a dumb blonde, either."

"Intelligence goes both ways," De Gier said. The radio crackled.

"Sergeant De Gier?"

"Right here."

"Your parties are staying at the Victoria Hotel. We checked with the desk and they are in their room. Should I tell them to expect you?"

"Please," De Gier said. He pushed the microphone back under the dashboard.

"We aren't being silly now?" Sudema asked. "If we are, I might want to phone my wife."

De Gier unhooked the microphone. "Headquarters? De Gier again. Please phone the State Police station at Dingjum, Friesland, and tell the constable to phone Lieutenant Sudema's wife to tell her that her husband may be late for dinner."

"Thanks," Sudema said.

De Gier shook hands; Lieutenant Sudema saluted.

"Please sit down," Mr. Wang said.

"Cup of tea?" Mr. Tzu asked. He poured. The four men raised their cups and smiled politely at each other.

"We're sorry to hear about Mr. Dzung's death," Wang said. "Very sorry. To die in a foreign country is unpleasant experience. Perhaps his body can go home, yes?"

"If a request is made," Sudema said, "I'm sure we would be happy to oblige. To be murdered is also an unpleasant experience."

"Very sad," Tzu said. Tzu stooped; a hearing aid hid in the tufted white hairs sprouting from his ear. He also wore thick glasses. Wang's belly rested comfortably on his thighs. Wang would be a little younger than Tzu.

"We represent Mustang Electrics," Wang said. "We deal in advanced computer technology. Mr. Dzung and Dr. Haas are known to us and we thought that Dzung might help us to do business with Philips, on commission, of course."

"Or take over our idea," Tzu said, "for money, but he wasn't interested. So, instead, we made contact with Phillips directly."

"Successfully?" De Gier asked.

"Hopefully," Wang said. "Likely," Tzu said. "Very likely, yes; our suggestions were well received."

"We hear," De Gier said, smiling apologetically, "that you and Mr. Tzu did, eh, disagree with Mr. Dzung while visiting him in Dingjum? There was, perhaps, some expression of anger during your brief get-together?"

"Hmm?" Wang asked. He spoke in Chinese to Tzu. Tzu shook his head.

"No," Wang said. "Not at all. It's very rude to be angry with a business relation. Besides, it doesn't pay."

Tzu polished his glasses with the tip of his tie. "Now, who would have told you that Dzung and us had disagreement?"

De Gier reached absent-mindedly for his teaspoon but his movement was awkward and the spoon slithered across the table into Wang's lap. The sergeant apologized. "Hmm?" Wang asked.

"Sorry sir, I dropped my spoon on your side."

Wang picked up the spoon with some effort, as he had to bend down. He gave it back.

"Talking about Dr. Haas," De Gier said, "you say you knew him. Dr. Haas was in Taiwan, perhaps?"

Tzu nodded. "Oh yes, for many years. Quite an expert on things Chinese. Very bright, this Dr. Haas."

"Like what things Chinese?" Lieutenant Sudema asked.

Tzu replaced his glasses. "Chinese table-tennis. He was very good. He beat my twice-removed nephew, an expert in Kung Fu."

"Kung Fu equates with table-tennis?" De Gier asked.

Wang smiled. "No."

"Many-sided man, this Dr. Haas," Tzu whispered.

De Gier smiled over the rim of his cup. "And what are you doing in Amsterdam now?"

Wang smiled broadly. "Very little, Sergeant. Bit of a holiday. The negotiations with Philips were straightforward, no time was wasted, so now we waste it here, a few days of . . ."

"Museums," Mr. Tzu said.

"Museums, Sergeant," Wang nodded enthusiastically.

De Gier got up. "I hope you're enjoying your stay in the city." He stumbled as he went to shake Mr. Tzu's hand. Mr. Tzu tried to move away but bumped heavily against a chair. Sudema steadied De Gier's sliding body.

"I'm sorry," De Gier said.

"My fault entirely," Tzu said, smiling.

Grijpstra was waiting at the State Police station. De Gier bounded through the door. "That didn't take long did it? Did you see Dr. Haas?"

"I did," Grijpstra said. "Lieutenant Sudema? Sir?"

Sudema snapped to attention. "Yes, Adjutant, at your orders. I hope we didn't hold you up."

"Lieutenant," Grijpstra said heavily, "why didn't you tell me that Dr. Haas has an alibi?"

Sudema slid behind his desk and threw his cap at a hook attached to the wall. The cap missed the hook. "I didn't? I thought I had."

De Gier sat down. "A good alibi?"

"Pretty good, Sergeant." Grijpstra smiled sadly. "We may have wasted time and effort. What were your Chinese ninjas like?"

"They never threw any steel stars, I would think." De Gier stretched. "Boy, I'm surprised we weren't caught for speeding. A hundred miles an hour all the way up that wonderful straight dike. Wasn't that fun, Lieutenant?"

"Yes," Sudema said. "I rather agree with your sergeant, Grijpstra. Maybe Wang and Tzu are excellent actors but I would think they're what they say they are, businessmen trying to make a profit and, at present, have a little holiday in sexy Amsterdam."

"They're clumsy," De Gier said. "Definitely no sportsmen. Uncoordinated movements and entirely unaware of their physical positions. They couldn't drop a brick on a rabbit in a trap."

"Could Dr. Haas do better?" Sudema asked.

Grijpstra arranged his hands on his stomach and slid a little further down in his chair. "Yes."

"You tested him?" De Gier asked.

"Dr. Haas," Grijpstra said ponderously, "is an agile athlete. A fly buzzed by him and he caught it with two fingers, without paying much attention. I threw him my lighter and he plucked it from the air. I bumped him on the staircase and I swear he was ready to do a somersault and drop to the landing below on his feet."

"But he didn't throw a *shuriken* at Mr. Dzung?" De Gier asked. "Isn't that hard to believe?"

"Wasn't Dzung killed at eleven-o-five A.M. last Friday morning?" Grijpstra asked.

"Yes," Sudema said brightly.

"At that time, Dr. Haas claims he was in his office and," Grijpstra said as he raised a menacing finger, "he produced two witnesses to prove that fact." His finger dropped to accuse Sudema. "You never told me that."

"The beeper stuff?" Sudema asked. "State Security believed it. Why shouldn't I?"

"So why didn't you tell me?"

"I forgot," Sudema said. "Adjutant, you're in the country now. We're all bumpkins here, vegetating in rustic retardation."

Grijpstra's hand became a fist that shook and trembled. "No, sir. You didn't believe that beeper stuff yourself and you're testing me now. Am I right? Confess."

Sudema bowed his head. "I believed the alibi at the time, but later I wondered, and when you came here to shine your dazzling light, I thought I might not mention the detail to see what you might make of it."

"What beeper stuff?" De Gier asked.

"Bah," Grijpstra said. "You know about beepers, Sergeant. A gadget you keep in your pocket and it beeps when you're wanted. So you run along and find out what you're wanted for. They use beepers at Dzung's computer factory. Some of the employees wander about and may be out of reach of a phone, so they get beeped and respond."

"At eleven A.M. last Friday, Dr. Haas beeped two of his wandering employees?" De Gier asked.

"And they both answered by phone," Grijpstra said. "They made use of inside phones connected to Dr. Haas' center of command. He spoke to them, gave them instructions, listened to their comments, commented on their comments—there were conversations. Both employees confirm that fact. Dr. Haas provided himself with a very nice alibi, alright."

"Can you crack it?" Sudema asked. "Dr. Haas was very confident when State Security questioned him as to his whereabouts at the time of Dzung's death. Too confident, maybe?"

"Now the lieutenant tells us," Grijpstra complained.

"You weren't here at the time," Sudema said.

"Grijpstra?" De Gier asked. "Can you crack that alibi or not? If you can't, we're going home. I've got to feed my cat sometime. She's waiting for me at my apartment right now."

Grijpstra took off his coat and waistcoat. He linked his fingers behind striped suspenders and began to pace the floor. Sudema stared.

"He's thinking," De Gier said. "Would you like to help? Are you wearing suspenders?"

"Are you?" Sudema asked.

"I'm not," De Gier said, "but maybe you can lend me a pair."

Sudema opened a wardrobe, took a pair of suspenders from his spare uniform, and passed it to De Gier. De Gier snapped them to his trousers. He nodded to the lieutenant. Lieutenant Sudema took off his uniform jacket and slid his hands behind the narrow strips that kept up his pants. "Like this? You are both crazy! Am I humoring you properly?"

"When conventional methods fail," De Gier said, "and time presses, we explore the beyond. You don't mind dancing a little now, do you?"

"Oh shit," Sudema said. "Do I have to?"

"THINK," Grijpstra roared, interrupting his self-induced trance. "THINK, IF YOU PLEASE."

"THINK," shouted De Gier.

"Think," squeaked the lieutenant.

They walked in a circle, chanting "Think," Grijpstra sonorously, De Gier in a normal voice, and the lieutenant in a falsetto. The constable from the office next door came in to see if everything was alright. The contemplators ignored him. The constable withdrew, whistling his disbelief. He whistled rhythmically, in time with the chant.

Grijpstra skipped his feet at every fourth measure. De Gier did likewise. The lieutenant imitated his examples. The dance didn't take long. Grijpstra stopped at his chair and sat down. De Gier dropped down on the next chair. Sudema hopped behind his desk.

"That must have done it," Grijpstra said. "You first, Sergeant. Did anything occur?"

"Let's hear the lieutenant," De Gier said. "Our method is new to him and may have worked spectacularly on his unsuspecting brain. What thoughts popped up, sir?"

"I thought," Sudema said dreamily, "that Dr. Haas is a computer expert. He analyzes what goes on in normal communcation, then apes it with his machines. All communication can be analyzed and classified."

"Foreseen?" Grijpstra asked. "Programmed into a phone at proper intervals?"

"But," De Gier said, "not when the communication is too complicated. The number of possible responses to a given question is fairly large, and one response to one question wouldn't even satisfy a numbskull of State Security. There would have to be several responses, and responses to the responses, and proper timing of them all."

"Ah," Sudema said. He patted the top of his desk. "Ah. Now I know what bothered me when Dr. Haas presented his alibi. Both workers who were willing to swear that they had communicated with him, proving thereby that Haas was in his office, were numbskulls."

"Are numbskulls employed by a factory turning out superchips for advanced computers?" De Gier asked.

Sudema waved a hand. "The two witnesses were of the fetch-and-carry variety. They open and close heavy boxes, put them on trucks, or take them off trucks, as the case may be; that sort of thing. They were usually busy outside the main building, running about between storage sheds; that's why they carried beepers."

"So," Grijpstra said, "Dr. Haas would give them simple commands. First he beeps them. They run to the nearest phone and dial the chief's number. He answers. 'Hello.'"

"Yes," De Gier said, "and the man says, 'Hi boss, it's me, Frank,' and Haas says, 'Hi Frank, would you carry box X from storage station Z,' and Frank says, 'There are no more boxes X, boss.'"

"Right," Sudema said, "and Haas says, 'Sure Frank, there's still a box X in shed A, in the rear.'"

Grijpstra rubbed his hands. "Yes. But Frank might be saying more than he is expected to say; the message becomes longer, and if Haas gives a pre-recorded answer, it cuts into what Frank has to say and Frank becomes bewildered."

Sudema rubbed his hands, too. "And Frank wasn't right? Frank testified to me and the State Security yoyos that he was conducting a normal conversation with Dr. Haas while that very same Dr. Haas, our athletic friend who kills flies on the wing between thumb and finger, was throwing a, what do you call it again?"

"*Shuriken?*" De Gier asked.

"Yep," Sudema nodded vigorously. "No matter, however. Dr. Haas holds PhDs in science. He must have used a device that wouldn't permit his pre-recorded messages, commands, orders, to get into the phone before the line was void of Frank's response."

Lieutenant Sudema sighed. "Pretty tricky."

De Gier shrugged. "Isn't Dr. Haas supposed to be a wizard? He's got a factory filled with tricky equipment. Surely it won't be too difficult for him to devise a gadget that wouldn't let the recorded messages out before Frank could finish phrasing his simple comments?"

Grijpstra rubbed out his soggy cigar butt. "Listen, Lieutenant, Frank and the other witness who holds up Dr. Haas' alibi, are predictable men. Dr. Haas was their boss so they wouldn't gab too much at him. First he gives them an order, then they say that it can't be done. Haas knows that, beforehand. He has manipulated the situation. His device waited for Frank, or the other feller, to stop talking, and then released another pre-recorded message in Dr. Haas' voice. He tells them that they are mistaken and that they *can* obey his order if they do this or that. They say 'Yes, Sir,' and hang up. Thinking back, it may seem to them that they had quite a conversation."

De Gier checked his watch. "It's getting late. Minny says that Dr. Haas likes to work late, but he may, by now, be ready to leave his office. Are we doing something? If not, I'd rather go back. I've got to feed my cat."

"Would you," Grijpstra asked Sudema, "own one of those mini-cassette players that also records?"

Sudema jumped up, rushed across his office, yanked the door open and pointed accusingly at the constable reclining behind his desk. "Ha!"

The constable was listening to his casette player, connected to his ears by tiny phones. "Give," Sudema barked, holding out his hand. "And find me a spare tape."

He ran back. "Here you are, Adjutant."

Grijpstra explained. Sudema applauded. "Clever," De Gier said, raising his eyebrows. "Amazing. You thought of that yourself?"

"Sit in the corner there," Grijpstra said, "and fill up that tape. You may not be equipped with a lot of furniture upstairs but you are a good actor."

De Gier spoke into the cassette recorder. Grijpstra put on his waistcoat and jacket. Sudema practiced fast draws with his pistol.

"Now," Grijpstra said. "That sounds fine. Return the lieutenant's suspenders and go talk to the constable. Make sure that he knows what to do."

Sudema's gun was stuck again in its holster. He yanked it free. "Pow!" He pointed it at a cupboard. He shook his head. "Can't we give this thing a little time? I could call in an arrest team."

"Nah," Grijpstra said.

"Gentlemen," Dr. Haas said. "I was just on my way out. You might not have caught me."

"You're using the right verb," Grijpstra said in a cold, menacing voice. "You're under arrest, sir. Anything you say from now on, we'll most definitely use against you. Isn't that right, Lieutenant?"

"Absolutely," Sudema said. "You're ordered, Dr. Haas, to return to your office forthwith. I, a ranking officer of the State Police, accuse you of foully murdering your employer, Lee Dzung. A despicable deed for which you will be tried in due course."

"You're joking," Dr. Haas said bravely. He looked at De Gier.

De Gier arranged his face into an expression of stern contempt.

"Sergeant," Grijpstra said, "you can go outside and guard the building."

De Gier turned and left.

"Now, Sudema said, "let's not waste time. Back to your office, sir, where you can confess to your heinous crime."

Dr. Haas sat down in his office. The lieutenant and Grijpstra looked at him expectantly. "Are you crazy?" Dr. Haas said. "What are you trying to do? What *is* this charade? *Me* kill my good friend Lee? My beneficent employer?"

"Your alibi is not good," Sudema barked. "You never fooled *us*, I'll have you know. Anyone can turn rings around State Security, dear sir. Espionage? Foreign killers? Selling of contraband killing machines to the red devils lurking nearby? Ha!" Sudema laughed harshly for a while.

"You're dealing with the Police now," Grijpstra said. "The State Police. The lieutenant saw through your ruse from the start."

Dr. Haas smiled. "Really, Adjutant. I can prove to you that quite a lot of equipment left this factory with a dubious destination. I warned Lee many a time. I'm sorry he died, of course, but he had it coming. Believe me, the Taiwanese Secret Service doesn't play around. You underestimate our State Security, too. Once they know what was on, they wisely decided not to pursue the matter."

Grijpstra peeled a cigar. He looked up. "Bah. Really, Dr. Haas. I'm a police officer, too. Your true motivations can be spelled out easily enough. What were you after? Money? How to get it? Well now . . .?" Grijpstra sucked smoke. "Well now, my crafty doctor, you seduced poor Minny, arranged to divorce your wife, promised Minny you would marry her, planned to procure Dr. Dzung's millions that way."

"What would I want with Minny?" Dr. Haas shouted.

"Leaving out the pornography," Sudema said quietly, "we know exactly what you'd like to do to the hapless girl. A sex object framed in pure gold?"

Dr. Haas folded his arms. "I do have an alibi, Lieutenant. You've heard it before and the judge will hear it, too. I beg you, for your own sake, not to make an idiot of yourself."

The phone rang. Dr. Haas picked it up. "Who? Segeant De Gier? Who's Sergeant De Gier?"

The voice on the phone said he was the tall man with the magnificent moustache whom Dr. Haas had just met.

"I see," Dr. Haas said. "What do you want? I'm busy."

The voice said that he wanted Dr. Haas to confess to killing Lee Dzung, a multimillionaire, so that he could marry Mrs. Dzung and collect the multimillions.

"You're out of your poor mind," snarled Dr. Haas.

The voice on the phone said that he was out of the phone, and that, in fact, he was coming into Dr. Haas' office.

De Gier walked into the room. "See?"

Dr. Haas looked at De Gier.

The voice on the phone said that it was surprising, was it not? How could Dr. Haas be speaking to Sergeant De Gier on the phone while Sergeant De Gier was standing right before him? Now wasn't that weird?

Dr. Haas slammed down the phone.

Silence filled the office.

"How did you do that?" Dr. Haas finally asked.

"You know how," Lieutenant Sudema said darkly. "Same way you fabricated your alibi. We don't have your advanced equipment so we used my constable to make the call and to activate the recorder at the appropriate moments. The device you have around will be tracked down by experts. Should be easy enough. Your proof will be destroyed."

Dr. Haas hid his face in his hands.

"Or you can show it to us now," Grijpstra said kindly. "It'll shorten your agony, poor man."

"You pathetic asshole," De Gier said kindly. "Minny doesn't love you anyway. You would have lost without our non-interference. What a risk to take." The sergeant spread his hands. "You really think she would go for you? She thinks you're boring. What a senseless rigmarole you set up. You merely did her a service that she planned you to perform. You really think Minny would hand you the loot?"

"Poor sucker," Sudema whispered.

"She abused you," Grijpstra said, nodding sadly.

Dr. Haas dropped his hands. "Minny loves me as much as I love her. I liberated that poor innocent girl. We'll be happy together forever after."

"Yes?" De Gier asked. "You were planning to see her tonight?"

Dr. Haas glared at the sergeant.

Grijpstra jumped up. "At what time?" Grijpstra roared. He sat down heavily again. "Not that it matters, as she won't be seeing you. Even at such short notice, with Mr. Dzung turning in his recently dug grave, she's soliciting another lover."

"Not you," Sudema said helpfully. "Oh, no!"

"Impossible!" Dr. Haas grabbed the phone. De Gier's hand grabbed the doctor's wrist. "Allow me, sir," De Gier said. "I'll make that call. What's her number?"

Dr. Haas mumbled the number. De Gier dialed. "Minny?" De Gier asked shyly. "It's me, Rinus De Gier. The sergeant you played ball with this afternoon. Remember?"

"Oh, Rinus," Minny moaned.

Grijpstra sneaked up to the phone. He pressed a button on its side. Minny's voice became audible to all parties concerned.

"Of course I remember," Minny said weakly.

"I was wondering," De Gier said. "I'm supposed to stay in Dingjum tonight. Not on what I came to see you about this afternoon, that's all over now. I was just wondering . . ."

"Oh, do come," Minny said. "That would be nice. I'm so lonely in this big house. Could you see me in an hour or so? I do want to receive you in style."

Grijpstra smiled gleefully at Sudema. Sudema winked back. Dr. Haas listened with round eyes.

"I'll be there," De Gier said. "Goodbye, dear Minny."

"Goodbye Rinus," Minny said softly. "Thanks for calling."

De Gier replaced the phone.

Grijpstra rubbed his hands while looking at the doctor. "See? You got trapped in your own greed. She has no use for you now that Mr. Dzung's vast wealth is available to her. She'll have the time of her life with more attractive men."

"You may be smart, Doctor," Lieutenant Sudema said, "but your looks are regular, to say the least. You really thought that a beauty queen would fall for you?" Sudema laughed harshly.

The phone rang. Dr. Haas picked it up. Minny's voice once again penetrated to the far corners of the office. "Haas? Listen Haas, something has come up. I don't want to see you tonight. Okay?"

"But Minny," Haas said. "Please, we have an appointment; there's so much to discuss; our future . . ."

"What future?" Minny asked shrilly. "Perhaps you should never come to see me again. If you do, you might be in trouble."

"Minny?" Dr. Haas shrieked. The phone clicked dryly.

"Now, make your confession," Sudema said briskly. "Let's get this over with."

Dr. Haas looked at the blotter on his desk. His face became calm. His deeply recessed eyes behind the gold-rimmed spectacles began to sparkle.

A smile pushed up the corners of his thin lips.

"What's up?" Grijpstra asked.

"If you won't talk," Sudema said, "I have to remind you that you are under arrest. Please stand up, turn and face the wall with your hands above your head. Spread your legs, Dr. Haas. I have to frisk you now."

Dr. Haas smiled. "Just a minute, Lieutenant. Let's go through this again. What did I do?"

"You killed a man, Doctor," Sudema said.

"I exterminated a dangerous criminal," Dr. Haas corrected. "A flaw in our society who supplied the enemy with lethal machinery that will be used to do away with the free world. I also removed an alien sadist who beat up one of the most beautiful women with a whip split in seven thongs. I saved both democracy and a rare specimen of local female beauty. Is that a crime?"

"Sure," De Gier said. "Undemocratic, too. Did you ask for a vote?"

Dr. Haas kept smiling. "You're such a joker, Sergeant. Allow me to finish my plea. If you arrest me, nothing is gained and much will be lost. Maybe Minny will get the present available loot, and good luck to her, I say. Dzung's wealth will soon be replaced. I have, together with the wicked alien, developed an almost unimaginable improvement that will make intercontinental missiles all-seeing. Only I know how these inventions work. Let me go free and I will set up a fresh company that will control patents I can apply for alone. All three of you will be my partners. Your investment only involves your friendship and, in return, I'll hand over ten percent of the shares. My millions will soon be made. I assure you, the profits of our new venture will be immense."

"And Minny?" Sudema asked.

"Who cares about Minny?" Dr. Haas asked.

"Have her," Dr. Haas presented Minny to De Gier on the palm of his hand. "You're so clever, Sergeant, maybe you can marry her, too. It would be nice if you can bring in some of our present equipment. It will save me some time."

"Won't Minny be a problem?" De Gier asked.

"How could she be, Sergeant? It was she who suggested I do away with Lee. As an accomplice, she'll have to stay mum."

"A bribe?" Sudema asked. Grijpstra kicked him gently. "Ah," Sudema said, "Well, maybe not."

"You wouldn't want to see Minny waste away in jail," De Gier said, "would you, Lieutenant?"

Sudema grinned helpfully. "Absolutely not. But only ten percent for me and you get Minny, too . . ."

"Weren't you married?" De Gier asked. "Of course, you could ignore that illusionary bond—not too often, of course—and if you happened to share a growing experience with my wife, and if I was away that evening, spending a million here or there . . ."

The lieutenant's left eyelid trembled nervously. "You mean you wouldn't mind?"

"I spent my formative years in Amsterdam," De Gier said.

Dr. Haas looked up. "Let's be serious, gentlemen." He turned to De Gier. "And would you mind sitting down, Sergeant? You make me nervous. When I was in the Far East, I practiced some of the martial arts, and if there's one thing I learned it was the art of always being aware. Now, let's go through this again. I'm a scientist, too, and my mind is trained to make optimal use of any available situation." He smiled at his audience. "For mutual benefit, of course; it's the object of science to make this a better world. I could raise my offer to fifteen percent to the lieutenant and adjutant and nothing extra for the sergeant provided he marries Minny. If not . . ." The doctor made an appeasing gesture. ". . . well, that's fine, too. The sergeant gets fifteen percent, too. Money, and a lot of it, will flow in either case."

"You *are* a businessman," Grijpstra said. "We were misinformed."

"Interesting," Sudema said.

De Gier moved toward a chair. "I agree. Shall we call it a deal? The sooner I can free myself from my tedious present routine . . ." He looked at Dr. Haas. The doctor wasn't paying attention. De Gier turned and leaped. Grijpstra's gun pointed at Dr. Haas. Sudema was still trying to yank his pistol free.

Both Dr. Haas' hands fled under his jacket. "HEY!" shouted De Gier. His flat hands hit the doctor's wrists. One came back and flew out again, this time against the doctor's chin. The doctor tumbled out of his chair and De Gier fell on top of him. The sergeant's nimble hands quickly frisked the doctor's body. De Gier got up, holding several metal stars in each hand.

Dr. Haas was coming to. Sudema gave up trying to get to his pistol, rolled the suspect over, yanked his arms to the rear and connected them with handcuffs.

The constable was waiting at the State Police station. He waved his cassette recorder. "Did I do all right?"

"Splendid job," Sudema said. "Now you know why I allowed you to listen to Beethoven during office hours. I knew your gadget would come in handy one day. Lock up this suspect, Constable. Be careful, he's a dangerous gent."

"Well," De Gier said, "we'd better drive back while there's still light. We can watch the cormorants land on the lake at sunset. Didn't we have an instructive day? I thank you, Lieutenant, for showing us the way you work."

"What about my report?" Sudema asked.

"You don't need us for mere paperwork," Grijpstra said. "Suspect will provide you with a detailed confession. You made the arrest. There's circumstantial evidence; those star shaped discs, for instance."

"We don't want to interefere," De Gier said. "Are you coming, Grijpstra?"

Sudema blocked the door. "We still have to catch Minny."

"She's all yours," De Gier said. "Bring her in, confront her with Dr. Haas. They'll yell at each other. Their mutual accusations will add up to evidence. That's all normal routine."

"But she's waiting for you, dolled up and all." Sudema patted the sergeant's shoulder. "You bring her in, Sergeant, after you've reaped your reward. Your chief and I will be at my house, having a late supper."

"I have to go," De Gier said. "I'm really not very good with women. My cat is female, too; she wipes the floor with me. I might release your suspect and interfere with your case."

"Don't want to interefere with your routine here, sir," Grijpstra said, pushing the lieutenant gently aside. "Thanks for the lunch. Your tomato salad was very tasty."

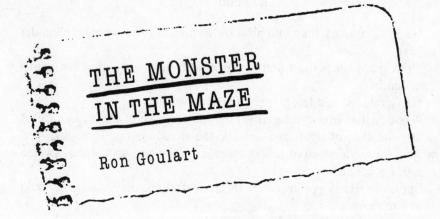

THE MONSTER IN THE MAZE

Ron Goulart

IT WAS EARLY in October of 1896 that Harry Challenge arrived in England and before many days had passed was nearly assassinated by bow and arrow, confronted on the misty moors of Sussex by a legendary monster and informed that the future of the British Empire depended on him.

He reached London early on a chill, misty evening, after making a reluctant, and choppy, trip across the Channel. A cablegram from New York had caused him to leave Paris four days ahead of schedule.

Dear Son: Off your duff and over to London. See Human Kangaroo, Crystal Theatre. This loon thinks ladyfriend carried off by monster. Big fee looms. Your loving father, the Challenge International Detective Agency.

The thick grey mist tightened around Harry as he went striding along Tottenham Court Road, causing the bracketed gas lanterns above the entrance of the public house he passed to look blurred and fuzzy. The hoofbeats of the Hansom cab horses were muffled and the figures in the posters slapped on the dingy brick wall next to the Crystal Theatre loomed vague and ghostlike.

Glancing back over his shoulder, the detective turned down the alley leading to the stage door. He was a lean, clean-shaven man of thirty, a shade above average height, and dressed in a dark, fairly conservative suit. The sort of suit his father firmly believed made a good impression on the clients of their detective agency.

The heavy stage door came flying open and yellow electric light spilled out into the fog.

Harry halted, reaching into his coat for his .38 revolver in his shoulder holster.

"'Ow many times must I tell yer Buckskin Sal hain't partial ter gentleman admirers."

Harry relaxed and left his gun where it was.

A pudgy man in a checkered yellow suit flew out of the theater, sailed across the slice of light, and fell into the shadowy fog. In his lopsided wake followed a bunch of yellow roses, a bowler hat, and a satin-covered box of chocolates.

Sprinting, Harry got inside the theater before the burly doorman could shut him out.

"'Ere now. Won't you blokes ever learn that Buckskin Sal's dazzlin' beauty hain't for the likes of—"

"I have an appointment with Alfie Quint, the Human Kangaroo."

The doorman eyed him. "An' what might yer name be?"

"Harry Challenge."

Loud, excited brassy music was drifting back from the orchestra pit. The audience was applauding enthusiastically and a hollow thumping was coming from the stage Harry couldn't as yet see.

After scrutinizing him again, the stage doorman said, "Gor, I've 'eard of you. Yer the detective chap, hain't yer? Internationally famed sleuth'ound."

"That I am," admitted Harry. "Where can I find Quint?"

"Blimey, 'e's on the bloomin' stage now, behavin' like a ruddy jumpin' jack." He pointed in the direction of the stage. "Yer can wait in the wings."

Nodding, Harry moved across the dimlit backstage area. He stopped near an open trunk full of Indian clubs to watch Alfie Quint's act out on the stage.

" . . .with your humble indulgence, ladies and gentlemen, I shall conclude my performance this evening with a feat of agility and endurance that has helped earn me the nickname of the Human Kangaroo," a muscular, fairhaired young man in crimson tights was announcing. "You will note that my assistant is arranging these straightback chairs in a ring. You will further take notice that each chair is a full ten feet from its mate. Yes, ladies and gentlemen, I said ten feet. You will realize at. . . ."

Harry became aware of a small growling sound behind him.

There was a collie dog standing on his hind legs, eying Harry in a far from cordial way. He carried a toy trombone in his forepaws and was clad in a yellow checkered suit and bowler hat.

"A gent dressed very much like you just got tossed out of here," Harry informed the dog in a low voice. "I'd watch myself."

The collie snarled.

A bulldog in a grey pinstripe suit came walking over, dragging a toy bullfiddle. When he noticed Harry, he began to make whimpering sounds.

"Boys, boys," whispered the small wrinkled man who trotted over. "Is this, I ask you, mannerly? Don't go being rude to Mr. Challenge just because he's standing where you usually stand before going on."

Out on the stage, the Human Kangaroo had successfully leaped from one chair bottom to the next, accompanied by applause and agitated music.

Harry grinned. "Professor Bascom, isn't it?"

The small man's right hand shot out from within the sleeve of his too large tailcoat. "It is, indeed. Professor Bascom and His Famous Dog Orchestra. We all met while playing on the same bill with your friend, the Great Lorenzo, in New York City a few years back.

"Paddy, mind your manners."

A terrier trumpet player in a tweedy Norfolk suit had joined the group in the wings. More unsettled by Harry's presence than his fellow orchestra members, he let go of his gilded instrument, dropped to all fours, and commenced chewing at Harry's trouser leg.

Harry squatted and took the unhappy dog musician by the coat collar. "I'll go wait in Quint's dressing room, sport, that way—"

Something came whizzing through the space where he'd been standing. It stuck with a thunk in a post immediately behind him.

"Well, fancy that!" Bascom glanced from the quivering arrow that had dug into the wood at about heart level up into the catwalks high above.

Harry extricated himself from the dog's grip and looked upward, too.

He was in time to catch a glimpse of a young woman in a skirt of fringed leather as she went running along a metal walkway high above. "Looks like I'm going to be pursuing Buckskin Sal, after all," he said.

He ran over to a metal ladder that climbed up the brick wall of the dark backstage area and went swiftly up. When Harry reached the catwalk, there was no sign of the young woman in the buckskin outfit.

Drawing his .38 revolver, he started along the narrow walkway. Midway along, he found another arrow. "Authentic Navajo," he muttered, and moved on.

At the far end of the catwalk, fog came swirling in at him. A small window leading to an outside fire ladder was open wide. Nodding to himself, Harry holstered his gun.

Down below, on the bright stage, Alfie Quint leaped from the final chair to the stage.

* * *

"I'm definitely non-plussed," confessed Quint as he removed his makeup.

Harry was occupying the small dressing room's only other chair. "Before we chat about why Buckskin Sal tried to do me in," he suggested, "explain why you want to hire the Challenge International Detective Agency."

"I fear I'll appear a coward in your eyes; or worse," said the performer, watching Harry's reflection in his mirror. "Let me try, though, to explain as best I can. England is not as democratic a country as your own United States, Mr. Challenge. Although I am known far and wide as *The Greatest Jumper in the World*, and though I am able to earn a princely income in my chosen profession, I am of humble origin. There are those who look down on me because I am not a born gentleman. One such is Sir Peveril Plumm."

"The diplomat." Harry took out one of the thin dark cigars he favored. "He's involved right now with the Lusitania-Great Britain Mutual Defense Treaty."

"You're even better informed than I anticipated."

"I hear things," replied Harry. "Would your young lady be Esmeralda Plumm?"

Quint gasped, then sighed. "She is the dearest thing in all the world to me. But my lowly station—her stubborn father is unrelenting—has kept us apart."

Harry's wax match sputtered and gave off a punky smell as he struck it and lit his cigar. "The Plumm estate is in Sussex somewhere, isn't it?" he inquired exhaling puffs of smoke. "Yes . . . and there's a famous maze there. One that's rumored to be haunted by some kind of monster."

Sitting up in his chair, Quint said, "I say, you are a well-informed fellow."

Harry'd paid a rundown British journalist, now going swiftly to ruin in Paris, twenty dollars for information on Alfie Quint and his romantic entanglements before catching a boat for Dover. He saw no need to share that fact with his client. "Is it this legendary monster who has carried off Esmeralda Plumm?"

Quint said, "Usually I am an extremely level-headed man. Unimaginative is what dear Esmeralda often—"

"But you saw something?"

Nodding forlornly, the Human Kangaroo said, "Sunday, not having to perform, I traveled by rail to Blackmarsh, which is a small coastal town near Eastbourne. The meetings between dear Esmeralda and myself must be, I regret to say, furtive. Especially now, when Sir Peveril is entertaining the Lusitanian Ambassador at Stumbleford Court, his palatial estate in Blackmarsh."

"You and the girl met secretly?"

"We arranged to meet in the maze itself at the hour of midnight this past Sunday."

"Doesn't sound too cheerful."

"It was not, I can assure you, cheerful at all. Yet, when lovers are separated by social boundaries so wide that even the World's Greatest Jumper can't clear them, their meetings needs must be clandestine and uncomfortable." Quint slumped in his chair. "I arrived at the rendezvous a few minutes short of the witching hour, having trudged afoot across the grim moorlands surrounding the isolated Plumm estate. The fog hung oppressively thick all around and I, who know the intricate paths of the maze as well as I know the streets of London, took more than one wrong turning before I reached the iron bench near the heart of the labyrinth where we were to meet. The time was by now a few minutes beyond midnight, and yet she was not there. Finally, at nearly a quarter past the hour, Esmeralda came running up to me from out the surrounding mist. She was quite obviously much upset and agitated. When I clasped her to me, I could feel her dear heart beating in a highly excited manner."

"What was wrong?" Harry took a puff of his stogie.

"I fear I never obtained the whole and entire story from her," explained Quint. "She was quite upset about something she had recently discovered. It had to do with the Lusitania-Great Britain Treaty and defense plans. That much Esmeralda was able to convey to me. I have the impression, Mr. Challenge, that she feared someone in the Stumbleford Court household was about to—or, indeed, already had, betrayed England to her enemies by passing copies of the treaty and plans on to foreign agents."

"Her brother, for instance?"

Sighing again, Quint said, "You've heard of Wild Jack Plumm, her eldest brother, then?"

"He was expelled from the Wastrel Club here in London only last month for cheating at cards," said Harry. "He's rumored to be 50,000 pounds in debt and Sir Peveril will no longer bail him out."

"And yet," said the Human Kangaroo, bitterness filling his voice, "he's considered a gentleman and I am not."

Harry asked, "What else did Miss Plumm say?"

"Not a deuced lot. She..." He straightened, snapping his fingers. "Now there's a coincidence—though I imagine, actually, it isn't. Esmeralda was asking me how well I knew Buckskin Sal, and if I'd ever seen her brother visiting Sal here at the theater."

"How'd you answer?"

"Never got the chance, though if I had I'd have explained that I am not close to Sal, whom I find rather uncouth and immodest. I've never seen hide nor hair of Wild Jack Plumm anywhere near the Crystal."

Harry leaned forward. "Tell me about the monster."

"The legend itself goes back to the late 17th century. The residents of Blackmarsh still give credence to it, although the monster has been seldom seen in recent times. Supposedly, it was old Kingsmill Plumm who made a pact with the Devil in 1693 and thereby unleashed a dark creature from the bowels of the—"

"How about what you saw on Sunday?"

Quint licked his upper lip. "Esmeralda, poor dear, saw him first. She moved free of my arms, stood up, and screamed," he said. "Turning I saw him. He was large, shrouded in a black cloak, and his face. . . well, it wasn't much of a face. It resembled the visage of a corpse who's languished in the mouldering ground for a year or more. Not that I've seen many corpses, but I'm sure you get my general drift."

"What happened then?"

"The brute spoke not a word. Instead, he rushed for Esmeralda. Grabbing her up in a loathsome embrace, he carried her off along a hedgerow."

"While you did what?"

Quint wiped at the corner of his eye. "Nothing," he answered ruefully. "That is, I took one step toward the foul creature and I was struck from behind. A stunning blow that rendered me unconscious for several precious minutes."

"You didn't see who conked you?"

"Not so much as a fleeting glimpse," Quint answered. "As I came to myself, I heard Esmeralda cry out from some distance away. Maddened by rage, I leaped over the hedge tops—they're only seven feet high—and managed to reach the spot I was certain she had called from. It was in the exact center of the maze, a small clearing with a sundial. Of Esmeralda or the monster there was no trace."

"What'd you do next?"

"I searched the maze until dawn with absolutely no luck."

"And then?"

Quint spread his hands wide. "That is when I behaved rather like a coward. I fled."

"You were afraid to tell Sir Peveril?"

"He'd vowed to horsewhip me should I ever so much as speak to his daughter again," explained the forlorn performer. "Going to the local police was of no use, since they are little more than toadies of Sir Peveril."

"So you engaged us."

"I had been informed that the Challenge Agency is one of the best and most efficient in the world," Quint said. "And that you have been especially effective in solving cases with a possible supernatural element. Since a recent legacy from a great aunt in Australia puts me in a position to pay your far from modest fees, I immediately—"

"I can see why my father was so interested in your case." Harry stood. "This is Thursday. You haven't heard anything from Esmeralda since Sunday, or anything from her family?"

"Nothing, alas, no."

Harry frowned. "Sort of odd."

"How so? I fail to see—"

"Well, if I were Sir Peveril and my daughter'd disappeared," Harry said, "first thing I'd do would be to check and see if she'd run off with you."

Harry left Victoria Station the next morning on a train bound for Eastbourne. The day was bleak and a fine rain hit at the windows of his first class carriage.

Twenty some minutes after the train had departed, the corridor door slid open to admit two fellow passengers.

The first was a sun-browned man of fifty with a neat cropped moustache so white it almost seemed to glow. Although he wore a tweedy Norfolk suit, there was something decidedly military about his bearing and he swung his Mallaca cane as though it were a swagger stick.

His companion was a huge muffled fellow, carrying an immense wicker picnic basket up in front of his broad chest. He was decked out in a billowing Inverness cape, wore his broad-brimmed felt hat pulled down low on his forehead, a paisley scarf pulled up high over most of his face, and a pair of rimless dark-tinted spectacles. He sat down opposite Harry, plumped the picnic basket onto the seat and dipped a gloved hand into it. Extracting the latest copy of *The Strand* magazine, he opened it and brought it up in front of his face.

The gentleman of military bearing sat near the window. "Beastly weather," he remarked. "Nothing at all like Rangoon."

"True," agreed Harry, who returned to going over the pages of the notebook resting on his knee.

The train rattled on through the grim, rain-swept morning.

Over half an hour later, while they were passing through sparsely populated, rural countryside, the gentleman with the moustache said, "Jove, I do believe I know who you are, sir."

Harry glanced across at him. "Oh, so?"

"Harry Challenge, ain't you? By way of being a detective."

"I am," he admitted. "I don't think we've ever—"

"Met? No, we never have." He gave a small shrug. "Just wanted to make sure I had the proper chap before giving Tizzo the nod to do you in."

The other passenger shed his magazine and rose up. His hat fell from his shaggy head and he made a rumbling, growling noise.

"Your friend seems to be a gorilla." Harry reached for his .38.

"Ah, none of that now, Challenge." The cane whistled as it swung out to whack Harry's hand. "Yes, and he's been taught to kill in quite brutal ways. Once Tizzo's finished with you, you'll cease worrying about the treaty any longer."

Harry's right hand went numb. "You and your pet have made a mist—"

"No more chatter," interrupted the military gentleman. "Do him in, Tizzo."

"Unk," replied the gorilla, and grabbed for Harry.

Harry, however, was no longer where he had been. He'd dropped to the floor between the facing seats.

He kicked up, getting the well-dressed gorilla first in the kneecaps and then in the groin.

Tizzo roared, swatting down with a gloved paw.

Legs together and braced on his back, Harry sunk both feet into Tizzo's furry mid-section. He lifted him up and over, tossing him right into the outside door of the railroad carriage.

With another unhappy roar, the gorilla hit the door, ripped it clear of its moorings, and went cannonballing out into the rain. He was already out of sight when they heard the damp thud that signalled his landing in a slanting field beyond the tracks.

Harry started to reach for his revolver with his left hand.

The military gentleman's cane struck again. "I'm deuced miffed at what you've done to Tizzo, I don't mind saying," he said. "He and I have been through a lot together."

Harry's left hand was clutched into a claw shape and scarcely functioning. Using his elbows, he got free of the floor and managed to sit down. "There's really no reason for any roughhousing," he said amiably. "The case I'm working on here in England has absolutely nothing to do with treaties or—"

"Bosh. I know full well what you're about, Challenge." Twisting the gilded handle of his cane, he drew out a glittering, thin-bladed sword. "Once I do for you, I'll heave you out. Much the same rude way you treated poor. . . Ah!"

A pistol shot echoed in the compartment.

The military gentleman staggered, lurched, and, with a helpful kick from Harry, fell off the fast-moving train.

"I do hope, Harry, you won't take my action as an intrusion into your affairs. I know how proud you are of your own prowess in dangerous situations such as this, yet I couldn't merely stand by and watch that scoundrel skewer you with his wicked blade."

"Not offended in the least, Victoria."

A handsome, blonde young woman, dressed in a modest traveling suit and holding an ivory-handled .32 pistol in her left hand, was standing just inside the corridor door. "That's awfully decent of you, Harry."

"Sit down and we'll talk," he invited, flexing his fingers.

Victoria Steele shivered slightly. "If you don't mind, I'd much prefer moving to my own compartment," she said. "Your's is a bit airy now it hasn't a door."

Harry got to his feet. "Yours'll be cozier." Pausing to gather up Tizzo's abandoned basket of fruit and magazines, he then followed the young woman down the swaying corridor.

"Yes, the fate of the British Empire," repeated Victoria Steele as she efficiently peeled an orange.

Harry sat watching her, the rain pelting on the window beside him. "You tend to see just about everything," he told her, "as a threat to the Empire."

"I must disagree, Harry," she responded. "For while I am a dedicated agent of Her Majesty's Secret Service, I have never allowed that fact to cloud my vision nor warp my judgment."

"And you really think this treaty with Lusitania is that important?

"In the wrong hands the details of the defense plan could do my country most serious harm." She ate an orange section. "Let me ask you this, Harry. Don't you realize that an unfriendly nation that can afford to employ a trained gorilla to discourage interference means business?"

"Been thinking about that. The gorilla is just the sort of touch that'd appeal to a master spy I've run into before."

"Really?" She concentrated on the orange.

"Come on, Victoria, Count Dragonthorpe is involved in this, isn't he?"

She didn't meet his eyes. "Dragonthorpe is one of those who *might* be," she conceded.

"He usually works for England's major rivals, especially Germany."

"As do others."

Harry leaned back. "Why are you going to Blackmarsh?"

"That much I can tell you," she said, looking up. "We have reason to believe that Esmeralda Plumm has been kidnapped. I am assuming you're interested in the very same abduction."

He nodded. "Reason to believe? Hasn't Sir Peveril gone to the authorities or—"

"He has not, no. Our information comes from... Well, since Ambassador Lazarillo of Lusitania is Sir Peveril's house-guest, we've seen to it that our interests are represented on the household staff." Frowning, she studied Harry's face for a few seconds. "Didn't Sir Peveril hire you?"

"Nope."

Victoria thoughtfully ate another slice of orange. "What can be the old gentleman's reasons for keeping silent?"

"Most likely the kidnappers warned him," said Harry. "Any idea who they are?"

She hesitated before answering, "None whatsoever. I've been dispatched to Blackmarsh to assist our agents already in the vicinity. As you can imagine, we haven't as yet approached Sir Peveril directly and, therefore, must conduct our investigation without his knowledge or cooperation."

"You obviously think her disappearance ties in with an attempt to get the details of the treaty."

"It may, yes. Though I needn't caution you about the dangers in jumping to conclu—"

"What details of her kidnapping do you have?"

"Precious few," replied the blonde secret agent. "Esmeralda Plumm slipped out of Stumbleford Court fairly close to the hour of midnight this past Sunday. She has not returned."

"Has anyone contacted Sir Peveril?"

"That we do not know," said Victoria. "Might I ask who your client is and how much you know about the girl's vanishment?"

Harry grinned. "Can't tell you who our client is," he said. "And I don't know much more about what happened to Esmeralda Plumm than you people do."

"Must I remind you again, Harry, that your failure to be helpful in this investigation may jeopardize the entire British—"

"I'll find her," he said, on my own."

"I had entertained the hope, most especially after I prevented that vile pair of foreign agents from doing away with you, that you'd be willing to work with me."

Harry reached across to pick an apple from the basket. "Only up to a point," he said.

As midnight neared, Harry was climbing across the Blackmarsh downs, wearing an oilskin coat and carrying a bull's-eye lantern. At his back, a mile or more downhill, were the chalky cliffs that dropped down to the black foamy water of the Channel. The beam of the Blackmarsh lighthouse was sweeping the rainy night and the roar of the sea carried this far.

High grass grew all around, along with heather and gorse. Harry turned up the collar of the coat he'd bought in the village that afternoon. Illuminating the way ahead with his lantern, he trudged through the night toward the maze at the edge of the Plumm estate.

Another wet and windy mile and he was at the two stone lions that guarded the entrance to the maze. It covered, according to research Harry'd done in both London and the village of Blackmarsh, over three acres. An intricate labyrinth of twisting paths and trimmed hedges that were near seven feet high and two feet thick.

Giving the lefthand lion a lazy salute with his free hand, Harry entered the maze. He had the momentary impression that the sound of the hardfalling rain had diminished.

He walked straight ahead for fifty yards, then turned into a lane on his right to walk another hundred yards. He hung his lantern on a hedge at chest level. Silently he moved back to the mouth of the lane, pressed his back to the high, thick hedge, and waited.

In just three minutes, a figure in a night-black slicker stepped into the lane. Lunging, Harry caught the follower in a hammerlock.

"My gracious, Harry. There's no need for all this viol—"

"We're not working on this, Victoria," he reminded, letting the pretty secret agent loose. "So quit tailing—"

"One doesn't talk to a representative of Her Majesty's government in such a rude way," Victoria informed him. "Let me, however, explain why I tailed you—to use your vulgarism."

"Do. Swiftly."

"I was perplexed," she confided. "I must own that I have followed you for several hours, curious as to what you were up to in Blackmarsh." She gave a puzzled shrug. "You haven't gone near Stumbleford Court until now. Instead, you prowled the village, talking to fisher-folk, loafers, even a youth I'm certain is the village idiot or—"

"Actually he's a noted author of novels of mystery and detection, vacationing here and dressed in what he fancies to be rustic style. Continue."

"You spent a good two hours in the town hall, then you sat around in the cottage of a retired professor from a small college in Eastbourne and chatted endlessly."

"Your agents should've been doing the same."

"For the life of me, Harry."

"Loafers see a lot," he explained. "Such things as at least three meetings on the beach between Wild Jack Plumm—he of the enormous gambling debts—and Buckskin Sal. I'd bet she's working for Count Dragonthorpe, using her mobility as an internationally known Wild West sharpshooter and trick shot to cover her espionage activities."

"Ah, that confirms a suspicion of mine." Victoria nodded her head and rain came splashing off her hat. "Jack Plumm is the weak link, the one who agreed to get copies of the treaty and defense plans from Ambassador Lazarillo during his stay at Stumbleford Court."

"Seems like."

"But where does that ancient scholar fit into—"

"He happens to be a keen student of local history," answered Harry as rain trickled down his neck. "I figured that Blackmarsh, like many a town on this coast, was up to its ears in the smuggling trade in the 17th and 18th Centuries. It was, the professor assured me, and several of the Plumms were involved. Hence, they created the legend about the monster so that folks would stay away from this—"

Harry, your lantern just vanished!"

He shoved her aside, spun, and yanked out his .38 revolver.

Standing in front of the dangling lantern and masking much of its glow was a large cloaked figure. What Harry could see of its head indicated that this was none other than the celebrated monster of the maze.

"Vicky, cover our rear." Harry ran right toward the monster.

"Begone!" it warned. "Lest death be thy fate."

"Carrying on in the family tradition, huh, Jack?" Harry shot him in the leg.

"I say, old man, that was hardly sporting." The monster swayed, slumped, fell over in a faint. He made a soggy sound when he hit the ground.

Behind Harry, two shots were fired.

"Got them, Harry," called Victoria. "Two low rascals bent on coshing us. Who's that you have?"

Harry lifted the mask from the unconscious man's face. "Looks a good deal like Wild Jack."

She came hurrying over, held the lantern close. "Yes, that's he," she agreed. "What a pity he betrayed his native land and aided in the abduction of his sister."

"They had to keep her quiet for a while."

"But even so, he—"

"I hate to suggest this, but it could be Jack's simply not a gentleman."

"Shame he's passed out, for now he can't lead us to where his poor sister is hidden."

Reaching out, Harry took hold of her hand. "Come along," he invited, "and I'll show you."

Harry pointed at the sundial in the center of the clearing at the heart of the rain-swept maze. "Shine the light on this piece that casts the shadow. Notice the stuff tangled around it?"

"Some sort of moss or—"

"Nope, it's crepe hair. From Wild Jack's fright-wig. Means he's been fooling with this thing." Harry crouched slightly, taking hold of the copper part. He tried twisting it to the left, got no results and twisted it to the right.

A great rumbling commenced directly beneath them. Slowly, a marble slab just beyond the base of the venerable sundial began to slide open.

"A secret stairway leading underground," exclaimed Victoria, shining the lantern beam on the mossy stone steps.

"Built by the smugglers on the Plumm family tree." Harry got his pistol out again and started descending the stairway. "More than likely there's a tunnel leading from here to a cave down near the shore."

"This must be where they're holding Esmeralda Plumm."

"That's how I. . . duck!" He dropped to one knee at the foot of the stairs, firing his pistol into the dimness ahead.

An arrow came whispering in his direction, missed him and grated against the stone wall of the musty tunnel.

"Hot dang," muttered someone in the tunnel.

Harry moved on, then swung out with his left hand and landed a solid punch on the jaw of Buckskin Sal before she could fit another arrow to her bow.

"Son of a gun!" the dark-haired lady grunted before she tumbled over into unconsciousness.

"You really ought to have allowed me the opportunity punching her." Victoria caught up with him. "After all, hitting a woman isn't exactly—"

"Didn't bother me at all," he assured her, as he stopped to gather up the bow and a quiver of arrows.

They found Esmeralda Plumm all alone in a small stonewalled room. She was trussed up with old rope, gagged with a soiled red bandana, and propped against a wine barrel atop of which a stubby candle sputtered.

"I'd rather been hoping and praying," Esmeralda said after Harry removed the gag and started cutting away the oily ropes, "that Alfred Quint would be the one to rescue me from this den of spies. That might well have impressed my father and—"

"Alfie hired me," explained Harry. "Where are the rest of the spies?"

"Oh, I'm glad you reminded me," said the pretty golden-haired girl. "That wicked Count Dragonthorpe departed only moments ago to meet a submarine boat down on the beach. My wicked brother obtained a copy of the Lusitania Great Britain Treaty. They've had the papers for several days but the exchange with foreign agents could not be made until tonight. Thus, when they thought I might betray them before they could complete their evil scheme, they abducted me and—"

"You can tell us all the details later." Harry folded his jackknife and dropped it into a pocket.

"My unfortunate, though often pigheaded, father was helpless to act, even though he suspected what had happened, because he was warned I'd come to serious harm unless he kept absolutely silent and allowed—"

"Stay with her, Vicky." Carrying the borrowed bow and arrow, Harry started off along the tunnel that would lead him down to the sea and the narrow Blackmarsh beach.

Harry saw the submarine before he saw the count. The craft was rising up out of the night sea about half a mile off the narrow gritty strip of beach. It was the first such he'd ever encountered and he was impressed by the bulky ugliness of the thing. He spotted Count Dragonthorpe then, a small man in a grey suit and a bowler hat that looked to be about a size too small. The master spy was about a hundred yards down the beach from the mouth of the small cave from which Harry had emerged.

Dragonthorpe was facing the rising submarine, signaling to it with a lantern. A portmanteau rested on the sand beside his feet.

"Jig's up," called Harry.

The count flinched. That caused his hat to rise off his head and go cartwheeling away on the rainy wind. Dragonthorpe touched at his crinkly blond hair, glanced back at Harry with a deep frown, and, snatching up the black portmanteau, started running.

"Halt!" warned Harry.

The spy kept running.

Following, Harry fit an arrow to the bow. He stopped, took careful aim, quickly calculated the effect the wind and rain would have on the flight, and shot at the fleeing Dragonthorpe.

The arrow flew true, hitting the escaping spy square in the backside. He howled, flapped his arms, and dropped the portmanteau. He stumbled and dropped to his knees on the night beach.

"*Right this way, lads! A dozen men to the boats, another dozen for the count!*"

Gunshots sounded.

Ignoring everything, Harry ran along the beach.

The felled count was struggling to reach inside his coat for a weapon, though a tap on the skull from the butt of Harry's pistol discouraged that and put the crinkly-haired spy to sleep.

"That was absolutely marvelous, if you don't mind my saying." Victoria joined him. Kneeling, he pried open the portmanteau. "Yes, as we suspected, this contains copies of the treaty and the defense plans."

"What was the shooting and hollering about?"

"I decided to follow you in case a ruse was needed," she explained, standing and brushing sand from her rainslicker. "It was, and, I must say, it worked handsomely. Those rogues were about to lower a boat from that underwater dreadnaught. Believing that a large force had arrived, they have turned tail."

Glancing seaward, Harry saw that the submarine was sinking from view. "You were damned convincing apparently."

Victoria smiled at him, then rose on tiptoe to kiss him politely on the cheek. "That was to express my deep-felt gratitude."

Harry eyed her. "Well, it's a start," he said.

The night Harry took his leave of London, it was raining. The platforms inside Victoria Station were crowded with departing travelers carrying dripping umbrellas or trying to furl them without losing any luggage.

Harry was still some distance from his first class compartment on the Continental boat-train when he became aware that he was being trailed by someone unusual. The passengers walking toward him were gazing around him, blinking, gasping, chuckling or feigning indifference.

Halting, reaching unobtrusively inside his coat, Harry turned.

A terrier pup in a tweedy suit was walking in his wake, balanced on its hind legs and clutching a toy trumpet.

Kneeling, Harry let go of the handle of his .38 revolver and extended his hand toward the dog. "Going on the road, Paddy?"

The dog musician, dropping his instrument, went on all fours and ran up to Harry. He snapped, got hold of the detective's coat cuff with his teeth, and started tugging.

"Paddy! Paddy, you rogue! What's become of you?"

"He's seeing me off, Professor Bascom." Harry stood, with the terrier dangling from his left sleeve, and waved his right hand.

The professor emerged from behind a plump lady with an immense feather boa encircling her. "Ah, this is a pleasant surprise," he said, catching hold of Paddy and tugging. "Must I remind you again, you rascal, that Mr. Challenge is a friend of ours?"

"You and your dog orchestra leaving London?"

"Not at all." The terrier came loose, taking a small swatch of Harry's coat with him. "Look what you've done, Paddy! For shame! We're here, along with some of the other performers from the Crystal Theatre, to see Alfie Quint and his bride off on their European honeymoon."

"Bride?" Harry rubbed his torn coat.

"Come along and exchange a few pleasantries."

Following the professor and the forlorn Paddy, and carrying the dog's trumpet, Harry backtracked to another compartment. Its doors stood open and it was crowded with flowers, hampers of food, travel rugs and people. A tall, lean young man was standing on the damp platform juggling three bottles of champagne.

The golden-haired Esmeralda Plumm caught sight of Harry, cried out, and pushed free of the compartment. Hugging him, she said, "How very nice of you to come wish us *bon voyage*, Mr. Challenge. For had it not been for you we—"

"Actually, I'm departing myself," he explained as he moved back from her grasp and turned the trumpet over to Professor Bascom. "Going back to Paris for a few—"

"We're bound for Paris ourselves, my dear Alfred and I. The first stop on our honeymoon will. . . Alfred! Over here, my darling." She called and waved to someone moving down the platform.

Quint, wearing a conservative grey suit and a bowler hat, came bounding over. He cleared a high stack of luggage and landed beside Harry and Esmeralda. "I purchased *The Strand* for you, my love, as well as the *Pall Mall* and . . . I say, Challenge, it's quite thoughtful of you to have come out on a foul night like this to—"

"He didn't," said Esmeralda. "Mr. Challenge is journeying to Dover to catch a boat to Paris."

Nodding, the Human Kangaroo said, "We owe you a good deal, Challenge, more than we can ever repay in—"

"You did pay the bill my father sent, didn't you?"

"To be sure, two days ago."

"Then you don't owe us anything."

Quint said, "I was alluding to intangible feelings, such as deep gratitude. Not only did you save dear Esmeralda's life and aid the British government, but you made smooth the way for us to wed."

Harry frowned. "How did I do that exactly?"

Esmeralda inclined her head toward the left. "Have you chanced to notice that woebegone figure down there near the obese opera diva in the unsightly furs? A frail old gentleman all muffled up in an overcoat and scarf?"

"Would that be your father, Sir Peveril Plumm?"

"It is he, yes. Or rather a shadow of his former self."

"He's not sharing your—"

"Not at all," said Quint quickly.

"Father is going into exile, actually," explained Esmeralda. "He's severed his connections with our government and intends to live on the Continent for some time to come. He feels he's been disgraced."

"Because your brother was in cahoots with the spies?"

"Exactly." The young woman sighed. "Despite all my wild brother's follies up to now, my father remained fond of him. He firmly believed that I should be the one to disgrace him finally."

"Wild Jack's arrest in this espionage matter quite took the wind out of the old duffer's sails," said Quint, shaking his head. "So much so that he gave us his consent to be married."

"Plus a substantial dowry," added Esmeralda, smiling faintly. "It is my theory that father feels so deeply ruined by what Jack's done that my marrying beneath my class no longer seems important. The Plumm name is so tarnished that nothing else matters."

"Not exactly flattering to me," said Quint, slipping an arm around his bride's slim waist, "yet I'm willing to put up with a bit of a slight so long as I can have Esmeralda as mine."

"Father will come around in time," said Esmeralda confidently. "Why a moment ago I do believe I noticed his glancing in our direction with fondness in his tear-stained old eyes. Did you notice, Mr. Challenge?"

"I did," Harry lied. "Sir Peveril seems to be mellowing even as he stands there." Grinning, he shook hands with the groom, wished them both well, and took his leave.

He was nearly to his compartment again when an arm was linked with his.

"What a most satisfying coincidence," said Victoria Steele, smiling up at him as they walked side by side. "Don't tell me, Harry, you are bound for the Continent?"

"I'm going back to Paris. And you?"

"Why, I am bound for Paris, too," she replied, "on a most important errand. Would I be imposing, do you think, if I shared your compartment with you?"

Harry opened the door for her.

"Not at all."

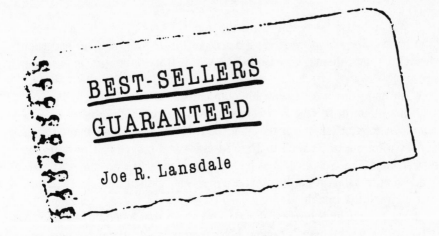

BEST-SELLERS GUARANTEED

Joe R. Lansdale

LARRY HAD A headache, as he often did. It was those all night stints at the typewriter, along with his job and his boss, Fraggerty, yelling for him to fry the burgers faster, to dole them out lickity-split on mustard-covered sesame seed buns.

Burgers and fries, typing paper and typewriter ribbons—the ribbons as grey and faded as the thirty-six years of his life. There really didn't seem to be any reason to keep on living. Another twenty to thirty years of this would be foolish. Then again, that seemed the only alternative. He was too cowardly to take his own life.

Washing his face in the bathroom sink, Larry jerked a rough paper towel from the rack and dried off, looking at himself in the mirror. He was starting to look like all those hacks of writer mythology. The little guys who turned out the drek copy. The ones with the blue veined, alcohol noses and the eyes like volcanic eruptions.

"My God," he thought, "I look forty easy. Maybe even forty-five."

"You gonna stay in the can all day?" a voice yelled through the door. it was Fraggerty, waiting to send him back to the grill and the burgers. The guy treated him like a bum.

A sly smile formed on Larry's face as he thought: "I am a bum. I've been through three marriages, sixteen jobs, eight typewriters, and all I've got to show for it are a dozen articles, all of them in obscure magazines that either paid in copies or pennies." He wasn't even as good as the hack he looked like. The hack could at least point to a substantial body of work, drek or not. And I've been at this . . . God, twelve years! An article a year. Some average. Not even enough to pay back his typing supplies.

He thought of his friend Mooney—or James T. Mooney, as he was known to his fans. Yearly, he wrote a bestseller.

It was a bestseller before it hit the stands. And except for Mooney's first novel, *The Goodbye Reel*, a detective thriller, all of them had been dismal. In fact, dismal was too kind a word. But the public lapped them up.

What had gone wrong with his own career? He used to help Mooney with his plots; in fact he had helped him work out his problems on *The Goodbye Reel*, back when they had both been scrounging their livings and existing out of a suitcase. Then Mooney had moved to Houston, and a year later *The Goodbye Reel* had hit the stands like an atomic bomb. Made record sales in hardback and paper, and gathered in a movie deal that boggled the imagination.

Being honest with himself, Larry felt certain that he could say he was a far better writer than Mooney. More commercial, even. So why had Mooney gathered the laurels while he bagged burgers and ended up in a dirty restroom contemplating the veins in his nose?

It was almost too much to bear. He would kill to have a bestseller. Just one. That's all he'd ask. Just one.

"Tear the damned crapper out of there and sit on it behind the grill!" Fraggerty called through the door. "But get out here. We got customers lined up down the block."

Larry doubted that, but he dried his hands, combed his hair and stepped outside.

Fraggerty was waiting for him. Fraggerty was a big fat man with bulldog jowls and perpetual blossoms of sweat beneath his meaty arms. Mid-summer, dead of winter—he had them.

"Hey," Fraggerty said, "you work here or what?"

"Not any more," Larry said. "Pay me up."

"What?"

"You heard me, fat ass. Pay up!"

"Hey, don't get tough about it. All right. Glad to see you hike."

Five minutes later, Larry was leaving the burger joint, a fifty dollar check in his pocket.

He said aloud: "Job number seventeen."

The brainstorm had struck him right when he came out of the restroom. He'd go see Mooney. He and Mooney had been great friends once, before all that money and a new way of living had carried Mooney back and forth to Houston and numerous jet spots around the country and overseas.

Maybe Mooney could give him a connection, an *in*, as it was called in the business. Before, he'd been too proud to ask, but now he didn't give a damn if he had to crawl and lick boots. He had to sell his books;

had to let the world know he existed.

Without letting the landlord know, as he owed considerable back rent, he cleaned out his apartment.

Like his life, there was little there. A typewriter, copies of his twelve articles, a few clothes and odds and ends. There weren't even any books. He'd had to sell them all to pay his rent three months back.

In less than twenty minutes, he snuck out without being seen, loaded the typewriter and his two suitcases in the trunk of his battered Chevy, and looked up at the window of his dingy apartment. He lifted his middle finger in salute, climbed in the car and drove away.

Mooney was easy to find. His estate looked just the part for the residence of a bestselling author. A front lawn the size of a polo field, a fountain of marble out front, and a house that looked like a small English castle. All this near downtown Houston.

James T. Mooney looked the part, too. He answered the door in a maroon smoking jacket with matching pajamas. He had on a pair of glossy leather bedroom slippers that he could have worn with a suit and tie. His hair was well-groomed with just the right amount of grey at the temples. There was a bit of a strained look about his eyes, but other than that he was the picture of health and prosperity.

"Well, I'll be," Mooney said. "Larry Melford. Come in."

The interior of the house made the outside look like a barn. There were paintings and sculptures and shelves of first edition books. On one wall, blown up to the size of movie posters and placed under glass and frame, were copies of the covers of his bestsellers. All twelve of them. A thirteenth glass and frame stood empty beside the others, waiting for the inevitable.

They chatted as they walked through the house, and Mooney said, "Let's drop off in the study. We can be comfortable there. I'll have the maid bring us some coffee or iced tea."

"I hope I'm not interrupting your writing,'" Larry said.

"No, not at all. I'm finished for the day. I usually just work a couple of hours a day."

"A couple hours a day?" thought Larry. A serpent of envy crawled around in the pit of his stomach. For the last twelve years, he had worked a job all day and had written away most of the night, generally gathering no more than two to three hours sleep a day. And here was Mooney writing these monstrous bestsellers and he only wrote a couple of hours in the mornings.

Mooney's study was about the size of Larry's abandoned apartment.

And it looked a hell of a lot better. One side of the room was little more than a long desk covered with a word processor and a duplicating machine. The rest of the room was taken up by a leather couch and rows of bookshelves containing nothing but Mooney's work. Various editions of foreign publications, special collectors' editions, the leather-bound Christmas set, the paperbacks, the bound galleys of all the novels. Mooney was surrounded by his success.

"Sit down; take the couch," Mooney said, hauling around his desk chair. "Coffee or tea? I'll have the maid bring it."

"No, I'm fine."

"Well then, tell me about yourself."

Larry opened his mouth to start, and that's when it fell out. He just couldn't control himself. It was as if a dam had burst open and all the water of the world was flowing away. The anguish, the misery, the years of failure found expression.

When he had finished telling it all, his eyes were glistening. He was both relieved and embarrassed. "So you see, Mooney, I'm just about over the edge. I'm craving success like an addict craves a fix. I'd kill for a bestseller."

Mooney's face seemed to go lopsided. "Watch that kind of talk."

"I mean it. I'm feeling so small right now, I'd have to look up to see a snake's belly. I'd lie, cheat, steal, kill—anything to get published in a big way. I don't want to die and leave nothing of me behind."

"And you don't want to miss out on the good things either, right?"

"Damned right. You've got it."

"Look, Larry, worry less about the good things and just write your books. Ease up some, but do it your own way. You may never have a big bestseller, but you're a good writer, and eventually you'll crack and be able to make a decent living."

"Easy for you to say, Mooney."

"In time, with a little patience . . ."

"I'm running out of time and patience. I'm emotionally drained, whipped. What I need is an *in*, Mooney, an *in*. A name. Anything that can give me a break."

"Talent is the name of the game, Larry, not an *in*," Mooney said very softly.

"Don't give me that garbage. I've got talent and you know it. I used to help you with the plots of your short stories. And your first novel—remember the things I worked out for you there? I mean, come on, Mooney. You've read my writing. It's good. Damned good! I need help. An *in* can't hurt me. It may not help me much, but it's got to give me a damn sight better chance than I have now."

Larry looked at Mooney's face. Something seemed to be moving there behind the eyes and taut lips. He looked sad, and quite a bit older than his age. Well, okay. So he was offended by being asked right out to help a fellow writer. That was too bad. Larry just didn't have the pride and patience anymore to beat around the bush.

"An *in*, huh?" Mooney finally said.

"That's right."

"You sure you wouldn't rather do it your way?"

"I've been doing it my way for twelve years. I want a break, Mooney."

Mooney nodded solemnly. He went over to his desk and opened a drawer. He took out a small, white business card and brought it over to Larry.

It read:

BESTSELLERS GUARANTEED

Offices in New York, Texas, California
and
Overseas

The left hand corner of the card had a drawing of an open book, and the right hand corner had three phone numbers. One of them was a Houston number.

"I met a lady when I first moved here," Mooney said, "a big name author in the romance field. I sort of got this thing going with her . . . finally asked her for . . . an *in*. And she gave me this card. We don't see each other anymore, Larry. We stopped seeing each other the day she gave it to me."

Larry wasn't listening. "This an editor?"

"No."

"An agent?"

"No."

"Publisher, book packager?"

"None of those things and a little of all, and a lot more."

"I'm not sure . . ."

"You wanted your *in*, so there it is. You just call that number. And Larry, do me a favor. Never come here again."

The first thing Larry did when he left Mooney's was find a telephone booth. He dialed the Houston number and a crisp female voice answered: "Bestsellers Guaranteed."

"Are you the one in charge?"

"No sir, just hold on and I'll put you through to someone who can help you."

Larry tapped his quarter on the phone shelf till a smooth-as-well-water male voice said: "B.G. here. May I be of assistance?"

"Uh . . . yes, a friend of mine . . . a Mr. James T. Mooney—"

"Of course, Mr. Mooney."

"He suggested . . . he gave me a card. Well, I'm a writer. My name is Larry Melford. To be honest, I'm not exactly sure what Mooney had in mind for me. He just suggested I call you."

"All we need to know is that you were recommended by Mr. Mooney. Where are you now?"

Larry gave the address of the *Seven Eleven* phone booth.

"Why don't you wait there . . . oh, say . . . twenty minutes, and we'll send a car to pick you up? That suit you?"

"Sure, but . . ."

"I'll have an agent explain it to you when he gets there, okay?"

"Yes, yes, that'll be fine." Larry hung up and stepped outside to lean on the hood of his car. By golly, he thought, that Mooney does have connections, and now after all these years, my thirteenth year of trying, maybe, just maybe, I'm going to get connected, too.

He lit a cigarette and watched the August heat waves bounce around the *Seven Eleven* lot, and twenty minutes later, a tan, six-door limousine pulled up next to his Chevy.

The man driving the limo wore a chauffeur's hat and outfit. He got out of the car and walked around to the tinted, far backseat window and tapped gently on the glass. The window slid down with a short whoosh. A man dressed in black with black hair, a black mustache and thick-rimmed black shades, looked out at Larry. He said, "Mr. Melford?"

"Yes," Larry said.

"Would you like to go around to the other side? Herman will open the door for you."

After Larry had slid onto the seat and Herman had closed the door behind him, his eyes were drawn to the plush interior of the car. Encased in the seat in front of them was a phone, a television set and a couple of panels that folded out. Larry felt certain one of them would be a small bar. Air-conditioning hummed softly. The car was nice enough and large enough to live in.

He looked across the seat at the man in black, who was extending his hand. They shook. The man in black said, "Just call me James, Mr. Melford."

"Fine. This is about . . . writing? Mooney said he could give me a . . . connection. I mean, I have work, plenty of it. Four novels, a couple of dozen short stories, a novella—of course I know that length is a dog to sell, but . . ."

"None of that matters," James said.

"This *is* about writing?"

"This is about bestsellers, Mr. Melford. That is what you want, isn't it? To be a bestselling author?"

"More than anything."

"Then you're our man and we're your organization."

Herman had eased in behind the wheel. James leaned forward over the seat and said firmly, "Drive us around." Leaning back, James touched a button on the door panel and a thick glass rose out of the seat in front of them and clicked into place in a groove in the roof.

"Now," James said, "shall we talk?"

As they drove, James explained. "I'm the agent assigned to you, and it's up to me to see if I can convince you to join our little gallery. But, if you should sign on with us, we expect you to remain loyal. You must consider that we offer a service that is unique, unlike any offered anywhere. We can guarantee that you'll hit the bestseller list once a year, every year, as long as you're with us.

"Actually, Mr. Melford, we're not a real old organization, and though I have a hard time remembering the exact year we were founded, it predated the Kennedy assassination by a year."

"That would be sixty-two," Larry said.

"Yes, yes, of course. I'm terrible at years. But it's only lately that we've come into our own. Consider the bad state of publishing right now, then consider the fact that our clients have each had a bestseller this year—and they will next year, no matter how bad publishing may falter. Our clients may be the only ones with books, but each of their books will be a bestseller, and their success will, as it does every year, save the industry."

"You're a packager?"

"No. We don't actually read the books Mr. Melford, we just make sure they're bestsellers. You can write a book about the Earth being invaded by giant tree toads from the moon, if you like, and we will guarantee it will be a bestseller."

"My God, you are connected."

"You wouldn't believe the connections we have."

"And what does your organization get out of this? How much of a percentage?"

"We don't take a dime."

"What?"

"Not a dime. For our help, for our guarantee that your books will be bestsellers, we ask only one thing. A favor. One favor a year. A favor for each bestseller."

"What's the favor?"

"We'll come to that in a moment. But before we do, let me make sure you understand what we have to offer. I mean, if you were successful— and I mean no offense by this—then you wouldn't be talking to me now. You need help. We can offer help. You're in your mid-thirties, correct? Yes, I thought so. Not really old, but a bit late to start a new career plan. People do it, but it's certainly no piece of cake, now, is it?"

Larry found that he was nodding in agreement.

"So," James continued, "what we want to do is give you success. We're talking money in the millions of dollars, Mr. Melford. Fame. Respect. Most anything you'd want would be at your command. Exotic foods and wines? A snap of the fingers. Books? Cars? Women? A snap of the fingers. Anything your heart desires and it's yours."

"But I have to make a small, initial investment, right?'"

"Ah, suspicious by nature, are you?"

"Wouldn't you be? My God, you're offering me the world."

"So I am. But no . . . no investment. Picture this, Mr. Melford. You might get lucky and sell your work, might even have a bestseller. But the slots are getting smaller and smaller for new writers. And one reason for that is that our writers, our clients, are filling those slots, Mr. Melford. If it's between your book and one of our client's, and yours is ten times better written, our client will still win out. Every time."

"What you're saying is, the fix is in?"

"A crude way of putting it, but rather accurate. Yes."

"What about talent, craftsmanship?"

"I wouldn't know about any of that. I sell success, not books."

"But it's the public that puts out its money for these books. They make or break an author. How can you know what they'll buy?"

"Our advertising system is the best in the world. We know how to reach the public and how to convince. We also use subliminals, Mr. Melford. We flash images on television programs, theater films; we hide them in the art of wine and cigarette ads. Little things below conscious perception, but images that lock tight to the subconscious mind. People who would not normally pick up a book will buy our bestsellers."

"Isn't that dishonest?"

"Who's to tell in this day and age what's right and wrong? It's relative, don't you think, Mr. Melford?"

Larry didn't say anything.

"Look. The public pictures writers as rich, all of them. They don't realize that the average full-time writer makes four thousand dollars or less a year. Most of them are out there starving and for what? Get on the winning side for a change, Mr. Melford. Otherwise, spend the rest of your life living in roach motels and living off the crumbs tossed you by the publishing world. And believe me, Mr. Melford, if you fail to join up with us, crumbs are all you'll get. If you're lucky."

The limousine had returned to the *Seven Eleven* parking lot. They were parked next to Larry's car.

"I suppose," James said, "we've come to that point that the bullfighters call 'the moment of truth.' You sign on with us and you'll be on Easy Street for the rest of your life."

"But we haven't talked terms."

"No, we haven't. It's at this point that I must ask you to either accept or turn down our offer, Mr. Melford. Once I've outlined the terms, you must be in full agreement with us."

"Accept before I hear what this favor you've talked about is?"

"That's correct. Bestseller or Bohemian, Mr. Melford. Which is it? Tell me right now. My time is valuable."

Larry paused only a moment. "Very well. Count me in. In for a penny, in for a pound. What's the favor?"

"Each year, you assassinate someone for us."

Larry dove for the door handle, but it wouldn't open. It had been locked electronically. James grabbed him by the wrist and held him tightly, so tightly Larry thought his bones would shatter.

"I wouldn't," James said. "After what I've told you, you step out of this car and they'll find you in a ditch this afternoon, obviously the victim of some hit and run driver."

"That's . . . that's murder."

"Yes, it is." James said. "Listen to me. You assassinate whomever we choose. We're not discriminating as far as sex, color, religion or politics goes. Anyone who gets in our way dies. Simple as that. You see, Mr. Melford, we are a big organization. Our goal is world domination. You, and all our clients, are little helpers toward that goal. Who is more respected than a bestselling author? Who is allowed in places where others would not be allowed? Who is revered by public figures and the general public alike? An author—a bestselling author."

"But . . . it's murder."

"There will be nothing personal in it. It'll just be your part of the contract. One assassination a year that we'll arrange."

"But, if you're so connected . . . why do it this way? Why not just hire a hit man?"

"In a sense, I have."

"I'm not an assassin. I've never even fired a gun."

"The amateur is in many ways better than the professional. He doesn't fall into a pattern. When the time comes, we will show you what you have to do. If you decide to be with us, that is."

"And if not?"

"I told you a moment ago. The ditch. The hit and run driver."

Suddenly, Herman was standing at the door, his hand poised to open it.

"Which is it, Mr. Melford? I'm becoming impatient. A ditch or a bestseller? And if you have any ideas about going to the police, don't. We have friends there, and you might accidently meet one. Now, your decision."

"I'm in," Larry said, softly. "I'm in."

"Good," James said, taking Larry's hand. "Welcome aboard. You get one of those books of yours out, pick out a publisher, and mail it in. And don't bother with return postage. We'll take care of the rest. Congratulations."

James tapped the window at Herman. The door opened. Larry got out. And just before the door closed, James said, "If you should have trouble coming up with something, getting something finished, just let me know and we'll see that it gets written for you."

Larry stood on the sidewalk nodding dumbly. Herman returned to the driver's seat, and a moment later the tan limo from *Bestsellers Guaranteed* whispered away.

James was as as good as his word. Larry mailed off one of his shop-worn novels, a thriller entitled *Texas Backlash*, and a contract for a half million dollars came back, almost by return mail.

Six months later, the book hit the bestseller list and rode there for a comfortable three months. It picked up a two million dollar paperback sale and a bigshot movie producer purchased it for twice that amount.

Larry now had a big mansion outside of Nacogdoches, Texas, with a maid, a cook, two secretaries and a professional yard man. Any type of food he wanted was his for the asking. Once he had special seafood flown in from the East Coast to Houston and hauled from there to his door by refrigerated truck.

Any first edition book he wanted was now within his price range. He owned four cars, two motorcycles, a private airplane and a yacht.

He could own anything—even people. They hopped at his every word, his most casual suggestion. He had money and people wanted to satisfy those with money. Who knows, maybe it would rub off on them.

And there were women. Beautiful women. There was even one he had grown to care for, and believed cared for him instead of his money and position. Lovely Luna Malone.

But in the midst of all this finery, there was the favor. The thought of it rested on the back of his mind like a waiting vulture. And when a year had gone by, the vulture swooped in.

On a hot August day, the tan limo from *Bestsellers Guaranteed* pulled up the long, scenic drive to Larry's mansion. A moment later, Larry and James were in his study and Herman stood outside the closed door with his arms akimbo, doing what he did best. Waiting, silently.

James was dressed in black again. He still wore the thick-framed sun shades. "You know what I've come for, don't you?"

Larry nodded. "The favor."

"On March fifteenth, *Bestsellers Guaranteed* will arrange for an autograph party in Austin for your new bestseller, whatever that may be. At eleven-fifteen, you will excuse yourself to go upstairs to the men's room. Next door to it is a janitor's lounge. It hasn't been used in years. It's locked but we will provide you with the key.

"At the rear of the lounge is a restroom. Lift off the back of the commode and you will discover eight small packages taped to the inside. Open these and fit them together and you'll have a very sophisticated air rifle. One of the packages will contain a canister of ice, and in the middle, dyed red, you will find a bullet-shaped projectile of ice. The air gun can send that projectile through three inches of steel without the ice shattering.

"You will load the gun, go to the window, and at exactly eleven-twenty five, the Governor will drive by in an open car in the midst of a parade. A small hole has been cut in the window. It will exactly accommodate the barrel of the rifle and the scope will fit snugly against the glass. You will take aim, and in a matter of seconds, your favor for this year will be done."

"Why the Governor?"

"That is our concern."

"I've never shot a rifle."

"We'll train you. You have until March. You won't need to know much more than how to put the rifle together and look through the scope. The weapon will do the rest."

"If I refuse?"

"The bestselling author of *Texas Backlash* will be found murdered in his home by a couple of burglars, and a couple of undesirables will be framed for the crime. Don't you think that has a nicer ring to it than the hit and run program I offered you before? Or perhaps, as a warning, we'll do something to your lady friend. What's her name . . . Luna?"

"You wouldn't!"

"If it would offer incentive or achieve our desired goals, Mr. Melford, we would do anything."

"You bastard!"

"That'll be quite enough, Mr. Melford. You've reaped the rewards of our services, and now we expect to be repaid. It seems a small thing to ask for your success—and certainly you wouldn't want to die at the hands of other bestselling authors, the ones who will ultimately be your assassins."

In spite of the air-conditioning, Larry had begun to sweat. "Just who are you guys, really?"

"I've told you. We're an organization with big plans. What we sponsor more than anything else, Mr. Melford, is moral corruption. We feed on those who thrive on greed and ego; put them in positions of power and influence. We belong to a group, to put it naively, who believe that once the silly concepts of morality and honor break down, then we, who really know how things work, can take control and make them work to our advantage. To put it even more simply, Mr. Melford. We will own it all."

"I . . . I can't just cold-bloodedly murder someone."

"Oh, I think you can. I've got faith in you. Look around you, Mr. Melford. Look at all you've got. Think of what you've got to lose, then tell me if you can murder from a distance someone you don't even know. I'll wait outside with Herman for your answer. You have two minutes."

From the March fifteenth edition of *The Austin Statesman*, a front page headline: "GOVERNOR ASSASSINATED, ASSASSIN SOUGHT"

From the same issue, page 4B: "BESTSELLING AUTHOR, LARRY MELFORD, SIGNS BOOKS"

Six months later, in the master bedroom of Larry Melford's estate, Larry was sitting nude in front of the dresser mirror, clipping unruly nose hairs. On the bed behind him, nude, dark, luscious, lay Luna Malone. There was a healthy glow of sweat on her body as she lay with two pillows propped under her head, her raven hair like an explosion of ink against their whiteness.

"Larry," she said, "you know, I've been thinking . . . I mean there's something I've been wanting to tell you, but haven't said anything about because . . . well, I was afraid you might get the wrong idea. But now that we've known each other a while, and things look solid . . . Larry, I'm a writer."

Larry quit clipping his nose hairs. He put the clipper on the dresser and turned very slowly. "You're what?"

"I mean, I want to be. And not just now, not just this minute. I've always wanted to be. I didn't tell you, because I was afraid you'd laugh, or worse, think I'd only got to know you so you could give me an *in*, but I've been writing for years and have sent book after book, story after story in, and just know I'm good, and well . . . ."

"You want me to look at it?"

"Yeah, but more than that, Larry. I need an *in*. It's what I've always wanted. To write a bestseller. I'd kill for . . . ."

"Get out! Get the hell out!"

"Larry, I didn't meet you for that reason . . . ."

"Get the hell out or I'll throw you out."

"Larry . . . ."

"Now!" He stood up from the chair, grabbed her dressing gown. "Just go. Leave everything. I'll have it sent to you. Get dressed and never let me see you again."

"Aren't you being a little silly about this? I mean . . . ."

Larry moved as fast as an eagle swooping down on a field mouse. He grabbed her shoulder and jerked her off the bed onto the floor.

"All right, you bastard, all right." Luna stood. She grabbed the robe and slipped into it. "So I did meet you for an *in*; what's wrong with that? I bet you had some help along the way. It sure couldn't have been because you're a great writer. I can hardly force myself through that garbage you write."

He slapped her across the cheek so hard she fell back on the bed.

Holding her face, she got up, gathered her clothes and walked stiffly to the bathroom. Less than a minute later, she came out dressed, the robe over her shoulder.

"I'm sorry about hitting you," Larry said. "But I meant what I said about never wanting to see you again."

"You're crazy, man. You know that? Crazy. All I asked you for was an *in*, just . . . ."

Luna stopped talking. Larry had lifted his head to look at her. His eyes looked as dark and flat as the twin barrels of a shotgun.

"Don't bother having Francis drive me home. I'll call a cab from downstairs, Mr. Bigshot Writer."

She went out, slamming the bedroom door. Larry got up and turned off the light, went back to the dresser chair and sat in the darkness for a long time.

Nearly a year and a half later, not long after completing a favor for *Bestsellers Guaranteed*, and acquiring a somewhat rabid taste for alcoholic beverages, Larry was in the Houston airport waiting to catch a plane for Hawaii for a long vacation, when he saw a woman in the distance who looked familiar. She turned and he recognized her immediately. It was Luna Malone. Still beautiful, a bit more worldly looking, and dressed to the hilt.

She saw him before he could dart away. She waved. He smiled. She came over and shook hands with him. "Larry, you aren't still mad are you?"

"No, I'm not mad. Good to see you. You look great."

"Thanks."

"Where're you going?"

"Italy. Rome."

"Pope country," Larry said with a smile, but at his words, Luna jumped.

"Yes . . . Pope country."

The announcer called for the flight to Rome, Italy. Luna and Larry shook hands again and she went away.

Larry, to kill time, went to the airport bookstore. He found he couldn't even look at the big cardboard display with his latest bestseller in it. He didn't like to look at bestsellers by anyone. But something did catch his eye. It was the cardboard display next to his. The book was called *The Little Storm*, and appeared to be one of those steamy romance novels. But what had caught his eyes was the big, emblazoned name of the author—LUNA MALONE.

Larry felt like a python had uncoiled inside of him. He felt worse than he had ever felt in his life.

"Italy. Rome," she had said.

"Pope country," he had said, and she jumped.

Larry stumbled back against the rack of his books, and his clumsiness knocked it over. The books tumbled to the floor. One of them slid between his legs and when he looked down he saw that it had been turned over to its back. There was his smiling face looking up at him. Larry Melford, big name author, bestseller, a man whose books found their way into the homes of millions of readers.

Suddenly, Hawaii was forgotten and Larry was running, running to the nearest pay phone. What had James said about moral corruption? "We feed on those who thrive on greed and ego . . . once silly concepts of morality and honor break down . . . we will own it all."

The nightmare had to end. *Bestsellers Guaranteed* had to be exposed. He would wash his hands with blood and moral corruption no more. He would turn himself in.

With trembling hand, he picked up the phone, put in his change, and dialed the police.

From today's *Houston Chronicle*, front page headline: "POPE ASSASSINATED"

From the same edition, the last page before the "Want Ads," the last paragraph: "BESTSELLING AUTHOR MURDERED IN HOME." The story follows: "Police suspect the brutal murder of author Larry Melford occurred when he surprised burglars in the act. Thus far, police have been unable to. . . ."

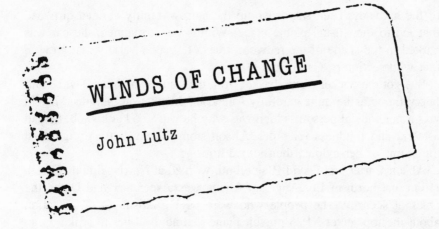

WINDS OF CHANGE

John Lutz

"LAST NIGHT WHEN I was with my wife I accidentally spoke your name."

Alison didn't answer David immediately. Slanted sunlight blasted from between the clouds in the California sky and glinted off the highly polished gray hood of her 1936 Chevy convertible. Tommy Dorsey's band was playing swing on the dashboard radio. The car was five years old, but Alison regarded it as if it were the newest model. She had only recently been able to afford such a luxury.

"What was your wife's reaction?" she asked at last, shifting gears for a steep grade in the twisting road.

David threw back his handsome head, his blond hair whipping forward in the turmoil of wind, and laughed. "None. She didn't understand me, I'm sure. There's so much she doesn't understand about me."

Alison didn't caution him to be more discreet, as she usually did. She seemed lulled by their motion through the warm, balmy evening. Her long auburn hair flowed gracefully where it curled from beneath the scarf that covered her head and was knotted beneath her chin. She knew that she and David were an enviable young couple in her sleek convertible, speeding along the coast road in mountainous Big Sur Country, with the shaded, thick redwood forest on their right and the sea, charging the shore and crashing sun-shot against the rocks on their left.

He extended a long arm and languidly, affectionately, dragged his fingertips across the shoulder of her wool sweater. She felt her heart accelerate at his touch.

"My wife doesn't know you're a spy," he said.

Alison turned her head toward him and smiled. "Let's hope not."

She braked the convertible, shifted gears again, and pulled to the side of the highway. Then she drove up the narrow, faintly defined dirt road that led to their usual picnic place. Within a few minutes, the car was parked in the shade of the redwood trees of smaller variety that grew in that wild section of California.

She got the wicker picnic basket from the trunk, watching David's tall, lanky frame as he quite carefully spread the blanket on the grass. David was a methodical person, which was why he was good at his job; he had a talent and fondness for order. Alison stopped and deftly straightened the seams of her nylons, then joined him.

Alison Carter and David Blaine both worked at Norris Aircraft Corporation just north of Los Angeles. Alison was a secretary and David the chief of security. The people who were paying Alison for information about the top-secret XP25 pursuit plane had advised her to strike up an acquaintance with the plant security chief. If she were caught, the relationship would be a valuable insurance policy.

Of course Alison had followed their advice. She believed everything they told her. She had been barely eighteen when Karl Prager had first approached her, had first become her lover. Nineteen when their affair was over and she was in too deeply as an informer ever to hope she might get out.

Not that it had bothered Alison to sell "industrial information." Oh, she knew she was working for the Germans, actually, but what difference did that make? It wasn't as if America was at war. Politics didn't interest Alison in the slightest, and the money Karl paid her more than doubled her meager salary earned as a secretary.

Alison hadn't had to think of a way to meet David. Her rather extravagant habits, considering her salary, prompted him to ask her some routine questions one day. When she'd told him she was the beneficiary of her late father's will, he'd believed her.

They'd seen each other again, after business hours, despite the fact that David was married. Apparently he and his wife, Glenda, were having difficulties. For Alison, the business of seducing the shy and precise David Blaine quickly became pleasure. And by the time he found out she was violating company rules, he was willing to overlook her transgressions.

On Saturdays, David would often give Glenda an excuse, that probably even she didn't believe, and he and Alison would drive up the coast road in Alison's convertible and picnic with sandwiches and champagne in their private, lover's hideaway.

Alison sat down beside David on the blanket. She untied and removed her head scarf, plucking out the bobby pins helping to hold it in place. Through the trees, the undulating blue-green sea was barely visible, but she could hear its enigmatic whisper on the rocky beach.

David paused in unwrapping the sandwiches. He dug into his shirt pocket and handed Alison a folded sheet of paper patterned with scrawled numbers. "Here," he said casually, "these are the performance specifications you asked for."

The figures represented the data on the experimental plane's latest test flight. Alison accepted the paper with a smile and slipped it into a pocket of her skirt. She knew that David took the business of revealing company information no more seriously than she did. He didn't know to whom she was giving the information—probably he assumed it was a rival aircraft manufacturer—and he didn't care. It was his love affair that was important to him, that had consumed his very soul, and not dry columns of figures that meant nothing except to an aeronautical engineer. He knew he'd be fired if the company found out about Alison and him, but he could always get another job of some sort. And he'd still have Alison.

After they'd eaten the ham sandwiches and finished the champagne, David looked at her with his level blue eyes. His head was resting in her lap, and she was stroking his fine blond hair that was just beginning to thin at the crown of his head. Alison had thought the first time she saw David that he looked very much like movie star Richard Widmark.

"There's so much I want to say to you today," he told her

"Not now," she said, bending her body and kissing him on the lips. "Let's not talk now."

As usual, David saw her point of view, and agreed with it.

An hour later, in the purpling twilight, Alison lay on her back and watched a plane drone high overhead in the direction of the sea. A U.S. Navy plane, she noted, on a routine nighttime training mission.

David was asleep beside her, his deep, regular breathing merging with the sounds of the plane and the eternal sighing of the sea. Though her body was very still alongside his sleeping form, Alison's mind was tortured and turning.

Not that she had any real choice. Her time of choices was over. She wished David had never told her about speaking her name in front of his wife. But he had. And Alison knew that he might speak her name again in the wrong circumstances, even if tomorrow he still saw things her way.

Quietly, she rose from the blanket and fished in her straw purse for her key ring. She walked to her car, the tall grass tickling her bare feet and ankles, thinking *tomorrow, tomorrow* . . .

She unlocked and opened the car's trunk, and left it open as she returned to stand over David. She was holding a small revolver that she'd gotten from the trunk, the gun they had given her.

Alison didn't want to miss where she was aiming, didn't want to hurt him more than necessary. She did love him.

She knelt beside David, placing the gun barrel inches from his temple, and glanced in all directions to make certain they were alone. In the sudden chill breeze rushing in from the ocean, she drew in her breath sharply and squeezed the trigger.

The crack of the gun seemed feeble in the vastness of mountains and sea.

Alison sat with her eyes clenched shut until the sound of David moving on the blanket ceased. Then, still not looking at him, she returned to the car and got a shovel from the trunk.

She wrapped David's still body in the blanket and dragged it deeper into the forest. She began to dig.

In a very few hours, halfway around the world, a signal would be given, and the Japanese would attack Pearl Harbor. War would immediately be declared, not only against Japan but against Germany and Italy as well. The rules of the game Alison was being forced to play would abruptly change. Who knew if David would have been willing to continue to play if the stakes were real? Who could say what else he might have accidentally let slip to his wife? Alison knew that much more than her job, and perhaps a criminal record, depended on David's silence now. Her survival was at stake.

As she cast loose earth over the huddled, motionless form in the blanket, Alison didn't realize she was burying a ring in David's pocket, the engagement ring he had intended to give her when he awoke. The ring with her initials engraved inside the band. The ring wrapped loosely in a copy of the letter he had written to his wife, confessing everything and explaining why he was leaving her.

Alison worked frantically with the shovel, feeling her tears track hotly down her cheeks. At least David's war was over. He was at peace. Her war was just beginning, and look what it had already forced her to do.

She would be one of the first to realize why hers was a losing cause.

CHARLIE'S GAME

Brian Garfield

WHEN I TURNED the corner I saw Leonard Ross going into Myerson's office ahead of me. By the time I reached the door I heard Ross say, "Where's Charlie?"

"Late. As usual. Shut the door."

Late. As usual. As far as I could remember—and I have phenomenal recall—there had been only one time when I had been late arriving in Myerson's office and that had been the result of a bomb scare that had grounded everything for three hours at Tempelhof. His acidulous remark had been a cheap shot. But then that was Myerson.

Ross was shutting the door in my face when I pushed in past him and kicked it closed. Ross said, "Hello, Mr. Dark."

Myerson only glanced up from the desk. Then he went on pretending to read something in a manila file folder. I said, "Welcome back, Charlie," in an effort to prompt him but he ignored it and I decided to play his silly game so I dropped my raincoat across a chair and squeezed into one of the tubular steel armchairs and perused the photos on the wall, waiting him out.

The room was stale with Myerson's illegal Havana smoke; it was a room that obviously was unnerving to youngsters like Leonard Ross because among Myerson's varied and indeterminate functions was that of hatchet man. Any audience with him might turn out to be one's last: fall into disfavor with him and one could have a can tied to one's tail at any time, Civil Service or no Civil Service; and as junior staff, Ross had no illusions about his right to tenure. I had none myself: I was there solely at Myerson's sufferance, but that was something else—he could fire me at any time he chose to but he was never going to choose to because he needed me too much and he knew it.

His rudeness meant nothing; that was what passed for amiability with Myerson. I gave Ross a glance and switched it meaningfully toward a chair and finally Ross sat down, perched uneasily on the edge of it.

The view from Myerson's window isn't terribly impressive. An enormous parking lot and, beyond it, a hedgerow of half-wilted trees. Here and there you can see the tops of the high-rises around Langley.

Finally he closed the file and looked at me. "You're late."

"Would you care for a note from my mother explaining my tardiness?"

"Your sarcasms seldom amuse me."

"Then don't provoke them."

"You are," he said, "preposterously fat."

"And you are a master of the non sequitur."

"You disgust me, do you know that?" He turned to young Ross. "He disgusts me. Doesn't he disgust you?"

Ross made embarassed gestures and I said, "Don't put the kid on the spot. What's on?"

Myerson wasn't in a particularly savage mood, obviously, because he gave up trying to goad me with no more prompting than that. He tapped the manila folder with a fingertip. "We've got a signal from Arbuckle."

"Where's Arbuckle?"

"East Africa. You really ought to try to keep up on the postings in your own department."

Ross explained to me, "Arbuckle's in Dar-es-Salaam."

"Thank-you."

Ross's impatience burst its confines and he turned to Myerson: "What's the flap, then?"

Myerson made a face. "It distresses me, Ross, that you're the only drone in this department who doesn't realize that words like 'flap' became obsolete sometime before you were born."

I said, "If you're through amusing yourself maybe you could answer the young man's question."

Myerson squinted at me; after a moment he decided not to be affronted. "As you may know, affairs in Tanzania remain sensitive. Especially since the Uganda affair. The balance is precarious—a sort of three-sided teeter-totter: ourselves, the Soviets and the Chinese. It would require only a slight upheaval to tip the bal—"

"Can't you spare us the tiresome diplomatic summaries and get down to it?"

Myerson coolly opened the file, selected a photograph and held it up on display. "Recognize the woman?"

To Ross I suppose it was only a badly focused black-and-white of a thin woman with attractive and vaguely Oriental features, age indeterminate. But I knew her well enough. "Marie Lapautre."

"Indeed."

Ross leaned forward for a closer look. I imagine it may have been the first time he'd ever seen a likeness of the dragon lady, whose reputation in our world was something like that of John Wesley Harding in the days of gunslingers.

"Arbuckle reports she's been seen in the lobby of the Kilimanjaro in Dar. Buying a picture post card," Myerson added drily.

I said, "Maybe she's on vacation. Spending some of the blood money on travel like any well-heeled tourist. She's never worked that part of the world, you know."

"Which is precisely why someone might hire her if there were a sensitive job to be done there."

"That's all we've got? Just the one sighting? No evidence of a caper in progress?"

"If we wait for evidence it could arrive in a pine box. I'd prefer not to have that sort of confirmation." He scowled toward Ross. "Fidel Castro, of course, has been trying to persuade Tanzania to join him in leading the Third World toward the Moscow sphere of influence, but up to now the Nyerere regime has maintained strict neutrality. We have every reason to wish that it continiue to do so. We want the status to remain quo. That's both the official line and the under-the-counter reality."

Ross was perfectly aware of all that, I'm sure, but Myerson enjoys exposition. "The Chinese aren't as charitable as we are toward neutralists," Myerson went on, "particularly since the Russian meddlings in Angola and Ethiopia. The Chinese want to increase their influence in Africa—that's confirmed in recent signals from the Far East. Add to this background the presence of Marie Lapautre in Dar-es-Salaam and I believe we must face the likelihood of an explosive event. Possibly you can forecast the nature of it as well as I can?"

The last question was addressed to me, not Ross. I rose to meet it without much effort. "Assuming you're right, I'd buy a scenario in which Lapautre's been hired to assassinate one of the top Tanzanian officials. Not Nyerere—that would provoke chaos. But one of the others. Probably one who leans toward the Russian or Chinese line."

Ross said, "What?"

I told him, "They'd want to make the assasination look like an American plot."

Myerson said, "It wouldn't take any more than that to tilt the balance over toward the East."

"Deal and double deal," Ross said under his breath in disgust.

"It's the way the game is played," Myerson told him. "If you find it repugnant I'd suggest you look for another line of work." He turned to me: "I've booked you two on the afternoon flight by way of Zurich. The assignment is to prevent Lapautre from embarrasing us."

"All right." This was the sum of my response; I didn't ask any questions. I pried myself out of the chair and reached for my coat.

Ross said, "Wait a minute. Why not just warn the Tanzanians? Tell them what we suspect. Wouldn't that get us off the hook if anything did happen?"

"Hardly," Myerson said. It would make things worse. Don't explain it to him, Charlie—let him reason it out for himself. It should be a useful exercise for him. On your way now—you've barely got time to make your plane."

By the time we were belted into our seats Ross thought he had it worked out. "If we threw them a warning and then somebody got assassinated, it would look like we did it ourselves and tried to alibi it in advance. Is that what Myerson meant?"

"Go to the head of the class." I gave him the benediction of my saintly smile. Ross is a good kid: not stupid, merely inexperienced. He has sound instincts and good moral fibre, which is more than can be said for most of the Neanderthals in the Company. I explained, "Things are touchy in Tanzania. There's an excess of suspicion toward *auslanders*—they've been raided and occupied by Portuguese slave traders and German soldiers and British colonialists and you can't blame them for being xenophobes. You can't tell them things for their own good. Our only option is to neutralize the dragon lady without anyone knowing about it."

He gave me a sidewise look. "Can we pin down exactly what we mean by that word 'neutralize'?"

I said, "Have you ever killed a woman?"

"No. Nor a man, for that matter."

"Neither have I. And I intend to keep it that way."

"You never even carry a piece, do you, Charlie?"

"No. Any fool can shoot people."

"Then how can we do anything about it? We can't just ask her to go away. She's not the type that scares."

"Let's just see how things size up first." I tipped my head back against the paper antimacassar and closed my eyes and reviewed what I knew about Marie Lapautre—fact, rumor and legend garnered from various briefings and shoptalk along the corridors in Langley.

She had never been known to botch an assignment.

French father, Vietnamese mother. Born 1934 on a plantation west of Saigon. Served as a sniper in the Viet Minh forces at Dienbienphu. Ran with the Cong in the late 1960s with assignments ranging from commando infiltration to assassinations of village leaders and then South Vietnamese officials. Seconded to Peking in 1969 for specialized terrorist instruction. Detached from the Viet Cong, inducted into the Chinese Army and assigned to the Seventh Bureau—a rare honor. Seconded as training cadre to the Japanese Red Army, a terrorist gang. It was rumored Lapautre had planned the tactics for the bombings at Tel Aviv Airport in 1975. During the past seven or eight years Lapautre's name had cropped up at least a dozen times in reports I'd seen dealing with unsolved assassinations in Laos, Syria, Turkey, Libya, West Germany, Lebanon and elsewhere.

Marie Lapautre's weapon was the rifle. At least seven of the unsolved assassinations had been effected with long-range fire from Kashkalnikov sniper rifles—the model known to be Lapautre's choice.

She was forty-five years old, five feet four, one hundred and five pounds, black hair and eyes, mottled burn scar on back of right hand. Spoke five languages, including English. Ate red meat barely cooked when the choice was open. She lived between jobs in a 17th century villa on the Italian Riviera—a home she had bought with funds reportedly acquired from hire-contract jobs as a freelance. Five of the seven suspected assassinations with Kashkalnikovs had been bounty jobs and the other two probably had been unpaid because she still held a commission in Peking's Seventh Bureau.

We had met, twice and very briefly; both times on neutral ground— once in Singapore, once in Teheran. In Singapore it had been a diplomatic reception; the British attaché had introduced us and stood by watching with amusement while we sized up each other like rival gladiators but it had been nothing more than a few minutes of inconsequential pleasantries and then she had drifted off on the arm of a Malaysian black marketeer.

The files on her were slender and all we really knew was that she was a professional with a preference for the 7.62mm Kashkalnikov and a reputation for never missing a score. By implication I added one other thing: if Lapautre became aware of the fact that two Americans were moving in to prevent her from completing her present assignment she wouldn't hesitate to kill us—and naturally she would kill us with proficient dispatch.

The flight was interminable. I ate at least five meals. We had to change planes in Zurich and from there it was another nine hours. I noticed that

Ross was having trouble keeping his eyes open by the time we checked into the New Africa Hotel.

It had been built by the Germans when Tanganyika had been one of the Kaiser's colonies and it had been rebuilt by Africans to encourage business travel; it was comfortable enough and I'd picked it mainly for the food, but it happened to be within easy walking distance of the Kilimanjaro, where Lapautre had been spotted. Also, unlike the luxurious Kilimanjaro, the New Africa had a middle-class businessman's matter of factness and one didn't need to waste time trying to look like a tourist.

The change in time zones seemed to bewilder Ross. He stumbled groggily when we went along to the shabby export office that housed the front organization for Arbuckle's soporific East Africa station.

A fresh breeze came off the harbor. I've always liked Dar; it's a beautiful port, ringed by palm-shaded beaches and colorful villas on the slopes. Some of the older buildings bespeak a dusty poverty but the city is more modern and energetic than anything you'd expect to find near the equator on the shore of the Indian Ocean. There are jams of hooting traffic on the main boulevards. Businessmen in various shadings: Europeans, turbaned Arabs, madrassed Asians, black Africans in tribal costumes. Now and then a four-by-four lorry growls by carrying a squad of soldiers but the place hasn't got that air of police-state tension that makes the hairs crawl on the back of my neck in countries like Paraguay and East Germany. It occured to me as we reached Arbuckle's office that we hadn't been accosted by a single beggar.

It was crowded in among cubbyhole curio shops selling African carvings and cloth. Arbuckle was a tall man, thin and bald and nervous; inescapably he was known in the Company as Fatty. He had one item to add to the information we'd arrived with: Lapautre was still in Dar.

"She's in room four-eleven at the Kilimanjaro but she takes most of her dinners in the dining room of the New Africa. They've got better beef."

"I know."

"Yeah, you would. Watch out you don't bump into her there. She must have seen your face in dossiers."

"We've met a couple of times. But I doubt she'd know Ross by sight."

Ross was grinding knuckles into his eye sockets. "Sometimes it pays to be unimportant."

"Hang onto that thought," I told him. When we left the office I added, "You'd better go back to the room and take the cure for that jet lag."

"What about you?"

"Chores and snooping. And dinner, of course. I'll see you at breakfast. Seven o'clock."

"You going to tell me what the program is?"

"I see no point discussing anything at all with you until you've had a night's sleep."

"Don't *you* ever sleep?

"When I've got nothing better to do."

I watched him slouch away under the palms. Then I went about my business.

The breakfast layout was a nice array of fruits, juices, breads, cold cuts. I had heaped a plate full and begun to consume it when Ross came puffy-eyed down to the second-floor dining room and picked his way through the mangoes and sliced ham. He eats like a bird.

The room wasn't crowded; a sprinkling of businessmen and a few Americans in safari costumes that appeared to have been tailored in Hollywood. I said mildly to Ross when he sat down, "I picked this table at random," by which I meant that it probably wasn't bugged. I tasted the coffee and made a face; you'd think they could make it better—after all they grow the stuff there. I put the cup down. "All right. We've got to play her cagey and careful. If anything blows loose there won't be any cavalry to rescue us."

"Us?"

"Did you think you were here just to feed me straight lines, Ross?"

"Well, I kind of figured I was mainly here to hold your coat. On-the-job training, you know."

"It's a two-man job. Actually it's a six-man job but the two of us have got to carry it."

"Wonderful. Should I start practicing my quick draw?"

"If you'd stop asking droll questions we'd get along a little faster."

"All right. Proceed, my general."

"First the backgrounding. We're jumping to a number of conclusions based on flimsy evidence but it can't be helped." I enumerated them on my fingers. "We assume, one, that she's here on a job and not just to take pictures of elephants. Two, that it's a Seventh Bureau assignment. Three, that the job is to assassinate someone—after all, that's her principal occupation. Four, that the target may be a government leader here, but not Nyerere. We don't know the timetable so we have to assume, five, that it could happen at any moment. Therefore we must act quickly. Are you with me so far?"

"So far, sure."

"We assume, six, that the local Chinese station is unaware of her mission."

"Why should we assume that?"

"Because they're bugging her room."

Ross gawked at me.

I am well past normal retirement age and I'm afraid it is not beneath me to gloat at the weaknesses of the younger generations. I said, "*I* didn't waste the night sleeping."

He chewed a mouthful, swallowed, squinted at me. "All right. You went through the dragon lady's room, you found a bug. But what makes you think it's a Chinese bug?"

"I found not one bug but three. One was ours—up-to-date equipment and I checked it out with Arbuckle. Had to get him out of bed; he wasn't happy but he admitted it's our bug. The second was American-made but obsolescent. Presumably placed in the room by the Tanzanian secret service—we sold a batch of that model to them about ten years ago. The third mike was made in Sinkiang Province, one of those square little numbers they must have shown you in tech briefings. Satisfied?"

"Okay. No Soviet agent worth his vodka would stoop to using a bug of Chinese manufacture, so that leaves the Chinese. So the local Peking station is bugging her room and that means either they don't know why she's here or they don't trust her. Go on."

"They're bugging her because she's known to freelance. Naturally they're nervous. But you're mistaken about one thing. They definitely don't know why she's here. The Seventh Bureau never tells anyone anything. So the local station wants to find out who she's working for and who she's gunning for. The thing is, Ross, as far as the local Chinese are concerned she could easily be down here on a job for Warsaw or East Berlin or London or Washington or some Arab oil sheikh. They just don't know, do they?"

"Go on."

Now the Tanzanians are bugging her as well and that means they know who she is. She's under surveillance. That means we have to act circumspectly. We can't make waves that might splash up against the presidential palace. When we leave here we leave everything exactly as we found it, all right? Now then. More assumptions. We assume, seven, that Lapautre isn't a hipshooter. If she were she wouldn't have lasted this long. She's careful, she cases the situation before she steps into it. We can use that caution of hers. And finally, we assume, eight, that she's not very well versed in surveillance technology." Then I added, "That's a crucial assumption, by the way."

"Why? How can we assume that?"

"She's never been an intelligence gatherer. Her experience is in violence. She's a basic sort of creature—a carnivore. I don't see her as a scientific whiz. She uses an old-fashioned sniper's rifle because she's comfortable with it—she's not an experimenter. She'd know the rudiments of electronic eavesdropping but when it comes to sophisticated devices I doubt she's got much interest. Apparently she either doesn't know her room is bugged or knows it but doesn't care. Either way it indicates the whole area is outside her field of interest. Likely there are types of equipment she doesn't even know about."

"Like for instance?"

"Parabolic reflectors. Long-range directionals."

"Those are hardly ultrasophisticated. They date back to World War II."

"But not in the Indochinese jungles. They wouldn't be a part of her experience."

"Does it matter?"

"I'm not briefing you just to listen to the sound of my dulcet baritone voice, Ross. The local Chinese station is equipped with parabolics and directionals."

"I see." He said it but he obviously didn't see. Not yet. It was getting a bit tedious leading him along by the nose but I liked him and it might have been worse: Myerson might have sent along one of the idiot computer whiz-kids who are perfectly willing to believe the earth is flat if an IBM machine says it is.

I said, "You're feeding your face and you look spry enough but are you awake? You've got to memorize your lines fast and play your part perfectly the first time out."

"What are you talking about?"

According to plan Ross made the phone call at nine in the morning from a coin box in the cable office. He held the receiver out from his ear so I could eavesdrop. A clerk answered and Ross asked to be connected to extension four-eleven; it rang three times and was picked up. I remembered her voice right away: low and smoky. "*Oui?*"

"Two hundred thousand dollars, in gold, deposited to a Swiss account." That was the opening line because it was unlikely she'd hang up on us right away after that teaser. "Are you interested?"

"Who is this?"

"Clearly, Mademoiselle, one does not mention names on an open telephone line. I think we might arrange a meeting, however. It's an urgent matter."

Ross's palm was visibly damp against the receiver. I heard the woman's voice: "For whom are you speaking, M'sieur?"

"I represent certain principals." Because she wouldn't deal directly with anyone fool enough to act as his own front man. Ross said, "You've

been waiting to hear from me, *N'est-ce-pas?*" That was for the benefit
of those who were bugging her phone; he went on quickly before she
could deny it: "At noon today I'll be on the beach just north of the fishing
village at the head of the bay. I'll be wearing a white shirt, short sleeves;
khaki trousers and white plimsolls. I'll be alone and of course without
weapons." I saw him swallow quickly.

The line seemed dead for a while but finally the woman spoke.
"Perhaps."

Click.

"Perhaps," Ross repeated dismally, and cradled it.

Driving us north in the rent-a-car he said to me, "She didn't sound
enthusiastic, did she. You think she'll come?"

"She'll come."

"What makes you think so?"

"Without phone calls like that she wouldn't be able to maintain her
standard of living."   "But if she's in the middle of setting up a caper
here—"

"It doesn't preclude her from discussing the next job. She'll come."

"Armed to the teeth, no doubt," Ross muttered.

"No. She's a pro. A pro never carries a gun when he's not on a job—a
gun can get you into too much trouble if it's discovered. But she's probably capable of dismantling you by hand in a hundred different ways so
try not to provoke her until we've sprung the trap."

"You can be incredibly comforting sometimes, you know that?"

"You're green, Ross, and you have a tendency to be flip and you'd
better realize this isn't a matter for frivolous heroics. You're not without
courage and it's silly to pretend otherwise. But don't treat this thing with
childish bravado. There's a serious risk you may end up facedown in the
surf if you don't treat the woman with all the caution in the world. Your
job's simple and straightforward and there's nothing funny about it—just
keep her interested and steer her to the right place. And for God's sake,
remember your lines."

We parked off the road and walked through the palms toward the edge
of the water. The beach was a narrow white strip of perfect sand curving
away in a crescent. There was hardly any surf. At the far end of the curve
I saw a scatter of thatched huts and a few dilapidated old piers to which
were tethered a half dozen primitive outrigger fishing boats. It was pleasantly warm and the air was clear and dry: the East African coast has none
of the muggy tropicality of the West one. Two small black children ran

up and down the distant sand and their strident voices carried weakly to my ears. The half mile of beach between was empty of visible life. A tourist-poster scene, I thought, but clearly a feeling of menace was preoccupying Ross; I had to steady him with a hand on his shoulder.

Out on the open water, beyond a few small boats floating at anchor, a pair of junks drifted south with the mild wind in their square sails. A dazzling white sport-fisherman with a flying bridge rode the swells in a lazy figure-eight pattern about four hundred yards offshore; two men in floppy white hats sat in the stern chairs trolling lines. Beyond, on the horizon, a tramp prowled northward—a coaster: Tanga next, then Mombasa, so forth. And there was a faint spiral of smoke even farther out— probably the Zanzibar ferry.

I put my back to the view and spoke in a voice calculated to reach no farther than Ross's ears: "Spot them?"

Ross was searching the beach. "Not a soul. Maybe they didn't get the hint."

"The sport fisherman, Ross. They've got telescopes and long-range microphones focused on this beach right now and if I were facing them they'd hear every word I'm saying."

That was why we'd given it several hours' lead time after making the phone call. To give the Chinese time to get in position to monitor the meeting.

"They've taken the bait," I said. "It remains to be seen whether the dragon lady will prove equally gullible."

Ross was carrying the rifle and I crooked a finger and he gave it to me. We were still in the palms, too shadowed for the watchers on the fishing boat to get much of a look at us. I slid back into the deeper shadows and watched Ross begin to walk out along the beach, kicking sand with his toes. He had his hands in his pockets but then thought the better of that and took them out again and I applauded him for that—he was making it obvious his hands were empty.

I saw him look at his watch. It was eleven fifty-five. *Don't get too nervous, Ross.* He walked out to the middle of the crescent of sand and stood there looking back inland and I had some idea what he was going through: trying to ignore the fishing boat a quarter of a mile behind him, trying to talk himself out of the acute feeling that someone's telescopic crosshairs were centered between his shoulder blades.

I watched him begin to walk around in an aimless little circle—perhaps he felt they'd have a harder time hitting a moving target. He hadn't much to worry about, actually; they had no reason to take potshots at him— they'd be curious, not murderous—but perhaps Ross was no longer in a state of mind where logic was the ruling force. I trusted him to do his part, though. I knew a little about him. He'd come right into the Company after college, seeking adventure and challenge, and if he'd been worried by the stink of the Company's growing notoriety he'd balanced it with a naïve notion that the Company needed people like him to keep it clean. Mainly what I knew about him was that Joe Cutter gave him very high marks and there's nobody in Langley whose judgment I'd sooner trust than Joe's. This caper should have been Joe's by rights—it was more in his line than mine, I'm more of a troubleshooter and rarely get picked for front-line counter-espionage capers because I'm too visible—but Joe hates Myerson even more than I do and he'd managed to get himself posted out to the Near East away from Myerson's influence.

I heard the putt-putt of an engine and watched a little outboard come in sight around the headland and beat its way forward, its bow gently slapping the water, coming at a good clip. Ross saw it too—looked at it, then looked away, back into the palm trees—probably wondering when the woman would show up. He hadn't yet realized she was already here. I saw him do a slow take and turn on his heel again. Then we both watched the outboard come straight in onto the beach.

It was the dragon lady and she was alone at the tiller. She tipped the engine up across the transom, jumped overside and came nimbly ashore, dragging the boat up onto the sand a bit. Then she turned to look at Ross across the intervening forty yards of sand. I had a good view of her in profile. Ross was trying to meet her stare without guile. Her eyes left him after a bit and began to explore the trees. I didn't stir; I was in among a cluster of palm boles and the thing she'd spot first would be movement.

She made a thorough job of it before she turned toward Ross. She walked with lithe graceful strides: petite but there was nothing fragile about her. She wore an *ao dai,* the simple formfitting dress of Indochina; it was painted to her skin and there was no possibility she could have concealed a weapon under it. Perhaps she wore it for that reason.

Ross didn't move. He let her come to him. It was in his instructions.

I was near enough to hear them because the offshore breeze carried their voices to me.

"Well then, M'sieur."

"The money," Ross began, and then he stopped, tongue-tied.

Christ. He'd forgotten his lines.

"*Oui?*"

He looked away from her. Perhaps it was the glimpse of the white sport boat out there that galvanized him. I heard him speak clearly and calmly. "The money's on deposit and we have the receipt and the numbered account book. If you do the job you'll be given both of them. Two hundred thousand American dollars in gold. That works out to something over half a million Swiss francs at the current rate."

She said, "I would need a bit more information than that."

"The name of the target, of course. The deadline date by which the assignment must be completed. More than that you don't need." Ross kept his face straight. I had a feeling he was feverishly rehearsing the rest of his lines.

She said, "You've left out one thing."

"I don't think so, Mlle. Lapautre."

"I must know who employs me."

"Not included in the price of your ticket, I'm afraid."

"Then we've wasted our morning, both of us."

"For two hundred thousand dollars we expected a higher class of discretion than you seem inclined to exercise." It was a line I had drilled into him and apparently he hadn't liked it—it went against his usual mode of expression—but I had insisted on the precise wording, and now she responded as I'd said she would: it was as if I'd written her dialogue as well as Ross's.

She said, "Discretion costs a little more, M'sieur, especially if it concerns those whom I might regard as my natural enemies. You *are* American."

"I am. That's not to say my principals are."

The thing is, Ross, you don't want to close the door, you want to keep her talking. String her along, whet her curiosity. She's going to insist on more information. Stall. Stretch it out. Don't give her the name of the target until she's in position.

Casually Ross put his hands in his pockets and turned away from her. I watched him stroll very slowly toward me. He didn't look back to see if she was following him. He spoke in a normal tone so that she'd have trouble hearing him against the wind if she let him get too far ahead of her. "My principals are willing to discuss the matter more directly with you if you agree to take the job on. Not a face-to-face meeting, of course, but one of them may be willing to speak to you on a safe line. Coin telephones at both ends—you know the drill."

It was working. She was trailing along, moving as casually as he was. Ross threw his head back and stared at the sky. I saw what she couldn't see—Ross wetting his lips nervously. "The target isn't a difficult one. The security measures aren't too tough."

"But he's important, isn't he? Visible. Otherwise the price would not be so high."

It was something I hadn't forecast for him and I wasn't sure Ross would know how to handle it but he did the right thing: he made no reply at all. He just kept drifting toward the palms, off on a tangent from me now, moving in seemingly aimless half circles. After a moment he said, "Of course you weren't followed here." It was in the script.

"Why do you think I chose to come by open boat? No one followed me. Can you say the same?"

Position.

Ross turned and she moved alongside. She had, as I predicted, followed his lead: it was Indochinese courtesy, inbred and unconscious—the residue of a servile upbringing.

She stood beside him now a few feet to his right; like Ross she was facing the palm trees.

Ross dropped his voice and spoke without turning his head; there was no possibility the microphones on the boat would hear him. I barely caught his words myself, and I was only about thirty feet downwind of him. "Don't speak for a moment now, Mademoiselle. Look slightly to your right—the little cluster of palm trees."

She was instantly alert and suspicious; I saw her face come around and I stirred a bit and it was enough to make her spot me. Then I leveled the rifle, aiming down the sights.

In the same guarded low voice Ross said, "It's a Mannlicher bolt action with high-speed ammunition. Hollowpoint bullets and he's an expert marksman. You'd stand no chance at all if you tried to run for it." Ross kept stepping back because I'd told him not to let her get close enough to jump him and use him for a shield. Yet he had to stay within voice range because if he lifted his tone or turned his head the fine-focus directional mike on the sport fishing boat would pick up his words immediately.

I saw her shoulders drop half an inch and felt relief.

If she doesn't break for it in the first few seconds she won't break at all.
She's a pro and a pro doesn't fight the drop.

"You're in a box, Mlle. Lapautre. You've got one way to get out of it alive. Are you listening to me?"

"Certainly."

"Don't try to figure it out because there are parts of it you'll never know. We're playing out a charade, that's all you need to keep in mind.

Play your part as required and you'll walk away alive."

"What do you want, then?"

It was evident that her cool aplomb amazed Ross, even though I'd told him to expect it.

I knew she couldn't have recognized me; most of me was behind one of the palms and all she really could see was a heavyset fellow with a rifle. Because of the angle I was hidden completely from the view of those on board the sport fishing boat. All they'd be able to tell was that Ross and Lapautre were having a conversation in tones too low for their equipment to record. They'd be frustrated and angry but they'd hang on hoping to pick up scraps of words that they could later edit together and make some sense out of.

Ross answered her, *sotto voce:* "I want you to obey my instructions now. In a moment I'm going to step around and face you. The man in the trees will kill you if you make any sudden move, so pay attention . . . . Now I'm going to start talking to you in a loud voice. The things I say may not make much sense to you. I don't care what you say by way of response—but say it quietly so that nobody hears your answers. And I want you to nod your head 'yes' now and then to make it look as if you're agreeing with whatever proposition I make to you. Understand?"

"No," she said. "I do not understand."

"But you'll do as I say, won't you."

"I seem to have little choice." She was looking right at me when she said that.

"That's good enough. Here we go."

Then Ross stepped off to the side and made a careful circle around her, keeping his distance, looking commendably casual. He started talking midway around: "Then we've got a deal. I'm glad you agreed to take it on."

He stopped when he was facing her from her port bow. The woman didn't speak; she only watched him. Ross enunciated clearly and I appreciated that; we both were mindful of the shotgun microphone focused on his lips from four hundred yards offshore.

"I'm glad," he said again. "You're the best in the business, I think everybody knows that."

Her lip curled ever so slightly: an expression exquisite in its subtle contempt. "And just what is it I'm supposed to have agreed to?"

Ross nodded vigorously. "Exactly. When you talk to my principals you'll recognize the Ukranian accents immediately but I hope that won't deter you from putting your best effort into it."

"This is absurd." But she kept her voice right down. I was aiming the thing straight at her heart.

"That's right," Ross said cheerfully. "There will be no official Soviet record of the transaction. If they're accused of anything naturally they'll deny it so you can see that it's in your best interests to keep absolutely silent."

"This is pointless. Who can possibly benefit from this ridiculous performance?"

"I think they'll find that acceptable," Ross said. "Now then, about the target. He must be taken out within the next twelve days because that's the deadline for a particular international maneuver the details of which needn't concern you. The target is here in Dar-es-Salaam, so you'll have plenty of time to set up the assassination. Do you recognize the name Chiang Hsien?"

She laughed then. She actually laughed. "Incredible."

Ross managed to smile. "Yes. The chief of the Chinese station in Dar. Now there's just one more detail."

"Is that all? Thank goodness for that."

Ross nodded pleasantly. "Yes, that's right. You've go to make it look as if it's the work of Americans. I'd suggest you use an American rifle. I leave the other details in your hands, but the circumstantial evidence must point to an American plot against the Chinese people's representative. You understand?"

"Is that all then?"

"If you still want confirmation I'll arrange for a telephone contact between you and my principals. I think that covers everything, then. It's always pleasant doing business with a professional." With a courtly bow—he might have been Doug Fairbanks himself—Ross turned briskly on his heel and marched away toward the trees without looking back.

I watched the woman walk back to her open boat. The junks had disappeared past the point of land to the south; the outriggers were still tethered in the water by the village; the coastal steamer was plowing north, the Zanzibar ferry's smoke had disappeared—and the two white-hatted men in the stern of the sport fishing boat were packing up their rods and getting out of their swivel chairs. The dragon lady pushed her boat into the surf, climbed over the gunwale, made her way aft and hooked the outboard engine over the transom. She yanked the cord a few times. It sputtered and roared; and she went chugging out in a wide circle toward the open water, angling to starboard to clear the headland.

When she'd gone a couple hundred yards Ross came through the trees beside me and said, "What happens now?"

"Watch." I smiled at him. "You did a beautiful job, you know."

"Yeah, I know I did."

I liked him for that. I hate false modesty.

The sport fisherman was moving, its engines whining, planing the water: collision course. Near the headland it intercepted the little open outboard boat. The woman tried to turn away but the big white boat leaped ahead of her and skidded athwart her course.

"That skipper knows how to handle her," Ross commented without pleasure.

With no choice left, the woman allowed her boat to be drawn alongside by a long-armed man with a boathook. One of the men in the stern—one of the two with white hats—gave her a hand aboard. She didn't put up a struggle; she was a pro. I saw them push her toward the cabin—they went below, out of sight, and then the two boats disappeared around the headland, one towing the other.

Ross and I walked back to the car; I tossed the rifle into the back seat—we'd drop it off at Arbuckle's. It wasn't loaded. If she'd called our bluff I'd have let her run for it. (There's always another day.)

I said, "They'll milk her of course, but they won't believe a word of it. They've got the evidence on tape and they won't buy her denials. They wouldn't believe the truth in a thousand years and it's all she's got to offer."

Ross leaned against the car, both arms against the roof, head down between his arms. "You know what they'll do to her, don't you. After they squeeze her dry."

I said, "It'll happen a long way from here and nobody will ever know about it."

"And that makes it right?"

"No. It adds another load to whatever we've already got on our consciences. If it makes you feel a little better it's a form of justice—think of the people she's murdered. She may survive this, you know. She may come out of it alive. But if she does she'll never get another job in that line of work. Nobody'll trust her again."

"It hasn't solved a thing," he complained. He gave me a petulant little boy look. "They'll just send somebody to take her place, won't they? Next week or next month."

"Maybe they will. If they do we'll have to deal with it when it happens. You may as well get used to it, Ross—you play one game, you finish it, you add up the score and then you put the pieces back onto the board and start the next game. That's all there is to it—and that's the fun of it. As long as you stay lucky there's always another game."

Ross stared at me. "I guess there is," he said reluctantly.

We got in the car and Ross turned the key. I smiled briefly, trying to reassure him. The starter meshed and he put it in gear. He said with sudden savagery, "But it's not all that much fun for the losers, is it."

"That's why you should always play to win," I replied.

Ross fishtailed the car angrily out into the road.